David Baldacci is the author of international bestsellers *Absolute Power*, *Total Control*, *The Winner*, *The Simple Truth*, *Wish You Well*, *Last Man Standing*, *The Christmas Train*, *Split Second*, *Hour Game* and *The Camel Club*. He lives in his native state of Virginia.

For more information visit his official website at www.david-baldacci.com

DAVID BALDACCI

absolute power
&
total control

PAN BOOKS

Absolute Power first published 1996 by Warner Books USA.
First published in Great Britain 1996 by Simon and Schuster UK.
First published in paperback 2003 by Pan Books.
Total Control first published 1997 by Warner Books USA.
First published in Great Britain 1997 by Simon and Schuster UK.
First published in paperback 2003 by Pan Books.

This omnibus first published 2006 by Pan Books
an imprint of Pan Macmillan Ltd
Pan Macmillan, 20 New Wharf Road, London N1 9RR
Basingstoke and Oxford
Associated companies throughout the world
www.panmacmillan.com

ISBN-13: 978-0-330-44664-8
ISBN-10: 0-330-44664-9

absolute power

To Michelle,
my dearest friend, my loving wife, my partner in crime,
without you this dream would have remained a feeble
glint in a weary eye

To my mother and father,
no parents could have done any more

To my brother and sister,
for putting up with a lot from their younger sibling and
still always being there for me

"Absolute power corrupts absolutely."
—LORD ACTON

ONE

He gripped the steering wheel loosely as the car, its lights out, drifted slowly to a stop. A few last scraps of gravel kicked out of the tire treads and then silence enveloped him. He took a moment to adjust to the surroundings and then pulled out a pair of worn but still effective night-vision binoculars. The house slowly came into focus. He shifted easily, confidently in his seat. A duffel bag lay on the front seat beside him. The car's interior was faded but clean.

The car was also stolen. And from a very unlikely source.

A pair of miniature palm trees hung from the rear-view mirror. He smiled grimly as he looked at them. Soon he might be going to the land of palms. Quiet, blue, see-through water, powdery salmon-colored sunsets and late mornings. He had to get out. It was time. For all the occasions he had said that to himself, this time he felt sure.

Sixty-six years old, Luther Whitney was eligible to collect Social Security, and was a card-carrying member of AARP. At that age most men had settled down into second careers as grandfathers, part-time raisers of their children's children, when weary joints were eased down into familiar recliners and arteries finished closing up with the clutter of a lifetime.

Luther had had only one career his entire life. It involved breaking and entering into other people's homes and places of business, usually in the

1

nighttime, as now, and taking away as much of their property as he could feasibly carry.

Though clearly on the wrong side of the law, Luther had never fired a gun or hurled a knife in anger or fear, except for his part in a largely confusing war fought where South and North Korea were joined at the hip. And the only punches he had ever thrown were in bars, and those only in self-defense as the suds made men braver than they should have been.

Luther only had one criterion in choosing his targets: he took only from those who could well afford to lose it. He considered himself no different from the armies of people who routinely coddled the wealthy, constantly persuading them to buy things they did not need.

A good many of his sixty-odd years had been spent in assorted medium- and then maximum-security correctional facilities along the East Coast. Like blocks of granite around his neck, three prior felony convictions stood to his credit in three different states. Years had been carved out of his life. Important years. But he could do nothing to change that now.

He had refined his skills to where he had high hopes that a fourth conviction would never materialize. There was absolutely nothing mysterious about the ramifications of another bust: he would be looking at the full twenty years. And at his age, twenty years was a death penalty. They might as well fry him, which was the way the Commonwealth of Virginia used to handle its particularly bad people. The citizens of this vastly historic state were by and large a God-fearing people, and religion premised upon the notion of equal retribution consistently demanded the ultimate payback. The commonwealth succeeded in disposing of more death row

2

criminals than all but two states, and the leaders, Texas and Florida, shared the moral sentiments of their Southern sister. But not for simple burglary; even the good Virginians had their limits.

Yet with all that at risk he couldn't take his eyes off the home — mansion, of course, one would be compelled to call it. It had engrossed him for several months now. Tonight that fascination would end.

Middleton, Virginia. A forty-five-minute drive west on a slingshot path from Washington, D.C. Home to vast estates, obligatory Jaguars, and horses whose price tags could feed the residents of an entire inner-city apartment building for a year. Homes in this area sprawled across enough earth with enough splendor to qualify for their own appellation. The irony of his target's name, the Coppers, was not lost upon him.

The adrenaline rush that accompanied each job was absolutely unique. He imagined it was somewhat like how the batter felt as he nonchalantly trotted the bases, taking all the time in the world, after newly bruised leather had landed somewhere in the street. The crowd on its feet, fifty thousand pairs of eyes on one human being, all the air in the world seemingly sucked into one space, and then suddenly displaced by the arc of one man's glorious swing of the wood.

Luther took a long sweep of the area with his still sharp eyes. An occasional firefly winked back at him. Otherwise he was alone. He listened for a moment to the rise and fall of the cicadas and then that chorus faded into the background, so omnipresent was it to every person who had lived long in the area.

He pulled the car further down the blacktop road and backed onto a short dirt road that ended in a mass of thick trees. His iron-gray hair was covered with a black ski hat. His leathery face was smeared black with camouflage cream; calm, green eyes hovered

3

above a cinder block jaw. The flesh carried on his spare frame was as tight as ever. He looked like the Army Ranger he had once been. Luther got out of the car.

Crouching behind a tree, Luther surveyed his target. The Coppers, like many country estates that were not true working farms or stables, had a huge and ornate wrought iron gate set on twin brick columns but had no fencing. The grounds were accessible directly from the road or the nearby woods. Luther entered from the woods.

It took Luther two minutes to reach the edge of the cornfield adjacent to the house. The owner obviously had no need for home-grown vegetables but had apparently taken the country squire role to heart. Luther wasn't complaining, since it afforded him a hidden path almost to the front door.

He waited a few moments and then disappeared into the embracing thickness of the corn stalks.

The ground was mostly clear of debris and his tennis shoes made no sound, which was important, for any noise carried easily here. He kept his eyes straight ahead; his feet, after much practice, carefully picked their way through the slender rows, compensating for the slight unevenness of the ground. The night air was cool after the debilitating heat of another stagnant summer, but not nearly cool enough for breath to be transformed into the tiny clouds that could be seen from a distance by restless or insomniac eyes.

Luther had timed this operation several times over the past month, always stopping at the edge of the field before stepping into the front grounds and past no-man's-land. In his head, every detail had been worked and reworked hundreds of times until a precise script of movement, waiting, followed by more movement was firmly entrenched in his mind.

He crouched down at the edge of the front grounds and took one more long look around; no need to rush. No dogs to worry about, which was good. A human, no matter how young and fleet, simply could not outrun a dog. But it was the noise they made that stopped men like Luther cold. There was also no perimeter security system, probably because of the innumerable false alarms that would be caused by the large populations of deer, squirrel and raccoon roaming over the area. However, Luther would shortly be faced with a highly sophisticated defense package that he would have thirty-three seconds to disarm – and that included the ten seconds it would take him to remove the control panel.

The private security patrol had passed through the area thirty minutes earlier. The cop clones were supposed to vary their routines, making sweeps through their surveillance sectors every hour. But after a month of observations, Luther had easily discerned a pattern. He had at least three hours before another pass would be made. He wouldn't need nearly that long.

The grounds were pitch black, and thick shrubs, the lifeblood of the burglary class, clung to the brick entryway like a caterpillar nest to a tree branch. He checked each window of the house: all black, all silent. He had watched the caravan carrying the home's occupants parade out two days ago to points south, and carefully took inventory of all owners and personnel. The nearest estate was a good two miles away.

He took a deep breath. He had planned everything out, but in this business, the simple fact was that you could never account for everything.

He loosened the grips on his backpack and then glided out from the field in long, smooth strides across the lawn, and in ten seconds was facing the

5

thick, solid-wood front door with reinforced steel framing together with a locking system that was rated at the top of the charts for holding force. None of which concerned Luther in the least.

He slipped a facsimile front-door key out of his jacket pocket and inserted it into the keyhole without, however, turning it.

He listened for another few seconds. Then he slipped off his backpack and changed his shoes so there would be no traces of mud. He readied his battery-operated screwdriver, which could reveal the circuitry he needed to fool ten times faster than he could by hand.

The next piece of equipment he carefully pulled from his backpack weighed exactly six ounces, was slightly bigger than a pocket calculator and other than his daughter was the best investment he had ever made in his life. Nicknamed "Wit" by its owner, the tiny device had assisted Luther in his last three jobs without a hitch.

The five digits comprising this home's security code had already been supplied to Luther and programmed into his computer. Their proper sequence was still a mystery to him, but that obstacle would have to be eradicated by his tiny metal, wire and microchip companion if he wanted to avoid the ear-piercing shriek that would instantly emit from the four sound cannons planted at each corner of the ten-thousand-square-foot fortress he was invading. Then would follow the police call dialed by the nameless computer he would battle in a few moments. The home also had pressure-sensitive windows and floor plates, in addition to tamperproof door magnets. All of which would mean nothing if Wit could tear the correct code sequence from the alarm system's grasp.

He eyed the key in the door and with a practiced motion hooked Wit to his harness belt so that it hung

6

easily against his side. The key turned effortlessly in the lock and Luther prepared to block out the next sound that he would hear, the low beep of the security system that warned of impending doom for the intruder if the correct answer was not fed into it in the allotted time and not a millisecond later.

He replaced his black leather gloves with a pair of more nimble plastic ones that had a second layer of padding on the fingertips and palms. It was not his practice to leave any evidence behind. Luther took one deep breath, then opened the portal. The shrill beep of the security system met him instantly. He quickly moved into the enormous foyer and confronted the alarm panel.

The automatic screwdriver whirled noiselessly; the six metal pieces dropped into Luther's hands and then were deposited in a carrier on his belt. Slender wires attached to Wit flashed against the sliver of moonlight seeping through the window beside the door, and then Luther, probing momentarily like a surgeon through a patient's chest cavity, found the correct spot, clipped the strands into place and then flipped on the power source to his companion.

From across the foyer, a slash of crimson stared down at him. The infrared detector had already locked on Luther's thermal offset. As the seconds ticked down, it patiently waited for the security system's "brain" to pronounce the intruder friend or foe.

Faster than the eye could follow, the numbers flashed across Wit's digital screen in neon amber; the allotted time blinked down in a small box at the top-right-hand corner of the same screen.

Five seconds elapsed and then the numbers 5, 13, 9, 3 and 11 appeared on Wit's tiny glass face and locked.

The beep stopped on cue as the security system was

disarmed, the red light flashed off and was replaced with the friendly green, and Luther was in business. He removed the wires, screwed the plate back on and repacked his equipment, then carefully locked the front door.

The master bedroom was on the third floor, which could be reached by an elevator down the main first-floor hallway to the right, but Luther chose the stairs instead. The less dependent he was on anything he did not have complete control over the better. Getting stuck in an elevator for several weeks was not part of his battle plan.

He looked at the detector in the corner of the ceiling as its rectangular mouth smiled at him, its surveillance arc asleep for now. Then he headed up the staircase.

The master bedroom door was not locked. In a few seconds he had his low-power, nonglare work lamp set up and took a moment to look around. The green glow from a second control panel mounted next to the bedroom door broke the darkness.

The house itself had been built within the last five years; Luther had checked the records at the courthouse and had even managed to gain access to a set of blueprints of the place from the planning commissioner's office, it being large enough to require special blessing from the local government as though they would ever actually deny the rich their wishes.

There were no surprises in the building plans. It was a big, solid house more than worth the multi-million-dollar price tag that had been paid in cash by its owner.

Indeed, Luther had visited this home once before, in broad daylight, with people everywhere. He had been in this very room and he had seen what he needed to see. And that was why he was here tonight.

Six-inch crown molding peered down at him as he

knelt next to the gigantic, canopied bed. Next to the bed was a nightstand. On it were a small silver clock, the newest romance novel of the day and an antique silver-plated letter opener with a thick leather handle.

Everything about the place was big and expensive. There were three walk-in closets in the room, each about the size of Luther's living room. Two were occupied by women's clothes and shoes and purses and every other female accoutrement one could rationally or irrationally spend money on. Luther glanced at the framed prints on the nightstand and wryly observed the twenty-something "little woman" next to the seventy-something husband.

There were many types of lotteries in the world and not all of them state-run.

Several of the photos showed off the lady of the house's proportions to almost maximum degree, and his quick examination of the closet revealed that her dressing pleasures leaned to the downright sleazy.

He looked up at the full-length mirror, studying the ornate carvings around its edges. He next surveyed the sides. It was a heavy, nifty bit of work, built right into the wall, or so it seemed, but Luther knew that hinges were carefully hidden into the slight recess six inches from the top and bottom.

Luther looked back at the mirror. He had the distinct advantage of having seen a target like this full-length model a couple of years ago although he hadn't planned to crack it. But you didn't ignore a second golden egg just because you had the first in hand, and that second golden egg had been worth about fifty thou'. The prize on the other side of this private looking glass he figured would be about ten times that.

Using brute force and the aid of a crowbar he could overcome the locking system built into the mirror's carvings but that would take precious time. And, more than that, it would leave behind obvious signs of the place having been violated. And although the house was supposed to be empty for the next several weeks, one never knew. When he left the Coppers there would be no obvious evidence he had ever been there. Even upon their return the owners might not check the vault for some time. In any event, he did not have to take the hard route.

He walked quickly over to the large-screen TV located against one wall of the vast chamber. The area was set up as a sitting room with matching chintz-covered chairs and a large coffee table. Luther looked at the three remotes lying there. One to work the TV, one for the VCR and one that would cut his night's work by ninety percent. Each had a brand name on it, each looked pretty much like the other, but a quick experiment showed that two worked their appropriate apparatus and one did not.

He walked back across the room, pointed the control at the mirror and pushed the lone red button located at the bottom of the hardware. Ordinarily that action meant the VCR was recording. Tonight, in this room, it meant the bank was opening for business for its one fortunate customer.

Luther watched the door swing open easily, silently on the now-revealed no-maintenance hinges. From long habit, he replaced the control exactly where it had been, pulled a collapsible duffel bag out of his backpack and entered the vault.

As his light swept through the darkness he was surprised to see an upholstered chair sitting in the middle of the room, which looked to be about six feet by six feet. On the chair's arm rested an identical remote, obviously a safeguard against being locked in by accident. Then his eyes took in the shelves down each side.

The cash, bundled neatly, went in first, then the

contents of the slender boxes that were definitely not costume jewelry. Luther counted about two hundred thousand dollars' worth of negotiable bonds and other securities, and two small boxes of antique coins and another of stamps, including one of an inverted figure that made Luther swallow hard. He ignored the blank checks and the boxes full of legal documents, which were worthless to him. His quick assessment ended at almost two million dollars, probably more.

He took one more look around, taking care not to miss any stray nook. The walls were thick — he figured they had to be fireproof, or as fireproof as man could make something. The place wasn't hermetically sealed; the air was fresh, not stale. Somebody could stay in here for days.

The limo moved quickly down the road followed by the van, each driver expert enough to accomplish this feat without the benefit of headlights.

Inside the spacious back seat of the limo were a man and two women, one of whom was close to being drunk and who was doing her best to undress the man and herself right there, despite the gentle defensive efforts of her victim.

The other woman sat across from them tight-lipped, ostensibly trying to ignore the ridiculous spectacle, which included girlish giggling and much panting, but in reality she closely observed every detail of the pair's efforts. Her focus was on a large book that sat open in her lap where appointments and notes battled each other for space and the attention of the male sitting across from her, who took the opportunity of his companion wrenching off her spike heels to pour himself another drink. His capacity for alcohol was enormous. He could drink twice the amount he had already consumed tonight and there would be no outward signs, no slurring of speech or impeded motor functions – which would have been deadly for a man in his position.

She had to admire him, his obsessions, his truly raw edges, while at the same time his being able to project an image to the world that cried out purity and strength, normalcy but, at the same time, greatness. Every woman in America was in love with him, enamored with his classic good looks, immense self-assurance and also what he represented, for all of them. And he returned that universal admiration with a passion, however misplaced, that astonished her.

Unfortunately, that passion had never pointed itself in her direction despite her subtle messages, the touches that lingered a shade too long; how she maneuvered to see him first thing in the morning when she looked her best, the sexual references used in their strategy sessions. But until that time came – and it would come, she kept telling herself – she would be patient.

She looked out the window. This was taking too long; it threw everything else off. Her mouth curled up in displeasure.

Luther heard the vehicles enter the front drive. He flitted to a window and followed the mini-caravan as it went around back, where it would be hidden from view from the front drive. He counted four people alighting from the limo, one from the van. His mind scrolled swiftly through possible identities. Too small a party for it to be the owners of the house. Too many for it to be someone simply checking on the place. He could not make out any faces. For one ironic instant Luther debated whether the home was destined to be burgled twice on the same night. But that was too enormous a coincidence. In this business, like a lot of others, you played the percentages. Besides, criminals did not march up to their targets wearing clothing more suitable for a night on the town.

He thought quickly as noises filtered up to him, presumably from outside the rear of the house. It took him a second to realize that his retreat was cut off and to calculate what his plan of action would be.

Grabbing his bag, he raced to the alarm panel next to the bedroom door and activated the home's security system, silently thanking his memory for numbers. Then Luther slipped across to the vault and entered it, carefully closing the door behind him. He pushed himself as far back into the little room as he could. Now he had to wait.

He cursed his misfortune; everything had been going so smoothly. Then he shook his head clear, forced himself to breathe regularly. It was like flying. The longer you did it, the greater your chance of something bad happening. He would just have to hope that the house's most recent arrivals would have no need to make a deposit in the private bank he was now occupying.

A burst of laughter and then the drum of voices filtered up to him, together with the loud beep from the alarm system, which sounded like a jet plane screeching directly over his head. Apparently there was slight confusion about the security code. A bead of sweat appeared on Luther's forehead as he envisioned the alarm exploding and the police wanting to examine every inch of the house just in case, starting with his little roost.

He wondered how he would react as he listened to the mirrored door being opened, a light blazing in, without the slightest possibility of missing him. The strange faces peering in, the drawn guns, the reading of his rights. He almost laughed. Trapped like a fucking rat, nowhere to go. He hadn't had a cigarette in almost thirty years, but now he desperately craved a smoke. He put his bag down quietly and slowly let his legs out straight so they wouldn't go to sleep.

Heavy steps on the oak plank staircase. Whoever they were they didn't care who knew they were there. Luther counted four, possibly five. They turned left and headed his way.

The door to the bedroom opened with a slight squeak. Luther searched his mind. Everything had been picked up or put back in its place. He'd only touched the remote, and he had replaced it right in line with the slight dust pattern. Now Luther could only hear three voices, a man and two women. One of the females sounded drunk, the other was all business. Then Ms. Business disappeared, the door closed but wasn't locked, and Ms. Drunk and the man were alone. Where were the others? Where had Ms. Business gone? The giggles continued. Footsteps came closer to the mirror. Luther scrunched down in the corner as far as he could, hoping that the chair would shield him from view but knowing that it couldn't possibly.

Then a burst of light hit him right in the eyes and he almost gasped at the suddenness of his little world going from inky black to broad daylight. He blinked rapidly to adjust to the new level of brightness, his pupils going from almost full dilation to pinpoints in seconds. But there were no screams, no faces, no guns.

Finally, after a full minute had passed, Luther peered around the corner of the chair and received another shock. The vault door seemed to have disappeared; he was staring right into the goddamned room. He almost fell backward but caught himself. Luther suddenly understood what the chair was for.

He recognized both of the people in the room. The woman he had seen tonight already, in the photos: the little wife with the hooker taste in clothes.

The man he knew for an altogether different reason; he certainly wasn't the master of this house. Luther slowly shook his head in amazement and let out his breath. His hands shook and a queasiness crept over him. He fought back the grip of nausea and stared into the bedroom.

The vault door also served as a one-way mirror. With the light on outside and darkness in his little space, it was as though he were watching a giant TV screen.

Then he saw it and a fist of breath kicked out of his lungs: the diamond necklace on the woman's neck. Two hundred thou' to his practiced eye, maybe more. And just the sort of bauble one would routinely put away in a home vault before retiring for the evening. Then his lungs relaxed as he watched her take the piece off and casually drop it on the floor.

His fear receded enough to where he rose and inched over to the chair and slowly eased himself into it. So the old man sat here and watched his little woman get her brains screwed out by a procession of men. From the looks of her, Luther figured that some members of that procession included young guys making minimum wage or hanging on to freedom by the width of a green card. But her gentleman caller tonight was in an altogether different class.

He looked around, his ears focused for any sound of the other inhabitants of the house. But what could he really do? In over thirty years of active larceny, he had never encountered anything like this, so he decided to do the only thing he could. With only an inch of glass separating him from absolute destruction, he settled down quietly into the deep leather and waited.

TWO

Three blocks from the broad white bulk of the United States Capitol, Jack Graham opened the front door of his apartment, threw his overcoat on the floor and went straight to the fridge. Beer in hand he flopped down on the threadbare couch in his living room. His eyes quickly perused the tiny room as he took a drink. Quite a difference from where he'd just been. He let the beer stand in his mouth and then swallowed. The muscles of his square jaw tensed and then relaxed. The nagging prickles of doubt slowly drained away, but they would reappear; they always did.

Another important dinner party with Jennifer, his soon-to-be wife, and her family and circle of social and business acquaintances. People at that level of sophistication apparently didn't have mere friends they hung with. Everyone served a particular function, the whole being greater than the sum of the parts. Or at least that was the intent, although Jack had his own opinion on the matter.

Industry and finance had been well represented, brandishing names Jack read about in the *Wall Street Journal* before he chucked it for the sports pages to see how the 'Skins or Bullets were doing. The politicos had been out in full force, scrounging future votes and current dollars. The group was rounded out by the ubiquitous lawyers of which Jack was one, the occasional doctor to show ties to the old ways and a couple of public-interest types to demonstrate that

16

the powers that be had sympathy for the plight of the ordinary.

He finished the beer and flipped on the TV. His shoes came off, and the forty-dollar patterned socks his fiancée had bought for him were carelessly flung over the back of the lamp shade. Given time she'd have him in two-hundred-dollar braces with matching hand-painted ties. Shit! Rubbing his toes, he seriously considered a second beer. The TV tried but failed to hold his interest. He pushed his thick, dark hair out of his eyes and focused for the thousandth time on where his life was hurtling, seemingly with the speed of the space shuttle.

Jennifer's company limo had driven the two of them to her Northwest Washington townhouse where Jack would probably move after the wedding; she detested his place. The wedding was barely six months off, apparently no time at all by a bride's standards, and he was sitting here having severe second thoughts.

Jennifer Ryce Baldwin possessed instant head-turning beauty to such a degree that the women stared as often as the men. She was also smart and accomplished, came from serious money and was intent on marrying Jack. Her father ran one of the largest development companies in the country. Shopping centers, office buildings, radio stations, entire subdivisions, you name it, he was in it, and doing better than just about anyone else. Her paternal great-grandfather was one of the original Midwest manufacturing tycoons, and her mother's family had once owned a large chunk of downtown Boston. The gods had smiled early and often on Jennifer Baldwin. There wasn't one guy Jack knew who wasn't jealous as hell of him.

He squirmed in his chair and tried to rub a kink out of his shoulder. He hadn't worked out in a week. His six-foot-one body, even at thirty-two, had the same hard edge it had enjoyed all through high school where he was a man among boys in virtually every sport offered, and in college where the competition was a lot rougher but where he still managed to make first-string varsity as a heavyweight wrestler and first-team All-Academic. That combination had gotten him into the University of Virginia School of Law, where he made *Law Review*, graduated near the top of his class and promptly settled down as a public defender in the District of Columbia's criminal justice system.

His classmates had all grabbed the big-firm option out of law school. They had routinely called with phone numbers of psychiatrists who could help coax him out of his insanity. He smiled and then went and grabbed that second beer. The fridge was now empty.

Jack's first year as a PD had been rough as he learned the ropes, losing more than he won. As time went on, he graduated to the more serious crimes. And as he poured every ounce of youthful energy, raw talent and common sense he had into each of those cases, the tide began to turn.

And then he started kicking some serious ass in court.

He discovered he was a natural at the role, as talented at cross-examination as he had been at throwing men much bigger than he across a two-inch-thick mat. He was respected, liked as an attorney if you could believe that.

Then he had met Jennifer at a Bar function. She was vice president of development and marketing at Baldwin Enterprises. Dynamic in presence, she had the added skill of making whomever she was talking to feel important; their opinions were listened to if not necessarily followed. She was a beauty who had no need to rely solely on that asset.

When you got past the eye-catching looks, there was a lot more there. Or seemed to be. Jack would have been less than human had he not been attracted to her. And she had made it clear, early on, that the attraction was mutual. While being ostensibly impressed at his dedication in defending the rights of those accused of crimes in the Capital City, little by little Jennifer had convinced Jack that he had done his bit for the poor, dumb and unfortunate, and that maybe he should start thinking about himself and his future, and that maybe she wanted to be a part of that future. When he finally left PD, the U.S. Attorney's office had given him quite a send-off party, and good riddance. That should have told him then and there that there were a lot more of the poor, dumb and unfortunate who needed his help. He didn't expect to ever top the thrill he had felt being a PD; he figured times like that came around once in life and then they were gone. It was time to move on; even little boys like Jack Graham had to grow up someday. Maybe it was just his time.

He turned off the TV, grabbed a bag of corn chips and went to his bedroom, stepping over the piles of dirty laundry strewn in front of the doorway. He couldn't blame Jennifer for not liking his place; he was a slob. But what bothered him was the dead certainty, that, even spotless, Jennifer would not consent to live here. For one thing it was in the wrong neighborhood; Capitol Hill to be sure, but not a gentrified part of Capitol Hill, actually not even close.

Then there was the size. Her townhouse must have run five thousand square feet, not counting the live-in maid's quarters and the two-car garage that housed her Jag and brand new Range Rover, as if anybody living in D.C., with its traffic-strangled roads, needed a vehicle capable of driving up the vertical side of a twenty-thousand-foot-high mountain.

He had four rooms if you counted the bathroom. He reached his bedroom, stripped off his clothes and dropped into bed. Across the room, on a small plaque that had once hung in his office at work until he had grown embarrassed looking at it, was the announcement of his joining Patton, Shaw & Lord. PS&L was the Capital City's number-one corporate firm. Legal caterer to hundreds of blue-chip companies, including his soon-to-be father-in-law's, representing a multimillion-dollar account that he was credited with bringing to the firm and that, in turn, guaranteed him a partnership at the next review. Partnerships at Patton, Shaw were worth, on average, at least half a million dollars a year. That was tip money for the Baldwins, but then he wasn't a Baldwin. At least not yet.

He pulled the blanket over him. The building's insulation left a lot to be desired. He popped a couple of aspirin and washed them down with the rest of a Coke that was sitting on his nightstand, then looked around the cramped, messy bedroom. It reminded him of his room growing up. It was a warm, friendly memory. Homes should look lived in; they should always give way to the screams of kids as they dashed from room to room in search of new adventures, of fresh objects to break.

That was the other thing with Jennifer: she had made it clear that the sound of little feet was a distant project that was far from certain. Her career at her father's company was first and foremost in her mind and heart – maybe more so, Jack felt, than he was.

He rolled over and tried to close his eyes. The wind pushed against the window and he glanced in that direction. He looked away, but then with a resigned air, his eyes drifted back over to the box.

It held part of his collection of old trophies and awards from high school and college. But those items

20

were not the object of his focus. In the semidarkness he reached out a long arm for the framed photo, decided against it, and then changed his mind again.

He pulled it out. This had almost become a ritual. He never had to worry about his fiancée stumbling onto this particular possession of his because she absolutely refused to enter his bedroom for longer than a minute. Whenever they slid between the sheets it was either at her place, where Jack would lie on the bed staring up at the twelve-foot ceiling where a mural of ancient horsemen and young maidens shared space while Jennifer amused herself until she collapsed and then rolled over for him to finish on top of her. Or at her parents' place in the country where the ceilings were even higher and the murals had been taken from some thirteenth-century church in Rome, all of which made Jack feel that God was watching him being ridden by the beautiful and absolutely naked Jennifer Ryce Baldwin and that he would languish in eternal hell for those few moments of visceral pleasure.

The woman in the photo had silky brown hair that curled slightly at the ends. Her smile looked up at Jack and he remembered the day he had taken the picture.

A bike ride far into the countryside of Albemarle County. He was just starting law school; she was in her second year of college at Mr. Jefferson's university. It was only their third date but it was like they had never lived without each other.

Kate Whitney.

He said the name slowly; his hand instinctively traced the curves of her smile, the lone dimple right above the left cheek that gave her face a slightly lopsided look. The almond-shaped cheekbones bordered a dainty nose that sloped toward a pair of sensual lips. The chin was sharp and screamed out

21

"stubborn." Jack moved back up the face and stopped at the large teardrop-shaped eyes that always seemed full of mischief.

Jack rolled back over and lay the photo on his chest so that she stared directly at him. He could never think of Kate without seeing an image of her father, with his quick wit and crooked smile.

Jack had often visited Luther Whitney at his little row house in an Arlington neighborhood that had seen better days. They spent hours drinking beer and telling stories, mostly Luther telling and Jack listening.

Kate never visited her father, and he never attempted to contact her. Jack had found his identity almost by accident, and despite Kate's objections, Jack had wanted to get to know the man. It was a rare thing for her face to hold anything but a smile, but that was one thing she never smiled about.

After he graduated they moved to D.C. and she enrolled in law school at Georgetown. Life seemed idyllic. She came to his first few trials as he worked the butterflies from his stomach and the squeak from his throat and tried to remember which counsel table to sit at. But as the seriousness of the crimes his clients were accused of committing grew, her enthusiasm diminished.

They had split up his first year in practice.

The reasons were simple: she couldn't understand why he had chosen to represent people who broke the law, and she could not tolerate that he liked her father.

At the very last breath of their lives together he remembered sitting with her in this very room and asking, pleading, for her not to leave. But she had and that was four years ago, and he hadn't seen or heard from her since.

He knew that she had taken a job with the

Commonwealth Attorney's office in Alexandria, Virginia, where she was no doubt busily putting former clients of his behind bars for stomping on the laws of her adopted state. Other than that Kate Whitney was a stranger to him.

But lying there with her staring at him with a smile that told him a million things that he had never learned from the woman he was supposed to marry in six months, Jack wondered if Kate would remain a stranger to him; whether his life was destined to become far more complicated than he ever intended. He grabbed the phone and dialed.

Four rings and he heard the voice. It had an edge that he didn't remember, or maybe it was new. The beep came and he started to leave a message, something funny, right out of the blue, but then right on cue he got nervous and quickly hung up, his hands shaking, his breathing accelerated. He shook his head. Jesus Christ! He had done five murder one cases and he was shaking like a goddamned sixteen-year-old sucking up the courage to call his first date.

Jack put the picture away and imagined what Kate was doing right that very minute. Probably still in her office pondering over how many years to take off somebody's life.

Then Jack wondered about Luther. Was he at this very minute on the wrong side of someone's door-step? Or leaving with another bundle of financial joy slung over his back?

What a family, Luther and Kate Whitney. So different and so much the same. As focused a pair as he had ever encountered, but their respective focuses occupied different galaxies. That last night, after Kate had walked out of his life, he had gone around to Luther's to say good-bye and to drink a last beer. They had sat in the small well-tended garden, watching the clematis and ivy cling to the fence; the scent of lilacs and roses lay thick like a net over them.

The old man had taken it all right, asked few questions, and wished Jack well. Some things did not work out; Luther understood that as well as anyone. But as Jack left that night he had noticed the glistening in the old man's eyes – and then the door closed on that part of his life.

Jack finally put out the light and closed his eyes with the knowledge that another tomorrow was close upon him. His pot of gold, his once-in-a-lifetime payoff, was one day closer to reality. It did not make for easy sleep.

THREE

As Luther stared through the glass, the thought struck him that the two made a very attractive couple. It was an absurd opinion to have under the circumstances, but that didn't make the conclusion any less valid. The man was tall, handsome, a very distinguished mid-forties. The woman could not have ventured far into her twenties; the hair was full and golden, the face oval and lovely, with a pair of enormous deep blue eyes that now looked up lovingly into the man's elegant countenance. He touched her smooth cheek; she nestled her lips against his hand.

The man had two tumblers and filled them with the contents of the bottle he had brought with him. He handed the woman one. After a clink of glasses, their eyes firmly set on each other, he finished his drink in one swallow while she only managed a small sip of hers. Glasses put down, they embraced in the middle of the room. His hands slid down her backside and then back up to the bare shoulders. Her arms and shoulders were tanned and well-toned. He grasped her limbs admiringly as he leaned down to kiss her neck.

Luther averted his eyes, embarrassed to be viewing this very personal encounter. A strange emotion to have when he was still clearly in danger of being caught. But he was not so old that he could not appreciate the tenderness, the passion that was slowly unfolding in front of him.

As he raised his eyes up, he had to smile. The couple was now engaged in a slow dance around the room. The man was obviously well-practiced at the endeavor; his partner was less so, but he gently led her through the simple paces until they again ended up beside the bed.

The man paused to fill his glass again and then quickly drained it. The bottle was now empty. As his arms encircled her once more, she leaned into him, pulled at his coat, started to undo his tie. The man's hands drifted to the zipper of her dress and slowly headed south. The black dress slid down and she slowly stepped out of it, revealing black panties and thigh-high stockings, but no bra.

She had the sort of body that made other women who didn't instantly jealous. Every curve was where it was supposed to be. Her waist Luther could have encircled with both hands touching. As she turned to the side to slide out of her stockings, Luther observed that the breasts were large, round and full. The legs were lean and defined, probably from hours of daily exercise under the watchful eyes of a personal trainer.

The man quickly undressed down to his boxers and sat on the side of the bed watching the woman as she took her time slipping out of her underwear. Her rear end was round and firm and creamy white against the backdrop of a flawless tan. With her last piece of clothing shed, a smile cut across the man's face. The white teeth were straight and thick. Despite the alcohol, his eyes seemed clear and focused.

She smiled at his attention and slowly advanced. As she drew within his reach, his long arms gripped her, pulled her to him. She rubbed up and down against his chest.

Again, Luther began to avert his eyes, wishing more than anything else that this spectacle would soon be over and that these people would leave. It

26

would only take him a few minutes to return to his car, and this night would be filed away in his memory as a unique, if potentially disastrous, experience.

That's when he saw the man grip the woman's buttocks hard and then slap them, again and again. Luther winced in vicarious pain at the repeated blows; the white skin now glowed red. But either the woman was too drunk to feel the pain or she enjoyed this sort of treatment, because her smile didn't fade. Luther felt his gut clinch again as the man's fingers dug into the soft flesh.

The man's mouth danced across her chest; she ran her finger through his thick hair as she positioned her body inside his legs. She closed her eyes, her mouth gathered into a contented smile; she arched her head back. Then she opened her eyes and attacked his mouth with hers.

His strong fingers moved up from the abused buttocks and started to gently massage her back. Then he dug in hard until she winced and pulled back from him. She half-smiled and he stopped as she touched his fingers with hers. He turned his attention back to her breasts and suckled them. Her eyes closed once again, as her breathing turned perceptibly to a low moan. The man moved his attention again to her neck. His eyes were wide open, looking across at where Luther sat but with no idea of his presence.

Luther stared at the man, at those eyes, and didn't like what he saw. Pools of darkness surrounded by red, like some sinister planet seen through a telescope. The thought struck him that the naked woman was in the grip of something not so gentle, not so loving as she probably anticipated.

The woman finally grew impatient and pushed her lover down on the bed. Her legs straddled the man, giving Luther a view from behind that should have been reserved for her gynecologist and husband. She

27

hoisted herself up, but then with a sudden burst of energy he roughly pushed her aside and went on top of her, grabbing her legs and lifting them up until they were perpendicular with the bed.

Luther stiffened in his chair at the man's next movement. He grabbed her by the neck and jerked her up, pulling her head between his legs. The suddenness of the act made her gasp, her mouth a bare inch from him there. Then he laughed and threw her back down. Dazed for a moment, she finally managed a weak smile and sat up on her elbows as he towered over her. He grabbed his erection with one hand, spreading her wide with the other. As she lay placidly back to accept him, he stared wildly at her.

But instead of plunging between her legs, he grabbed her breasts and squeezed, apparently a little too hard, because, finally, Luther heard a yelp of pain and the woman abruptly slapped the man. He let go and then slapped her back, viciously, and Luther saw a patch of blood emerge at the corner of her mouth and spill onto the thick, lipstick-coated lips.

"You fucking bastard." She rolled off the bed and sat on the floor rubbing her mouth, tasting her blood, her drunken brain momentarily lucid. The first words Luther had clearly heard spoken the entire night hit his brain like a sledgehammer. He stood up, inched toward the glass.

The man grinned. Luther froze when he saw it. It was more like the snarl of a wild animal close to a kill than a human being.

"Fucking bastard," she said again, a little more quietly, the words slurred. As she stood up he grabbed her arm, twisted it, and she fell hard to the floor. The man sat on the bed and looked down triumphantly.

His breathing accelerating, Luther stood before the

glass, his hands clenching and unclenching as he continued to watch and hoped that the other people would come back. He eyed the remote on the chair and then his eyes shot back to the bedroom. The woman had raised herself half off the floor, the wind slowly coming back to her. The romantic feelings she had been experiencing had vanished. Luther could see that in her body movements, wary and deliberate. Her companion apparently failed to notice the change in her movements and the flash of anger in the blue eyes, or else he would not have stood up and put out a hand for her to take, which she did.

The man's smile abruptly vanished as her knee caught him squarely between the legs, doubling him over and ending any arousal he had been experiencing. As he crumpled to the floor, no sound came from his lips, except for his labored breathing while she grabbed her panties and started to put them on.

He caught her ankle, threw her to the floor, her underwear halfway up her legs.

"You little cunt." The words came out in short gasps as he tried to get his breath back, all the time holding on to that ankle, drawing her closer to him.

She kicked at him, again and again. Her feet thudded against his rib cage, but still he hung on. "You fucking little whore," he said.

At the menace he heard in those words, Luther stepped toward the glass, one of his hands flying to its smooth surface as if to reach through it, to grab the man, make him let go.

The man painfully dragged himself up and his look made Luther's flesh turn cold.

The man's hands gripped the woman's throat.

Her brain, clouded by the alcohol, snapped back to high gear. Her eyes, now completely filled with fear, darted to the left and right as the pressure on her neck increased and her breath started to weaken. Her fingers clawed at his arms, scratching deeply.

Luther saw the blood rise to the man's skin where she attacked him but his grip did not loosen.

She kicked and jerked her body, but he was almost twice her weight; her attacker didn't budge.

Luther again looked at the remote. He could open the door. He could stop this. But his legs would not move. He stared helplessly through the glass, sweat poured from his forehead, every pore in his body seemed to be erupting; his breath came in short bursts as his chest heaved. He placed both hands against the glass.

Luther's breath stopped as the woman fixed on the nightstand for an instant. Then, with a frantic motion, she grabbed the letter opener, and with one blinding stroke she slashed the man's arm.

He grunted in pain, let go and grabbed his bloody arm. For one terrible instant he looked down at his wound, almost in disbelief that he had been damaged like that. Pierced by this woman.

When the man looked back up, Luther could almost feel the murderous snarl before it escaped from the man's lips.

And then the man hit her, harder than Luther had seen any man hit a woman. The hard fist connected with the soft flesh and blood flew from her nose and mouth.

Whether it was all the booze she had consumed or what, Luther didn't know, but the blow that ordinarily would have crippled a person merely incensed her. With convulsive strength she managed to stagger up. As she turned toward the mirror, Luther watched the horror in her face as she suddenly viewed the abrupt destruction of her beauty. Eyes widening in disbelief, she touched the swollen nose; one finger dropped down and probed the loosened teeth. She had become a smeared portrait, her major attribute had vanished.

She turned around to face the man, and Luther saw the muscles in her back tense so hard they looked like small pieces of wood. With lightning quickness, she again slammed her foot into the man's groin. Instantly the man was weak again, his limbs useless as nausea overcame him. He collapsed to the floor, rolled over onto his back, moaning. His knees curled upward, his hand protectively at his crotch.

With blood streaming down her face, with eyes that had gone from stark horror to homicidal in an instant, the woman dropped to her knees beside him and raised the letter opener high above her head.

Luther grabbed the remote, took a step toward the door, his finger almost on the button.

The man, seeing his life about to end as the letter opener plunged toward his chest, screamed with every bit of strength he had left. The call did not go unheeded.

His body frozen in place, Luther's eyes darted to the bedroom door as it flew open.

Two men, hair cropped short, crisp business suits not concealing impressive physiques, burst into the room, guns drawn. Before Luther could take another step they had assessed the situation and made their decision.

Both guns fired almost simultaneously.

Kate Whitney sat in her office going over the file one more time.

The guy had four priors, and had been arrested but ultimately not charged on six other occasions because witnesses had been too frightened to talk or had ended up in trash Dumpsters. He was a walking time bomb ready to explode on another victim, all of whom had been women.

The current charge was murder during the commission of robbery and rape, which met the criteria for capital murder under Virginia's laws. And this time she decided to go for the home run: death. She had never asked for it before, but if anybody deserved it, this guy did, and the commonwealth was not squeamish about authorizing it. Why allow him life when he had cruelly and savagely ended the one given to a nineteen-year-old college student who made the mistake of going to a shopping mall in broad daylight to pick up some nylons and a new pair of shoes?

Kate rubbed her eyes and, using a rubber band from the pile on her desk, pulled her hair back into a rough ponytail. She looked around her small, plain office; the case files were piled high around the room and for the millionth time she wondered if it would ever stop. Of course it wouldn't. If anything it would get worse, and she could only do what she could do to stem the flow of blood. She would start with the execution of Roger Simmons, Jr., twenty-two years old, and as hardened a criminal as she had ever confronted, and she had already faced an army of them in her as yet short career. She remembered the look he had given her that day in court. It was a countenance totally without remorse or caring or any other positive emotion. It was also a face without hope, an observation substantiated by his background history, which read like a horror story of a childhood. But that was not her problem. It seemed like the only one that wasn't.

She shook her head and checked her watch: well after midnight. She went to pour some more coffee; her focus was starting to wander. The last staff attorney had left five hours ago. The cleaning crew had been gone for three. She moved down the hallway in her stocking feet to the kitchen. If Charlie

Manson were out and doing his thing now, he'd be one of her milder cases; an amateur compared to the monsters roaming loose today.

Cup of coffee in hand, she walked back into her office and paused for a moment to look at her reflection in the window. With her job looks were really unimportant; hell, she hadn't been on a date in over a year. But she couldn't pull her eyes away. She was tall and slender, perhaps too skinny in certain areas, but her routine of running four miles every day had not changed while her caloric intake had steadily dwindled. Mostly she subsisted on bad coffee and crackers, although she limited herself to two cigarettes a day and was hoping with luck to quit altogether.

She felt guilty about the abuse her body was taking with the endless hours and stress of moving from one horrific case to another, but what was she supposed to do? Quit because she didn't look like the women on the cover of *Cosmopolitan*? She consoled herself with the fact that their job twenty-four hours a day was to make themselves look good. Hers was to ensure that people who broke the law, who hurt others, were punished. Under any criteria she reasoned she was doing far more productive things with her life.

She swiped at her own mane; it needed to be cut, but where was the time to do that? The face was still relatively unmarked by the burden she found increasingly difficult to carry. Her twenty-nine-year-old face, after four years of nineteen-hour days and countless trials, had held its own. She sighed as she realized that probably would not last. In college she had been the gracious recipient of turned heads, the cause of raised heartbeats and cold sweats. But as she got ready to enter her thirties, she realized that what she had taken for granted for so many years, that what she had, in fact, derided on so many occasions, would not be with her that much longer. And like so many things you took for granted or dismissed as unimportant, being able to quiet a room by your mere entrance was one she knew she was going to miss.

That her looks had remained strong over the last few years was remarkable considering she had done relatively little to preserve them. Good genes, that must be it; she was fortunate. But then she thought of her father and decided that she wasn't very lucky at all in the genes department. A man who stole from others and then pretended to live a normal life. A man who deceived everyone, including his wife and daughter. A man you could not depend on to be there.

She sat at her desk, took a quick sip of the hot coffee, poured in more sugar and looked at Mr. Simmons while she stirred the black depths of her nighttime stimulus.

She picked up the phone, called home to check messages. There were five, two from other lawyers, one from the policeman she would put on the stand against Mr. Simmons and one from a staff investigator who liked to call her at odd hours with mostly useless information. She should change her telephone number. The last message was a hang-up. But she could hear very low breathing on the end, she could almost make out a word or two. Something in the sound was familiar, but she couldn't place it. People with nothing better to do.

The coffee flowed through her veins, the file came back into focus. She glanced up at her little bookshelf. On top was an old photo of her deceased mother and ten-year-old Kate. Cut out from the picture was Luther Whitney. A big gap next to mother and daughter. A big nothing.

"Jesus fucking Christ!" The President of the United States sat up, one hand covering his limp and damaged privates, the other holding the letter opener that a moment before was to have been the instrument of his death. It had more than just his blood on it now. "Jesus fucking Christ, Bill, you fucking killed her!" The target of his barrage stooped to help him up while his companion checked the woman's condition: a perfunctory examination, considering two heavy-caliber bullets had blown through her brain.

"I'm sorry, sir, there wasn't time. I'm sorry, sir."

Bill Burton had been a Secret Service agent for twelve years, and a Maryland state trooper for eight years before that, and one of his rounds had just blown apart a beautiful young woman's head. Despite all his intense training, he was shaking like a pre-schooler just awakened from a nightmare.

He had killed before in the line of duty: a routine traffic stop gone wrong. But the deceased had been a four-time loser with a serious vendetta against uniformed officers and wielding a Glock semiautomatic pistol in a sincere attempt to lift Burton's head from his shoulders.

He looked down at the small, naked body and thought he would be sick. His partner, Tim Collin, looked across at him, grabbed his arm. Burton swallowed hard and nodded his head. He would make it.

They carefully helped up Alan J. Richmond, President of the United States, a political hero and leader to young, middle-aged and old alike, but now simply naked and drunk. The President looked up at them, the initial horror finally passing as the alcohol worked its effects. "She's dead?" The words were a little slurred; the eyes seemed to roll back in the head like loose marbles.

"Yes, sir," Collin answered crisply. You didn't let a question from the President go unanswered, drunk or not.

Burton hung back now. He glanced at the woman again and then looked back at the President. That was their job, his job. Protect the goddamned President. Whatever it took, that life must not end, not like that. Not stuck like a pig by some drunken bitch.

The President's mouth curled up into what looked like a smile, although neither Collin nor Burton would remember it that way later. The President started to rise.

"Where are my clothes?" he demanded.

"Right here, sir." Burton, snapping back to attention, stooped to pick up the clothes. They were heavily spotted — everything in the room seemed to be — with her.

"Well, get me up, and get me ready, goddammit. I've got a speech to give for somebody, somewhere, don't I?" He laughed shrilly. Burton looked at Collin and Collin looked at Burton. They both watched as the President passed out on the bed.

At the sound of the explosions, Chief of Staff Gloria Russell had been in the bathroom on the first floor, as far away from that room as she could get.

She had accompanied the President on many of these assignations, but rather than growing used to them, they disgusted her more each time. To imagine her boss, the most powerful man on the face of the earth, bedding all these celebrity whores, these political groupies. It was beyond comprehension, and yet she had almost learned to ignore it. Almost.

She had pulled her pantyhose back up, grabbed her purse, flung open the door, run down the hallway and even in heels took the steps two at a time. When she reached the bedroom door Agent Burton stopped her.

"Ma'am, you don't want to see this, it's not pretty."

She pushed past him and then stopped. Her first thought was to run back out, down the stairs, into the limo, out of there, out of the state, out of the miserable country. She wasn't sorry for Christy Sullivan, who'd wanted to get screwed by the President. That had been her goal for the last two years. Well, sometimes you don't get what you want; sometimes you get a lot more.

Russell steadied herself and faced off with Agent Collin.

"What the hell happened?"

Tim Collin was young, tough and devoted to the man he was assigned to protect. He was trained to die defending the President, and there was no question in his mind that if the time came he would. Several years had passed since he had tackled an assailant in the parking lot of a shopping center where the then presidential candidate Alan Richmond had been making an appearance. Collin had had the potential assassin down on the asphalt and completely immobile before the guy had even gotten his gun fully out of his pocket, before anyone else had even reacted. To Collin, his only mission in life was to protect Alan Richmond.

It took Agent Collin one minute to report the facts to Russell in succinct, cohesive sentences. Burton solemnly confirmed the account.

"It was either him or her, Ms. Russell. There was no other way to cut it." Burton instinctively glanced at the President, who still lay on the bed oblivious to anything. They had covered the more strategic portion of his body with a sheet.

"Do you mean to tell me you heard nothing? No

sounds of violence before, before this?" She waved at the mess of the room.

The agents looked at each other. They had heard many sounds emanating from bedrooms where their boss happened to be. Some might be construed as violent, some not. But everybody had always come out okay before.

"Nothing unusual," Burton replied. "Then we heard the President scream and we went in. That knife was maybe three inches from going into his chest. Only thing fast enough was a bullet."

He stood as erect as he could and looked her right in the eye. He and Collin had done their job, and this woman wasn't going to tell them otherwise. No blame would be put on his shoulders.

"There was a goddamned knife in the room?" She looked at Burton incredulously.

"If it was up to me, the President wouldn't go out on these, these little excursions. Half the time he won't let us check anything out beforehand. We didn't get a chance to scope the room." He looked at her. "He's the President, ma'am," he added, for good measure, as if that justified everything. And for Russell it usually did, a fact Burton was well aware of.

Russell looked around the room, taking in everything. She had been a tenured professor of political science at Stanford with a national reputation before answering the call in Alan Richmond's quest for the presidency. He was such a powerful force, everybody wanted to jump on his bandwagon.

Currently Chief of Staff, with serious talk of becoming Secretary of State if Richmond won re-election, which everyone expected him to do with ease. Who knew? Maybe a Richmond-Russell ticket might be in the making. They made a brilliant combination. She was the strategist, he was the consummate campaigner. Their future grew brighter every day. But now? Now she had a corpse and a drunken President inside a home that was supposed to be vacant.

She felt the express train coming to a halt. Then her mind snapped back. Not over this little piece of human garbage. Not ever!

Burton stirred. "You want me to call the police now, ma'am?"

Russell looked at him like he had lost his mind. "Burton, let me remind you that our job is to protect the President's interests at all times and nothing – absolutely nothing – takes precedence over that. Is that clear?"

"Ma'am, the lady's dead. I think we—"

"That's right. You and Collin shot the woman, and she's dead." After exploding from Russell's mouth, the words hung in the air. Collin rubbed his fingers together; a hand went instinctively to his holstered weapon. He stared at the late Mrs. Sullivan as if he could will her back to life.

Burton flexed his burly shoulders, moved an inch closer to Russell so that the significant height difference was at its maximum.

"If we hadn't fired, the President would be dead. That's our job. To keep the President safe and sound."

"Right again, Burton. And now that you have prevented his death, how do you intend to explain to the police and the President's wife and your superiors, and the lawyers and the media and the Congress and the financial markets and the country and the rest of the goddamned world, why the President was here? What he was doing while he was here? And the circumstances that led up to you and Agent Collin having to shoot the wife of one of the wealthiest and most influential men in the United States? Because if you call the police, if you call anybody, that is exactly what you will have to do. Now if you are prepared to accept full responsibility for that undertaking, then pick up that phone over there and make that call."

Burton's face changed color. He backed up a step, his superior size useless to him now. Collin was frozen, watching the two square off. He had never seen anyone talk that way to Bill Burton. The big man could have snapped Russell's neck with a lazy thrust of his arm.

Burton looked down at the corpse one more time. How could you explain that so that everybody came out all right? The answer was simple: you couldn't.

Russell watched his face carefully. Burton looked back at her. His eyes twitched perceptibly; they would not meet hers now. She had won. She smiled benignly and nodded. The show was hers to run.

"Go make some coffee, a whole pot," she ordered Burton, momentarily relishing this switching of roles. "And then stay by the front door just in case we get any late-night visitors.

"Collin, go to the van, and talk to Johnson and Varney. Don't tell them anything about this. For now just tell them there was an accident, but that the President's okay. That's all. And that they're to stay put. Understood? I'll call when I want you. I need to think this out."

Burton and Collin nodded and headed out. Neither had been trained to ignore orders so authoritatively given. And Burton didn't want to be calling the shots on this one. They couldn't pay him enough to do that.

Luther hadn't moved since the shots had blown apart the woman's head. He was afraid to. His feelings of shock had finally passed, but he found his eyes continually wandering to the floor and to what had

40

once been a living, breathing human being. In all his years as a criminal he had only seen one other person killed. A thrice-convicted pedophile whose spinal cord had collided with a four-inch shiv wielded by an unsympathetic fellow inmate. The emotions sweeping over him now were totally different, as though he were the sole passenger on a ship that had sailed into a foreign harbor. Nothing looked or seemed familiar at all. Any sound now would do him no good, but he slowly sat back down before his trembling legs gave way.

He watched as Russell moved around the room, stooped next to the dead woman, but did not touch her. Next she picked up the letter opener, holding it by the end of the blade with a handkerchief she pulled from her pocket. She stared long and hard at the object that had almost ended her boss's life and had played a major role in ending someone else's. She carefully put the letter opener in her leather purse, which she had placed on the nightstand, and put the handkerchief back in her pocket. She glanced briefly at the contorted flesh that had recently been Christine Sullivan.

She had to admire the way Richmond accomplished his extracurricular activities. All his "companions" were women of wealth and social position, and all were married. This ensured that no exposé of his adulterous behavior would appear in any of the tabloids. The women he bedded had as much to lose if not more than he, and they understood that fact very well.

And the press. Russell smiled. In this day and age the President lived under a never-ending barrage of scrutiny. He couldn't pee, smoke a cigar or belch without the public knowing all of the most intimate details. Or so the public thought. And that was based largely on the overestimation of the press and their abilities to nudge out every morsel of a story from its hiding place. What they failed to understand was that while the office of the President might have lost some of its enormous power over the years as the problems of a troubled globe soared beyond the ability of any one person to confront them on an equal basis, the President was surrounded by absolutely loyal and supremely capable people. People whose skill level at covert activities were in another league from the polished, cookie-cutter journalists whose idea of trailing down a tough story was asking puffball questions of a congressman who was more than willing to talk for the benefit of the evening news coverage. It was a fact that, if he so desired, President Alan Richmond could move about without fear that anyone would be successful in tracking his where-abouts. He could even disappear from public view for as long as he wished, although that was the antithesis of what a successful politician hoped to accomplish in a day's work. And that privilege boiled down to one common denominator.

The Secret Service. They were the best of the best. This elite group had proved it time and again over the years, as they had in planning this most recent activity.

A little after noon, Christy Sullivan had walked out of her beauty salon in Upper Northwest. After walking one block she had stepped into the foyer of an apartment building and thirty seconds later she had walked out encased in a full-length hooded cloak pulled from her bag. Sunglasses covered her eyes. She had walked for several blocks, randomly window-shopping, then taken a redline Metro train to Metro Center. Exiting the Metro she had walked two more blocks and entered an alley between two buildings scheduled for demolition. Two minutes later, a car with tinted windows had emerged from the alley.

Collin had been driving. Christy Sullivan was in the back seat. She had been sequestered in a safe place with Bill Burton until the President had been able to join her later that night.

The Sullivan estate had been chosen as the perfect spot for the planned interlude because, ironically, her home in the country was the last place anyone would expect Christy Sullivan to be. And Russell knew it would also be perfectly empty, guarded by a security system that was no barrier to their plans.

Russell sat down in a chair and closed her eyes. Yes, she had two of the most capable members of the Secret Service in this house with her. And, for the first time, that fact troubled the Chief of Staff. The four agents with her and the President tonight had been handpicked, out of the approximately one hundred agents assigned to the presidential detail, by the President himself for these little activities. They were all loyal and highly skilled. They took care of the President and held their tongues, regardless of what was asked of them. Up until tonight President Richmond's fascination with married women had spawned no overwhelming dilemmas. But tonight's events clearly threatened all of that. Russell shook her head as she forced herself to think of a plan of action.

Luther studied the face. It was intelligent, attractive but also a very hard face. You could almost see the mental maneuvering as the forehead alternately wrinkled and then went lax. Time slipped by and she didn't budge. Then Gloria Russell's eyes opened and moved across the room, not missing any detail.

Luther involuntarily shrank back as her gaze swept by him like a searchlight across a prison-yard. Then her eyes came to the bed and stopped. For a long minute she stared at the sleeping man, and then she got a look on her face that Luther could not figure

43

out. It was halfway between a smile and a grimace.

She got up, moved to the bed and looked down at the man. A Man of the People, or so the people thought. A Man for the Ages. He did not look so great right now. His body was half on the bed, legs spread, feet nearly touching the floor; an awkward position to say the least when one was wearing no clothes.

She ran her eyes up and down the President's body, lingering on some points, an activity that was amazing to Luther considering what was lying on the floor. Before Gloria Russell had entered the room and faced off with Burton, Luther had expected to hear sirens and to be sitting there watching policemen and detectives, medical examiners and even spin doctors swarming everywhere; with news trucks piling up in vast columns outside. Obviously, this woman had a different plan.

Luther had seen Gloria Russell on CNN and the major networks, and countless times in the papers. Her features were distinctive. A long, aquiline nose set between high cheekbones, the gift from a Cherokee ancestor. The hair was raven black and hung straight, stopping at her shoulders. The eyes were big and so dark a blue that they resembled the deepest of ocean water, twin pools of danger for the careless and unwary.

Luther carefully maneuvered in the chair. Watching the woman in front of a stately fireplace inside the White House pontificating on the latest political concerns was one thing. Watching her move through a room containing a corpse and examining a drunk, naked man who was the leader of the Free World was an entirely different matter. It was a spectacle Luther did not want to watch anymore but he could not pull his eyes away.

Russell glanced at the door, walked quickly across

the room, took out her handkerchief, and closed and locked it. She swiftly returned to again stare down at the President. Her hand went out and for a moment Luther cringed in anticipation, but she simply stroked the President's face. Luther relaxed, but then stiffened again as her hand moved down to his chest, lingering momentarily on the thick hair, and then dropped still lower to his flat stomach, which rose and fell evenly in his deep sleep.

Then her hand moved lower and she slowly pulled the sheet away and let it drop to the floor. Her hand reached down to his crotch and held there. Then she glanced at the door again and knelt down in front of the President. Now Luther had to close his eyes. He did not share the peculiar spectator interests of the house's owner.

Several long minutes passed, and then Luther opened his eyes.

Gloria Russell was now shedding her pantyhose, laying them neatly on a chair. Then she carefully climbed on top of the slumbering President.

Luther closed his eyes again. He wondered if they could hear the bed squeak downstairs. Probably not, as it was a very large house. And even if they did, what could they do?

Ten minutes later Luther heard a small, involuntary gasp from the man, and a low moan from the woman. But Luther kept his eyes closed. He wasn't sure why. It seemed to be from a combination of raw fear and disgust at the disrespect shown to the dead woman.

When Luther finally opened his eyes, Russell was staring directly at him. His heart stopped for a moment until his brain told him it was okay. She quickly slipped on her pantyhose. Then, in confident, even strokes, she reapplied her lipstick in the looking glass.

A smile clung to her face; the cheeks were flushed.

45

She looked younger. Luther glanced at the President. He had returned to a deep sleep, the last twenty minutes probably filed away by his mind as an especially realistic and pleasant dream. Luther looked back at Russell.

It was unnerving to see this woman smile directly at him, in this room of death, without knowing he was there. There was power in that woman's face. And a look Luther had already seen once in this room. This woman, too, was dangerous.

"I want this entire place sanitized, except for that." Russell pointed to the late Mrs. Sullivan. "Wait a minute. He was probably all over her. Burton, I want you to check every inch of her body, and anything that looks remotely like it doesn't belong there I want you to make disappear. Then put her clothes on."

Hands gloved, Burton moved forward to carry out this order.

Collin sat next to the President, forcing another cup of coffee down the man's throat. The caffeine would help clear away the grogginess, but only the passage of time would clean the slate completely. Russell sat down next to him. She took the President's hand in hers. He was fully clothed now although his hair was in disarray. His arm hurt, but they had bandaged it as best they could. He was in excellent health; it would heal quickly.

"Mr. President? Alan? *Alan*?" Russell gripped his face and pointed it toward her.

Had he sensed what she had done to him? She doubted it. He had so desperately wanted to get laid tonight. Wanted to be inside a woman. She had given him her body, no questions asked. Technically she had committed rape. Realistically she was confident she had fulfilled many a male's dream. It didn't matter if he had no recollection of the event, of her sacrifice.

46

But he would damn sure know what she was going to do for him now.

The President's eyes came in and out of focus. Collin rubbed his neck. He was coming around. Russell glanced at her watch. Two o'clock in the morning. They had to get back. She slapped his face, not hard, but enough to get his attention. She felt Collin stiffen. God, these guys had tunnel vision.

"Alan, did you have sex with her?"

"Wha . . ."

"Did you have sex with her?"

"Wha . . . No. Don't think so. Don't remem . . ."

"Give him some more coffee, pour it down his damned throat if you have to, but get him sober." Collin nodded and went to work. Russell walked over to Burton, whose gloved hands were dexterously examining every inch of the late Mrs. Sullivan.

Burton had been involved in numerous police investigations. He knew exactly what detectives looked for and where they looked for it. He never imagined himself using that specialized knowledge to inhibit an investigation, but then he had never imagined anything like this ever happening either.

He looked around the room, his mind calculating which areas would need to be gone over, what other rooms they had used. They could do nothing about the marks on the woman's throat and other microscopic physical evidence that was no doubt imbedded in her skin. The Medical Examiner would pick those up regardless of what they tried to do. However, none of those things could be realistically traced to the President unless the police identified the President as a suspect, which was pretty much beyond the realm of possibility.

The incongruity of attempted strangulation of a small woman with death caused by gunshot was

47

something they would have to leave to the police's imagination.

Burton turned his attention back to the deceased and started to carefully slide her underwear up her legs. He felt a tap on his shoulder.

"Check her."

Burton looked up. He started to say something.

"Check her!" Russell's eyebrows were arched. Burton had seen her do that a million times with the White House staff. They were all terrified of her. He wasn't afraid of her, but he was smart enough to cover his ass whenever she was around. He slowly did as he was told. Then he positioned the body exactly as it had fallen. He reported back with a single shake of his head.

"Are you sure?" Russell looked unconvinced, although she knew from her interlude with the President that chances were he had not entered the woman, or that if he had he hadn't finished. But there might be traces. It was scary as hell, the things they could determine these days from the tiniest specimens.

"I'm not a goddamned ob-gyn. I didn't see anything and I think I would have, but I don't carry a microscope around with me."

Russell would have to let that one go. There was still a lot to do and not much time.

"Did Johnson and Varney say anything?"

Collin looked over from where the President was ingesting his fourth cup of coffee. "They're wondering what the hell's going on, if that's what you mean."

"You didn't te—"

"I told them what you said to tell them and that's all, ma'am." He looked at her. "They're good men, Ms. Russell. They've been with the President since the campaign. They're not going to do anything to mess things up, okay?"

48

Russell rewarded Collin with a smile. A good-looking kid and, more important, a loyal member of the President's personal guard; he would be very useful to her. Burton might be a problem. But she had a strong trump card: he and Collin had pulled the trigger, maybe in the line of duty, but who really knew? Bottom line: they too were in this all the way.

Luther watched the activity with an appreciation that he felt guilty about under the circumstances. These men were good: methodical, careful, thought things through, and didn't miss anything. Dedicated lawmen and professional criminals were not so different. The skills, the techniques were much the same, just the focus was different, but then the focus made all the difference, didn't it?

The woman was now completely dressed, lying exactly where she had fallen. Collin was finishing with her fingernails. A solution had been injected under each, and a small suction device had cleaned away traces of skin and other incriminating remnants.

The bed had been stripped and remade; the evidence-laden sheets were already packed in a duffel bag for their ultimate destination in a furnace. Collin had already scoped the downstairs area.

Everything any of them had touched, except for one item, had been wiped clean. Burton was now vacuuming parts of the carpet and he would be the last one to leave, backing out, as he painstakingly extinguished their trail.

Earlier Luther had watched the agents ransack the room. Their obvious goal made him smile in spite of himself. Burglary. The necklace had been deposited in a bag along with her plethora of rings. They would make it appear as if the woman had surprised a burglar in her house and he had killed her, not knowing that six feet away a real-life burglar was watching and listening to everything they were doing.

An eyewitness!

Luther had never been an eyewitness to a burglary other than those he had committed. Criminals hated eyewitnesses. These people would kill Luther if they knew he was there; there was no question about that. An elderly criminal, a three-time loser, was not much to sacrifice for the Man of the People.

The President, still groggy but with Burton's aid, slowly made his way out of the room. Russell watched them go. She did not notice Collin frantically searching the room. Finally, his sharp eyes fixed on Russell's purse on the nightstand. Poking out from the bag was about an inch of the letter opener's handle. Using a plastic bag, Collin quickly pulled out the letter opener and prepared to wipe it off. Luther involuntarily jerked as he watched Russell race over and grab Collin's hand.

"Don't do that, Collin."

Collin wasn't as sharp as Burton, and certainly wasn't in Russell's league. He looked puzzled.

"This has his prints all over it, ma'am. Hers too, plus some other stuff if you know what I mean — it's leather, it's soaked right in."

"Agent Collin, I was retained by the President as his strategic and tactical planner. What appears to you an obvious choice appears to me to require much more thought and deliberation. Until that analysis has been completed you will not wipe that object down. You will put it in a proper container, and then you will give it to me."

Collin started to protest but Russell's menacing stare cut him off. He dutifully bagged the letter opener and handed it to her.

"Please be careful with that, Ms. Russell."

"Tim, I am always careful."

She rewarded him with another smile. He smiled back. She had never called him by his first name before; he had been unsure if she even knew it. He also observed, and not for the first time, that the Chief of Staff was a very good-looking woman.

"Yes, ma'am." He began to pack up the equipment.

"Tim?"

He looked back at her. She moved toward him, looked down, and then her eyes caught his. She spoke in low tones; she almost seemed embarrassed, Collin felt.

"Tim, this is a very unique situation we're faced with. I need to feel my way a little bit. Do you understand?"

Collin nodded. "I'd call this a unique situation. Scared the hell out of me when I saw that blade about to go into the President's chest."

She touched his arm. Her fingernails were long and perfectly manicured. She held up the letter opener. "We need to keep this between us, Tim. Okay? Not the President. Not even Burton."

"I don't know—"

She gripped his hand. "Tim, I really need your support on this. The President has no idea what happened and I don't think Burton is looking at this too rationally right now. I need someone I can depend on. I need you, Tim. This is too important. You know that, don't you? I wouldn't ask you if I didn't think you could handle it."

He smiled at the compliment, then looked squarely at her.

"Okay, Ms. Russell. Whatever you say."

As Collin finished packing up, Russell looked at the bloody seven-inch piece of metal that had come so close to ending her political aspirations. If the President had been killed, there could have been no

51

cover-up. An ugly word — cover-up — but often necessary in the world of high politics. She shivered slightly at the thought of the headlines. "PRESIDENT FOUND DEAD IN BEDROOM OF CLOSE FRIEND'S HOME. WIFE ARRESTED IN SLAYING. CHIEF OF STAFF GLORIA RUSSELL HELD RESPONSIBLE BY PARTY LEADERS." But that had not happened. Would not happen.

This thing she held in her hand was worth more than a mountain of weapons-grade plutonium, more than the total oil production of Saudi Arabia.

With this in her possession, who knew? Perhaps even a *Russell*-Richmond ticket? The possibilities were absolutely infinite.

She smiled and put the plastic bag inside her purse.

The scream made Luther whip his head around. The pain shot through his neck and he almost cried out.

The President ran into the bedroom. He was wide-eyed, but still half-drunk. The memory of the last few hours had come back like a Boeing 747 landing on his head.

Burton ran up behind him. The President started toward the body; Russell dropped her purse on the nightstand, and she and Collin met him halfway.

"Goddammit! She's dead. I killed her. Oh sweet Jesus help me. I killed her!" He screamed and then cried and then screamed again. He tried to push through the wall in front of him but was still too weak. Burton pulled at the President from behind.

Then with convulsive strength, Richmond tore loose and launched himself across the room and slammed into the wall, rolling into the nightstand. And finally the President of the United States crumpled to the floor and curled up like a fetus, whimpering, next to the woman he had intended to have sex with that night.

Luther watched in disgust. He rubbed at his neck and slowly shook his head. The incredibility of the entire night's events was becoming too much to endure.

The President slowly sat up. Burton looked like Luther felt, but said nothing. Collin eyed Russell for instructions. Russell caught the look and smugly accepted this subtle changing of the guard.

"Gloria?"

"Yes, Alan?"

Luther had seen the way Russell had looked at the letter opener. He also knew something now that no one else in the room knew.

"Will it be okay? Make it okay, Gloria. Please. Oh God, Gloria!"

She rested her hand on his shoulder in her most reassuring manner, as she had done across hundreds of thousands of miles of campaign dust. "Everything's under control, Alan. I've got *everything* under control."

The President was far too intoxicated to catch the meaning, but she didn't really care.

Burton touched his radio earpiece, listening intently for a moment. He turned to Russell.

"We better get the hell out of here. Varney just scoped a patrol car coming down the road."

"The alarm . . . ?" Russell looked puzzled.

Burton shook his head. "It's probably just a rent-a-cop on routine, but if he sees something . . ." He didn't need to say anything else.

Leaving in a limo in this land of wealth was the best cover they could have. Russell thanked God for the routine she had developed for using rented limos without the regular drivers for these little adventures. The names on all the forms were dummies, the rental fee and deposit paid in cash, the car picked up and dropped off after hours. There were no faces

53

associated with the transaction. The car would be sterilized. That would be a dead end for the police if they ever snagged that line, which was highly doubtful.

"Let's go!" Russell was now slightly panicked.

The President was helped up. Russell went out with him. Collin grabbed the bags. Then stopped cold.

Luther swallowed hard.

Collin turned back, grabbed Russell's purse off the nightstand and headed out.

Burton started up the small vacuum, completed the room and then left, closing the door and turning off the light.

Luther's world returned to inky darkness.

This was the first time he had been alone in the room with the dead woman. The rest of them had apparently grown used to the bloody figure lying on the floor, unconsciously stepping over or around the now inanimate object. But Luther had not grown accustomed to the death barely eight feet away.

He could no longer see the pile of stained clothing and the lifeless body inside of them, but he knew it was there. "Sleazy rich bitch" would probably be her informal epitaph. And, yes, she had cheated on her husband, not that he seemed to care about that. But she hadn't deserved to die like that. He would've killed her, there was no question about that. Except for her swift counterattack, the President would've committed murder.

The Secret Service men he could not really fault. That was their job and they did it. She had picked the wrong man to attempt to kill in the heat of whatever she had been feeling. Maybe it was better. If her hand had been a little faster or the agents' response a little slower, she might be spending the rest of her life in jail. Or she'd probably get death for killing a President.

Luther sat down in the chair. His legs were almost numb. He forced himself to relax. Soon he would be getting the hell out of there. He needed to be ready to run.

He had a lot to think through, considering that they were unwittingly setting up Luther Whitney to be the number-one suspect in what would no doubt be deemed a heinous and gruesome crime. The wealth of the victim would demand that enormous law enforcement resources be expended in finding the perpetrator. But there was no way they would be looking to 1600 Pennsylvania Avenue for the answer. They would search elsewhere, and despite Luther's intense preparations, they might very well find him. He was good, very good, but then he had never faced the types of forces that would be unleashed to solve this crime.

He quickly thought back through his entire plan leading up to tonight. He could think of no obvious holes, but it was the not-so-obvious ones that usually did you in. He swallowed, curled and uncurled his fingers, stretched his legs to calm himself. One thing at a time. He still wasn't out of here. Many things could go wrong, and one or two undoubtedly would.

He would wait two more minutes. He ticked off the seconds in his head, visualized them loading the car. They would probably wait for any further sight or sound of the patrol car before heading out.

He carefully opened his bag. Inside were much of the contents of this room. He had almost forgotten that he had come here to steal and in fact had stolen. His car was a good quarter mile away. He thanked God he had quit smoking all those years ago. He would need every ounce of lung capacity he could muster. How many Secret Service Agents was he confronted with? At least four. Shit!

The mirrored door slowly opened and Luther stepped out into the room. He hit the remote one more time and then tossed it back onto the chair as the door swung closed.

He eyed the window. He had already planned an alternate escape through that aperture. A hundred-foot coil of extremely strong nylon rope, knotted every six inches, was in his bag.

He made a wide berth around the body, careful not to step in any of the crimson, the position of which he had programmed into his memory. He glanced only once at the remains of Christine Sullivan. Her life could not be brought back. Luther was now faced with keeping his own intact.

It took him a few seconds to reach the nightstand, and probe down behind it.

Luther's fingers clutched the plastic bag. The President's collision with the furniture had toppled Gloria Russell's purse on its side. The plastic bag and its immensely valuable occupant had fallen out and slid down behind the nightstand.

Luther's finger nudged the blade of the letter opener through the plastic before secreting it in his duffel bag. He went quickly over to the window and carefully peered out. The limo and van were still there. That wasn't good.

He went across to the other side of the room, took out his rope, secured it under the leg of the enormously heavy chest of drawers, and ran the line across to the other window, which would drop him at the opposite end of the house, hidden from the road. He carefully opened the window, praying for a well-oiled track, and was rewarded.

He played out the rope and watched it snake down the brick sides of the house.

*

Gloria Russell looked up at the massive face of the mansion. There was real money there. Money and position that Christine Sullivan did not deserve. She had won it with her boobs and artfully displayed ass and her trashy mouth that had somehow inspired the elderly Walter Sullivan, awakening some emotion buried deep within his complex depths. In six months he would not miss her anymore. His world of rock-solid wealth and power would hurtle on.

Then it struck her.

Russell was halfway out of the limo before Collin caught her arm. He held up the leather bag she had bought in Georgetown for a hundred bucks and was now worth incalculably more to her. She settled back down in her seat, her breath normalized. She smiled, almost blushed at Collin.

The President, slumped in a semicatatonic state, didn't notice the exchange.

Then Russell peeked inside her bag, just to be sure. Her mouth dropped open, her hands frantically tore through the few contents of the bag. It took all her willpower not to shriek out loud as she stared horror-stricken at the young agent. The letter opener was not there. It must still be in the house.

Collin tore back up the stairs, a thoroughly confused Burton racing after him.

Luther was halfway down the wall when he heard them coming.

Ten more feet.

They burst in the bedroom door.

Six more feet.

Stunned, the two Secret Service men spotted the rope; Burton dove for it.

Two more feet, and Luther let go, hitting the ground running.

Burton flew to the window. Collin threw the

57

nightstand aside: nothing. He joined Burton at the window. Luther had already disappeared around the corner. Burton started to head out the window. Collin stopped him. The way they had come would be faster.

They bolted out the door.

Luther crashed through the cornfield, no longer concerned with leaving a trail, now only worried about surviving. The bag slowed him down slightly, but he had worked too hard over the last several months to walk away empty-handed.

He exploded out from the friendly cover of the crops and hit the most dangerous phase of his flight: a hundred yards of open field. The moon had disappeared behind thickening clouds and there were no streetlights in the country; in his black clothing he would be almost impossible to spot. But the human eye was best at spotting movement in the darkness, and he was moving as fast as he could.

The two secret service agents stopped momentarily at the van. They emerged with Agent Varney and raced across the field.

Russell rolled down the window and watched them, shock on her face. Even the President was somewhat awake, but she quickly calmed him and he returned to his half-slumber.

Collin and Burton slipped on their night-vision goggles and their view instantly resembled a crude computer game. Thermal images registered in red, everything else was dark green.

Agent Travis Varney, tall and rangy, and only vaguely aware of what was going on, was ahead of them. He ran with the easy motion of the collegiate miler he used to be.

In the Service three years, Varney was single,

committed entirely to his profession, and looked to Burton as a father figure to replace the one killed in Vietnam. They were looking for someone who had done something in that house. Something that involved the President and that therefore involved him. Varney pitied whoever he was chasing if he caught up to him.

Luther could hear the sounds of the men behind him. They had recovered faster than he had thought. His head start had dwindled but it still should be enough. They had made a big mistake by not jumping in the van and running him down. They had to have known he would have transportation. It wasn't like he would have coptered in. But he was grateful that they weren't quite as smart as they probably should have been. If they had he would not be alive to see the sun come up.

He took a shortcut through a path in the woods, spotted on his last walk-through. It gained him about a minute. His breath came in quick bursts, like machine-gun fire. His clothes felt heavy on him; as in a child's dream, his legs seemed to move in slow motion.

Finally he broke free from the trees, and he could see his car and was again grateful for having taken the precaution to back in.

A hundred yards behind, a thermal figure other than Varney's finally came alive on Burton's and Collin's screens. A man running, and running hard. Their hands flew to their shoulder holsters. Neither weapon was effective long-range but they couldn't worry about that now.

Then an engine roared to life and Burton and Collin ran like a tornado was raging at their heels.

Varney was still ahead of them and to the left. He

would have a better line of fire, but would he shoot? Something told them he would not; that was not part of his training, to fire at a fleeing person who was no longer a danger to the man he was sworn to protect. However, Varney did not know that at stake here was more than a mere beating heart. There was an entire institution that would never be the same, in addition to two Secret Service agents who were certain they had done nothing wrong, but were intelligent enough to realize that the blame would fall heavily on their shoulders.

Burton was never much of a runner, but he picked up his pace as these thoughts flew through his head, and the younger Collin was hard-pressed to keep up with him. But Burton knew it was too late. His legs started to slow down as the car exploded out and turned away from them. In moments it was already two hundred yards down the road.

Burton stopped running, dropped to his knee, aimed his gun, but all he could see was the dust kicked up by the fleeing vehicle. Then the taillights went out and in a moment he lost the target entirely.

He turned to see Collin next to him, looking down at him, the reality of the whole event starting to set in. Burton slowly got up and put his gun away. He took off his goggles; Collin did likewise.

They looked at each other.

Burton sucked air in; his limbs shook. His body was finally reacting to the recent exertions now that the adrenaline had stopped flowing. It was over, wasn't it?

Then Varney came running up. Burton was not too distraught to note with an envious twinge and a small measure of pride that the younger man wasn't even out of breath. He would see to it that Varney and Johnson didn't suffer with them. They didn't deserve that.

He and Collin would go down, but that was all. He felt bad about Collin; however, there was nothing he could do about that. But when Varney spoke, Burton's thoughts of the future went from complete and absolute doom to a small glimmer of hope.

"I got the license plate number."

"Where the hell was he?" Russell looked incredulously around the bedroom. "What? Was he under the goddamned bed?"

She tried to stare Burton down. The guy hadn't been under the bed, not in any of the closets. Burton had examined all those spaces when he was sanitizing the room. He told her so in no uncertain terms.

Burton looked at the rope and then the open window. "Jesus, it was like the guy was watching us the whole time, knew right when we left the house." Burton looked around for other possible bogeymen hovering nearby. His eyes rested on the mirror, then moved on, stopped and went back.

He looked down at the carpet in front of the mirror.

He had gone over that area repeatedly with the vacuum until it was smooth; the carpet nape, already plush and expensive, had been a good quarter inch thicker by the time he was finished. No one had walked there since they had come back into the room.

And yet now as he stooped down, his eye discerned very rough traces of footprints. He hadn't noticed them before because now the whole section was matted down, as if something had swept out. . . . He slapped on his gloves, rushed to the mirror, pulling and prying around its edges. He yelled to Collin to get some tools while Russell looked on stunned.

Burton inserted the crowbar about midway down

the side of the mirror and he and Collin threw all
their weight against the tool. The lock was not that
strong, depending on deception rather than brute
strength to safeguard its secrets.

There was a grinding sound and then a tear and a
pop and the door swung open.

Burton plunged inside with Collin right behind. A
light switch was on the wall. The room turned bright
and the men looked around.

Russell peered in, saw the chair. As she looked
around, her face froze on the inner side of the mirror
door. She was staring right at the bed. The bed where
a little while before . . . She rubbed her temples as a
searing pain ripped through her skull.

A one-way mirror.

She turned to find Burton looking over her
shoulder and through the mirror. His earlier remark
about someone watching them had just proven itself
prophetic.

Burton looked helplessly at Russell. "He must have
been right here the whole time. The whole goddamned time. I can't fucking believe this." Burton
looked at the empty shelves inside the vault. "Looks
like he took a bunch of stuff. Probably cash and
untraceables."

"Who cares about that!" Russell exploded, pointing at the mirror. "This guy saw and heard everything, and you let him get away."

"We got his license plate." Collin was hoping for
another rewarding smile. He didn't get it.

"So what? You think he's going to wait around for
us to run his tag and go knock on his door?"

Russell sat down on the bed. Her head was
spinning. If the guy had been in there he had seen
everything. She shook her head. A bad but controllable situation had suddenly become an incomprehensible disaster, and totally out of her control.

Particularly considering the information Collin had relayed to her when she had entered the bedroom.

The sonofabitch had the letter opener! Prints, blood, everything, straight to the White House.

She looked at the mirror and then at the bed, where a short time before she had been on top of the President. She instinctively pulled her jacket tighter around herself. She was suddenly sick to her stomach. She braced herself against the bedpost.

Collin emerged from the vault. "Don't forget he committed a crime being here. He can get in big-time trouble if he goes to the cops." That thought had struck the young agent while he peered around the vault.

He should have thought a little more.

Russell pushed back a strong urge to vomit. "He doesn't have to exactly go and turn himself in to cash in on this. Have you ever heard of the goddamned phone? He's probably calling the *Post* right now, *Dammit!* And then next the tabloids and by the end of the week we'll be watching him on Oprah and Sally being shot on remote from whatever little island he's retired to with his face blurred. And then comes the book and after that the movie. *Shit!*"

Russell envisioned a certain package arriving at the *Post* or the J. Edgar Hoover Building or the U.S. Attorney's office or the Senate Minority Leader's office, all possible depositories promising maximum political damage — not to mention the legal repercussions.

The note accompanying it would ask them to please match the prints on it and the blood with specimens of the President of the United States. It would sound like a joke, but they would do it. Of course they would do it. Richmond's prints were already on file. His DNA would be a match. Her body would be found, her blood would be checked

63

and they would be confronted with more questions than they could possibly have answers to.

They were dead, they were all dead. And that bastard had just been sitting in there, waiting for his chance. Not knowing that tonight would bring him the biggest payoff of his life. Nothing as simple as dollars. He would bring down a President, in flames and tatters, crashing to earth without a chance of survival. How often did someone get to do that? Woodward and Bernstein had become supermen, they could do no wrong. This topped the hell out of Watergate. This was too fucking much to deal with.

Russell barely made it to the bathroom. Burton looked over at the corpse and then back at Collin. They said nothing, their hearts pounding with increased frequency as the absolute enormity of the situation settled down on them like the stone lid of a crypt. Since they could think of nothing else to do, Burton and Collin dutifully retrieved the sanitizing equipment while Russell emptied the contents of her stomach. In an hour they were packed and gone.

The door closed quietly behind him.

Luther figured he had a couple of days at best, maybe less. He risked turning on a light and his eyes went quickly over the interior of the living room.

His life had gone from normal, or close to it, straight to horror land.

He took off the backpack, switched off the light, and stole over to the window.

Nothing – everything was quiet. Fleeing from that house had been the most nerve-racking experience of his life, worse than being overrun by screaming North Koreans. His hands still twitched. All the way back, every passing car seemed to bore its headlights into his face, searching out his guilty secret. Twice, police cars had passed him, and the sweat had poured off his forehead, his breathing constricted.

The car had been returned to the impoundment lot where Luther had "borrowed" it earlier that night. The plate would get them nowhere, but something else could.

He doubted they had gotten a look at him. Even if they had, they would only know generally his height and build. His age, race and facial features would still be a mystery, and without that they had nothing. And as fast as he had run, they probably figured him for a younger man. There was one open end, and he had thought about how to handle that on the ride back. For now, he packed up as much of the last thirty years as he could into two bags; he would not be coming back here.

He would clear out his accounts tomorrow morning; that would give him the resources to run far away from here. He had faced more than his share of danger during his long life. But the choice between going up against the President of the United States or disappearing was a no-brainer. The night's haul was safely hidden away. Three months of work for a prize that could end up getting him killed. He locked the door and disappeared into the night.

FOUR

At seven A.M. the gold–colored elevator doors opened, and Jack stepped into the meticulously decorated expanse that was Patton, Shaw's reception area.

Lucinda wasn't in yet, so the main reception desk, solid teakwood and weighing about a thousand pounds, and costing about twenty dollars for each of those pounds, was unmanned.

He walked down the broad hallways under the soft lights of the neoclassical wall sconces, turned right, and then left and in one minute opened the solid–oak door to his office. In the background, a smattering of ringing phones could be heard as the city woke up for business.

Six floors, well over one hundred thousand square feet in one of the best addresses downtown, housing over two hundred highly compensated attorneys, with a two–story library, fully equipped gymnasium, sauna, women's and men's showers and lockers, ten conference rooms, a supporting staff of several hundred and, most important, a client list coveted by every other major firm in the country, that was the empire of Patton, Shaw & Lord.

The firm had weathered the miserable end to the 1980s, and then picked up speed after the recession had finally subsided. Now it was going full–bore as many of its competitors had downsized. It was loaded with some of the best attorneys in virtually every field of law, or at least the fields that paid the best. Many had been scooped from other leading firms, enticed by signing bonuses and promises that no dollar would be spared when chasing a new piece of business.

Three senior partners had been tapped by the current administration for top-level positions. The firm had awarded them severance pay in excess of two million dollars each, with the implicit understanding that after their government stint they would be back in harness, bringing with them tens of millions of dollars in legal business from their newly forged contacts.

The firm's unwritten, but strictly adhered to, rule was that no new client matter would be accepted unless the minimum billing would exceed one hundred thousand dollars. Anything less, the management committee had decided, would be a waste of the firm's time. And they had no problem sticking to that rule, and flourishing. In the nation's capital, people came for the best and they didn't mind paying for the privilege.

The firm had only made one exception to that rule, and ironically it had been for the only client Jack had other than Baldwin. He told himself he would test that rule with increasing frequency. If he was going to stick this out, he wanted it to be on his terms as much as that was possible. He knew his victories would be small at first, but that was okay.

He sat down at his desk, opened his cup of coffee and glanced over the *Post*. Patton, Shaw & Lord had five kitchens and three full-time housekeepers with their own computers. The firm probably consumed five hundred pots of coffee a day, but Jack picked up his morning brew at the little place on the corner because he couldn't stand the stuff they used here. It was a special imported blend and cost a fortune and tasted like dirt mixed in with seaweed.

He tipped back in his chair and glanced around his

67

office. It was a good size by big-firm associate standards, about fourteen by fourteen, with a nice view up Connecticut Avenue.

At the Public Defenders Service, Jack had shared an office with another attorney and there had been no window, only a giant poster of a Hawaiian beach Jack had tacked up one repulsively cold morning. Jack had liked the coffee at PD better.

When he made partner he would get a new office, twice this size – maybe not a corner just yet, but that was definitely in the cards. With the Baldwin account he was the fourth biggest rainmaker in the firm, and the top three were all in their fifties and sixties, looking more toward the golf courses than to the inside of an office. He glanced at his watch. Time to start the meter.

He was usually one of the first ones in, but the place would soon be stirring. Patton, Shaw matched top New York firm wages, and for the big bucks, they expected big-time efforts. The clients were enormous and their legal demands were of equal size. Making a mistake in this league might mean a four-billion-dollar defense contract went down the tubes or a city declared bankruptcy.

Every associate and junior partner he knew at the firm had stomach problems; a quarter of them were in therapy of one kind or another. Jack watched their pale faces and softening bodies as they marched daily through the pristine hallways of PS&L bearing yet another Herculean legal task. That was the trade-off for compensation levels that put them in the top five percent nationwide among all professionals.

He alone among them was safe from the partnership gauntlet. Control of clients was the great equalizer in law. He had been with Patton, Shaw about a year, was a novice corporate attorney, and was accorded the respect of the most senior and experienced members of the firm.

All of that should have made him feel guilty, undeserving – and it would have if he hadn't been so miserable about the rest of his life.

He popped the final miniature doughnut into his mouth, leaned forward in his chair and opened a file. Corporate work was often monotonous and his skill level was such that his tasks were not the most exciting in the world. Reviewing ground leases, preparing UCC filings, forming limited liability companies, drafting memorandums of understanding and private placement documents, it was all in a day's work, and the days were growing longer and longer, but he was learning fast; he had to in order to survive. His courtroom skills were virtually useless to him here.

The firm traditionally did no litigation work, preferring instead to handle the more lucrative and steady corporate and tax matters. When litigation did arise it was farmed out to select, elite litigation-only firms, who in turn would refer any nontrial work that came their way to Patton, Shaw. It was an arrangement that had worked well over the years.

By lunchtime he had moved two stacks of drift from his in to his out basket, dictated three closing checklists and a couple of letters, and received four calls from Jennifer reminding him about the White House dinner they would be attending that night.

Her father was being honored as Businessman of the Year by some organization or other. It spoke volumes about the President's close nexus to big business that such an event would be worthy of a White House function. But at least Jack would get to see the man up close. Getting to meet him was probably out of the question, but then you never knew.

"Got a minute?" Barry Alvis popped his balding

head in the door. He was a senior staff associate, meaning he had been passed over for partner more than three times and in fact would never successfully complete that next step. Hardworking and bright, he was an attorney any firm would be fortunate to have. His schmooz skills and hence his client-generating prospects, however, were nil. He made a hundred sixty thousand a year, and worked hard enough to earn another twenty in bonuses each year. His wife didn't work, his kids went to private schools, he drove a late-model Beemer, was not expected to generate business and had little to complain about.

A very experienced attorney with ten years of intense and high-level transactional work behind him, he should have resented the hell out of Jack Graham, and he did.

Jack waved him in. He knew Alvis didn't like him, understood why, and didn't push it. He could take his lumps with the best of them, but then he would only allow himself to be pushed so far.

"Jack, we've got to get cranking on the Bishop merger."

Jack looked blank. That deal, a real pain in the ass, had died, or at least he thought it had. He took out a legal pad, his hands twitching.

"I thought Raymond Bishop didn't want to get into bed with TCC."

Alvis sat down, placed the fourteen-inch file he was carrying on Jack's desk and leaned back.

"Deals die, then they come back to haunt you. We need your comments on the secondary financing documents by tomorrow afternoon."

Jack almost dropped his pen. "That's fourteen agreements and over five hundred pages, Barry. When did you find out about this?"

Alvis stood up and Jack caught the beginnings of a smile tugging at the other man's face.

"Fifteen agreements, and the official page count is six hundred and thirteen pages, single-spaced, not counting exhibits. Thanks, Jack. Patton, Shaw really appreciates it." He turned back. "Oh, have a great time with the President tonight, and say hello to Ms. Baldwin."

Alvis walked out.

Jack looked at the bundle in front of him and rubbed his temples. He wondered when the little sonofabitch had really learned the Bishop deal had been resurrected. Something told him it wasn't this morning.

He checked the time. He buzzed his secretary, managed to clear his schedule for the rest of the day, picked up the eight-pound file and headed for conference room number nine, the firm's smallest and most secluded, where he could hide and work. He could do six intense hours, go to the party, come back, work all night, hit the steam room, shower and shave here, finish up the comments and have them on Alvis's desk by three, four at the latest. The little shit.

Six agreements later, Jack ate the last of his chips, finished off his Coke, pulled on his jacket and ran the ten flights down to the lobby.

The cab dropped him at his apartment. He stopped cold.

The Jag was parked in front of his building. The vanity plate SUCCESS told him his soon-to-be date for life was up there waiting. She must be upset with him. She never condescended to come to his place unless she was upset with him about something and wanted to let him know it.

He checked his watch. He was running a little late, but he was still okay. He unlocked his front door, rubbing his jaw; maybe he could get by without shaving. She was sitting on the couch, having first draped a sheet across it. He had to admit, she looked stunning; a real blue blood, whatever that meant these days. Unsmiling, she stood up and looked at him.

"You're late."

"I'm not my own boss you know."

"That's no excuse. I work too."

"Yeah, but the difference is your boss has the same last name, and is wrapped around his daughter's pretty little finger."

"Mother and Dad went on ahead. The limo will be here in twenty minutes."

"Plenty of time." Jack undressed and jumped in the shower. He pulled the curtain aside. "Jenn, can you get out my blue double-breasted?"

She walked into the bathroom, looked around in ill-concealed disgust. "The invitation said black tie."

"Black tie optional," he corrected her, rubbing the soap out of his eyes.

"Jack, don't do this. It's the White House for godsakes, it's the President."

"They give you an option, black tie or not. I'm exercising my right to forgo the black tie. Besides, I don't have a tux." He grinned at her and pulled the curtain closed.

"You were supposed to get one."

"I forgot. C'mon, Jenn, for chrissakes. Nobody's going to be watching me, nobody cares what I'll be wearing."

"Thank you, thank you very much, Jack Graham. I ask you to do one little thing."

"Do you know how much those suckers cost?"

The soap was stinging his eyes. He thought of Barry Alvis and having to work all night and having to explain that fact to Jennifer and then to her father, and his voice got angrier. "And how many times am I going to wear the goddamned thing? Once or twice a year?"

"After we're married we'll be attending a lot of

72

functions where black tie isn't optional, it's mandatory. It's a good investment."

"I'd rather put my retirement funds into baseball cards." He poked his head out again to show her he was kidding, but she wasn't there.

He rubbed a towel through his hair, wrapped it around his middle and walked into the tiny bedroom where he found a new tux hanging on the door. Jennifer appeared, smiling.

"Compliments of Baldwin Enterprises. It's an Armani. It'll look wonderful on you."

"How'd you know my size?"

"You're a perfect forty-two long. You could be a model. Jennifer Baldwin's personal male model." She wrapped her perfumed arms around his shoulders and squeezed. He felt her considerable breasts push into his back and inwardly cursed that there wasn't time to take advantage of the moment. Just once without the goddamn murals, without the cherubs and chariots, maybe it would be different.

He looked longingly at the small, untidy bed. And he had to work all night. Goddamned Barry Alvis and the wishy-washy Raymond Bishop.

Why was it every time he saw Jennifer Baldwin he hoped that things could be different between them? Different meaning better. That she would change, or he would, or they both would meet somewhere in the middle? She was so beautiful, had everything in the world going for her. Jesus, what was wrong with him anyway?

The limo moved easily through the dregs of post-rush-hour traffic. Past seven o'clock on a weeknight, downtown D.C. was pretty much deserted.

Jack looked over at his fiancée. Her light but very expensive coat didn't conceal the plunging neckline. The perfectly chiseled features were covered by flawless skin that occasionally flashed a perfect smile. Her thick auburn hair was piled high on top of her head; she usually wore it down. She looked like one of those one-name supermodels.

He moved closer to her. She smiled at him, checked her makeup, which was immaculate, and patted his hand.

He stroked her leg, slid her dress up; she pushed him away.

"Later, maybe," she whispered so the driver wouldn't hear.

Jack smiled and mouthed that later he might have a headache. She laughed and then he remembered there would be no "later" tonight.

He slumped back in the thickly padded seat and stared out the window. He had never been to the White House; Jennifer had, twice before. She didn't look nervous; he was. He tugged at his bow tie, and smoothed his hair as they turned onto Executive Drive.

The White House guards checked them methodically; Jennifer as usual got second and third looks from all of the men and women present. When she bent down to adjust her high heel, she almost spilled out of her five-thousand-dollar dress and made several White House staffers far happier men for it. Jack got the usual envious looks from the guys. Then they moved into the building and presented their engraved invitations to the Marine sergeant who escorted them through the lower-level entry corridor and then up the stairs to the East Room.

"Dammit!" The President had bent down to pick up a copy of his speech for the night's event and the pain had shot up to his shoulder. "I think it nicked a tendon, Gloria."

Gloria Russell sat in one of the wide, plush chairs

with which the President's wife had decorated the Oval Office.

The First Lady had good taste if not a lot else. She was nice to look at, but a little light in the intellect department. No challenge to the President's power, and an asset in the polls.

Her family background was impeccable: old money, old ties. The President's connection to the conservative wealth and influence segment of the country had not hurt his standing with the liberal contingent in the least, however, owing mainly to his charisma and skills at consensus-building. And his good looks, which counted for a lot more than anyone cared to admit.

A successful President had to be able to talk a good game, and this President's batting average was up there with Ted Williams's.

"I think I need to see a doctor." The President was not in the best of moods, but then neither was Russell.

"Well, Alan, then exactly how would you explain a stab wound to the White House press?"

"What the hell ever happened to doctor-patient confidentiality?"

Russell rolled her eyes. He could be so stupid sometimes.

"You're like a Fortune 500 company, Alan, everything about you is public information."

"Well, not everything."

"That remains to be seen, doesn't it? This is far from over, Alan." Russell had smoked three packs of cigarettes, and drunk two pots of coffee since last night. At any moment their world, her career, could come crashing down. The police knocking on the door. It was all she could do to keep herself from running screaming from the room. As it was, nausea continuously swept over her in vast waves. She clenched her teeth, gripped the chair. The image of total destruction would not budge from her mind.

The President scanned the copy, memorizing some, the rest he would ad-lib; his memory was phenomenal, an asset that had served him well.

"That's why I have you, Gloria, isn't it? To make it all better?"

He looked at her.

For a moment she wondered if he knew. If he knew what she had done with him. Her body stiffened and then relaxed. He couldn't know, that was impossible. She remembered his drunken pleadings; oh how a bottle of Jack could change a person.

"Of course it is, Alan, but some decisions have to be made. Some alternative strategies have to be developed depending on what we find ourselves faced with."

"I can't exactly cancel my schedule. Besides, this guy can't do anything."

Russell shook her head. "We can't be sure of that."

"Think about it! He'll have to admit to burglary to even place himself there. Can you see him trying to get on the evening news with that story? They'll put him in a rubber room in a New York minute." The President shook his head. "I'm safe. This guy cannot touch me, Gloria. Not in a million years."

They had worked out a threshold strategy on the limo ride back to town. Their position would be simple: categorical denial. They would let the absurdity of the allegation, if it ever came, do their work for them. And it was an absurd story despite the fact that it was absolutely true. Sympathy from the White House for the poor, unbalanced and admitted felon and his shamefaced family.

There was, of course, another possibility, but Russell had chosen not to address that with the

President just yet. In fact she concluded it was the more likely scenario. It was really the only thing allowing her to function.

"Stranger things have happened." She looked at him.

"The place was cleaned, right? There's nothing left to find, right, except her?" There was a hint of nervousness in his voice.

"Right." Russell licked her lips. The President didn't know that the letter opener with his prints and blood on it was now in the possession of their felonious eyewitness.

She stood up and paced. "Of course I can't speak about certain traces of sexual contact. But that wouldn't be linked to you in any event."

"Jesus, I can't even remember if we did it or not. It seems like I did."

She couldn't help smiling at his remark.

The President turned and looked at her. "What about Burton and Collin?"

"What about them?"

"Have you talked to them?" His message was clear enough.

"They have as much to lose as you, don't they, Alan?"

"As *us*, Gloria, as us." He fixed his tie in the mirror. "Any clue to the Peeping Tom?"

"Not yet; they're running the plate."

"When do you think they'll realize she's missing?"

"As warm as it's been during the day, soon I hope."

"Real funny, Gloria."

"She'll be missed, inquiries will be made. Her husband will be called, they'll go to the house. The next day, maybe two, maybe three tops."

"And then the police will investigate."

"There's nothing we can do about that."

"But you'll keep on top of it?" A trace of concern

crossed the President's brow as he thought swiftly through various scenarios. *Had he fucked Christy Sullivan? He hoped that he had. At least the night wouldn't have been a total disaster.*

"As much as we can without arousing too much suspicion."

"That's easy enough. You can use the angle that Walter Sullivan is a close friend and political ally of mine. It would be natural for me to have a personal interest in the case. Think things through, Gloria, that's what I pay you for."

And you were sleeping with his wife, Russell thought. *Some friend.*

"That rationale had already occurred to me, Alan."

She lit a cigarette, blew the smoke out slowly. That felt good. She had to keep ahead of him on this. Just one small step ahead and she would be fine. It wouldn't be easy; he was sharp, but he was also arrogant. Arrogant people habitually overestimated their own abilities and underestimated everyone else's.

"And nobody knew she was meeting you?"

"I think we can assume she was discreet, Gloria. Christy didn't have too much upstairs, her gifts were slightly lower, but she understood economics with the best of them." The President winked at his Chief of Staff. "She had about eight hundred million to lose if her husband found out she was screwing around, even with the President."

Russell knew about Walter Sullivan's odd viewing habits from the mirror and chair, but then again, for the assignations he didn't know about, didn't get to watch, who knew what his reaction would've been? Thank God it hadn't been Sullivan sitting there in the dark.

"I warned you, Alan, that one day your little extracurricular activities would get us into trouble."

78

Richmond looked at her, disappointment on his features. "Listen, you think I'm the first guy to hold this office to catch a little action on the side? Don't be so goddamned naive, Gloria. At least I'm a helluva lot more discreet than some of my predecessors. I take the responsibilities of the job . . . and I take the perks. Understand?"

Russell nervously rubbed at her neck. "Completely, Mr. President."

"So it's just this one guy, who can't do anything."

"It only takes one to bring the house of cards tumbling down."

"Yeah? Well there are a lot of people living in that house. Just remember that."

"I do, Chief, every day."

There was a knock at the door. Russell's deputy assistant leaned in. "Five minutes, sir." The President nodded and waved him off.

"Great timing on this presentation."

"Ransome Baldwin contributed heavily to your campaign, as did all of his friends."

"You don't have to explain political paybacks to me, sweetheart."

Russell stood up and moved over to him. She took his good arm, looked intently at him. On his left cheek was a small scar. A souvenir from some shrapnel during a brief stint in the Army toward the end of the Vietnam War. As his political career had taken off, the female consensus was that the tiny imperfection greatly enhanced his attractiveness. Russell found herself staring at that scar.

"Alan, I will do whatever it takes to protect your interest. You will get through this, but we need to work together. We're a team, Alan, we're a helluva team. They can't take us down, not if we act together."

The President studied her face for a brief moment,

and then rewarded her with the smile that routinely accompanied front-page headlines. He pecked her on the cheek, squeezed her against him; she clung to him.

"I love you, Gloria. You're a trouper." He picked up his speech. "It's showtime." He turned and walked out. Russell stared after his broad back, carefully rubbed at her cheek and then followed him out.

Jack looked around the overstated elegance of the immense East Room. The place was full of some of the most powerful men and women in the country. Skillful networking was taking place all around him, and all he could do was stand and gawk. He looked across the room and spied his fiancée cornering a congressman from some state out West, no doubt plying Baldwin Enterprises's needy case for the good legislator's assistance on riparian rights.

His fiancée spent much of her time gaining access to holders of power at all levels. From county commissioners to Senate Committee chairmen, Jennifer stroked the right egos, fed the right hands, and made certain that all the important players were in place when Baldwin Enterprises wanted another mammoth deal orchestrated. The doubling of the assets of her father's company during the last five years was due in no small part to her excelling at that task. In truth, what man was really safe from her?

Ransome Baldwin, all six feet five inches, thick white hair and baritone voice, made his rounds, solidly shaking hands with politicians he already owned and rubbing elbows with the few he didn't as yet.

The award ceremony had been mercifully brief. Jack glanced at his watch. He would need to be getting back to the office soon. On the way over Jennifer had mentioned a private party at the Willard Hotel at eleven. He rubbed his face. Of all the friggin' luck.

He was about to pull Jennifer aside to explain his early exit, when the President walked up to her, was joined by her father, and a moment later all three headed his way.

Jack put his drink down and cleared his throat so he wouldn't sound like a complete fool when the words stumbled out of his mouth. Jennifer and her father were talking to the President like old friends. Laughing, chatting, touching elbows like he was Cousin Ned in from Oklahoma. But this wasn't Cousin Ned, this was the President of the United States for godsakes!

"So you're the lucky fellow?" The President's smile was immediate and pleasant. They shook hands. He was as tall as Jack, and Jack admired that he had kept trim and fit with a job like his.

"Jack Graham, Mr. President. It's an honor to meet you, sir."

"I feel like I already know you, Jack, Jennifer's told me so much about you. Most of it good." He grinned.

"Jack's a partner at Patton, Shaw & Lord." Jennifer still held on to the President's arm. She looked at Jack and smiled a cutesy smile.

"Well, not a partner yet, Jenn."

"Matter of time is all." Ransome Baldwin's voice boomed out. "With Baldwin Enterprises as a client, you could name your price at any firm in this country. Don't you forget that. Don't let Sandy Lord pull the wool over your eyes."

"Listen to him, Jack. The voice of experience." The President raised his glass and then involuntarily jerked it back. Jennifer stumbled, letting go of his arm.

81

"I'm sorry, Jennifer. Too much tennis. Damn arm's giving me problems again. Well, Ransome, you look like you've got yourself a fine protégé here."

"Hell, he'll have to fight my daughter for the empire. Maybe Jack can be queen and Jenn can be the king. How's that for equal rights?" Ransome laughed a big laugh that swept everybody up with it.

Jack felt himself redden. "I'm just a lawyer, Ransome; I'm not necessarily looking for an empty throne to occupy. There are other things to do in life."

Jack picked up his drink. This wasn't exactly going as well as he would have liked. He felt on the defensive. Jack crunched an ice cube. And what did Ransome Baldwin really think about his future son-in-law? Especially right now? The point was Jack didn't really care.

Ransome stopped laughing and eyed him steadily. Jennifer cocked her head the way she did when he said something she thought was inappropriate, which was most of the time. The President looked at all three of them, smiled quickly and excused himself. He went over to the corner where a woman was standing.

Jack watched him go. He had seen the woman on TV, defending the President's position on a myriad of issues. Gloria Russell did not look very happy right now, but with all the crises in the world, happiness was probably a rare commodity in her line of work.

That was an afterthought. Jack had met the President, had shaken hands with him. He hoped his arm got better. He pulled Jennifer aside and made his regrets. She was not pleased.

"This is totally unacceptable, Jack. Do you realize how special a night this is for Daddy?"

"Hey, I'm just a working stiff. You know? Billable hours?"

"That's ridiculous! And you know it. No one at that firm can make those demands of you, let alone some nothing associate."

"Jenn, it's not that big a deal. I had a great time. Your dad got his little award. Now it's time to go back to work. Alvis is okay. He's kicking my butt a little bit, but he works just as hard, if not harder than I do. Everybody has to take their lumps."

"This isn't fair, Jack. This is not convenient for me."

"Jenn, it's my job. I said don't worry about it, so don't worry about it. I'll see you tomorrow. I'm gonna grab a cab back."

"Daddy will be very disappointed."

"Daddy won't even miss me. Hey, hoist one for me. And remember what you said about later? I'll take a rain check on that. Maybe we can make it my place for a change?"

She allowed herself to be kissed. But when Jack was gone she stormed over to her father.

83

FIVE

Kate Whitney pulled into the parking lot of her building. The grocery bag clunked against one leg, her overflowing briefcase against the other as she jogged up the four flights of stairs. Buildings in her price range had elevators, just not ones that worked on a consistent basis.

She changed quickly into her running outfit, checked her messages, and headed back out. She stretched the cramps and kinks out of her long limbs in front of the Ulysses S. Grant statue and started her run.

She headed west, past the Air and Space Museum, and then by the Smithsonian castle that, with its towers and battlements and twelfth-century-style Italian architecture, looked more like a mad scientist's home than anything else. Her easy, methodical strides took her across the Mall at its widest point and she circled the Washington Monument twice.

Her breath was coming a little quicker now; the sweat began to seep through her T-shirt and blot the Georgetown Law sweatshirt she was wearing. As she made her way along the fringes of the Tidal Basin, the crowds of people grew thicker. The early fall brought plane-, bus- and carloads of people from across the country hoping to miss the summer crush of tourists and the infamous Washington heat.

As she swerved to avoid one errant child she collided with another runner coming the other way. They went down in a tangle of arms and legs.

"Shit." The man rolled over quickly and then sprang back up. She started to get up, looked at him, an apology on her lips, and then abruptly sat back down. A long moment went by as camera-toting clans of Arkansans and Iowans danced around them.

"Hello, Kate." Jack gave her a hand up and helped her to a spot under one of the now bare cherry blossom trees that encircled the Tidal Basin. The Jefferson Memorial sat big and imposing across the calm water, the tall silhouette of the country's third President clearly visible inside the rotunda.

Kate's ankle was starting to swell. She took off her shoe and sock and began to rub it out.

"I didn't think you'd have time to run anymore, Jack."

She looked over at him: no receding hairline, no paunch, no lines on the face. Time had stood still for Jack Graham. She had to admit it, he looked great. She, on the other hand, was an absolute and total disaster.

She silently cursed herself for not getting that haircut and then cursed herself again for even thinking that. A drop of sweat plunged down her nose, and she brushed it away with an irritable swipe of her hand.

"I was wondering the same thing about you. I didn't think they let prosecutors go home before midnight. Slacking off?"

"Right." She rubbed her ankle, which really hurt. He saw the pain, leaned over and took her foot in his hands. She flinched back. He looked at her.

"Remember I used to almost do this for a living and you were my best and only client. I have never seen a woman with such fragile ankles, and the rest of you looks so healthy."

She relaxed and let him work the ankle and then the foot, and she soon realized he had not lost his

85

touch. Did he mean that about looking healthy? She frowned. After all, she had dumped him. And she had been absolutely right in doing so. Hadn't she?

"I heard about Patton, Shaw. Congratulations."

"Aw shucks. Any lawyer with millions in legal business could've done the same thing." He smiled.

"Yeah, I read about the engagement in the paper too. Congratulations twice." He didn't smile at that one. She wondered why not.

He quietly put her sock and shoe back on. He looked at her. "You're not going to be able to run for a day or two, it's pretty swollen. My car's right over there. I'll give you a lift."

"I'll just take a cab."

"You trust a D.C. cabbie over me?" He feigned offense. "Besides, I don't see any pockets. You going to negotiate a free ride? Good luck."

She looked down at her shorts. Her key was in her sock. He had already eyed the bulge. He smiled at her dilemma. Her lips pressed together, her tongue slid along the bottom one. He remembered that habit from long ago. Although he hadn't seen it for years, it suddenly seemed like he had never been away.

He stretched out his legs and stood up. "I'd float you a loan, but I'm busted too."

She got up, put an arm against his shoulder as she tested the ankle.

"I thought private practice paid better than that."

"It does, I've just never been able to handle money. You know that." That was true enough; she had always balanced the checkbook. Not that there was much to balance back then.

He held on to one of her arms as she limped to his car, a ten-year-old Subaru wagon. She looked at it amazed.

"You never got rid of this thing?"

"Hey, there's a lot of miles left on it. Besides, it's

full of history. See that stain right over there? Your Dairy Queen butterscotch-dipped ice cream cone, 1986, the night before my tax final. You couldn't sleep, and I wouldn't study anymore. You remember? You took that curve too fast."

"You have a bad case of selective memory. As I recall you poured your milkshake down my back because I was complaining about the heat."

"Oh, that too." They laughed and got in the car.

She examined the stain more closely, looked around the interior. So much coming back to her in big, lumpy waves. She glanced at the back seat. Her eyebrows went up. If that space could only talk. She turned back to see him looking at her, and found herself blushing.

They pulled off into the light traffic and headed east. Kate felt nervous, but not uncomfortable, as if it were four years ago and they had merely jumped in the car to get some coffee or the paper or have breakfast at the Corner in Charlottesville or at one of the cafés sprinkled around Capitol Hill. But that was years ago, she had to remind herself. That was not the present. The present was very different. She rolled the window down slightly.

Jack kept one eye on traffic, and one eye on her. Their meeting hadn't been accidental. She had run on the Mall, that very route in fact, since they had moved to D.C. and lived in that little walk-up in Southeast near Eastern Market.

That morning Jack had woken up with a desperation he had not felt since Kate had left him four years ago when it dawned on him about a week after she had gone that she wasn't coming back. Now with his wedding looming ahead, he had decided that he had to see Kate, somehow. He would not, could not, let that light die out, not yet. It was quite likely that he was the only one of the

87

two who sensed any illumination left. And while he might not have the courage to leave a message on her answering machine, he had decided that if he was meant to find her out here on the Mall amidst all the tourists and locals, then he would. He had let it go at that.

Until their collision, he had been running for an hour, scanning the crowds, looking for the face in that framed photo. He had spotted her about five minutes before their abrupt meeting. If his heart rate hadn't already doubled because of the exercise, it would've hit that mark as soon as he saw her moving effortlessly along. He hadn't meant to sprain her ankle, but then that was why she was sitting in his car; it was the reason he was driving her home.

Kate pulled her hair back and tied it in a ponytail, using a braid that had been on her wrist. "So how's work going?"

"Okay." He did not want to talk about work. "How's your old man?"

"You'd know better than me." She did not want to talk about her father.

"I haven't seen him since . . ."

"Lucky you." She lapsed into silence.

Jack shook his head at the stupidity of bringing up Luther. He had hoped for a reconciliation between father and daughter over the years. That obviously had not happened.

"I hear great things about you over at the Commonwealth's Attorney."

"Right."

"I'm serious."

"Since when."

"Everyone grows up, Kate."

"Not Jack Graham. Please, God, no."

He turned right onto Constitution, and made his way toward Union Station. Then he caught himself.

He knew which direction to go, a fact he did not want to share with her. "I'm kind of rambling here, Kate. Which way?"

"I'm sorry. Around the Capitol, over to Maryland and left on 3rd Street."

"You like that area?"

"On my salary, I like it just fine. Let me guess. You're probably in Georgetown, right, one of those big federal townhouses with maid's quarters, right?"

He shrugged. "I haven't moved. I'm in the same place."

She stared at him. "Jack, what do you do with all of your money?"

"I buy what I want; I just don't want that much." He stared back. "Hey, how about a Dairy Queen butterscotch-dipped ice cream cone?"

"There's none to be had in this town, I've tried." He did a U-turn, grinned at the honkers, and roared off.

"Apparently, counselor, you didn't try hard enough."

Thirty minutes later he pulled into her parking lot. He ran around to help her out. The ankle had stiffened a little more. The butterscotch cone was almost gone.

"I'll help you up."

"You don't have to."

"I busted your ankle. Help me relieve some of my guilt."

"I've got it, Jack." That tone was very familiar to him, even after four years. He smiled wearily and stepped back. She was halfway up the stairs, moving slowly. He was getting back in his car when she turned around.

"Jack?" He looked up. "Thanks for the ice cream." She went into the building.

Driving off, Jack did not see the man standing near the little cluster of trees at the entrance to the parking lot.

Luther emerged from the shadows of the trees and looked up at the apartment building.

His appearance from two days ago had drastically changed. It was lucky his beard grew fast. His hair had been cut very short, and a hat covered what was left. Sunglasses obscured his intense eyes and a bulky overcoat concealed the lean body.

He had hoped to see her one more time before he left. He had been shocked to see Jack, but that was all right. He liked Jack.

He huddled in his coat. The wind was picking up, and the chill was more than Washington usually carried at this time of year. He stared up at his daughter's apartment window.

Apartment number fourteen. He knew it well; had even been inside it on a number of occasions, unbeknownst to his daughter, of course. The standard front-door lock was child's play for him. It would've taken longer for someone with a key to open it. He would sit in the chair in her living room and look around at a hundred different things, all of them carrying years of memories, some good times, but mostly disappointments.

Sometimes he would just close his eyes and examine all the different scents in the air. He knew what perfume she wore – very little and very non-descript. Her furniture was big, solid and well-worn. Her refrigerator was routinely empty. He cringed when he viewed the meager and unhealthy contents of her cabinets. She kept things neat, but not perfect; the place looked lived in as it should have.

And she got a lot of calls. He would listen to some of them leaving messages. They made him wish she had picked a different line of work. Being a criminal himself, he was well aware of the number of real crazy bastards out there. But it was too late for him to recommend a career change to his only child.

He knew that it was a strange relationship to have with one's offspring, but Luther figured that was about all he deserved. A vision of his wife entered his mind; a woman who had loved him and stood by him all those years and for what? For pain and misery. And then an early death after she had arrived at her senses and divorced him. He wondered again, for the hundredth time, why he had continued his criminal activities. It certainly wasn't the money. He had always lived simply; much of the proceeds of his burglaries had been simply given away. His choice in life had driven his wife mad with worry and forced his daughter from his life. And for the hundredth time he came away with no compelling answer to the question of why he continued to steal from the well-protected wealthy. Perhaps it was only to show that he could.

He looked up once again at his daughter's apartment. He hadn't been there for her, why should she be there for him? But he could not sever the bond entirely, even if she had. He would be there for her if she so desired, but he knew that she never would.

Luther moved quickly down the street, finally running to catch a Metro bus heading toward the subway at Union Station. He had always been the most independent of people, never relying to any significant degree on anyone else. He was a loner and had liked that. Now, Luther felt very alone, and the feeling this time was not so comforting.

The rain started and he stared out the back window of the bus as it meandered its way to the great rail terminus, which had been saved from extinction by an ambitious railway-shopping mall renovation. The water bubbled up on the smooth surface of the window and clouded his view of where he had just been. He wished he could, but he couldn't go back there now.

He turned back in his seat, pulled his hat down tighter, blew into his handkerchief. He picked up a discarded newspaper, glancing down its old headlines. He wondered when they would find her. When they did, he would know about it immediately; everyone in this town would know that Christine Sullivan was dead. When rich people got themselves killed, it was front-page news. Poor people and Joe Average were stuck in the Metro section. Christy Sullivan would most certainly be on page one, front and center.

He dropped the paper on the floor, hunched down in his seat. He needed to see a lawyer, and then he would be gone. The bus droned on, and his eyes finally closed, but he wasn't sleeping. He was, for the moment, sitting in his daughter's living room, and this time, she was there with him.

92

SIX

Luther sat at the small conference room table in the very plainly furnished room. The chairs and table were old and carried a thousand scrapes. The rug was just as ancient and not very clean. A card holder was the only thing on the table other than his file. He picked up one of the cards and thumbed it. "Legal Services, Inc." These people weren't the best in the business; they were far from the halls of power downtown. Graduates of third-rate law schools with no shot at the traditional firm practice, they eked out their professional existence hoping for some luck down the road. But their dreams of big offices, big clients and, most important, big money faded a little more with the passage of each year. But Luther did not require the best. He only required somebody with a law degree and the right forms.

"Everything is in order, Mr. Whitney." The kid looked about twenty-five, still full of hope and energy. This place was not his final destination. He still clearly believed that. The tired, pinched, flabby face of the older man behind him held out no such hope. "This is Jerry Burns, the managing attorney, he'll be the other witness to your will. We have a self-proving affidavit, so we won't have to appear in court as to whether or not we witnessed your will." A stern-looking, forty-something woman appeared with her pen and notary seal. "Phyllis here is our notary, Mr. Whitney." They all sat down. "Would you like me to read the terms of your will out to you?"

Jerry Burns had been sitting at the table looking bored to death, staring into space, dreaming of all the other places he would rather be. Jerry Burns, managing attorney. He looked like he would rather be shoveling cow manure on some farm in the Midwest. Now he glanced at his young colleague with disdain.

"I've read it," Luther replied.

"Fine," said Jerry Burns. "Why don't we get started?"

Fifteen minutes later Luther emerged from Legal Services, Inc., with two original copies of his last will and testament tucked in his coat pocket.

Fucking lawyers, couldn't piss, shit or die without them. That was because lawyers made all the laws. They had the rest of them by the balls. Then he thought of Jack and smiled. Jack was not like that. Jack was different. Then he thought of his daughter and his smile faded. Kate was not like that either. But then Kate hated him.

He stopped at a camera shop and purchased a Polaroid OneStep camera and a pack of film. He didn't plan to let anyone else develop the pictures he was going to be taking. He arrived back at the hotel. An hour later he had taken a total of ten photos. These were wrapped in paper and placed in a manila folder that was then secreted far down into his backpack.

He sat down and looked out the window. It was almost an hour before he finally moved, sliding over and then collapsing onto the bed. Some tough guy he was. Not so indifferent that he could not flinch at death, not be horrified by an event that had ripped the life out of someone who should've lived a lot longer. And on top of it all was the fact that the President of the United States was involved in all of it. A man Luther had respected, had voted for. A man who held the country's highest office had almost murdered a woman with his own drunken hands. If he had seen his closest relative bludgeon someone in cold blood, Luther would not have been any more sickened or shocked. It was as though Luther himself had been invaded, as though those murderous hands had been around his throat.

But something else gripped at him; something he could not confront. He turned his face to the pillow, closed his eyes in a futile effort to sleep.

"It's great, Jenn." Jack looked at the brick and stone mansion that stretched more than two hundred feet from end to end and had more rooms than a college dorm, and wondered why they were even there. The winding driveway ended in a four-car garage behind the massive structure. The lawns were groomed so perfectly that Jack felt he was staring at an enormous jade pool. The rear grounds were triple-terraced, with each terrace sporting its own pool. It had the standard accoutrements of the very wealthy: tennis courts and stables, and twenty acres – a veritable land empire by Northern Virginia standards – on which to roam.

The realtor waited by the front door, her late-model Mercedes parked by the large stone fountain covered with fist-size roses carved out of granite. Commission dollars were being swiftly calculated and recalculated. Weren't they a terrific young couple? She had said that enough to where Jack's temples throbbed.

Jennifer Baldwin took his arm and two hours later their tour was finished. Jack walked over to the edge of the broad lawn and admired the thick woods, where an eclectic grouping of elm, spruce, maple, pine and oak jostled for dominance. The leaves were beginning to turn and Jack observed the beginnings of reds, yellows and oranges dance across the face of the property they were considering.

"So how much?" He felt he was entitled to ask that question. But this had to be out of their ballpark. His ballpark anyway. He had to admit it was convenient. Only forty-five rush-hour minutes from his office. But they couldn't touch this place. He looked expectantly at his fiancée.

She looked nervous, played with her hair. "Three million eight."

Jack's face went gray. "Three million eight hundred thousand? Dollars?"

"Jack, it's worth three times that."

"Then why the hell are they selling it for three million eight? We can't afford it, Jenn. Forget it."

She answered him by rolling her eyes. She waved reassuringly to the realtor, who sat in her car writing up the contract.

"Jenn, I make a hundred twenty thou' a year. You make about the same, maybe a little more."

"When you make partner—"

"Right. My salary goes up, but not enough for this. We can't make the mortgage payments. I thought we were moving into your place, anyway.

"It's not right for a married couple."

"Not right? It's a friggin' palace." He walked over to a forest-green-painted garden bench and sat down.

She planted herself in front of him, arms crossed, a determined look on her face. Her summer tan was starting to fade. She wore a creamy brown fedora from under which her long hair tumbled across her shoulders. Her pants were perfectly tailored to her elegantly slender form. Polished leather boots encased her feet and disappeared under the pant legs.

"We won't be carrying a mortgage, Jack."

He looked up at her. "Really? What, are they

giving us the place because we're such a terrific young couple?"

She hesitated, then said, "Daddy is paying cash for it, and we're going to pay him back."

Jack had been waiting for that one.

"Pay him back? How the hell are we going to pay him back, Jenn?"

"He's suggested a very liberal repayment plan, which takes into account future earnings expectations. For godsakes, Jack, I could pay for this place out of accumulated interest on one of my trusts, but I knew you'd object to that." She sat down next to him. "I thought if we did it this way, you'd feel better about the whole thing. I know how you are about the Baldwin money. We *will* have to pay Daddy back. It's not a gift. It's a loan *with interest*. I'm going to sell my place. I'll net about eight from that. You're going to have to come up with some money too. This is not a free ride." She playfully stuck a long finger into his chest, driving home her point. She looked back at the house. "It's beautiful, isn't it, Jack? We'll be so happy here. We were meant to live here."

Jack looked over at the front of the house but without really seeing it. All he saw was Kate Whitney, in every window of the monolith.

Jennifer squeezed his arm, leaned against him. Jack's headache moved into the panic zone. His mind was refusing to function. His throat went dry and his limbs felt stiff. He gently disengaged his arm from his fiancée's, got up and walked quietly back to the car.

Jennifer sat there for several moments, disbelief chief among the emotions registering across her face, and then angrily followed him.

The realtor, who had intently watched the exchange between the two while seated in her

Mercedes, stopped writing up the contract, her mouth pursed in displeasure.

It was early morning when Luther emerged from the small hotel hidden in the cluttered residential neighborhoods of Northwest Washington. He hailed a cab to the Metro Center subway, asking the driver to take a circuitous route on the presumption of seeing various D.C. landmarks. The request did not surprise the cabbie and he automatically went through the motions to be replicated a thousand times before the tourist season was officially over, if it was ever truly over for the town.

The skies threatened rain but you never knew. The unpredictable weather systems swirled and whipped across the region either missing the city or falling hard on it before sliding into the Atlantic. Luther looked up at the darkness, which the newly risen sun could not penetrate.

Would he even be alive six months from now? Maybe not. They could conceivably find him, despite his precautions. But he planned to enjoy the time he had left.

The Metro took him to Washington National Airport, where he took a shuttle bus across to the Main Terminal. He had prechecked his luggage onto the American Airlines flight that would take him to Dallas/Fort Worth, where he would change airlines and then head to Miami. He would stay there overnight and then another plane would drop him in Puerto Rico and then a final flight would deposit him in Barbados. Everything was paid for in cash; his passport proclaimed him to be Arthur Lanis, age sixty-five, from Michigan. He had a half-dozen such identifying documents, all professionally crafted and official-looking and all absolutely phony. The passport was good for eight more years and showed him to be well-traveled.

He settled into the waiting area and pretended to scan a newspaper. The place was crowded and noisy, a typical weekday for the busy airport. Occasionally Luther's eyes would rise over the paper to see if anyone was paying more than casual attention to him, but nothing registered. And he had been doing this long enough that something would have clicked if he had anything to worry about. His flight was called, his boarding pass was handed over and he trudged down the ramp to the slender projectile that within three hours would deposit him in the heart of Texas.

The Dallas/Fort Worth run was a busy one for American, but surprisingly he had an empty seat next to him. He took his coat off and laid it across the seat daring anyone to trespass. He settled himself in and looked out the window.

As they began to taxi to the takeoff runway, he could make out the tip of the Washington Monument over the thick, swirling mist of the clammy morning. Barely a mile from that point his daughter would be getting up shortly to go to work while her father was ascending into the clouds to begin a new life somewhat ahead of schedule and not exactly easy in his mind.

As the plane accelerated through the air, he looked at the terrain far below, noted the snaking of the Potomac until it was left behind. His thoughts went briefly to his long-dead wife and then back to his very much alive daughter.

He glanced up at the smiling, efficient face of the flight attendant and ordered coffee and a minute later accepted the simple breakfast handed to him. He drank down the steaming liquid and then reached over and touched the surface of the window with its queer streaks and scratches. Wiping his glasses clean, he noted that his eyes were watering freely. He looked around quickly; most passengers were finishing up their breakfast or reclining for a short nap before they landed.

He pushed his tray up, undid his seat belt and made his way to the lavatory. He looked at himself in the mirror. The eyes were swollen, red-blotched. The bags hung heavy, he had perceptibly aged in the last thirty-six hours.

He ran water over his face, let the droplets gather around his mouth and then splashed on some more. He wiped his eyes again. They were painful. He leaned against the tiny basin, tried to get his twitching muscles under control.

Despite all his willpower, his mind wandered back to that room where he had seen a woman savagely beaten. The President of the United States was a drunk, an adulterer and a woman beater. He smiled to the press, kissed babies and flirted with enchanted old women, held important meetings, flew around the world as his country's leader, and he was a fucking asshole who screwed married women, then beat them up and then got them killed.

What a package.

It was more knowledge than one person should be carrying around.

Luther felt very alone. And very mad.

And the sorry thing was the bastard was going to get away with it.

Luther kept telling himself if he were thirty years younger he would take this battle on. But he wasn't. His nerves were still stronger than most, but, like river rock, they had eroded over the years; they were not what they were. At his age battles became someone else's to fight, and win or lose. His time had finally come. He wasn't up to it. Even he had to understand that, to accept that reality.

Luther looked at himself in the tiny mirror again.

100

A sob swelled in his throat before it reached the surface and filled the small room.

But no excuse would justify what he had not done. He had not opened that mirrored door. He had not flung that man off Christine Sullivan. He could have prevented the woman's death, that was the simple truth. She would still be alive if he had acted. He had traded his freedom, perhaps his life, for another's. For someone who could have used his help, who was fighting for her very life while Luther just watched. A human being who had barely lived a third of Luther's years. It had been a cowardly act, and that fact gripped him like some savage anaconda, threatening to explode every organ in his body.

He bent low over the sink as his legs began to fail him. He was grateful for the collapse. He could not look at his reflection anymore. As choppy air buffeted the plane he was sick to his stomach.

A few minutes elapsed and he wet a paper towel with cold water and wiped it across his face and the back of his neck. He finally managed to stumble back to his seat. As the plane thundered on his guilt grew with each passing mile.

The phone was ringing. Kate looked at the clock. Eleven o'clock. Normally she would screen her calls. But something made her hand dart out and pick it up before the machine engaged.

"Hello."

"Why aren't you still at work?"

"Jack?"

"How's your ankle?"

"Do you realize what time it is?"

"Just checking on my patient. Doctors never sleep."

"Your patient is fine. Thanks for the worry." She smiled in spite of herself.

"Butterscotch cone, that prescription has never failed me."

"Oh, so there were other patients?"

"I've been advised by my attorney not to answer that question."

"Smart counsel."

Jack could visualize her sitting there, one finger playing with the ends of her hair, the same way she had done when they studied together; he laboring through securities regulations, she through French.

"Your hair curls enough at the ends without you helping it."

She pulled her finger back, smiled, then frowned. That statement had brought a lot of memories back, not all good ones.

"It's late, Jack. I've got court tomorrow."

He stood up and paced with the cordless, thinking rapidly. Anything to hold her on the phone for a few more seconds. He felt guilty, as though he were sneaking around. He involuntarily looked over his shoulder. There was no one there, at least no one he could see.

"I'm sorry I called late."

"Okay."

"And I'm sorry I hurt your ankle."

"You already apologized for that."

"Yeah. So, how are you? I mean except for your ankle?"

"Jack, I really need to get some sleep."

He was hoping she would say that.

"Well tell me over lunch."

"I told you I've got court."

"After court."

"Jack, I'm not sure that's a good idea. In fact, I'm pretty sure it's a lousy idea."

He wondered what she meant by that. Reading

too much into her statements had always been a bad habit of his.

"Jesus, Kate. It's just lunch. I'm not asking you to marry me." He laughed, but knew he'd already blown it.

Kate was no longer fiddling with her hair. She too stood up. Her reflection caught in the hallway mirror. She pulled at the neck of her nightgown. The frown lines were prominent on her forehead.

"I'm sorry," he said quickly. "I'm sorry, I didn't mean that. Look, it'll be my treat. I have to spend all that money on something." He was met with silence. In fact, he wasn't sure if she was still on the line.

He had rehearsed this conversation for the last two hours. Every possible question, exchange, deviation. He'd be so smooth, she so understanding. They would hit it off so well. So far, absolutely nothing had gone according to plan. He fell back on his alternate plan. He decided to beg.

"Please, Kate. I'd really like to talk to you. Please."

She sat back down, curled her legs under her, rubbed at her long toes. She took a deep breath. The years hadn't changed her as much as she had thought. Was that good or bad? Right now she had no way to deal with that question.

"When and where?"

"Morton's?"

"For lunch?"

He could see her incredulous face at the thought of the ultra-expensive restaurant. Wondering what type of world he now lived in. "Okay, how about the deli in Old Town near Founder's Park around two? We'll miss the lunchtime crowd."

"Better. But I can't promise. I'll call if I can't make it."

He slowly let out his breath. "Thanks, Kate."

He hung up the phone and collapsed on the couch.

Now that his plan had worked, he wondered what the hell he was doing. What would he say? What would she say? He didn't want to fight. He hadn't been lying, he did just want to talk to her, and to see her. That was all. He kept telling himself that.

He went to the bathroom, plunged his head into a sink of cold water, grabbed a beer and went up to the rooftop pool and sat there in the darkness, watching the planes as they made their approach up the Potomac into National. The twin, bright red lights of the Washington Monument blinked consolingly at him. Eight stories down, the streets were quiet except for the occasional police or ambulance siren.

Jack looked at the calm surface of the pool, put his foot in the now cool water and watched as it rippled across. He drank his beer, went downstairs and fell asleep in a chair in the living room, the TV droning in front of him. He did not hear the phone ring, no message was left. Almost one thousand miles away, Luther Whitney hung up the phone and smoked his first cigarette in over thirty years.

The Federal Express truck pulled slowly down the isolated country road, the driver scanning the rusty and leaning mailboxes for the correct address. He had never made a delivery out here. His truck seemed to ride ditch to ditch on the narrow road.

He pulled into the driveway of the last house and started to back out. He just happened to look over and saw the address on the small piece of wood beside the door. He shook his head and smiled. Sometimes it was just luck.

The house was small, and not very well kept up. The weathered aluminum window awnings, popular about twenty years before the driver had been born, sagged down, as if they were tired and just wanted to rest.

104

The elderly woman who answered the door was dressed in a pullover flowered dress, a thick sweater wrapped around her shoulders. Her thick red ankles told of poor circulation and probably a host of other ailments. She seemed surprised by the delivery, but readily signed for it.

The driver glanced at the signature on his pad: Edwina Broome. Then he got in his truck and left. She watched him leave before shutting the door.

The walkie-talkie crackled.

Fred Barnes had been doing this job for seven years now. Driving around the neighborhoods of the rich, seeing the big houses, manicured grounds, the occasional expensive car with its mannequinlike occupants coming down the perfect asphalt drive and through the massive gates. He had never been inside any of the homes he was paid to guard, and never expected to be.

He looked up at the imposing structure. Four to five million dollars, he surmised. More money than he could make in five lifetimes. Sometimes it just didn't seem right.

He checked in on his walkie-talkie. He would take a look around the place. He didn't exactly know what was going on. Only that the owner had called and requested a patrol car check.

The cold air in his face made Barnes think about a hot cup of coffee and a danish, to be followed by eight hours of sleep until he had to venture out again in his Saturn for yet another night of protecting the possessions of the wealthy. The pay wasn't all that bad, although the benefits sucked. His wife worked full-time too, and with three kids, their combined incomes were barely enough. But then everybody had it tough. He looked at the five-car garage in back, the pool and the tennis courts. Well, maybe not everybody.

As he rounded the corner, he saw the dangling rope and thoughts of coffee and a creamy danish disappeared. He crouched down, his hand flying to his sidearm. He grabbed his mike and reported in, his voice cracking embarrassingly. The real police would be here in minutes. He could wait for them or investigate himself. For eight singles an hour he decided to stay right where he was.

Barnes's supervisor arrived first in the stark white station wagon with the company's logo on the door panel. Thirty seconds later the first of five patrol cars pulled down the asphalt drive until they were stacked like a waiting train in front of the house.

The window was covered by two officers. It was probable that the perps had long since exited the premises, but assumptions were dangerous in the police business.

Four officers went to the front, two more covered the back. Working in pairs, the four policemen proceeded to make their way in. They noted that the front door was unlocked, the alarm off. They satisfied themselves with the downstairs and cautiously moved up the broad staircase, their ears and eyes straining for any trace of sound or movement.

By the time they reached the second-floor landing, the nostrils of the sergeant in charge told him that this would not be a routine burglary.

Four minutes later they stood in a circle around what had recently been a young, beautiful woman. The healthy coloring of each of the men had faded to dull white.

The sergeant, fiftyish and a father of three, looked at the open window. Thank God, he thought to himself; even with the outside air the atmosphere inside the room was stupefying. He looked once more at the corpse, then strode quickly to the window and sucked in deep gulps of the crisp air.

He had a daughter about that age. For a moment he imagined her on that floor, her face a memory, her life brutally over. The matter was out of his bailiwick now, but he wished for one thing: he wished to be there when whoever had done this atrocious thing was caught.

SEVEN

Seth Frank was simultaneously munching a piece of toast and attempting to tie his six-year-old daughter's hair ribbons for school when the phone call came. His wife's look told him all he needed. She finished the ribbon. Seth cradled the phone while he finished knotting his tie, listening all the while to the calm, efficient tones of the dispatcher. Two minutes later he was in his car; the official bubble light needlessly stuck to the top of his department-issued Ford and aqua blue grille lights flashing ominously as he roared through the nearly deserted back roads of the county.

Frank's tall, big-boned frame was beginning its inevitable journey to softness, and his curly black hair had seen more affluent days. At forty-one years old, the father of three daughters who grew more complex and bewildering by the day, he had come to realize that not all that much in life made sense. But overall he was a happy man. Life had dealt him no knockout punches. Yet. He had been in law enforcement long enough to know how abruptly that could change.

Frank wadded up a piece of Juicy Fruit and slowly chewed it while compact rows of needle pines flew past his window. He had started his law enforcement career as a cop in some of the worst areas of New York City where the statement "the value of life" was an oxymoron and where he had seen virtually every way one person could kill another. He had eventually made detective, which had thrilled his wife. At least now he would arrive at crime scenes after the bad guys had departed. She slept better at night, knowing that the dreaded phone call would probably not come to destroy her life. That was as much as she could hope for being married to a cop.

Frank had finally been assigned to homicide, which was pretty much the ultimate challenge in his line of work. After a few years, he decided he liked the job and the challenge, but not at the rate of seven corpses a day. So he had made the trek south to Virginia.

He was senior homicide detective for the County of Middleton, which sounded better than it actually was, since he also happened to be the only homicide detective the county employed. But the relatively innocuous confines of the rustic Virginia county had not lent itself to much demanding work over that time. The per capita income levels in his jurisdiction were off the scale. People were murdered, but other than wives shooting husbands or vice versa or inheritance-minded kids popping off their parents, there hadn't been much excitement. The perps in those cases were pretty self-evident, less mental work than legwork. The dispatcher's phone call promised to change all that.

The road snaked past a wooded area and then opened out onto fenced, green fields where leggy thoroughbreds lazily faced the new morning. Behind impressive gates and long, winding driveways, were the residences of the fortunate few, who were actually very plentiful in Middleton. Frank concluded that he wasn't going to get any help from the neighbors on this one. Once inside their fortresses they probably saw or heard nothing on the outside. Which was undoubtedly the way they wanted it and paid dearly for that privilege.

As Frank approached the Sullivan estate he

straightened his tie in the rearview mirror and pushed back some stray wisps of hair. He had no particular affinity for the wealthy, nor did he dislike them. They were parts of the puzzle. A conundrum that was as far from a game as you could get. Which led to the most satisfying part of his job. For amidst all the twists, turns, red herrings and plain mistakes, there lurked an undeniable truism: if you killed another human being, you came within his domain and you would be ultimately punished. What that punishment was, Frank usually did not care. What he did care about was that someone stand trial and, if convicted, that someone receive the meted penalty. Rich, poor or in-between. His skills may be somewhat dulled, but the instincts were still there. In the long run, he'd always go with the latter.

As he pulled in the drive he noticed a small combine chewing under the adjacent cornfield, its driver watching the police activity with a keen eye. That information would soon be passing through the area in rapid movements. The man had no way to know he was destroying evidence, evidence of a flight. Neither did Seth Frank as he climbed out of his car, threw on his jacket and hustled through the front door.

Hands deep in his pockets, his eyes moved slowly around the room, taking in each detail of the floor, walls, and venturing to the ceiling before coming back to the mirrored door and then to the spot where the deceased had lain for the last several days.

Seth Frank said, "Take a lot of pics, Stu, looks like we'll need it."

The crime unit photographer paced through the room in discrete grids outward from the corpse in his effort to reproduce on film every aspect of the room including its lone occupant. This would be followed by a videotaping of the entire crime scene complete with a narrative. Not necessarily admissible in court, but it was invaluable to the investigation. As football players watched game films, detectives were more and more scrutinizing the videos for additional clues that might only be seized upon on the eighth, tenth or hundredth examination.

The rope was still tied to the bureau and still disappeared out the window. Only now it was covered with black fingerprint powder, but there wouldn't be much there. One usually wore gloves to climb down a rope, even a knotted one.

Sam Magruder, the officer in charge, approached, having just spent two minutes leaning out the window sucking in air. Fiftyish with a shock of red hair that topped a plump, hairless face, he was having a hard time keeping his breakfast down. A large portable fan had been brought in and the windows were fully open. All the CU personnel wore floater masks, but the stench was still oppressive. Nature's parting laugh to the living. Beautiful one minute, rotting the next.

Frank checked Magruder's notes, noted the greenish tint to the OIC's face.

"Sam, if you'd stay away from the window, your sense of smell would go dead in about four minutes. You're just making it worse."

"I know that, Seth. My brain tells me that, but my nose won't listen."

"When did the husband phone in?"

"This morning, seven-forty-five local time."

Frank tried to make out the cop's scribbles. "And he's where?"

"Barbados."

Frank's head inclined. "How long?"

"We're confirming it."

"Do that."

111

"How many calling cards they leave, Laura?" Frank looked over at his ident technician, Laura Simon.

She glanced up. "I'm not finding much, Seth."

Frank walked over to her. "Come on, Laura, she's gotta be all over the place. How about her husband? The maid? There's gotta be usables everywhere."

"Not that I'm finding."

"You're shitting me."

Simon, who took her work very seriously and was the best print lifter Frank had ever worked with, including at NYPD, looked almost apologetic. Carbon dusting powder was everywhere, and there was nothing? Contrary to popular belief, a lot of criminals left their prints at the scene of the crime. You just had to know where to look. Laura Simon knew where to look and she was getting zip. Hopefully they would get something after analysis back at the lab. Many latents just weren't visible no matter how many angles you hit them with the light. That's why they called them latents. You just powdered and taped everything you thought the perps might have touched. And you might get lucky.

"I've got a few things packaged to take back to the lab. After I use the ninhydrin and hit the rest with the Super Glue I might have something for you." Simon dutifully returned to her work.

Frank shook his head. Super Glue, a cyanoacrylate, was probably the best method of fuming and could pull prints off things you couldn't believe. The problem was the damn process took time to work its magic. Time they didn't have.

"Come on, Laura, from the looks of the body the bad guys have had enough of a head start."

She looked at him. "I've got another cyanoacrylate ester I've been wanting to use. That's faster. Or I can always speed-burn the Super Glue." She smiled.

The detective grimaced. "Right. The last time you

tried that we had to evacuate the building."

"I didn't say it was a perfect world, Seth."

Magruder cleared his throat. "Looks like we're dealing with some real professionals."

Seth looked at the OIC sternly. "They're not professionals, Sam, they're criminals, they're killers. It's not like they went to goddamned college to learn how to do this."

"No, sir."

"We sure it's the lady of the house?" Frank inquired.

Magruder pointed to the photo on the nightstand. "Christine Sullivan. Of course, we'll get a positive ID."

"Any witnesses?"

"No obvious ones. Haven't canvassed the neighbors yet. Gonna do that this morning."

Frank proceeded to make copious notes of the room and its occupant's condition and then made a detailed sketch of the room and its contents. A good defense attorney could make any unprepared prosecution witness look like a candidate for the Silly Putty factory. Being unprepared meant guilty people went free.

Frank had learned the only lesson he would ever need on the subject as a rookie cop and the first on the scene of a breaking and entering. He had never been more embarrassed or depressed in his life as he had when he had gotten off the witness stand, his testimony torn to shreds and actually used as the basis to get the defendant off. If he had been able to wear his .38 in court, the world would have had one fewer lawyer that day.

Frank crossed the room to where the Deputy Medical Examiner, a beefy, white-haired man who was perspiring heavily despite the morning chill outside, was lowering the skirt on the corpse. Frank knelt down and examined one of the small Baggie-clad hands, then glanced at the woman's face. It looked like it had been beaten black and blue. The clothing was soaked through with her body fluids. With death comes an almost immediate relaxing of the sphincters. The resulting smell combination was not pleasant. Luckily the insect infestation was minimal, despite the open window. Even though a forensic entomologist could usually ascertain time of death more accurately than could a pathologist, no detective, despite the increased accuracy, ever relished the thought of examining a human body that had become an insect buffet.

"Got an approximate yet?" Frank asked the Medical Examiner.

"My rectal thermometer isn't going to be much use to me, not when body temperature drops one and a half degrees an hour. Seventy-two to eighty-four hours. I'll have a better number for you after I open her up." The ME straightened up. "Gunshot wounds to the head," he added, although there was no doubt about the woman's cause of death to anyone in the room.

"I noticed the marks on her neck."

The Medical Examiner looked at Frank keenly for a moment and then shrugged. "They're there. I don't know what they mean yet."

"I'd appreciate a quick turnaround on this one."

"You'll get it. Not many murders out this way. They usually get a priority, y'know."

The detective winced slightly at the remark.

The Medical Examiner looked at him. "Hope you enjoy dealing with the press. They'll be on this like a swarm of honeybees."

"More like yellowjackets."

The Medical Examiner shrugged. "Better you than me. I'm way too old for that crap. She's ready to go whenever."

The Medical Examiner finished packing up and left.

Frank held the small hand up to his face, looked at the professionally manicured nails. He noted several tears in two of the cuticles, which seemed likely enough if there was a struggle before she'd gotten popped. The body was grossly distended; bacteria raged everywhere as the putrefaction process raced on. Rigor had passed long ago, which meant she had been dead well over forty-eight hours. The limbs were supple as the body's soft tissue dissolved. Frank sighed. She had indeed been here awhile. That was good for the killer, bad for the cops.

It still amazed him how death changed a person. A bloated wreck barely recognizable as a human, when just days before . . . Had his sense of smell not already gone dead, he would have been unable to do what he was doing. But that came with being a homicide detective. All your clients were dead.

He carefully held the deceased's head up, turning each side to the light. Two small entry wounds on the right side, one large, ragged exit hole on the left. They were looking at heavy-caliber stuff. Stu had already gotten pictures of the wounds from several different angles, including from directly overhead. The circular abrasion collars and the absence of burns or tattooing on the skin's surface led Frank to conclude that the shots had been fired from over two feet away.

Small-caliber contact wounds, those fired muzzle to flesh, and near-contact wounds fired from a distance of less than two inches from the target, could duplicate the types of entry wounds present on the victim. But there would be powder residue deep in the tissues along the bullet track if they were looking at a contact wound. The autopsy would definitively answer that question.

Next Frank looked at the contusion on the left side of her jaw. It was partially hidden by the natural blistering of the body as it decomposed but Frank had seen enough corpses to tell the difference. The surface of the skin there was a curious amalgamation of green, brown and black. A big blow had done that. A man? That was confusing. He called Stu over to take pictures of the area with a color scale. Then he laid the head back down with the reverence the deceased deserved even under the largely clinical circumstances.

The medico-legal autopsy to follow would not be so deferential.

Frank slowly lifted the skirt. Underwear intact. The autopsy protocol would answer the obvious question.

Frank moved around the room as the CU members continued their work. One thing about living in a rich, although largely rural county, the tax base was more than enough to support a first-rate if relatively small crime scene unit complete with all the latest technology and devices that theoretically made catching bad people easier.

The victim had fallen on her left side, away from the door. Knees tucked partially under her, left arm stretched out, the other against her right hip. Her face was pointed east, perpendicular with the right side of the bed; she was almost in a fetal position. Frank rubbed his nose. From beginning to end, back to the beginning. Nobody ever knew how they were going to eventually exit this old world, did they?

With Simon's help he did the triangulation of the body's location; the tape measure made a screeching sound as it unwound. It sounded somehow unholy in this room of death. He looked at the doorway and the position of the body. He and Simon performed a preliminary trajectory path of the shots. That indicated the shots most probably came from the doorway, which with a burglary you'd expect the other way around if the perp was caught in the act. However, there was another piece of evidence that would pretty much confirm which way the slugs had traveled.

Frank again kneeled next to the body. There were no drag marks across the carpet and the bloodstains and spray patterns indicated the deceased was shot at the spot she had fallen. Frank carefully turned to the body, again lifting up the skirt. Postmortem, blood settles to the lowest portions of the body, a condition called livor mortis. After four to six hours, the livor mortis remains fixed in position. Consequently, movement of the body does not lead to a change in distribution of blood. Frank laid the body back down. All indications were strong that Christine Sullivan had died right here.

The spray patterns also reinforced the conclusion that the deceased was probably facing toward the bed when she met her end. If so, what the hell had she been looking at? Normally a person about to be shot would look in the direction of the assailant, pleading for their life. Christine Sullivan would have begged, Frank was certain of that. The detective looked at the opulent surroundings. She had a lot to live for.

He eyed the carpet carefully, his face barely inches from its surface. The spray patterns were irregularly distributed as though something had been lying in front of or to the side of the deceased. That could prove to be important later on. Much had been written about spray patterns. Frank respected their usefulness, but tried not to read too much into them. But if something had partially shielded the carpet from the blood, he would want to know what that something was. Also the absence of spotting on her dress puzzled him. He would catalogue that one away; it might mean something too.

Simon opened her rape kit and with Frank's assistance swabbed the deceased's vagina. Next they combed through both the hair on her head and her pubic hair with nothing readily apparent in the way of foreign substances. Next they bagged the victim's clothing.

Frank looked over the body minutely. He glanced at Simon. She read his mind.

"There's not going to be any, Seth."

"Indulge me, Laurie."

Simon dutifully lugged her print kit over and applied powder to the corpse's wrists, breasts, neck and inside upper arms. After a few seconds she looked at Frank and slowly shook her head. She bagged what they did find.

He watched as the body was wrapped in a white sheet, deposited in a body pouch and taken outside where a silent ambulance would transport Christine Sullivan to a place everyone prayed they would never have to go.

He next viewed the vault, noted the chair and remote. Dust patterns on the floor of the vault had been disturbed. Simon had already covered the area. There was a smudge of dust on the chair seat. The vault had been forced though; the door and wall were heavily marked where the lock had been broken. They would cut out the levered piece of evidence, see if they could get a tool print. Frank looked back through the vault door and shook his head. One-way mirror. That was real nice. In the bedroom too. He couldn't wait to meet the man of the house.

He went back into the room, looked down at the picture on the nightstand. He looked over at Simon.

"I've already got it, Seth," she said. He nodded and picked up the picture. Nice-looking woman, he

118

thought to himself, real nice-looking in a come–fuck–me kind of way. The photo had been taken in this very room, the recently departed seated in the chair next to the bed. Then he noticed the mark on the wall. The place had real plaster walls instead of the usual drywall, but the mark was still deep. Frank noted the nightstand had been moved slightly; the thick carpet betrayed its original position. He turned to Magruder.

"Looks like somebody slammed into this."

"Probably during the struggle."

"Probably."

"Find the slug yet?"

"One's still in her, Seth."

"I mean the other one, Sam." Frank impatiently shook his head. Magruder pointed to the wall beside the bed where a small hole was barely visible.

Frank nodded. "Cut the section and let the lab boys pull it out. Don't screw with it yourself." Twice in the last year ballistics had been rendered useless because an overzealous uniform had scraped a bullet out of a wall, ruining the striations.

"Any brass?"

Magruder shook his head. "If the murder weapon ejected any spent shells, they've been picked up."

He turned to Simon. "Any treasures from the E-vac?" The evidence vacuum was a highly powerful machine that, utilizing a series of filters, was used to comb the carpet and other materials for fibers, hairs and other small objects that more often than not turned out big dividends because if the perps couldn't see 'em, they weren't going to try to remove 'em.

Magruder tried to joke. "My carpet should be that clean."

Frank looked at his CU team. "Did we find any trace, people?" They all looked at one another not knowing if Frank was kidding or not. They were still

119

wondering when he walked out of the room and went downstairs.

A representative from the alarm company was talking with a uniformed officer at the front door. A CU member was packing the plate and wires in plastic evidence bags. Frank was shown where the paint had been slightly chipped and an almost microscopic metal shard indicated that the panel had been removed. On the wiring were small toothlike indentations. The security rep looked admiringly at the lawbreaker's handiwork. Magruder joined them, his color slowly returning.

The rep was nodding his head. "Yep, they probably used a counter. Looks that way anyway."

Seth looked at him. "What's that?"

"Computer-assisted method of ramming massive numbers of combinations into the system's recognition bank until they hit the right combo. You know, like they do to bust the ATMs.'

Frank looked at the gutted panel and then back at the man. "I'm surprised a place like this wouldn't have a more sophisticated system."

"It is a sophisticated system." The rep sounded defensive.

"Lotta crooks using computers these days."

"Yeah, but the thing is, this baby has a fifteen-digit base, not a ten, and a forty-three-second delay. You don't hit it, the gate comes crashing down."

Frank rubbed his nose. He would have to go home and shower. The stench of death warmed over several days in a hot room left its indelible mark on your clothes, hair and skin. And sinuses.

"So?" Frank asked.

"So, the portable models you'd most likely have to use on a job like this can't crunch enough combos through in thirty seconds or so. Shit, based on a fifteen-digit configuration you're looking at over a

120

trillion-three in possibles. It's not like the guy's gonna be lugging around a PC."

The OIC piped in. "Why thirty seconds?"

Frank answered. "They needed some time to get the plate off, Sam." He turned back to the security man. "So what are you saying?"

"I'm saying that if he knocked this system over with a numbers cruncher then he had already eliminated some of the possible digits from the process. Maybe half, maybe more. I mean, maybe you got a system that'll do it all right, or they might've rigged something up that could pop this cage. But you're not talking cheap hardware and you're not talking some bozos off the street that walked into a Radio Shack and came out with a calculator. I mean, they're making computers faster and smaller every day but you gotta realize that the speed of *your* hardware doesn't solve the problem. You gotta factor in how fast the security system's computer will respond back to all the combos flowing in. It's probably gonna be a lot slower than your equipment. And then you gotta big problem. Bottom line if I were these guys I'd want a nice comfort zone, you know what I'm saying? In their line of work, you don't get second chances."

Frank looked at the man's uniform and then back at the panel. If the guy was right he knew what that meant. His line of thinking had already moved in that direction by virtue of the fact that the front door had not been forced or even nominally tampered with.

The security company rep continued, "I mean, we could eliminate the possibility entirely. We have systems that refuse to react to massive combos being forced down their throat. Computers would be jack-shit useless. Problem is, those systems are so sensitive to interference they were also routinely slamming down on owners who couldn't seem to remember

121

their numbers on the first or second try. Hell, we were getting hit with so many false alarms the police departments were starting to fine us. Go fucking figure."

Frank thanked him and then moved through the rest of the house. Whoever had committed these crimes knew what they were doing. This was not going to be a quick one. Good pre-crime planning usually meant equally good post-planning. But they probably hadn't counted on blowing away the lady of the house.

Frank suddenly leaned against a doorway and pondered the word used by his friend the Medical Examiner: *wounds*.

EIGHT

Jack was early. His watch showed one-thirty-five. He had taken the day off, spending much of it deciding what to wear; something he had never concerned himself with before, but which now seemed vitally important.

He pulled at his gray tweed jacket, fingered a button on his white cotton shirt and adjusted the knot in his tie for the tenth time.

He walked down to the dock and watched the deck hands clean the *Cherry Blossom*, a tour ship built to resemble an old Mississippi riverboat. He and Kate had gone on it their first year in D.C. during a rare afternoon off from work. They had tried to hit all the touristy attractions. It had been a warm day like today, but clearer. Gray clouds were now rolling in from the west; afternoon thunderstorms were almost a given this time of year.

He sat on the weathered bench near the dockmaster's small hut and followed the lazy drift of the sea gulls across the choppy water. The Capitol was visible from his vantage point. Lady Liberty, minus the collective filth of over a hundred and thirty years of residing outdoors thanks to a recent cleaning, stood imperiously on top of the famous dome. People in this town were encased in grime over time, Jack thought to himself. It just came with the territory.

Jack's musings turned to Sandy Lord, the firm's most prolific rainmaker, and the biggest ego Patton, Shaw had ever seen. Sandy was close to being an institution in the legal and political circles of D.C. The other partners dropped his name as though he had just that moment stepped down from Mount Sinai with his own version of the Ten Commandments, which would have commenced with "Thou Shalt Make Patton, Shaw and LORD Partners As Much Money As Possible."

Ironically, Sandy Lord was part of the attraction when Ransome Baldwin had mentioned the firm. Lord was one of the best, if not the best example of a power lawyer the city had to offer, and it had dozens in that league. The possibilities were limitless for Jack. Whether those possibilities included his personal happiness, he was far from certain.

He was also not certain what he expected from this lunch. What he was sure about was that he wanted to see Kate Whitney. He wanted that very much. It seemed as though the closer his marriage came, the more he was emotionally retreating. And where more likely a spot to retreat than to the woman he had asked to marry him over four years ago? He shuddered as that memory engulfed him. He was terrified of marrying Jennifer Baldwin. Terrified that his life would soon become unrecognizable to him.

Something made him turn, he wasn't sure what exactly. But she was standing there, at the edge of the pier, watching him. The wind whipped her long skirt around her legs, the sun battled the darkening clouds, but still provided enough light to sparkle across her face as she moved the long strands of hair from her eyes. The calves and ankles were summer brown. The loose blouse bared her shoulders, showing off the freckles, and the tiny half-moon birthmark Jack had the habit of tracing after they had finished making love, she asleep and he watching her.

He smiled as she walked toward him. She must have gone home to change. This was clearly not her courtroom armor; these clothes represented a far more feminine side to Kate Whitney than any of her legal opponents would ever witness.

They walked down the street to the small deli, ordered and spent the first few minutes alternately staring out the window watching the approaching rain as it whipped the trees around, and exchanging awkward glances, as if on a first date and afraid to make steady eye contact.

"I appreciate your making the time, Kate."

She shrugged. "I like it here. Haven't been for a while. It's nice to get out for a change. I usually eat at my desk."

"Crackers and coffee?" He smiled and stared at her teeth. The funny one that curved inwardly slightly, like it was giving a quick hug to its neighbor. He liked that tooth the best. It was the only flaw he had ever noticed about her.

"Crackers and coffee." She smiled back. "Down to two cigarettes a day."

"Congratulations." The rain came at the same time their orders did.

She looked up from her plate, her eyes swept over to the window and then abruptly to Jack's face. She caught him staring at her. Jack smiled awkwardly and took a quick gulp of his drink.

She put her napkin on the table.

"The Mall's a big place to accidentally run into someone."

He didn't look at her. "I've been having a run of good luck lately." Now he met her eye. She waited. His shoulders finally collapsed.

"Okay, so it was less of an accident and more premeditated. You can't argue with the results."

"What are the results? Lunch?"

"I'm not looking ahead. I'm just taking it one step at a time. New life resolution. Change is good."

She said with more than a little contempt, "Well, at least you're not defending rapists and murderers anymore."

"And burglars?" he shot back, and then instantly regretted it.

Kate's face turned gray.

"I'm sorry, Kate. I didn't mean that."

She pulled out a cigarette and matches, lit up and blew smoke in his face.

He waved the cloud away. "Your first or second of the day?"

"Third. For some reason you always make me feel daring." She stared at the window, crossed her legs. Her foot touched his knee and she quickly jerked it back. She stabbed out her cigarette and stood up, grabbing her purse.

"I have to get back to work. How much do I owe you?"

He stared at her. "I invited *you* to lunch. Which you haven't even eaten."

She pulled out a ten and tossed it down on the table and headed for the door.

Jack threw another ten down and raced after her.

"Kate!"

He caught up to her just outside the deli. The rain had stiffened and despite holding his jacket over their heads they were quickly soaked. She didn't seem to notice. She climbed in her car. He jumped in the passenger side. She looked at him.

"I really have to get back."

Jack took a deep breath, wiped the moisture off his face. The heavy rain drummed on the car's exterior. He felt it all slipping away. He was far from sure how to handle this situation. But he had to say something.

"Come on, Kate, we're dripping wet, it's almost three o'clock. Let's go get cleaned up and hit a movie. No, we can drive out to the country. Remember the Windsor Inn?"

She looked at him, absolute astonishment on her features. "Jack, by any chance, have you discussed this with the woman you're engaged to marry?"

Jack looked down. What was he supposed to say? That he was not in love with Jennifer Baldwin despite having asked her to marry him? Right at that moment, he could not even recall asking her.

"I'd just like to spend some time with you, Kate. That's all. There's nothing wrong with that."

"There is everything wrong with that, Jack. *Everything!*" She started to put the key in the ignition but he held her hand back.

"I'm not looking to make this a battle."

"Jack, you've made your decision. It's a little late for this now."

His face curled into disbelief. "Excuse me? My decision? I made a decision to marry you over four years ago. That was my decision. It was your decision to end it."

She pushed wet hair out of her eyes. "Okay, it was my decision. Now what?"

He turned to face her, gripped both her shoulders. "Look, it suddenly occurred to me last night. Oh what the hell! It's been every night since you left. I knew it was a mistake, goddammit! I'm not at PD anymore. You're right, I don't defend criminals anymore. I make a good, respectable living. I, we . . ." As he looked at her astonished face, his entire mind went blank. His hands were shaking. He let go of her, slumped back in the seat.

He stripped off his drenched tie, stuffed it in his pocket, and stared at the little clock on the dashboard. She checked out the motionless speedometer, then glanced at him. There was kindness in her tone, although the pain was evident in her eyes.

127

"Jack, lunch was very nice. It was good to see you. But that's as far as we can go. I'm sorry." She bit her lip, a movement he didn't see because he was getting out of the car.

He poked his head back in. "Have a good life, Kate. You ever need anything, call me."

She watched his thick shoulders as he walked through the steady rain, got in his car and drove off. She sat for several minutes. A tear traced its way down her cheek. She angrily flicked it away, put the car in gear and drove off in the opposite direction.

The next morning, Jack picked up the phone and then slowly put it back down. What was the point really? He had been in the office since six, wiped out his backlog of high-priority work and moved on to projects that had been on the back burner for weeks. He looked out the window. The sun ricocheted off the concrete and brick edifices. He rubbed the glare out of his eyes and pulled the blinds down.

Kate was not going to suddenly plunge back into his life and he had to adjust to that. He had spent the night turning every possible scenario over in his head, most wildly unrealistic. He shrugged. Things like this happened to men and women every day in every country in the world. Things sometimes did not work out. Even if you wanted them to more than anything else. You couldn't will someone to love you back. You had to move on. He had plenty to move on to. Maybe it was time for him to enjoy the future he knew he did have.

He sat down at his desk and methodically moved through two more projects, a joint venture for which he was doing low-level, no-brain grunt work, and a project for the only client he had other than Baldwin, Tarr Crimson.

Crimson owned a small audiovisual company, was

a genius with computer-generated graphics and images, and made a very good living running AV conferences for companies at area hotels. He also rode a motorcycle, dressed in cutoff jeans, smoked everything including an occasional cigarette, and looked like the biggest burnt-out druggie in the world.

Jack and he had met when a friend of Jack's had prosecuted Tarr for drunk and disorderly, and lost. Tarr had come in dressed in a three-piece suit, briefcase and neatly trimmed hair and beard, and argued persuasively that the officer's testimony was biased because the bust was outside a Grateful Dead concert, that the field test was inadmissible because the cop had not given the proper verbal warnings and lastly because an improperly functioning piece of equipment had been used to administer the test.

The judge, burdened with over a hundred D&Ds from the concert, had dismissed the case after admonishing the officer to adhere strictly to the rules in the future. Jack had watched the entire affair in amazement. Impressed, Jack walked out of the courtroom with Tarr, had a beer with him that night, and they quickly became friends.

Except for occasional, relatively innocuous brushes with the law, Crimson was a good, if unwelcome, client to the halls of Patton, Shaw. It had been part of Jack's deal that Tarr, who had fired his last attorney, would be allowed to follow Jack to Patton, Shaw – as if the firm would have actually said no to their new four-million-dollar man.

He put down his pen and moved once again to the window as his thoughts drifted back to Kate Whitney. An idea lumbered across the forefront of his mind. When Kate had left him originally, Jack had gone to see Luther. The old man had had no words of wisdom, no instant solution to Jack's dilemma.

Indeed, Luther Whitney was the unlikeliest person in the world to have the answer that would reach to his daughter's heart. And yet Jack had always been able to talk to Luther. About anything. The man listened. He really listened. He didn't merely wait for you to pause with your own story so he could plunge in with his own troubles. Jack wasn't sure what he was going to say to the man. But whatever it was he was certain Luther would listen. And that was probably going to have to be good enough.

One hour later Jack's computerized calendar buzzed a warning. He checked the time and threw on his jacket.

Jack moved quickly down the hallway. Lunch with Sandy Lord in twenty minutes. Jack was uncomfortable about being with the man, alone. Legions had been spoken about Sandy Lord, mostly true, Jack assumed. He wanted lunch with Jack Graham, Jack's secretary had told him this morning. And what Sandy Lord wanted he got. Jack's secretary also reminded him of that in a hushed whisper that made Jack slightly repulsed.

Twenty minutes, but first Jack had to check with Alvis on the Bishop documents. Jack smiled as he remembered Barry's face when the drafts had been placed carefully on his desk, thirty minutes before the deadline. Alvis had scanned them, the astonishment clear on his features.

"This looks pretty good. I realize I gave you a tough deadline. I don't usually like to do that." His eyes were averted. "I really appreciate the hustle, Jack. I'm sorry if I screwed up your plans."

"No sweat, Barry, that's what they pay me for." Jack had turned to leave. Barry had risen from his desk.

"Jack, uh, we really haven't had a chance to talk since you've been here. Place is so damn big. Let's have lunch one day, soon."

"Sounds great, Barry, have your secretary give mine some dates."

At that moment Jack realized that Barry Alvis wasn't such a bad guy. He had dinged Jack, but so what? Compared to how the senior partners ran their underlings, Jack had gotten off easy. Besides, Barry was a first-rate corporate attorney and Jack could learn a lot from him.

Jack passed Barry's secretary's desk but Sheila was not there.

Then Jack noticed the boxes stacked against the wall. Barry's door was closed. Jack knocked, but there was no answer. He looked around and then opened the door. His eyes closed and reopened as he looked at the empty bookcases, at the rectangular patches of unfaded wallpaper where a slew of diplomas and certificates had hung.

What the hell? He closed the door, turned and bumped into Sheila.

Normally professional and precise in her manner, without a hair out of place and glasses set firmly on the bridge of her nose, Sheila was a wreck. She had been Barry's secretary for ten years. She stared at Jack, fire flashed through her pale blue eyes, and then was gone. She turned around, walked quickly back to her cubicle and started packing up boxes. Jack stared blankly at her.

"Sheila, what's going on? Where's Barry?" She did not respond. Her hands moved faster until she was literally throwing things into the box. Jack moved over next to her, looked down at the petite frame.

"Sheila? What the hell's going on? Sheila!" He grabbed her hand. She slapped him, which shocked her so badly she abruptly sat down. Her head slowly went down to her desk and stayed there. She began to quietly sob.

Jack looked around again. Was Barry dead? Had

there been a terrible accident and no one had bothered to tell him? Was the firm that big, that callous? Would he read about it in a firm memo? He looked at his hands. They were trembling.

He perched on the edge of the desk, gently touched Sheila's shoulder, trying to bring her out of it, but without success. Jack looked around helplessly as the sobs continued, rising higher and higher in their intensity. Finally, two secretaries from around the corner appeared and quietly led Sheila away. Each of them gave Jack a not very friendly glance.

What the hell had he done? He looked at his watch. He had to meet Lord in ten minutes. Suddenly he was very much looking forward to this lunch. Lord knew everything that happened at the firm, usually before it actually did happen. Then a thought tickled the back of his head, a truly horrible thought. His mind went back to the White House dinner and his irate fiancée. He had mentioned Barry Alvis by name to her. But she wouldn't have . . . ? Jack practically sprinted down the hallway, the back of his jacket flapping behind him.

Fillmore's was a Washington landmark of fairly recent vintage. The doors were solid mahogany and bedecked with thick, weighty brass; the carpets and drapes were handwoven and supremely costly. Each table area was a self-contained haven of intense meal-time productivity. Phone, fax and copier services were readily available and widely used. The ornately carved tables were surrounded by richly upholstered chairs in which sat the truly elite of Washington's business and political circles. The prices ensured that the clientele would remain that way.

While crowded, the pace of the restaurant was unhurried; its occupants unused to being dictated to, they moved at their own level of intensity. Sometimes their very presence at a particular table, a raised eyebrow, a stifled cough, a knowing look, was a full day's work for them, and would reap huge rewards for them personally or for those whom they represented. Money and raw power floated through the room in distinct patterns, coupling and uncoupling.

Waiters in stiff shirts and neat bow ties appeared and then disappeared at discreetly placed intervals. Patons were coddled and served and listened to or left alone as the particular occasion called for. And the gratuities reflected the clientele's appreciation.

Fillmore's was Sandy Lord's favorite lunch spot. He peered over his menu, briefly, but methodically surveyed with his intense, gray eyes the broad expanse of the dining room for potential business or perhaps something else. He moved his heavy bulk gracefully in his chair and carefully coaxed a few gray hairs back into place. The trouble was, familiar faces kept disappearing as time moved forward, stolen away by death or retirement to points south. He removed a fleck of dust from one of his monogrammed shirt cuffs and sighed. Lord had picked this establishment, maybe this town, clean.

He punched on his cellular phone and checked his messages. Walter Sullivan hadn't called. If Sullivan's deal came through, Lord could land a former Eastern Bloc country as a client.

A whole goddamned country! How much could you charge a country for legal work? Normally a lot. The problem was the ex-communists had no money, unless you counted rubles and coupons and kopecks and whatever else they were using these days, all of which might as well be used for toilet paper.

That reality did not trouble Lord. What the ex-commies had in abundance was raw materials that Sullivan was salivating to acquire. That was the reason Lord had spent three godforsaken months there. But it would be worth it if Sullivan came through.

Lord had learned to have his doubts about everyone. But if anyone could pull this deal off, Walter Sullivan could. Everything he had touched seemed to multiply to global proportions, and the droppings that went to his cohorts were truly awe-inspiring. And at almost eighty, the old man hadn't slowed a step. He worked fifteen-hour days, was married to a twenty-something babe right out of a drive-in movie. He was right this minute in Barbados where he had flown the three highest-ranking politicos for a little business and entertainment Western style. Sullivan would call. And Sandy's short but select client list would grow by one, but what a one it would be.

Lord took note of the young woman in the painfully short skirt and tiptoe heels strolling across the dining room.

She smiled at him; he returned the look with slightly elevated eyebrows, a favorite signal of his because of its ambiguity. She was a congressional liaison for one of the big 16th Street associations, not that he cared about her occupation. She was excellent in bed, that he did care about.

The view brought back a number of pleasant memories. He would have to call her soon. He jotted a note to that effect in his electronic notebook. Then he turned his attention, as did most of the ladies in the room, to the tall, angular figure of Jack Graham striding across the room, heading straight for him.

Lord rose and extended his hand. Jack didn't take it.

"What the hell happened to Barry Alvis?"

Lord introduced one of his blank stares to the confrontation and sat back down. A waiter appeared and then was dismissed by a short wave of Lord's hand. Lord eyed Jack, who remained standing.

"You don't give a person a chance to catch their breath, do you? Straight out the mouth and into the fire. Sometimes that strategy is smart, sometimes it isn't."

"I'm not kidding, Sandy, I want to know what is going on. Barry's office is empty, his secretary is looking at me like I personally ordered a hit on him. I want some answers." Jack's voice was rising, and with it the stares increased.

"Whatever you have on your mind, I am sure we can discuss it with a little more dignity than you're mustering right now. Why don't you have a seat and start acting like a partner at the best damned law firm in this city."

Their eyes stayed locked for a full five seconds until Jack slowly sat down.

"Drink?"

"Beer."

The waiter reappeared and went away with an order for beer and Sandy's potent gin and tonic. Sandy lit a Raleigh and casually looked out the window, then back at Jack.

"You know about Barry then."

"All I know is he's gone. Why he's gone is what I want you to tell me."

"Not much to tell. He was let go, effective today."

"Why?"

"What's it to you?"

"Barry and I were working together."

"But you weren't friends."

"We didn't have a chance to be friends yet."

"Why on God's earth would you want to be friends with Barry Alvis? Man was permanent associate material if ever I saw one, and I've seen plenty."

"He was a helluva lawyer."

"No, technically, he was a highly competent attorney, proficient in the area of corporate transactional matters and tax, with a sub-specialty in health care acquisitions. He's never generated a dime in business, and never would. Thus he was not a 'helluva lawyer.'"

"Goddammit, you know what I mean. He was a very valuable asset to the firm. You need somebody to do the friggin' work."

"We have roughly two hundred attorneys who are very well suited to do the friggin' work. On the other hand, we have only a dozen or so partners who bring in any material clients. That is not the proportion one should strive for. Plenty of soldiers, not enough chiefs. You see Barry Alvis as an asset, we saw him as a high-priced liability without the talent to leverage himself. He billed enough to keep himself very highly compensated. That is not how we, the partners, make the most money. Thus a decision was made to sever our relationship."

"And you're telling me you didn't get a little nudge from Baldwin?"

Lord's face contained genuine surprise. A lawyer with over thirty-five years' experience blowing smoke in people's faces, he was a consummate liar. "What the hell do the Baldwins care about Barry Alvis?"

Jack scrutinized the corpulent face for a full minute and then let his breath out slowly. He looked around the restaurant suddenly feeling silly and embarrassed. All this for nothing? But if Lord was lying? He glanced again at the man, but the face was impassive. But why would he lie? Jack could think of several reasons, but none of them made too much sense. Could he have been wrong? Had he just made a complete ass out of himself in front of the firm's most powerful partner?

136

Lord's voice was softer now, almost consoling. "Barry Alvis was let go as part of an ongoing effort to clear out the deadwood near the top. We want more attorneys who can do the work *and* produce the rain. Hell, like you. Simple as that. Barry wasn't the first and he won't be the last. We've been working on this for a long time, Jack. Long before you ever came to the firm." Lord paused and looked keenly at Jack. "Is there something you're not telling me? We're going to be partners soon, you can't keep things from your partners."

Lord chuckled inwardly. The list of secret deals he had had with clients was a long one.

Jack was close to biting, but decided not to.

"I'm not a partner yet, Sandy."

"Pure formality."

"Things don't happen till they happen."

Lord shifted uncomfortably in his chair, waved his cigarette smoke like a wand. So maybe the rumors that Jack was contemplating jumping ship were true. Those rumors were the reason Lord was sitting here with the young lawyer. They looked at each other. A smile tugged at Jack's mouth. Jack's four million in legal business was an irresistible carrot. Particularly because it meant another four hundred grand to Sandy Lord, not that he needed it, but not that he would turn it down either. He had the reputation of being a big spender. And lawyers didn't retire. They worked until they dropped. The best made a lot of money, but compared to CEOs, rock stars and actors they were strictly minor-league compensation-wise.

"I thought you liked our shop."

"I do."

"So?"

"So what?"

Sandy's eye roamed the dining room again. He spotted another female acquaintance encased in a

137

sleek and costly business suit under which Sandy had good reason to believe she wore absolutely nothing. He swallowed the rest of his gin and tonic, looked at Jack. Lord grew more and more irritated. The stupid, green sonofabitch.

"You ever been to this place before?"

Jack shook his head, surveyed the thick menu, searching for a burger and fries and not finding it. Then the menu was yanked out of his hand and Lord leaned into him, his breath heavy and saggy in Jack's face.

"Well, why don't you take a look around then?"

Lord lifted a finger for the waiter and ordered a Dewar's and water, which appeared a minute later. Jack leaned back in his chair, but Lord inched closer, almost straddling the ornately carved table.

"I've been in restaurants before, Sandy, believe it or not."

"Not this one though, right? You see that little lady over there?" Lord's surprisingly slender fingers sliced through the air. Jack's gaze fell on the congressional liaison. "I've fucked that woman five times in the past six months." Lord could not help but smile as Jack appraised the subject and came away duly impressed.

"Now ask yourself why a creature like that would condescend to sleep with a big old bag of fat like me."

"Maybe she feels sorry for you." Jack smiled.

Lord did not. "If you actually believe that, then you possess a naïveté that borders on incompetence. Do you really believe women in this town are any more pure than the men? Why should they be? Just because they have tits and a skirt doesn't mean they won't take what they want and use any means at their disposal to do so.

"You see, son, it's because I can give her what she wants, and I don't mean between the sheets. She knows that, I know that. I can open doors in this

138

town only a handful of men can. And the quid pro quo for that is she lets me fuck her. It's a straight commercial transaction entered into by intelligent, highly sophisticated parties. How about that?"

"How about it?"

Lord sat back in his chair, lit a fresh cigarette and blew precise rings to the ceiling. He picked at his lip and chuckled to himself.

"Something funny, Sandy?"

"I was just now thinking how you probably got a kick out of people like me when you were in law school. Thinking how you were never going to be like me. Gonna go defend illegal aliens wanting political asylum or do death row appeals for poor sonofabitches who've butchered a few too many people and blamed it on getting spanked by their momma when they were bad. Now come on, tell the truth, you did that, didn't you?"

Jack loosened his tie, took a sip of beer. He had seen Lord in action before. He smelled a setup.

"You're one of the best lawyers around, Sandy, everybody says so."

"Shit, I haven't practiced law in years."

"Whatever works for you."

"What works for you, Jack?"

Jack felt a slight but perceptible clinch in his gut as he heard his name pass through Lord's lips. It suggested a coming intimacy that had startled him, despite his knowledge of its inevitability. Partner? Jack took a breath and shrugged.

"Who knows what they want to be when they grow up?"

"But see you are grown up, Jack, and it's time to pay the man at the door. So what's it gonna be?"

"I'm not following this."

Lord leaned in again, hands clenched, like a heavyweight pressing the exchange, looking for the tiniest

139

opening. Indeed, for a moment, an attack seemed imminent. Jack tensed.

"You think I'm an asshole, don't you?"

Jack picked up his menu again. "Recommend anything?"

"Come on, kid, you think I'm a greedy, ego-centric, power-happy asshole who doesn't give a shit about anything or anybody that can't do something for me. Ain't that right, Jack!" Lord's voice was rising, his thick body half out of his chair. He pushed Jack's menu back down to the table.

Jack nervously scanned the room, but no one seemed to be paying attention, which meant every word of the exchange was being carefully absorbed and dissected. Lord's red eyes focused directly on Jack's, pulling them to him.

"I am, you know. That's exactly what I am, Jack."

Lord settled back in his chair, triumphant. He grinned. Jack felt inclined to smile in spite of the repulsiveness.

Jack relaxed a notch. Almost as if sensing that slight release, Lord slid his chair over next to Jack's, crowding him. For a moment Jack seriously con-templated decking the older man — enough was enough.

"That's right, I'm all those things, Jack, all those things and more, much more. But you know what, Jack? That's who I am. I don't try to disguise it or explain it. Every sonofabitch that has ever met me has come away knowing exactly who and what I was. I believe in what I do. There's no bullshit there." Lord took a deep breath, and then slowly let it out. Jack shook his head, trying to clear it.

"What about you, Jack?"

"What about me?"

"Who are you, Jack? What do you believe in, if anything?"

"I've got twelve years of Catholic school, I've got to believe in something."

Lord shook his head wearily. "You're disappointing me. I heard you were a bright kid. Either my reports are wrong, or you've got that shit-eating grin on your face because you're afraid of what you might say."

Jack grasped Lord's wrist in a viselike grip.

"What the fuck do you want from me?"

Lord smiled and gently rapped Jack's hand until the grip was released.

"You like these kinds of places? With Baldwin as a client you'll be eating in places like this until your arteries are hard as drill bits. In about forty years, you'll keel over in some sand trap in the Caribbean and leave behind some young and suddenly rich third-time-around honey; but you'll die happy, believe me."

"One place is the same as another to me."

Lord's hand came down hard on the table. This time several heads did turn. The maitre d' glanced in their direction, trying to conceal his apprehension behind his thick mustache and quiet air of competence.

"That's my whole goddamned point, son, that goddamned ambivalence of yours." His voice lowered, but he continued to lean into Jack, crowding him. "One place is definitely not the same as another. You have the key to this place, you know. Your key is Baldwin and that nice-looking daughter of his. Now the question becomes: will you or won't you open that door? Which query interestingly enough leads us right back to my original question. What do you believe in, Jack? Because if you do not believe in this" – Lord spread his arms wide – "if you do not want to become the Sandy Lord of the next generation, if you wake up at night and laugh at or

141

curse my little idiosyncrasies, my assholeness if you will, if you really and truly believe you are above that, if you really hate whaling away at Ms. Baldwin and if you don't see one single item on that menu that you care for, then why don't you tell me to fuck off? And get up and walk out that door there, your head high, your conscience clear, and your beliefs intact? Because frankly this game is far too important and intensely played for the uncommitted."

Lord slumped back in his chair, his mass extrapolating outward until it fully engulfed the space.

Outside the restaurant a truly beautiful fall day was unfolding. Neither rain nor excessive humidity marred the blue sky's perfectness; the gentle breeze rustled discarded newspapers. The torrid pace of the city seemed to have momentarily slowed a notch. Down the street at LaFayette Park, sunseekers lay in the grass, hoping for a few more moments of tan before the really cold weather set in. Bike messengers on break prowled the area looking for unconcealed legs and blouses open just a peek.

Inside the restaurant Jack Graham and Sandy Lord were staring at each other.

"You don't pull any punches, do you?"

"I don't have time for that, Jack. Not for the last twenty years. If I didn't believe you could handle the direct approach, I would've just bullshit with you and let it go."

"What do you want me to say?"

"All I want to know is whether you're in or out. The truth is, with Baldwin, you could go to any other shop in town. You chose us, I'm presuming, because you like what you saw."

"Baldwin recommended you."

"He's a smart man. Lots of people would follow his lead. You've been with us one year. If you choose to stay, you'll be made a partner. Frankly, the twelve-

142

month wait was purely a formality, to see if we were a good fit. After that you will never have any financial concerns, not counting your future wife's considerable monies. Your main occupation will be to keep Baldwin happy, and to expand that piece of business, and to bring in anybody else you can. Because let's face it, Jack, the only security any lawyer has are the clients he controls. They never tell you that in law school and it's the most important lesson you have to learn. Never, never lose sight of that fact. Even doing the work should take a back seat to that. There'll always be bodies to do the work. You will be given carte blanche to chase more business. You will have no one supervising you, except Baldwin. You will not have to monitor the legal work being done for Baldwin, we have others who will do that for you. All in all, not such a terrible life."

Jack looked down at his hands. Jennifer's face appeared there. So perfect. He felt guilty for having assumed she had had Barry Alvis fired. Then he thought of the numbing hours as a PD. His thoughts finally turned to Kate, and then quickly stopped. What was there? The answer was nothing. He looked up.

"Stupid question. Do I get to keep practicing law?"

"If that's what you want." Lord eyed him closely. "So do I take that as a yes?"

Jack glanced down at the menu. "The crab cakes look good."

Sandy exhaled smoke to the ceiling and smiled broadly. "I love 'em, Jack. I goddamn love 'em."

Two hours later, Sandy stood in the corner of his massive office suite staring out onto the busy street below, while a conference call plodded forward on the speaker phone.

Dan Kirksen walked in the door, his stiff bow tie

and crisp shirt concealing a slender jogger's body. Kirksen was the firm's managing partner. He had unwavering control over everyone in the place except Sandy Lord. And now perhaps Jack Graham.

Lord glanced at him with uninterested eyes. Kirksen sat down and waited patiently until the conference call participants said their good-byes. Lord clicked the phone off and sat down in his chair. Leaning back, he eyed the ceiling and lit up. Kirksen, a health fanatic, inched back from the desk.

"You want something?" Lord's eyes had finally come to rest on Kirksen's lean, hairless face. The man consistently controlled a shade under six hundred thousand in business, which guaranteed him a long, secure home at PS&L, but those numbers were chickenshit to Lord and he did nothing to hide his dislike of the firm's managing partner.

"We were wondering how the lunch went."

"You can handle the softballs. I don't have time to play fucking softball."

"We had heard unsettling rumors, and then with Alvis having to be terminated when Ms. Baldwin called."

Lord waved a hand through the air. "That's taken care of. He loves us, he's staying. And I wasted two hours."

"The amount of money at stake, Sandy, we all felt it would be better, it would convey the strongest possible impression if you—"

"Yeah. I understand the numbers, Kirksen, better than you, I understand the numbers. Okay? Now, Jacky boy is staying put. With luck he might double his fishing line in ten years, and we can all retire early." Lord looked over at Kirksen, who seemed to grow smaller and smaller under the big man's gaze. "He's got balls, you know. More balls than any of my other partners."

144

Kirksen winced.

"In fact, I kind of like the kid." Lord stood up and moved over to the window, where he watched a procession of preschoolers attached together with rope cross the street ten stories below.

"Then I can report a positive to the committee?"

"You can report any goddamn thing you like. Just remember one thing: don't you boys ever bother me with one of these things again, unless it's really, really important, you understand me?"

Lord glanced once more at Kirksen and then his eyes returned to the window. Sullivan still had not called. That was not good. He could see his country slipping away, like the little bodies disappearing around the corner. Gone.

"Thank you, Sandy."

"Yeah."

NINE

Walter Sullivan stared at the face, or what was left of it. The exposed foot showed the official morgue toe tag. While his entourage waited outside, he quietly sat alone with her. The identification had already been formally made. The police had gone off to update their records, the reporters to file their stories. But Walter Sullivan, one of the most powerful men of his era, who had made money from nearly everything he had touched since he was fourteen, now suddenly found himself bereft of energy, of any will whatsoever.

The press had had a field day with him and Christy after his marriage of forty-seven years had ended in the death of his first wife. But at almost eighty years old, he had just wanted something young and alive. After so much death, he had wanted something that would most certainly outlive him. With close friends and loved ones dying around him, he had passed his tolerance level as a mourner. Growing old was not easy, even for the very rich.

But Christy Sullivan had not survived him. And he was going to do something about that. It was fortunate that he was largely ignorant of what lay ahead for the remains of his late wife. It was a necessary process that was not in the least designed to comfort the victim's family.

As soon as Walter Sullivan left the room, a technician would enter and wheel the late Mrs. Sullivan into the autopsy room. There she would be weighed and have her height confirmed. She would be photographed, first fully clothed, and then in the nude. Then X-rayed and fingerprinted. A complete external exam would be conducted, with the intent of noting and obtaining as much usable evidence and as many clues as possible from the body. Fluids would be taken and sent to toxicology for drug and alcohol screens and other testing. A Y incision would split her body shoulder to shoulder, chest to genitals. A horrific chasm for even the veteran observer. Every organ would be analyzed and weighed, her genitalia checked for signs of sexual intercourse or damage. Every trace of semen, blood or foreign hair would be sent for DNA typing.

Her head would be examined, wound patterns traced. Then a saw would make an intermastoid incision over the top of the skull, cutting through the scalp and down to the bone. Next, the front quadrant of the skull would be cut away and the brain removed through the frontal craniotomy and examined. The one slug would be extracted, marked for chain-of-custody purposes and held for ballistics.

Once that process was completed, Walter Sullivan would be given back his wife.

Toxicology would verify the contents of her stomach and traces of foreign substances in her blood and urine.

The autopsy protocol would be prepared, listing the cause and mechanism of death and all relevant findings, and the official opinion of the Medical Examiner.

The autopsy protocol, together with all photographs, X-rays, fingerprints, toxicology reports and any other information constituting the entire case file would be deposited with the detective in charge.

Walter Sullivan finally rose, covered the remains of his deceased wife and left.

From behind yet another one-way mirror, the detective's eyes followed the bereaved husband as he left the room. Then Seth Frank put on his hat and quietly exited.

Conference room number one, the largest in the firm, held a prominent center position right behind the reception area. Now, behind the thick sliding doors, a meeting of the entire partnership had just convened.

Between Sandy Lord and another senior partner sat Jack Graham; his partnership not yet official, but protocol was not important today and Lord had insisted.

Coffee was poured by the housekeeping staff, danishes and muffins were distributed around, and then the help retreated, closing the doors behind them.

All heads turned to Dan Kirksen. He sipped his juice, tapped his mouth affectedly with his napkin and rose.

"As I'm sure you've heard by now, a terrible tragedy has befallen one of our most" – Kirksen glanced quickly at Lord – "or I should say, our most significant client." Jack looked around the sixty-foot marble-top table. Most heads remained trained on Kirksen, a few others were filled in on the events by whispers from their neighbor. Jack had seen the headlines. He had never worked on any of Sullivan's matters but he knew they were extensive enough to occupy forty attorneys at the firm on almost a full-time basis. He was, by far, Patton, Shaw's biggest client.

Kirksen continued, "The police are investigating the matter thoroughly. As yet there have been no developments in the case." Kirksen paused, glanced again at Lord, and then continued, "As one can imagine, this is a very distressing time for Walter. To make matters as easy as possible for him during this time, we are asking all attorneys to pay particular attention to any Sullivan-related matters, and, hopefully, to nip any potential problem in the bud before it escalates. Further, while we do not believe that this is anything other than a routine burglary with a very unfortunate result, and is in no way connected to any of Walter's business affairs, we are asking each of you to be alert for any unusual signs in any of the dealings in which you are engaged on Walter's behalf. Any suspicious activity is to be reported immediately to either myself or Sandy."

A number of heads turned toward Lord, who was looking at the ceiling in his customary fashion. Three cigarette butts lay in the ashtray in front of him, the remains of a Bloody Mary beside it.

Ron Day, from the international law section, spoke up. His neatly trimmed hair framed an owlish face partially obscured by slender oval spectacles. "This isn't a terrorist thing, is it? I've been putting together a string of Middle Eastern joint ventures for Sullivan's Kuwaiti subsidiary, and those people operate under their own rules, I can tell you that. Should I be worried for my personal safety? I'm on a flight this evening for Riyadh."

Lord swiveled his head around until his eyes fell on Day. Sometimes it surprised him how myopic if not downright idiotic many of his partners were. Day was a service partner whose main, and in Lord's mind only, strength was his ability to speak seven languages and politely kiss the ass of the Saudis.

"I wouldn't worry about that, Ron. If this is an international conspiracy, you're not important enough to dick around with, and if they do target you, you'll be dead before you ever see it coming."

Day fiddled with his necktie as an uneasy mirth quietly circled the table.

"Thank you for the clarification, Sandy."

"You're welcome, Ron."

Kirksen cleared his throat. "Rest assured that everything that can be done to solve this heinous crime is being done. There's even talk that the President himself will authorize a special investigative task force to look into the matter. As you know, Walter Sullivan has served in various capacities in several administrations, and is one of the President's closest friends. I think we can assume that the criminals will be in custody shortly." Kirksen sat down.

Lord looked around the table, elevated his eyebrows and crushed out his last cigarette. The table cleared.

Seth Frank swiveled around in his chair. His office was a six-by-six pen, the Sheriff warranting the only spacious area in the small headquarters building. The Medical Examiner's report was on his desk. It was only seven-thirty in the morning but Frank had already read every word of the report three times.

He had attended the autopsy. It was just something detectives had to do, for a lot of reasons. Although he had been present at literally hundreds of them, he had never grown comfortable with seeing the dead tinkered with like the animal remains every college biology student has sunk their digits into. And although he no longer became ill at the sight, it usually took him two or three hours of driving around aimlessly before he could attempt to settle back down to work.

The report was thick and neatly typed. Christy Sullivan had been dead at least seventy-two hours, probably longer. The swelling and blistering of the body, and the bacteria and gaseous onset in her organs, substantiated that time range with pretty good accuracy. However, the room had been very warm, which had accelerated the postmortem putrefaction of the body. That fact, in turn, made ascertaining the actual time of death increasingly difficult. But not less than three days, the Medical Examiner had been firm on that. Frank also had ancillary information that led him to believe that Christine Sullivan had met her death on Monday night, which would put them smack in the three-to-four-day range.

Frank felt himself frowning. A minimum of three days meant he was facing a very cold trail. Someone who knew what they were doing could disappear from the face of the earth in three or four days. Added to that was the fact that now Christine Sullivan had been dead a while now and his investigation was really no further along than when he started. He could not remember a case where the trail was so nonexistent.

As far as they could ascertain there were no witnesses to the incidents at the Sullivan estate, other than the decedent and whoever had murdered her. Notices had been placed in the papers, at banks and shopping centers. No one had come forward.

They had talked to every homeowner within a three-mile radius. They had all expressed shock, outrage and fear. Frank had seen the latter in the twitch of an eyebrow, hunched shoulders and the nervous rubbing of hands. Security would be even tighter than ever in the little county. All those emotions, however, yielded no usable information. The staffs of each of the neighbors had also been thoroughly questioned. There was nothing there. Telephone interviews had been conducted of Sullivan's household staff, who had accompanied him to Barbados, with nothing earth-shattering to report

151

back. Besides, they all had ironclad alibis. Not that that was insurmountable. Frank filed that away in the back of his mind.

They also did not have a good snapshot of Christine Sullivan's last day of life. She was murdered in her house, presumably late at night. But if she had indeed been murdered on Monday night, what had she been doing during the day? Frank believed that information had to lend them something to go on.

At nine-thirty in the morning on that Monday, Christine Sullivan had been seen in downtown Washington at an upscale salon where it would cost Frank two weeks' pay to send his wife for a pampering. Whether the woman was gearing up for some late-night fun or this was something the rich did on a regular basis was something Frank would have to find out. Their inquiries had turned up nothing on Sullivan's whereabouts after she had left the salon around noon. She had not returned to her apartment in the city, nor had she taken a taxicab anywhere that they could determine.

If the little woman had stayed behind when everyone else went to the sunny south, she had to have a reason, he figured. If she had been with someone that night, that was someone Frank wanted to talk to, and maybe handcuff.

Ironically, murder in the commission of a burglary did not constitute capital murder in Virginia, although, interestingly enough, murder during the course of an armed robbery did. If you robbed and killed, you could be sentenced to death. If you burgled and killed, the most you'd be looking at was life, which wasn't that great a choice given the barbaric conditions of most state prisons. But Christine Sullivan had worn much jewelry. Every report the detective had received indicated she was a great lover of diamonds, emeralds, sapphires; you

152

name it, she wore it. There was no jewelry on the body, although it was easy enough to see the marks on the skin the rings had made. Sullivan had also confirmed that his wife's diamond necklace was missing. The beauty salon owner also remembered seeing that particular piece on Monday.

A good prosecutor could make out a case of robbery on those facts, Frank was sure of it. The perps were lying in wait, premeditation the whole way. Why should the good people of Virginia have to pay thousands of dollars a year to feed, clothe and house a coldblooded killer? Burglary? Robbery? Who the fuck really cared? The woman was dead. Blown away by some sick goon. Legal distinctions like that did not sit well with Frank. Like many law enforcement people, he felt the criminal-justice system was weighted far too heavily in favor of the defendant. It often seemed to him that lost in the entire convoluted process with its intricate deals, technical traps and ultrasmooth defense attorneys was the fact that someone had actually broken the law. That someone had been hurt, raped or killed. That was just flat-out wrong. Frank had no way to change the system, but he could peck around its edges.

He pulled the report closer, fumbling with his reading glasses. He took another sip of the thick, black coffee. Cause of death: lateral gunshot wounds to the cephalic region caused by high-velocity, large-caliber firearm(s) firing one expanding, softnose bullet causing a perforating wound, and a second slug of unknown composition from an unidentified weapon source causing a penetrating wound. Which, in ordinary English, meant her brain had been blown apart by some heavy-duty hardware. The report also stated that the manner of death was homicide, which was the only clear element Frank could see in the entire case. He noted that he had been correct in his

153

conclusion of the distance from which the shots had come. There were no traces of powder in the wound track. The shots had come from over two feet away: Frank surmised that the distance was probably closer to six feet, but that was only his gut talking. Not that suicide had ever been a consideration. But murders for hire were usually of the barrel-to-flesh variety. That particular method cut down considerably on the margin of error.

Frank leaned closer to his desk. Why more than one shot? The woman most certainly was killed with the first round. Was the assailant a sadist, pumping round after round into a dead body? And yet they could account for only two entries into the body, hardly the lead barrage of some madman. Then there was the issue of the slugs. A dumdum and a mystery bullet.

He held up a bag with his mark on it. Only one round had been recovered from the body. It had entered below the right temple, flattened and expanded on impact, penetrated the skull and brain, causing a shock wave of the soft brain tissue, like rolling up a carpet.

He carefully nudged the caged creature or what was left of it. A gruesome projectile that was designed to flatten upon impact and then proceed to rip apart everything in its path, it had worked as designed on Christine Sullivan. Problem was dumdums were everywhere now. And the projectile deformity had been immense. Ballistics had been next to useless.

The second round had entered a half-inch above the other, traversed the entire brain, and exited the other side, leaving a gaping hole much larger than the entrance wound. The bone and tissue damage had been considerable.

This bullet's resting place had given them all a surprise. A half-inch hole in the wall against the bed.

Ordinarily after having cut out the piece of plaster, the lab personnel, using special tools, would have extracted the slug, being careful to preserve the grooving of the bullet, which would enable them to narrow down the make of gun from which it was fired and hopefully to eventually match it to a particular piece of ordnance. Fingerprints and ballistics identification were as close to certain as you got in this business.

Except in this case, while the hole was there, there was no slug in the hole, and no other slug in the room. When the lab had called him to report that finding, Seth Frank had gone down to see for himself. That was as angry as he had gotten in a long time.

Why go to the trouble of digging out a slug when you still had one in the corpse? What would the second slug show that the first wouldn't? There were possibilities.

Frank made some notes. The missing bullet could be a different caliber or type, which probably would show there were at least two assailants. Strong as his imagination was, Frank could not realistically envision one person wielding a gun in each hand and popping off at the woman. So now he had a probable two suspects. That would also explain the different entry, exit and internal wound patterns. The tumbling dumdum's entry hole was larger than the other slug's. So the second slug wasn't a hollow or softnose. It had blown right through her head, leaving a tunnel half the width of a pinkie in its wake. Projectile deformity had probably been minimal, which was meaningless since he didn't have the damn slug.

He looked over his initial scene notes. He was in the collection-of-information stage. He hoped he would not be stuck there forever. At least he didn't have to worry about the statute of limitations expiring on this one.

He looked at the report one more time, and his frown returned.

He picked up his phone and dialed. Ten minutes later he was sitting across from the Medical Examiner in the latter's office.

The big man pried at his cuticles with an old scalpel and finally glanced up at Frank.

"Strangulation marks. Or at least *attempted* strangulation. Understand, the trachea wasn't crushed, although there was some swelling and hemorrhaging in the tissue, and I found evidence of a slight fracture of the hyoid bone. Got traces of petechia in the conjunctiva of the eyelids too. Nonligature. It's all in the protocol."

Frank turned that over in his mind. Petechia, or tiny hemorrhages in the conjunctiva, or mucous membrane, of the eyes and eyelids, could be caused by strangulation and the resulting pressure on the brain.

Frank leaned forward in his chair, looked at the degrees lining the wall proclaiming the man opposite from him to be a long-dedicated student of forensic pathology.

"Man or woman?"

The Medical Examiner shrugged at the inquiry.

"Hard to tell. Human skin isn't a stellar surface for prints, as you know. In fact it's pretty impossible except in a few discrete areas, and after about half a day, if there was anything there, it won't be anymore. Hard to imagine, though, a woman trying to strangle another woman with her bare hands, but it's happened. Doesn't take much pressure to crush a trachea, but bare-handed strangling's usually a macho method of inflicting death. In a hundred strangling cases, I've never seen one where it was proved that a woman committed it. This was from the front too," he added. "*Mano a mano*. You'd have to be pretty

156

damn confident of your strength advantage. My educated guess? It was a man, for what a guess is worth."

"The report also says there were contusions and bruises on the left side of her jaw, loosened teeth and cuts on the inside of her mouth?"

"Looks like somebody belted her a good one. One of the molars almost penetrated her cheek."

Frank glanced at his case file. "The second bullet?"

"The damage inflicted leads me to believe it's a large caliber, just like the first."

"Any guesses on the first?"

"That's all it would be. Maybe .357, .41. Could've been a 9mm too. Jesus, you saw the slug. Damn thing was flat as a pancake with half of it dispersed through her brain tissue and fluid. No lands, grooves, twists. Even if you find a probable firearm you're not going to get a match there."

"If we can find the other one, we might be in business."

"Maybe not. Whoever dug it out of that wall probably messed up the markings. Ballistics won't be happy with that."

"Yeah, but it might just have some of the deceased's hair, blood and skin imbedded in the nose. That's some trace I'd love to get my hands on."

The ME rubbed his chin thoughtfully. "That's true. But you've got to find it first."

"Which we probably won't." Frank smiled.

"You never know."

The two men looked at each other, knowing full well that there was no way in hell they were going to find the other slug. Even if they did, they couldn't place it at the murder scene unless it had trace evidence of the deceased on it, or they could find the gun that had fired it and placed the weapon at the murder scene. A potential double whammy.

157

"Find any brass?"

Frank shook his head.

"Then you got no pinprick either, Seth." The Medical Examiner was referring to the unique imprint left by the firing pin of a gun on the base of the shell casing.

"Never said it would be easy. By the way, state guys giving you room to breathe on this one?"

The Medical Examiner smiled. "Remarkably silent. Now if it had been Walter Sullivan getting whacked, who knows? I already filed my report in Richmond."

Then Frank said the question he had really come to ask.

"Why two shots?"

The Medical Examiner stopped picking his cuticle, put down his scalpel and looked at Frank.

"Why not?" His eyes crinkled. He was in the unenviable position of being more than competent for the opportunities presented him in the quiet county. One of approximately five hundred Deputy Medical Examiners in the commonwealth, he enjoyed a thriving general practice but had a personal fascination with both police investigations and forensic pathology. Before settling into a quiet life in Virginia he had served as a deputy coroner for Los Angeles County for almost twenty years. It didn't get much worse than L.A. for homicides. But this was one he could get his teeth into.

Frank looked at him intently and said, "Either shot would have obviously been fatal. No question. So why fire a second? You wouldn't for a lot of reasons. Number one being the noise. Number two, if you want to get the hell out of there, why take the time to pump another round into her? On top of that, why leave behind another slug that could ID you later on? Did Sullivan startle them? If so, why did the shot

158

come from the doorway into the room, and not the other way around? Why was the firing line descending? Was she on her knees? She probably was or else the shooter was off the scale height-wise. If she was on her knees, why? Execution-style? But there were no contact wounds. And then you have the marks on the neck. Why try to strangle her first, then stop, pick up a gun and blow her head off? And then blow it off again. One slug's taken. Why? A second gun? Why try to hide that? What's significant about that?"

Frank stood up and moved around the room, his hands stuck deep into his pockets, a habit of his when thinking intently. "And the crime scene was so fucking clean I couldn't believe it. There was nothing left. And I mean nothing. I'm surprised they didn't operate on her and pull out the other slug.

"I mean, come on, this guy was a burglar or maybe that's what he wants us to believe. But the vault *was* cleaned out. About four and a half million taken. And what was Mrs. Sullivan doing there? She was supposed to be sunning in the Caribbean. Did she know the guy? Was she screwing around on the side? If she was, are the two incidents related in any way? And why the hell would you waltz in the front door, knock out the security system, and then use a rope to climb out the window? Every time I ask myself one question another one pops up." Frank sat back down, looking slightly bewildered at his outpouring.

The Medical Examiner leaned back in his chair, twirled the case file around and took a minute to read over it. He took off his glasses and wiped them on his sleeve, tugged at a corner of his lip with his thumb and index finger.

Frank's nostrils quivered as he watched the ME. "What?"

"You mentioned nothing being left at the crime

scene. I've been thinking about that. You're right. It was *too* clean." The Medical Examiner took his time in lighting up a Pall Mall — unfiltered, Frank noted. Every pathologist he had ever worked with had smoked. The Medical Examiner blew rings in the air, obviously enjoying this mental exercise.

"Her fingernails were too clean."

Frank looked puzzled.

The Medical Examiner continued, "I mean, there was no dirt, nail polish — although she was wearing it, bright red stuff — none of the ordinary residues you'd expect to find. Nothing. It was like they had been scoped out, you know what I mean?" He paused and then continued, "I also found minute traces of a solution." He paused again. "Like a cleansing solution."

"She'd been to some fancy beauty salon that morning. For a nail job and all that."

The ME shook his head. "Then you'd expect to find more residue, not less, with all the chemicals they use."

"So what are you saying? That her nails were deliberately cleaned out?"

The Medical Examiner nodded. "Someone was real careful not to leave any ident material behind."

"Which means they were paranoid about being identified, somehow, by the physical evidence."

"Most perps are, Seth."

"To a degree. But squirting out fingernails and leaving a place so clean our E-vac came up basically empty is a little much."

Frank scanned the report. "You also found traces of oil on her palms?"

The ME nodded, looked closely at the detective. "A preservative/protective compound. You know, like you'd use on fabrics, leathers, stuff like that."

"So she may have been holding something and the residue was left there?"

160

"Yep. Although we can't be sure exactly when the oil came to be on her hands." The Medical Examiner put his glasses back on. "You think she knew the person, Seth?"

"None of the evidence points that way, unless she invited him over to burglarize the place."

The Medical Examiner had a sudden inspiration. "Maybe she set up the burglary. You know? Tired of the old man, brings in the new bedroom buddy to conveniently steal their nest egg and it's off to Fairy Tale Land?"

Frank considered the theory. "Except they have a falling out or there's a double cross all along, and she gets the business end of some serious lead?"

"It fits the facts, Seth."

Frank shook his head. "From all accounts the deceased loved *being* Mrs. Walter Sullivan. More than the money, if you know what I mean. She got to rub shoulders, and probably other parts of her anatomy, with famous people all over the world. Pretty heady for somebody who used to flip burgers at a Burger King."

The ME stared at him. "You're kidding?"

The detective smiled. "Eighty-year-old billionaires sometimes get strange ideas. It's like where does the eight-hundred-pound gorilla sit? Anywhere he damn well pleases."

The Medical Examiner grinned and shook his head. Billionaire? What would he do with a billion dollars? He looked down at the ink blotter on his desk. Then he put out his cigarette and looked back at the report, then at Frank. He cleared his throat.

"I think the second slug was a semi- or full-metal jacket."

Frank loosened his tie, put his elbows on the desk. "Okay."

The Medical Examiner went on. "It blew through

the right temporal bone of the cranium and burst through the left pareital bone, leaving an exit wound over twice the size of the entry."

"So you're saying definitely two guns."

"Not unless the guy was chambering different types of ammo in the same gun." He looked keenly at the detective. "That doesn't seem to surprise you, Seth."

"It would have an hour ago. It doesn't now."

"So we probably have two perps."

"Two perps with two guns. And a lady how big?"

The Medical Examiner didn't need to refer to his notes. "Sixty-two inches tall, one hundred and five pounds."

"So a little woman and two probable male perps with heavy-caliber hardware who try to strangle her, beat her up and then both open fire on her, killing her."

The Medical Examiner rubbed at his chin. The facts were more than a little puzzling.

Frank glanced at the report. "You're sure the strangulation marks and beating came before death?"

The Medical Examiner looked offended. "Positive. Pretty mess, isn't it?"

Frank flipped through the report, making notes as he went. "You could say that. No attempted rape. Nothing like that?"

The Medical Examiner didn't answer.

Finally Frank looked up at him, took off his glasses, put them down on the desk and leaned back, sipping the black coffee he had been offered earlier.

"The report doesn't say anything about a sexual assault," he reminded his friend.

The Medical Examiner finally stirred. "The report's correct. There was no sexual assault. No trace of seminal fluid, no evidence of penetration, no overt bruising. All that leads me to conclude,

162

officially, that no sexual assault occurred."

"So? You're not satisfied with that conclusion?" Frank looked at him expectantly.

The Medical Examiner took a sip of coffee, stretched out his long arms until he felt a comforting pop deep within the confines of his aging body and then leaned forward.

"Your wife ever go in for a gynecological exam?"

"Sure, doesn't every woman?"

"You'd be surprised," the Medical Examiner replied dryly, then continued. "Thing is, you go in for an exam, no matter how good the ob-gyn is, there's usually some slight swelling and small abrasions in the genitalia. It's the nature of the beast. To be thorough, you have to get in there and dig around."

Frank put down his coffee, shifted in his chair. "So what are you saying, she had her gynecologist visit her in the middle of the night right before she got popped?"

"The indications were slight, very slight, but they were there." The Medical Examiner paused, choosing his words carefully. "I've been thinking about it ever since I handed in the protocol. Understand, it could be nothing. She could have done it herself, you understand what I'm saying? To each their own. But from the looks of it, I don't think it was self-inflicted. I think somebody examined her shortly *after* her death. Maybe two hours after, maybe earlier."

"Checked her for what? To see if something had happened?" Frank did not try to hide his incredulity.

The Medical Examiner eyed him steadily. "Not much else to check a woman for down there in that particular situation, is there?"

Frank stared at the man for a long moment. This information merely added to his already increasing temple throbber. He shook his head. The balloon theory again. Push one side in and it bulges out somewhere else. He scribbled down some notes, his eyebrows bunched together, the coffee sipped unconsciously.

The Medical Examiner looked him over. This was not an easy one, but so far, the detective had punched all the right buttons, asked good questions. He was puzzled, but then that was a big part of the process. The good ones never solved them all. But then they also didn't remain puzzled forever. Eventually, if you were lucky and diligent, maybe more of some on one case than on another, you would break it open, and the pieces would come tumbling into place. The Medical Examiner hoped this was one of those cases. Right now, it didn't look all that good.

"She was pretty drunk when she bought it." Frank was examining the toxicology report.

"Point two-one. I haven't personally seen that number since my college frat days."

Frank smiled. "Well I'm wondering where she got that point two-one."

"Plenty of booze in a place like that."

"Yeah, except there were no dirty glasses, no open bottles, and no discards in the trash."

"So, maybe she got drunk somewhere else."

"So how'd she get home?"

The Medical Examiner thought for a moment, rubbed the sleep from his eyes. "Drove. I've seen people with higher percentages behind the wheel."

"You mean in the autopsy room, don't you?" Frank continued: "The problem with that theory is that none of the cars in the garage had been driven from the time the household left for the Caribbean."

"How do you know that? An engine isn't going to be warm after three days."

164

Frank perused the pages of his notebook, found what he wanted and slid it around to his friend.

"Sullivan has a full-time chauffeur. Old guy named Bernie Kopeti. Knows his cars, anal as a tax lawyer, and he keeps meticulous records on Sullivan's fleet of automobiles. Has the mileage for every one of them in a log book, updated daily, if you can believe it. At my request he checked the odometer on each of the cars in the garage, which presumably were the only ones the wife would have access to, and in fact were the only cars in the garage at the time of the discovery of the body. On top of that Kopeti confirmed that no vehicles were missing. There was no additional mileage on any of them. They hadn't been driven since everyone cleared out for the Caribbean. Christine Sullivan didn't drive home in one of those cars. So how did she get home?"

"Cab?"

Frank shook his head. "We've talked to every cab company that operates out here. No fare was dropped off at the Sullivan address on that night. It'd be pretty hard to forget the place, wouldn't you think?"

"Unless maybe the cabbie whacked her, and isn't talking."

"You're saying she invited a cabbie into her house?"

"I'm saying she was drunk and probably didn't know what the hell she was doing."

"That doesn't jibe with the fact that the alarm system was tampered with, or that there was a rope dangling outside her window. Or that we're probably talking about two perps. I've never seen a cab driven by two cabbies."

A thought struck Frank and he scribbled in his notebook. He was certain Christine Sullivan had been driven home by someone she knew. Since that person or persons had not come forward, Frank thought he had a pretty good idea why they hadn't. And exiting out the window via a rope instead of the way they'd entered – through the front door – meant that something had caused the killers to rush. The most obvious reason was the private security patrol, but the security guard on duty that night had not reported anything out of the ordinary. The perps didn't know that, however. The mere sight of the patrol car might have prompted such a hasty exit.

The Medical Examiner leaned back in his chair, unsure of what to say. He spread out his hands. "Any suspects?"

Frank finished writing. "Maybe."

The Medical Examiner looked sharply at him. "What's her husband's story? One of the richest guys in the country."

"The world." Frank put his notebook away, picked up the report, drained the last of his coffee. "She decided to opt out on the way to the airport. Her husband believes she went to stay at their Watergate apartment in town. That fact has been confirmed. Their jet was scheduled to pick her up in three days and take her down to the Sullivan estate outside of Bridgetown, Barbados. When she didn't show at the airport, Sullivan got worried and started calling. That's his story."

"She give him any reason for the change in plan?"

"Not that he's telling me."

"Rich guys can afford the best. Make it look like a burglary while they're four thousand miles away swinging in a hammock sipping island bug juice. Think he's one of them?"

Frank stared at the wall for a long moment. His thoughts went back to the memory of Walter Sullivan sitting quietly next to his wife at the morgue. How he looked when he had no reason to believe anyone was watching.

Frank looked at the Medical Examiner, then got up to leave.

"No. I don't."

TEN

Bill Burton was sitting in the White House Secret Service command post. He slowly put down the newspaper, his third of the morning. Each carried a follow-up account of the murder of Christine Sullivan. The facts were virtually the same as the initial stories. Apparently there were no new developments.

He had talked to Varney and Johnson. At a cookout over the weekend at his place. Just him, Collin and their two fellow agents. The guy had been in the vault, seen the President and the Mrs. The man had come out, knocked out the President, killed the lady and gotten away despite the best efforts of Burton and Collin. That story didn't exactly match the actual sequence of events that night but both men had unfailingly accepted Burton's version of the occurrence. Both men had also expressed anger, indignation that anyone had laid a hand on the man they were dedicated to protect. The perp deserved what was coming to him. No one would hear of the President's involvement from them.

After they had left, Burton had sat in his backyard sipping a beer. If they only knew. The trouble was, he did. An honest man his entire life, Bill Burton did not savor his new role as prevaricator.

Burton swallowed his second cup of coffee and checked his watch. He poured himself another cup and looked around the White House Secret Service quarters.

He had always wanted to be a member of an elite security force, protecting the most important individual on the planet: the quiet resourcefulness, strength and intelligence of the Secret Service agent, the close camaraderie. The knowledge that at any moment you would be expected to and in fact would sacrifice your life for that of another man, for the benefit of the common good, made for a supremely noble act in a world more and more devoid of anything remotely virtuous. All that had allowed Agent William James Burton to get up with a smile each morning and sleep soundly at night. Now that feeling was gone. He had simply done his job, and the feeling was gone. He shook his head, sneaked a quick smoke.

Sitting on a keg of dynamite. That's what they all were doing. The more Gloria Russell explained it to him, the more impossible he thought it was.

The car had been a disaster. Very discreet inquiries had traced it directly to the goddamned D.C. police impoundment lot. That was too dangerous to push. Russell had been pissed. But let her be. She said she had this under control. Bullshit.

He folded up the paper, placed it neatly away for the next agent.

Fuck Russell. The more Burton thought about it the madder he became. But it was too late to go back now. He touched the left side of his jacket. His .357, filled with cement, along with Collin's 9mm, was at the bottom of the Severn River at the most remote point they could find. To most perhaps an unnecessary precaution, but to Burton, no precaution was unnecessary. The police had one useless slug and would never find the other. Even if they could, the barrel on his new pistol would be squeaky clean. Burton wasn't worried about the ballistics department of the local Virginia police bringing him down.

Burton hung his head as the events of that night raced through his mind. The President of the United States was an adulterer who had roughed up his lay for the night so badly she had tried to kill him and Agents Burton and Collin had to blow her away.

And then they had covered it all up. That's what made Burton wince every time he looked in the mirror. The cover-up. They had lied. By their silence they had lied. But hadn't he lied all this time? All these late-night trysts? When he greeted the First Lady each morning? When he played with their two kids on the rear lawn? Not telling them that her husband and their father was not nearly so nice and kind and good as they probably believed he was. As the whole country believed he was.

The Secret Service. Burton grimaced. It was an apt title for an unlikely reason. The crap he had seen going on over the years. And Burton had looked the other way. Every agent had, at one time or another. They all joked or complained about it in private, but that was all. That particular, if unwelcome, function came with the job. Power made people crazy; it made them feel invincible. And when something bad happened it was the working staff of the Secret Service who were expected to clean up the mess.

Several times Burton had picked up the phone to call the Director of the Secret Service. Tell him the whole story, try to cut his losses. But each time he had put the phone back down, unable to say the words that would end his career and, in essence, his life. And with each passing day, Burton's hopes grew a little brighter that it might all blow over, even though his common sense told him that could not possibly happen. Now it was too late to tell the truth, he felt. Calling in a day or two later with the story might be explained away, but not now.

His thoughts turned back to the investigation of

Christine Sullivan's death. Burton had read with great interest the findings of the autopsy, courtesy of the local police at the request of the President, who was so, so distraught over the tragedy. Fuck him too.

A shattered jaw and strangulation marks. His and Collin's shots had not inflicted those injuries. She had good reason to want to kill him. But Burton couldn't let that happen, under no circumstances could he let that happen. There were few absolutes anymore, but that was sure as hell one of them.

He had done the right thing. Burton told himself that a thousand times. The very action he had trained virtually his entire adult life for. The ordinary person couldn't understand, could never possibly comprehend how an agent would think or feel if something bad went down on their watch.

He had talked to one of Kennedy's agents a long time ago. The man had never gotten over Dallas. Walking right beside the President's limo, nothing he could do. And the President had died. Right in front of his eyes, the President's head had been blown apart. Nothing he could do, but there was always something. Always another precaution you could have taken. Turned to the left instead of the right, watched one building more closely than you had. Scanned the crowd with a little more intensity. Kennedy's guy had never been the same. Quit the Service, divorced, finished his human existence in obscurity in some rat's hole in Mississippi, but still living in Dallas for the last twenty years of his life.

That would never happen to Bill Burton. That was why he had hurled his body in front of Alan Richmond's predecessor six years ago and caught twin .38 caliber steel jackets for his trouble despite his body armor; one through the shoulder, the other through the forearm. Miraculously, neither had struck any vital organs or arteries, leaving Burton

171

only with a number of scars and the heartfelt gratitude of an entire country. And, more important, the adulation of his fellow agents.

And that was why he had fired upon Christine Sullivan. And he would do the same thing today. He would kill her, kill her as often as it took. Pull the trigger, watch the one-hundred-sixty-grain bullet slam into the side of the head at over twelve hundred feet per second, the young life over. Her choice, not his. Dead.

He went back to work. While he still could.

Chief of Staff Russell walked briskly down the corridor. She had just finished briefing the President's press secretary on the appropriate spin for the Russia–Ukraine conflict. The bare politics of the matter dictated backing Russia, but bare politics rarely controlled the decision-making process in the Richmond administration. The Russian Bear had all the intercontinental nuclear forces now, but Ukraine was in a much better position to become a major trade player with the Western countries. What had tipped the scales in Ukraine's favor was the fact that Walter Sullivan, the good and now grieving friend of the President, was homing in on a major deal with that country. Sullivan and friends, through various networks, had contributed approximately twelve million dollars to Richmond's campaign, and garnered him virtually every major endorsement he needed in his quest for the Oval Office. There was no way he could not make a significant payback on that kind of effect. Hence, the United States would back Ukraine.

Russell looked at her watch, counting her blessings that there were independent reasons for siding with Kiev over Moscow, although she felt sure Richmond would have come out the same way regardless. He did not forget loyalty. Favors must be returned. A President just happened to be in a position to return them on a massive, global scale. One major problem out of the way, she settled down at the desk and turned her attention to a growing list of crises.

Fifteen minutes into her political juggling, Russell rose and slowly walked over to the window. Life went on in Washington, much like it had for two hundred years. Factions were scattered everywhere, pouring money, massive intellects and established heavyweights into the business of politics, which essentially meant screwing others before they got around to screwing you. Russell understood that game, better than most. She also loved and excelled at it. This was clearly her element, and she was as happy as she'd been in years. Being unmarried and childless had started to worry her. The piles of professional accolades had grown monotonous, and hollow. And then Alan Richmond had come into her life. Made her see the possibility of moving up to the next level. Perhaps to a level where no woman had ever gone. That thought weighed so powerfully inside her head that she sometimes shook with anticipation.

And then a goddamned hunk of metal exploded in her face. Where was he? Why hadn't he come forward? He must, had to know what he had in his possession. If it was money he wanted, she would pay it. The slush funds at her disposal were more than adequate for even the most unreasonable demands, and Russell expected the worst. That was one of the wonderful things about the White House. No one really knew how much money it actually took to run the place. That was because so many agencies contributed parts of their budget and personnel to help the White House function. With so much financial confusion, administrations rarely had to worry about

173

finding money for even the most outrageous purchases. No, Russell thought to herself, money would be the least of her worries. She had many others to concern herself with, however.

Did the man know that the President was totally oblivious to the situation? That was what was tearing Russell's stomach apart. What if he tried to communicate with the President directly, and not with her? She started to shake, and plopped down in a chair by the window. Richmond would immediately recognize Russell's intentions, there was no question of that. He was arrogant but no fool. And then he would destroy her. Just like that. And she would be defenseless. There would be no good exposing him. She couldn't prove a thing. Her word against his. And she would be relegated to the political toxic waste dump, condemned and then, worst of all, forgotten.

She had to find him. Somehow get a message to him, that he must work through her. There was only one person who could help her do that. She sat back down at her desk, collected herself and resumed working. This was no time to panic. Right now she needed to be stronger than she had ever been in her life. She could still make it, still control the outcome if she just kept her nerves in check, used the first-rate mind God had bestowed upon her. She could get out of this mess. She knew where she had to start.

The mechanism that she had chosen to use would strike anyone who knew Gloria Russell as particularly odd. But there was a side to the Chief of Staff that would surprise those few who claimed to know her well. Her professional career had always come foremost to the detriment of every other facet of her life, including the personal, and the sexual relationships that were spawned from that area of one's life. But Gloria Russell considered herself a very desirable woman; indeed, she possessed a feminine side that was in the sharpest contrast to her official shroud. That the years were going by, and rapidly, only increased the apprehension she had been starting to feel regarding this imbalance in her life. Not that she was necessarily planning anything, especially in light of the potential catastrophe she was confronted with, but she believed she knew the best way to accomplish this mission. And confirm her desirability in the process. She could not escape her feelings, no more than she could her shadow. So why try? Anyway, she also felt that subtlety would be lost on her intended target.

Several hours later she clicked off her desk lamp and called for her car. Then she checked the Secret Service staffing for the day and picked up her phone. Three minutes later Agent Collin stood before her, his hands clasped in front of him in a pose standard to all the agents. She motioned for him to wait a moment. She checked her makeup, performing a perfect oval with her lips as she reapplied her lipstick. Out of the corner of her eye she studied the tall, lean man standing next to her desk. The magazine-cover looks would've been difficult for any woman to consciously ignore. That his profession also dictated that he lived on the brink of danger and could, indeed, be dangerous himself, only added favorably to the total package. Like the bad boys in high school girls always seemed to be drawn to, if only to escape, momentarily, the dullness of their own existence. Tim Collin, she surmised with reasonable confidence, must have broken many a female heart in his relatively short life.

Her calendar was clear tonight, a rarity. She pushed her chair back and slipped into her heels. She didn't see Agent Collin as his eyes shifted to her legs and then quickly back to stare straight ahead. Had she seen, she would have been pleased, not least of all for the obvious reason.

"The President will be giving a press conference next week at the Middleton Courthouse, Tim."

"Yes, ma'am, nine-thirty-five A.M. We're working on the preliminaries right now." His eyes stared straight ahead.

"Do you find that a little unusual?"

Collin looked at her. "How so, ma'am?"

"It's after working hours, you can call me Gloria."

Collin shifted uncomfortably from one foot to another. She smiled at him, at his obvious awkwardness.

"You understand what the press conference is for, don't you?"

"The President will be addressing the" – Collin swallowed perceptibly – "the killing of Mrs. Sullivan."

"That's right. A President conducting a press conference regarding the homicide of a private citizen. Don't you find that curious? I believe it's a first in presidential history, Tim."

"I wouldn't know about that, ma— Gloria."

"You've spent a lot of time with him lately. Have you noticed anything unusual about the President?"

"Like what?"

"Like has he appeared overly stressed or worried? More than the usual?"

Collin slowly shook his head, not knowing where this conversation was intended to go.

"I think we might have a slight problem, Tim. I think the President might need our help. You're ready to help him, aren't you?"

"He's the President, ma'am. That's my job, to take care of him."

Rummaging in her bag, she said, "Are you busy tonight, Tim? You're off at the regular time tonight, aren't you? I know the President's staying in."

He nodded.

"You know where I live. Come over as soon as you're off duty. I'd like to talk to you privately, continue this discussion. Would you mind helping me, and the President?"

Collin's answer was immediate. "I'll be there, Gloria."

Jack knocked on the door again. No answer. The blinds were drawn and no light emitted from the house. He was either asleep or not home. He checked the time. Nine o'clock. He remembered Luther Whitney to rarely be in bed before two or three A.M. The old Ford was in the driveway. The tiny garage door was shut. Jack looked in the mailbox beside the door. It was overflowing. That didn't look good. Luther was what now, mid-sixties? Would he find his old friend on the floor, cold hands clutching at his chest? Jack looked around and then lifted up a corner on a terra-cotta planter next to the front door. The spare key was still there. He looked around once more, then put the key in the door and went in.

The living room was neat and spare. Everything was stacked where it should be.

"Luther?" He moved through the hallway, his memory steering him through the simple configurations of the house. Bedroom on the left, toilet on the right, kitchen at the rear of the house, small screened porch off that, garden in the back. Luther was in none of these rooms. Jack entered the small bedroom, which, like the rest of the house, was neat and orderly.

On the nightstand a number of picture frames containing various photos of Kate looked at him as he sat on the side of the bed. He turned quickly away and left the room.

The tiny rooms upstairs were mostly bare. He listened intently for a moment. Nothing.

He sat down in the small wire and plastic kitchen chair, looked around. He didn't turn on a light, but sat in the darkness. He leaned across and popped open the refrigerator. He grinned. Two six-packs of Bud looked back at him. You could always count on Luther for a cold brew. He took one and opened the back door to step outside.

The small garden looked beaten down. The hostas and ferns drooped even in the shade of a thick oak and the Nelly Moser clematis clinging to the board-on-board fence was painfully withered. Jack looked at Luther's prized annuals flowerbed and noted more victims than survivors of the Washington late-summer heat furnace.

He sat down, put the beer to his lips. Luther had clearly not been here for a while. So? He was an adult. He could go where he wanted, when he wanted. But something just felt wrong. But it had been several years. Habits change. He reflected a moment more. But Luther's habits would not have changed. The man was not like that. He was rock-solid, as dependable a person as Jack had ever met in his life. Stacked-up mail, dead flowers, car not in the garage, that was not how he would have voluntarily left things. *Voluntarily.*

Jack went back inside. The answering machine tape was blank. He went back into the small bedroom, the musty air hitting him again as he opened the door. He scanned the room once more, then started to feel a little silly. He wasn't a goddamned detective. Then he laughed to himself. Luther was probably living it up on some island for a couple of weeks, and here he was playing the nervous parent. Luther was one of the most capable men Jack had ever met. Besides, it was no business of his anymore.

The Whitney family were not his concern, father or daughter. In fact, why was he even here? Trying to relive old times? Trying to get to Kate through her old man? That was the most unlikely scenario one could imagine.

Jack locked the door on the way out, replaced the key under the planter. He glanced back at the house and then walked to his car.

Gloria Russell's home occupied a cul-de-sac in a quiet upper-brackets Bethesda suburb off River Road. Her consulting work on behalf of many of the country's largest corporations coupled with her sizable professorship, and now Chief of Staff salary and many years of careful investing, had left her with a deep purse, and she liked to be surrounded by beautiful things. The entrance was framed by an aged arbor interlaced with strong, thick ivy. The entire front yard was enclosed by a waist-high brick and mortar serpentine wall and set up as a private garden complete with tables and umbrellas. A small fountain bubbled and hissed in a darkness broken only by the shallow light thrown from the big bay window in the front of the house.

Gloria Russell was sitting at one of the garden tables when Agent Collin pulled up in his convertible, back ramrod straight, suit still crisp, tie knotted rigidly. The Chief of Staff had not changed either. She smiled at him and they walked up the front walk together and into the house.

"Drink? You look like a bourbon-and-water person." Russell looked at the young man and slowly drained her third glass of white wine. It had been a long time since she had a young man over. Maybe too long, she was thinking, although the alcohol guaranteed that she wasn't thinking that clearly.

"Beer, if you have it."

179

"Coming up." She stopped to kick off her heels and padded into the kitchen. Collin looked around the expanse of the living room with its billowy professionally done curtains, textured wallpaper and tasteful antiques and wondered what he was doing here. He hoped she hurried with the beer. A star athlete, he had been seduced by women before, from high school on up. But this was not high school and Gloria Russell was no cheerleader. He decided he would not be able to endure the night without a heavy buzz. He had wanted to tell Burton about it, but something had made him keep quiet. Burton had been acting aloof and moody. What they had done was not wrong. He knew the circumstances were awkward, and an action that would ordinarily have brought them praise from the entire country had to be kept secret. He had regretted killing the woman, but there were no other options. Death happened, tragedies occurred all the time. It was her time. Christine Sullivan's number had just come up.

A few moments later he was sipping his beer and checking out the Chief of Staff's derriere as she fluffed up a pillow on the broad couch before sitting down. She smiled at him, delicately sipped her wine.

"How long have you been in the Service, Tim?"

"Almost six years."

"You've risen quickly. The President thinks quite a lot of you. He's never forgotten that you saved his life."

"I appreciate that. I really do."

She took another sip of wine and ran her eyes over him. He sat erect; his obvious nervousness amused her. She finished her examination and came away very impressed. Her attention had not been lost on the young agent, who was now hiding his discomfort by examining the numerous paintings that adorned the walls.

"Nice stuff." He pointed at the artwork.

She smiled at him, watched him hurriedly gulp his beer. *Nice stuff.* She had been thinking the same thing.

"Let's go sit where it's more comfortable, Tim." Russell stood up and looked down at him. He was led from the living room through a long, narrow hallway and then through double doors into a large sitting room. The lights came on by themselves, and Collin noted that through another set of double doors the Chief of Staff's bed was clearly visible.

"Would you mind if I take a minute to change? I've been in this suit long enough."

Collin watched as she went into her bedroom. She did not close the doors all the way. A sliver of the room was visible from where he was sitting. He turned his head away, tried to focus all his attention on the scrolls and designs of an antique fireplace screen that would be seeing activity soon. He finished his beer and instantly wanted another one. He lay back in the thick cushions. He tried not to but he could hear every sound she made. Finally, he couldn't resist it. He turned his head and looked straight through the open doorway. With a pinch of regret he saw nothing. At first. Then she moved across the opening.

It was only a moment, as she lingered by the end of the bed, to pick up some article of clothing. Chief of Staff Gloria Russell parading naked in front of him sent a jolt through Collin, although he had been expecting it, or something close to it.

The night's agenda confirmed, Collin turned his head away, more slowly than he probably should have. He licked the top of the beer can, absorbing the last few drops of the amber liquid. He felt the butt of his new weapon dig against his chest. Normally the mass of metal felt comforting against his skin. Now it just hurt.

He wondered about fraternization rules. Members of the First Family had been known to become quite attached to their Secret Service agents. Over the years there had always been talk of fooling around, but the official policy was clear on that point. Were Collin discovered in this room with a naked Chief of Staff in her bedroom, his career would be short-lived.

He thought rapidly. He could leave right now, report in to Burton. But how would that look? Russell would deny it all. Collin would look like a fool, and his career would probably be over anyway. She had brought him here for a reason. She said the President needed his help. He wondered now who he would really be helping. And for the first time Agent Collin felt trapped. Trapped. Where his athleticism, his quick wits and his 9mm were useless to him. Intellectually he was no match for the woman. In the official power structure he was so far below her, it was like he stared up from an abyss with a telescope and still couldn't glimpse the bottom of her high heels. It promised to be a long night.

Walter Sullivan paced while Sandy Lord watched. A bottle of Scotch occupied a prominent position on the corner of Lord's desk. Outside, the darkness was marred by the dull glow of street lamps. The heat had returned for a short spell and Lord had ordered the air conditioning to remain on at Patton, Shaw for his very special visitor tonight. That visitor stopped his pacing and stared down the street where a half-dozen blocks away sat the familiar white building, home to Alan Richmond, and one of the keys to Sullivan and Lord's grand scheme. Sullivan, however, was not thinking about business tonight. Lord was. But he was far too cunning to show it. Tonight he was here for his friend. To listen to the grief, the outpouring, to let Sullivan mourn his little hooker. The quicker that was done, the sooner they could get down to what really mattered: the next deal.

"It was a beautiful service, people will remember it for a long time." Lord chose his words carefully. Walter Sullivan was an old friend, but it was a friendship built on an attorney–client relationship and thus its underpinning could experience some unexpected shifting. Sullivan was also the only person in Lord's acquaintance who made him nervous, where Lord knew he was never in complete control, that the man he was dealing with was at least his equal and probably more.

"Yes it was." Sullivan continued to look down the street. He believed that he had finally convinced the police that the one-way mirror was not connected to the crime. Whether they were completely convinced was another matter. In any event it had been quite an embarrassing moment for a man not accustomed to such. The detective, Sullivan couldn't remember his name, had not given Sullivan the respect he deserved and that had angered the older man. If anything, he had earned the respect of everyone. It did not help matters that Sullivan did not feel the least bit confident in the local police's abilities to find the persons responsible.

He shook his head as his thoughts returned to the mirror. At least it had not been disclosed to the press. That was attention Sullivan could not tolerate. The mirror had been Christine's idea. But he had to admit he had gone along with it. Now as he looked back, it seemed ludicrous. At first it had fascinated him, watching his wife with other men. He was beyond the age where he could satisfy her himself, but he could not reasonably deny her the physical pleasures that were beyond him. But it had all been absurd, including the marriage. He saw that now. Trying to recapture his youth. He should have known that

183

nature bowed to no one, regardless of their monetary worth. He was embarrassed and he was angry. He finally turned to Lord.

"I'm not certain that I have confidence in the detective in charge. How can we get the federals involved?"

Lord put his glass down, lifted a cigar from a box hidden within the recesses of his desk and slowly unwrapped it.

"Homicide of a private citizen isn't grounds for a federal investigation."

"Richmond is getting involved."

"Fluff, if you ask me."

Sullivan shook his massive head. "No. He seemed genuinely concerned."

"Maybe. Don't count on that concern lingering for too long. He has a thousand cans of worms to handle."

"I want the people responsible for this caught, Sandy."

"I understand that, Walter. Of all people, I understand that. They will be. You have to be patient. These guys weren't nickel-and-dimers. They knew what they were doing. But everybody makes mistakes. They'll go to trial, mark my words."

"And then what? Life imprisonment, correct?" Sullivan said contemptuously.

"It's probably not going to be a capital murder case, so life is what they'll end up getting. But no chance of parole, Walter, believe me. They'll never breathe another drop of free air. And getting a little prick in the arm might seem real desirable after a few years of getting bent over every night."

Sullivan sat down and stared at his friend. Walter Sullivan wanted no part of any trial. Where all the details of the crime would be revealed. He winced at the thought of all of it being rehashed. Strangers knowing intimate details of his life and that of his deceased wife. He could not bear that. He just wanted the men caught. He would arrange the rest. Lord had said the Commonwealth of Virginia would imprison for life the persons responsible. Walter Sullivan decided right then and there that he would save the commonwealth the cost of that lengthy incarceration.

Russell curled up on the end of the couch, bare feet tucked under a loose-fitting cotton pullover that stopped slightly above her calves. Her ample cleavage peeked at him where the fabric suddenly dipped. Collin had fetched himself two more beers and poured her another glass of wine from the bottle he had brought with him. His head was now slightly warm, as though a small fire were burning inside. The necktie was now loosened, the jacket and gun lay on the opposite couch. She had fingered it as he had taken it off.

"It's so heavy."

"You get used to it." She did not ask the question he was usually confronted with. She knew he had killed someone.

"Would you really take a bullet for the President?" She looked at him through drooping eyelids. She had to remain focused, she kept telling herself. That had not stopped her from leading the young man to the very threshold of her bed. She felt a large measure of her control slipping away. With a masterful effort she started to regain it. What the hell was she doing? At a crisis point in her life and she was acting like a prostitute. She needn't approach the issue in this way. She knew that. The tugging she was feeling from another sector of her being was disrupting her decision-making processes. She could not allow that, not now.

She should go change again, retreat back to the living room, or perhaps to her study where the dark oak paneling and walls of books would quash the unsettling rumblings.

He eyed her steadily. "Yes."

She was about to get up but never made it.

"I'd take one for you too, Gloria."

"For me?" Her voice quavered. She looked at him again, her strategic plans forgotten, her eyes wide.

"Without thinking. Lot of Secret Service agents. Only one Chief of Staff. That's the way it works." He looked down and said quietly, "It's not a game, Gloria."

When he went again for more beer he noticed that she had moved close enough that her knee touched his thigh when he sat down. She stretched her legs out, rubbing against his, and then she rested them on the table across from them. The pullover had somehow worked itself up, revealing thighs that were full and creamy white; they were the legs of an older woman, and a damned attractive one. Collin's eyes moved slowly across the display of skin.

"You know I've always admired you. I mean all of the agents." She almost seemed embarrassed. "I know sometimes you get taken for granted. I want you to know that I appreciate you."

"It's a great job. Wouldn't trade it for anything." He chugged another beer, and felt better. His breathing relaxed.

She smiled at him. "I'm glad you came tonight."

"Anything to help, Gloria." His confidence level was going up as his alcohol intake increased. He finished the beer and she pointed with an unsteady finger to a stand of liquor over by the door. He mixed drinks for them, sat back down.

"I feel I can trust you, Tim."

"You can."

186

"I hope you don't take this the wrong way, but I don't feel that way with Burton."

"Bill's a top agent. The best."

She touched his arm, left it there.

"I didn't mean it that way. I know he's good. I just don't know about him sometimes. It's hard to explain. It's just an instinct on my part."

"You should trust your instincts. I do." He looked at her. She looked younger, much younger, like she should be graduating college, ready to take on the world.

"My instincts tell me that you're someone I can depend on, Tim."

"I am." He drained his drink.

"Always?"

He stared at her, touched his empty glass to hers. "Always."

His eyes were heavy now. He thought back to high school. After scoring the winning touchdown in the state championship, Cindy Purket had looked at him just like that. An all-giving look on her face.

He laid his hand on her thigh, rubbed it up and down. The flesh was just loose enough to be intensely womanly. She didn't resist but instead inched closer. Then his hand disappeared under the pullover, tracing over her still firm belly, just nicking the undersides of her breasts, and then returning into view. The other arm encircled her waist, drawing her closer to him; his hand dropped down to her bottom and gripped hard. She sucked in air and then let it out slowly, as she leaned into his shoulder. He felt her chest push into his arm, up and down. The floating mass was soft, and warm. She dropped her hand to his hardening crotch and squeezed, then lingered her mouth over his, slowly pulling back and looking at him, her eyelids moving up and down in slow rhythms.

187

She put her drink down, and slowly, almost teasingly, slid out of the pullover. He exploded against her, hands digging under the bra strap until he felt it give way and she poured out to him, his head buried in the loose mounds. Next, the last remaining piece of clothing, a pair of black lace panties, was ripped from her body; she smiled as it was sent sailing against the wall. Then she caught her breath as he lifted her effortlessly and carried her into the bedroom.

ELEVEN

The Jaguar drove slowly up the long drive, stopped, and two people got out.

Jack turned up the collar on his coat. The evening was brisk as rain-heavy clouds marched into the area.

Jennifer walked around the car and settled in next to him as they leaned against the luxury car.

Jack looked up at the place. Thick sheets of ivy swept across the top of the entrance. The house had a heavy substance to it, real and committed. Its occupants probably would absorb a good measure of that. He could use that in his life right now. He had to admit, it was beautiful. What was wrong with beautiful things anyway? Four hundred thou' as a partner. If he started bringing in other clients, who knew? Lord made five times that, two million dollars a year, and that was his base.

Compensation figures of partners were strictly confidential and were never discussed even under the most informal circumstances at the firm. However, Jack had guessed correctly on the computer password to the partner comp file. The code word was "greed." Some secretary must have laughed her ass off over that one.

Jack looked over a front lawn the size of a carrier flight deck. A vision galloped across. He looked at his fiancée.

"It has plenty of space to play touch football with the kids." He smiled.

189

"Yes, it does." She smiled back at him, kissed his cheek gently. She took his arm and encircled her waist with it.

Jack looked back at the mansion; soon to be his three-point-eight-million-dollar home. Jennifer continued to look at him, her smile broadening as she gripped his fingers. Her eyes seemed to glisten, even in the darkness.

As Jack continued to stare at the structure, he felt a rush of relief. This time he only saw windows.

At thirty-six thousand feet, Walter Sullivan leaned back in the deep softness of his cabin chair and glanced out the window of the 747 into the darkness. As they moved east to west, Sullivan was adding a number of hours to his day, but time zones had never bothered him. The older he became the less sleep he needed, and he had never needed very much to begin with.

The man sitting across from him took the opportunity to examine the older man closely. Sullivan was known throughout the world as a legitimate, although sometimes bullying, global businessman. Legitimate. That was the key word running itself through Michael McCarty's head. Legitimate businessmen typically had no need of, nor desire to speak with, gentlemen in McCarty's profession. But when one is alerted through the most discreet channels that one of the wealthiest men on earth desires a meeting with you, then you attend. McCarty had not become one of the world's foremost assassins because he particularly enjoyed the work. He particularly enjoyed the money and with it the luxuries that money inspired.

McCarty's added advantage was the fact that he appeared to be a businessman himself. Ivy League good looks, which wasn't too far afield, since he held a degree in international politics from Dartmouth. With his thick, wavy blond hair, broad shoulders and wrinkle-free face he could be the hard-charging entrepreneur on the way up or a film star at his peak. The fact that he killed people for a living, at a per-hit fee of in excess of one million dollars, did nothing to dampen his youthful enthusiasm or his love of life.

Sullivan finally looked at him. McCarty, despite an enormous confidence in his abilities and a supreme coolness under pressure, began to grow nervous under the billionaire's scrutiny. From one elite to another.

"I want you to kill someone for me," Sullivan said simply. "Unfortunately, at the present time, I do not know who that person is. But with any luck, one day I will. Until that time comes, I will place you on a retainer so that your services will always be available to me until such time as I need them."

McCarty smiled and shook his head. "You may be aware of my reputation, Mr. Sullivan. My services are already in great demand. My work carries me all over the world, as I'm sure you know. Were I to devote my full time to you until this opportunity arose, then I would be forgoing other work. I'm afraid my bank account, along with my reputation, would suffer."

Sullivan's reply was immediate. "One hundred thousand dollars a day until that opportunity arises, Mr. McCarty. When you successfully complete the task, double your usual fee. I can do nothing to preserve your reputation; however, I trust that the per diem arrangement will forestall any damage to your financial status."

McCarty's eyes widened just a bit and then he quickly regained his composure.

"I think that will be adequate, Mr. Sullivan."

"Of course you realize I am placing considerable

confidence not only in your skills at eliminating subjects, but also in your discretion."

McCarty hid his smile. He had been picked up in Sullivan's plane in Istanbul at midnight local time. The flight crew had no idea who he was. No one had ever identified him, thus someone recognizing him was not a concern. Sullivan meeting him in person eliminated one thing. An intermediary who would then have Sullivan in his control. McCarty, on the other hand, had no earthly reason to betray Sullivan and every motivation not to.

Sullivan continued, "You will receive particulars as they become available. You will assimilate yourself into the Washington, D.C., metropolitan area, although your task may take you anywhere in the world. I will need you to move on a moment's notice. You will make your location known to me at all times and will check in with me daily on secured communication lines that I will establish. You will pay your own expenses out of the per diem. A wire transfer will be set up to funnel the fee to an account of your choosing. My planes will be available to you if the need arises. Understood?"

McCarty nodded, a little put off by his client's series of commands. But then you didn't get to be a billionaire without being somewhat commanding, did you? On top of that McCarty had read about Christine Sullivan. Who the hell could blame the old man?

Sullivan pushed a button on the armrest of his chair.

"Thomas? How long until we're stateside?"

The voice was brisk and informed. "Five hours and fifteen minutes, Mr. Sullivan, if we maintain present air speed and altitude."

"Make sure that we do."

"Yes, sir."

192

Sullivan pressed another button and the cabin attendant appeared and efficiently served them the sort of dinner that McCarty had never had on a plane before. Sullivan said nothing to McCarty until the dinner was cleared and the younger man rose and was being directed to his sleeping quarters by the attendant. Registering on a sweep of Sullivan's hand, the attendant disappeared within the recesses of the aircraft.

"One more thing, Mr. McCarty. Have you ever failed on a mission?"

McCarty's eyes turned to slits as he stared back at his new employer. For the first time it was evident that the Ivy Leaguer was extremely dangerous.

"Once, Mr. Sullivan. The Israelis. Sometimes they seem more than human."

"Please don't make it twice. Thank you."

Seth Frank was roaming the halls of the Sullivan home. The yellow police lines were still up outside, fluttering softly in the increasing breeze and thickening bank of dark clouds that promised more heavy rain. Sullivan was staying at his Watergate penthouse downtown. His domestic staff were at their employer's residence on Fisher Island, Florida, catering to members of Sullivan's family. He had already interviewed each of them in person. They were being flown home shortly for more detailed questioning.

He took a moment to admire the surroundings. It was as though he were touring a museum. All that money. The place reeked of it, from the superlative antiques to the broadbrush paintings that casually hung everywhere, with real signatures at the bottom. Hell, everything in the house was an original.

He wandered into the kitchen and then into the dining room. The table resembled a bridge spanning

193

the pale blue rug spread over the refinished parquet flooring. His feet seemed to be sucked into the thick, heavy fibers. He sat down at the head of the table, his eyes constantly roaming. As far as he could tell nothing had happened in here. Time was slipping by and progress was not coming easily.

Outside, the sun momentarily pushed through the heavy clouds and Frank got his first break on the case. He wouldn't have noticed it if he hadn't been admiring the moldings around the ceiling. His father had been a carpenter. Joints smooth as a baby's cheek.

That's when he observed the rainbow dancing across the ceiling. As he admired the parallels of color, he began to wonder about its source, like the folklore of tracking the pot of gold at the end of the striped apparition. His eye scanned the room. It took him a few seconds, but then he had it. He quickly knelt down beside the table and peered under one of the legs. The table was a Sheraton, eighteenth century, which meant it was as heavy as a semi. It took him two tries, and perspiration broke across his forehead, a trickle entering his right eye and making him tear for a moment, but he finally managed to budge the table and pull it out.

He sat back down and looked at his new possession, maybe his little pot of gold. The little piece of silver-colored material acted as a barrier between the furniture to prevent the wet carpet from causing damage to wood or upholstery and also stopped leaching into the damp fibers. With the aid of sunlight, its reflective surface also made for a nice rainbow. He had had similar ones in his own house when his wife had gotten particularly nervous about a visit from her in-laws and decided some serious household cleaning had to be done.

He took out his notebook. The servants arrived at

Dulles at ten tomorrow morning. Frank doubted in this house if the small piece of foil he was holding would have been allowed to remain in its resting place for very long. It could be nothing. It could be everything. A perfect way to gauge the lay of the land. It would probably fall somewhere in between, if he were very, very lucky.

He hit the floor again and sniffed the carpet, ran his fingers through the fibers. The stuff they used nowadays, you could never tell. No odor, dried in a couple of hours. He would know soon enough how long it had been; if it could tell him anything. He could call Sullivan, but for some reason, he wanted to hear it from someone other than the master of the house. The old man was not high on the list of suspects, but Frank was smart enough to realize that Sullivan remained on that list. Whether his place descended or ascended depended on what Frank could find out today, tomorrow, next week. When you boiled it down, it was that simple. That was good, because up to now nothing about the death of Christine Sullivan had been simple. He wandered out of the room, thinking about the whimsical nature of rainbows and police investigations in general.

Burton scanned the crowd, Collin beside him. Alan Richmond made his way to the informal podium set up on the steps of the Middleton Courthouse, a broad block of mortar-smeared brick, stark white dentil moldings, weather-beaten cement steps and the ubiquitous American flag alongside its Virginia counterpart swooping and swirling in the morning breeze. Precisely at nine-thirty-five the President began to speak. Behind him stood the craggy and expressionless Walter Sullivan with the ponderous Herbert Sanderson Lord beside him.

195

Collin moved a little closer to the crowd of reporters at the bottom of the courthouse steps as they strained and positioned like opposing teams of basketball players waiting for the foul shot to swish or bang off the rim. He had left the Chief of Staff's home at three in the morning. What a night it had been. What a *week* it had been. As ruthless and unfeeling as Gloria Russell seemed in public life, Collin had seen another side of the woman, a side that he was strongly attracted to. It still seemed like a careless daydream. He had slept with the President's Chief of Staff. That simply did not happen. But it had happened to Agent Tim Collin. They had planned to see each other tonight as well. They had to be careful, but they were both cautious by nature. Where it would lead, Collin did not know.

Born and raised in Lawrence, Kansas, Collin had a good set of Midwestern values to fall back upon. You dated, fell in love, married and had four or five kids, strictly in that order. He didn't see that happening here. All he knew was he wanted to be with her again. He glanced across and eyed her where she stood behind and to the left of the President. Sunglasses on, wind lifting her hair slightly, she seemed in complete control of everything around her.

Burton had his eyes on the crowd, then glanced at his partner in time to see the latter's gaze riveted for an instant on the Chief of Staff. Burton frowned. Collin was a good agent who did his job well, maybe to the point of overzealousness. Not the first agent to suffer from that, and not necessarily a bad trait in their line of work. But you kept your eyes on the crowd, everything out *there*. What the hell was going on? Burton made a sideways glance at Russell, but she stared straight ahead, seemingly oblivious to the men assigned to protect her. Burton looked at Collin once more. The kid now scanned the crowd, changing his pace every now and then, left to right, right to left, sometimes up, occasionally he would stare straight ahead, no trace of a pattern a potential assailant could count on. But Burton could not forget the look he had given the Chief of Staff. Behind the sunglasses Burton had seen something he did not like.

Alan Richmond finished his speech by staring stonily out at the cloudless sky as the wind whipped through his perfectly styled hair. He seemed to be looking to God for help, but in actuality he was trying to remember if he was meeting the Japanese ambassador at two or three that afternoon. But his faraway, almost visionary look would carry well on the evening news.

On cue he snapped back to attention and turned to Walter Sullivan and gave the bereaved husband a hug befitting someone of his stature.

"God, I am so sorry, Walter. My deepest, deepest condolences. If there is anything, anything that I can do. You know that."

Sullivan held on to the hand that was offered to him, and his legs began to shake until two of his entourage invisibly supported him with a quick thrust of sinewy arms.

"Thank you, Mr. President."

"Alan, please, Walter. Friend to friend now."

"Thank you, Alan, you have no idea how much I appreciate your taking the time to do this. Christy would have been so moved by your words today."

Only Gloria Russell, who was watching the pair closely, noticed the slight twinge of a smirk at the corner of her boss's cheek. Then, in an instant it was gone.

"I know there are really no words I can say to do

justice to what you're feeling, Walter. It seems more and more that things in this world happen for no purpose. Except for her sudden illness, this never would've happened. I can't explain why things like this occur, no one can. But I want you to know that I am here for you, when you need me. Anytime, anyplace. We've been through so much together. And you've certainly helped me through some pretty rough times."

"Your friendship has always been important to me, Alan. I won't forget this."

Richmond slid an arm around the old man's shoulders. In the background microphones dangled on long poles. Like giant rods and reels, they surrounded the pair despite the collective efforts of the men's respective entourages.

"Walter, I'm going to get involved in this. I know some people will say it's not my job and in my position I can't become personally involved with anything. But goddammit, Walter, you're my friend and I'm not going to just let this slide away. The people responsible for this are going to pay."

The two men embraced once more as the photographers popped away. The twenty-foot antennas sprouting from the fleet of news trucks dutifully broadcast this tender moment to the world. Another example of President Alan Richmond being more than just a President. It made the White House PR staff giddy thinking about the initial pre-election polls.

The television channel-hopped from MTV to Grand Ole Opry to cartoons, to QVC to CNN to Pro Wrestling and then back to CNN. The man sat up in bed and put out his cigarette, laid the remote down. The President was giving a press conference. He looked stern and appropriately appalled at the abominable murder of Christine Sullivan, wife of billionaire Walter Sullivan, one of the President's closest friends, and its symbolism of the growing lawlessness in this country. Whether the President would have made the same pitch if the victim had been a poor black, Hispanic or Asian found with their throat cut in an alley in Southeast D.C. was never addressed. The President spoke in firm, crisp tones with the perfect trace of anger, of toughness. The violence must stop. The people must feel safe in their homes, or at their estates in this particular case. It was an impressive scene. A thoughtful and caring President.

The reporters were eating it up, asking all the right questions.

The television showed Chief of Staff Gloria Russell, dressed in black, nodding approvingly when the President hit key points in his views on crime and punishment. The police fraternity and AARP vote was locked up for the next election. Forty million votes, well worth the morning drive out.

She would not have been so happy if she knew who was watching them right this minute. Whose eyes bored into every inch of flesh on both her and the President's faces, as the memories of that night, never far from the surface, welled up like an oil fire spewing heat and potential destruction in all directions.

The flight to Barbados had been uneventful. The Airbus was a vast ship whose massive engines had effortlessly ripped the plane from the ground in San Juan, Puerto Rico, and in a few minutes they had hit their cruising altitude of 36,000 feet. The plane was packed, San Juan acting as a feeder for tourists bound for the clusters of islands that made up the Caribbean vacation strip. Passengers from Oregon and New York and all points in between looked at the wall of black clouds as the plane banked left and moved away from the remnants of an early-season tropical storm that had never hit hurricane status.

A metal stairway met them as they departed the aircraft. A car, tiny by American standards, shepherded five of them on the wrong side of the road as they left the airport and headed into Bridgetown, the capital of the former British colony, which had retained strong traces of its long colonialism in its speech, dress and mannerisms. In melodious tones the driver informed them of the many wonders of the tiny island, pointing out the pirate ship tour as the skull and crossbones ship pounded through still rough seas. On its deck, pale but reddening tourists were plied with rum punch in such levels that they would all be very drunk and/or very sick by the time they returned to the dock later that afternoon.

In the back seat two couples from Des Moines made excited plans in chirrupy patters of conversation. The older man who sat in the front seat staring out the windshield had his thoughts mired two thousand miles north. Once or twice he checked where they were headed, instinctively craving the lay of the land. The major landmarks were relatively few; the island was barely twenty-one miles long and fourteen miles across at its widest point. The near constant eighty-five-degree heat was ameliorated by the continual breeze, its sound eventually disappearing into one's subconscious but always nearby like a faded but still potent dream.

The hotel was an American standard Hilton built on a manmade beach that jutted out on one end of the island. Its staff was well-trained, courteous and more than willing to leave you alone if that was desired. While most of the guests gave themselves wholeheartedly to the pampering efforts, one patron shunned contact, leaving his room only to wander to isolated areas of the white beach or the mountainous Atlantic Ocean side of the island. The rest of the time was spent in his room, lights set low, TV on, room service trays littering the carpet and wicker furnishings.

On the first day there Luther had grabbed a cab from in front of the hotel and taken a ride north, almost to the edge of the ocean, where atop one of the island's numerous hills stood the Sullivan estate. Luther's selection of Barbados had not been arbitrary.

"You know Mr. Sullivan? He's not here. Went back to America." The cabbie's lyrical tones had brought Luther out of his trance. The massive iron gates at the bottom of the grassy hill hid a long, winding drive up to the mansion, which, with its salmon-colored stucco walls and eighteen-foot-high white marble columns, looked strangely appropriate in the lush greenery, like an enormous pink rose jutting out from the bushes.

"I've been to his place," Luther answered. "In the States."

The cabbie looked at him with new respect.

"Is anyone home? Any of the staff maybe?"

The man shook his head. "All gone. Dis morning."

Luther sat back in his seat. The reason was obvious. They had found the mistress of the house.

Luther spent the next several days on the broad white beaches watching cruise ships unload their population into the duty-free shops that littered the downtown area. Dreadlocked residents of the island made their rounds with their battered briefcases housing watches, perfumes and other counterfeit paraphernalia.

For five American dollars, you could watch an

201

islander cut up an aloe leaf and pour its rich liquid into a small glass bottle for use when the sun started to nip at tender white skin that had lain dormant and unblemished behind suits and blouses. Your own handwoven corn rows cost you forty dollars and took about an hour, and there were many women with flabby arms and thick, crumpled feet who patiently lay in the sand while this operation was performed upon them.

The island's beauty should have served to free Luther, to some degree, from his melancholy. And, finally, the warming sun, gentle breezes and low-key approach to life of the island populous had eroded his nervous agitation to where he occasionally smiled at a passerby, spoke monosyllables to the bartender and sipped his mixed drinks far into the night while lying on the beach, the surf pounding into the darkness and gently lifting him away from his nightmare. He planned to move on in a few days. Where to, he wasn't quite sure.

And then the channel-hopping stopped at the CNN broadcast and Luther, like a battered fish on an unbreakable line, was sent reeling toward what he had spent several thousand dollars and traveled several thousand miles trying to escape.

Russell stumbled out of bed and walked over to the bureau, fumbled for a pack of cigarettes.

"They'll cut ten years off your life." Collin rolled over and watched her naked machinations with amusement.

"This job's already done that." She lit up, inhaled deeply for several seconds, put the smoke out and climbed back in bed, snuggling butt-first to Collin, smiling contentedly as she was wrapped up in his long, muscular arms.

"The press conference went well, don't you

202

think?" She could feel him thinking it through. He was fairly transparent. Without the sunglasses they all were, she felt.

"As long as they don't find out what really happened."

She turned to face him, traced her finger along his neck, making a V against his smooth chest. Richmond's chest had been hairy, some of the tufts turning gray, curling at the edges. Collin's was like a baby's bottom, but she could feel the hard muscle beneath the skin. He could break her neck with no more than a passing motion. She wondered, briefly, how that would feel.

"You know we have a problem."

Collin almost laughed out loud. "Yeah, we've got some guy out there with the President's and a dead woman's prints and blood on a knife. That qualifies as a big problem I'd say."

"Why do you think he hasn't come forward?"

Collin shrugged. If he were the guy he would've disappeared. Taken the stash and gone. Millions of dollars. As loyal as Collin was, what he could do with that kind of money. He would disappear too. For a while. He looked at her. With that kind of money would she condescend to go with him? Then he turned his thoughts back to the discussion at hand. Maybe the guy was a member of the President's political party, maybe he had voted for him. In any event, why bring yourself that kind of trouble?

"Probably scared to," he finally replied.

"There are ways of doing it anonymously."

"Maybe the guy's not that sophisticated. Or maybe there's no profit in that. Or maybe he doesn't give a shit. Take your pick. If he was going to come forward, he probably would have. If he does, we'll sure know soon enough."

She sat up in bed.

"Tim, I'm really worried about this." The edge in her voice made him sit up too. "I made the decision to keep that letter opener as is. If the President were to find out . . ." She looked at him. He read the message in her eyes and stroked her hair and then cupped her cheek with his hand.

"He's not going to find out from me."

She smiled. "I know that, Tim, I really believe that. But if he, this person, were to somehow try to communicate with the President directly."

Collin looked puzzled. "Why would he do that?"

Russell shifted to the side of the bed, let her feet dangle several inches from the floor. For the first time Collin noticed the small reddish oval birthmark, half the size of a penny, at the base of her neck. Next he noticed that she was shivering, even though the room was warm.

"Why would he do that, Gloria?" Collin edged closer.

She spoke to the bedroom wall. "Has it occurred to you that that letter opener represents one of the most valuable objects in the world?" She turned to him, rubbed his hair, smiled at the vacant expression that was slowly coming to a conclusion.

"Blackmail?"

She nodded at him.

"How do you blackmail the goddamned President?"

She got up, threw a loose robe around her shoulders and poured another drink from the almost-empty decanter.

'Being President doesn't make you immune from blackmail attempts, Tim. Hell, it just gives you that much more to lose . . . or gain."

She slowly stirred her drink, sat down on a couch and tipped her glass back, the liquid warm and soothing going down. She had been drinking much

204

more than usual lately. Not that her performance had been impaired, but she would have to watch it, especially at this level, at this critical point. But she decided she would watch it tomorrow. Tonight, with the weight of political disaster lurking above her shoulders, and a young, handsome man in her bed, she would drink. She felt fifteen years younger. Every passing moment with him made her feel more beautiful. She would not forget her primary goal, but who was to say she couldn't enjoy herself?

"What do you want me to do?" Collin looked at her.

Russell had been waiting for that. Her young, handsome Secret Service agent. A modern white knight like the kind she read about as a wide-eyed girl. She looked at him as the drink dangled from her fingers. She used her other hand to slowly pull off her robe and let it drop to the floor. There was time enough, especially for a thirty-seven-year-old woman who had never had a serious relationship with a man. Time enough for everything. The drink soothed away her fear, her paranoia. And with it her cautiousness. All of which she needed in abundance. But not tonight.

"There is something you can do for me. But I'll tell you in the morning." She smiled, lay back on the couch and put out her hand. Obediently he rose and went to her. A few moments later the only sounds were intermingled groans and the persistent squeaks of the overwrought couch.

A half-block down the street from Russell's home, Bill Burton sat in his wife's nondescript Bonneville and cradled a can of Diet Coke between his knees. Occasionally he would glance at the house that he had observed his partner entering at 12:14 A.M. and where he'd caught a glimpse of the Chief of Staff in

205

attire that didn't indicate the visit was a business one. With his long-range lens he had gotten two pictures of that particular scene that Russell would have killed to get her hands on. The lights in the house had moved progressively from room to room until they reached the east side of the place, when all lights were dramatically extinguished.

Burton looked at the dormant taillights of his partner's car. The kid had made a mistake. Being here. This was a career ender, maybe for both him and Russell. Burton thought back to that night. Collin racing back to the house. Russell white as a sheet. Why? In all the confusion Burton had forgotten to ask. And then they were smashing through cornfields after someone who shouldn't have been there but sure as hell had been.

But Collin had gone back in that house for a reason. And Burton decided it was time he found out what that reason was. He had a dim feeling of a conspiracy slowly evolving. Since he had been excluded from participating, he naturally concluded that he was probably not intended to benefit from that conspiracy. Not for one moment did he believe that Russell was interested solely in what was behind his partner's zipper. She was not that type, not by a long shot. Everything she did had a purpose, an important purpose. A good fuck from a young buck was not nearly important enough.

Another two hours passed. Burton looked at his watch and then stiffened as he saw Collin open the front door, move slowly down the walk and get in his car. As he drove by, Burton ducked down in his seat, feeling slightly guilty at this surveillance of a fellow agent. He watched the wink of a turn signal as the Ford made its way out of the high-priced area.

Burton looked back up at the house. A light came on in what probably was the living room. It was late, but apparently the lady of the house was still going strong. Her stamina was legendary around the White House. Burton briefly wondered if she exhibited that same endurance between the sheets. Two minutes later the street was empty. The light in the house remained on.

TWELVE

The plane landed and thundered to a stop on the short strip of tarmac constituting National Airport's main runway, hit an immediate left a few hundred yards from the tiny inlet that accessed the Potomac for the swarms of weekend boat enthusiasts, and taxied to gate number nine. An airport security officer was answering questions from a group of anxious, camera-toting tourists and did not observe the man walking rapidly past him. Not that identification was going to be made anyway.

Luther's return trip had followed the circuity of his exit. A stopover in Miami, and then Dallas/Fort Worth.

He grabbed a cab and watched the south-moving rush-hour traffic on the George Washington Parkway as weary commuters threaded their way home. The skies promised more rain, and the wind whipped through the tree-lined parkway meandering lazily on its parallel course with the Potomac. Planes periodically rocketed into the air, banking left and rapidly disappearing into the clouds.

One more battle beckoned Luther. The image of a righteously indignant President Richmond pounding the lectern in his impassioned speech against violence, his smug Chief of Staff by his side, was the one constant in Luther's life now. The old, tired and fearful man who had fled the country was no longer tired, no longer fearful. The overriding guilt at

208

allowing a young woman to die had been replaced with an overriding hate, an anger that surged through every nerve in his body. If he was to be, of sorts, Christine Sullivan's avenging angel, he would perform that task with every ounce of energy and every shred of ingenuity he had left.

Luther settled back into his seat, munched on some crackers saved from the plane trip, and wondered if Gloria Russell was any good at playing chicken.

Seth Frank glanced out the car window. His personal interviews of Walter Sullivan's household staff had revealed two things of interest, the first of which was the business enterprise Frank was now parked in front of; the second could keep. Housed in a long, gray concrete building in a heavy commercial area of Springfield just outside the Beltway, Metro Steam Cleaner's sign proclaimed that it had been in business since 1949. That was stability that meant nothing to Frank. A lot of long-standing legitimate businesses were now money-laundering fronts for organized crime, both Mafia, Chinese and America's own homegrown versions. And a carpet cleaner firm that catered to affluent homeowners was in a perfect position to scope alarm systems, cash and jewelry nests and patterns of behavior of the intended victims and their households. Whether he was dealing with a loner or an entire organization Frank didn't know. It was more likely that he was headed toward a dead end, but then you never knew. There were two patrol cars stationed three minutes away. Just in case. Frank got out of his car.

"That would have been Rogers, Budizinski and Jerome Pettis. Yep, August 30, nine A.M. Three floors. Damn house was so big, it took all day even with three guys." George Patterson consulted his record book while Frank's eyes took in the grimy office.

"Can I speak to them?"

"You can to Pettis. The other two are gone."

"Permanently?" Patterson nodded. "How long had they been with you?"

Patterson's eyes scanned his employment log. "Jerome's been with me five years. He's one of my best people. Rogers was about two months. I think he moved out of the area. Budizinski had been with us about four weeks."

"Pretty short stays."

"Hell, that's the nature of the business. Spend a thousand bucks training these guys and wham they're gone. It's not a career-type job, you know what I mean? It's hot, dirty work. And the pay ain't exactly going to put you on the Riviera, you hear what I'm saying?"

"You got addresses for them?" Frank took out his notebook.

"Well, like I said, Rogers moved. Pettis is in today, if you want to talk to him. He's got a job to do out in McLean in about a half hour. He's back loading his truck now."

"Who decides which crew goes to which house?"

"I do."

"All the time?"

Patterson hesitated. "Well, I got guys who specialize in different stuff."

"Who specializes in the high-dollar areas?"

"Jerome. Like I said, he's my best guy."

"How did the other two get assigned to him?"

"I don't know, we juggle stuff like that. Depends on who shows up for work sometimes."

"You remember any of those three being particularly interested in visiting the Sullivan place?"

Patterson shook his head.

210

"What about Budizinski? You got an address on him?"

Patterson consulted a notebook crammed with paper and wrote on a slip of paper. "It's over in Arlington. Don't know if he's still there."

"I'll want their employment file. Social Security numbers, birthdates, job history, all that stuff."

"Sally can get that for you. She's the gal up front."

"Thanks. You got photos of these guys?"

Patterson looked at Frank like he was nuts. "Are you kidding. This ain't the FBI, for crying out loud."

"Can you give me a description?" Frank asked patiently.

"I've got sixty-five employees and a turnover rate of over sixty percent. I usually don't even see the guy after he's hired. Everybody starts to look the same after a while anyway. Pettis'll remember."

"Anything else you think might help me?"

Patterson shook his head. "You think one of them might have killed that woman?"

Frank stood up and stretched. "I don't know. What do you think?"

"Hey, I get all kinds in here. Nothing surprises me anymore."

Frank turned to leave, then turned back. "Oh by the way, I'll want records of all homes and establishments cleaned by your firm in Middleton in the last two years."

Patterson exploded out of his chair. "What the fuck for?"

"You have the records?"

"Yeah, I got 'em."

"Good, let me know when they're ready. Have a good one."

Jerome Pettis was a tall, cadaverous black man in his

early forties with a perpetual cigarette hanging from his mouth. Frank watched admiringly as the man methodically loaded the heavy cleaning equipment with a practiced hand. His blue jumpsuit announced that he was a senior technician with Metro. He didn't look at Frank, kept his eyes on his work. All around them in the huge garage white vans were being similarly loaded. A couple of men stared over at Frank but quickly returned to their work.

"Mr. Patterson said you had some questions?"

Frank parked himself on the van's front bumper. "A few. You did a job at Walter Sullivan's home in Middleton on August 30 of this year."

Pettis's brow furrowed. "August? Hell, I do about four homes a day. I don't remember them cuz they aren't that memorable."

"This one took you all day. Big house out in Middleton. Rogers and Budizinski were with you."

Pettis smiled. "That's right. Biggest goddamned house I'd ever seen and I've seen some bad places, man."

Frank smiled back. "That's the same thing I thought when I saw it."

Pettis straightened up, relit his cigarette. "Problem was all that furniture. Had to move every damn piece, and some of that shit was heavy, heavy like they don't make no more."

"So you were there all day?" Frank hadn't meant the question to come out that way.

Pettis stiffened, sucked on his Camel and leaned against the door of the van. "So how come the cops are interested in how the carpets were cleaned?"

"Woman was murdered in the house. Apparently she mixed it up with some burglars. Don't you read the papers?"

"Just the sports. And you're wondering if I'm one of them dudes?"

"Not right now. I'm just collecting information. Everybody who was near that house recently interests me. I'll probably talk to the mailman next."

"You're funny for a cop. You think I killed her?"

"I think if you did, you're smart enough not to stick around here waiting for me to ring your doorbell. These two men who were with you, what can you tell me about them?"

Pettis finished his smoke and looked at Frank without answering. Frank started to close his notebook.

"You want a lawyer, Jerome?"

"Do I need one?"

"Not as far as I'm concerned, but it's not my call. I don't plan on pulling out my Miranda card if that's what you're worried about."

Pettis finally looked at the concrete floor, crushed out his cigarette, looked back at Frank. "Look, man, I've been with Mr. Patterson a long time. Come to work every day, do my job, take my paycheck and go home."

"Then it sounds like you have nothing to worry about."

"Right. Look, I did some stuff a while back. Did some time. You can pull it off your computers in five seconds. So I'm not gonna sit here and bullshit you, okay?"

"Okay."

"I've got four kids and no wife. I didn't break into that house and I didn't do anything to that woman."

"I believe you, Jerome. I'm a lot more interested in Rogers and Budizinski."

Pettis eyed the detective for several seconds. "Let's take a walk."

The two men left the garage and walked over to an ancient Buick as big as a boat that had more rust than metal. Pettis got inside. Frank followed.

213

"Big ears in the garage, you know?"

Frank nodded.

"Brian Rogers. Called him Slick cuz he was a good worker, picked up things fast."

"What'd he look like?"

"White guy about fifty, maybe older. Not too tall, five eight, maybe a buck fifty. Talkative. Worked hard."

"And Budizinski?"

"Buddy. Everybody here has a nickname. I'm Ton. For skele*ton*, you know." Frank smiled at that one. "He was a white guy too, a little bigger. Maybe a little older than Slick. He kept to himself. Did what he was told and nothing more."

"Which one did the master bedroom?"

"We all did. We had to lift the bed and the bureau. They weighed a couple tons each. Back still hurts." Jerome reached in the rear seat and pulled out a cooler. "No time for breakfast this morning," he explained as he pulled out a banana and an egg biscuit.

Frank shifted uncomfortably in the worn seat. A piece of metal jabbed into his back. The car reeked of cigarette smoke.

"Were either of them ever alone in the master bedroom or the house?"

"Always somebody in the house. Man had a lot of people working there. They coulda gone upstairs by themselves. I never kept a watch on them. Wasn't my job, you know?"

"How'd Rogers and Budizinski come to be working with you that day?"

Jerome thought for a moment. "I'm not sure, come to think of it. I know it was an early job. It might've just been they were the first ones here. Sometimes that's all it takes."

"So if they knew ahead of time you were going to

do a place like that early, and they got here before everyone else, they could hook on with you?"

"Yeah, I guess they could. Man, we just look for bodies, you know what I'm saying? Don't take no brain surgeon to do this shit."

"When was the last time you saw them?"

The other man scrunched up his face, bit into his banana.

"Couple of months ago, maybe longer. Buddy left first, never said why. Guys come and go all the time. I've been here longer than anybody except Mr. Patterson. Slick moved away, I think."

"Know where?"

"I remember him saying something about Kansas. Some construction work. He used to be a carpenter. Got laid off up here when commercial went belly up. Good with his hands."

Frank wrote this information down while Jerome finished his breakfast. They walked back to the garage together. Frank looked inside the van, at all the hoses, power handles, bottles and heavy cleaning equipment.

"This the van you used to do the Sullivan place?"

"This been my van for three years. Best one in the place."

"You keep the same equipment in the van?"

"Damn straight."

"Then you better get a new van for a while."

"What?" Jerome slowly climbed out of the driver's seat.

"I'll talk to Patterson. I'm impounding this one."

"You're shitting me."

"No, Jerome, I'm afraid I'm not."

"Walter, this is Jack Graham. Jack, Walter Sullivan." Sandy Lord sat down heavily in his chair. Jack shook hands with Sullivan and then the men sat around the

215

small table in conference room number five. It was eight o'clock in the morning and Jack had been in the office since six after pulling two all-nighters. He had already consumed three cups of coffee and proceeded to pour himself out a fourth from the silver coffee pot.

"Walter, I've told Jack about the Ukraine deal. We've gone over the structure. The Hill word looks real good. Richmond pushed all the right buttons. The Bear's dead. Kiev got the glass slipper. Your boy came through."

"He's one of my best friends. I expect that from my friends. But I thought we had enough lawyers on this deal. Padding the bill, Sandy?" Sullivan heaved himself up and looked out the window at the pristine early-morning sky that promised a beautiful fall day. Jack glanced sideways at the man as he made notes from the crash course on Sullivan's latest deal. Sullivan didn't look all that interested in completing the multibillion international monolith. Jack didn't know that the old man's thoughts hung back at a morgue in Virginia, remembering a face.

Jack had caught his breath when Lord had ceremoniously appointed him to play second chair to Lord on the biggest transaction currently going on in the firm, leapfrogging over several top partners and a host of associates senior to Jack. Hard feelings had already started to roll through the plush hallways. At this point Jack didn't care. They didn't have Ransome Baldwin as a client. Regardless of how he had gotten it, he had rain, substantial rain. He was tired of feeling guilty for his position. This was Lord's test case on Jack's abilities. He had as good as said it. Well, if he wanted the deal rammed through, Jack would deliver. Philosophical, politically correct ivory tower babble didn't cut it here. Only results.

"Jack is one of our best attorneys. He's also Baldwin's legal eagle."

Sullivan looked over at them. "Ransome Baldwin?"

Sullivan appraised Jack in a different light and then turned once more to the window.

"Our window of opportunity, however, is growing more narrow by the day," Lord continued. "We need to firm up the players and make sure Kiev knows what the hell they're supposed to do."

"Can't you handle it?"

Lord looked at Jack and then back at Sullivan. "Of course I can handle it, Walter, but don't assume you can abdicate right now. You still have a major role to play. You sold this deal. Your continued involvement is absolutely necessary from the point of view of all sides." Sullivan still did not stir. "Walter, this is the crowning glory of your career."

"That's what you said about the last one."

"Can I help it if you keep topping yourself?" Lord shot back.

Finally, almost imperceptibly, Sullivan smiled, for the first time since the telephone call from the States had come to shatter his life.

Lord relaxed a bit, looked over at Jack. They had rehearsed this next step several times.

"I'm recommending that you fly over there with Jack. Shake the right hands, pat the right shoulders, let them see you're still in control of this tiger. They need that. Capitalism is still a new game for them."

"And Jack's role?"

Lord motioned to Jack.

Jack stood up, went over to the window. "Mr. Sullivan, I've spent the last forty-eight hours learning every aspect of this deal. All the other lawyers here have just been working on a piece of it. Except for Sandy, I don't think there's anyone at the firm who knows what you want to accomplish better than I do."

Sullivan slowly turned to Jack. "That's a pretty big statement."

"Well, it's a pretty big deal, sir."

"So you know what I want to accomplish?"

"Yes, sir."

"Well, why don't you enlighten me as to what you think that is." Sullivan sat down, crossed his arms and stared expectantly up at Jack.

Jack didn't bother to swallow or catch his breath. "Ukraine has massive natural resources, all the things that heavy industry around the world use and want. The issue becomes how to get the resources out of Ukraine at minimal cost and minimal risk, considering the political situation over there."

Sullivan uncrossed his arms, sat up and sipped at his coffee.

Jack continued, "The hook is, you want Kiev to believe that the exports your company will be making will be matched by investments in Ukraine's future. A long-term investment, I gather, you do not want to commit to."

"I spent the bulk of my adult life being scared to death of the reds. I have about as much belief in perestroika and glasnost as I do in the tooth fairy. I consider it my patriotic duty to strip the communists of as much as I can. Leave them without the means to dominate the world, which is their long-term plan, despite this latest hiccup of democracy."

Jack said, "Exactly, sir. 'Strip' being the key word. Strip the carcass before it self-destructs . . . or attacks." Jack paused to check both men's reactions. Lord stared at the ceiling, his features unreadable.

Sullivan stirred. "Go on. You're getting to the interesting part."

"The interesting part is how to leverage the deal so

218

that Sullivan and Company has little or no downside exposure and the maximum upside potential. You'll either broker the deal or you'll buy direct from Ukraine and you'll sell to the multinationals. You sprinkle a little of those proceeds around in Ukraine."

"That's right. Eventually the country will be almost cleaned out, and I'll walk away with at least two billion net."

Jack again looked at Lord, who now sat straight in his chair, listening intently. This was the hook. Jack had thought of it only yesterday.

"But why not take from Ukraine what really makes them dangerous?" Jack paused. "And triple your net at the same time."

Sullivan stared intently at him. "How?"

"IRBMs. Intermediate-Range Ballistic Missiles. Ukraine has a shitload of them. And now that the '94 Nonproliferation Treaty fell apart, those nukes are a major headache for the West again."

"So what are you suggesting? That I buy the god-damn things? What the hell would I do with them?"

Jack watched Lord finally lean forward, then continued. "You buy them for bottom dollar, maybe a half-billion, using a portion of the proceeds from the raw materials sales. You will buy them using dollars, which can then be used by Ukraine to purchase other necessities in the world markets."

"Why bottom-dollar? Every Middle Eastern country will be bidding on them."

"But Ukraine can't sell to them. The G-7 countries would never allow it. If Ukraine did, they'd be cut out of the EU and other Western markets, and if that happens, they're dead."

"So I buy them and sell them to whom?"

Jack couldn't help but grin. "To us. The United States. Six billion is a conservative estimate on their worth. Hell, the weapons-grade plutonium those babies contain is priceless. The rest of the G-7s would probably pitch in a few billion. It's your relationship with Kiev that makes this whole thing work. They look to you as their savior."

Sullivan looked stunned. He started to rise and then thought better of it. Even to him the amounts of money potentially out there were staggering. But he had enough money, more than enough. But to remove part of the nuclear equation from the collective miseries of the world . . .

"And this was whose idea?" Sullivan looked at Lord as he asked the question. Lord pointed at Jack.

Sullivan leaned back in his chair and looked up at the young man. Then he rose with a swiftness that startled Jack. The billionaire took Jack's hand in an iron grip. "You're going places, young man. Mind if I tag along?"

Lord beamed like a father. Jack couldn't stop smiling. He had started to forget what it was like to hit one out of the park.

After Sullivan departed, Jack and Sandy sat at the table.

Finally Sandy said, "I recognize it was not an easy assignment. How do you feel?"

Jack couldn't help but grin. "Like I just slept with the prettiest girl in high school, kind of tingling all over."

Lord laughed and stood up. "You'd better go home and get some rest. Sullivan's probably calling his pilot from the car. At least we got his mind off the bitch."

Jack didn't hear the last part as he quickly left the room. For now, for once in a long time, he felt good. No worries, just possibilities. Endless possibilities.

That night he sat up late telling a very enthusiastic

220

Jennifer Baldwin all about it. Afterward, over a very chilled bottle of champagne and a platter of oysters specially delivered to her townhouse, the couple had the most gratifying sex of their courtship. For once, the high ceilings and murals did not bother Jack. In fact, he was growing to like them.

THIRTEEN

The White House receives millions of pieces of nonofficial mail each year. Each item is carefully screened and appropriately processed, the whole task handled by an in-house staff with assistance and supervision by the Secret Service.

The two envelopes were addressed to Gloria Russell, which was somewhat unusual since most of this type of correspondence was addressed to the President or members of the First Family, or frequently the First Pet, which currently happened to be a golden retriever named Barney.

The handwriting on each was in block letters, the envelopes white and cheap and thus widely available. Russell got to them about twelve o'clock on a day that had been going pretty well up until then. Inside one was a single sheet of paper and inside the other was an item she had stared at for some minutes. Written on the paper, again in block letters, were the words:

> Question: What constitutes high crimes and misdemeanors? Answer: I don't think you want to find out. Valuable item available, more to follow, chief, signed not a secret admirer

Even though she had expected it, in fact had desperately wanted to receive it, she still could feel her heartbeat increase to where it pounded against the wall of her chest; her saliva dwindled down to where she reached for and gulped down a glass of water and repeated the procedure until she could hold the letter without shaking. Then she looked at the second item. A photograph. The sight of the letter opener had brought the nightmare events rushing back to her. She gripped the sides of her chair. Finally the attack subsided.

"At least he wants to deal." Collin put down the note and photo and returned to his chair. He noted the extreme pallor of the woman and wondered if she was tough enough to make it through this one.

"Maybe. It could also be a setup."

Collin shook his head. "Don't think so."

Russell sat back in her chair, rubbed at her temples, downed another Tylenol. "Why not?"

"Why set us up this way? In fact, why set us up at all? He's got the stuff to bury us. He wants money."

"He probably got millions from the Sullivan heist."

"Maybe. But we don't know how much of it was liquid. Maybe he stashed it and can't get back to it. Maybe he's just an extremely greedy person. World is full of those."

"I need a drink. Can you come over tonight?"

"The President is having dinner at the Canadian embassy."

"Shit. Can't you get someone to replace you?"

"Maybe, if you pulled some strings."

"Consider them pulled. How soon do you think we'll hear from him again?"

"He doesn't seem too anxious, although he might just be acting cautious. I would in his situation."

"Great. So I can smoke two packs of menthols a day until we hear from him. By then I'll be dead of lung cancer."

"If he wants money, what are you going to do?" he asked.

"Depending on how much he wants, it can be

accomplished without too much difficulty." She seemed calmer now.

Collin rose to go. "You're the boss."

"Tim?" Russell went over to him. "Hold me for a minute."

He felt her rub against his pistol as he gripped her.

"Tim, if it comes down to more than money. If we can't get it back."

Collin looked down at her.

"Then I'll take care of it, Gloria." He touched his fingers to her lips, turned and left.

Collin found Burton waiting in the hallway.

Burton looked the younger man up and down. "So how's she holding up?"

"All right." Collin continued to walk down the hallway, until Burton grabbed his arm, spun him around.

"What the fuck's going on, Tim?" Collin loosened his partner's grip.

"This isn't the time or the place, Bill."

"Well, tell me the time and the place, and I'll be there because we need to talk."

"What about?"

"You gonna fucking play stupid with me?" He roughly pulled Collin to a corner.

"I want you to think real clearly about that woman in there. She doesn't give a shit about you or me or anybody else. The only thing she cares about is saving her own little ass. I don't know what kind of story she's spinning on you, and I don't know what you two are cooking up, but I'm telling you to be careful. I don't want to see you throw everything away over her."

"I appreciate the concern but I know what I'm doing, Bill."

"Do you, Tim? Does fucking the Chief of Staff

come within the purview of a Secret Service agent's responsibilities? Why don't you show me where that is in the manual? I'd like to read it for myself. And while we're talking about it, why don't you enlighten me about what the hell we went back into that house for. Because we ain't got it, and I guess I know who does. My ass is on the line here too, Tim. If I'm going down I'd like to know why."

An aide passed by in the hallway and stared strangely at the two men. Burton smiled and nodded and then returned his attention to Collin.

"Come on, Tim, what the hell would you do if you were me?"

The young man looked at his friend and his face slowly relaxed from the hard line he normally wore while on duty. If he were in Burton's position what would he do? The answer was easy. He'd kick some ass until people started talking. Burton was his friend, had proven it time and again. What the man was saying about Russell was probably true. Collin's reasoning hadn't totally evaporated in the presence of silk lingerie.

"You got time for a cup of coffee, Bill?"

Frank walked down the two flights of stairs, turned right and opened the door to the crime lab. Small and in need of paint, the room was surprisingly well-organized due in large measure to the fact that Laura Simon was a very compulsive person. Frank imagined her home to be every bit as neat and well-kept despite the presence of two preschoolers that kept her sufficiently haggard. Around the room were stacked unused evidence kits with their unbroken orange seals creating a bit of color against the drab, chipping gray walls. Cardboard boxes, carefully labeled, were piled in another corner. In yet another corner was a small floor safe that held the few physical items requiring additional security measures. Next to it was a refrigerator that housed evidence requiring a temperature-controlled environment.

He watched her small back as it curved over a microscope at the far end of the room.

"You rang?" Frank leaned over. On the glass slide were small fragments of some substance. He couldn't imagine spending his days looking at microscopic pieces of who knew what, but he was also fully aware that what Laura Simon did was an enormously important contribution to the conviction process.

"Look at this." Simon motioned him over to the lens. Frank removed his eyeglasses, which he had forgotten were still on. He glanced down and then raised his head back up.

"Laura, you know I never know what I'm looking at. What is it?"

"It's a sample of carpet taken from the Sullivans' bedroom. We didn't get it on the initial search, picked it up later."

"So, what's significant about it?" Frank had learned to listen very attentively to this tech.

"The carpet in the bedroom is one of those very high-priced models that cost about two hundred dollars a square foot. The carpet just for the bedroom must have run them almost a quarter mil."

"Jesus Christ!" Frank popped another piece of gum in his mouth. Trying to quit smoking was rotting his teeth and adding to his waistline. "Two-fifty for something you walk on?"

"It's incredibly durable; you could roll a tank across it and it would just spring back. It's only been there about two years. They did a bunch of renovation back then."

"Renovation? The house is only a few years old."

"That's when the deceased married Walter Sullivan."

226

"Oh."

"Women like to make their own statement about those things, Seth. Actually, she had good taste in carpets."

"Okay, so where does her good taste get us?"

"Look at the fibers again."

Frank sighed but obeyed the request.

"You see at the very tips? Look at the cross section. They've been cut. Presumably with not very sharp scissors. The cut is pretty ragged, although like I said these fibers are like iron."

He looked at her. "Cut? Why would anyone do that? Where'd you find them?"

"These particular samples were found on the bed skirt. Whoever cut them probably wouldn't have noticed a few fibers clinging to his hand. Then he brushed against the skirt and there you are."

"You find a corresponding part on the carpet?"

"Yep. Right under the left side of the bed if you're looking toward it about ten centimeters away at a perpendicular angle. The cut was slight but verifiable."

Frank straightened back up and sat down on one of the stools next to Simon.

"That's not all, Seth. On one of the fragments I also found traces of a solvent. Like a stain remover."

"That might be from the recent carpet cleaning. Or maybe the maids spilled something."

Simon shook her head. "Uh-uh. The cleaning company uses a steam system. For spot cleaning they use a special organic-based solvent. I checked. This one is a petroleum-based, off-the-shelf cleaner. And the maids use the same cleanser as recommended by the manufacturer. It's an organic base too. They have a whole supply of it at the house. And the carpet is chemically treated to prevent stains from soaking in. Using a petroleum-based solvent probably made it

227

worse. That's probably why they ended up snipping out pieces."

"So presumably the perp takes the fibers because they show something. Do they?"

"Not on the sample I got, but he might have cut around the area just to make sure he didn't miss anything and we got one of the clean specimens."

"What would be on the carpet that someone would go to the trouble of cutting one-centimeter fibers out? It must've been a pain in the ass."

Both Simon and Frank had the same thought and indeed had it for several moments.

"Blood," Simon said simply.

"And not the deceased's either. If I remember correctly, hers wasn't anywhere near that spot." Frank added, "I think you got one more test to run, Laura."

She hooked a kit off the wall. "I was just getting ready to go do it, thought I'd better buzz you first."

"Smart girl."

The drive out took thirty minutes. Frank rolled down his window and let the wind course over his face. It also helped dispel the cigarette smoke. Simon was constantly giving him a hard time about that.

The bedroom had remained sealed under Frank's orders.

Frank watched from the corner of Walter Sullivan's bedroom as Simon carefully mixed the bottles of chemicals and then poured the result into a plastic sprayer. Frank then helped her stuff towels under the door and tape brown packing paper to the windows. They closed the heavy drapes, cutting out virtually all traces of natural light.

Frank surveyed the room once again. He looked at the mirror, the bed, the window, the closets and then his eyes rested on the nightstand and at the gaping hole behind where the plaster had been removed. Then his eyes moved back to the picture. He picked it up. He was reminded again that Christine Sullivan had been a very beautiful woman, as far removed as one could get from the destroyed hulk he had viewed. In the photograph she was sitting in the chair beside the bed. The nightstand was clearly visible to her left. The corner of the bed made its way into the right side of the picture. Ironically so, considering all the use she had probably made of that particular vehicle. The springs were probably due for their sixty-thousand-mile checkup. After that, they probably wouldn't have much to do. He remembered the look on Walter Sullivan's face. Not much left there.

He put the photo down and continued to observe Simon's fluid movements. He glanced back at the photo, something bothering him, but whatever it was popped out of his head as quickly as it had sprung into it.

"What's that stuff called again, Laura?"

"Luminol. It's sold under a variety of names, but it's the same reagent stuff. I'm ready."

She positioned the bottle over the section of carpet where the fibers had been cut from.

"Good thing you don't have to pay for this carpet." The detective smiled at her.

Simon turned to look at him. "Wouldn't matter to me. I'd just declare bankruptcy. They could garnishee my wages from here until eternity. It's the poor person's great equalizer."

Frank hit the light, plunging the room into pitch-black darkness. Swishes of air were heard as Simon squeezed the trigger on the spray bottle. Almost immediately, like a mass of lightning bugs, a very small portion of the carpet started to glow a pale blue and then disappeared. Frank turned on the overhead light and looked at Simon.

"So we got somebody else's blood. Helluva pickup, Laura. Any way you can scrape up enough to analyze, get a blood type? DNA typing?"

Simon looked dubious. "We'll pull the carpet to see if any leaked through, but I doubt it. Not much soaks into a treated carpet. And any residue has been mixed with a lot of stuff. So don't count on it."

Frank thought out loud. "Okay, one perp wounded. Not a lot of blood, but some." He looked for confirmation from Simon on that point and received an affirmative nod of the head. "Wounded, but with what? She had nothing in her hand when we found her."

Simon read his mind. "And as sudden as her death was, we're probably talking cadaveric spasm. To get it out of her hand they would've almost had to break her fingers."

Frank finished the thought. "And there was no sign of that on the autopsy."

"Unless the impact of the slugs caused her hand to fly open."

"How often does that happen?"

"Once is enough for this case."

"Okay, let's assume she had a weapon, and now that weapon is missing. What kind of weapon might it have been?"

Simon considered this as she repacked her kit.

"You probably could rule out a gun; she should've been able to get a round off, and there were no powder burns on her hands. They couldn't have scraped those off without leaving a trail."

"Good. Plus there's no evidence she ever had a gun registered to her. And we've already confirmed that there are no guns in the house."

"So no gun. Maybe a knife then. Can't tell what kind of wound it made, but maybe a slash, probably superficial. The number of fibers that were snipped

230

out was small, so we're not talking life-threatening."

"So she stabbed one of the perps, maybe in the arm or leg. Then they backed up and shot her? Or she stabbed as she was dying?" Frank corrected himself. "No. She died instantly. She stabs one of them in another room, runs in here and then gets shot. Standing over her, the wounded perp drips some blood."

"Except the vault's in here. The more likely scenario is that she surprised them in the act."

"Right, except remember the shots came from the doorway *into* the room. And fired *down*. Who surprised who? That's what keeps bugging the ever-loving shit out of me."

"So why take the knife, if that's what it was?"

"Cause it IDs somebody, somehow."

"Prints?" Simon's nostrils quivered as she thought of the physical evidence lurking out there.

Frank nodded. "That's how I read it."

"Was the last Mrs. Sullivan in the habit of keeping a knife with her?"

Frank responded by slapping his hand to his forehead so hard it made Simon wince. She watched as he rushed over to the nightstand and picked up the photo. He shook his head and handed it to her.

"There's your goddamned knife."

Simon looked at the photo. In it, resting on the nightstand was a long, leather-handled letter opener.

"The leather also explains the oily residue on the palms."

Frank paused at the front door on the way out. He looked at the security control panel, which had been restored to its operating condition. Then he broke into a smile as an elusive thought finally trickled to the surface.

"Laura, you got the fluorescent lamp in the trunk?"

"Yeah, why?"

"You mind getting it?"

Puzzled, Simon did so. She returned to the foyer and plugged it in.

"Shine it right on the number keys."

What was revealed under the fluorescent light made Frank smile again.

"Goddamn, that's good."

"What does it mean?" Simon looked at him, her brow furrowed.

"It means two things. First, we definitely got us somebody on the inside and, second, our perps are real creative."

Frank sat in the small interrogation room and decided against another cigarette and opted instead for a cherry Tums. He looked at the cinder block walls, cheap metal table and beat-up chairs and decided this was a very depressing place to be interrogated in. Which was good. Depressed people were vulnerable people, and vulnerable people, given the appropriate prodding, tended to want to talk. And Frank wanted to listen. He would listen all day.

The case was still extremely muddled, but certain elements were becoming clearer.

Buddy Budizinski still lived in Arlington and now worked at a car wash in Falls Church. He had admitted being in the Sullivan house, had read about the murder, but beyond that knew nothing. Frank tended to believe him. The man was not particularly bright, had no previous police record and had spent his adult life performing menial tasks for a living, no doubt compelled by his having finished only the fifth grade. His apartment was modest to the point of near poverty. Budizinski was a dead end.

Rogers, on the other hand, had produced a treasure trove. The Social Security number he had given on his employment application was real enough, only it

232

belonged to a female State Department employee who had been assigned to Thailand for the last two years. He must have known the carpet cleaning company wouldn't have checked. What did they care? The address on the application was a motel in Beltsville, Maryland. No one by that name had registered at the motel in the last year and no one fitting Rogers's description had been seen there. The state of Kansas had no record of him. On top of that he had never cashed any of the payroll checks given to him by Metro. That in itself spoke volumes.

An artist's sketch based on Pettis's recollection was being made up down the hallway and would be distributed throughout the area.

Rogers was the guy, Frank could feel it. He had been in the house, and he had disappeared leaving behind a trail of false information. Simon was right this minute painstakingly examining Pettis's van in the hopes that Rogers's prints were still lurking somewhere within. They had no prints to match at the crime scene, but if they could ident Rogers, then dollars to donuts he had priors, and Frank's case would finally be forming. It would take a great leap forward if the person he was waiting for would decide to cooperate.

And Walter Sullivan had confirmed that an antique letter opener from his bedroom was indeed missing. Frank feverishly hoped to be able to lay his hands on that potential evidentiary gold mine. Frank had imparted his theory to Sullivan about his wife stabbing her attacker with that instrument. The old man hadn't seemed to register the information. Frank had briefly wondered if Sullivan was losing it.

The detective checked his list of employees at Sullivan's residence once more, although by now he knew them all by heart. There was only one he was really interested in.

The security company rep's statement kept coming back to him. The variations generated by fifteen digits to get a five-digit code in the correct sequence was impossible for a portable computer to crunch in the very brief time allowed, particularly if you factored in a less than blazing fast response from the security system's computer. In order to do it, you had to eliminate some of the possibles. How did you do that?

An examination of the keypad showed that a chemical – Frank couldn't remember the exact name although Simon had recognized it – which was revealed only under fluorescent light, had been applied to each of the number keys.

Frank leaned back and envisioned Walter Sullivan – or the butler, or whoever's job it was to set the alarm – going down and entering the code. The finger would hit the proper keys, five of them, and the alarm would be set. The person would walk away, completely unaware that he or she now had a small tracing of chemical, invisible to the naked eye, and odorless, on their finger. And, more important, they would be totally ignorant of the fact that they had just revealed the numbers comprising the security code. Under fluorescent light, the perps would be able to tell which numbers had been entered because the chemical would be smeared on those keys. With that information, it was up to the computer to deliver the correct sequence, which the security rep was certain it could do in the allotted time, once given the elimination of 99.9 percent of the possible combos.

Now the question remained: who had applied the chemical? Frank at first had considered that Rogers, or whatever his real name was, might have done it while at the house, but the facts against that conclusion were overwhelming. First, the house was always filled with people and to even the most unobservant a stranger lurking around an alarm panel would arouse suspicion. Second, the entry foyer was large and open and the most unsecluded spot in the house. Lastly, the application would take some time and care. And Rogers didn't have that luxury. Even the slightest suspicion, the most fleeting glance and his whole plan could be ruined. The person who had thought this one up was not the type to take that sort of risk. Rogers hadn't done it. Frank was pretty sure he knew who did.

Upon first glance, the woman appeared so thin as to convey the impression of emaciation perhaps due to cancer. On second glance, the good color in the cheeks, the light bone structure and the graceful way she moved led to the conclusion that she was very lean but otherwise healthy.

"Please sit down, Ms. Broome. I appreciate your coming down."

The woman nodded and slid into one of the seats. She wore a flowery skirt that ended midcalf. A single strand of large fake pearls encircled her neck. Her hair was tied in a neat bun; some of the strands at the top of her forehead were beginning to turn a silvery gray, like ink leaching onto paper. Going on the smooth skin and absence of wrinkles, Frank would have put her age at about thirty-nine. Actually she was some years older.

"I thought you were already done with me, Mr. Frank."

"Please call me Seth. You smoke?"

She shook her head.

"I've just got a few follow-up questions, routine. You're not the only one. I understand you're leaving Mr. Sullivan's employment?"

She noticeably swallowed, looked down and then back up. "I was close, so to speak, to Mrs. Sullivan.

It's hard now, you know . . ." Her voice trailed off.

"I know it is, I know it is. It was terrible, awful." Frank paused for a moment. "You've been with the Sullivans how long now?"

"A little over a year."

"You do the cleaning and . . .?"

"I help do the cleaning. There's four of us, Sally, Rebecca and me. Karen Taylor, she does the cooking. I also looked after Mrs. Sullivan's things for her too. Her clothes and what-not. I was sort of her assistant, I guess you could say. Mr. Sullivan had his own person, Richard."

"Would you like some coffee?"

Frank didn't wait for her to answer. He got up and opened the door to the interrogation room.

"Hey Molly, can you bring me a couple of javas?" He turned to Ms. Broome. "Black? Cream?"

"Black."

"Make it two pures, Molly, thanks."

He shut the door and sat back down.

"Damn chill in the air, I can't seem to stay warm." He tapped the rough wall. "This cinder block doesn't help much. So you were saying about Mrs. Sullivan?"

"She was really nice to me. I mean she would talk to me about things. She wasn't – she wasn't, you know, from that class of people, the upper class I guess you could say. She went to high school where I did right here in Middleton."

"And not too far apart in years I'm thinking."

His remark brought a smile to Wanda Broome's lips and a hand unconsciously moved to cajole back into place an invisible strand of hair.

"Further than I'd like to admit."

The door opened and their coffee was delivered. It was gratefully hot and fresh. Frank had not been lying about the chill.

"I won't say she fit in real well with all those types

236

of people, but she seemed to hold her own. She didn't take anything from anybody if you know what I mean."

Frank had reason to believe that was true. From all accounts the late Mrs. Sullivan had been a hellion in many respects.

"Would you say the relationship between the Sullivans was . . . good, bad, in between?"

She didn't hesitate. "Very good. Oh I know what people say about the age difference and all, but she was good for him, and he was good for her. I truly believe that. He loved her, I can tell you that. Maybe more like a father loves his daughter, but it was still love."

"And she him?"

Now there was perceptible hesitation. "You've got to understand that Christy Sullivan was a very young woman, maybe younger in a lot of ways than other women her age. Mr. Sullivan opened up a whole new world for her and—" She broke off, clearly unsure of how to continue.

Frank changed gears. "What about the vault in the bedroom? Who knew about it?"

"I don't know. I certainly didn't. I assume that Mr. and Mrs. Sullivan knew. Mr. Sullivan's valet, Richard, he may have known. But I'm not sure about that."

"So Christine Sullivan or her husband never indicated to you that there was a safe behind the mirror?"

"My goodness no. I was her friend of sorts, but I was still just an employee. And only with them a year. Mr. Sullivan never really spoke to me. I mean that's not the sort of thing you would tell someone like me, is it?"

"No, I guess not." Frank was certain she was lying, but he had been unable to unearth any evidence to the contrary. Christine Sullivan was the very type to show off her wealth to someone she could identify with, if only to show how far she had suddenly risen in the world.

"So you didn't know the mirror was a one-way looking into the bedroom?"

This time the woman showed visible surprise. Frank noticed a blush under the light application of makeup.

"Wanda, can I call you Wanda? Wanda, you understand, don't you, that the alarm system in the house was deactivated by the person who broke in? It was deactivated by the appropriate code being put in. Now, who set the alarm at night?"

"Richard did," she replied promptly. "Or sometimes Mr. Sullivan did it himself."

"So everyone in the house knew the code?"

"Oh no, of course not. Richard did. He's been with Mr. Sullivan for almost forty years. He was the only one other than the Sullivans who knew the code that I know of."

"Did you ever see him set the alarm?"

"I was usually already in bed when the system was set."

Frank stared at her. *I'll bet you were, Wanda, I'll bet you were.*

Wanda Broome's eyes widened. "You're, you're not suspecting that Richard had anything to do with it?"

"Well, Wanda, somehow, somebody who wasn't supposed to be able to, disarmed that alarm system. And naturally suspicion falls on anyone who had access to that code."

Wanda Broome looked like she might start to cry, then composed herself. "Richard is almost seventy years old."

"Then he's probably in need of a nice little nest

egg. You understand what I'm telling you is to be held in the strictest confidence of course?"

She nodded and at the same time wiped her nose. The coffee, untouched, was now sipped in quick little bursts.

Frank continued, "And until someone can explain to me how that security system was accessed, then I'm going to have to explore the avenues that make the most sense to me."

He continued to look at her. He had spent the past day finding out everything he could about Wanda Broome. It was a fairly average story except for one twist. She was forty-four years old, twice divorced with two grown children. She lived in the servants' wing with the rest of the in-house staff. About four miles away her mother, aged eighty-one, lived in a modest, somewhat run-down home, existing comfortably on Social Security and her husband's railroad pension. Broome had been employed by the Sullivans, as she said, for about a year, which was what initially had drawn Frank's attention: she was by far the newest member of the house's staff. That in itself didn't mean much, but by all accounts Sullivan treated his help very well, and there was something to be said for the loyalty of long-standing, well-paid employees. Wanda Broome looked like she could be very loyal too. The question was to whom?

The twist was that Wanda Broome had spent some time in prison, more than twenty years ago, for embezzlement when she had worked as a bookkeeper for a doctor in Pittsburgh. The other servants were squeaky-clean. So she was capable of breaking the law, and she had spent time on the inside. Her name back then had been Wanda Jackson. She had divorced Jackson when she got out, or rather he had dropped her. There was no record of arrest since then. With the name change and the conviction far in the past, if the Sullivans had done a background check, they might not have turned up anything, or maybe they didn't care. From all sources Wanda Broome had been an honest, hardworking citizen these last twenty years. Frank wondered what had changed that.

"Is there anything you can remember or think of that might help me, Wanda?" Frank tried to look as innocent as possible, opening his notebook and pretending to jot down some notes. If she were the inside person, the one thing he didn't want was Wanda running back to Rogers, which would result in his going even further underground. On the other hand, if he could get her to crumble, then she just might jump sides.

He envisioned her dusting the entrance hall. It would have been so easy, so easy to apply that chemical to the cloth, then casually brush it against the security panel. It would all look so natural, no one, even staring directly at her while she did it, would have given it a thought. Just a conscientious servant doing her job. Then sneaking down when everyone was asleep, a quick sweep of the light and her part was done.

Technically, she would probably be an accomplice to murder, since homicide was a reasonably likely result when you burglarized someone's home. But Frank was far less interested in sending Wanda Broome away for a large portion of the rest of her life than he was in bagging the trigger man. The woman sitting across from him had not concocted this plan, he believed. She had played a role, a small, albeit important role. Frank wanted the master of ceremonies. He would get the Commonwealth's Attorney to cut a deal with Wanda to accomplish that goal.

"Wanda?" Frank leaned across the table and

earnestly took one of her hands. "Can you think of anything else? Anything that will help me catch the person who murdered your friend?"

Frank finally received a small shake of the head in return and he leaned back. He hadn't expected much on this go-round, but he had made his point. The wall was beginning to crumble. She wouldn't warn the guy, Frank was certain of that. He was getting to Wanda Broome, little by little.

As he would discover, he had already gone too far.

FOURTEEN

Jack threw his carry-on into the corner, tossed his overcoat on the sofa and fought the impulse to pass out right there on the carpet. Ukraine and back in five days had been a killer. The seven-hour time difference had been bad enough, but for someone closing in on octogenarian status, Walter Sullivan had been indefatigable.

They had been whisked through the security checkpoints with the alacrity and respect Sullivan's wealth and reputation commanded. From that point forward a series of endless meetings had commenced. They toured manufacturing facilities, mining operations, office buildings, hospitals and then had been taken to dinner and gotten drunk with the Mayor of Kiev. The President of Ukraine had received them on the second day, and Sullivan had him eating out of his hand within the hour. Capitalism and entrepreneurship were respected above all else in the liberated republic and Sullivan was a capitalist with a capital *C*. Everyone wanted to talk to him, shake his hand, as if some of his money-making magic would rub off on them, producing untold wealth in a very short time.

The result had been more than they could have hoped for as the Ukrainians fell in line on the business deal with glowing praise for its vision. The pitch for dollars for nukes would come later at the appropriate time. Such an asset. An unnecessary asset that could be turned into liquidity.

Sullivan's retrofitted 747 had flown nonstop from Kiev to BWI and his limo had just dropped Jack off. He made his way into the kitchen. The only thing in the fridge was soured milk. The Ukrainian food had been good but was heavy, and after the first couple of days he only picked at his meals. And there had been way too much booze. Apparently business could not be conducted without it.

He rubbed his head, tussling with sleep deprivation of massive proportion. In fact he was too tired to sleep. But he was hungry. He checked his watch. His internal clock said it was almost eight A.M. His watch proclaimed that it was well after midnight. While D.C. was not the Big Apple in its ability to cater to any appetite or interest no matter the time of day or night, there were a few places where Jack could get some decent food on a weeknight despite the lateness of the hour. As he struggled into his overcoat, the phone rang. The machine was on. Jack started to go out, then hesitated. He listened to the perfunctory message followed by the beep.

"Jack?"

A voice swarmed up on him, from out of the past, like a ball held underwater until it's free and explodes to the surface. He snatched up the phone.

"Luther?"

The restaurant was hardly more than a hole in the wall, which made it one of Jack's favorites. Any reasonable concoction of food could be gotten there at any time, day or night. It was a place that Jennifer Baldwin would never set foot inside and one that he and Kate had frequented. A short time ago, the results of that comparison would have disturbed him, but he had made up his mind, and he didn't intend on revisiting the question. Life was not perfect, and you could spend your entire life waiting

243

for that perfection. He was not going to do that.

Jack wolfed down scrambled eggs, bacon and four pieces of toast. The fresh coffee burned his throat going down. After five days of instant java and bottled water, it tasted wonderful.

Jack looked across at Luther, who sipped on his coffee and alternated between looking out the dirty plate-glass window onto the dark street and passing his eye around the small, grimy interior.

Jack put his coffee down. "You look tired."

"So do you, Jack."

"I've been out of the country."

"Me too."

That explained the condition of the yard and the mail. A needless worry. Jack pushed the plate away and waved for a refill on his coffee.

"I went by your place the other day."

"Why was that?"

Jack had expected the question. Luther Whitney had never taken anything other than the direct approach. But anticipation was one thing, having a ready answer another. Jack shrugged.

"I don't know. Just wanted to see you, I guess. It's been a while."

Luther nodded agreement.

"You seeing Kate again?"

Jack swallowed a mouthful of coffee before answering. His temples started to throb.

"No. Why?"

"I thought I saw you two together a while back."

"We sort of ran into each other. That's all."

Jack couldn't tell exactly, but Luther looked upset with that answer. He noticed Jack watching him closely, then smiled.

"Used to be, you were the only way I could find out if my little girl was doing okay. You were my pipeline of information, Jack."

244

"You ever consider just talking to her directly, Luther? You know that might be worth a shot. The years are going by."

Luther waved the suggestion off and stared out the window again.

Jack looked him over. The face was leaner than usual, the eyes puffy. There were more wrinkles on the forehead and around the eyes than Jack remembered. But it had been four years. Luther was at the age now where the onslaught of age hit you quickly, deterioration was more and more evident every day.

He caught himself staring into Luther's eyes. Those eyes had always fascinated Jack. Deep green, and large, like a woman's, they were supremely confident eyes. Like you see on pilots, an infinite calmness about life in general. Nothing rattled them. Jack had seen happiness in those eyes, when he and Kate announced their engagement, but more often he had seen sadness. And yet right beneath the surface Jack saw two things he had never seen in Luther Whitney's eyes before. He saw fear. And he saw hatred. And he wasn't sure which one bothered him the most.

"Luther, are you in trouble?"

Luther took out his wallet and, despite Jack's protests, paid for the food.

"Let's take a walk."

A taxi cab ride took them to the Mall and they walked in silence to a bench across from the Smithsonian castle. The chilly night air settled in on them and Jack pulled up the collar of his coat. Jack sat while Luther stood and lit a cigarette.

"That's new." Jack looked at the smoke curving up slowly in the clear night air.

"At my age who gives a shit?" Luther flung the match down and buried it in the dirt with his foot. He sat down.

"Jack, I want you to do me a favor."

"Okay."

"You haven't heard the favor yet." Luther suddenly stood up. "You mind walking? My joints are getting stiff."

They had passed the Washington Monument and were headed toward the Capitol when Luther broke the silence.

"I'm in kind of a jam, Jack. It's not so bad now, but I got a feeling it's going to get worse and that might happen sooner rather than later." Luther didn't look at him, he seemed to be staring ahead at the massive dome of the Capitol.

"I'm not sure how things are going to play out right now, but if it goes the way I think it's gonna go, then I'm going to need a lawyer, and I want you, Jack. I don't want no bullshitter and I don't want no baby lawyer. You're the best defense lawyer I've ever seen and I've seen a lot of them, up close and personal."

"I don't do that anymore, Luther. I push paper, do deals." It struck Jack at that moment that he was more a businessman than a lawyer. That thought was not an especially pleasing one.

Luther did not seem to hear him. "It won't be a freebie. I'll pay you. But I want someone I can trust, and you're the only one I trust, Jack." Luther stopped walking and turned to the younger man, waiting for an answer.

"Luther, you want to tell me what's going on?"

Luther shook his head vigorously. "Not unless I have to. That wouldn't do you or anybody else any good." He stared at Jack intently until it made him uncomfortable.

"I gotta tell you, Jack, if you're my lawyer on this, it's gonna get kinda hairy."

"What do you mean?"

246

"I mean people could get hurt on this one, Jack. Really hurt, like not-coming-back hurt."

Jack stopped walking. "If you've got some guys like that on your butt it might be better to cut a deal now, get immunity and disappear in a Witness Protection Program. Lots of people do. It's not an original idea."

Luther laughed out loud. Laughed until he choked and ended up doubled over, coughing up the little that was in his stomach. Jack helped him back up. He could feel the older man's limbs trembling. He did not realize they were trembling with rage. This outburst was so out of character for the man that Jack felt his flesh crawl. He realized he was perspiring despite watching his breath produce small clouds in the late-night chill.

Luther composed himself. He took a deep breath and looked almost embarrassed.

"Thanks for the advice, send me a bill. I gotta go."

"Go? Where the hell are you going? I want to know what's going on, Luther."

"If something should happen to me——"

"Goddammit, Luther, I'm growing real tired of this cloak-and-dagger shit."

Luther's eyes became slits. The confidence suddenly returned with a touch of ferocity. "Everything I do is for a reason, Jack. If I'm not telling you the whole scoop now you better believe it's for a goddamned good reason. You may not understand it now, but the way I'm doing it is to keep you as safe as I can. I wouldn't be involving you at all except I needed to know if you'd go to bat for me when and if I needed you. Because if you won't, forget this conversation ever happened, and forget you ever knew me."

"You can't be serious."

"Serious as shit, Jack."

The men stood looking at each other. The trees behind Luther's head had shed most of their leaves. Their bare branches reached to the skies, like bursts of dark lightning frozen in place.

"I'll be there, Luther." Luther's hand swiftly settled into Jack's and the next minute Luther Whitney disappeared into the shadows.

The cab dropped Jack off in front of the apartment building. The pay phone was right across the street. He paused for a moment, gathering energy and the nerve he would need for what he was about to do.

"Hello?" The voice was full of sleep.

"Kate?"

Jack counted the seconds until her mind cleared and identified the voice.

"Jesus Christ, Jack, do you know what time it is?"

"Can I come over?"

"No, you cannot come over. I thought we had settled all of this."

He paused, steeled himself. "It's not about that." He paused again. "It's about your father."

The extended silence was difficult to interpret.

"What about him?" The tone was not as cold as he would have thought.

"He's in trouble."

Now the familiar tone returned. "So? Why the hell does that still surprise you?"

"I mean he's in serious trouble. He just proceeded to scare the living shit out of me without really telling me anything."

"Jack, it's late and whatever my father is involved in—"

"Kate, he was scared, I mean really scared. So scared he threw up."

Again there was a long pause. Jack tracked her mental processes as she thought about the man they

248

both knew so well. Luther Whitney scared? That didn't make sense. His line of work necessarily demanded someone with steel nerves. Not a violent person, his entire adult life had been spent right on the edge of danger.

She was terse. "Where are you?"

"Right across the street."

Jack looked up as he saw a slender figure move to a window of the building and look out. He waved.

The door opened to Jack's knock and he saw her retreating into the kitchen where he heard a pot clattering, water being poured and the gas on the stove being lit. He looked around the room, and then stood just inside the front door feeling a little foolish.

A minute later she walked back in. She had on a thick bathrobe that ended at her ankles. She was barefoot. Jack found himself staring at her feet. She followed his gaze and then looked at him. He jolted back.

"How's the ankle? Looks fine." He smiled.

She frowned and said tersely, "It's late, Jack. What about him?"

He moved into the tiny living room and sat down. She sat across from him.

"He called me up a couple hours ago. We grabbed some food at that little dive next to Eastern Market and then started walking. He told me he needed a favor. That he was in trouble. Serious trouble with some people who could do some permanent damage to him. Real permanent."

The tea kettle started whistling. She jumped up. He watched her go, the sight of her perfectly shaped derriere outlined against the bathrobe bringing back a flood of memories he wished would just leave him the hell alone. She came back with two cups of tea.

"What was the favor?" She sipped her tea. Jack left his where it was.

"He said he needed a lawyer. He *might* need a lawyer. Although things might turn out so he wouldn't. He wanted me to be that lawyer."

She put her tea down. "Is that it?"

"Isn't that enough?"

"Maybe for an honest, respectable person, but not for him."

"My God, Kate, the man was scared. I've never seen him scared before, have you?"

"I've seen all I need to see of him. He chose his lifestyle and now apparently it's catching up to him."

"He's your father for chrissakes."

"Jack, I don't want to have this conversation." She started to get up.

"What if something happens to him? Then what?"

She looked at him coldly. "Then it happens. That's not my problem."

Jack got up and started to leave. Then he turned back, his face red with anger. "I'll tell you how the funeral service goes. On second thought, what the hell would you care? I'll just make sure you get a copy of the death certificate for your scrapbook."

He didn't know she could move that quickly, but he would feel the slap for about a week, like someone had poured acid across his cheek, a truer description than he realized at the moment.

"How dare you?" Her eyes blazed at him as he slowly rubbed his face.

Then the tears erupted from her with so much force that they spilled onto the front of the robe.

He said quietly, as calmly as he could, "Don't shoot the messenger, Kate. I told Luther and I'm telling you, life is way too short for this crap. I lost both my parents a long time ago. Okay, you have reasons for not liking the guy, fine. That's up to you. But the old man loves you and cares about you and regardless of how you think he's screwed up your life you have to

250

respect that love. That's my advice to you, take it or leave it."

He moved toward the door but she again got there before him.

"You don't know anything about it."

"Fine, I don't know anything about it. Go back to bed, I'm sure you'll fall right asleep, nothing important on your mind."

She grabbed his coat with such force that she jerked him around, even though he outweighed her by eighty pounds.

"I was two years old when he went to prison for the last time. I was nine when he got out. Do you understand the incredible shame of a little girl whose dad is in prison? Whose dad *steals* other people's property for a living? When you had show-and-tell at school and the one kid's dad is a doctor and another's is a truck driver and it comes to your turn and the teacher looks down and tells the class that Katie's dad had to go away because he did something bad and then she'd skip to the next kid?

"He was never there for us. *Never!* Mom worried sick about him all the time. But she always kept the torch, right up until the end. She made it easy for him."

"She finally divorced him, Kate," Jack gently reminded her.

"Only because that was the only choice she had left. And right when she was just getting her life turned around, she finds a lump in her breast and in six months she's gone."

Kate leaned back against the wall. She looked so tired, it was painful to witness. "And you know what the really crazy thing is? She never once stopped loving him. After all the incredible shit he put her through." Kate shook her head, having a hard time believing the words she had just spoken.

251

She looked up at Jack, her chin trembling slightly.

"But that's okay, I have enough hate for both of us." She stared at him, a mixture of pride and righteousness on her features.

Jack didn't know if it was the complete exhaustion he was feeling or the fact that for so many years what he was about to say had been pent up inside him. Years of watching this charade. And brushing it aside in favor of the beauty and vivaciousness of the woman across from him. His vision of perfection.

"Is that your idea of justice, Kate? Enough hate balanced against enough love, and everything equals out?"

She stepped back. "What are you talking about?"

He moved forward as she continued to retreat into the small room. "I've listened to this goddamned martyrdom of yours until I'm sick of it. You think you're some perfect defender of the hurt and victimized. Nothing comes above that. Not you, not me, not your father. The only reason you're out there prosecuting every sonofabitch that comes into your sights is because your father hurt you. Every time you convict somebody that's another nail in your old man's heart."

Her hand flew to his face. He caught it, gripped it. "Your whole adult life has been spent getting back at him. For all the wrongs. For all the hurt. For never being there for you." He squeezed her hand until he heard her gasp. "Did you ever once stop to think that maybe you were never there for him?"

He let go of her hand as she stood there, staring at him, a look on her face he had never seen before.

"Do you understand that Luther loves you so much that he's never tried to contact you, never tried to be a part of your life, because he knows that's how you want it? His only child living a few miles away from him and he's completely cut out of her life. Did you ever think about how he feels? Did your hate ever let you do that?"

She didn't answer.

"Don't you ever wonder why your mother loved him? Is your picture of Luther Whitney so goddamned distorted that you can't see why she loved him?"

He grabbed her shoulders, shook her. "Does your goddamned hatred ever let you be compassionate? Does it ever let you love anything, Kate!"

He pushed her away. She stumbled backward, her eyes locked on his face.

He hesitated for a moment. "The fact is, lady, you don't deserve him." He paused and then decided to finish. "You don't deserve to be loved."

In one furious instant her teeth gnashed, her face contorted into rage. She screamed and flew at him, hammering her fists into his chest, slapping his face. He felt none of her blows as the tears slid down her cheeks.

Her assault stopped as quickly as it started. Her arms like lead, they clutched at his coat, holding on. That's when the heaves started and she sank to the floor, the tears bursting from her, the sobs echoing through the tiny space.

He lifted her up and placed her gently on the couch.

He knelt beside her, letting her cry, and she did so for a long time, her body repeatedly tensing and then going limp until he felt himself growing weak, his hands clammy. He finally wrapped his arms around her, laid his chest against her side. Her thin fingers clutched tightly to his coat as both their bodies shook together for a long time.

When it was over she sat up slowly, her face red, splotchy.

Jack stepped back.

She refused to look at him. "Get out, Jack."

"Kate—"

"Get *out!*" Despite her scream the voice was fragile, battered. She covered her face in her hands.

He turned and walked out the door. As he headed down the street he turned to look at her building. Her silhouette was framed in the window, looking out, but she wasn't looking at him. She was looking for something, he wasn't sure what. Probably she didn't even know. As he continued to watch, she turned from the window. A few moments later the light in her apartment went out.

Jack wiped at his eyes, turned and walked slowly down the street, heading home after one of the longest days he could ever remember.

"*Goddammit!* How long?" Seth Frank stood next to the car. It was not quite eight in the morning.

The young Fairfax County patrolman didn't know the significance of the event and was startled by the detective's outburst.

"We found her about an hour ago; an early-morning jogger saw the car, called it in."

Frank walked around the car and peered in from the passenger side. The face was peaceful, much different from the last corpse he had viewed. The long hair was undone, streamed down the sides of the car seat and flowed across the floorboard. Wanda Broome looked like she was asleep.

Three hours later the crime scene investigation was completed. Four pills had been found on the car seat. The autopsy would confirm that Wanda Broome had died from a massive overdose of digitalis, from a prescription she had filled for her mother but obviously had never delivered. She had been dead for about two hours when her body was discovered on the secluded dirt path that ran around a five-acre pond about eight miles from the Sullivan place just over the county line. The only other piece of tangible evidence was in a plastic bag that Frank was carrying back to headquarters after getting the okay from his sister jurisdiction. The note was on a piece of paper torn from a spiral ring notepad. The handwriting was a woman's, flowing and embellished. Wanda's last words had been a desperate plea for redemption. A shriek of guilt in four words.

I am so sorry.

Frank drove on past the rapidly fading foliage and misty swamp that paralleled the winding back road. He had fucked that one up royally. He never would have figured the woman for a suicide candidate. Wanda Broome's history pegged her as a survivor. Frank couldn't help but feel sorry for the woman, but also raged at her stupidity. He could've gotten her a deal, a sweetheart deal! Then he reflected on the fact that his instincts had been right on one count. Wanda Broome *had* been a very loyal person. She had been loyal to Christine Sullivan and could not live with the guilt that she had contributed, however unintentionally, to her death. An understandable, if regrettable, reaction. But with her gone, Frank's best, and perhaps only, opportunity to land the big fish had just died too.

The memory of Wanda Broome faded into the background as he focused on how to bring to justice a man who had now caused the death of two women.

"Damn, Tarr, was it today?" Jack looked at his client in the reception area of Patton, Shaw. The man looked as out of place as a junkyard mutt at a dog show.

"Ten-thirty. It's eleven-fifteen now, does that mean I get forty-five minutes free? By the way, you look like hell."

Jack looked down at his rumpled suit and put a hand through his unkempt hair. His internal clock was still on Ukraine time, and a sleepless night had not helped his appearance.

"Believe me, I look much better than I feel."

The two men shook hands. Tarr had dressed up for the meeting, which meant his jeans didn't have holes in them, and he wore socks with his tennis shoes. The corduroy jacket was a relic from the early 1970s, and the hair was its usual tangle of curls and mats.

"Hey, we can do it another day, Jack. Me, I understand hangovers."

"Not when you got all dressed up. Come on back. All I need is some grub. I'll take you to lunch and won't even bill you for the tab."

As the men walked down the hallway, Lucinda, prim and proper in keeping with the firm's image, breathed a sigh of relief. More than one Patton, Shaw partner had walked through her turf with absolute horror on their face at the sight of Tarr Crimson. Memos would fly this week.

"I'm sorry, Tarr, I'm running on about twelve cylinders lately." Jack tossed his overcoat over a chair and settled down miserably behind a stack of pink message slips about six inches high on his desk.

"Out of the country, so I heard. Hope it was someplace fun."

"It wasn't. How's business?"

"Booming. Pretty soon, you might be able to call me a legitimate client. Make your partners' stomachs feel a lot better when they see me sitting in the lobby."

"Screw 'em, Tarr, you pay your bills."

"Better to be a big client and pay some of your bills than a teeny client who pays all of his."

Jack smiled. "You got us all figured out, don't you?"

256

"Hey, man, you seen one algorithm, you've seen 'em all."

Jack opened Tarr's file and perused it quickly.

"We'll have your new S corp set up by tomorrow. Delaware incorporation with a qualification in the District. Right?"

Tarr nodded.

"How're you planning on capitalizing it?"

Tarr pulled out a legal pad. "I've got the list of potentials. Same as the last deal. Do I get a reduced rate?" Tarr smiled. He liked Jack, but business was business.

"Yeah, this time you won't pay for the learning curve of an overpriced and underinformed associate."

Both men smiled.

"I'll cut the bill to the bone, Tarr, just like always. What's the new company for, by the way?"

"Got the inside track on some new technology for surveillance work."

Jack looked up from his notes. "Surveillance? That's a little off the mark for you, isn't it?"

"Hey, you gotta go with the flow. Corporate business is down. But when one market dries up, being the good entrepreneur that I am, I look around for other opportunities. Surveillance for the private sector has always been hot. Now the new twist is big brother in the law enforcement arena."

"That's ironic for somebody who got thrown in jail in every major city in the country during the 1960s."

"Hey, those causes were good ones. But we all grow up."

"How does it work?"

"Two ways. First, low-level orbit satellites are downlinked to metropolitan police tracking stations. The birds have preprogrammed sweep sectors. They spot trouble and they send an almost instantaneous signal to the tracking station, giving precise incident information. It's real time for the cops. The second method involves placing military–style surveillance equipment, sensors and tracking devices on top of telephone poles, or underground with surface sensors or on the outside of buildings. Their exact locations will be classified, of course, but they'll be deployed in the worst crime areas. If something starts to go down, they'll call in the cavalry."

Jack shook his head. "I can think of a few civil rights that might be trampled."

"Tell me about it. But it's effective."

"Until the bad guys move."

"Kinda hard to outrun a satellite, Jack."

Jack shook his head and turned back to his file.

"Hey, how're the wedding plans coming?"

Jack looked up. "I don't know, I try to keep out of the way."

Tarr laughed. "Shit, Julie and I had a total of twenty bucks to get married on, including the honeymoon. We got a Justice of the Peace for ten dollars, bought a case of Michelob with the rest, and rode the Harley down to Miami and slept on the beach. Had a helluva good time."

Jack smiled, shook his head. "I think the Baldwins have something a little more formal in mind. Although your way sounds like a lot more fun to me."

Tarr looked at him quizzically, remembering something. "Hey, whatever happened to that gal you were dating when you were defending the criminal elements of this fair city? Kate, right?"

Jack looked down at his desk. "We decided to go our separate ways," he said quietly.

"Huh, I always thought you two made a nice-looking couple."

Jack looked across at him, licked his lips and then

closed his eyes for a moment before answering. "Well, sometimes looks can be deceiving."

Tarr studied his face. "You sure?"

"I'm sure."

After lunch and finishing up some overdue work, Jack returned half of his phone messages and decided to leave the rest until the following day. Looking out the window, he turned his thoughts fully to Luther Whitney. What he could be involved in, Jack could only guess. The most puzzling aspect was that Luther was a loner in private life and with his work. Back when he was with the PD, Jack had checked on some of Luther's priors. He worked alone. Even on the cases where he hadn't been arrested but had been questioned, there was never an issue of more than one person involved. Then who could these other people be? A fence Luther had somehow ripped off? But Luther had been in the business much too long to do something like that. It wasn't worth it. His victim perhaps? Maybe they couldn't prove Luther had committed the crime but nevertheless held a vendetta against him. But who held that sort of grudge for getting burglarized? Jack could understand if someone had been hurt or killed, but Luther was not capable of that.

He sat down at his small conference table and thought back for a moment to the night before with Kate. It had been the most painful experience of his life, even more so than when Kate had left him. But he had said what needed to be said.

He rubbed his eyes. At this moment in his life the Whitneys weren't especially welcome. But he had promised Luther. Why had he done that? He loosened his tie. At some point he would have to draw the line, or cut the cord, if only for his own mental well-being. Now he was hoping that his promised favor would never come due.

He went down and got a soda from the kitchen, sat back down at his desk and finished up the bills for last month. The firm was invoicing Baldwin Enterprises roughly three hundred thou' a month and the work was accelerating. While Jack had been gone, Jennifer had sent over two new matters that would occupy a regiment of associates for about six months. Jack quickly calculated his profit sharing for the quarter and whistled under his breath when he got an approximate. It was almost too easy.

Things were really improving between Jennifer and him. His brain told him not to screw that up. The organ in the center of his chest wasn't so sure, but he was thinking that his brain should start taking command of his life. It wasn't that their relationship had changed. It was only that his expectation of that relationship had. Was that a compromise on his part? Probably. But who said you could manage to get through life without compromise? Kate Whitney had tried and look what it had gotten her.

He phoned Jennifer's office, but she wasn't there. Gone for the day. He checked his watch. Five-thirty. When she wasn't traveling, Jennifer Baldwin rarely left the office before eight. Jack looked at his calendar. She was in town the whole week. When he had tried her from the airport last night there had been no answer either. He hoped nothing was wrong.

As he was contemplating leaving and heading over to her house, Dan Kirksen popped his head in.

"Could I trouble you for a minute, Jack?"

Jack hesitated. The little man and his bow ties irritated Jack, and he knew exactly why. Deferential as hell, Kirksen would have treated Jack like a piece of manure had he not controlled millions in business.

On top of that, Jack knew that Kirksen desperately wanted to treat him like a piece of shit anyway, and he hoped to accomplish that goal one day.

"I was thinking about heading out. I've been hitting it pretty heavy lately."

"I know." Kirksen smiled. "The whole firm's been talking about it. Sandy better watch out — by all accounts Walter Sullivan is very enamored with you."

Jack smiled to himself. Lord was the only person whom Kirksen wanted to kick in the ass more than Jack. Lord without Sullivan would be vulnerable. Jack could read all those thoughts as they passed behind the spectacles of the firm's managing partner.

"I don't think Sandy has anything to worry about."

"Of course not. It'll just take a few minutes. Conference room number one." Kirksen disappeared as quickly as he had appeared.

What the hell was all this about? Jack wondered. He grabbed his coat and walked down the hallway. As he passed a couple of fellow associates in the hallway, they gave him sidelong glances that only increased his puzzlement.

The sliding doors to the conference room were closed, which was unusual unless something was going on inside. Jack slid back one of the thick doors. The dark room confronting him exploded into bright light, and Jack looked on in amazement as the party came into focus. The banner on the far wall said it all: CONGRATULATIONS PARTNER!

Lord presided over the lavish affair of drinks and an expensive, catered spread. Jennifer was there, along with her father and mother.

"I am so proud of you, sweetie." She had already consumed several drinks and her soft eyes and gentle caresses told Jack things would only get better later that night.

"Well, we can thank your dad for this partnership."

"Uh-uh, lover. If you weren't doing a good job, Daddy would cut you loose in a New York minute. Give yourself some credit. You think Sandy Lord and Walter Sullivan are easy to please? Honey, you pleased Walter Sullivan, stunned him even, and there's only a handful of attorneys who have ever done that."

Jack swallowed the rest of his drink and contemplated that statement. It sounded plausible. He had scored big with Sullivan, and who was to say Ransome Baldwin wouldn't have taken his business elsewhere if Jack hadn't been up to the task?

"Maybe you're right."

"Of course I'm right, Jack. If this firm were a football team, you'd be MVP or rookie of the year, maybe both." Jennifer took another drink and slid her arm around Jack's waist.

"And on top of that, you can now afford to support me in the lifestyle I've grown accustomed to." She pinched his arm.

"Grown accustomed to. Right! Try, from birth." They stole a quick kiss.

"You'd better mingle, superstar." She pushed him away and went in search of her parents.

Jack looked around. Every person in this room was a millionaire. He was easily the poorest of them all, but his prospects probably surpassed all of theirs. His base income had just quadrupled. His profit sharing for the year would easily be double that. It occurred to him that he too was now, technically, a millionaire. Who would've thought it, when four years ago a million dollars seemed to be more money than existed on the planet?

He had not entered law to become rich. He had spent years working as hard as he ever had for what amounted to pennies. But he was entitled now, wasn't he? This was the typical American Dream, wasn't it? But what was it about that dream that made you feel guilty when you finally attained it?

He felt a big arm around his shoulder. He turned to look at Sandy Lord, red eyes and all staring at him.

"Surprised the hell out of you, didn't we?"

Jack had to agree with that. Sandy's breath was a mixture of hard liquor and roast beef. It reminded Jack of their very first encounter at Fillmore's, not a pleasant memory. He subtly distanced himself from his intoxicated partner.

"Look around this room, Jack. There's not a person here, with the possible exception of yours truly, who wouldn't love to be in your shoes."

"It seems a little overwhelming. It happened so fast." Jack was talking more to himself than to Lord.

"Hell, these things always do. For the fortunate few, wham, zero to the top in seconds. Improbable success is just that: improbable. But that's what makes it so damn satisfying. By the way, let me shake your hand for taking such good care of Walter."

"Pleasure, Sandy. I like the man."

"By the way, I'm having a little get-together at my place on Saturday. Some people are going to be there you should meet. See if you can persuade your extremely attractive Significant Other to attend. She might find some marketing opportunities. Girl's a natural hustler just like her daddy."

Jack shook the hand of every partner in the place, some more than once. By nine o'clock he and Jennifer were headed home in her company limo. By one o'clock they had already made love twice. By one-thirty Jennifer was sound asleep.

Jack wasn't.

He stood by the window looking out at the few stray snowflakes that had started to fall. An early

263

winter storm system had settled in over the area although accumulations were not supposed to be significant. Jack's thoughts were not on the weather, however. He looked over at Jennifer. She was dressed in a silk nightgown, nestled between satin sheets, in a bed the size of his apartment's bedroom. He looked up at his old friends the murals. Their new place was supposed to be ready by Christmas, although the very proper Baldwin family would never allow patent cohabitation until the vows were exchanged. The interiors were being redone under the sharp eye of his fiancée to suit their individual tastes and to boldly cast their own personal statement – whatever the hell that meant. As he studied the medieval faces on the ceiling it occurred to Jack that they were probably laughing at him.

He had just made partner in the most prestigious firm in town, was the toast of some of the most influential people you could imagine, every one of them eager to advance his already meteoric career even further. He had it all. From the beautiful princess, to the rich, old father-in-law, to the hallowed if utterly ruthless mentor, to serious bucks in the bank. With an army of the powerful right behind him and a truly limitless future, Jack never felt more alone than he did that night. And despite all his willpower, his thoughts continually turned to an old, frightened and angry man, and his emotionally spent daughter. With those twin beauties swirling in his head he silently watched the gentle fall of snowflakes until the softened edges of daybreak greeted him.

The old woman watched through the dusty Venetian blinds that covered the living room window as the dark sedan pulled into her driveway. The arthritis in both grossly swollen knees made getting up difficult, much less trying to move herself around. Her back was permanently bent and the lungs were dense and unforgiving after fifty years of tar and nicotine bombardment. She was counting down to the end; her body had carried her about as far as it could. Longer than her daughter's had.

She fingered the letter that she kept in the pocket of her old, pink dressing gown that failed to completely cover the red, blistered ankles. She figured they would show up sooner or later. After Wanda had come back from the police station, she knew it was a matter of time before something like this happened. The tears welled up in her eyes as she thought back to the last few weeks.

"It was my fault, Momma." Her daughter had sat in the tiny kitchen where, as a little girl, she had helped her mother bake cookies and can tomatoes and stringbeans harvested from the strip of garden out back. She had repeated those words over and over as she slumped forward on the table, her body convulsing with every word. Edwina had tried to reason with her daughter but she was not eloquent enough to dent the shroud of guilt that surrounded the slender woman who had started life as a roly-poly baby with thick dark hair and horseshoe legs. She had shown Wanda the letter but it had done no good. It was beyond the old woman to make her child understand.

Now she was gone and the police had come. And now Edwina had to do the right thing. And at eighty-one and God-fearing, Edwina was going to lie to the police, which was to her the only thing she could do.

"I'm sorry about your daughter, Mrs. Broome." Frank's words rang sincere to the old woman's ears. A trickle of a tear slipped down the deep crevices of her aged face.

The note Wanda had left behind was given to Edwina Broome and she looked at it through a thick

265

magnifying glass that lay on the table within easy reach. She looked at the earnest face of the detective. "I can't imagine what she was thinking when she wrote this."

"You understand that a robbery took place at the Sullivan home? That Christine Sullivan was murdered by whoever it was that broke in?"

"I heard that on the television right after it happened. That was terrible. Terrible."

"Did your daughter ever talk to you about the incident?"

"Well of course she did. She was so upset by it all. She and Mrs. Sullivan got along real well, real well. It broke her up."

"Why do you think she took her own life?"

"If I could tell you, I would."

She let that ambiguous statement hang in front of Frank's face until he folded the paper back up.

"Did your daughter tell you anything about her work that might shed some light on the murder?"

"No. She liked her job pretty much. They treated her real well from what she said. Living in that big house, that's real nice."

"Mrs. Broome, I understand that Wanda was in trouble with the law a while back."

"A *long* while back, Detective. A *long* while back. And she lived a good life since then." Edwina Broome's eyes had narrowed, her lips set in a firm line, as she stared down Seth Frank.

"I'm sure she did," Frank added quickly. "Did Wanda bring anyone by to see you in the last few months. Someone you didn't know perhaps?"

Edwina shook her head. That much was the truth.

Frank eyed her for a long moment. The cataract-filled eyes stared straight back at him.

"I understand your daughter was out of the country when the incident happened?"

"Went down to that island with the Sullivans. They go every year I'm told."

"But Mrs. Sullivan didn't go."

"I suppose not, since she was murdered up here while they were down there, Detective."

Frank almost smiled. This old lady wasn't nearly as dumb as she was making out to be. "You wouldn't have any idea why Mrs. Sullivan didn't go? Something Wanda might have told you?"

Edwina shook her head, stroked a silver and white cat that jumped up on her lap.

"Well, thank you for talking to me. Again I'm sorry about your daughter."

"Thank you, I am too. Very sorry."

As she wrenched herself up to see him to the door, the letter fell out of her pocket. Her weary heart skipped a beat as Frank bent down, picked it up without glancing at it and handed it to her.

She watched him pull out of the driveway. She slowly eased herself back down in the chair by the fireplace and unfolded the letter.

It was in a man's hand she knew well: *I didn't do it. But you wouldn't believe me if I told you who did.*

For Edwina Broome that was all she needed to know. Luther Whitney had been a friend for a long time, and had only broken into that house because of Wanda. If the police caught up to him, it would not be with her assistance.

And what her friend had asked her to do she would. God help her, it was the only decent thing she could do.

Seth Frank and Bill Burton shook hands and sat down. They were in Frank's office and the sun was barely up.

"I appreciate your seeing me, Seth."

"It is a little unusual."

267

"Damn unusual if you ask me." Burton grinned. "Mind if I light one up?"

"How about I join you?" Both men pulled out their packs.

Burton bent his match forward as he settled back in his chair.

"I've been with the Service a long time and this is a first for me. But I can understand it. Old man Sullivan is one of the President's best friends. Helped get him started in politics. A real mentor. They both go way back. Just between you and me, I don't think the President actually wants us to do much more than give an impression of involvement. We are in no way looking to step on your toes."

"Not that you have jurisdiction to do that anyway."

"Exactly, Seth. Exactly. Hell, I was a state trooper for eight years. I know how police investigations go. The last thing you need is somebody else looking over your goddamned shoulder."

The wariness started to fade from Frank's eyes. An ex-state trooper turned Secret Service agent. This guy was really a career law enforcement person. In Frank's book you didn't get much better than that.

"So what's your proposal?"

"I see my role as an information pipeline to the President. Something breaks, you give me a call and I'll fill in the President. Then when he sees Walter Sullivan he can speak intelligently about the case. Believe me, it's not all smoke and mirrors. The President is genuinely concerned about the case." Burton smiled inwardly.

"And no interference from the feds? No second-guessing?"

"Hell, I'm not the FBI. It's not a federal case. Look at me as the civilian emissary of a VIP. Not much more than a professional courtesy really."

Frank looked around his office as he slowly absorbed the situation. Burton followed that gaze and tried to size up Frank as precisely as possible. Burton had known many detectives. Most had average capabilities, which, coupled with an exponentially increasing caseload, resulted in a very low arrest and much lower conviction rate. But he had checked out Seth Frank. The guy was former NYPD with a string of citations a mile long. Since his coming to Middleton County, there had not been one unsolved homicide. Not one. It was a rural county to be sure, but a one hundred percent solve rate was still pretty impressive. All those facts made Burton very comfortable. For although the President had requested that Burton keep in contact with the police in order to fulfill his pledge to Sullivan, Burton had his own reason for wanting access to the investigation.

"If something breaks really fast, I might not be able to apprise you right away."

"I'm not asking for miracles, Seth, just a little info when you get a chance. That's all." Burton stood up, crushing out his cigarette. "We got a deal?"

"I'll do my best, Bill."

"A man can't ask for more than that. So, you got any leads?"

Seth Frank shrugged. "Maybe. Might peter out, you never know. You know how that goes."

"Tell me about it." Burton started to leave and then looked back. "Hey, as some quid pro quo if you need any red tape cut during your investigation, access to databases, stuff like that, you let me know and your request gets a top priority. Here's my number."

Frank took the offered card. "I appreciate that, Bill."

Two hours later Seth Frank lifted up his phone and

nothing happened. No dial tone, no outside line. The phone company was called.

An hour later, Seth Frank again picked up his phone and the dial tone was there. The system was fixed. The phone closet was kept locked at all times, but even if someone had been able to look inside, the mass of lines and other equipment would have been indecipherable to the layperson. Not that the police force ordinarily worried about someone tapping their lines.

Bill Burton's lines of communication were open now, a lot wider than Seth Frank had ever dreamed they would be.

FIFTEEN

"I think it's a mistake, Alan. I think we should be distancing ourselves, not trying to take over the investigation." Russell stood next to the President's desk in the Oval Office.

Richmond was seated at the desk going over some recent health care legislation; a quagmire to say the least and not one he planned to expend much political capital on before the election.

"Gloria, get with the program, will you?" Richmond was preoccupied; well ahead in the polls, he thought the gap should be even greater. His anticipated opponent, Henry Jacobs, was short, and not particularly good-looking or a great speaker. His sole claim to fame was thirty years of toiling on behalf of the country's indigent and less fortunate. Consequently, he was a walking media disaster. In the age of sound bites and photo ops, being able to look and talk a big game was an absolute necessity. Jacobs was not even the best among a very weak group that had seen its two leading candidates knocked out over assorted scandals, sexually based and otherwise. All of which made Richmond wonder why his thirty-two-point lead in the polls wasn't fifty.

He finally turned to look at his Chief of Staff.

"Look, I promised Sullivan I'd keep on top of it. I said that to a goddamned national audience that got me a dozen points in the polls that apparently your well-oiled re-election team can't improve upon. Do

I need to go out and start a war to get the polls where they should be?"

"Alan, the election's in the bag; we both know that. But we have to play not to lose. We have to be careful. That person is still out there. What if he's caught?"

Exasperated, Richmond stood up. "Will you forget him! If you'd stop to think about it for a second, the fact that I have closely associated myself with the case takes away the only possible shred of credibility the guy might have had. If I hadn't publicly proclaimed my interest some nosy reporter might have pricked up his ears at an allegation that the President was somehow involved in the death of Christine Sullivan. But now that I've told the nation that I'm mad and determined to bring the perpetrator to justice, if the allegation is made, people will think the guy saw me on TV and he's a whacko."

Russell sat down in a chair. The problem was Richmond didn't have all the facts. If he knew about the letter opener would he have taken these same steps? If he knew about the note and photo Russell had received? She was withholding information from her boss, information that could ruin both of them, absolutely and completely.

As Russell walked down the hallway back to her office, she didn't notice Bill Burton staring at her from a passageway. The look was not one of affection, not anywhere close.

Stupid, stupid bitch. From where he was standing he could've popped three slugs into the back of her head. No sweat. His talk with Collin had cleared up the picture completely. If he had called the police that night, there would have been trouble, but not for him and Collin. The President and his skirted sidekick would've taken all the heat. The woman had

272

snookered him. And now he was barely hanging on the edge of all that he had worked for, sweated for, taken bullets for.

He knew far better than Russell what they were all confronted with. And it was because of that knowledge that he had made his decision. It had not been an easy one, but it was the only one he could make. It was the reason he had visited Seth Frank. And it was also the reason he had had the detective's phone line tapped. Burton knew his course of action was probably a long shot, but they were all well outside the range of guarantees of any kind now. You just had to go with the cards you had and hope Lady Luck would smile on you at some point.

Again Burton shook with anger at the position the woman had put him in. The decision her stupidity had caused him to make. It was all he could do not to run down the stairs and break her neck. But he promised himself one thing. If he lived to do nothing else, he would ensure that this woman would suffer. He would rip her from the safe confines of her power career and hurl her right into the shit of reality – and he would enjoy every minute of it.

Gloria Russell checked her hair and lipstick in the mirror. She knew she was acting like a damned love-struck teenager, but there was something so naive and yet so masculine about Tim Collin that it was actually starting to distract her attention from her work, something that had never happened before. But it was a historical fact that men in power positions usually got some action on the side. Not an ardent feminist, Russell saw nothing wrong with emulating her male counterparts. As she saw it, it was just another perk of the position.

As she slipped out of her dress and underwear and

into her most transparent nightgown, she kept reminding herself of why she was seducing the younger man. She needed him for two reasons. One, he knew about her blunder with the letter opener and she needed absolute assurance that he keep quiet about that, and, second, she needed his help to get that piece of evidence back. Compelling, rational reasons and yet tonight, like all the nights before, they were the furthest things from her mind.

At that moment she felt she could fuck Tim Collin every night for the rest of her life and never tire of the feelings that flooded through her body after each encounter. Her brain could rationalize a thousand reasons why she should stop, but the remainder of her body was, for once, not listening.

The knock on the door came a little early. She finished primping her hair, quickly checked her makeup again, and then awkwardly slipped into her heels as she hurried down the hallway. She opened the front door and it felt like someone had plunged a knife between her breasts.

"What the hell are you doing here?"

Burton put one foot inside the half-opened door and one massive hand against the door itself.

"We need to talk."

Russell unconsciously checked behind him for the man she had expected to make love to her tonight.

Burton noted the glance. "Sorry, lover-boy ain't coming, Chief."

She tried to slam the door closed, but couldn't budge the two-hundred-and-forty-pound Burton an inch. With maddening ease he pushed open the door and went inside, shutting the door behind him.

He stood in the entranceway looking at the Chief of Staff, who was now desperately trying to under-stand what he was doing there at the same time she was trying to cover up strategic parts of her anatomy.

She was not succeeding with either.

"Get out, Burton! How dare you come barging in here? You're through."

Burton moved past her into the living room, barely brushing against her as he walked by.

"Either we talk here or we talk someplace else. It's up to you."

She followed him into the living room. "What the hell are you talking about? I told you to get out. You're forgetting your place in the official hierarchy, aren't you?"

He turned to face her. "You always answer the door dressed like that?" He could understand Collin's interest. The nightgown did nothing to hide the Chief of Staff's voluptuous figure. Who would've thought? He might have been aroused despite twenty-four years with the same woman and four children spawned from that marriage, except for the fact that he was absolutely repulsed by the half-naked woman standing across from him.

"Go to hell! Go straight to hell, Burton."

"That's probably where we're all going to end up, so why don't you go get on some clothes and then we're going to talk and then I'll leave. But until then I ain't going anywhere."

"Do you realize what you're doing? I can crush you."

"Right!" He pulled out the photos from his jacket pocket and tossed them down on the table. Russell tried to ignore them, but finally picked them up. She steadied her trembling legs by placing a hand on top of a table.

"You and Collin make a beautiful couple. You really do. I don't think the media will lose sight of that fact. Might make for an interesting movie of the week. What do you think? Chief of Staff gets brains screwed out by young Secret Service agent. You could call it *The Fuck Heard 'Round the World*. That's catchy, don't you think?"

She slapped him, as hard as she had ever slapped anyone. Pain shot through her arm. It had been like hitting a piece of wood. Burton took her hand and twisted it sideways until she screamed.

"Listen, lady, I know every fucking thing that's going on here. Everything. The letter opener. Who's got it. Most importantly, how he got it. And now this recent correspondence from our little larcenous voyeur. Now any way you cut it, we got us a big problem, and seeing that you've screwed everything up from the get-go, I think a change of command is in order. Now go get out of the hooker clothes, and come back in here. If you want me to save your horny little ass, you'll do exactly what I tell you to do. Do you understand? Because if you don't then I suggest we go have a little chat with the President. It's up to you, Chief!" Burton spat out the last word, communicating unequivocally his absolute disgust with her.

Burton slowly let go of her arm but still towered over her like a mountain. His massive bulk seemed to block out her ability to think. Russell gingerly rubbed her arm and almost timidly looked up at him as the hopelessness of her situation started to sink in.

She went immediately to the bathroom and threw up. It seemed like she was spending an increasing amount of her time doing that. The cold water on her face finally started to work through the throes of nausea until she was able to sit up and then walk slowly to her bedroom.

Her head spinning, she changed into long pants and a thick sweater, dropping the negligee on the bed, too ashamed to even look at it as the garment floated down; her dreams for a night of pleasure

276

shattered with terrifying abruptness. She replaced her red stilettos with a pair of brown flats.

Patting her cheeks down as she sensed the rush of blood there, she felt like she had just been caught by her father with a boy's hands far up her dress. That event had actually occurred in her life and probably contributed to her absolute focus on her career to the detriment of everything else, so embarrassed had she been by the entire episode. Her father had called her a whore and beaten her so badly that she had missed a week of school. She had prayed her entire life that she would never feel such embarrassment again. Until tonight that prayer had been answered.

She forced herself to breathe regularly and when she went back into the living room she noted that Burton had taken his jacket off and a pot of coffee sat on the table. She eyed the thick holster with its deadly occupant.

"Cream and sugar, right?"

She managed to meet his gaze. "Yes."

He poured out the coffee and she sat down across from him.

She looked down at her cup. "How much did Ti . . . Collin tell you?"

"About the two of you? Nothing really. He's not the kind of guy who would. I think he's fallen for you pretty hard. You've fucked with his head and his heart. Nice going."

"You don't understand anything, do you?" She almost exploded out of her chair.

Burton was maddeningly calm. "I understand this much. We're about one inch from the edge of the cliff and where we're headed I can't even see the bottom. Frankly, I don't give a shit who you're sleeping with. That's not why I'm here."

Russell sat back down and forced herself to drink the coffee. Her stomach started to finally settle down.

Burton leaned across and held her arm as gently as he could. "Look, Ms. Russell. I'm not going to sit here and bullshit and tell you I'm here because I think the world of you and I want to get you out of a jam, and you don't have to pretend to love me either. But the way I look at it, like it or not, we're in this thing together. And the only way I see us making it through is to work as a team. That's the deal I'm offering." Burton sat back and watched her.

Russell put down her coffee and dabbed a napkin against her lips.

"All right."

Burton immediately leaned forward. "Just to recount, the letter opener still has both the President's and Christine Sullivan's prints on it. And their blood. Correct?"

"Yes."

"Any prosecutor would be salivating for that thing. We've got to get it back."

"We'll buy it. He wants to sell it. The next communication will tell us how much."

Burton shocked her for the second time. He tossed the envelope across.

"The guy's savvy, but at some point he has to tell us a drop point."

Russell took out the letter and read it. The writing was block print as before. The message was brief:

Coordinates coming soon. Recommend advance steps be taken for financial backing. For such prime property suggest mid seven figures. Would suggest consequences of default be considered thoroughly. Respond via Post personals if interested.

"He's got quite a writing style, doesn't he? Succinct, but he gets his point across." Burton poured another cup of coffee. Then he tossed across

278

another photograph of what Russell was desperately hoping to retrieve.

"He sure likes to tease, doesn't he, Ms. Russell?"

"At least it sounds like he's ready to deal."

"We're talking some big bucks. You prepared for that?"

"Let me worry about that piece, Burton. Money won't be the problem." Her arrogance was returning just in time.

"Probably not," he agreed. "By the way, why the hell didn't you let Collin wipe that thing clean?"

"I don't have to answer that."

"No, actually you don't, *Madam* President."

Russell and Burton actually smiled at each other. Maybe she had been wrong. Burton was a pain in her ass, but he was cunning and careful. She realized now that she needed those qualities more than Collin's gallant naîveté even if it was accompanied by a fresh, hard body.

"There's one more piece to the puzzle, Chief."

"And that is?"

"When it comes time to kill this guy, are you gonna get squeamish on me?"

Russell choked on her coffee and Burton had to literally pound her on the back until she started breathing normally again.

"I guess that answers that."

"What the hell are you talking about, Burton — killing him?"

"You still don't understand what's going on here, do you? I thought you were some brilliant professor somewhere. Ivory towers ain't what they used to be, I guess. Or maybe you need a little dose of common sense. Let me explain this real simply for you. This guy was an eyewitness to the President trying to murder Christine Sullivan, Sullivan trying to return the favor, and me and Collin doing our job and taking her out before the President gets stuck like a side of beef. An eyewitness! Remember that term. Before I found out about this little piece of evidence you left behind, I figured our asses were cooked anyway. Guy leaks the story somehow, some way and it snowballs from there. Some things we just can't explain, right?

"But nothing happens and I figure maybe we all got lucky and this guy is too afraid to come forward. Now I find out about this blackmail shit and I ask myself what does that mean."

Burton looked questioningly at Russell.

She answered, "It means he wants money in exchange for the letter opener. It's his lottery. What else could it mean, Burton?"

Burton shook his head. "No, it means this guy is fucking with us. Playing mind games. It means we got an eyewitness out there who's getting a little daring, a little adventurous. On top of that it took a real professional to crack the Sullivan nest. So this guy is not the type who's gonna scare too easily."

"So? If we get back the letter opener aren't we home free?" Russell was dimly beginning to see what Burton was getting at, but it still wasn't clear.

"If he doesn't keep photos of it, which might end up on the front page of the *Post* any day now. An enlarged photo of the President's palm print on a letter opener that came from Christine Sullivan's bedroom on page one. Probably make for an interesting series of articles. Grounds enough for the papers to start digging around. Even the slightest hint of a connection between the President and Sullivan's murder and it's over. Sure, we can argue the guy's a whacko and the picture's a clever forgery, and maybe we'll succeed. But one of those photos showing up at the *Post* doesn't concern me half as much as our other problem."

"Which is?" Russell sat forward now, her voice low, almost husky, as something terrible was beginning to dawn on her.

"You seem to have forgotten that this guy saw everything we did that night. Everything. What we were wearing. Everybody's name. How we wiped the place clean, which I'm sure the police are still scratching their heads over. He can tell them how we arrived and how we left. He can tell them to check the President's arm for traces of a knife wound. He can tell them how we dug one slug out of the wall and where we were standing when we fired. He can tell them everything they want to know. And when he does, they'll at first think he knows all about the crime scene because he was there and was actually the trigger man. But then the cops will start to realize that this was more than a one-man show. They'll wonder how he knows all this other stuff. Some of which he couldn't have made up and which they can verify. They'll begin to wonder about all those little details that just don't make sense but that this guy can explain."

Russell stood up and went over to the bar and poured herself a Scotch. She poured one for Burton too. She thought about what Burton had said. The man *had* seen everything. Including her and an unconscious President having sex. Miserable, she pushed the thought from her mind.

"Why would he come forward after he'd been paid off?"

"Who says he actually has to come forward? Remember like you said that night? He could do it from a distance. Laugh all the way to the bank and take down an administration. Hell, he can write it all down and fax it to the cops. They'll have to investigate it and who's to say they won't find something? If they got any physical evidence from

281

that bedroom, hair root, saliva, seminal fluid, all they need is a body to match it against. Before, there was no reason for them to look our way, but now, who the hell knows? You get a DNA match against Richmond, we're dead. Dead.

"And so what if the guy never comes forward voluntarily? The detective on the case is no bonehead. And my gut tells me that, given time, he's gonna find the sonofabitch. And a guy looking at life in prison or maybe the ultimate penalty will talk his head off, believe me. I've seen it happen too many times."

Russell felt a sudden chill. What Burton said made absolute sense. The President had sounded so convincing. Neither of them had even considered this line.

"Besides, I don't know about you, but I don't plan on spending the rest of my life looking over my shoulder waiting for that shoe to drop."

"But how can we find him?"

It amused Burton that the Chief of Staff had fallen in with his plans without much argument. The value of life apparently did not mean much to this woman when her personal well-being was threatened. He hadn't expected less.

"Before I knew about the letters, I thought we had no chance. But with blackmail, at some point you gotta have the payoff. And then he's vulnerable."

"But he'll just ask for a wire transfer. If what you say is true, this guy's too smart to be looking for a bag of money in a Dumpster. And we won't know where the letter opener will be until long after he's gone."

"Maybe, maybe not. You let me worry about that. What is imperative is that you string the guy along just a bit. If he wants the deal done in two days, you make it four. Whatever you put in the personals make it sincere. I'll leave that up to you, Professor.

But you've got to buy me some time." Burton got up. She grabbed his arm.

"What are you going to do?"

"The less you know about it the better. But you do understand that if the whole thing blows up, we all go down, including the President? There's nothing at this point I could or would do to prevent that. As far as I'm concerned you both deserve it."

"You don't sugarcoat things, do you?"

"Never found it useful." He put on his coat. "By the way, you realize that Richmond beat Christine Sullivan up bad, don't you? From the autopsy report it looks like he tried to turn her neck into a spaghetti loop."

"So I understand. Is that important to know?"

"You don't have any children, do you?"

Russell shook her head.

"I've got four. Two daughters, not much younger than Christine Sullivan. As a parent you think about things like that. Loved ones getting messed up by some asshole like that. Just wanted you to know the kind of guy our boss is. That is, if he ever gets frisky, you might want to think twice."

He left her sitting in the living room contemplating her wrecked life.

As he climbed into his car, he took a moment to light a cigarette. Burton had spent the last few days reviewing the preceding twenty years of his life. The price being paid to preserve those years was heading into the stratosphere. Was it worth it? Was he prepared to pay it? He could go to the cops. Tell them everything. His career would be over, of course. The police could get him on obstruction of justice, conspiracy to commit murder, maybe some bullshit manslaughter charge for popping Christine Sullivan and other assorted nickel-and-dime stuff. It would all add up, though. Even cutting a deal he was going to do some serious time. But he could do the time. He could also endure the scandal. All the shit the papers would write. He'd go down in history as a criminal. He'd be inextricably linked to the notoriously corrupt Richmond administration. And yet he could take that, if it came to it. What the hard-as-rock Bill Burton could not take was the look in his children's eyes. He would never again see pride and love. And the absolute and complete trust that their daddy, this big hulk of a man, was, indisputably, one of the good guys. That was something that was too tough even for him.

Those were the thoughts that had been racing through Burton's head ever since his talk with Collin. A part of him wished he hadn't asked. That he had never found out about the blackmail attempt. Because that had given him an opportunity. And opportunities were always accompanied by choices. Burton had finally made his. He wasn't proud of it. If things worked out according to plan, he would do his best to forget it had ever happened. If things didn't work out? Well, that was just too bad. But if he went down, so would everyone else.

That thought triggered another idea. Burton reached across and popped open the car's glove compartment. He pulled out a mini-cassette recorder and a handful of tapes. He looked back up at the house as he puffed on his cigarette.

He put the car in gear. As he passed Gloria Russell's house, he figured the lights there would remain on for a long time.

SIXTEEN

L aura Simon had just about given up hope of finding it.

The exterior and interior of the van had been minutely dusted and then fumed for prints. A special laser from the state police headquarters in Richmond had even been brought up, but every time they found a match, it was someone else's prints. Someone they could account for. She knew Pettis's prints by heart now. He was unfortunate enough to have all arches, one of the rarest of fingerprint compositions, as well as a tiny scar on his thumb that had in fact led to his arrest years earlier for grand-theft auto. Perps with scars across their fingertips were an ident tech's best friend.

Budizinski's prints had shown up once because he'd stuck his finger in a solvent and then pressed it against a piece of plywood kept in the back of the van, a print as perfect as if she had fingerprinted him herself.

All told, she had found fifty-three prints, but none were of any use to her. She sat in the middle of the van and glumly looked around its interior. She had gone over every spot where a print could reasonably be expected to exist. She had hit every nook and cranny of the vehicle with the handheld laser and was running out of ideas where else to look.

For the twentieth time she went through the motions of men loading the truck, driving it – the rearview mirror was an ideal spot for prints – moving the equipment, lifting the bottles of cleaners, dragging the hoses, opening and closing the doors. The difficulty of her task was increased by the fact that prints tended to disappear over time, depending on the surface containing them and the surrounding climate. Wet and warm were the best preservatives, dry and cool, the worst.

She opened the glove compartment and went through the contents again. Every item had already been inventoried and dusted. She idly flipped through the van's maintenance log. Purplish stains on the paper reminded her that the lab's stock of ninhydrin was low. The pages were well-worn although the van had had very few breakdowns the three years it had been in commission. Apparently the company believed in a rigorous maintenance program. Each entry was carefully noted, initialed and dated. The company had its own in-house maintenance crew.

As she scanned the pages, one entry caught her eye. All the other entries had been initialed by either a G. Henry or an H. Thomas, both mechanics employed by Metro. This entry had J.P. initialed beside it. Jerome Pettis. The entry indicated that the van had run low on oil and a couple of quarts had been added. All that was terribly unexciting except that the date was the day the Sullivan place had been cleaned.

Simon's breathing accelerated slightly as she crossed her fingers and got out of the van. She popped the hood and began looking at the engine. She shone her light around and within a minute she found it. An oily thumbprint that preened back at her from the side of the windshield washer fluid reservoir. Where someone would naturally rest their hand when they were applying leverage to open or close the oil cap. And a glance told her it wasn't Pettis's.

Nor was it either of the two mechanics. She grabbed a file card with Budizinski's prints on it. She was ninety-nine percent sure they weren't his and she turned out to be right. She carefully dusted and lifted the print, filled out a card and nearly ran the entire way to Frank's office. She found him with his hat and overcoat on, which he quickly removed.

"You're shitting me, Laura."

"You want to check with Pettis to see if he remembers Rogers adding the oil that day?"

Frank called the cleaning company, but Pettis had already gone for the night. Calls to his home went unanswered.

Simon looked at the lift card like it was the most precious jewel in the world. "Forget it. I'll run it through our files. Stay all night if I have to. We can get Fairfax to access the state police AFIS, our damn terminal's still down." Simon was referring to the Automated Fingerprint Identification System housed in Richmond, where latent prints found at crime scenes could be compared against the ones on the state's computerized database.

Frank thought for a moment. "I think I can do one better."

"How's that?"

Frank pulled a card out of his pocket, picked up the phone and dialed. He spoke into the phone. "Agent Bill Burton please."

Burton picked up Frank and they drove down together to the FBI's Hoover Building, located on Pennsylvania Avenue. Most tourists know the building as bulky and rather ugly and as a place not to miss on a visit to D.C. Housed here was the National Crime Information Center, a computerized information system operated by the FBI, consisting of fourteen centralized-distributed types of databases and two subsystems that constituted the world's largest collection of data on known criminals. The Automated Identification System (AIS) component of NCIC was a cop's best friend. With tens of millions of criminal print cards on file, Frank's chances of a hit were measurably increased.

After depositing the print with FBI technicians — who had clear instructions that this assignment was to be moved to as near the top of the pile as possible — Burton and Frank stood outside in the hallway nervously sipping coffee.

"This is gonna take a little while, Seth. The computer's gonna kick out a bunch of probables. The techs will still have to make the ident manually. I'll hang out and let you know as soon as a match comes back."

Frank checked his watch. His youngest was in a school play that started in forty minutes. Her role was only that of a vegetable, but was right now the most important thing on earth to his little girl.

"You sure?"

"Just leave me a number where I can reach you."

Frank did so and hurried out. The print could turn out to be nothing, a gas station attendant, but something told Frank that was not the case. Christine Sullivan had been dead a while now. Trails that cold usually stayed as cold as the victim resting six feet under, the longest six feet any of them would ever have to face. But a cold trail had suddenly turned blazing hot; whether it would flicker out remained to be seen. For now, Frank was going to enjoy the warmth. He smiled, and not just at the thought of his six-year-old running around dressed as a cucumber.

Burton stared after him, smiling for a very different reason. The FBI used a sensitivity and reliability factor in excess of ninety percent when processing latents through the AFIS. That meant that no more than two probables, and most likely only one, would be kicked out of the system. In addition, Burton had obtained a higher priority for the search than he had told Frank. All of which gained Burton time, precious time.

Later that night, Burton stared down at a name that was totally unfamiliar to him.

LUTHER ALBERT WHITNEY.

DOB 8/5/29. His Social Security number was also listed; the first three digits were 179, indicating it had been issued in Pennsylvania. Whitney's physical description was given as five foot eight, a buck sixty, with a two-inch scar on his left forearm. That comported with Pettis's description of Rogers.

Using NCIC's Triple I (Interstate Identification Index) database, Burton had also gotten a good snapshot of the man's past. The report listed three prior felony convictions for burglary. Whitney had records in three different states. He had done lengthy time, last coming out of prison in the mid-1970s. Nothing since then. At least nothing the authorities knew about. Burton had known men like that before. They were career guys who just kept getting better and better at their chosen profession. He was betting Whitney was one of those types.

One hitch, the last known address was in New York and was almost twenty years old.

Taking the point of least resistance, Burton walked down the hallway to a phone cubicle and grabbed up all the phone books for the area. He tried D.C. first; surprisingly it was a blank. Northern Virginia was next. There were three Luther Whitneys listed. His next phone call went to the Virginia State Police, where he had a longtime contact. Division of Motor Vehicles records were accessed by computer. Two of the Luther Whitneys were twenty-three and eighty-five years old respectively. However, Luther

Whitney of 1645 East Washington Avenue, Arlington, had been born on August 5, 1929, and his Social Security number, used in Virginia as the driver's license number, confirmed that he was the man. But was he Rogers? There was one way to find out.

Burton pulled out his notebook. Frank had been very courteous in letting Burton go through the investigation file. The phone rang three times and then Jerome Pettis answered. Vaguely identifying himself as being with Frank's office, Burton asked the question. Five long seconds followed while Burton tried to keep his nerves intact as he listened to the shallow breathing of the man on the other end of the line. The response was worth the short wait.

"Damn, that's right. Engine almost locked up. Somebody had left the oil cap loose. Got Rogers to do it cuz he was sitting on the case of oil we carry in the back."

Burton thanked him and hung up. He checked his watch. He still had time before he would have to leave Frank the message. Despite the mounting evidence, Burton still couldn't be absolutely certain Whitney had been the guy in the vault, but Burton's gut told him Whitney was the man. And although there was no way in hell Luther Whitney would have gone anywhere near his house after the murder, Burton wanted to get a better feel for the guy and maybe get some indication of where he'd gone. And the best way to do that was to check out where he lived. Before the cops did. He walked as quickly as he could to his car.

The weather had turned wet and cold again as Mother Nature toyed with the most powerful city on earth. The wipers flapped relentlessly across the windshield. Kate didn't exactly know why she was there. She had visited the place exactly once in all these years. And on that occasion she had sat out in the car while Jack had gone in to see him. To tell him that he and Luther's only child were getting married. Jack had insisted, despite her maintaining that the man wouldn't care. Apparently he had. He had come out on the front porch and looked at her, smiling, an awkward thrust to his body that proclaimed his hesitation in approaching her. Wanting to congratulate but not knowing exactly how, given their peculiar circumstances. He had shaken Jack's hand, pounded him on the back, then looked over at her as if for approval.

She had resolutely looked away, arms folded, until Jack had climbed back in and they had driven off. She had caught the reflection of the small figure in the side mirror as they pulled away. He looked much smaller than she remembered, almost tiny. In her mind her father would forever represent an enormous monolith of all that she resented and feared in the world, that filled all space around it and dragged one's breath away with its sheer, overpowering bulk. That creature obviously never existed, but she refused to admit that fact. But while she had not wanted to deal with that image ever again, she could not look away. For more than a minute as the car gathered speed her eyes dipped into the reflection of the man who had given her life and then taken it and her mother's away with brutal finality.

As the car pulled away he had continued to look at her, a mixture of sadness and resignation on his features that had surprised her. But she had rationalized it away, as another of his tricks to make her feel guilty. She could not attribute benign qualities to any of his actions. He was a thief. He had no regard for the law. A barbarian in a civilized society. There was no possible room in his shell for sincerity. Then they had turned the corner and his image had disappeared, like it had been on a string and was suddenly pulled away.

Kate pulled into the driveway. The house was pitch dark. As she sat there her headlights reflected off the rear of the car parked in front of her and the glare hurt her eyes. She switched off the lights, took a deep breath to steady her nerves and climbed out into the cold and wetness.

The previous snowfall had been light, and what little residue there was crunched under her feet as she made her way up to the front door. The temperature promised icy conditions developing overnight. She placed one hand against the side of his car to balance herself as she walked. Despite not expecting to find her father home, she had washed and styled her hair, was encased in one of her suits normally reserved for court and had actually applied more than a dab of makeup. She was successful, in her own way, and if chance brought them face-to-face, she wanted him to realize that despite his maltreatment she had not only survived, she had flourished.

The key was still where Jack had told her it was so many years ago. It had always seemed ironic to her that a consummate burglar should leave his own property so accessible. As she unlocked the door and slowly went inside, she did not notice the car that had pulled to a stop on the other side of the street or the driver who watched her intently, and who was already writing down her license plate number.

The house had the built-up musty odor of a long-abandoned place. She had occasionally imagined what the place would look like on the inside. She had figured it to be neat and orderly and she was not disappointed.

In the darkness she sat down in a chair in the living room, not realizing it was her father's favorite and totally unaware that Luther had unconsciously done the same thing when he had visited her apartment.

The photo was on the mantel. It must've been almost thirty years old. Kate, held in her mother's arms, was swaddled from head to toe, a few wisps of tar-colored hair visible from under the pink bonnet; she had been born with a remarkably thick head of hair. Her father, calm-faced and wearing a snap-brim, was standing next to mother and daughter, his muscular hand touching Kate's tiny outstretched fingers.

Kate's mother had kept that same photo on her dressing table until her death. Kate had thrown it away the day of the funeral, cursing the intimacy between father and daughter that the image displayed. She had hurled it away right after her father had come by the house where she had exploded at him with a fury, an outburst that became more and more out of control since its target did not respond, did not fight back, but stood there and accepted the barrage. And the quieter he had become, the more angry she became until she had slapped him, with both hands, until others had pulled her away and held her down. And only then did her father put his hat back on, lay the flowers he had brought down on the table and, with an inflamed face from her pounding and water-filled eyes, he had walked out the door, closing it quietly behind him.

And it occurred to Kate as she sat in her father's chair that he too had been grieving that day. Grieving for a woman he had presumably loved for a good portion of his life and who certainly had loved him. She felt a catch in her throat and rushed to forestall it with pressure from her fingers.

She got up and moved through the house, peering cautiously into each room and then backing away, growing more and more nervous as she penetrated further and further into her father's domain. The bedroom door was ajar, and she finally decided to push it open all the way. As she moved into the room, she risked turning on a light, and as her eyes adjusted to the exit from darkness they fell upon the nightstand and she drew nearer, finally sitting down on the bed.

The collection of photographs was, in essence, a small shrine to her. From the earliest age upward, her life was retold here. Each night as her father went to sleep, the last thing he saw was her. But what shocked her the most were the photos from later in life. Her graduation from college and law school. Her father had certainly not been invited to these events, but they were recorded here. None of the photos were posed. She was either walking or waving to someone or just standing there obviously unaware of the camera's presence. She moved on to the last photo. She was walking down the steps of the Alexandria Courthouse. Her first day in court, nervous as hell. A petty-misdemeanor case, General District Court Mickey Mouse stuff, but the big smile on her face proclaimed nothing less than absolute victory.

And she wondered how in the world she had never seen him. And then she wondered if she had but just would not admit it.

Her immediate reaction was anger. Her father had been spying on her all these years. All those special moments of her life. He had violated them. Violated her with his uninvited presence.

Her second reaction was more subtle. And as she felt it rising through her she abruptly jumped up from the bed and turned to flee the room.

That's when she thudded right into the big man standing there.

★

294

"Again, I'm sorry, ma'am, I didn't mean to startle you."

"Startle me? You scared the living hell out of me." Kate sat on the side of the bed, trying to regain her nerves, to stop shaking, but the chill in the house didn't help.

"Excuse me, but why is the Secret Service interested in my father?"

She looked at Bill Burton with something akin to fear in her eyes. At least he read it as fear. He had watched her in the bedroom, swiftly gauging her motives, her intent from her subtle body movements. A skill he had spent years developing, scanning endless crowds for the one or two true dangers that might be lurking there. His conclusions: estranged daughter and father. She had finally come looking for him. Things started to add up, and maybe in a very positive way for his purposes.

"We're not really, Ms. Whitney. But the police in Middleton County sure as hell are."

"Middleton?"

"Yes, ma'am. I'm sure you've read about the Christine Sullivan homicide." He let that statement hang out there to test her reaction. He got the expected one. Complete disbelief.

"You think my father had something to do with that?" It was a legitimately asked question. And not one framed particularly defensively. Burton deemed that significant and another positive for his plan, which had been forming the minute he'd laid eyes on her.

"The detective in charge of the case does. Apparently your father, as part of a carpet cleaning crew, and using a false name, was in the Sullivans' house a short time before the murder."

Kate caught her breath. Her father cleaning carpets? Of course, he had been casing the place.

Figuring its weaknesses, just like before. Nothing had changed. But murder?

"I can't believe he killed that woman."

"Right, but you can believe he was trying to burgle that house can't you, Ms. Whitney? I mean this isn't the first time, is it, or the second?"

Kate looked down at her hands. Finally she shook her head.

"People change, ma'am. I don't know how close you've been to your father lately" – Burton noted the small but discernible jerk in her expression – "but the evidence is pretty strong that he was involved somehow. And the woman is dead. You've probably gotten a conviction on less evidence that that."

Kate looked at him suspiciously. "How do you know about me?"

"I see a woman sneaking into the house of a man the police are looking for, I do what any law enforcement officer would do: I ran your license plate. Your reputation precedes you, Ms. Whitney. The state police think the world of you."

She looked around the room. "He's not here. It doesn't look like he's been here for a while."

"Yes, ma'am, I know. You wouldn't happen to know where he is, would you? He hasn't tried to contact you or anything?"

Kate thought of Jack and his late-night visitor. "No." The answer was quick, a little too quick for Burton's taste.

"It'll be better if he turns himself in, Ms. Whitney. You get some trigger-happy beat cop out there . . ." Burton expressively raised his eyebrows.

"I don't know where he is, Mr. Burton. My father and I . . . we haven't been close . . . for a long time."

"But you're here now and you knew where he kept the spare key."

Her voice rose an octave. "This is the first time I've stepped foot in this house."

Burton scrutinized her expression and decided she was telling the truth. Her unfamiliarity with the house had already led him pretty much to that conclusion, and also that she and her father were estranged.

"Is there any way you can get in touch with him?"

"Why? I really don't want to get involved in this, Mr. Burton."

"Well, I'm afraid you already are, to a degree. It'd be better if you'd cooperate."

Kate slung her purse over her arm and stood up.

"Listen, Agent Burton, you can't bluff me, I've been in the business too long. If the police want to waste their time questioning me, I'm in the phone book. The government phone book under Commonwealth's Attorney. See you around."

She headed for the door.

"Ms. Whitney?"

She whirled round, ready for some verbal sparring. Secret Service or not, she wasn't going to take any crap from this guy.

"If your father committed a crime, then he should be tried by a jury of his peers and convicted. If he's innocent, he goes free. That's how the system's supposed to work. You know that better than I do."

Kate was about to respond when her eye caught the photos. Her first day in court. It seemed a century ago and was, in a lot more ways than she could ever admit to herself. That smile, the pie-in-the-sky dreams everybody starts with, nothing less than perfection the only goal. She had dropped back to earth a long time ago.

Whatever barbed remark she was going to come back with had just escaped her, lost in the smile of a pretty young woman with a lot she wanted to do with her life.

Bill Burton watched her turn and leave. He looked over at the photos and then back at the empty doorway.

SEVENTEEN

"Shouldn't have fucking done that, Bill. You said you were not going to interfere in the investigation. Hell, I ought to throw your keester right in jail. That'd go over real well with your boss." Seth Frank slammed his desk drawer and stood up, eyes blazing at the big man.

Bill Burton stopped pacing and sat down. He had expected to take some lumps over this one.

"You're right, Seth. But Jesus I was a cop for a long time. You were unavailable, I go over there just to reconnoiter the place, I see some skirt slipping in. What would you have done?"

Frank didn't answer.

"Look, Seth, you can kick me in the ass, but I'm telling you, friend, this woman is our ace up the sleeve. With her we can nail this guy."

Frank's tensed face relaxed, his anger subsiding.

"What are you talking about?"

"The girl is his daughter. His friggin' daughter. In fact his only child. Luther Whitney is a three-time loser, a career crim who's apparently gotten better with age. His wife finally divorced him, right? Couldn't take it anymore. Then when she starts to get her life in order, she dies from breast cancer."

He paused.

Seth Frank was all attention now. "Go on."

"Kate Whitney is devastated by her mother's death. Her father's betrayal as she sees it. So devastated that she totally breaks off from him. Not

299

only that, she goes to law school and then goes to work as an Assistant Commonwealth's Attorney where she has the reputation of being one hard-assed prosecutor, especially for property-related crimes – burglary, theft, robbery. She goes for the max on all those guys. And usually gets it, I might add."

"Where the hell did you get all that info?"

"A few well-placed phone calls. People like to talk about other people's misery; it makes them feel their own life is somehow better when it usually isn't."

"So where does all this family turmoil get us?"

"Seth, look at the possibilities here. This girl hates her old man. Hates with a capital H underscored."

"So you want to use her to get to him. If they're estranged that badly, how do we do it?"

"That's the twist. By all accounts, all the hate and misery is on her side. Not his. He loves her. Loves her more than anything else. He's got a goddamned shrine to her in his bedroom. I'm telling you the guy is ripe for this."

"If, and it's still a big if in my mind, if she's willing to cooperate, how does she get in touch with him? He sure as hell isn't going to be hanging around his phone at home."

"No, but I bet he checks in for messages. You should see his house. This guy is very orderly, everything in its place, bills probably paid ahead of time. And he's got no idea we're on his ass. Not yet anyway. He probably checks his machine once or twice a day. Just in case."

"So she leaves him a message, arranges a meeting and we nail him?"

Burton stood back up, flushed two cigarettes from his pack and flipped one over to Frank. They both took a moment to light up.

"Personally, that's how I see it going down, Seth. Unless you got a better idea."

300

"We still have to convince her to do it. From what you said, she didn't seem too willing."

"I think you need to talk to her. Without me there. Maybe I came down a little too hard on her. I have a tendency to do that."

"I'll hit it first thing in the morning."

Frank put on his hat and coat and then paused.

"Look, I didn't mean to jump all over your butt, Bill."

Burton grinned. "Sure you did. I would've done the same thing if I were you."

"I appreciate the assistance."

"Anytime."

Seth started to walk out.

"Hey, Seth, little favor to an old-fart ex-cop."

"What's that?"

"Let me in on the kill. I wouldn't mind seeing his face when the hammer comes down."

"You got it. I'll call you after I talk to her. This cop's going home to his family. You should do the same, Bill."

"After I finish this smoke I'm outta here."

Frank left. Burton sat down, slowly finished his cigarette, then drowned it out in a half cup of coffee.

He could've withheld Whitney's name from Seth Frank. Told him there had been no match by the FBI. But that was too dangerous a game to play. If Frank ever found out, and the detective could through a myriad of independent channels, Burton would be stone-cold dead. Nothing could explain that deception other than the truth, which wasn't an option. Besides, Burton needed Frank to know Whitney's identity. The Secret Service agent's plan all along was to have the detective hunt the ex-con down. Find him, yes; arrest him, no.

Burton stood up, put on his coat. Luther Whitney. Wrong place, wrong time, wrong people.

Well, if it were any solace he wouldn't see it coming. He'd never even hear the shot. He'd be dead before the synapses could fire the impulse to his brain. Those were the breaks. Sometimes they went for you and sometimes against you. Now if he could only think of a way to leave the President and his Chief of Staff high and dry, he would've done a good day's work.

But that one, he was afraid, was beyond even him.

Collin parked his car down the street. The few remaining multicolored leaves gently cascaded down on him, nudged along by the breeze that lazily made its way past. He was dressed casually: jeans, cotton pullover and leather jacket. There was no bulge under his jacket. His hair was still damp from a hasty shower. His bare ankles protruded from his loafers. He looked like he should be heading to the college library for a late-night study session or hitting the party circuit after playing in the Saturday afternoon football game. As he made his way up to the house, he started getting nervous. It had surprised him, her phone call. She had sounded normal, there was no strain, no anger in her voice. Burton said she had taken it pretty well, considering. But he knew how abrasive Burton could be and that was why he was worried. Letting him keep Collin's appointment with the lady probably was not the smartest thing Collin had ever done. But the stakes were high. Burton had made him see that.

The door opened to his knock and he walked in. As he turned, the door closed and she was standing there. Smiling. Dressed in a sheer white negligee that was too short and too tight everywhere that counted, she stood tiptoe in her bare feet to kiss him gently on the lips. Then she took his hand and led him into the bedroom.

She motioned for him to lie down on the bed. Standing in front of him she undid the straps holding up the flimsy garment and let it drop to the floor. Next her underwear slid down her legs. He started to rise up, but she gently pushed him back down.

She slowly climbed on top of him, running her fingers through his hair. She slid a hand down to his erection and nicked at it through his jeans with the tip of her fingernail. He almost screamed as the confines of his pants became too painful. Again he tried to touch her but she held him down. She slid his belt off and then undid his pants. They dropped to the floor. Next she freed his explosion of flesh. It sprung up at her and she cradled it between her legs, squeezing it tightly between her thighs.

She dipped her mouth down to his and then nestled her lips against his ear.

"Tim, you want me, don't you? You want to fuck me so bad, don't you?"

He groaned and clutched at her buttocks, but she quickly moved his hands away.

"Don't you?"

"Yes."

"I wanted you so bad too, the other night. And then he showed up."

"I know, I'm sorry about that. We talked and—"

"I know, he told me. That you didn't say anything about us. That you were a gentleman."

"That part was none of his business."

"That's right, Tim. It was none of his business. And now you want to fuck me, don't you?"

"Jesus Christ yes, Gloria. Of course I do."

"So bad it hurts."

"It's killing me. It's goddamn killing me."

"You feel so good, Tim, God, you feel so good."

"Just wait, baby, just wait. You don't know what good is."

"I know, Tim. All I seem to think about is making love to you. You know that, don't you?"

"Yes." Collin was in so much pain now his eyes watered.

She licked at the drops, amused.

"And you're sure you want me? You're absolutely sure?"

"Yes!"

Collin felt it before his mind actually registered the fact. Like a blast of cold air.

"Get out." The words were spoken slowly, deliberately, as though practiced a number of times, to get just the right tone, the correct inflection; the speaker savoring each syllable. She climbed off him, taking care to apply enough force to his erection that he gasped for breath.

"Gloria—"

His jeans hit him in the face as he lay there. When he pulled them away and sat up, her body was covered in a thick, full-length robe.

"Get out of my house, Collin. Now."

He dressed quickly, embarrassed, as she stood there watching him. She followed him to the front door and as it opened and he stepped across the portal, she abruptly pushed him through and then slammed it behind him.

He looked back for a moment, wondering if she were laughing or crying behind the door or maybe displaying any emotion at all. He hadn't meant to hurt her. He had clearly embarrassed her. He shouldn't have done it that way. She had certainly paid him back for that embarrassment, bringing him to the threshold like that, manipulating him like some laboratory experiment and then bringing the curtain crashing down on top of him.

But as he walked to his car the memory of that look on her face made him relieved their brief relationship had ended.

For the first time since joining the Commonwealth's Attorney's office, Kate called in sick. Bedcovers pulled up to her chin, she sat propped up on pillows staring out at a bleak morning. Every time she had tried to get out of bed, the image of Bill Burton loomed up in front of her like a mass of sharp-edged granite, threatening to crush or impale her.

She slid down lower in the bed, sinking into the soft mattress like immersing herself in warm water, just below the surface where she could neither hear nor see anything that transpired around her.

They would be coming soon. Just like with her mother. All those years ago. People pushing their way in and firing off questions Kate's mother couldn't possibly answer. Looking for Luther.

She thought of Jack's outburst from the other night and tightly closed her eyes, trying to hurl those words away.

Goddamn him.

She was tired, more tired than any trial had ever made her. And he had done it to her, just like he had to her mother. Drawn her into the web even though she wanted no part of it, detested it, would destroy it if she could.

She sat up again, unable to breathe. She held her throat with her fingers, tightly, trying to prevent another attack. When it subsided, she turned over on her side and stared at the photo of her mother.

He was all she had left. She almost laughed. Luther Whitney was all the family she had left. God help her.

She lay on her back and waited. Waited for the knock at the door. From mother to daughter. It was her turn now.

At that moment, barely ten minutes away, Luther stared again at the old newspaper article. A cup of coffee sat near his elbow, forgotten. The small refrigerator hummed in the background. In the corner CNN droned on. Otherwise the room was absolutely quiet.

Wanda Broome had been a friend. A good friend. Ever since their accidental meeting in a Philadelphia halfway house after Luther's last prison term and Wanda's first and only. And now she was dead too. Had taken her own life, the newspaper article said, slumped over in the front seat of her car with a bunch of pills stuffed down her throat.

Luther had never operated in the mainstream, and yet, even to him, this was all a little much to take. It could have been some continuing nightmare except that every time he awoke and stared in the mirror, cold water dripping from features that grew more and more grizzled, more and more sunken with each passing day, he knew he was not going to wake up from this one.

What was ironic, in the shadow of Wanda's tragic death, was that the Sullivan job had been *her* idea. A miserable, terrible idea looking back, but one that had leapt from her surprisingly fertile mind. And an idea to which she had held doggedly, despite warnings from both Luther and her mother.

And they had planned it and he had done it. It was really that simple. And in the cold face of retro-spection he had wanted to do it. It was a challenge, and a challenge combined with a huge payoff was too tough to resist.

How Wanda must have felt when Christine Sullivan hadn't gotten on that plane. And no way for her to let Luther know that the coast was not nearly so clear as they thought it would be.

She had been Christine Sullivan's friend. That part had been absolutely sincere. A last reminder of real people in the midst of the sybaritic life Walter Sullivan lived. Where everyone was not only beautiful, like Christine Sullivan was, but educated, well-connected and sophisticated, all things Christine Sullivan was not and never would be. And because of that burgeoning friendship Christine Sullivan had begun to tell Wanda things she shouldn't have, including, finally, the location and contents of the vault constructed behind a mirrored door.

Wanda was convinced that the Sullivans had so much, they couldn't possibly miss so little. The world did not work that way, Luther knew, and Wanda probably did too, but that didn't matter now.

After a lifetime of hardship, where money was always too scarce, Wanda had gone for her lottery win. Just like Christine Sullivan had, neither of them realizing just how high the price for such things really was.

Luther had flown to Barbados, would have gotten a message to Wanda there if she hadn't already left. He had sent the letter to her mother. Edwina would have shown it to her. But had she believed him? Even if she had, Christine Sullivan's life had still been sacrificed. Sacrificed, as Wanda would have seen it, to Wanda's greed and desire to have things she had no right to. Luther could almost see those thoughts running through his friend's mind as she drove out, alone, to that deserted spot; as she unscrewed the cap to get at those pills, as she drifted into permanent unconsciousness.

And he had not even been able to attend the funeral. He could not tell Edwina Broome how sorry he was, without risking getting her pulled into this nightmare. He had been as close to Edwina as he had to Wanda, in some ways even closer. He and Edwina

307

had spent many nights trying to dissuade Wanda from her plan, to no avail. And only when it dawned on them that she would do it with or without Luther did Edwina ask Luther to take care of her daughter. Not let her go to prison again.

His eyes finally turned to the personals in the newspaper and it took him only a few seconds to find the one he was looking for. He did not smile when he read it. Like Bill Burton, Luther did not believe Gloria Russell had any redeeming qualities.

He hoped they believed this was only about money. He pulled out a piece of paper and began to write.

"Trace the account." Burton sat across from the Chief of Staff in her office. He sipped on a Diet Coke but wished for something stronger.

"I'm already doing that, Burton." Russell put her earring back on as she replaced the phone in its cradle.

Collin sat quietly in a corner. The Chief of Staff had not yet acknowledged his presence although he had walked in with Burton twenty minutes ago.

"When does he want the money again?" Burton looked at her.

"If a wire transfer does not reach the designated account by close of business, there will be no tomorrow for any of us." She swept her eyes across to Collin and then returned them to Burton.

"Shit." Burton stood up.

Russell glowered at him. "I thought you were taking care of this, Burton."

He ignored the stare. "How does he say he's going to work the drop?"

"As soon as the money is received he'll provide the location where the item will be."

"So we gotta trust him?"

"So it would seem."

"How does he know you've even gotten the letter yet?" Burton started to pace.

"It was in my mailbox this morning. My mail is delivered in the afternoon."

Burton collapsed in a chair. "Your fucking mailbox! You mean he was right outside your house?"

"I doubt if he would have allowed someone else to deliver this particular message."

"How'd you know to check the mailbox?"

"The flag was up." Russell almost smiled.

"This guy has got balls, I'll give him that, Chief."

"Apparently bigger ones than either of you." She concluded the statement by staring at Collin for a full minute. He cringed under the gaze, finally looking down at the floor.

Burton smiled to himself at the exchange. That was okay, the kid would thank him in a few weeks. For pulling him out of this black widow's web.

"Nothing really surprises me, Chief. Not anymore. How about you?" He looked at her and then at Collin.

Russell ignored the remark. "If the money is not transferred out, then we can expect him to go public somehow soon thereafter. What exactly are we going to do about it?"

The Chief of Staff's calm demeanor was no sham. She had decided that she was through crying, through vomiting every time she turned around, and that she had been hurt and embarrassed enough to last the rest of her life. Come what may, she felt almost numb to anything else. It felt surprisingly good.

"How much does he want?" Burton asked.

"Five million," she replied simply.

Burton went wide-eyed. "And you got that kind of money? Where?"

"That doesn't concern you."

"Does the President know?" Burton asked the question knowing full well the answer.

"Again, that doesn't concern you."

Burton didn't push it. What did he care anyway?

"Fair enough. Well, in answer to your question, we are doing something about it. If I were you I'd find a way to pull that money back somehow. Five million dollars isn't going to do much to someone not among the living."

"You can't kill what you can't find," Russell shot back.

"That's true, that's so true, Chief." Burton sat back and recounted his conversation with Seth Frank.

Kate was fully dressed when she answered the door, thinking, somehow, that if she were in her bathrobe the interview would endure longer, that she would appear more and more vulnerable as each question came her way. The last thing she wanted to appear was vulnerable, which was exactly how she felt.

"I'm not sure what you want from me."

"Some information, that's all, Ms. Whitney. I realize you're an officer of the court, and believe me, I hate to put you through this, but right now your father is my number-one suspect in a very high-profile case." Frank looked at her with a pair of earnest eyes.

They were sitting in the tiny living room. Frank had his notebook out. Kate sat erect on the edge of the couch trying to remain calm, although her fingers kept fluttering to her small chain necklace, twisting and turning it into small knots, tiny centers of bedlam.

"From what you've told me, Lieutenant, you don't have much. If I were the ACA on that case I don't think I'd even have enough to get an arrest warrant issued, much less a bill of indictment returned."

"Maybe, maybe not." Frank eyed the way she played with the chain. He wasn't really there to gather information. He probably knew more about her father than she did. But he had to ease her into the trap. Because, as he thought about it, that's what it was, a trap. For someone else. Besides, what did she care? It made his conscience feel better anyway, to think that she didn't really care at all.

Frank continued, "But I'll tell you some interesting coincidences. We have your father's print on a cleaning van that we *know* was at the Sullivan place a short time before the murder. The fact that we know he was in the house, and in the very bedroom where the crime was committed, a short time before. We have two eyewitnesses to that. And the fact that he used an alias and a false address and Social Security number when applying for the job. And the fact that he seems to have disappeared."

She looked at him. "He had priors. He probably didn't use his real info because he didn't think he'd get the job otherwise. You say he's disappeared. Did you ever think he just may have taken a trip? Even ex-cons go on vacation." Her instincts as a trial lawyer found her defending her father, an unbelievable thought. A sharp pain shot through her head. She rubbed at it distractedly.

"Another interesting discovery is that your father was good friends with Wanda Broome, Christine Sullivan's personal maid and confidante. I checked. Your father and Wanda Broome had the same parole officer back in Philly. According to certain sources, they've apparently kept in touch all these years. My bet is Wanda knew about the safe in the bedroom."

"So?"

"So I talked with Wanda Broome. It was obvious she knew more about the matter than she was letting on."

311

"So why aren't you talking to her instead of sitting here with me? Maybe she committed the crime herself."

"She was out of the country at the time, a hundred witnesses to that effect." Frank took a moment to clear his throat. "And I can't talk to her anymore because she committed suicide. Left behind a note that said she was sorry."

Kate stood up and looked blankly out the window. Bands of cold seemed to close around her.

Frank waited for some minutes, staring at her, wondering how she must feel, listening to the growing evidence against the man who had helped create her and then apparently abandoned her. Was there love left there? The detective hoped not. At least his professional side did. As a father of three, he wondered if that feeling could ever really be killed, despite the worst.

"Ms. Whitney, are you all right?"

Kate slowly turned away from the window. "Can we go out somewhere? I haven't eaten for a while and there's no food here."

They ended up at the same place Jack and Luther had met. Frank started to devour his food, but Kate touched nothing.

He looked across at her plate. "You picked the place, I figured you must like the food. You know, nothing personal, but you could stand to put on some weight."

Kate finally looked at him, a half-smile breaking through. "So you're a health consultant on the side?"

"I've got three daughters. My oldest is sixteen going on forty and she swears she's obese. I mean she probably goes one-ten and she's almost as tall as me. If she didn't have such rosy cheeks, I'd think she was anorexic. And my wife, Jesus, she's always on some

312

diet or another. I mean, I think she looks great, but there must be some perfect shape out there that every woman strives for."

"Every woman except me."

"Eat your food. That's what I tell my daughters every day. *Eat.*"

Kate picked up her fork and managed to consume half her meal. As she sipped her tea and Frank fingered a big trough of coffee, they both settled themselves in as the discussion wound its way back to Luther Whitney.

"If you think you have enough to pick him up, why don't you?"

Frank shook his head, put down his coffee. "You were at his house. He's been gone for a while. Probably blew out right after it happened."

"If he did it. Your party bag is all circumstantial. That doesn't come close to being beyond a reasonable doubt, Lieutenant."

"Can I play straight with you, Kate? Can I call you Kate, by the way?"

She nodded.

Frank put his elbows on the table, stared across at her. "All bullshit outside, why do you find it so hard to believe that your old man popped this woman? He's been convicted of three prior felonies. The guy's apparently lived on the edge his whole life. He's been questioned in about a dozen other burglaries, but they couldn't pin anything on him. He's a career crim. You know the animal. Human life doesn't mean shit to them."

Kate finished sipping her tea before answering. A career criminal? Of course her father was that. She had no doubt he had continued to commit crimes all these years. It was in his damn blood apparently. Like a coke addict. Incurable.

"He doesn't kill people," she said quietly. "He may

313

steal from them, but he's never hurt anyone. It's not the way he does things."

What had Jack said specifically? Her father was scared. Terrified so badly he was sick to his stomach. The police had never scared her father. But if he *had* killed the woman? Perhaps just a reflex, the gun fired and the bullet ended Christine Sullivan's life. All that would have transpired in a matter of seconds. No time to think. Just to act. To prevent him from going to prison for good. It was all possible. If her father had killed the woman, he would be scared, he would be terrified, he *would* be sick.

Through all the pain, the most vivid memories she held of her father was his gentleness. His big hands encircling hers. He was quiet to the point of rudeness with most people. But with her he talked. To her, not above her, or below her as most adults managed to do. He would speak to her about things a little girl was interested in. Flowers and birds and the way the sky changed color all of a sudden. And about dresses and hair ribbons and wobbly teeth that she constantly fiddled with. They were brief but sincere moments, between a father and daughter, smashed between the sudden violence of convictions, of prison. But as she had grown up those talks somehow became gibberish, as the occupation of the man behind the funny faces and the big but gentle fingers came to dominate her life, her perspective of Luther Whitney.

How could she say that this man could not kill?

Frank watched the eyes as they blinked rapidly. There was a crack there. He could feel it.

Frank fingered his spoon as he scooped more sugar into his coffee. "So you're saying it's inconceivable that your father killed this woman? I thought you said the two of you hadn't really kept in touch?"

Kate jolted back from her musings. "I'm not saying it's inconceivable. I'm just saying . . ." She was really blowing this. She had interviewed hundreds of witnesses and she couldn't remember one who had performed as badly as she was right now.

She hurriedly rummaged through her purse for her pack of Benson & Hedges. The sight of the cigarette made Frank reach for his pack of Juicy Fruit.

She blew the smoke away from him, eyed the gum. "Trying to quit too?" A flicker of amusement crossed her face.

"Trying and failing. You were saying?"

She slowly exhaled the smoke, willed her nerves to cease their cartwheels. "Like I told you, I haven't seen my father in years. We aren't close. It's possible that he could have killed the woman. Anything's possible. But that doesn't work in court. Evidence works in court. Period."

"And we're attempting to build a case against him."

"You have no tangible physical evidence tying him to the actual crime scene? No prints? No witnesses? Nothing like that?"

Frank hesitated, then decided to answer. "No."

"Have you been able to trace any of the stuff from the burglary to him?"

"Nothing's turned up."

"Ballistics?"

"Negative. One unusable slug and no gun."

Kate sat back in her chair, more comfortable as the conversation centered on a legal analysis of the case.

"That's all you've got?" Her eyes squinted at him.

He hesitated again, then shrugged. "That's it."

"Then you got nothing, Detective. Nothing!"

"I've got my instincts and my instincts tell me Luther Whitney was in the house that night and he was in that bedroom. Where he is now is what I want to know."

315

"I can't help you there. That's the same thing I told your buddy the other night."

"But you did go to his house that night. Why?"

Kate shrugged. She was determined not to mention her conversation with Jack. Was she withholding evidence? Maybe.

"I don't know." That, in part, was true.

"You strike me, Kate, as someone who always knows why she does something."

Jack's face flashed across her mind. She angrily pushed it out. "You'd be surprised, Lieutenant."

Frank ceremoniously closed his notebook and hunched forward.

"I really need your help."

"For what?"

"This is off the record, unofficial, whatever you want to call it. I'm more interested in results than in legal niceties."

"Funny thing to tell a state prosecutor."

"I'm not saying I don't play by the rules." Frank finally caved in and pulled out his cigarettes. "All I'm saying is I go for the point of least resistance when I can get it. Okay?"

"Okay."

"My information is that while you may not be wild about your father, he is still out there pining for you."

"Who told you that?"

"Jesus I'm a detective. True or not?"

"I don't know."

"Goddammit, Kate, don't play fucking games with me. True or not?"

She angrily stabbed out her cigarette. "True! Satisfied?"

"Not yet, but I'm getting there. I've got a plan to flush him out, and I'm looking for you to help me."

"I don't see that I'm in any position to help you."

Kate knew what was coming next. She could see it in Frank's eyes.

It took him ten minutes to lay out his plan. She refused three times. A half hour later they were still sitting at the table.

Frank leaned back in his chair and then abruptly lurched forward. "Look, Kate, if you don't do it, then we don't have a chance in hell of laying our hands on him. If it's like you say and we don't have a case, he goes free. But if he did do it, *and* we can prove it, then you've got to be the last goddamned person in the world that should tell me he should get away with it. Now, if you think I'm wrong about that, I'll drive you back to your place and forget I ever saw you, and your old man can go right on stealing . . . and maybe killing." He stared directly at her.

Her mouth opened but no words came out. Her eyes drifted over his shoulder where a misty image from the past beckoned to her, but then suddenly faded away.

At almost thirty years of age Kate Whitney was far removed from the toddler who giggled as her father twirled her through the air, or the little girl who divulged important secrets to her father she would tell no other. She was all grown up, a mature adult, out on her own for a long time now. On top of that she was an officer of the court, a state prosecutor sworn to uphold the law and the Constitution of the Commonwealth of Virginia. It was her job to ensure that persons who broke those laws were appropriately punished regardless of who they were and regardless of to whom they were related.

And then another image invaded her mind. Her mother watching the door, waiting for him to come home. Wondering if he were okay. Visiting him in prison, making up lists of things to talk to him about, making Kate dress up for those encounters, getting all

317

excited as his release date came closer. As if he were some goddamned hero out saving the world instead of a thief. Jack's words came back to her, biting hard. He had called her entire life a lie. He expected her to have sympathy for a man who had abandoned her. As if Luther Whitney had been wronged instead of Kate. Well, Jack could go straight to hell. She thanked God she had decided against marrying him. A man who could say those awful things to her did not deserve her. But Luther Whitney deserved everything coming to him. Maybe he hadn't killed that woman. But maybe he had. It wasn't her job to make that decision. It was her job to make sure that decision had an opportunity to be made by men and women in a jury box. Her father belonged in prison anyway. At least there he could hurt no one else. There he could ruin no more lives.

And it was with that last thought that she agreed to help deliver her father into the hands of the police.

Frank felt a twinge of guilt as they got up to leave. He had not been entirely truthful with Kate Whitney. In fact, he had downright lied to her about the most critical piece of the case other than the million-dollar question of where Luther Whitney happened to be. He wasn't pleased with himself right now. Law enforcement people had to occasionally lie, just like everybody else. It didn't make it any easier to swallow, especially considering the recipient was someone the detective had instantly respected and now heavily pitied.

318

EIGHTEEN

Kate had placed the call that night; Frank had wanted to waste no time. The voice on the machine stunned her; it was the first time in years she had heard those tones. Calm, efficient, measured like the practiced stride of an infantryman. She actually began to tremble as the tone sounded and it took all her will to summon the simple words that were designed to trap him. She kept reminding herself how cunning he could be. She wanted to see him, wanted to talk to him. As soon as possible. She wondered if the wily old mind would smell a trap, and then she recalled their last face-to-face meeting, and she realized that he would never see it coming. He would never attribute deceit to the little girl who confided in him her most precious information. Even she had to give him that.

It was barely an hour later when the phone rang. As she reached out for it, she wished to God she had never agreed to Frank's request. Sitting in a restaurant hatching a plan to catch a suspected murderer was quite different from actually participating in a charade designed solely to deliver your father to the authorities.

"Katie." She sensed the slight break in the voice. A tinge of disbelief blended in.

"Hello, Dad." She was grateful that the words had come out on their own. At that moment she seemed incapable of articulating the simplest thought.

Her apartment was not good. He could understand

that. Too close, too personal. His place, she knew, would be unworkable for obvious reasons. They could meet on neutral grounds, he suggested. Of course they could. She wanted to talk, he certainly wanted to listen. Desperately wanted to listen.

A time was reached, tomorrow, four o'clock, at a small café near her office. At that time of day it would be empty, quiet; they could take their time. He would be there. She was sure nothing short of death would keep him away.

She hung up and called Frank. She gave him the time and the place. Listening to herself it finally dawned on her what she had just done. She could feel everything suddenly giving way and she could not stop it. She flung down the phone and burst into tears; so hard did her body convulse that she slumped to the floor, every muscle twitching, her moans filling the tiny apartment like helium into a balloon; it all threatened to violently explode.

Frank had stayed on the phone a second longer and wished he hadn't. He yelled into the phone but she could not hear him; not that it would have made a difference if she had. She was doing the right thing. She had nothing to be ashamed about, nothing to feel guilty about. When he finally gave up and cradled the receiver, his moment of euphoria at growing ever closer to his quarry was over like a flamed-out match.

So his question had been answered. She loved him still. That thought for Lieutenant Seth Frank was troubling but controllable. For Seth Frank, father of three, it made his eyes water and he suddenly didn't like his job very much anymore.

Burton hung up the phone. Detective Frank had been true to his promise to let the agent in on the kill.

Minutes later Burton was in Russell's office.

"I don't want to know how you're going to do it."
Russell looked worried.

Burton smiled to himself. Getting squeamish, just like he predicted. Wanted the job done, just didn't want to get her pretty nails dirty.

"All you have to make sure you do is tell the President where it's going down. And then you make damn sure he tells Sullivan before the fact. He has *got* to do that."

Russell looked puzzled. "Why?"

"Let me worry about that. Just remember, do what I tell you." He was gone before Russell had a chance to explode at him.

"Are the police sure he's the one?" There was a hint of anxiousness in the President's voice as he looked up from his desk.

Russell, pacing the room, stopped to look at him. "Well, Alan, I'm assuming that if he weren't they wouldn't be going to all the trouble to arrest him."

"They've made mistakes before, Gloria."

"No argument there. Just like us all."

The President closed the binder he had been examining and stood up, surveyed the White House grounds from the window.

"So the man will shortly be in custody?" He turned to look at Russell.

"So it would seem."

"What's that supposed to mean?"

"Only that the best-laid plans sometimes go awry."

"Does Burton know?"

"Burton seems to have orchestrated the entire thing."

The President walked over to Russell; put his hand on her arm.

"What are you talking about?"

Russell relayed the events of the last few days to her

boss. The President rubbed his jaw. "What is Burton up to?" The question was said more to himself than to Russell.

"Why don't you buzz him and ask him yourself? The only point he was absolutely insistent on was your relaying the message to Sullivan."

"Sullivan? Why the hell would . . ." The President did not finish his thought. He rang for Burton but was told he had suddenly become ill and gone to the hospital.

The President's eyes bored into his Chief of Staff. "Is Burton going to do what I think he's going to do?"

"Depends on what you're thinking."

"Cut the games, Gloria. You know exactly what I mean."

"If you mean does Burton intend on making sure that this individual is never taken into custody, yes, that thought had crossed my mind."

The President fingered a heavy letter opener on his desk, sat down in his chair and faced out the window. Russell shuddered when she looked at it. She had thrown the one on her desk away.

"Alan? What do you want me to do?" She stared at the back of his head. He was the President and you had to sit and wait patiently, even if you wanted to reach across and throttle him.

Finally he swiveled around. The eyes were dark, cold and commanding. "Nothing. I want you to do nothing. I better get in touch with Sullivan. Give me the location and time again."

Russell thought the same thing she had earlier as she recounted the information. *Some friend.*

The President picked up his phone. Russell reached across and put her hand on top of his. "Alan, the reports said Christine Sullivan had bruises on her jaw and had been partially strangled."

322

The President didn't look up. "Oh really?"

"What exactly happened in that bedroom, Alan?"

"Well, from the small pieces I can remember she wanted to play a bit rougher than I did. The marks on her neck?" He paused and put down the phone. "Let's just put it this way: Christy was into a lot of kinky things, Gloria. Including sexual asphyxiation. You know, people get off when they're gasping for air and climaxing at the same time."

"I've heard of it, Alan, I just didn't think you'd be into something like that." Her tone was harsh.

The President snapped back: "Remember your place, Russell. I do not answer to you or anyone else for my actions."

She stepped back, and quickly said, "Of course, I'm sorry, Mr. President."

Richmond's face relaxed; he stood up and spread his arms resignedly. "I did it for Christy, Gloria, what can I say. Women sometimes have strange effects on men. I'm certainly not immune to it."

"So why did she try to kill you?"

"Like I said, she wanted to play rougher than I did. She was drunk and she just went out of control. Unfortunate, but those things happen."

Gloria looked past him out the window. The encounter with Christine Sullivan did not just "happen." The time and planning that had gone into that rendezvous had eventually taken on the elements of a full-blown election campaign. She shook her head as the images from that night poured back to her.

The President came up behind her, gripped her shoulders, turned her to him.

"It was an awful experience for everyone, Gloria. I certainly didn't want Christy to die. It was the last thing in the world I wanted. I went there to have a quiet, romantic evening with a very beautiful

323

woman. My God, I'm no monster." A disarming smile emerged across his face.

"I know that, Alan. It's just, all those women, all those times. Something bad was bound to happen."

The President shrugged. "Well, as I told you before, I'm not the first man to hold this office to engage in those types of extracurricular activities. Nor will I be the last." He cupped her chin in his hand. "You know the demands of the office I hold, Gloria, better than most. There's no other job like it in the world."

"I know the pressures are enormous. I realize that, Alan."

"That's right. It's a job that really requires more than is humanly possible to deliver. Sometimes you have to deal with that reality by relieving some of that pressure, from pulling yourself out from between the vise occasionally. How I deal with that pressure is important, because it dictates how well I can serve the people who have elected me, who have placed their trust in me."

He turned back to his desk. "And besides, enjoying the company of beautiful women is a relatively innocuous way of combating that stress."

Gloria stared angrily at his back. As if he expected her, of all people, to be swayed by the rhetoric, by a bullshit patriotic speech.

"It certainly wasn't innocuous for Christine Sullivan," she blurted out.

Richmond turned back to her; he was no longer smiling. "I really don't want to talk about this anymore, Gloria. What's past is past – start thinking about the future. Understand?"

She bowed her head in formal assent and stalked from the room.

The President again picked up the phone. He would deliver all the necessary details about the police sting to his good friend Walter Sullivan. The President smiled to himself as the call was being placed. It sounded like it wouldn't be long now. They were almost there. He could count on Burton. Count on him to do the right thing. For all of them.

Luther checked his watch. One o'clock. He showered, brushed his teeth and then trimmed his newly grown beard. He lingered over his hair until it met with his satisfaction. His face looked better today. The phone call from Kate had worked wonders. He had cradled the phone in his ear playing the message over and over again, just to hear the voice, the words he had never expected to hear again. He had risked going to a men's store downtown where he bought a new pair of slacks, sports coat and patent leathers. He had considered and then discarded the notion of a tie.

He tried on his new coat. It felt good. The pants were a little loose on him; he had lost weight. He would have to eat more. He might even start with buying his daughter an early dinner. If she'd let him. He'd have to think about that one; he didn't want to push it.

Jack! It must've been Jack. He had told her of their meeting. That her father had been in trouble. That was the connection. Of course! He had been stupid not to see it right away. But what did that mean? That she cared? He felt a tremble start in his neck and it ended at his knees. After all these years? He swore under his breath at the timing. The fucking timing! But he had made up his mind and nothing could change that decision now. Not even his little girl. Something terribly wrong had to be set right.

Luther was certain Richmond knew nothing about his correspondence with the Chief of Staff. Her only hope was to quietly buy back what Luther had and then make sure no one ever laid eyes on it again. Buy him off, hoping he'd disappear forever and the world would never know. He had verified that the money had arrived in the designated account. What happened to that money would be their first surprise.

The second surprise, though, would make them forget all about the first. And the best part was that Richmond would never see it coming. He seriously doubted that the President would actually do any time. But if this didn't meet the criteria for impeachment he didn't know what did. This made Watergate look like a third-grade prank. He wondered what impeached ex-Presidents did. Withered in the flames of their own destruction, he hoped.

Luther pulled the letter out of his pocket. He would arrange for her to receive it right about the time she'd be expecting the last set of instructions. The payoff. She would get her payoff. They all would. It was worth it, letting her squirm like he knew she had all this time.

No matter how often he tried he couldn't erase the memory of the woman's leisurely sexual encounter in the presence of a still warm body, as though the dead woman was a pile of trash, not to be bothered with. And then Richmond. The drunken, slobbering bastard! Again the visions made Luther seethe. He clenched his teeth, then abruptly smiled.

Whatever deal Jack could cut him he would take. Twenty years, ten years, ten days. He didn't care anymore. Fuck the President and everybody around him. Fuck the whole town, he was taking them down.

But first he was going to spend some time with his daughter. After that he really didn't care anymore.

As he walked over to the bed, Luther's body took a jolt. Something else had just occurred to him. Something that hurt, but which he could understand.

He sat on the bed and sipped a glass of water. If it were true could he really blame her? And besides, he could just kill two birds with one stone. As he lay back on the bed, it occurred to him that things that looked too good to be true usually were. Did he deserve any better from her? The answer was absolutely clear. He did not.

When the money transfer had reached District Bank, automatic prewire instructions kicked in and the funds were immediately transferred out of the account to five different area banks, each in the amount of one million dollars. From there the funds followed a circuitous route until the total sum was once again assembled in one place.

Russell, who had put a tracer on the flow of money from her end, would find out soon enough what had happened. She would not be particularly pleased about it. She would be far less pleased about the next message she received.

The Café Alonzo had been open about a year. It had the usual array of outdoor tables with colorful umbrellas in a small space on the sidewalk enclosed by a waist-high black iron railing. The coffee was varied and strong; the on-premises bakery was popular among the morning and lunch crowds. At five minutes to four only one person sat at the outdoor table. In the chilly air the umbrellas were collapsed down resembling a column of giant drinking straws.

The café was located in the ground floor of a modern office building. Two stories up hung a scaffolding. Three workers were replacing a glass panel that had cracked. The entire facade of the building consisted of mirrored panels that gave a complete image of the area directly opposite it. The panel was heavy and even the burly men struggled with the weight and bulk.

Kate bundled her coat around her and sipped her coffee. The afternoon sun was warming in spite of the chill, but it was fading rapidly. Long shadows had commenced to creep over the tables. She felt the rawness in her eyes as she squinted at the sun suspended directly over the tops of a number of dilapidated row houses that sat diagonally across the street from the café. They were destined for demolition to make room for the continued renovation of the area. She did not notice that the upper-story window on one of the row houses was now open. The row house next door had two windows smashed out. The front door on another was partially caved in.

Kate looked at her watch. She had been sitting there for approximately twenty minutes. Used to the frenetic pace of the prosecutor's office, the day had dragged interminably. She had no doubt there were dozens of police officers in the vicinity waiting to pounce once he walked up to her. Then she thought about it. Would they even have a chance to say anything to each other? What the hell could she say anyway? Hi Dad, you're busted? She rubbed her raw cheeks and waited. He would be there right at four. And it was too late for her to change any of it. Too damned late for anything. But she was doing the right thing, despite the guilt she was feeling, despite breaking down like that after calling the detective. She angrily squeezed her hands together. She was about to hand her father over to the police, and he deserved it. She was through debating it. She now just wanted it to be over.

McCarty did not like it. Not at all. His usual routine was to follow his target, sometimes for weeks, until the assassin understood the victim's patterns of behavior better than the victim did. It made the killing so much easier. The additional time also allowed McCarty to plan his escape, to allow for worst-case scenarios. He had none of those luxuries on this job. Sullivan's message had been terse. The man had already paid him an enormous sum on his per diem, with another two million to follow upon completion. Under any yardstick he had been compensated – now he had to deliver. Except for his first hit many years ago, McCarty could not remember being this nervous. It didn't help matters that the place was crawling with cops.

But he kept telling himself things would be okay. In the time he had, he had planned well. He had reconnoitered the area right after Sullivan's phone call. The row house idea had hit him immediately. It was really the only logical place. He had been here since four in the morning. The back door to the house opened into an alleyway. His rental car was parked at the curb. It would take him exactly fifteen seconds from the moment the shot was fired to drop his rifle, make his way down the stairs, out the door and into his car. He would be two miles away before the police even fully understood what had happened. A plane was leaving in forty-five minutes from a private airstrip ten miles north of Washington. Its destination was New York City. It would carry one passenger, and in a little over five hours McCarty would be a pampered passenger on board the Concorde as it descended into London.

He checked his rifle and scope for the tenth time, automatically flicking away a grain of dust on the barrel. A suppressor would have been nice, but he had yet to find one that worked on a rifle, especially one that was chambered with supersonic ammo as his weapon was. He would count on the confusion to mask the shot and his subsequent departure. He looked across the street and checked his watch. Almost time.

McCarty, while being a very accomplished killer, could not have possibly known that another rifle would be trained on his target's head. And behind that rifle would be a pair of eyes as sharp if not sharper than his own.

Tim Collin had qualified as an expert marksman in the Marine Corps, and his master sergeant had written in his evaluation that he had never seen a better shot. The focus of that accolade was now sighting through his scope; then he relaxed. Collin looked around the confines of the van he was in. Parked down the street on the curb opposite from the café, he had a straight shot to the target. He sighted through his rifle again, Kate Whitney appearing fleetingly in the crosshairs. Collin slid open the side window of the van. He was under shadow of the buildings behind him. No one could notice what he was doing. He also had the added advantage of knowing that Seth Frank and a contingent of county police were stationed to the right of the café while others were in the office building lobby where the café was located. Unmarked cars were stationed at various locations up and down the street. If Whitney ran he wouldn't get far. But then Collin knew the man wasn't going to run anywhere.

After the shot Collin would quickly disassemble the rifle and secrete it in the van, emerge with his sidearm and badge and join the other authorities in pondering what the hell had happened. No one would think to check a Secret Service van for the firearm or shooter who had just wasted their target.

Burton's plan made a lot of sense to the young agent. Collin had nothing against Luther Whitney but there was a lot more at stake than a sixty-six-year-old career criminal's life. A helluva lot more. Killing the old man was not something Collin was going to enjoy; in fact, he would do his best to forget it once done. But that was life. He was paid to do a job, had in fact sworn to do that job, above all else. Was he breaking the law? Technically he was committing murder. Realistically he was just doing what had to be done. He assumed the President knew about it; Gloria Russell knew about it; and Bill Burton, a man he respected more than anyone else, had instructed him to do it. Collin's training simply did not permit him to ignore those instructions. Besides, the old guy had broken into the place. He was going to do twenty years. He'd never make twenty years. Who wanted to be in prison at eighty years old? Collin was just saving him a lot of misery. Given those choices, Collin would've taken the round too.

Collin glanced up at the workmen on the scaffolding above the café as they struggled to right the replacement panel. One man grabbed the end of a rope connected to a block and tackle. Slowly the piece began to rise.

Kate looked up from studying her hands and her eyes locked on him.

He moved gracefully along the sidewalk. The fedora and muffler hid most of his features but the walk was unmistakable. Growing up she had always wanted to be able to glide along the ground like her father, so effortlessly, so confidently. She started to rise and thought better of it. Frank had not said at what point he would move in, but Kate didn't expect him to wait very long.

Luther stopped in front of the café and looked at her. He had not been this close to his daughter for over a decade, and he was a little unsure how to proceed. She felt his uncertainty and forced a smile to

331

her lips. He immediately went to her table and sat down, his back to the street. Despite the chill he took off his hat and put his sunglasses away in his pocket.

McCarty sighted through his rifle scope. The iron-gray hair came into focus and his finger flipped off the safety and then floated to the trigger.

Barely a hundred yards away, Collin was mirroring those actions. He was not as hurried as McCarty since he had the advantage of knowing when the police were going to move in.

McCarty's trigger finger crooked back. Earlier, he had noticed the workmen on the scaffolding once or twice but then had put them out of his mind. It was only the second mistake he had ever committed in his line of work.

The mirrored panel suddenly jerked upward as the rope was pulled down and the panel cocked in McCarty's direction. Catching the falling sun directly on its surface, the panel threw the reflection, red and glimmering, full in McCarty's eyes. Momentary pain shot through his pupils and his hand jerked involuntarily as the rifle fired. He cursed and flung down the gun. He made it to the back door five seconds ahead of schedule.

The bullet struck the umbrella pole and severed it before ricocheting off and imbedding into the concrete pavement. Both Kate and Luther went down, father instinctively shielding daughter. A few seconds later Seth Frank and a dozen uniforms, guns drawn, formed a semicircle around the pair, facing out, their eyes scanning every nook and cranny of the street.

"Shut this whole fucking area down," Frank screamed to the sergeant, who barked orders into his radio. Uniforms spread out, unmarked cars moved in.

332

The workmen stared down at the street, completely oblivious to the unwitting role they had played in the events unfolding below.

Luther was pulled up and handcuffed and the entire party hustled into the lobby of the office building. An excited Seth Frank stared at the man for one satisfying moment and then read him his rights. Luther looked across at his daughter. Kate at first could not meet his gaze, but then decided he at least deserved that. His words hurt her more than anything she had prepared for.

"Are you all right, Katie?"

She nodded and the tears started to pour, and this time, despite squeezing her throat in an iron grip, she could not stop them as she crumpled to the floor.

Bill Burton stood just inside the lobby doorway. When an astonished Collin came in, Burton's look threatened to disintegrate the younger man. That is until Collin whispered in his ear.

To his credit Burton assimilated the information rapidly and hit upon the truth a few seconds later. Sullivan had hired a hit man. The old man had actually done what Burton had intended to falsely set him up for.

The wily billionaire rose a notch in Burton's estimation.

Burton walked over to Frank.

Frank looked at him. "Any idea what the fuck that was all about?"

"Maybe," Burton answered back.

Burton turned around. For the first time he and Luther Whitney actually looked at each other. For Luther, memories of that night again came hurtling back to him. But he was calm, unruffled.

Burton had to admire that. But it also was a great source of concern for him. Whitney was obviously not overly distressed at being arrested. His eyes told

333

Burton – a man who had participated in literally thousands of arrests, which normally involved adults blubbering like babies – all he needed to know. The guy was planning to go to the cops all along. For what reason Burton was unsure and he really didn't care.

Burton continued to look at Luther while Frank checked in with his men. Then Burton looked over at the huddled mass in the corner. Luther had already struggled with his captors in an attempt to go to her, but they were having no part of it. A policewoman was making awkward efforts to console Kate but with little success. Traces of tears worked their way down the thick wrinkles in the old man's cheeks as he watched each sob wrack his little girl.

When he noticed Burton right at his elbow, Luther finally flashed fire at the man until Burton led the old man's eyes back over to Kate. The men's eyes locked again. Burton raised his eyebrows a notch and then settled them back down with the finality of a round being fired into Kate's head. Burton had stared down some of the worst criminals the area had to offer and his features could be menacing, but it was the absolute sincerity in those features that turned hardened men cold. Luther Whitney was no punk, that was easy enough to see. He was not one of the blubberers. But the wall of concrete that made up Luther Whitney's nerves had already started to crumble. It swiftly finished dissolving and the remnants trickled toward the sobbing woman in the corner.

Burton turned and walked out the door.

NINETEEN

Gloria Russell sat in her living room and held the epistle in her quavering hand. She looked at the clock. It had come right on time, via messenger; a turbaned older man in a beat-up Subaru. A Metro Rush Couriers logo on the passenger door. Thank you, ma'am. Say good-bye to your life. She had expected to finally have in her hand the key to wiping away all the nightmares she had suffered. All the risks she had taken.

The wind was starting to howl in the chimney. A cozy fire burned in the fireplace. The house was scrupulously clean thanks to the efforts of Mary, her part-time maid, who had just left. Russell was expected at Senator Richard Miles's home for dinner at eight. Miles was very important to her own personal political aspirations and he had started making all the right noises. Things had finally started to go right again. The momentum had shifted back to her. After all those torturous, humiliating moments. But now? But now?

She looked at the message again. The disbelief continued to sweep over her like an enormous fishing net, dragging her to the bottom, where she would remain.

Thanks for the charitable contribution. It will be greatly appreciated. Also appreciate the extra rope you just gave me to hang you. About that item we had discussed, it's no longer for sale. Now that I think

about it, the cops will probably need it for the trial.
Oh, by the way, FUCK YOU!

It was all she could do to stagger up. Extra rope? She couldn't think, she couldn't function. She first thought to call Burton, but then realized he would not be at the White House. Then it hit her. She raced to the TV. The six o'clock news was just recounting a late-breaking story. A daring police operation conducted jointly by the Middleton County Police Department and Alexandria City Police had netted a suspect in the Christine Sullivan murder case. A shot had been fired by an unknown gunman. The target was assumed to be the suspect.

Russell watched as footage from the Middleton police station was run. She saw Luther Whitney, staring straight ahead, not in any way attempting to hide his face, walk up the steps. He was far older than she had imagined he would be. He looked like a school principal. That was the man who had watched her . . . It never even occurred to her that Luther had been arrested for a crime she knew he had not committed. Not that that revelation would have prompted her to do anything. As the cameraman swung around, she glimpsed Bill Burton with Collin behind him as they stood listening to Detective Seth Frank make a statement to the press.

The goddamn incompetent bastards! He was in custody. He was in fucking custody and she had a message right there in her head that guaranteed the guy was going to make sure they were all brought down. She had trusted Burton and Collin, the President had trusted them, and they had failed, failed miserably. She could hardly believe how Burton could be standing there so calmly while their entire world was about to flame out, like a suddenly used-up star.

Her next thought surprised even her. She raced to the bathroom, tore open the medicine cabinet and grabbed the first bottle she saw. How many pills would be enough? Ten? A hundred?

She twisted at the cap but her shaking hands couldn't get it off. She continued to struggle; finally the pills spilled into the sink. She scooped up a handful and then stopped. In the mirror, her reflection stared back. For the first time she realized how much she had aged. The eyes were gaunt, her cheeks had caved in and her hair looked as if it were graying before her eyes.

She looked at the mass of green in her hand. She couldn't do it. Despite her world shattering in front of her, she could not do it. She flushed the pills, turned out the light. She telephoned the senator's office. Sickness would prevent her from attending. She had just lain down on the bed when the knock came.

At first it seemed like the distant beating of drums. Would they have a warrant? What did she have that could incriminate her? The note! She tore it out of her pocket and tossed it in the fireplace. As it ignited and a burst of flame sailed up the chimney, she smoothed down her dress, put on her pumps and walked out of the room.

For the second time a stab of pain seared her chest as her eyes fell upon Bill Burton at the front door. Without a word he walked in, threw off his coat and went straight to the liquor.

She slammed the door.

"Great job, Burton. Brilliant. You took care of everything beautifully. Where's your sidekick? Getting his damned eyes examined?"

Burton sat down with his drink. "Shut up and listen."

Ordinarily such a remark would have sent her off.

337

But his tone stopped her dead. She noted the holstered weapon. She suddenly realized she was surrounded by people carrying guns. They seemed to be everywhere. Shots were now being fired. She had thrown in her lot with some very dangerous people. She sat down and stared at him.

"Collin never fired his weapon."

"But—"

"But somebody did. I know that." He swallowed most of his drink. Russell thought about mixing herself one, but decided against it.

He looked at her. "Walter Sullivan. That sonofabitch. Richmond told him, right?"

Russell nodded. "You think Sullivan was behind this?"

"Who the fuck else could it be? He thinks the guy killed his wife. He has the money to hire the best shooters in the world. He was the only other person who knew exactly where it was going down." He looked at her and shook his head in disgust. "Don't be stupid, lady, we don't have time for stupid."

Burton stood up and paced.

Russell's thoughts went back to the TV. "But the man's in custody. He'll tell the police everything. I thought it was them at the door."

Burton stopped pacing. "The guy's going to say nothing to the police. At least for now."

"What are you talking about?"

"I'm talking about a man who will do anything so his little girl can keep on living."

"You, you threatened him?"

"I got my message across real clear."

"How do you know?"

"Eyes don't lie, lady. He knows the game. Talk and his daughter goes bye-bye."

"You, you wouldn't really—"

Burton reached down and grabbed the Chief of

338

Staff, effortlessly lifting her off the floor and holding her in midair so she was eye-level.

"I will kill any fucking person who is in a position to fuck with me, do you understand that?" His tone was chilling. He threw her back into the chair.

She stared up at him, the blood gone from her face, her eyes filled with terror.

Burton's face was crimson with fury. "You were the one who got me into this. I wanted to call the cops right from the get-go. I did my job. Maybe I killed the woman, but there ain't a jury in the world that would've found me guilty. But you suckerpunched me, lady, with all your global disaster talk and bullshit concern for the President, and stupid me, I fell for it. And right now I'm about one step away from pissing away twenty years of my life and I'm not happy about it. If you can't understand that, tough."

They sat without speaking for several minutes. Burton cradled his glass and studied the carpet, thinking intently. Russell kept one eye on him as she tried to stop shaking. She could not bring herself to tell Burton about the note she had received. What good would it do? For all she knew Bill Burton would pull out his gun and shoot her on the spot. The thought of violent death so close to her made her blood turn to ice.

Russell managed to sit back in her chair. A clock ticked in the background; it seemed to be counting down the last remaining moments of her life.

"You're sure he won't say anything?" She looked at Burton.

"I'm not sure of anything."

"But you said—"

"I said the guy will do anything to make sure his little girl doesn't get herself killed. If he takes that threat away, then we'll be waking up the next few years staring at the bottom of a bunk bed."

"But how can he take that threat away?"

"If I knew the answer to that, I wouldn't be so worried. But I can guarantee you that Luther Whitney is sitting in his cell block right now thinking of precisely how to do that."

"What can we do?"

He grabbed his coat and pulled her up roughly. "Come on, it's time to talk to Richmond."

Jack shuffled through his notes and then looked around the conference table. His transaction team consisted of four associates, three paralegals and two partners. Jack's coup with Sullivan had spread throughout the firm. Each of them looked at Jack with a mixture of awe, respect and a little fear.

"Sam, you'll coordinate the raw materials sales through Kiev. Our guy over there is a real hustler, plays close to the edge; keep an eye on him, but let him run with things."

Sam, a ten-year partner, snapped his briefcase shut. "You got it."

"Ben, I checked your report on the lobbying efforts. I agree, I think we should push hard on Foreign Relations, can't hurt to have them on our side." Jack flipped open another file.

"We've got approximately a month to get this operation up and running. Of chief concern is Ukraine's tenuous political status. If we're going to hit the brass ring we have to do it pretty quickly. The last thing we need is Russia annexing our client. Now I'd like to take a few minutes to go over—"

The door opened and Jack's secretary leaned in. She looked edgy.

"I'm terribly sorry to bother you."

"It's okay, Martha, what's up?"

"There's someone on the phone for you."

"I told Lucinda to hold my calls except for an

340

emergency. I'll get back to everybody tomorrow."

"I think this might be an emergency."

Jack swiveled around in his chair. "Who is it?"

"She said her name was Kate Whitney."

Five minutes later Jack was in his car: a brand-new copper-colored Lexus 300. His thoughts raced. Kate had been near hysterical. All he managed to understand was that Luther had been arrested. For what he didn't know.

Kate opened the door on the first knock and nearly collapsed into his arms. It was several minutes before she started breathing regularly.

"Kate, what is it? Where's Luther? What's he charged with?"

She looked at him, her cheeks so puffy and raw it looked like she'd been mugged.

When she finally managed to breathe the word out, Jack sat back stunned.

"Murder?" He looked around the room, his mind going too fast for him to register. "That's impossible. Who the hell is he supposed to have murdered?"

Kate sat up straight and pushed the hair out of her face. She looked directly at him. This time the words were clear, direct and cut into him like chunks of jagged glass.

"Christine Sullivan."

Frozen for a long moment, Jack exploded out of the chair. He looked down at her, tried to speak and found he couldn't. He staggered over to the window, threw it open and let the cold beat into him. His stomach churned pure acid; it reached up into his throat until he was barely able to push it back. His legs slowly regained their rigidity. He closed the window and sat back down next to her.

"What happened, Kate?"

She dabbed raw eyes with a ragged tissue. Her hair

341

was a mass of tangles. She had not taken off her overcoat. Her shoes lay next to the chair where she had kicked them off. She collected herself as best she could. She wiped a strand of hair from her mouth, and finally looked at him.

The words rolled out of her mouth in quiet bursts. "The police have him in custody. They, they think he broke into the Sullivans' home. No one was supposed to be there . . . But Christine Sullivan was." She paused and took a deep breath. "They think Luther shot her." As soon as she uttered those last words her eyes closed, the eyelids seemed to ram down by themselves under a terrible weight. She slowly shook her head, her forehead a stack of wrinkles as the throbbing pain clicked up a notch.

"That's crazy, Kate. Luther would never kill anybody."

"I don't know, Jack. I, I don't know what to think."

Jack stood up and took off his coat. He put a hand through his hair as he struggled to think. He looked down at her.

"How did you find out? How the hell did they catch him?"

In response, Kate's body shook. The pain seemed to be so strong as to be visible, hovering above before it plunged repeatedly into her lean frame. She took a moment to wipe her face with another tissue. It took her so long to turn to him, one inch at a time, that she seemed like an ancient grandmother. Her eyes were still closed, her breathing interrupted by gasps, as if the air was being trapped and was having to struggle mightily before escaping.

Finally her eyes opened. The lips moved but no words came out at first. Then she managed to say them, slowly, distinctly, as though she were forcing herself to absorb every blow that accompanied them as long as possible.

"I set him up."

Luther, dressed in an orange jail suit, sat in the same cinder block interrogation room that Wanda Broome had occupied. Seth Frank sat across from him watching him closely. Luther stared directly ahead. He wasn't zoned out. The guy was thinking about something.

Two other men came in. One carried a recorder that he placed in the middle of the table. He turned it on.

"You smoke?" Frank extended a cigarette. Luther accepted it and both men exhaled tiny clouds.

For the record, Frank repeated, verbatim, Luther's Miranda warning. There would be no procedural miscues on this one.

"So you understand your rights?"

Luther vaguely waved his cigarette in the air.

The guy was not what Frank had been expecting. His record was certainly a felonious one. Three priors, but the last twenty years were clean. That didn't mean much. But no assaults, no violent acts. That also didn't mean much, but there was something about the guy.

"I need a yes or no to that question."

"Yes."

"Okay. You understand that you've been arrested in connection with the murder of Christine Sullivan?"

"Yes."

"And you're sure you want to waive your right to have counsel present on your behalf? We can get a lawyer for you, or you can call your own."

"I'm sure."

"And you understand you do not have to make any

343

statement to the police? That any statement you make now can be used in evidence against you?"

"I understand."

Years of experience had taught Frank that confessions early on in the game could spell disaster for the prosecution. Even a confession given voluntarily could be shredded by the defense with the result often being that all evidence obtained through that confession was thrown out as tainted. The perp could have led you right to the goddamned body and the next day he walks free with his attorney smiling at you and hoping to God his client never shows up in his neighborhood. But Frank had his case. Whatever Whitney added to it was just gravy.

He focused intently on the prisoner. "Then I'd like to ask you some questions. Okay?"

"Fine."

Frank stated the month, day and year and time of day for the record and then asked Luther to state his full name. That was as far as they got. The door opened. A uniform leaned in.

"We got his lawyer outside."

Frank looked at Luther, turned off the recorder.

"What lawyer?"

Before Luther could answer, Jack burst past the officer and entered the room.

"Jack Graham, I'm the accused's attorney. Get that recorder out of here. I want to talk to my client alone, right now, gentlemen."

Luther stared at him. "Jack—" he began sharply.

"Shut up, Luther." Jack looked at the men. "Right now!"

The men began to clear the room. Frank and Jack did an eye-to-eye and then the door was closed. Jack put his briefcase down on the table but didn't sit.

"You want to tell me what the hell's going on?"

"Jack, you gotta keep out of this. I mean it."

"*You* came to me. *You* made me promise I'd be there for you. Well, goddammit, here I am."

"Great, you did your part, now you can go."

"Okay, I go, then what the hell do you do?"

"That doesn't concern you."

Jack leaned into his face. "What are you going to do?"

Luther's voice rose for the first time. "I'm pleading guilty! I did it."

"You killed her?"

Luther looked away.

"Did you kill Christine Sullivan?" Luther didn't answer. Jack grabbed him by the shoulder.

"Did you kill her?"

"Yes."

Jack scrutinized the face. Then grabbed his briefcase.

"I'm your lawyer whether you want me anymore or not. And until I figure out why you're lying to me don't even think about talking to the cops. If you do I'll have you declared insane."

"Jack, I appreciate what you're doing, but—"

"Look, Luther, Kate told me what happened, what she did and why she did it. But let me tell it to you straight. If you go down for this, your little girl is never going to recover. You hear me?"

Luther never finished what he was about to say. Suddenly the tiny room seemed about the size of a test tube. He never heard Jack leave. He sat there and stared straight ahead. For one of the few times in his life, he had no idea what he should do.

Jack approached the men standing in the hallway.

"Who's in charge?"

Frank looked at him. "Lieutenant Seth Frank."

"Fine, Lieutenant. Just for the record, my client doesn't waive his Miranda rights and you're not to

345

attempt to talk to him outside of my presence. Understood?"

Frank folded his arms across his chest. "Okay."

"Who's the ACA handling this?"

"Assistant Commonwealth's Attorney George Gorelick."

"I'm assuming you got an indictment?"

Frank leaned forward. "Grand jury returned a true bill last week."

Jack put his coat on. "I'm sure they did."

"You can forget about bail, I guess you know that."

"Well, from what I've heard, I think he might be safer hanging with you guys. Keep an eye on him for me, will you?"

Jack handed his card to Frank and then walked purposefully down the hallway. At the parting remark, the smile faded from Frank's lips. He looked at the card and then toward the interrogation room and back at the rapidly disappearing defense counsel.

TWENTY

K ate had showered and changed. Her damp hair was swept straight back and hung loosely down to her shoulders. She wore a thick indigo blue V-neck sweater with white T-shirt underneath. The faded blue jeans hung loosely around her narrow hips. Thick wool socks covered her long feet. Jack watched those feet as they moved up and down, propelling their lithe owner about the room. She had recovered somewhat from earlier. But the horror was still lurking in her eyes. She seemed to be battling it with physical activity.

Jack cradled a glass of soda and sat back in the chair. His shoulders felt like a two-by-four. As if sensing that, Kate stopped pacing and started massaging.

"He didn't tell me they had an indictment." Kate's voice was angry.

"You really think cops are above using people to get what they want?" he shot back.

"I can see you're getting back into the defense attorney state of mind."

She really dug into his shoulders; it felt wonderful to him. Her wet hair dipped into his face as she bore down on the stiffest points. He closed his eyes. On the radio Billy Joel's "River of Dreams" was playing. What was his dream? Jack asked himself. The target seemed to keep jumping on him, like spots of sunlight you tried to chase down as a kid.

"How is he?" Kate's question jarred him back. He swallowed the rest of his drink.

"Confused. Screwed up. Nervous. All the things I never thought he could be. They found the rifle, by the way. Upper-story room of one of those old townhouses across the street. Whoever fired that bullet, they're long gone by now. That's for sure. Hell, I don't even think the cops care."

"When's the arraignment?"

"Day after tomorrow, ten o'clock." He arched his neck and gripped her hand. "They're going for capital murder, Kate."

She stopped massaging.

"That's bullshit. Homicide in the commission of a burglary is a class one felony, murder in the first degree, tops. Tell the ACA to check the statute."

"Hey, that's my line isn't it?" He tried to make her smile, but didn't succeed. "The commonwealth's theory is that he broke into the house and was in the middle of the burglary when she caught him in the act. They're using the evidence of physical violence – strangulation, beating and two shots to the head – to sever it from the act of burglary. They believe that takes it into the realm of a vile and depraved act. Plus they have the disappearance of Sullivan's jewelry. Murder in the commission of armed robbery equals capital murder."

Kate sat down and rubbed her thighs. She wore no makeup and had always been one of those women who didn't need to. The strain was telling though, especially in and under her eyes, in the slope of her shoulders.

"What do you know about Gorelick? He's going to be trying this sucker." Jack popped an ice cube in his mouth.

"He's an arrogant asshole, pompous, bigoted and a terrific trial lawyer."

"Great." Jack got up from his chair and sat down next to Kate. He took her ankle and rubbed it. She

348

sunk down into the sofa and put her head back. It had always been that way with them, so relaxed, so comfortable in the company of each other, like the last four years had never happened.

"The evidence Frank told me he had wasn't even close to getting an indictment. I don't understand, Jack."

Jack slipped off her socks and rubbed her feet with both hands, feeling the fine, tiny bones. "The police got an anonymous tip on the license plate of a car seen near the Sullivan place on what was probably the night of the murder. It was traced to the D.C. impoundment lot on that night."

"So. The tip was wrong."

"No. Luther used to tell me how easy it was to pick up a car from the impoundment lot. Do a job and then return it."

Kate didn't look at him, she appeared to be studying the ceiling.

"Nice little chats you two used to have." Her tone held the familiar reproach.

"Come on, Kate."

"I'm sorry." Her voice was weary again.

"The police checked the floor matting. Rug fibers from the Sullivan bedroom were found there. Also present was a very peculiar soil mixture. Turns out that exact same soil mix was used by Sullivan's gardener in the cornfield next to the house. The soil was a special blend made up for Sullivan; you won't find that exact composition anywhere else. I had a chat with Gorelick. He's feeling pretty confident, I can tell you that. I haven't gotten the reports yet. I'll file my discovery motion tomorrow."

"Again, so what? How does that tie in to my father?"

"They got a search warrant for Luther's house and car. They found the same mixture on the floor mat in

349

the car. And another sample on the living room rug."

Kate slowly opened her eyes. "He was in the house cleaning the damn carpets. He could've picked up the fibers then."

"And then he took a run through the cornfield? Come on."

"It could've been tracked in the house by somebody else and he stepped in it."

"That's what I would've argued except for one thing."

She sat up. "Which is?"

"Along with the fiber and dirt, they found a petroleum-based solvent. The police pulled traces of it out of the carpet during their investigation. They think the perp tried to clean some blood away, his blood. I'm sure they've got a handful of witnesses ready to swear that there was no such thing used on that carpet prior to or at the time the carpets were cleaned. Therefore Luther could've picked up traces of the carpet cleaner only if he had been in the house *after* that. Soil, fibers and carpet cleaner. There's your tie."

Kate slumped back down.

"On top of that they traced the hotel where Luther was staying in town. They found a fake passport and through that tracked Luther to Barbados. Two days after the murder he flew to Texas, then Miami and then on to the island. Looks like a fleeing suspect, doesn't it? They've got a sworn statement from a cab driver down there who drove Luther to Sullivan's place on the island. Luther made a reference to having been in Sullivan's place in Virginia. On top of that they've got witnesses who will testify that Luther and Wanda Broome were seen together several times prior to the murder. One woman, a close friend of Wanda's, will testify that Wanda told her she needed money, badly. And that Christine Sullivan had told

350

her about the safe. Which shows Wanda Broome had lied to the police."

"I can see why Gorelick was so free with the info. But it's still all circumstantial."

"No, Kate, it's a perfect example of a case with no home-run direct evidence linking Luther to the crime, but enough indirect stuff to where the jury will be thinking 'come on who are you kidding you did it you sonofabitch.'

"I'll deflect everywhere I can, but they've got some pretty heavy stones to hit us with. And if Gorelick can get in your Dad's priors, we might be finished."

"They're too old. Their prejudicial value far out-weighs their probative. He'll never get them in." Kate's words sounded more sure than she felt. After all, how could you be sure of anything?

The phone rang. She hesitated to answer it. "Does anyone know you're here?"

Jack shook his head.

She picked up the phone. "Hello?"

The voice on the other end was crisp, professional. "Ms. Whitney, Robert Gavin with the *Washington Post*. I wonder if I could ask you some questions about your father? I'd prefer to see you in person if that could be arranged."

"What do you want?"

"Come on, Ms. Whitney, your father is front-page news. You're a state prosecutor. There's a helluva story there if you ask me."

Kate hung up. Jack looked at her.

"What?"

"A reporter."

"Christ, they move fast."

She sat down again with a weariness that startled him. He went to her, took her hand.

Suddenly, she turned his face toward hers. She looked frightened. "Jack, you can't handle this case."

351

"The hell I can't. I'm an active member of the Virginia Bar. I've handled a half-dozen murder trials. I'm eminently qualified."

"I don't mean that. I know you're qualified. But Patton, Shaw doesn't do criminal defense work."

"So? You have to start somewhere."

"Jack, be serious. Sullivan is a huge client of theirs. *You've* worked for him. I read about it in *Legal Times*."

"There's no conflict there. There's nothing I've learned in my attorney–client relationship with Sullivan that could be used on this case. Besides, Sullivan's not on trial here. It's us against the state."

"Jack, they're not going to let you do this case."

"Fine, then I'll quit. Hang up my own shingle."

"You can't do that. You've got everything going for you right now. You can't mess that up. Not for this."

"Then for what? I know your old man didn't beat up a woman and then calmly blow her head off. He probably went to that house to burgle it, but he didn't kill anybody, that I know. But you want to know something else? I'm pretty damn sure he knows who killed her and that's what's got him scared to death. He saw something in that house, Kate. He saw *someone*."

Kate slowly let out her breath as the words sunk in.

Jack sighed and looked down at his feet.

He got up and put on his coat. He playfully pulled at her waistband. "When's the last time you actually had a meal?"

"I can't remember."

"I recall when you filled out those jeans in a way that was a little more aesthetically pleasing to the male eye."

She did smile that time. "Thanks a lot."

"It's not too late to work on it."

352

She looked around the four corners of her apartment. It held no appeal whatsoever.

"What did you have in mind?"

"Ribs, slaw and something stronger than Coke. Game?"

She didn't hesitate. "Let me get my coat."

Downstairs, Jack held open the door of the Lexus. He saw her studying every detail of the luxury car.

"I took your advice. Thought I'd start spending some of my hard-earned money." He had just climbed inside the car when the man appeared at the passenger door.

He wore a slouch hat and had a gray-trimmed beard and skinny mustache. His brown overcoat was buttoned up to his neck. He held a minicassette recorder in one hand, a press badge in the other.

"Bob Gavin, Ms. Whitney. I guess we got cut off before."

He looked across at Jack. His brow furrowed. "You're Jack Graham. Luther Whitney's attorney. I saw you at the station."

"Congratulations, Mr. Gavin, you've obviously got twenty-twenty vision and a very winning smile. Be seeing you."

Gavin clung to the car. "Wait a minute, c'mon just a minute. The public is entitled to hear about this case."

Jack started to say something, but Kate stopped him.

"They will, Mr. Gavin. That's what trials are for. I'm sure you'll have a front-row seat. Good-bye."

The Lexus pulled away. Gavin thought about making a run for his car but then decided not to. At forty-six, he and his soft and abused body were clearly in heart attack country. It was early in the game yet. He'd get to them sooner or later. He pulled up his collar against the wind and stalked off.

It was nearing midnight when the Lexus pulled up in front of Kate's apartment building.

"Are you really sure you want to do this, Jack?"

"Hell I never really liked the murals, Kate."

"What?"

"Get some sleep. We're both going to need it."

She put her hand on the door and then hesitated. She turned back and looked at him, nervously flicked her hair behind her ear. This time there was no pain in her eyes. It was something else, Jack couldn't quite put his finger on. Maybe relief?

"Jack, the things you said the other night."

He swallowed hard and gripped the steering wheel with both hands. He had been wondering when this was going to surface. "Kate, I've been thinking about that—"

She put a hand to his mouth. A small breath floated from her lips. "You were right, Jack . . . about a lot of things."

He watched her walk slowly inside and then he drove off.

When he got home his answering machine had run out of tape. The blinking message indicator was so full the light was reduced to one continuous crimson beacon. He decided to do the most sensible thing he could think of so he pretended they weren't there. Jack unplugged the phone, turned out the lights and tried to go to sleep.

It wasn't easy.

He had acted so confident in front of Kate. But who was he kidding? Taking on this case, by himself, without talking with anyone at Patton, Shaw was akin to professional suicide. But what good would talking have done? He knew what the answer would have been. Given the choice, his fellow partners would have slit their collective flabby wrists rather

354

than taken on Luther Whitney as a client.

But he was a lawyer and Luther needed one. Major issues like this were never that simple, but that was why he fought so hard to keep things as black and white as possible. Good. Bad. Right. Wrong. It was not easy going for a lawyer perpetually trained to search for the gray in everything. An advocate of any position, just depended on who your client was, who was filling the meter on any given day.

Well, he had made his decision. An old friend was fighting for his life and he'd asked Jack to help him. It didn't matter to Jack that his client seemed to be growing unusually recalcitrant all of a sudden. Criminal defendants were seldom the most co-operative in the world. Well, Luther had asked for his help and he was sure as hell going to get it now. There was no gray in this issue anymore. There was no going back now.

TWENTY-ONE

Dan Kirksen opened the *Washington Post* and started to take a sip of his orange juice. It never reached his mouth. Gavin had managed to file a story on the Sullivan case consisting chiefly of the information that Jack Graham, newly ordained partner at Patton, Shaw & Lord, was the defendant's counsel. Kirksen immediately called Jack's home. There was no answer. He dressed, called for his car and at half past eight walked through the lobby of his firm. He passed Jack's old office where boxes and personal items were still clustered. Jack's new quarters were just down the hall from Lord's. A twenty-by-twenty beauty with a small wet bar, antique furnishings and a panoramic view of the city. Nicer than his, Kirksen recalled with a grimace.

The chair was swiveled around away from the doorway. Kirksen didn't bother to knock. He marched in and tossed the paper down on the desk.

Jack turned slowly around. He glanced at the paper.

"Well at least they got the firm's name spelled correctly. Great publicity. This could lead to some big ones."

Kirksen sat down without taking his eyes off Jack. He spoke slowly and deliberately, as though to a child. "Have you gone insane? We don't handle criminal defense work. We don't handle any litigation whatsoever." Kirksen stood up abruptly, his long forehead now a shiny pink, his diminutive body

356

shaking with rage. "Particularly when this animal has murdered the wife of the firm's largest client," he said shrilly.

"Well, that's not entirely correct. We didn't handle criminal defense work but now we do. And I learned in law school that the accused is innocent until proven guilty, Dan. Maybe you forgot that." Smiling, Jack eyed Kirksen steadily. *Four million versus six hundred thou', pal. So back off, dickhead.*

Kirksen slowly shook his head and rolled his eyes. "Jack, maybe you don't fully understand the procedures we have in place at this firm before any new matter is undertaken. I'll have my secretary provide you with the pertinent provisions. In the meantime, take the necessary steps to have yourself and this firm taken off this matter immediately."

With a dismissive air, Kirksen turned to leave. Jack stood up.

"Listen, Dan, I took the case and I'm going to try it and I don't care what you or the firm's policy has to say about it. Close the door on your way out."

Kirksen turned around slowly and looked at Jack with intense brown eyes. "Jack, tread cautiously. I am the managing partner of this firm."

"I know you are, Dan. So you should be able to manage to close the goddamned door on your way out."

Without another word, Kirksen spun on his heel, shutting the door behind him.

The pounding in Jack's head finally subsided. He returned to his work. His papers were just about completed. He wanted to get them filed first thing before anyone could try to stop him. He printed out the documents, signed them and called the courier himself. That done he sat back in his chair. It was almost nine o'clock. He would have to get going, he was seeing Luther at ten. Jack's entire brain was overflowing with questions to ask his client. And then he thought about that night. That chilly night on the Mall. The look in Luther's eyes. Jack could ask the questions, he just hoped he was ready to handle the answers.

He threw on his coat, and in another few minutes was in his car on his way to the Middleton County Jail.

Under the constitution of the Commonwealth of Virginia and its criminal procedure stature, the state must turn over to a defendant any exculpatory evidence. Failure to do so was a terrific way for an ACA to abruptly derail his or her career, not to mention getting a conviction thrown out and letting a defendant walk on appeal.

Those particular rules were giving Seth Frank a very large headache.

He sat in his office and thought about the prisoner sitting alone in a cell less than a minute's walk away. His calm and seemingly innocuous manner didn't trouble Frank. Some of the worst offenders he had ever arrested looked like they had stepped out of the church choir right after they had split open somebody's skull for a couple of laughs. Gorelick was putting together a good case, methodically collecting a bagful of little threads that when woven together in front of a jury would make a nice sturdy necktie for Luther Whitney to choke himself on. That also didn't trouble Frank.

What did trouble Frank was all the little things that still didn't add up. The wounds. Two guns. A bullet dug out of the wall. The place sanitized like an operating room. The fact that the guy was in Barbados and then came back. Luther Whitney was a pro. Frank had spent the better part of four days learning everything he could about Luther Albert

Whitney. He had pulled off a crackerjack crime that except for one glitch would probably have remained unsolved. Millions from his heist, a cold trail for the cops; he's out of the country, and the sonofabitch comes back. Professionals did not do those things. Frank would've understood him coming back because of his daughter, but Frank had checked with the airlines. Luther Whitney, traveling under an alias, had returned to the United States long before Frank had hatched his plot with Kate.

And the kicker was this: was he really supposed to believe that Luther Whitney had any reason on earth to check Christine Sullivan's vagina? And on top of that somebody had tried to kill the guy. This was one of the few times Frank actually had more questions *after* he had arrested his suspect than he had before taking his guy into custody.

He felt in his pocket for a cigarette. His gum stage had long since passed. He would try again next year. When he looked back up Bill Burton was standing in front of him.

"You understand, Seth, I can't prove anything but I'm just letting you know how I think it went down."

"And you're sure the President told Sullivan?"

Burton nodded, fiddled with an empty cup on Frank's desk. "I just came from meeting with him. I guess I should've told him to keep it mum. I'm sorry, Seth."

"Hell, he's the President, Bill. You gonna tell the President what to do?"

Burton shrugged. "So what do you think?"

"Makes sense. I'm not gonna let it lie, I can tell you that. If Sullivan was behind it I'll take him down too, I don't care what his justification was. That shot could've hit anybody."

"Well, knowing the way Sullivan probably operates, you ain't gonna find much. The shooter's probably on some island in the Pacific with a different face and a hundred people who'll swear he's never even been in the States."

Frank finished writing in his log book.

Burton studied him. "Get anything out of Whitney?"

"Right! His lawyer has him clammed shut."

Burton appeared nonchalant. "Who is he?"

"Jack Graham. Used to be with the Public Defenders Service in the District. Now he's a big-shot partner with some big-shot law firm. He's in with Whitney now."

"Any good?"

Frank twisted a swizzle stick into a triangle. "He knows what he's doing."

Burton stood up to go. "When's the arraignment?"

"Ten tomorrow."

"You taking Whitney over?"

"Yeah. You want to come along, Bill?"

Burton threw his hands over his ears. "I don't want to know anything about it."

"How come?"

"I don't want anything leaking back to Sullivan, that's how come."

"You don't think they'd try anything again?"

"The only thing I know is that I don't know the answer to that question and neither do you. If I were you I'd make some special arrangements."

Frank looked at him intently.

"Take care of our boy, Seth. He's got a date with the death chamber at Greensville."

Burton left.

Frank sat at his desk for some minutes. What Burton said made sense. Maybe they would try again. He picked up the phone, dialed a number and spoke for a bit and then hung up. He had taken all the precautions he could think of for transporting Luther. This time Frank was confident there would be no leak.

Jack left Luther sitting in the interrogation room and walked down the hallway to the coffee machine. In front of him was a big guy, nice suit and a graceful tilt to his body. The man turned around just as Jack passed him. They bumped.

"Sorry."

Jack rubbed his shoulder where the holstered gun had struck him.

"Forget it."

"You're Jack Graham, aren't you?"

"Depends on who wants to know." Jack sized the guy up; since he was carrying a gun he obviously wasn't a reporter. He was more like a cop. The way he held his hands, his fingers ready to move instantly. The way the eyes checked out every feature without seeming to.

"Bill Burton, United States Secret Service."

The men shook hands.

"I'm kind of the President's earpiece on this investigation."

Jack's eyes focused on Burton's features. "Right, the news conference. Well I guess your boss is pretty happy this morning."

"He would be if the rest of the world wasn't in such a godawful mess. About your guy, hey, my feeling is they're only guilty if the court says they are."

"I hear you. You want to be on my jury?"

Burton grinned. "Take it easy. Good talking to you."

Jack put the two cups of coffee down on the table and

361

looked at Luther. He sat down and looked at his empty legal pad.

"Luther, if you don't start saying something I'm going to have to just make it up as I go along."

Luther sipped the strong coffee, looked out the barred window at the single bare oak tree next to the station. A thick, wet snow was falling. The mercury was plunging and the streets were already a mess.

"What's to know, Jack? Cut me a deal, save everybody the hassle of a trial and let's get this over with."

"Maybe you don't understand, Luther. Here's their deal. *They* want to strap you onto a gurney, insert an IV into your arm, pump nasty little poisons into you and pretend you're a chemistry experiment. Or I think now the commonwealth actually gives the condemned a choice. So you can opt for having your brain fried in the electric chair. That's their deal."

Jack stood up and looked out the window. For a moment the flash of a blissful evening in front of a toasty fire in the huge mansion with the big front yard with little Jacks and Jennifers running around went through his head. He swallowed hard, shook his head clear and looked back at Luther.

"Do you hear what I'm saying?"

"I hear." Luther eyed Jack steadily for the first time.

"Luther, will you please tell me what happened? Maybe you were in that house, maybe you burgled the safe, but you will never, ever make me believe you had anything to do with that woman's death. I know you, Luther."

Luther smiled. "Do you, Jack? That's good, maybe you can tell me who I am one of these days."

Jack threw his pad in his briefcase and snapped it shut. "I'm going to plead you not guilty. Maybe you'll come around before we have to try this thing."

He paused and added quietly, "I hope you do."

He turned to leave. Luther's hand fell on Jack's shoulder. Jack turned back to see Luther's quivering face.

"Jack." He swallowed with difficulty, his tongue seemed as big as a fist. "If I could tell you I would. But that wouldn't do you or Kate or anybody else any good. I'm sorry."

"Kate? What are you talking about?"

"I'll see you, Jack." Luther turned and stared back out the window.

Jack looked at his friend, shook his head, and knocked for the guard.

The snow had changed from fat, sloppy flakes to pellets of ice that clattered against the broad windows like handfuls of slung gravel. Kirksen paid no attention to the weather but looked directly at Lord. The managing partner's bow tie was slightly askew. He noticed it in the reflection from the window and angrily straightened it. His long forehead was red with anger and indignation. The little fuck was going to get his. No one talked to him like that.

Sandy Lord studied the dark clusters making up the cityscape. A cigar smoldered in his right hand. His jacket was off and his immense belly touched the window. The twin streaks of his red suspenders jumped out from the background of his highly starched monogrammed white shirt. He peered intently out as a figure dashed across the street frantically chasing down a cab.

"He is undermining the relationship this firm, *you*, have with Walter Sullivan. I could only imagine what Walter must have thought when he read the paper this morning. His own firm, his own attorney actually representing this, this person. My God!"

Lord digested only a fraction of the little man's

speech. He hadn't heard from Sullivan for several days now. Calls to his office and home had gone unanswered. No one seemed to know where he was. That was not like his old friend, who kept himself in constant contact with an elite inner circle of which Sandy Lord was a longtime member.

"My suggestion, Sandy, is that we take immediate action against Graham. We can't let this lie. It would set a terrible precedent. I don't care if he has Baldwin as a client. Hell, Baldwin is an acquaintance of Walter's. He must be livid as well about this whole deplorable situation. We can convene a meeting of the management committee tonight. I don't think it will take long to arrive at a conclusion. Then—"

Lord finally held up one hand and cut off Kirksen's ramblings.

"I'll take care of it."

"But, Sandy, as managing partner I believe that—"

Lord turned to look at him. The red eyes on either side of the large and bulbous nose cut right into the slender frame.

"I said I'll handle it."

Lord turned to look back out the window. Kirksen's hurt pride was of absolutely no consequence to him. What concerned Lord was the fact that someone had tried to kill the man accused of murdering Christine Sullivan. And no one could reach Walter Sullivan.

Jack parked his car, looked across the street and closed his eyes. That didn't help since the vanity plates seemed to be imprinted on his brain. He jumped out of his car and dodged traffic as he made his way across the slippery street.

He inserted the key in the lock, took a quick breath, and turned the doorknob.

Jennifer sat in the small chair by the TV. Her short black skirt was matched by black heels and patterned black stockings. A white blouse was open at the collar where an emerald necklace fired dazzling color into the little room. A full-length sable was draped carefully on the sheet covering his ragged couch. She was clicking her nails against the TV set when he walked in. She looked at him without speaking. The thick ruby lips were set in a firm, vertical line.

"Hi, Jenn."

"You've certainly been a very busy boy the last twenty-four hours, Jack." She didn't smile, her nails continued to click.

"Gotta keep hustling, you know that."

He took off his coat, undid his tie and went into the kitchen for a beer. He re-emerged, and sat across from her on the couch.

"Hey, got a new piece of business today."

She reached in her handbag and tossed across the *Post*.

"I know."

He looked down at the headlines.

"Your firm won't let you do it."

"Too bad, I already did it."

"You know what I mean. What in God's name has gotten into you?"

"Jenn, I know the guy, okay? I know him, he's a friend of mine. I don't believe he killed the woman, and I'm going to defend him. Lawyers do that every day in every place where there are lawyers, and in this country that's basically everywhere."

She leaned forward. "It's Walter Sullivan, Jack. Think about what you're doing."

"I know it's Walter Sullivan, Jenn. What? Luther Whitney doesn't deserve a good defense because somebody *says* he killed Walter Sullivan's wife? Excuse me but exactly where is that written?"

365

"Walter Sullivan is your client."

"Luther Whitney is my friend and I've known him a lot longer than I've known Walter Sullivan."

"Jack, the man you're defending is a common criminal. He's been in and out of jails all his life."

"Actually he hasn't been in prison for over twenty years."

"He's a convicted felon."

"But he's never been convicted of murder," Jack fired back.

"Jack, there are more attorneys in this city than there are criminals. Why can't another lawyer handle it?"

Jack looked at his beer. "You want one?"

"Answer my question."

Jack stood up and hurled the beer bottle against the wall.

"Because he goddamn asked me!"

Jenn looked up at him, the frightened look that had crossed her face passing as soon as the glass fragments and beer hit the floor. She picked up her coat and put it on.

"You're making a huge mistake and I hope you come to your senses before you do *irreversible* damage. My father almost had a coronary when he read that story."

Jack put his hand on her shoulder, turned her face to his and said quietly, "Jenn, this is something I have to do. I would've hoped you could support me on this."

"Jack, why don't you stop drinking beer and start thinking about how you want to spend the rest of your life."

When the door closed behind her, Jack slumped against it, rubbing his head until he thought the skin would start to peel away under the pressure his fingers were exerting.

He watched from the tiny, dirty window as the vanity plates disappeared into the blur of snow. He sat down, looked at the headlines again.

Luther wanted to cut a deal but there was no deal to cut. The stage was set. Everyone wanted to see this trial. The TV news had given a detailed analysis of the case; Luther's photo must have been seen by several hundred million people. They already had public opinion polls about Luther's guilt or innocence, and he was running far behind in all of them. And Gorelick was licking his chops thinking that this was the vehicle to catapult him into the Attorney General's office in a few years. And in Virginia, Attorneys General often ran for, and won, the Governor's Mansion.

Short, balding, big-voiced, Gorelick was as deadly as a rattler on speed. Dirty tactics, questionable ethics, just waiting to bury the knife in your back at the first opportunity. That was George Gorelick. Jack knew he was in for a long, tough fight.

And Luther wasn't talking. He was scared. And what did Kate have to do with that fear? Nothing was adding up. And Jack was going to walk into court tomorrow and plead Luther not guilty when he had absolutely no way to prove that Luther wasn't. But proof was the state's job. The problem was they probably had just enough to put them over the top. Jack would peck and chip, but he had a three-time loser as a client, even though the record said Luther had remained clean for the last two decades. They wouldn't care about that. Why should they? His guy made for the perfect ending to a tragic story. A poster boy for the three-strikes rule. Three heavies and your life is over, starring Luther Whitney.

He tossed the newspaper across the room and cleaned up the broken glass and spilled beer. He rubbed the back of his neck, felt the underused muscles in his arms and went to his bedroom and changed into sweats.

The YMCA was ten minutes away. Amazingly Jack found a parking space right in front and went inside. The black sedan behind him wasn't as lucky. The driver had to circle the block several times and then pull down the street and park on the other side.

The driver wiped his passenger-side window clear and checked out the front of the Y. Then he made up his mind, climbed out of his car and ran to the steps. He looked around, glanced at the gleaming Lexus and then slowly walked inside.

Three pickup games later, the sweat was pouring down Jack's body. He sat down on the bench as the teenagers continued to run up and down the court with the inexhaustible energy of youth. Jack groaned as one of the lanky black kids dressed in loose gym shorts, tank shirt and oversized sneakers tossed the ball at him. He tossed it back.

"Hey man, you tired?"

"No, just old."

Jack stood up, rubbed the kinks out of his aching thighs and headed out.

As he was leaving the building he felt a hand on his shoulder.

Jack drove. He glanced at his new passenger.

Seth Frank looked over the interior of the Lexus. "I've heard great things about these cars. How much it run you, if you don't mind my asking?"

"Forty-nine-five, loaded."

"Like hell! I don't even come close to making that in a year."

"Neither did I until recently."

"Public defenders don't make the big bucks, I've heard."

"You heard right."

The men fell silent. Frank knew he was breaking more rules than they probably had written down and Jack knew that too.

Finally Jack looked at him. "Look, Lieutenant, I'm assuming you didn't just come out here to check my taste in automobiles. Is there something you want?"

"Gorelick's got a winning case against your guy."

"Maybe. Maybe not. I'm not throwing in the towel if that's what you're thinking."

"You pleading him not guilty?"

"No, I'm gonna drive him down to the Greensville Correctional Center and inject the shit into him myself. Next question."

Frank smiled. "Okay, I deserved that. I think you and I need to talk. Some things about this case don't add up. Maybe it helps or hurts your guy, I don't know. You willing to listen?"

"Okay, but don't think this flow of information is going to be a two-way street."

"I know a place where you can actually cut the meatloaf with a butter knife and the coffee's passable."

"Is it an out-of-the-way place? I don't think you'd look good in a deputy's uniform."

Frank looked over at him, grinning. "Next question."

Jack managed a smile and then drove home to change.

Jack ordered another cup of coffee while Frank played with his first. The meatloaf had been terrific and the place was so isolated, Jack wasn't even sure where they were. Rural, southern Maryland, he thought. He looked around at the few occupants of the rustic dining room. No one was paying them any undue attention. He turned back to his companion.

Frank looked at him in an amused fashion. "I

369

understand you and Kate Whitney had a thing going a while back."

"Did she tell you that?"

"Hell no. She came down to the station a few minutes after you left today. Her father wouldn't see her. I talked with her for a while. Told her I was sorry about how things had gone down."

Frank's eyes glistened for a moment and then he continued. "I shouldn't have done what I did, Jack. Using her to get to her old man. Nobody deserves that."

"It worked. Some people would say don't argue with success."

"Right. Well anyway the subject got around to you. I'm not so old yet that I can't see a gleam in a woman's eyes."

The waitress brought Jack's coffee. He sipped it. Both men looked out the window where the snow had finally stopped and the whole earth seemed to be covered with a soft, white blanket.

"Look, Jack, I know the case against Luther is just about all circumstantial. But that's sent plenty of people to jail."

"I'm not arguing with that."

"The truth is, Jack, there's an awful lot of shit that doesn't make any sense."

Jack put down his coffee and leaned forward.

"I'm listening."

Frank looked around the room and then back at Jack. "I know I'm taking a chance doing this, but I didn't become a cop to send people to jail for crimes they didn't commit. Plenty enough guilty people out there."

"So what doesn't add up?"

"You'll see some of it for yourself in the reports you'll get in your discovery, but the fact is I'm convinced Luther Whitney burgled that house and

I'm also convinced that he didn't kill Christine Sullivan. But—"

"But you think he saw who did."

Frank sat back in his chair and stared wide-eyed at Jack. "How long have you thought that?"

"Not long. Any ideas on the matter?"

"I'm thinking your guy almost got caught with his hand in the cookie jar and then had to actually hide in that cookie jar."

Jack looked puzzled. Frank took a few minutes to explain about the vault, the incongruity of the physical evidence and his own questions.

"So Luther's in the vault all this time watching whoever gets it on with Mrs. Sullivan. Then something happens and she gets popped. Then Luther watches whoever wipe away all traces."

"That's how I got it figured, Jack."

"So he doesn't go to the cops because he can't without incriminating himself."

"That explains a lot."

"Except who did it."

"The only obvious suspect is the husband, and I don't believe it was him."

Jack thought back to Walter Sullivan. "Agreed. So who's not so obvious?"

"Whoever she was meeting that night."

"From what you've told me about the deceased's sex life, that narrows it down to a couple million."

"I didn't say it would be easy."

"Well, my hunch is it's not some ordinary Joe."

"Why's that?"

Jack took a swallow of coffee and looked at his slice of apple pie. "Look, Lieutenant—"

"Make it Seth."

"Okay, Seth, I'm walking a fine line here. I hear where you're coming from and I appreciate the info. But . . ."

371

"But you're not absolutely sure you can trust me, and in any event, you don't want to say anything that might prejudice your client?"

"Something like that."

"Fair enough."

They paid the bill and left. Driving back, the snow started again with such velocity that the wipers were having a hard time keeping up.

Jack looked over at Frank, who stared straight ahead, lost in thought or maybe just waiting for Jack to start talking.

"Okay. I'll take the chance, I don't have a helluva lot to lose, do I?"

Frank continued to stare straight ahead. "Not that I can see."

"Let's assume for the moment that Luther was in the house and saw the woman murdered."

Frank looked over at Jack; there was relief in the detective's features.

"Okay."

"You've got to know Luther, know how he thinks, to understand how he would react to something like that. He's about as unshakable a person as I've ever met. And I know his record doesn't indicate it, but he's about as trustworthy and dependable as you can get. If I had kids and needed to leave them with someone I'd leave them with Luther because I know absolutely nothing bad would happen to them on his watch. He's incredibly capable. Luther sees everything. He's a control freak."

"Everything except his daughter leading him into a trap."

"Right, except for that. He wouldn't have seen that coming. Not in a million years."

"But I know the kind of guy you're talking about, Jack. Some of the guys I've busted, except for the little habit of taking other people's property, they're some of the most honorable people I've ever met."

"And if Luther saw this woman killed, I'm telling you he would've found some way to deliver the guy to the cops. He wouldn't have let it go. He just wouldn't!" Jack stared grimly out the window.

"Except?"

Jack looked over at him. "Except for a helluva good reason. Like maybe he knew the person or knew *of* him."

"You mean the kind of person people would have a hard time believing could do something like that so Luther figures why even bother?"

"There's more to it than that, Seth." Jack turned the corner and pulled up next to the YMCA. "I've never seen Luther scared before this all happened. And he's scared now. Terrified, in fact. He's resigned himself to take the rap for the whole thing and I don't know why. I mean he left the country for godsakes."

"And came back."

"Right, which I still cannot figure out. You have the date by the way?"

Frank flipped opened his notebook and told him the date.

"So what the hell happened after Christine Sullivan was killed and before then to get him to come back?"

Frank shook his head. "Could be anything."

"No, it was one thing and if we could find out what that was, we might be able to figure this whole thing out."

Frank put away his notebook, absently rubbed his hand across the dashboard.

Jack put the car in park and leaned back in his seat.

"And he's not just scared for himself. Somehow he's scared for Kate too."

Frank looked puzzled. "You think somebody threatened Kate?"

Jack shook his head. "No. She would've told me. I

think someone got the message to Luther that he either keeps quiet or else."

"You think the same people who tried to take him out?"

"Maybe. I don't know."

Frank made a fist with both hands and looked out the car window. He took a deep breath and looked back at Jack. "Look, you've got to get Luther to talk. If he can deliver us whoever did Christine Sullivan, I'll recommend probation and community service in return for his cooperation; he won't do any time. Hell, Sullivan would probably let him keep what he stole if we could nail the guy."

"Recommend?"

"Let's put it this way, I'll cram it down Gorelick's throat. Good enough?" Frank extended his hand.

Jack slowly took it, eyeing the policeman steadily. "Good enough."

Frank got out of the car and then poked his head back in. "For what it's worth, as far as I'm concerned, tonight never happened and everything you've said stays with me, no exceptions. Not even on the witness stand. I mean it."

"Thanks, Seth."

Seth Frank walked slowly back to his car as the Lexus pulled down the street, turned the corner and was gone.

He understood exactly the kind of guy Luther Whitney was. So what the hell could scare that kind of a guy so badly?

TWENTY-TWO

It was seven-thirty in the morning when Jack pulled into the parking lot of the Middleton police station. The morning had broken clear but bitterly cold. Amid a number of snow-covered police cars was a black sedan with a cold hood that told him Seth Frank was an early riser.

Luther looked different today; the orange prison clothes had been replaced with a brown two-piece suit, and his striped tie was conservative and professional. He could be an insurance salesman or a senior partner in a law firm, with his thick gray hair neatly trimmed, and the remnants of his island tan. Some defense attorneys saved the nice citizen clothes for the actual trial where the jury could see that the accused wasn't such a bad guy, just misunderstood. But Jack was going to insist on the suit throughout. It wasn't merely game playing; it was Jack's firm conviction that Luther didn't deserve to be paraded around in neon orange. He might be a criminal, but he wasn't the kind of criminal where if you got too close you might get a shiv in your ribs or find a set of criminally insane teeth on your throat. Those guys deserved to wear the orange if only to make sure you always knew where they were in proximity to everyone else.

Jack didn't bother to open his briefcase this time. The routine was familiar. The charges against Luther would be read to him. The judge would ask Luther if he understood the charges and then Jack would enter

375

the plea. Then the judge would take them through the dog-and-pony show to determine if Luther understood what a plea of not guilty entailed, and whether Luther was satisfied with his legal representation. The only problem was Jack had a nagging feeling that Luther might tell him to go to hell right in front of the judge and plead himself guilty. That was not unprecedented. And who knew? The damn judge might just accept it. But the judge would most likely follow the book closely, since, in a capital murder case, any screw-up along the way could be grounds for appeal. And death penalty appeals tended to last forever anyway. Jack would just have to take his chances.

With any luck the entire proceeding would take all of five minutes. Then a trial date would be set and the real fun would begin.

Since the commonwealth had gotten an indictment against him, Luther wasn't entitled to a preliminary hearing. Not that having one would have done Jack any good, but he would've gotten a quick look at the commonwealth's case and a crack at some of their witnesses on cross although the circuit court judges were usually diligent in not letting defense counsel use the prelim as a fishing expedition.

He also could have waived the arraignment, but Jack's thinking was to let them work for everything. And he wanted Luther in open court, for all to see, and he wanted that not guilty plea heard loud and clear. And then he was going to hit Gorelick with a change of venue motion and get this case the hell out of Middleton County. With any luck Gorelick would get bumped for a new ACA and Mr. Future Attorney General could stew on that disappointment for a few decades. Then Jack was going to make Luther talk. Kate would be protected. Luther would spill his story and then the deal of the century would be cut.

Jack looked at Luther. "You look good."

Luther's mouth curled up more in a smirk than a smile.

"Kate would like to see you before the arraignment."

The response shot out of Luther's mouth. "No!"

"Why not? My God, Luther, you've wanted a relationship with her forever and now that she's finally willing to come around, you clam up. Damn, I don't understand you sometimes."

"I don't want her anywhere near me."

"Look, she's sorry about what she did. It tore her up. I'm telling you."

Luther swiveled his head around. "She thinks I'm mad at her?"

Jack sat down. For the first time he finally had Luther's attention. He should have tried this before.

"Of course she does. Why else won't you see her?"

Luther looked down at the plain, wooden table and shook his head in disgust.

"Tell her I'm not mad at her. She did the right thing. You tell her that."

"Why don't *you* tell her?"

Luther abruptly stood up and walked around the room. He stopped in front of Jack.

"This place has a lot of eyes, you hear me? You understand me? Somebody sees her in here with me, then somebody might think she knows something she doesn't. And believe me, that is not good."

"Who are you talking about?"

Luther sat back down. "Just tell her what I said. Tell her I love her and I always have and always will. You tell her that, Jack. No matter what."

"So you're saying this somebody might think you told me something even if you haven't?"

"I told you not to take this case, Jack, but you wouldn't listen."

Jack shrugged, flipped open his briefcase and took out a copy of the *Post*. "Check out the lead story."

Luther glanced down at the front page. Then he angrily threw the paper against the wall. "Fucking bastard! Fucking bastard!" The words exploded out of the old man's mouth.

The door to the room flew open and a beefy guard poked his head in, one hand on his standard issue. Jack motioned that it was all right and the guy slowly backed out, his eyes glued on Luther.

Jack went over and picked up the paper. The cover story had a photo of Luther taken outside the police station. The headline was in bold three-inch letters normally reserved for when the 'Skins won the Super Bowl: SULLIVAN MURDER SUSPECT ARRAIGNMENT TODAY. Jack scanned the rest of the front page. More killings in the former Soviet Union as ethnic cleansing continued. The Defense Department was preparing for another budget hit. Jack's eyes glanced over but did not really register on President Alan Richmond announcing his intent to take another stab at welfare reform and a picture of him at a children's center in impoverished Southeast D.C. that made for a nice photo op.

The smiling face had hit Luther right between the temples. Holding poor black babies for all the world to see. Fucking, lying asshole. The fist hit Christine Sullivan again and again and again. Blood flew into the air. The hands wrapped around her neck like a wily serpent, crushing life without a thought. Stealing life, that's what he had done. Kissing babies and killing women.

"Luther? Luther?" Jack gently laid a hand on Luther's shoulder. The old man's frame was quaking like an engine in dire need of a tune-up, threatening to fly apart, no longer able to confine itself within a quickly eroding shell. For a terrible moment Jack wondered if Luther had killed the woman, if his old friend had perhaps gone over the edge. His fears were dispelled when Luther turned and looked at him. The calm had returned, the eyes were clear and focused once more.

"Just tell Kate what I said, Jack. And let's go get this over with."

The Middleton Courthouse had long been the centerpiece of the county. A hundred and ninety-five years old, it had survived the British in the War of 1812 and the Yankees and the Confederates in the War of Northern Aggression or the Civil War depending on what side of the Mason-Dixon the person you asked hailed from. A costly renovation in 1947 had given it new life and the good townspeople expected it to be around for their great-grandchildren to enjoy and occasionally go inside, hopefully for nothing more than a traffic ticket or a marriage license.

Where before it had stood alone at the end of the two-lane road that made up Middleton's business district, it now shared space with antique shops, restaurants, a grocery market, a huge bed-and-breakfast and a service station that was all-brick in keeping with the architectural tradition of the area. Huddled within walking distance was a row of offices where the shingles of many a respected county lawyer hung with simple grace.

Normally quiet except on Friday morning, which was motions day for the civil and criminal docket, the Middleton Courthouse now held a scene that would have caused the town's forefathers to do somersaults in their final resting places. At first glance one could almost imagine that the Rebels and the Union Blue had returned to settle, once and for all, the score.

Six television trucks with thick call letters

emblazoned on their white sides held forth directly in front of the courthouse steps. Their broadcast masts were already rising skyward. Crowds ten-deep pushed and prodded against the wall of sheriffs reinforced by grim members of the Virginia State Police who stared silently at the mass of reporters pushing pads, microphones and pens into their faces.

Fortunately, the courthouse had a side entrance, which was at this moment surrounded by a semicircle of police, riot guns and shields front and center, daring anyone to come near. The van carrying Luther would come here. Unfortunately, the courthouse did not have an inside garage. But the police still felt they had matters under control. Luther would only be exposed for a few seconds at most.

Across the street, rifle-toting police officers patrolled the sidewalks, eyes sweeping up and down, looking for the glint of metal, an open window that shouldn't be.

Jack looked out the small window of the courtroom that overlooked the street. The room was as large as an auditorium with a hand-carved bench that rose a full eight feet high and swept more than fifteen feet from end to end. The American and Virginia flags stood at attention on either side of the bench. A lone bailiff sat at a small table in front of the bench, a tug boat before the ocean liner.

Jack checked his watch, eyed the security forces in place, then looked at the crush of media. Reporters were a defense attorney's best friends or worst nightmare. A lot depended on what the reporters thought about a particular defendant and about a particular crime. A good reporter will cry loud and hard about his or her objectivity on a story at the same time they're trashing your client in the latest edition, long before any verdict is in. Women journalists tended to go easier on defendants accused of rape, as they tried to avoid even the appearance of gender-bias. For similar reasons, the men seemed to bend over backward for battered women who had finally struck back. Luther would have no such luck. Ex-cons who murder rich, young women would receive the battering rams of all wordsmiths involved, regardless of sex.

Jack had already received a dozen phone calls from Los Angeles-based production companies clamoring for Luther's story. Before the guy had even entered a plea. They wanted his story and would pay for it. Pay well. Maybe Jack should tell them yes, come on in, but only on one condition. If he tells you anything you have to let me in on it, 'cause right now man, I've got nothing. Zip.

He looked across the street. The armed guards gave him some comfort. Although there had been police everywhere last time and the shot was still fired. At least this time the police were forewarned. They had things pretty much under control. But they had not counted on one thing, and that one thing was now coming down the street.

Jack swung his head around as he watched the army of reporters and plain curious turn en masse and race to the motorcade. At first Jack thought it must be Walter Sullivan, until he saw the police motor-cyclists followed by the Secret Service vans and finally the twin American flags on the limo.

The army this man had brought with him dwarfed the one that was preparing to receive Luther Whitney.

He watched as Richmond exited the vehicle. Behind him stepped the agent he had talked to earlier. Burton. That was the guy's name. One tough, serious dude. His eyes swept the area like a radar beam. His hand within inches of the man, ready to pull him down in an instant. The Secret Service vans parked across the street. One pulled into an alleyway across from the courthouse and then Jack looked back at the President.

An impromptu podium was set up and Richmond began his own little news conference as cameras clicked and half a hundred grown adults with journalism degrees tried to push and pull past their neighbor. A few ordinary and saner citizens were hovering in the back, two with video cameras recording what to them was certainly a special moment.

Jack turned to find the bailiff, a granite wall of a black man, beside him.

"Been here twenty-seven years and never had the man out here before. Now he's been here twice in the same year. Go figure."

Jack smiled at him. "Well, if your friend had invested ten mil in your campaign you might be out here too."

"Lot of big boys against you."

"That's okay, I brought a big bat with me . . ."

"Samuel, Samuel Long."

"Jack Graham, Samuel."

"You gonna need it, Jack, hope you loaded it with lead."

"So what do you think, Samuel? My guy gonna get a fair shake in here?"

"You ask me that question two, three years ago I'd say yeah, damn straight you will. Yes sir." He looked out at the crush of people. "You ask me today, I say I don't know. I don't care what court you're in. Supreme Court, traffic court. Things are changing, man. Not just the courts either. Everything. Everybody. Whole goddamn world's changing and I just don't know anymore."

They both looked out the window again.

The door to the courtroom opened and Kate

entered. Instinctively, Jack turned around and looked at her. No courtroom attire today, she had on a black pleated skirt that tapered at the waist where a thin black belt encircled her. The blouse was simple and buttoned to the neck. Her hair was brushed back off her forehead and hung to her shoulders. Her cheeks were rosy from the bitter cold, a coat was draped over her arm.

They sat together at the counsel table. Samuel discreetly disappeared.

"It's almost time, Kate."

"I know."

"Listen, Kate, like I told you on the phone, it's not that he doesn't want to see you, he's afraid. He's afraid for you. The man loves you more than anything."

"Jack, if he doesn't start talking, you know what's going to happen."

"Maybe, but I've got some leads to go on. The state's case isn't as foolproof as everyone seems to think."

"How do you know that?"

"Trust me on that one. Did you see the President outside?"

"How could you miss him? It's okay with me though. No one paid a bit of attention to me walking in."

"He definitely relegates everybody else to wallflowers."

"Is he here yet?"

"Soon."

Kate opened her purse and fumbled for some gum. Jack smiled and pushed her quivering fingers out of the way and pulled the pack out for her.

"Couldn't I at least talk to him on the phone?"

"I'll see what I can do."

They both sat back and waited. Jack's hand slipped

over Kate's and they both looked up at the massive bench where in a few short minutes it would start. But for now they just waited. Together.

The white van rounded the corner, passed the semi-circle of police officers and came to a stop within a few feet of the side door. Seth Frank pulled up directly behind the van and got out, radio in hand. Two officers alighted from the van, scanned the area. This was good. The entire crowd was in the front gawking at the President. The officer in charge turned and nodded to another man inside the van. A few seconds later Luther Whitney, ankles and hands manacled, and his suit covered by a dark trench coat, emerged. His feet touched the ground and, with an officer in front and back, he started to make his way to the courthouse.

That's when the crowd hit the corner. They were following the President, who was purposefully striding down the sidewalk to where his limo was parked. As he passed the side of the courthouse, he looked up. As if sensing his presence, Luther, whose eyes had been pressed to the ground, also looked up. Their eyes locked for one terrible instant. The words escaped Luther's lips before he knew what was happening.

"Fucking bastard." It was said quietly, but each officer heard something, because they looked around as the President walked by a mere hundred feet away. They were surprised. And then their thoughts focused on one thing only.

Luther's knees buckled. At first both officers thought he was intentionally making their job harder until they saw the blood streaming down the side of his face. One of them shouted an expletive and grabbed Luther's arm. The other pulled his gun and swung it in wide arcs at where he thought the shot

384

had come from. The events that happened in the next few minutes seemed a blur to most people who were there. The sound of the shot was not entirely clear over the screams of the crowds. The Secret Service agents heard it, though. Burton had Richmond on the ground in a second. Twenty dark suits carrying automatic weapons made a human cocoon around them.

Seth Frank watched as the Secret Service van tore out of the alley and blocked off the now hysterical crowd from the President. One agent emerged wielding a machine gun and scanned the street, barking into a radio.

Frank directed his men to cover every square inch of the area; every intersection was cordoned off and a building-by-building search would commence. Truckloads of officers would arrive shortly, but somehow Frank knew it was too late.

In another second Frank was beside Luther. He looked on in disbelief as the blood drenched the snow, warming it into a sickening pool of crimson. An ambulance was called and would be there in minutes. But Frank also knew it was too late for ambulances. Luther's face had already gone white, the eyes stared blank, the fingers were curled tight. Luther Whitney had two new holes in his head and the damn round had put a hole in the van after exiting the man. Someone was taking no chances.

Frank closed the dead man's eyes and then looked around. The President was up and being hustled into his limo. In a few seconds the limo and the vans were gone. Reporters started to flock to the murder scene, but Frank motioned to his men and the journalists were met by a brick wall of infuriated and embarrassed police officers who brandished their batons and hoped somebody tried something.

Seth Frank looked down at the body. He took off

385

his jacket despite the cold and laid it across Luther's torso and face.

Jack had made it to the window a few seconds after the screams started. His pulse was off the chart and his forehead was suddenly drenched in sweat.

"Stay here, Kate." He looked at her. She was frozen, her face having already registered a fact that Jack hoped beyond hope wasn't true.

Samuel had emerged from the inner sanctum.

"What the hell's going on?"

"Samuel, keep an eye on her, please."

Samuel nodded and Jack hit the door running.

Outside there were more men with guns than Jack had ever seen outside of a Hollywood war flick. He ran to the side of the courthouse and was about to have his head cracked open by a two-hundred-and-fifty-pound baton-wielding trooper when Frank's voice boomed out.

Jack warily approached. Each of his steps in the tight-packed snow seemed to take a month. All eyes seemed to be on him. The crumpled figure under the coat. The blood soaking the once pristine snowfall. The anguished and at the same time disgusted look on Detective Seth Frank's features. He would remember each of these things for many sleepless nights, perhaps for the rest of his life.

When he finally crouched down beside his friend, he started to draw back the jacket but then stopped. He turned around and looked back from where he had just come. The sea of reporters had parted. Even the wall of cops had hinged back just enough to let her through.

Kate stood there for a long minute, no coat on, shivering in the wind that swept down through the funnel-like space between the buildings. She looked straight ahead, her eyes so focused they seemed to register on nothing and everything simultaneously.

386

Jack started to rise, to go to her, but his legs did not have the strength. Just a few minutes ago, juiced and prepared to do battle, mad as hell at his uncooperative client, now every scintilla of energy had been stripped from his being.

With Frank's help he rose on unsteady legs and went to her. For once in their lives, nosy reporters did not attempt to ask questions. Photographers seemingly forgot to take their requisite shots. As Kate knelt beside her father and gently laid her hand on his still shoulder, the only sounds were the wind and the distant whine of the approaching ambulance. For a couple of minutes the world had stopped right outside the Middleton County Courthouse.

As the limo whisked him back to town, Alan Richmond smoothed down his tie and poured a club soda. His thoughts ventured to the headlines that would drown the upcoming papers. The major news shows would be salivating for him, and he would milk it. He would continue on his normal schedule for the day. The rock-solid President. Shots fired around him and he doesn't flinch, goes on about the business of running the country, of *leading* the people. He could envision the polls. A good ten points at least. And it had all been too easy. When was he ever going to feel a real challenge?

Bill Burton looked over at the man as the limo neared the D.C. line. Luther Whitney had just caught the business end of the most deadly piece of ammo Collin could find to chamber his rifle with, and this guy was calmly sipping soda water. Burton felt sick to his stomach. And it still wasn't over. He could never in his wildest dreams put any of this behind him, but perhaps he could live the rest of his life as a free man. A man whose children respected him, even if he no longer respected himself.

As he continued to look at the President it occurred to Burton that the sonofabitch was proud of himself. He had seen such calmness before amidst extreme and calculated violence. No remorse because a human being's existence had just been sacrificed. Instead, a rush of euphoria. Of triumph. Burton thought back to the marks on Christine Sullivan's neck. To the busted jaw. To the ominous sounds he had heard from behind other bedroom doors. The Man of the People.

Burton thought back to the meeting with Richmond where he had filled in his boss on all the facts. Other than seeing Russell squirm it had not been a pleasant experience.

Richmond had stared at each of them. Burton and Russell sat side by side. Collin hovered next to the door. They were clustered in the First Family's private quarters. A component of the White House the eager public was never permitted to see. The rest of the First Family was on a brief holiday visiting relatives. It was best that way. The most important member of that family was not in a pleasant mood.

The President was, finally, fully cognizant of the facts, the most remarkable of which had been a letter opener bearing some particularly incriminating evidence, and which had ended up in the hands of their intrepid and felonious eyewitness. The blood had almost frozen in the President's veins when Burton had told him. As the words fell out of the agent's mouth, the President had swiveled his head in Russell's direction.

When Collin recounted Russell's instructions not to wipe the blade and handle clean, the President had stood up and hovered over his Chief of Staff, who had pushed herself so far back in her chair that she seemed to have become part of the fabric. His stare was crushing. She finally covered her eyes with her hand. The underarms of her blouse were soaked in perspiration. Her throat was devoid of saliva.

Richmond had sat back down and slowly crunched the ice from his cocktail and finally turned his gaze out the window. He was still dressed in a monkey suit from yet another engagement but the tie was undone. He was still looking out to nowhere when he spoke.

"How long, Burton?"

Burton stopped looking at the floor. "Who knows? Maybe forever."

"You know better than that. I want your professional assessment."

"Sooner rather than later. He's got a lawyer now. Somehow, some way the guy's gonna pop to somebody."

"Do we have any idea where 'it' is?"

Burton rubbed his hands together uneasily. "No, sir. The police searched his house, his car. If they had found the letter opener, I would've heard."

"But they know it's missing from Sullivan's house?"

Burton nodded. "The police realize it has significance. If it turns up they'll know what to do with it."

The President stood up and played his fingers across a particularly ugly gothic crystal collection of his wife's that was displayed on one of the tables. Next to them were photos of his family. He never actually registered their countenances. All he saw in their faces were the flames of his administration. His face seemed to redden before the invisible conflagration. History was in jeopardy of being rewritten and all because of a little smart bimbo and an overly ambitious and incredibly stupid Chief of Staff.

"Any idea who Sullivan employed?"

Burton again answered. Russell was no longer an equal. Collin was there only to be told what to do.

389

"Could be one of twenty or thirty high-priced hit men. Whoever it is he's long gone by now."

"But you've laid the mental trail with our friend the detective?"

"He knows that you 'innocently' told Walter Sullivan where and when. The guy's plenty smart enough to follow up on that."

The President abruptly picked up one of the crystal pieces and hurled it against the wall where it shattered, sending fragments all across the room; his face contorted into a mass of hate and anger that made even Burton shudder. "Dammit, if he hadn't missed, it would've been perfect."

Russell looked at the tiny shards of crystal on the carpet. That was her life. All those years of education, toiling, hundred-hour weeks. For this.

"The police are going to follow up with Sullivan. I made sure the detective on the case understood Sullivan's possible involvement." Burton continued, "But even though he's the most likely suspect, he'll deny everything. They won't be able to prove anything. I'm not sure where that gets us, sir."

Richmond strolled around the room. He could've been preparing for a speech or getting ready to shake hands with a troop of Boy Scouts from a Midwestern state. He was actually contemplating how to murder someone in a way that absolutely no blame, not even a hint of suspicion, would ever fall his way.

"What if he tried again? And this time succeeded."

Burton looked puzzled. "How do we control what Sullivan does?"

"By doing it ourselves."

No one said anything for a couple of minutes. Russell glanced incredulously at her boss. Her entire life had just gone straight to hell and now she was compelled to participate in a conspiracy to commit murder. She had felt emotionally numb since all of

390

this had started. She had been absolutely certain her situation could not get any worse. And she had been absolutely wrong about that.

Finally Burton ventured an analysis. "I'm not sure the police would believe Sullivan would be that crazy. He's gotta know they're on to him, but can't prove anything. If we pop Whitney, I'm not sure they'd look Sullivan's way."

The President stopped strolling. He stood directly in front of Burton. "So let the police reach that conclusion themselves, if they ever do."

The reality was that Richmond no longer needed Walter Sullivan to regain the White House. Perhaps more important, this was a perfect way to rid himself of the obligation to back Sullivan's Ukraine deal over Russia; a decision that was growing into more and more of a potential liability. If Sullivan were even remotely implicated in the death of his wife's killer, he would be doing no more global deals. Richmond's support would be discreetly withdrawn. Everyone who counted would understand that silent retreat.

"Alan, you want to set Sullivan up for a murder?" These were the first words Russell had spoken. Her face betrayed her complete astonishment.

He looked at her, with unconcealed contempt in his eyes.

"Alan, think about what you're saying. This is Walter Sullivan, this is not some two-bit crook no one gives a damn about."

Richmond smiled. Her stupidity amused him. She had seemed so bright, so incredibly capable when he first brought her on board. He had been wrong.

The President did some rough calculations. At best Sullivan had perhaps a twenty percent chance of going down for the killing. Given similar circumstances, Richmond would take those odds. Sullivan

391

was a big boy, he could take care of himself. And if he faltered? Well, that was why they had prisons. He looked at Burton.

"Burton, do *you* understand?"

Burton didn't answer.

The President said sharply, "You were certainly prepared to kill the man before, Burton. As far as I can determine, the stakes haven't changed. In fact they're probably higher. For *all* of us. Do you understand, Burton?" Richmond paused for a moment, then repeated his question.

Burton finally looked up and said quietly, "I understand."

For the next two hours they laid their plans.

As the two Secret Service agents and Russell rose to leave, the President looked at her. "So tell me, Gloria, what happened to the money?"

Russell looked straight at him. "It was donated, anonymously, to the American Red Cross. I understand it was one of their biggest single contributions ever."

The door closed and the President had smiled. *Nice parting shot. Enjoy it, Luther Whitney. Enjoy it while you can, you insignificant little nothing.*

392

TWENTY-THREE

Walter Sullivan settled into his chair with a book but never opened it. His mind wandered back. Back to events that seemed more ethereal, more wholly unconnected to his person than anything else that had ever happened in his life. He had hired a man to kill. To kill someone who stood accused of murdering his wife. The job had been botched. A fact for which Sullivan was quietly thankful. For his grief had subsided enough to where he knew what he had attempted to do was wrong. A civilized society must follow certain procedures unless it were to become uncivilized. And no matter how painful it would be to him, he was a civilized man. He would follow the rules.

It was then that he looked down at the newspaper. Many days old now, its contents continued to beat incessantly into his head. The thick, dark headlines shone back at him on the white background of the page. As he turned his attention to it, distant suspicions in his mind were starting to crystallize. Walter Sullivan was not only a billionaire, he possessed a brilliant and perceptive mind. One that saw every detail along with every landscape.

Luther Whitney was dead. The police had no suspects. Sullivan had checked the obvious solution. McCarty had been in Hong Kong on the day in question. Sullivan's last directive to the man had indeed been heeded. Walter Sullivan had called off his hunt. But someone else had taken up the chase in his place.

And Walter Sullivan was the only person who knew that for a fact, other than his bungling assassin.

Sullivan looked at his old timepiece. It was barely seven in the morning and he had been up for four hours already. The twenty-four hours in a day meant little to him anymore. The older he grew, the less important became the parameters of time. Four o'clock in the morning could find him wide awake on a plane over the Pacific while two in the afternoon might be the halfway point in his sleep for the day.

There were many facts that he was sifting through, and his mind worked rapidly. A CAT scan done at his last physical evidenced a brain with the youth and vigor of a twenty-year-old. And that splendid mind was now working toward the few undeniable facts that were leading its owner to a conclusion that would amaze even him.

He picked up the phone on his desk and looked around the highly polished cherry paneling of his study as he dialed the number.

In a moment he had been put through to Seth Frank. Unimpressed with the man early on, Sullivan had grudgingly given him his due with the arrest of Luther Whitney. But now?

"Yes sir, Mr. Sullivan, what can I do for you?"

Sullivan cleared his throat. His voice had a humble note to it that was as far from his customary tone as was possible. Even Frank picked up on it.

"I had a question regarding the information I had given you earlier about Christy, um, Christine's sudden departure on the way to the airport for our trip to the estate in Barbados."

Frank sat up in his chair. "Did you remember something else?"

"Actually I wanted to verify whether I had given

you any reason for her not going on the trip."

"I'm afraid I don't understand."

"Well, I suppose my age is catching up with me. My bones aren't the only thing deteriorating I'm afraid, though I don't care to admit it to myself much less anyone else, Lieutenant. More to the point I thought I had told you she had taken ill and had to return home. I mean I *thought* that's what I had told you in any event."

Seth took a moment to pull his file, although he was certain of the answer. "You said she didn't give a reason, Mr. Sullivan. Just said she wasn't going, and you didn't push it."

"Ah. Well, I guess that settles that. Thank you, Lieutenant."

Frank stood up. One hand lifted a cup of coffee and then put it back down. "Wait a minute, Mr. Sullivan. Why would you think you had told me that your wife was sick? Was she sick?"

Sullivan paused before answering. "Actually no, Lieutenant Frank. She was remarkably healthy. To answer your question, I believe I thought I had told you differently because, to tell you the truth, aside from my occasional memory lapses, I think I've spent these last two months trying to convince myself that Christine staying behind was for some reason. Any reason, I guess."

"Sir?"

"To, in my own mind, justify what happened to her. To not let it be just a damn coincidence. I don't believe in fate, Lieutenant. For me, everything has a purpose. I suppose I wanted to convince myself that Christine's staying behind did too."

"Oh."

"I apologize if an old man's foolishness has caused you any unnecessary perplexity."

"Not at all, Mr. Sullivan."

When Frank hung up the phone he ended up staring at the wall for a good five minutes. Now what the hell had all that been about?

Following up on Bill Burton's suggestion, Frank had made discreet inquiries into Sullivan having possibly hired a contract killer to make sure his wife's presumed killer never stood trial. Those inquiries were going slow; one had to tread cautiously in these types of waters. Frank had a career to think about, a family to support, and men like Walter Sullivan had an army of very influential friends in government who could make the detective's professional life miserable.

The day after the slug had ended Luther Whitney's life, Seth Frank had made immediate inquiries as to Sullivan's whereabouts at the time although Frank was under no delusions that the old man had pulled the trigger on the cannon that had propelled Luther Whitney into the hereafter. But murder for hire was a particularly wicked deed, and although perhaps the detective could understand the billionaire's motivation, the fact was he had probably gunned down the wrong guy. This latest conversation with Sullivan left him with even more questions and no new answers.

Seth Frank sat down and wondered briefly if this nightmare of a case would ever leave his watch.

A half hour later Sullivan placed a call to a local television station of which he happened to own a controlling interest. His request was simple and to the point. In an hour a package was delivered to his front door. After one of the staff handed him the square box he ushered her out, shut and locked the door to the room he was in, and pressed a small lever on a portion of the wall. The small panel slid down silently, revealing a very sophisticated audiocassette tape deck. Behind most of this wall rested a cutting-edge home theater system that Christine Sullivan had seen in a magazine one day and simply had to have, although her tastes in video entertainment ventured from pornography to soap opera, neither of which in any way taxed the electronic muscle of this monolithic system.

Sullivan carefully unwrapped the audiocassette and placed it inside the tape deck; the door automatically closed and the tape began to play. Sullivan listened for a few moments. When he heard the words, no emotion was revealed on his intricate features. He had expected to hear what he had. He had outright lied to the detective. His memory was excellent. If only his sight were half as good. For he had indeed been a blind idiot to this reality. The emotion that finally penetrated the inscrutable line of his mouth and the deep gray of his introspective eyes was anger. Anger like he had not felt in a long time. Not even at Christy's death. A fury that would only be relieved through action. And Sullivan firmly believed that your first salvo should be your last because that meant that either you got them, or they got you, and he was not in the habit of losing.

The funeral was conducted in humble surroundings and with only three people other than the priest in attendance. It had taken the utmost secrecy to avoid the obvious assaults by the armies of journalists. Luther's casket was closed. The remains of violent trauma to the head was not the lasting impression loved ones typically wanted to carry away with them.

Neither the background of the deceased nor the means of his demise mattered the slightest to the man of God, and the service was appropriately reverent. The drive to the nearby cemetery was short as was the procession. Jack and Kate drove over together; behind them was Seth Frank. He had sat in the back of the church, awkward and uncomfortable. Jack had shaken his hand; Kate had refused to acknowledge him.

Jack leaned against his car and watched Kate as she sat in the fold-up metal chair next to the earthen pit that had just accepted her father. Jack looked around. This cemetery was not home to grandiose monuments of tribute. It was rare to see a grave marker sticking up, most were the in-the-dirt variety; a dark rectangle with its owner's name, dates of entry and exit from the living. A few said "in loving memory," most ventured no parting remarks.

Jack looked back at Kate and he saw Seth Frank start toward her, then the detective apparently thought better of his decision and made his way quietly over to the Lexus.

Frank took off his sunglasses. "Nice service."

Jack shrugged. "Nothing's really nice about getting killed." Though miles away from Kate's position on the issue, he had not entirely forgiven Frank for allowing Luther Whitney to die like that.

Frank fell silent, studied the finish on the sedan, drew out a cigarette, then changed his mind. He stuck his hands in his pockets and stared off.

He had attended Luther Whitney's autopsy. The transient cavitation had been immense. The shock waves had dissipated radially out from the bullet track to such an extent that fully half the man's brain had literally disintegrated. And it was no small wonder. The slug they'd dug out of the seat of the police van was an eye-popper. A .460 Magnum round. The Medical Examiner had told Frank that type of ammo was often used for sports hunting, big game in particular. And it was no wonder, since the round had slammed into Whitney with stopping power

398

equal to over eight thousand pounds of energy. It was like someone had dropped a plane on the poor guy. Big game hunting. Frank shook his head wearily. And it had happened on his watch, right in front of him in fact. He would never forget that.

Frank looked over the green expanse of the final resting place for over twenty thousand dearly departed. Jack leaned back against the car and followed Frank's gaze.

"So any leads?"

The detective dug a toe in the dirt. "A few. None of them really going anywhere."

They both straightened up as Kate rose, laid a small arrangement of flowers on the mound of dirt, and then stood, staring off. The wind had died down, and although cold, the sun was bright and warming.

Jack buttoned his coat up. "So what now? Case closed? Nobody would blame you."

Frank smiled, decided he'd have that smoke after all. "Not by a fucking long shot, chief."

"So what are you gonna do?"

Kate turned and started to walk toward the car. Seth Frank put his hat back on, pulled out his car keys.

"Simple, find me a murderer."

"Kate, I know how you feel, but you have to believe me. He didn't blame you for anything. None of this was your fault. Like you said, you were pushed into the middle involuntarily. You didn't ask for any of this. Luther understood that."

They were in Jack's car driving back into the city. The sun was eye level and dropping perceptibly with each mile. They had sat in his car at the cemetery for almost two hours because she didn't want to leave. As though if she waited long enough he would climb out of his grave and join them.

She cracked the window and a narrow stream of air engulfed the interior, dispelling the new-car smell with the thick moistness that heralded another storm.

"Detective Frank hasn't given up on the case, Kate. He's still looking for Luther's killer."

She finally looked at him. "I really don't care what he says he's going to do." She touched her nose, which was red and swollen and hurt like hell.

"Come on, Kate. It's not like the guy wanted Luther to get shot."

"Oh really? A case full of holes that gets blown apart at trial leaving everyone involved, including the detective in charge, looking like complete idiots. Instead you have a corpse, and a closed case. Now tell me again what the master detective wants?"

Jack stopped for a red light and slumped back in his seat. He knew that Frank was shooting straight with him, but there was no way in hell he was going to convince Kate of that fact.

The light changed and he moved through traffic. He checked his watch. He had to get back to the office, assuming he had an office to go back to.

"Kate, I don't think you should be alone right now. How about I crash at your place for a few nights? You brew the coffee in the morning and I'll take care of the dinners. Deal?"

He had expected an immediate and negative response and had already prepared his rejoinder.

"Are you sure?"

Jack looked over at her, found wide, puffy eyes on him. Every nerve in her body seemed ready to scream. As he walked himself through the paces of what was, to both of them, a tragedy, he suddenly realized that he was still totally oblivious to the enormity of the pain and guilt she was experiencing. It stunned him, even more than the sound of the shot as he sat holding her hand. Knowing before their

400

fingers ever parted that Luther was dead.

"I'm sure."

That night he had just settled himself on the couch. The blanket was drawn up to his neck, his bulwark against the draft that hit him chest high from an invisible crevice in the window across from him. Then he heard a door squeak and she walked out of her bedroom. She wore the same robe as before, her hair drawn up tightly in a bun. Her face looked fresh and clean; only a slight red sheen hovering around her cheeks hinted at the internal trauma.

"Do you need anything?"

"I'm fine. This couch is a lot more comfortable than I thought it would be. I've still got the same one from our apartment in Charlottesville. I don't even think it has any springs left. I think they all retired."

She didn't smile, but she did sit down next to him. When they had lived together she had taken a bath every night. Coming to bed she had smelled so good it had nearly driven him mad. Like the breath of a newborn, there was absolutely nothing imperfect about it. And she had played dumb for a while until he lay exhausted on top of her and she would smile a decidedly wicked little smile and stroke him and he would ruminate for several minutes on how it was so crystal-clear to him that women ruled the world.

He found his baser instincts creeping firmly ahead as she leaned her head against his shoulder. But her exhausted manner, her total apathy, swiftly quelled his secular inclinations and left him feeling more than a little guilty.

"I'm not sure I'm going to be very good company."

Had she sensed what he was feeling? How could she? Her mind, everything about her, must be a million miles away from this spot.

"Being entertained was not part of the deal. I can look after myself, Kate."

"I really appreciate your doing this."

"I can't think of anything more important."

She squeezed his hand. As she rose to go the flap on her robe came undone exposing more than just her long, slender legs and he was glad she would be in another room that night. His ruminations until the early-morning hours ran the gamut from visions of white knights with large dark spots disfiguring their pristine armor to idealistic lawyers who slept miserably alone.

On the third night he had settled in again on the couch. And, as before, she came out of her bedroom; the slight squeak made him lay down the magazine he was reading. But this time she did not go to the couch. He finally craned his neck around and found her watching him. She did not look apathetic tonight. And tonight she was not wearing the robe. She turned and went back inside her bedroom. The door stayed open.

For a moment he did nothing. Then he rose, went to the door and peered in. Through the darkness he could make out her form on the bed. The sheet was at the foot of the bed. The contours of her body, once as familiar to him as his own, confronted him. She looked at him. He could just make out the ovals of her eyes as they focused on him. She did not put out her hand for him; he recalled that she had never done that.

"Are you sure about this?" He felt compelled to ask it. He wanted no hurt feelings in the morning, no crushed, confused emotions.

For an answer she rose and pulled him to the bed. The mattress was firm, and warm where she had been. In another moment he was as naked as she. He instinctively traced the half-moon, moved his hand around the crooked mouth, which now touched his. Her eyes were open and this time, and it had been a

402

long time, there were no tears, no swelling, just the look he had grown so used to, expected to have around forever. He slowly put his arms around her.

The home of Walter Sullivan had seen visiting dignitaries of incredibly high rank. But tonight was special even compared to past events.

Alan Richmond raised his glass of wine and gave a brief but eloquent toast to his host as the four other carefully selected couples clinked their glasses. The First Lady, radiant in a simple, black dress, ash blonde hair framing a sculpted face that had worn remarkably well over the years and made for delightful photo ops, smiled at the billionaire. Accustomed as she was to being surrounded by wealth and brains and refinement, she, like most people, was still in awe of Walter Sullivan and men like him, if only for their rarity on the planet.

Technically still in mourning, Sullivan was in a particularly gregarious mood. Over imported coffee in the spacious library the conversation ventured from global business opportunities, the latest maneuvering of the Federal Reserve Board, the 'Skins' chances against the Forty-niners that Sunday, to the election the following year. There were none in attendance who thought Alan Richmond would have a different occupation after the votes were counted.

Except for one person.

In saying his good-byes the President leaned into Walter Sullivan to embrace the older man and say a few private words. Sullivan smiled at the President's remarks. Then the old man stumbled slightly but righted himself by grasping the arms of the President.

After his guests had gone, Sullivan smoked a cigar in his study. As he moved to the window, the lights from the presidential motorcade quickly faded from view. In spite of himself, Sullivan had to smile. The image of the slight wince in the President's eye as Sullivan had gripped his forearm had made for a particularly victorious moment. A long shot, but sometimes long shots paid off. Detective Frank had been very open with the billionaire about the detective's theories regarding the case. One theory that had particularly interested Walter Sullivan was his wife having wounded her assailant with the letter opener, possibly in the leg or arm. It must have cut deeper than the police had thought. Possible nerve damage. A surface wound certainly would have had time to heal by now.

Sullivan slowly walked out of the study, turning off the light as he exited. President Alan Richmond had assuredly felt only a small pain when Sullivan's fingers had sunk into his flesh. But as with a heart attack, a small pain was so often followed by a much larger one. Sullivan smiled broadly as he considered the possibilities.

From atop the knoll Walter Sullivan stared at the little wooden house with the green tin roof. He pulled his muffler around his ears, steadied his weakened legs with a thick walking stick. The cold was bitter in the hills of Southwest Virginia this time of year and the forecast pointed unerringly to snow, and a lot of it.

He made his way down across the, for now, iron–hard ground. The house was in an excellent state of repair thanks to his limitless pocketbook and a deep sense of nostalgia that seemed to more and more consume him as he grew closer to becoming a thread of the past himself. Woodrow Wilson was in the White House and the earth was heavily into the First World War when Walter Patrick Sullivan had first seen the glimmer of light with the aid of a midwife and the grim determination of his mother, Millie,

404

who had lost all three previous children, two in childbirth.

His father, a coal miner – it seems everyone's father was a coal miner in that part of Virginia back then – had lived until his son's twelfth birthday and then had abruptly expired from a series of maladies brought on by too much coal dust and too little rest. For years the future billionaire had watched his daddy stagger into the house, every muscle exhausted, the face as black as their big Labrador's coat, and collapse on the little bed in the back room. Too tired to eat, or play with the little boy who each day hoped for some attention but ended up getting none from a father whose perpetual weariness was so painful to witness.

His mother had lived long enough to see her off-spring become one of the richest men in the world, and her dutiful son had taken great pains to ensure that she had every comfort his immense resources could provide. For a tribute to his late father, he had purchased the mine that had killed him. Five million cash. He had paid a fifty-thousand-dollar bonus to every miner in the place and then he had, with great ceremony, shut it down.

He opened the door and went inside. The gas fireplace threw warmth into the room without the necessity of firewood. The pantry was stocked with enough food for the next six months. Here he was entirely self-sufficient. He never allowed anyone to stay here with him. This had been his homestead. All with the right to be here, with the exception of himself, were dead. He was alone and he wanted it that way.

The simple meal he prepared was lingered over while he stared moodily out the window where in the failing light he could just make out the circle of naked elms near the house; the branches waved to him with slow, melodic movements.

405

The interior of the house had not been returned to its original condition or configuration. This was his birthplace but it had not been a happy childhood amid poverty that threatened never to go away. The sense of urgency spawned from that time had served Sullivan well in his career, for it fueled him with a stamina, a resolve before which many an obstacle had wilted.

He cleaned the plates, and went into the small room that had once been his parents' bedroom. Now it contained a comfortable chair, a table and several bookcases that housed an extremely select collection of reading material. In the corner was a small cot, for the room also served as his sleeping chamber.

Sullivan picked up the sophisticated cellular phone that lay on the table. He dialed a number known only to a handful of people. A voice on the other line came on. Then Sullivan was put on hold for a moment before another voice came on.

"Goodness, Walter, I know you tend to keep odd hours, but you really should try to slow down a bit. Where are you?"

"You can't slow down at my age, Alan. If you do, you might not start back up again. I'd much rather explode in a fireball of activity than recede faintly into the mists. I hope I'm not disturbing something important."

"Nothing that can't wait. I'm getting better about prioritizing world crises. Was there something you needed?"

Sullivan took a moment to place a small recording device next to the receiver. One never knew.

"I only had one question, Alan." Sullivan paused. It occurred to him that he was enjoying this. Then he thought of Christy's face in the morgue and his face became grim.

"What's that?"

"Why did you wait so long to kill the man?"

In the silence that followed, Sullivan could hear the pattern of breathing on the other end of the phone. To his credit Alan Richmond did not start to hyperventilate; in fact, his breathing remained normal. Sullivan came away impressed and a little disappointed.

"Come again?"

"If your men had missed, you might be meeting with your attorney right now, planning your defense against impeachment. You must admit you cut it rather close."

"Walter, are you all right? Has something happened to you? Where are you?"

Sullivan held the receiver away from his ear for a moment. The phone had a scrambling device that made any possible tracing of his location impossible. If they were trying to lock in his position right now, as he was reasonably certain they were, they would be confronted with a dozen locations from which the call was supposedly originating, and not one of them anywhere near where he actually was. The device had cost him ten thousand dollars. But, then, it was only money. He smiled again. He could talk as long as he wanted.

"Actually I haven't felt this good in a long while."

"Walter, you're not making any sense. Who was killed?"

"You know, I wasn't all that surprised when Christy didn't want to go to Barbados. Honestly, I figured she wanted to stay behind and do some alley-catting with a few of the young men she had targeted over the summer. It was funny when she said she wasn't feeling well. I remember sitting in the limo and thinking what her excuse would be. She wasn't all that creative, poor girl. Her cough was particularly phony. I suppose in school she used the dog-ate-my-homework excuse with alarming regularity."

"Walt—"

"The odd thing was that when the police questioned me regarding why she hadn't come with me, I suddenly realized I couldn't tell them that Christy had claimed illness. You may recall that there were rumors of affairs floating in the papers about that time. I knew if I reported her not feeling well, coupled with her not joining me on the island, that the tabloids would soon have her pregnant with another man's child even if the autopsy confirmed otherwise. People love to assume the worst and the juiciest, Alan, you understand that. When you're impeached they'll assume the worst of you, of course. And deservedly so."

"Walter, will you please tell me where you are? You are obviously not feeling well."

"Would you like me to play the tape for you, Alan? The one from the press conference where you gave me that particularly moving line about things that happen that have no meaning. It was quite a nice thing to say. A private comment between old friends that was picked up by several TV and radio stations in the area but that never made the light of day. It's a tribute to your popularity, I suppose, that no one picked up on it. You were being so charming, so supportive, who cared if you said Christy was sick. And you did say that, Alan. You told me that if Christy hadn't gotten sick she wouldn't have been murdered. She would've gone with me to the island and she would be alive today.

"I was the only one Christy told about being sick, Alan. And as I said, I never even told the police. So how did you know?"

"You must have told me."

"I neither met nor spoke with you prior to the

press conference. That much is easily confirmed. My schedule is monitored by the minute. As President your whereabouts and communications are pretty much known at all times. I say pretty much, because on the night Christy was killed you were certainly not among your usual haunts. You happened to be in my house, and more to the point, in my bedroom. At the press conference we were surrounded by dozens of people at all times. Everything we said to each other is on tape somewhere. You didn't learn it from me."

"Walter, please tell me where you are. I want to help you through this."

"Christy was never really good at keeping things straight. She must have been so proud of her subterfuge with me. She probably bragged to you, didn't she? How she had snookered the old man? Because in fact my late wife was the only person in the world who could've told you that she had feigned illness. And you carelessly uttered those words to me. I don't know why it took me so long to arrive at the truth. I suppose I was so obsessed with finding Christy's killer that I accepted the burglary theory without question. Perhaps it was also subconscious self-denial. Because I was never wholly ignorant of Christy's desires for you. But I guess I just didn't want to believe you could do that to me. I should have assumed the worst in human nature and I would not have found myself disappointed. But as they say, better late than never."

"Walter, why did you call me?"

Sullivan's voice grew more quiet but lost none of its force, none of its intensity. "Because, you bastard, I wanted to be the one to tell you of your new future. It will involve lawyers and courts and more public exposure than even as President you ever dreamed was possible. Because I didn't want you to be wholly surprised when the police presented themselves on your doorstep. And most of all, I wanted you to know exactly who to thank for all of it."

The President's voice became tense. "Walter, if you want me to help you, I will. But I am the President of the United States. And although you are one of my oldest friends, I will not tolerate this type of accusation from you or anyone else."

"That's good, Alan. Very good. You discerned that I would be taping the conversation. Not that it matters." Sullivan paused for a moment, then continued. "My protégé, Alan. Taught you everything I knew, and you learned well. Well enough to hold the highest office in the land. Fortunately, your fall will also be the steepest."

"Walter, you've been under a lot of stress. For the last time, please get some help."

"Funny, Alan, that's precisely my advice to you."

Sullivan clicked off the phone and turned off the recorder. His heart was beating abnormally fast. He put one hand against his chest, forced himself to relax. A coronary was not going to be allowed. He was going to be around to see this one.

He looked out the window and then at the inside of the room. His little homestead. His father had died in this very room. Somehow, that thought was comforting to him.

He lay back in the chair and closed his eyes. In the morning he would call the police. He would tell them everything and he would give them the tape. Then he would sit back and watch. Even if they didn't convict Richmond, his career was over. Which was to say the man was as good as dead, professionally, spiritually, mentally. Who cared if his physical carcass lingered? So much the better. Sullivan smiled. He had sworn that he would avenge his wife's killer. And he had.

It was the sudden sensation of his hand rising from his side that brought his eyes open. And then his hand was being closed around a cold, hard object. It wasn't until the barrel touched the side of his head that he really reacted. And by then it was too late.

As the President looked at the phone receiver, he checked his watch. It would be over right about now. Sullivan had taught him well. Too well, as it had turned out, for the teacher. He had been almost certain Sullivan would contact him directly prior to announcing the President's culpability to the world. That had made it relatively simple. Richmond rose and headed upstairs to his private quarters. The thought of the late Walter Sullivan had already passed from his mind. It was not efficient or productive to linger over a vanquished foe. It only set you back for your next challenge. Sullivan had also taught him that.

In the twilight the younger man stared at the house. He had heard the shot, but his eyes never stopped staring at the dim light in the window.

Bill Burton rejoined Collin in a few seconds. He could not even look at his partner. Two trained and dedicated Secret Service agents, killers of young women and old men.

On the drive back, Burton sank back in his seat. It was finally over. Three people dead, counting Christine Sullivan. And why not count her? That's what had started this whole nightmare.

Burton looked down at his hand, still barely able to comprehend that it had just curled around the grip of a gun, forced a trigger back and ended a man's life. With his other hand Burton had taken the cassette recorder and the tape. They were in his pocket headed for the incinerator.

411

When he had checked the telephone tap and listened to Sullivan's phone conversation with Seth Frank, Burton had no idea what the old man was getting at with Christine Sullivan's "illness." But when he reported the information to the President, Richmond had looked out the window for some minutes, a shade paler than he had been when Burton had entered the room. Then he had phoned the White House Media Department. A few minutes later they had both listened to the tape from the first press conference on the Middleton Courthouse steps. To the President commiserating with his old friend, about the whimsical nature of life; how Christine Sullivan would still be alive if she hadn't taken ill. Having forgotten that Christine Sullivan had told him that on the day of her death. A fact that could be proven. A fact that could possibly topple all of them.

Burton had slumped back in his chair, stared at his boss, who silently looked at the tape as if he were trying to erase its words with his thoughts. Burton shook his head incredulously. Caught up in his own mushy rhetoric, just like a politician.

"What do we do now, Chief? Make a run for it on Air Force One?" Burton was only half-joking as he studied the carpet. He was too numb to even think anymore.

He looked up to find the President's eyes full upon him. "Walter Sullivan is the only living person, other than ourselves, who knows the significance of this information."

Burton rose from his chair and returned the stare. "My job doesn't include popping people just because you tell me to."

The President would not take his eyes from Burton's face. "Walter Sullivan is now a direct threat to us. He is also fucking with us and I don't like people fucking with me. Do you?"

"He's got a damned good reason to, don't you think?"

Richmond picked up a pen from his desk and twirled it between his fingers. "If Sullivan talks we lose everything. Everything." The President snapped his fingers. "Gone. Just like that. And I will do everything possible to avoid it happening."

Burton dropped into his chair, his belly suddenly on fire. "How do you know he hasn't already?"

"Because I know Walter," the President said simply. "He'll do it in his own way. And it will be spectacular. But deliberate. He is not a man who rushes into anything. But when he does act, the results will be swift and crushing."

"Great." Burton put his head in his hands, his mind whirling faster than he thought possible. Years of training had instilled in him an almost innate ability to process information instantly, think on his feet, act a fraction of a second before anyone else could. Now his brain was a muddle, like day-old coffee, thick and soupy; nothing was clear. He looked up.

"But killing the guy?"

"I can guarantee you that Walter Sullivan is right this minute plotting how best to destroy us. That type of action does not invoke sympathy from me."

The President leaned back in his chair. "Plainly and simply this man has decided to fight us. And one has to live with the consequences of one's decisions. Walter Sullivan knows that better than anyone alive." The President's eyes again lasered in on Burton's. "The question is, are we prepared to fight back?"

Collin and Burton had spent the last three days following Walter Sullivan. When the car had dropped him off in the middle of nowhere, Burton both couldn't believe his luck and experienced deep sadness for his target, now, truly, a sitting duck.

Husband and wife wiped out. As the car sped back to the Capital City, Burton unconsciously rubbed at his hand, trying to whittle away the filth he felt in every crevice. What turned his skin cold was the realization that he could never wipe away the feelings he was having, the reality of what he had done. The rock-bottom emotional barometer would be with him every minute of every day of the rest of his days. He had traded his life for another. Again. His backbone, for so long a steel beam, had wilted to pitiful rubber. Life had given him the supreme challenge and he had failed.

He dug his fingers into the armrest and stared out the window into the darkness.

TWENTY-FOUR

The apparent suicide of Walter Sullivan rocked not only the community. The funeral was attended by the high and mighty from all over the world. In an appropriately solemn and lavish ceremony at Washington's St. Matthew's Cathedral, the man was eulogized by a half-dozen dignitaries. The most famous had gone on for a full twenty minutes about the great human being Walter Sullivan had been, and also about the great stress he had been under and how those under such strain sometimes do things they would otherwise never contemplate. When Alan Richmond had finished speaking, there was not a dry cheek in the place, and the tears that dampened his own face were seemingly genuine. He had always been impressed with his superb oratorical skills.

The long funeral procession streamed out, and, over three and one half hours later, ended at the tiny house where Walter Sullivan had begun, and ended, his life. As the limos scrambled for space on the narrow, snow-covered road, Walter Sullivan was carried down and interred next to his parents, on the little knoll where the view down the valley was by far the richest part of the place.

As the dirt covered the coffin, and the friends of Walter Sullivan made their way back to the realm of the living, Seth Frank studied every face. He watched as the President made his way back to his limo. Bill Burton saw him, registered surprise for an instant, and then nodded. Frank nodded back.

When all the mourners had gone, Frank turned his attention to the little house. The yellow police lines were still around the perimeter and two uniformed officers stood guard.

Frank walked over, flashed his badge and entered.

It seemed the height of irony that one of the wealthiest men in the world had chosen a place like this to die. Walter Sullivan had been a walking poster child for Horatio Alger tales. Frank admired a man who had risen in the world on his own merit, sheer guts and determination. Who wouldn't?

He looked again at the chair where the body had been found, the gun beside it. The weapon had been pressed against Sullivan's left temple. The stellate wound, large and ragged, had preceded the massive bursting fracture that had ended the man's life. The gun had fallen on the left side of the floor. The presence of the contact wound and powder burns on the deceased's palm had prompted the locals to file the case away as a suicide, the facts of which were simple and straightforward. A grieving Walter Sullivan had exacted revenge on his wife's killer and then taken his own life. His associates had confirmed that Sullivan had been out of touch for days, unusual for him. He rarely came to this retreat and whenever he did, someone knew his whereabouts. The newspaper found beside the body had proclaimed the death of his wife's suspected murderer. All the signs pointed to a man who had intended on ending his life.

What bothered Frank was one small fact that he had purposefully not shared with anyone. He had met Walter Sullivan the day he had come to the morgue. During that meeting, Sullivan had signed off on several forms related to the autopsy and an inventory of his wife's few possessions.

And Sullivan had signed those forms with his *right* hand.

It was inconclusive in itself. Sullivan could have held the gun in his left hand for any number of reasons. His fingerprints were on the gun clear as day, maybe too clear, Frank thought to himself.

The physical condition of the gun: it was untraceable; the serial numbers had been so expertly obliterated that even the scope couldn't pull up anything. A completely sterilized weapon. The kind you'd expect to find at a crime scene. But why would Walter Sullivan be concerned about anyone tracing a gun he was going to use to kill himself? The answer was he wouldn't. But again the fact was inconclusive since the person providing Sullivan with the weapon could have obtained it illegally, although Virginia was one of the easier states in which to purchase a handgun, much to the dismay of police departments in the northeast corridor of the country.

Frank finished with the interior and paced outside. The snow still lay thickly on the ground. Sullivan had been dead before the snow had started, the autopsy had confirmed that. It was fortunate that his people knew the location of the house. They had come looking for him and the body had been discovered within approximately twelve hours of death.

No, the snow would not help Frank. The entire place was so isolated there was no one even to ask if anything suspicious had been observed on the night of Sullivan's death.

His counterpart from the county sheriff's department climbed out of his car and hustled over to where Frank was standing. The man carried a file with some papers in it. He and Frank conversed for a few moments and then Frank thanked him, climbed in his car and drove off.

The autopsy report indicated that Walter Sullivan had died sometime between eleven P.M. and one o'clock in the morning. But at twelve-ten Walter Sullivan had called someone.

The hallways of PS&L were unsettlingly quiet. The capillaries of a thriving law practice are ringing phones, pealing faxes, mouths moving and keyboards clicking. Lucinda, even with the firm's individual direct–dialing lines, was normally the recipient of eight phone calls per minute. Today she leisurely read through *Vogue*. Most office doors were closed, shielding from view the intense and often emotional discussions going on among all but a handful of the firm's lawyers.

Sandy Lord's office door was not only closed, it was locked. The few partners with the temerity to attempt a knock on the thick portal were quickly on the biting end of an obscene verbal barrage from the room's lone and moody occupant.

He sat in his chair, shoeless feet on the polished desk, tieless, collar undone, unshaven, a nearly empty bottle of his strongest whiskey within easy reach. Sandy Lord's eyes were now mere blots of red. At the church he had used those eyes to stare long and hard at the shiny brass coffin containing Sullivan's body; essentially it contained both their earthly remains.

For many years Lord had anticipated Sullivan's demise and had, with the help of a dozen PS&L specialists, established an elaborate series of safeguards that included cultivation of a loyal contingent on the board of directors of the parent holding company of Sullivan Enterprises, all of which would ensure continual representation of the huge network of Sullivan entities far into the future by PS&L generally and by Lord in particular. Life would go on. The PS&L train would thrive with its chief diesel engine intact and even replenished. But an unexpected development had occurred.

That Sullivan's passing was inevitable, the financial markets understood. What the business and investment community apparently could not accept was the man's death, allegedly by his own hand, coupled with the increasing rumors that Sullivan had had his wife's alleged killer gunned down, something that once accomplished, had prompted him to put a bullet into his own brain. The market was not prepared for such revelations. A surprised market, some economists would predict, often reacts wildly and precipitately. Those economists were not disappointed. Shares of stock in Sullivan Enterprises plummeted sixty-one percent in value on the New York Stock Exchange the morning after his body was discovered, on the heaviest trading volume for a single stock in the last ten years.

With the stock selling a full six dollars a share below book value it had not taken long for the vultures to circle.

Centrus Corp.'s tender offer was, upon Lord's advice, rejected by the board of directors. However, all indications pointed to overwhelming acceptance of the offer by the shareholders, who had nervously watched as a large chunk of their investment had evaporated overnight. It was likely that the proxy battle would be complete and the takeover finalized in two months. Centrus's counsel, Rhoads, Director & Minor, was one of the largest law firms in the country, well-stocked in all areas of legal expertise.

The bottom line was clear. PS&L would not be needed. Its largest client, over twenty million dollars' worth, almost one-third of its legal business, would disappear. Already résumés were flying out of the firm. Practice groups were trying to cut deals with Rhoads, pleading their familiarity with Sullivan's business as a hedge against the dreaded and costly learning curve. Twenty percent of the heretofore loyal PS&L attorney ranks had submitted their resignation and there were no indications the tidal wave would subside anytime soon.

Lord's hand slowly meandered along his desk until the whiskey was tilted back and finished. He swiveled around, checked out the gloom of the winter's morning and had to smile to himself.

There was no deal awaiting him at Rhoads, Director & Minor and, thus, it had finally happened: Lord was vulnerable. He had seen clients bite the dust with alarming swiftness, especially in the last decade where you were a paper billionaire one minute and an impoverished felon the next. He had, though, never imagined that his own fall, if it ever came, would be as terrifyingly fast, as painfully complete.

That was the problem with an eight-figure gorilla of a client. It took all of your time and attention. Old clients dried up and died away. New clients were not cultivated. His complacency had come back to bite him right in the ass.

He calculated swiftly. Over the last twenty years he had netted roughly thirty million dollars. Unfortunately, he had managed somehow not only to spend the thirty mil but a good deal more than that. Over the years he had owned a string of luxurious homes, a vacation place in Hilton Head Island, a hideaway fuck nest in the Big Apple where he had taken his wedded prey. The luxury cars, the various collections that a man of taste and resources was supposed to accumulate, the small but select wine cellar, even his own helicopter – he had had all those things, but three divorces, none of them amicable, had deteriorated his asset base.

The residence he now had left was straight from the pages of *Architectural Digest* but its mortgage matched its stunning opulence stride for stride. And the thing he truly didn't have much of was cash.

Liquidity escaped him and at PS&L you ate what you killed and PS&L partners didn't tend to hunt in packs. That was why Lord's monthly draw was so much larger than everyone else's. That revised draw check would now barely cover his plastic bills; his monthly Am Ex alone routinely crept into the five-figure range.

He turned his now-racing gray cells for a moment to his non-Sullivan clients. A rough ballpark estimate gave him maybe a half-million in potential legal business at best, if he pumped them hard, made the circuit, which he didn't want to do, lacked any desire to do. That was beneath him now. Or it had been up until good old Walter had decided life just wasn't worth living despite his several billions. *Jesus Christ. All for a little dumbshit whore.*

Five hundred thou'! That was even less than the little prick Kirksen. Lord winced at that realization.

He wheeled around and studied the artwork on the far wall. Within the brush strokes of a minor nineteenth-century artist he found reason to smile once more. He had an option left to him. Though his biggest client had royally screwed up Lord's life, the rotund deal-maker had an asset left to mine. He punched his phone.

Fred Martin pushed the cart quickly down the hallway. Only his third day on the job, and his first delivering the mail to the firm's attorneys, Martin was anxious to complete his task quickly and accurately. One of ten gofers employed by the firm, Martin was already feeling pressure from his supervisor to pick up his pace. After banging the streets for four months with no weapons other than his B.A. in history from Georgetown, Martin had figured his only recourse was to attend law school. And what better place to plumb the possibilities of such a career than at one of

D.C.'s most prestigious? His endless trek of job interviews had convinced him that it was never too early to commence networking.

He consulted his map with the attorneys' names listed in each square representing that person's office. Martin had grabbed the map from on top of the desk in his cubicle, not noticing the updated version buried under a multinational transaction closing binder that rose five thousand pages high, the indexing and binding of which awaited him that afternoon.

As he rounded the corner he stopped and looked at the closed door. Everyone's door was closed today. He took the Federal Express package and checked the name on the map, and compared that to the scrawled handwriting on the packing label. It matched. He looked at the empty nameplate holder and his eyebrows converged in confusion.

He knocked, waited a moment, knocked again and then opened the door.

He looked around. The place was a mess. Boxes littered the floor, the furniture was in disarray. Some papers lay scattered on the desk. His first instinct was to check with his supervisor. Maybe there was a mistake. He looked at his watch. Already ten minutes late. He grabbed the phone, dialed his supervisor. No answer. Then he saw the photo of the woman on the desk. Tall, auburn-haired, very expensively dressed. Must be the man's office. Probably moving in. Who'd leave a looker like that behind? With that rationale established, Fred carefully laid the package on the desk chair, where it would be sure to be found. He closed the door on his way out.

"I'm sorry about Walter, Sandy. I really am." Jack checked the view across the cityscape. A penthouse apartment in Upper Northwest. The place must have

422

been enormously expensive, and the dollars had continued to flow for the interior design. Everywhere Jack looked were original paintings, soft leather and sculptured stone. He reasoned that the world didn't have many Sandy Lords and they had to live somewhere.

Lord sat by the fire that popped pleasantly in the grate, a loose paisley robe covering his bulky frame, bare feet comforted in leather slippers. A cold rain fell against the broad expanse of windows. Jack drew closer to the fire, his mind appeared to crackle and jump like the flames; a loose ember hit the marble surround, flamed and then quickly disappeared. Jack cradled his drink and looked at his partner.

The phone call hadn't been totally unexpected. "We need to talk, Jack, the sooner the better for me. Not at the office."

When he arrived, Lord's aged valet had taken his coat and gloves and then inconspicuously receded into the farther reaches of the home.

The two men were in Lord's mahogany-paneled study, a luxuriously masculine retreat that Jack felt guiltily envious of. A glimmer of the large stone house briefly came into focus. It had a library, much like this. With an effort he focused on Lord's back.

"I'm kinda fucked, Jack." The first words out of Lord's mouth had the effect of making Jack want to smile. You had to appreciate the man's candor. But he caught himself. The tone in Lord's voice demanded a certain respect.

"The firm'll be okay, Sandy. We're not going to lose many more. So we sublease some space, it's no big deal."

Lord finally stood up and went straight to the well-fed bar in the corner. The shot glass was filled to the rim and downed in a well-practiced motion.

"Excuse me, Jack, maybe I'm not making myself

423

real clear here. The firm took a blow, but not one that'll send it down for the count. You're right, Patton, Shaw will weather this broadside. But what I'm talking about is whether Patton, Shaw and *Lord* will live to fight another day."

Lord lurched across the room and wearily plunged himself on the burgundy leather couch. Jack traced the column of brass nails as they marched across the outline of the heavy piece. He sipped his drink and studied the wide face. The eyes were narrow, no more than penny-wide slits really.

"You're the firm's leader, Sandy. I don't see that changing, even if your client base took a hit."

Lord groaned from his horizontal perch.

"A hit? A hit? I took a goddamned A-bomb, Jack, right up my ass. The heavyweight champion of the world couldn't have hit me any harder. I'm going down for the count. The buzzards they are a circling, and Lord he is the main course; the stuffed hog with the apple in the mouth and a bull's-eye on the butt."

"Kirksen?"

"Kirksen, Packard, Mullins, fucking Townsend. Keep counting, Jack, the list goes on until you get to the end of the partnership roll. I have, I must admit, a most unusual, hate-hate relationship with my partners."

"But not Graham, Sandy. Not with Graham."

Lord slowly edged himself up, perching on one flabby arm as he looked at Jack.

Jack wondered why he liked the man as much as he did. The answer probably lay somewhere in the lunch at Fillmore's way back when. No bullshit. A real-world baptism where the sting of words made your gut clench and your brain hammer out responses you'd never have the nerve to actually deliver. Now the man was in trouble. Jack had the means to protect him. Or maybe he did; his

424

relationship with the Baldwins right now was far from solid.

"Sandy, if they want to get to you, they'll have to go through me first." There, he had said it. And he meant it. It was also true that Lord had given him his chance to shine with the big boys, thrown him right into the fire. But what other way would you know if you could actually pull it off or not? That experience was also worth something.

"The waters might get a little rocky for both of us, Jack."

"I'm a good swimmer, Sandy. Besides, don't look at this as purely altruistic. You're an investment of the firm in which I'm a partner. You're a top-grade rainmaker. You're down now, but you won't stay down. Five hundred bucks says within twelve months you're back in the number-one slot. I don't intend on letting an asset like that walk away."

"I won't forget this, Jack."

"I won't let you."

After Jack had left, Lord started to pour another drink but stopped. He looked down at his quivering hands and slowly put down the bottle and glass. He made it to the couch before his knees gave out. The federal-style mirror over the fireplace caught his image. It had been twenty years since a single tear had escaped the heavy face. That had been at his mother's passing. But now the outpourings were steadily coming on. He had cried for his friend, Walter Sullivan. For years Lord had duped himself into believing that the man meant nothing more to him than a solid-gold draw check each month. The price for that self-deception had come due at the funeral, where Lord had wept so hard that he had gone back to his car until it was time to go bury his friend.

Now he rubbed at the puffy cheeks once again, pushing away the salty liquid. Fucking young punk.

Lord had planned everything down to the last detail. His pitch would be perfect. He had envisioned every possible response except the one he had gotten. He had mistaken the younger man. Lord assumed that Jack would have done what Lord himself would have done: pressed for every advantage in exchange for the enormous favor being asked.

It wasn't only guilt that pulled at him. It was shame. He realized that as sickness enveloped him and he bent low over the thick, spongy carpet. Shame. He hadn't felt that one for a long time either. When the nausea subsided and he once again looked at the wreck in the mirror, Lord promised himself that he would not disappoint Jack. That he *would* rise back to the top. And he would not forget.

TWENTY-FIVE

Frank had never in his wildest fantasies expected to be sitting here. He looked around and quickly determined that it was indeed oval in shape. The furnishings tended to be solid, conservative, but with a splash of color here, a stripe there, a pair of expensive sneakers placed neatly on a lower shelf, that stated that the room's occupant was not nearly ready for retirement. Frank swallowed hard and willed himself to breathe normally. He was a veteran policeman and this was just another routine inquiry in a series of endless ones. He was just following up a lead, nothing more. A few minutes and he'd be out of here.

But then his brain reminded him that the person he was about to make inquiries of was the current President of the United States. As a new shock wave of nervousness rushed over him the door opened and he quickly stood, turned and stared for a long moment at the extended hand until his mind finally registered and he slowly moved his out to meet it.

'Thank you for coming down into my neck of the woods, Lieutenant."

"No trouble at all, sir. I mean you've got better things to do than sit in traffic. Although I guess you never really sit in traffic, do you, Mr. President?"

Richmond sat behind his desk and motioned for Frank to resume his seat. An impassive Bill Burton, invisible to Frank until that moment, closed the door and inclined his head toward the detective.

"My routes are pretty well laid out in advance, I'm afraid. It's true I don't end up in many traffic jams but it does stifle the hell out of spontaneity." The President grinned and Frank could feel his own mouth automatically turning up into a smile.

The President leaned forward and stared directly at him. He clasped his hands together, his brow wrinkled and he went from jovial to intensely serious in an instant.

"I want to thank you, Seth." He glanced at Burton. "Bill has told me how cooperative you were with the investigation of Christine Sullivan's death. I really appreciate that, Seth. Some officials would have been less than forthcoming or tried to turn it into a media circus for their own personal gain. I hoped for better from you and my expectations were exceeded. Again, thank you."

Frank glowed as though he had been awarded the fourth-grade spelling bee crown.

"It's terrible, you know. Tell me, have you learned of any connection between Walter's suicide and this criminal being gunned down?"

Frank shook the stars from his eyes and his pair of steady eyes came to rest on the chiseled features of the President.

"Come on, Lieutenant. I can tell you that all of official and unofficial Washington is right this very minute savagely attacking the issue of Walter Sullivan having hired an assassin to avenge his wife's death and then taking his own life in the aftermath. You can't stop people from gossiping. I would just like to know if your investigation has led to any fact to substantiate Walter having ordered the killing of his wife's murderer."

"I'm afraid that I really can't say one way or another, sir. I hope you understand, but this is an ongoing police investigation."

"Don't worry, Lieutenant, I'm not treading on your toes. But I can tell you that this has been a particularly distressing time for me. To think Walter Sullivan would end his own life. One of the most brilliant and resourceful men of his era, of any era."

"So I've heard an awful lot of people say."

"But just between you and me, knowing Walter as I did, it would not be out of the realm of possibility that he would have taken precise and concrete steps to have his wife's killer . . . dealt with."

"Alleged killer, Mr. President. Innocent until proven guilty."

The President looked at Burton. "But I was led to understand that your case was pretty much ironclad."

Seth Frank scratched his ear. "Some defense attorneys love ironclad cases, sir. See, you dump enough water on iron, it starts to rust and before you know it, you got holes everywhere."

"And this defense attorney was such a person?"

"And then some. I'm not a betting man, but I would've given us no more than a forty percent shot at getting a clean conviction. We were in for a real battle."

The President sat back as he absorbed this information and then looked back at Frank.

Frank finally noted the expression of expectancy on his face and flipped open his notebook. His heartbeat calmed down as he perused the familiar scribbles.

"Are you aware it was right before his death that Walter Sullivan called you here?"

"I know that I spoke with him. I was not aware that it immediately preceded his death, no."

"I guess I'm a little surprised that you didn't come forward with this information earlier."

The President's face fell. "I know. I guess I'm a little surprised myself. I suppose I believed I was shielding

429

Walter, or at least his memory, from further trauma. Although I knew the police would eventually discover the call was placed. I'm sorry, Lieutenant."

"I need to know the details of that phone conversation."

"Would you like something to drink, Seth?"

"A cup of coffee would be fine, thank you."

As if on cue, Burton picked up a phone in the corner and a minute later a silver-plated coffee tray was delivered in.

The steaming hot coffee was sipped; the President looked at his watch, then saw Frank staring at him.

"I'm sorry, Seth, I *am* treating your visit with the importance it deserves. However, I've got a congressional delegation coming to lunch in a few minutes and quite frankly I'm not looking forward to it. As funny as it sounds, I'm not particularly enamored of politicians."

"I understand. This will only take a few minutes. What was the purpose of the call?"

The President leaned back in his chair as if organizing his thoughts. "I would characterize the call as one of desperation. He was definitely not his usual self. He seemed unbalanced, out of control. For long periods of time he would say nothing. Very unlike the Walter Sullivan I knew."

"What did he talk about?"

"Everything, and nothing. Sometimes he just babbled. He talked about Christine's death. And then about the man, the man you arrested for the murder. How he hated him, how he had destroyed his life. It was truly awful to hear."

"What did you tell him?"

"Well, I kept asking him where he was. I wanted to find him, get him some help. But he wouldn't tell me. I'm not sure he heard a word I said, really, he was that distraught."

"So you think he sounded suicidal, sir?"

"I'm no psychiatrist, Lieutenant, but if I had to make a layman's guess about his mental state, yes, I would definitely say Walter Sullivan sounded suicidal that night. It's one of the few times during my presidency that I felt truly hopeless. Frankly, after the conversation I had with him, I was not surprised to learn that he was dead." Richmond glanced at Burton's impassive face, then looked at the detective. "That's also why I questioned you as to whether you had determined if there was any truth to the rumor that Walter had anything to do with this person being gunned down. After Walter's telephone call I have to admit that the thought certainly crossed my mind."

Frank looked over at Burton. "I suppose you don't have a recording of the conversation? I know that some of the communications here are recorded."

The President answered. "Sullivan called my private line, Lieutenant. It's a secure communication link and no recordings of conversations on that line are allowed."

"I see. Did he directly indicate to you that he was involved in the death of Luther Whitney?"

"Not directly, no. He obviously wasn't thinking clearly. But reading between the lines, the rage that I knew he was feeling – well, and I hate to make this statement of a man who's dead, I think it was pretty clear that he had had the man killed. I have no proof of that of course, but it was my strong impression."

Frank shook his head. "Pretty uncomfortable conversation to have."

"Yes, yes it was very uncomfortable. Now, Lieutenant, I'm afraid that official duty calls."

Frank didn't budge. "Why do you think he called you, sir? And at that time of night?"

The President sat back down, threw another quick glance at Burton. "Walter was one of my closest

431

personal friends. He kept odd hours, but then so do I. It would not be unusual for him to call at that hour. I hadn't heard very much from him for the last few months. As you know, he had been under a considerable personal strain. Walter was the sort to suffer in silence. Now Seth, if you will excuse me."

"It just strikes me as odd that out of all the people he could have called, he called you. I mean, the chances were pretty good that you wouldn't even be here. Presidents' travel schedules are pretty hectic. It makes me wonder what he was thinking."

The President leaned back, placed his fingers together, and studied the ceiling. *Cop wants to play games to show me how smart he is.* He looked back at Frank and smiled. "If I were a mind reader I wouldn't have to rely so heavily on the pollsters."

Frank smiled back. "I don't think you have to be telepathic to know you're going to be occupying that chair for another four years, sir."

"I appreciate that, Lieutenant. All I can tell you is that Walter called me. If he was planning on killing himself, who would he call? His family has been estranged from him since his marriage to Christine. He had many business acquaintances, but few people he would call true friends. Walter and I have known each other for years, and I considered him a surrogate father. I had taken a very active interest in the investigation of his wife's death, as you know. All of that together could explain why he wanted to talk to me, particularly if he was contemplating taking his life. That's really all I know. I'm sorry I can't be of more help."

The door opened. Frank did not see that it was in response to a tiny button on the underside of the President's desk.

The President looked at his secretary. "I'll be right there, Lois. Lieutenant, if there's anything I can do

432

for you, you let Bill know. Please."

Frank closed his notebook. "Thank you, sir."

Richmond stared at the doorway after Frank had departed.

"What was the name of Whitney's attorney, Burton?"

Burton thought for a moment. "Graham. Jack Graham."

"The name sounds familiar."

"Works at Patton, Shaw. He's a partner there."

The President's eyes froze on the agent's face.

"What's the matter?"

"I'm not sure." Richmond unlocked a drawer in his desk and took out a notebook he had compiled on this little extracurricular matter. "Don't lose sight of the fact, Burton, that one very important piece of incriminating evidence, for which we happened to have paid five million dollars, has never turned up."

The President flipped through the pages of his notebook. There were numerous individuals involved, to various degrees, in their little drama. If Whitney had given his attorney the letter opener along with an account of what had happened, the whole world would've known by now. Richmond thought back to the awards ceremony for Ransome Baldwin at the White House. Graham was clearly no shrinking violet. Clearly he didn't have it. But then who, if anyone, would Whitney have given it to?

As his mind spun out neat blocks of analysis and possible scenarios, one name suddenly stood out at the President from within the lines of precise writing. One person who had never really been accounted for.

Jack cradled the carry-out in one arm, his briefcase in the other, and managed to wiggle the key out of his

433

pocket. Before he could put it in the lock, though, the door opened.

Jack looked surprised. "I didn't expect you home yet."

"You didn't have to stop. I could've made something."

Jack went inside, dropped his briefcase on the coffee table and headed to the kitchen. Kate stared after him.

"Hey, you work all day too. Why should you have to cook?"

"Women do it every day, Jack. Just look around."

He emerged from the kitchen. "No argument there. You want sweet and sour or moo goo gai pan? I got extra spring rolls too."

"Whichever you don't want. I'm not that hungry really."

He withdrew and came back with two fully stocked plates.

"You know if you don't eat more you're going to blow away. I half feel like stuffing rocks in your pockets as it is now."

He sat cross-legged next to her on the floor. She picked at her plate while he devoured his.

"So how was work? You know you probably could have stood to take a few more days off. You're always pushing yourself too hard."

"Look who's talking." She picked up a spring roll and then put it back down.

He put down his fork and looked over at her.

"So I'm listening."

She pulled herself up onto the couch and sat there playing with her necklace. Still dressed in her work clothes, she looked exhausted, like a flower collapsed in the wind.

"I think a lot about what I did to Luther."

"Kate—"

434

"Jack, let me finish." Her voice snapped at him like a whip. In an instant her features relaxed. She continued more calmly. "I've come to decide that I'm never going to get over it, so I might as well accept that fact. Maybe what I did wasn't wrong for a lot of reasons. But it was definitely wrong for at least one reason. He was my father. As lame as that might sound, it should've been a good enough reason." She twisted her necklace some more until it congealed into a series of tiny clumps. "I think being a lawyer, at least the kind of lawyer I am, has made me become someone I don't really like a lot. That's not a real good revelation to arrive at when you're hitting thirty."

Jack reached out his hand to stop hers from shaking. She didn't move it. He could feel the blood pumping through the veins.

"With all that said, I think I'm due for a radical change. In my life, my career, everything."

"What are you talking about?" He got up and sat down beside her. His pulse had accelerated as he anticipated the line she was taking.

"I'm not going to be a prosecutor anymore, Jack. In fact I'm not going to be a lawyer anymore. I submitted my resignation this morning. I have to admit, they were pretty shocked. Told me to think about it. I told them I already had. As much as I'm going to."

The incredulity was stiff in his voice. "You quit your job? Jesus, Kate, you've put a helluva lot into your career. You can't just throw that away."

She suddenly rose and stood by the window, looking out.

"That's just it, Jack. I'm not throwing anything away. My memories of what I've done for the last four years add up to about a lifetime of horror films. That's not exactly what I had in mind sitting in Con

Law as a first-year debating grand principles of justice."

"Don't sell yourself short. The streets are a heckuva lot safer because of what you've done."

She turned to look at him. "I'm not even stemming the flow anymore. I got washed out to sea a long time ago."

"But what are you going to do? You're a lawyer."

"No. You're wrong. I've only been a lawyer a tiny fraction of my life. My life before that time I liked a whole lot better." She stopped and stared at him, her arms folded across her chest. "You made that very clear to me, Jack. I became a lawyer to pay back my father. Three years of school and four years of no life outside a courtroom is a pretty big price." A deep sigh emerged from her throat, her body teetered for a moment before she regained her composure. "Besides, I guess I really paid him back now."

"Kate, it wasn't your fault, none of it." His mouth stopped moving as she turned away from him.

Her next words rocked him.

"I'm going to move away, Jack. I'm not exactly sure where yet. I've got a little money saved. The Southwest sounds nice. Or maybe Colorado. I want as different from here as I can get. Maybe that's a start."

"Moving." Jack said the word more to himself than to her. "Moving." He repeated the word as if both trying to make it go away and trying to dissect and interpret it in a manner that was not as painful as it felt at the moment.

She looked down at her hands. "There's nothing keeping me here, Jack."

He looked at her and he more felt than heard the angry response rush past his lips.

"Goddamn you! How dare you say that?"

She finally looked at him. He could almost see the crack in her voice as she spoke. "I think you better leave."

Jack sat at his desk unwilling to face the mounds of work, the small mountain of pink messages, wondering if his life could possibly get any worse. That's when Dan Kirksen walked in. Jack inwardly groaned.

"Dan, I really don't—"

"You weren't at the partners meeting this morning."

"Well, no one told me we were having one."

"A memo was sent around, but then your office hours have been somewhat erratic of late." He looked disapprovingly at the shambles of Jack's desk. His own was unfailingly in pristine condition; more a testament to how little actual legal work he did than anything else.

"I'm here now."

"I understand you and Sandy met at his house."

Jack eyed him keenly. "I guess nothing's private anymore."

Kirksen flushed angrily. "Partnership matters should be discussed by the full partnership. What we don't need are factions developing that will decimate this firm any more than it already has been."

Jack almost laughed out loud. Dan Kirksen, the undisputed king of the faction-builders.

"I think we've seen the worst."

"Do you, Jack? Do you really?" Kirksen sneered. "I didn't know you had so much experience with this sort of thing."

"Well, if it bothers you so much, Dan, why don't you leave?"

The sneer quickly evaporated from the little man's face. "I've been with this firm for almost twenty years."

"Sounds like it's about time for a change then. Might do you good."

Kirksen sat down, removed a smudge from his glasses. "Piece of friendly advice, Jack. Don't throw your lot in with Sandy. If you do that, you'll be making a big mistake. He's through."

"Thanks for the advice."

"I'm serious, Jack, don't endanger your own position in some futile, however well-intentioned attempt to salvage him."

"Endanger my position? You mean the Baldwins' position, don't you?"

"They're your client . . . for now."

"Are you contemplating a change at the helm? If you are, good luck. You'd last about a minute."

Kirksen stood up. "Nothing is forever, Jack. Sandy Lord can tell you that as well as anybody. What goes around comes around. You can burn bridges in this town, you just have to make sure there's no one left alive on those bridges."

Jack came around the desk, towering over Kirksen. "Were you like this as a little boy, Dan, or did you just turn into a fungus during your adulthood?"

Kirksen smiled and started to leave. "Like I said, you never know, Jack. Client relationships are always so tenuous. Take yours, for example. It's primarily based on your future nuptials with Jennifer Ryce Baldwin. Now, if Ms. Baldwin happened to find out, for instance, that you had not been going home at night, but, instead, had been sharing quarters with a certain young woman, she might be less inclined to refer legal business to you, much less become your wife."

It only took an instant. Kirksen's back was flat against the wall and Jack was so close in his face the man's glasses were fogged.

"Don't do anything foolish, Jack. Regardless of

438

your status here, the partnership would not look kindly on a junior partner assaulting a senior one. We still have standards here at Patton, Shaw."

"Don't ever fuck with my life like that, Kirksen. Don't ever." Jack effortlessly threw him against the door and turned back to his desk.

Kirksen smoothed down his shirt and smiled to himself. So easily manipulated. The big, tall good-looking ones. As strong as mules and no smarter. About as sophisticated as a brick.

"You know, Jack, you should realize what you've gotten yourself into. For some reason you seem to implicitly trust Sandy Lord. Did he tell you the truth about Barry Alvis? Did he happen to do that, Jack?"

Jack turned slowly back around and stared dully at the man.

"Did he use the permanent–associate, no–rain–making-capabilities line? Or did he tell you Alvis had screwed up a big project?"

Jack continued to look at him.

Kirksen smiled triumphantly.

"One phone call, Jack. Daughter calls complaining that Mr. Alvis had inconvenienced her and her father. And Barry Alvis disappears. It's just the way the game works, Jack. Maybe you don't want to play that game. If you don't there's no one stopping *you* from leaving."

Kirksen had been crafting this strategy for a while now. With Sullivan gone, he could promise Baldwin that his work would be the firm's top priority, and Kirksen still had the core of one of the best army of attorneys in the city. And four million dollars of legal business coupled with his own existing business would make him the largest rainmaker at the place. And the name Kirksen would finally go on the door, in substitution for another that would be unceremoniously dropped.

The managing partner smiled at Jack. "You may not like me, Jack, but I'm telling you the truth. You're a big boy, it's up to you to deal with it."

Kirksen closed the door behind him.

Jack stood for a second longer and then collapsed back into his chair. He lunged forward, scattered his desk clear with quick, violent thrusts of his arms, and then slowly laid his head down on its surface.

TWENTY-SIX

Seth Frank looked at the old man. Short, with a soft felt cap covering his head, dressed in corduroy pants, a thick sweater and winter boots, the man looked both uncomfortable and greatly excited at being in the police station. In his hand was a rectangular object covered in brown paper.

"I'm not sure I understand, Mr. Flanders."

"You see I was out there. At the courthouse that day. You know, when the man got killed. Just went to see what all the fuss was about. Lived here all my life, nothing ever came close to that spectacle, I can tell you that."

"I can understand that," Frank said dryly.

"So anyway I had my new Camcorder, real nifty thing, got an image screen and all. Just hold, look at it and shoot. Great quality. So the wife said I should come down."

"That's terrific, Mr. Flanders. And the purpose of all this?" Frank looked at him inquiringly.

Realization spread over Flanders's features. "Oh. I'm sorry, Lieutenant. I'm standing here rambling, have a tendency to do that, just ask the missus. Retired for a year. Never talked much at work. Assembly line at a processing plant. Like to talk now. Listen too. Spend a lot of time down at that little café over behind the bank. Good coffee and the muffins are the real thing, no low-fat stuff."

Frank looked exasperated.

Flanders hurried on. "Well, I came down here to show you this. Give it to you, really. Kept a copy for myself of course." He handed across the package.

Frank opened it and looked at the videocassette. Flanders took off his cap, revealing a bald head with cottony tufts of hair clustered around his ears. He went on excitedly, "Got some really good shots, like I said. Like of the President and right when that fella was shot. Got all that. Jesus, did I. I was following the President, you see. Ran me right into all the fireworks."

Frank stared at the man.

"It's all there, Lieutenant. For what it's worth." He looked at his watch. "Huh. I gotta go. Late for my lunch. Wife doesn't like that." He turned to leave. Seth Frank stared down at the cassette.

"Oh, Lieutenant. One more thing."

"Yes?"

"If anything were to come from my tape, do you think they might use my name when they write about it?"

Frank shook his head. "Write about it?"

The old man looked excited. "Yeah. You know, the historians. They'd call it the Flanders Tape, wouldn't they, or something like that. The Flanders Video maybe. You know, like before."

Frank wearily rubbed his temples. "Like before?"

"Yeah, Lieutenant. You know, like Zapruder with Kennedy."

Frank's face finally sagged in recognition. "I'll be sure to let them know, Mr. Flanders. Just in case. For posterity."

"There you go." Flanders pointed a happy finger at him. "Posterity, I like that. Have a good one, Lieutenant."

"Alan?"

442

Richmond absently motioned for Russell to come in and then looked down once again at the notebook in front of him. Finished, he closed it and looked at his Chief of Staff; his stare was impassive.

Russell hesitated, studying the carpet, her hands clasped nervously in front of her. Then she hurried across the room and fell rather than sat in one of the chairs.

"I'm not sure what to say to you, Alan. I realize my behavior was inexcusable, absolutely inappropriate. If I could plead temporary insanity I would."

"So you're not going to attempt to explain it away as being somehow in my best interests?" Richmond sat back in his chair; his eyes remained on Russell.

"No, I'm not. I'm here to offer my resignation."

The President smiled. "Perhaps I did underestimate you, Gloria."

He stood up, went around the desk and leaned against it, facing her. "On the contrary, your behavior was absolutely appropriate. If I had been in your position I would've done the same thing."

She looked up at him. Her face betrayed her astonishment. "Don't misunderstand me, I expect loyalty, Gloria, like any leader. I do not, however, expect human beings to be anything more than that, meaning human, with all their associated weaknesses and survival instincts. We are, after all, animals. I have attained my position in life by never losing sight of the fact that the most important person in the world is myself. Whatever the situation, whatever the obstacle, I have never, *never* lost sight of that one simple truism. What you did that night displays that you also share that belief."

"You know what I intended?"

"Of course I do. Gloria, I don't condemn you for taking a situation and attempting to maximize its beneficial effect on you. My God, that's the basis

443

upon which this country and this city in particular are built."

"But when Burton told you—"

Richmond held up one hand. "I admit I felt certain emotions that night. Betrayal perhaps foremost among them. But in the time since, I have concluded that what you did evidenced strength, not weakness, of character."

Russell struggled to see where this was going. "Then may I correctly assume that you do not want my resignation?"

The President bent forward, took one of her hands. "I can't recall you ever mentioning the word, Gloria. I can't imagine breaking up our relationship after we've come to know each other so well. Shall we leave it at that?"

Russell rose to go. The President went back to his desk.

"Oh, Gloria. I do have a number of things I want to go over with you tonight. The family's out of town. So perhaps we can work in my private quarters."

Russell looked back at him.

"It might be a late night, Gloria. Better bring a change of clothes." The President didn't smile. His stare cut right through her, than he went back to his work.

Russell's hand trembled as she closed the door.

Jack pounded on the door so hard he could feel the thick, polished wood cut into his knuckles.

The housekeeper opened the door but Jack shot through before she could say a word.

Jennifer Baldwin swept down the curved staircase and into the marbled entrance foyer. Dressed in yet another expensive evening gown, her hair tumbled down her shoulders framing her significant cleavage. She was not smiling.

444

"Jack, what are you doing here?"

"I want to talk to you."

"Jack, I have plans. This will have to wait."

"*No!*" He grabbed her hand, looked around, pushed open a pair of carved doors and pulled her into the library, shutting the doors behind them.

She jerked her hand free. "Are you insane, Jack?"

He looked around the room with its huge bookcases and well-fed shelves of gilt-edged first editions. All for show, none of them had probably ever been opened. All for show.

"I've got one simple question for you to answer and then I'll leave."

"Jack—"

"*One question.* And then I'll leave."

She eyed him suspiciously, crossed her arms. "What is it?"

"Did you or did you not call my firm and tell them to fire Barry Alvis because he made me work the night we were at the White House?"

"Who told you that?"

"Just answer the question, Jenn."

"Jack, why is this so important to you?"

"So you did have him fired?"

"Jack, I want you to stop thinking about that and start realizing the kind of future we're going to have together. If we—"

"Answer the goddamned question!"

She exploded. "*Yes!* Yes, I had the little shit fired. So what? He deserved it. He treated you as an inferior. And he was dead wrong. He was nothing. He played with fire and he got burned and I don't feel the least bit sorry for him." She looked at him without a trace of remorse.

Having heard the answer he expected to hear, Jack sat down in a chair and stared at the massive desk at the other end of the room. The high-backed, leather

445

desk chair faced away from them. He looked at the original oils adorning the walls, the huge windows with perfectly pooled flowing drapes that probably cost more than he could even guess, the ornate woodwork, the omnipresent sculptures of metal and marble. The ceiling with yet another legion of medieval characters marching across it. The world of the Baldwins. Well, they were welcome to it. He slowly closed his eyes.

Jennifer swept back her hair, looked at him, more than a hint of anxiousness in her eyes. She vacillated for a moment and then went to him, knelt beside him, touched his shoulder. The scent of her perfumed body cascaded over him. She spoke low, close to his face. Her breath tickled his ear.

"Jack, I told you before, you don't have to put up with that sort of behavior. And now that this ridiculous murder case is out of the way we can go on with our lives. Our house is almost ready, it's gorgeous, it really is. And we have wedding plans to finalize. Sweetheart, now everything can go back to normal." She touched his face, turned it toward hers. She looked at him with her best pair of bedroom eyes and then she kissed him, long and deeply, letting her lips pull back slowly from his. Her eyes quickly searched his. She didn't find what she was looking for.

"You're right, Jenn. The ridiculous murder case is over. A man I respected and cared for got his brains blown apart. Case closed, time to move on. Got a fortune to build."

"You know what I mean. You never should have involved yourself in that thing in the first place. It wasn't your problem. If you would just open your eyes you'd realize that all of that was beneath you, Jack."

"And hardly convenient for you, right?"

446

Jack abruptly stood up. He was more exhausted than anything else.

"Have a great life, Jenn. I'd say I'd see you around but I really can't imagine that happening." He started to leave.

She grabbed his sleeve. "Jack, will you please tell me what I did that was so awful?"

He hesitated and then confronted her.

"The fact that you even have to ask. Jesus Christ!" He shook his head wearily. "You took a man's life, Jenn, a man you didn't even know, and you destroyed it. And why did you do that? Because something he did to me 'inconvenienced' you. So you took ten years' worth of a career and wiped it out. With one phone call. Never thinking about what it would do to him, his family. He could've blown his brains out, his wife could have divorced him for all you know. You didn't care about that. You probably never even thought about that. And the bottom line is I could never love, I could never spend my life with someone who could do something like that. If you can't understand that, if you really think what you did wasn't wrong, then that's all the more reason why we need to say good-bye right now. We might as well flesh out the irreconcilable differences *before* the wedding. Saves everybody a lot of time and trouble."

He turned the handle on the door and smiled. "Everybody I know would probably tell me how crazy I am for doing this. That you're the perfect woman, smart, rich, beautiful — and you are all of those things, Jenn. They'd say we'd have a perfect life together. That we'd have everything. How could we not be happy? But the thing is, I wouldn't make you happy because I don't care about the things you do. I don't care about the millions in legal business, or houses the size of apartment buildings or cars that cost a year's salary. I don't like this house, I don't like your lifestyle, I don't like your friends. And I guess the bottom line is, I don't like you. And right now I'm probably the only man on the planet who would say that. But I'm a pretty simple guy, Jenn, and the one thing I'd never do to you is lie. And let's face it, in a couple of days, about a dozen guys a lot better suited to you than Jack Graham are going to be knocking on your door. You won't be lonely."

He looked at her and felt a grimace of pain as he observed the absolute astonishment on her face.

"For what it's worth, anybody who asks, you dumped me. Not up to the Baldwin standard. Unworthy. Good-bye, Jenn."

She still stood there several minutes after he left. A series of emotions competed for space across her face, none, in the end, winning out. Finally she fled the room. The sounds of her high heels against the marble floor disappeared as she hurried up the carpeted stairs.

For a few seconds more the library was quiet. Then the desk chair swung around and Ransome Baldwin eyed the doorway where his daughter had been standing.

Jack checked the peephole, half-expecting to see Jennifer Baldwin standing there with a gun. His eyebrows raised a notch when he saw who it was.

Seth Frank walked in, shrugged off his coat, and looked around appreciatively at Jack's cluttered little apartment.

"Man, this brings back memories of another time in my life, I can tell you."

"Let me guess. Delta House '75. You were vice president in charge of bar operations."

Frank grinned. "Closer to the truth than I'd care to admit. Enjoy it while you can, my friend. Without meaning to sound politically incorrect, a good woman will not allow you to continue such an existence."

"Then I might be in luck."

Jack disappeared into the kitchen and came back with a brace of Sam Adamses.

They settled into the furniture with their drinks.

"Trouble in wedded-bliss-to-be-land, counselor?"

"On a scale of one to ten, a one or a ten depending on your perspective."

"Why am I thinking that it's not the Baldwin gal that's entirely gotten to you?"

"Don't you ever stop being a detective?"

"Not if I can help it. You want to talk about it?"

Jack shook his head. "I might bend your ear another night, but not tonight."

Frank shrugged. "Just let me know, I'll bring the beer."

Jack noticed the package on Frank's lap. "Present?"

Frank took out the tape. "I'm assuming you've got a VCR under some of this junk?"

As the video came on Frank looked at Jack.

"Jack, this is definitely not G-rated. And I'm telling you up front, it shows everything including what happened to Luther. You up to it?"

Jack paused for a moment. "You think we might see something in here that'll catch whoever did it?"

"That's what I'm hoping. You knew him a lot better than I did. Maybe you'll see something I don't."

"Then I'm up to it."

Even forewarned, Jack was not prepared. Frank watched him closely as the moment grew closer. When the shot rang out he saw Jack involuntarily jerk back, his eyes wide in horror.

Frank cut off the video. "Hang in there, I warned you." Jack was slumped over in his chair. His breathing was irregular, his forehead clammy. His entire body shuddered for an instant and then he slowly came around. He wiped his forehead.

"Jesus Christ!"

Flanders's passing remark to the Kennedy example had not been inappropriate. "We can stop right now, Jack."

Jack's lips set in a firm line. "The hell we can!"

Jack hit the rewind one more time. They had gone through the tape about a dozen times now. Watching his friend's head virtually explode was not getting any easier to watch. The only mitigating factor was that Jack's anger was increasing with each viewing.

Frank shook his head. "You know it's too bad the guy wasn't filming the other way. We might've gotten a flash from the shooter. I guess that would've been too easy. Hey, you got any coffee? I have a hard time thinking without caffeine."

"Got some pretty fresh stuff in the pot, you can bring me a cup. Dishes are over the sink."

When Frank returned with the steaming cups, Jack had rewound the tape to a demonstrative Alan Richmond saying his piece on the impromptu stage outside the courthouse.

"That guy's a dynamo."

Frank looked at the screen. "I met him the other day."

"Yeah? Me too. That was in my I'm-marrying-into-the-rich-and-famous-set days."

"What'd you think of the guy?"

Jack gulped his coffee, reached for a bag of peanut butter crackers that lay on the couch, offered one to Frank, who took it and then put his feet up on the rickety coffee table. The detective was slipping easily back into the less-structured domain of bachelor-hood.

Jack shrugged. "I don't know. I mean, he's the President. I always thought he was presidential. What do you think of him?"

"Smart. Really smart. The kind of smart you want to be real careful not to get into a battle of wits with unless you're real sure about your own abilities."

"I guess it's a good thing he's on America's side."

"Yeah." Frank looked back at the screen. "So anything grab your eye?"

Jack punched a button on the remote. "One thing. Check this out." The video leapt forward. The figures jerked around like actors in a silent movie.

"Watch this."

The screen showed Luther stepping out of the van. His eyes were turned toward the ground; the manacles were obviously making it difficult for him to walk. Suddenly, a column of people moved into the video, led by the President. Luther was partially obscured. Jack froze the frame.

"Look."

Frank scrutinized the screen, absently munching peanut butter crackers and draining his coffee. He shook his head.

Jack looked at him. "Look at Luther's face. You can see it right between the suits. Look at his face."

Frank bent forward, almost touching the screen with his face. He recoiled, his eyes wide.

"Damn, looks like he's saying something."

"No, it looks like he's saying something to somebody."

Frank looked across at Jack. "You're saying he's recognized somebody, like maybe the guy who popped him?"

"Under the circumstances, I don't think he'd just be making casual conversation with some stranger."

Frank looked back at the screen, studying it intently. Finally he shook his head. "We're going to

451

need some special talents on this." He rose. "Come on."

Jack grabbed his coat. "Where to?"

Frank smiled as he rewound the tape and then put on his hat.

"Well, first I'm gonna buy us some dinner. I'm married, and I'm also older and fatter than you. Consequently, crackers for dinner don't cut it. Then we're going down to the station. I've got somebody I want you to meet."

Two hours later Seth Frank and Jack walked into the Middleton police station, their bellies lined with surf and turf and a couple slices of pecan pie. Laura Simon was in the lab; the equipment was already set up.

After introductions, Laura popped the tape in. The images sprung to life on a forty-six-inch screen in the corner of the lab. Frank fast-forwarded to the appropriate spot.

"There," Jack pointed. "Right there."

Frank froze the tape.

Laura sat at a keyboard and typed in a series of commands. On the screen, the part of the frame containing Luther's image was blocked out and then magnified in increasingly large degrees, like a balloon being blown up. This process continued until Luther's face seemed to span the entire forty-six inches.

"That's as far as I can take it." Laura spun her chair around and nodded to Frank. He pushed a button on the remote and the screen again came to life.

The audio was choppy; screams, shouts, traffic noise and the blended sounds of hundreds of people served to make what Luther was saying incomprehensible. They watched as his lips moved open and closed.

"He's pissed. Whatever he's saying he is not

452

happy." Frank pulled out a cigarette, got a dirty look from Simon and put it back in his pocket.

"Anybody read lips?" Laura looked at each of them.

Jack stared at the screen. What the hell was Luther saying? The look on his face. Jack had seen that once before, if he could only remember when. It had been recently, he was sure of it.

"You see something we don't?" Frank asked. Jack looked over to see Frank staring at him.

Jack shook his head, rubbed his face. "I don't know. There's something there, I just can't place it."

Frank nodded to Simon to cut off the equipment. He stood up and stretched. "Well, sleep on it. Anything comes to you, let me know. Thanks for coming in, Laura."

The two men walked out together. Frank glanced over at Jack, then reached across and felt behind his neck. "Jesus, you are a stress grenade ready to explode."

"Christ, I don't know why I should be. The woman I was supposed to marry I'm not, the woman I wanted to marry just told me to get out of her life, and I'm reasonably sure I'm not going to have a job in the morning. Oh, not to mention, someone murdered a person I cared a lot about and we're probably never going to find out who it is. Hell, my life couldn't get any more perfect, could it?"

"Well, maybe you're due for some good luck."

Jack unlocked his Lexus. "Yeah, hey if you know anyone who wants an almost-brand-new car, let me know."

Frank's eyes twinkled as he looked at Jack. "Sorry, nobody I know could afford it."

Jack smiled back. "Me either."

Driving back, Jack looked at his car clock. It was

453

almost midnight. He passed the offices of Patton, Shaw, looked up at the stretch of darkened offices and wheeled his car around, turning into the garage. He slid his security card in, waved to the security camera posted outside the garage door, and a few minutes later was in the elevator heading up.

He didn't know exactly why he was here. His days at Patton, Shaw were now clearly numbered. Without Baldwin as a client, Kirksen would ride him out on a rail. He felt a little sorry for Lord. He had promised the man protection. But he wasn't going to marry Jennifer Baldwin simply to ensure Lord's mammoth draw check. And the man had lied to him about Barry Alvis's departure from the firm. But Lord would land on his feet. Jack hadn't been kidding about his faith in the man's resiliency. A number of firms would snap him up in a New York minute. Lord's future was far more assured than Jack's.

The elevator doors opened and Jack stepped into the firm's lobby. The wall lights were on low and the shadowy effect would have been a little unnerving if he hadn't been so completely preoccupied with his thoughts. He walked down the hallway toward his office, stopped at the kitchen and grabbed a glass of soda. Ordinarily, even at midnight, there were a few people beating their brains out over some impossible deadline. Tonight there was only stone-cold silence.

Jack turned on his light and closed his office door. He looked around at the domain of his personal partnership. His kingdom, if only for another day. It was impressive. The furniture was tastefully expensive, the carpet and wall coverings luxurious. He went down his line of diplomas. Some hard-earned, others freebies that you got for just being a lawyer. He noticed that the scattered papers had been picked up, the work of the meticulous and sometimes overzealous cleaning crew who were used to attorney sloppiness and the occasional full-blown tantrum.

He sat down, leaned back in his chair. The soft leather was more comfortable than his bed. He could visualize Jennifer talking with her father. Ransome Baldwin's face would flame red at what he would perceive as an unforgivable insult to his precious little girl. The man would lift the phone tomorrow morning and Jack's corporate career would be over.

And Jack couldn't have cared less. His only regret was not instigating that result sooner. Hopefully PD would take him back. That was where he belonged anyway. No one could stop him from doing that. No, his real troubles had started when he had tried being something and someone he wasn't. He would never make that mistake again.

His attention shifted to Kate. Where would she go? Had she really been serious about quitting her job? Jack recalled the fatalistic look on her face and concluded that, yes, she had been quite serious. He had pleaded with her once more. Just like four years before. Pleaded with her not to go, not to leave his life again. But there was something there he could not break through. Maybe it was the enormous guilt she carried. Maybe she simply did not love him. Had he ever really addressed that possibility? The fact was he hadn't. Consciously had not. The possible answer scared the hell out of him. But what did it matter now?

Luther dead; Kate leaving. His life hadn't really changed all that much, despite all the recent activity. The Whitneys were finally, irreversibly, gone from him.

He looked at the pink pile of messages on his desk. All routine. Then he hit a button on his phone to check his voice mail, which he hadn't done in a couple of days. Patton, Shaw let their clients have their choice of the antiquated written phone message

455

or the technologically advanced voice mail. The more demanding clients loved the latter. At least then they didn't have to wait to scream at you.

There were two calls from Tarr Crimson. He would find Tarr another lawyer. Patton, Shaw was too expensive for him anyway. There were several Baldwin-related matters. Right. Those could wait for the next guy Jennifer Baldwin set her laser sights on. The last message jolted him. It was a woman's voice. Small, hesitant, elderly, clearly uncomfortable with the concept of voice mail. Jack played it back again.

"Mr. Graham, you don't know me. My name is Edwina Broome. I was a friend of Luther Whitney." Broome? The name was familiar. The message continued. "Luther told me that if anything happened to him I was to wait a little bit and then I was to send the package on to you. He told me not to open it and I didn't. He said it was like a Pandora's box. If you looked you might get hurt. God rest his soul, he was a good man, Luther was. I hadn't heard from you, not that I expected to. But it just occurred to me that I should call and make sure that you got the thing. I've never had to send something like that before, overnight delivery they call it. And I think I did it right, but I don't know. If you didn't get it, please call me. Luther said it was very important. And Luther never said anything that wasn't true."

Jack listened to the phone number and wrote it down. He checked the time of the call. Yesterday morning. He quickly searched his office. There was no package lurking there. He jogged down the hallway to his secretary's workstation. There was no package there either. He went back to his office. *My God, a package from Luther. Edwina Broome?* He put his hand through his hair, assaulted his scalp, forced himself to think. Suddenly the name came to him. The mother of the woman who had killed herself.

Frank had told him about her. Luther's alleged partner.

Jack picked up the phone. It seemed to ring for an eternity.

"H–hello?" The voice was sleepy, distant.

"Mrs. Broome? This is Jack Graham. I'm sorry for calling you so late."

"Mr. Graham?" The voice was no longer sleepy. It was alert, sharp. Jack could almost envision her sitting up in bed, clutching at her nightgown, looking anxiously at the phone receiver.

"I'm sorry, I just got your message. I didn't get the package, Mrs. Broome. When did you send it?"

"Let me think for a minute." Jack could hear the labored breathing. "Why it was five days ago, counting today."

Jack thought furiously. "Do you have the receipt with a number on it?"

"The man gave me a piece of paper. I'll have to go get it."

"I'll wait."

He tapped his fingers against his desk, tried to stop his mind from flying apart. *Just hold on, Jack. Just hold on.*

"I've got it right here, Mr. Graham."

"Please call me Jack. Did you send it by Federal Express?"

"That's right. Yes."

"All right, what's the tracking number?"

"The what?"

"I'm sorry. The number on the upper–right–hand corner of the piece of paper. It should be a long series of numbers."

"Oh yes." She gave it to him. He scribbled the numbers down, read them back to her to confirm it. He also had her confirm the address of the law firm.

457

"Jack, is this very serious? I mean Luther dying the way he did and all."

"Has anyone called you, anyone you don't know? Besides me?"

"No."

"Well, if they do I want you to call Seth Frank, Middleton police department."

"I know him."

"He's a good guy, Mrs. Broome. You can trust him."

"All right, Jack."

He hung up and phoned Federal Express. He could hear the computer keys clicking on the other end of the line.

The female voice was professional and concise. "Yes, Mr. Graham, it was delivered at the law offices of Patton, Shaw & Lord on Thursday at ten-oh-two A.M. and signed for by a Ms. Lucinda Alvarez."

"Thank you. I guess it's around here somewhere." Bewildered, he was about to hang up.

"Has there been some special problem with this package delivery, Mr. Graham?"

Jack looked puzzled. "Special problem? No, why?"

"Well, when I pulled up the delivery history of this package it shows that we already had an inquiry about it earlier today."

Jack's whole body tensed. "Earlier today? What time?"

"Six-thirty P.M."

"Did they leave a name?"

"Well, that's the unusual part. According to my records, that person also identified himself as Jack Graham." Her tone made it clear she was far from certain of Jack's real identity.

Jack felt a chill invade every part of his body.

He slowly hung up the phone. Somebody else was very interested in this package, whatever it was. And

458

someone knew it was coming to him. His hands were shaking as he picked up the phone again. He quickly dialed Seth Frank, but the detective had gone home. The person would not give out Frank's home phone, and Jack had left that number back at his apartment. After some prodding by Jack the person tried the detective's home, but there was no answer. He swore under his breath. A quick call to directory assistance was useless; the home number was nonpub.

Jack leaned back in his chair, the breaths coming a little more rapidly. He felt his chest where his heart suddenly threatened to explode through his shirt. He had always considered himself a possessor of above-average courage. Now he wasn't so sure.

He forced himself to focus. The package had been delivered. Lucinda had signed for it. The routine at Patton, Shaw was precise; mail was vitally important to law firms. All overnight packages would be given to the firm's in-house gofer team to be distributed with the day's other mail. They brought it around in a cart. They all knew where Jack's office was. Even if they didn't, the firm printed out a map that was routinely updated. So long as you used the correct map . . .

Jack raced to the door, flung it open and sprinted down the hallway. Completely unbeknownst to him, around the corner, in the opposite direction, a light had just come on in Sandy Lord's office.

Jack clicked on the light in his old office and the room quickly came into focus. He frantically searched the desktop, then pulled out the chair to sit down and his eyes came to rest on the package. Jack picked it up. He instinctively looked around, noted the open blinds and hurriedly shut them.

He read the package label: Edwina Broome to Jack Graham. This was it. The package was boxy, but light. It was a box within a box, that's what she had

459

said. He started to open it, then stopped. They knew the package had been delivered here. *They?* That was the only label he could think to apply. If *they* knew the package was here, had in fact called about it this very day, what would they do? If whatever was inside was that important and it had already been opened, presumably they would already know about it. Since that hadn't happened, what would they do?

Jack sprinted back down the hallway to his office, the package held tightly under his arm. He flung on his coat, grabbed his car keys off his desk, almost knocking over his half-empty glass of soda, and turned to go out. He stopped cold.

A noise. He couldn't tell from where; the sound seemed to echo softly down the hallway, like water lapping through a tunnel. It wasn't the elevator. He was sure he would have heard the elevator. But would he really? It was a big place. The background noise produced by that mode of transportation was so everyday, would he have even noticed it? And he had been on the phone, all his attention had been so concentrated. The truth was he couldn't be sure. Besides it might just be one of the firm's attorneys, dropping in to work or pick up something. All his instincts told him that conclusion was the wrong one. But this was a secure building. But then again, how secure could any public building be? He softly closed his office door.

There it was again. His ears strained to pick up its location without success. Whoever it was, they were moving slowly, stealthily. No one who worked here would do that. He inched over to the wall and turned off the light, waited for an instant and then carefully opened the door.

He peered out. The hallway was clear. But for how long? His tactical problem was obvious. The firm's office space was configured such that if he started

460

down one way he was more or less committed to that path. And he would be totally exposed, the hallways were absolutely devoid of furnishings. If he met whoever it was going that way, he wouldn't have a chance.

A practical consideration struck him and he looked around the darkness of his office. His gaze finally fell upon a heavy, granite paperweight, one of the many knickknacks he had received upon making partner. It could do some real damage if wielded properly. And Jack was confident he could do so. If he was going down he wouldn't make it easy for them. That fatalist approach helped to stiffen his resolve and he waited another few seconds before venturing out into the hallway, closing the door behind him. Whoever it was probably would have to make a door-to-door search to find his office.

He crouched low as he came to a corner. Now he desperately wished the office was in total darkness. He took a deep breath and peered around. The way was clear, at least for now. He thought quickly. If there was more than one intruder, they would probably split up, cut their search time in half. Would they even know if he was in the building? Maybe he had been followed here. That thought was especially troubling. They might even at this moment be circling him, coming from both ways.

The sounds were closer now. Footsteps – he could make out at least one pair. His hearing was now raised to its highest level of acuteness. He could almost make out the person's breathing, or at least he imagined he could. He had to make a choice. And his eyes finally fell upon something on the wall, something that gleamed back at him: the fire alarm.

As he was about to make a run for it, a leg came around the corner at the other end of the hallway. Jack jerked back, not waiting for the rest of the body to catch up with the limb. He walked as swiftly as he could in the opposite direction. He turned the corner, made his way down the hall, and came to a stairwell door. He jerked it open and a loud creak hit him full in the face.

He heard the sounds of running feet.

"Shit!" Jack slammed the door closed behind him and clattered down the stairs.

A man hurtled around the corner. A black ski mask covered his face. A pistol was in his right hand.

An office door opened and Sandy Lord, dressed in his undershirt, with his pants halfway off, stumbled out and accidentally plowed into the man. They went down hard. Lord's flailing hands instinctively gripped the mask, pulling it off.

Lord rolled to his knees, sucking in blood from his battered nose.

"What the goddamn hell is going on? Who the hell are you?" Lord angrily looked eye-to-eye with the man. Then Lord saw the gun and froze.

Tim Collin looked back at him, shaking his head half in disbelief, half in disgust. There was no way around it now. He raised his gun.

"Jesus Christ! Please no!" Lord wailed and fell back.

The gun fired and blood spurted from the very center of the undershirt. Lord gasped once, his eyes glazed and his body landed back against the door. It fell the rest of the way open to reveal the nearly naked figure of the young legislative liaison, who stared in shock at the dead lawyer. Collin swore under his breath. He looked at her. She knew what was coming, he could see it in the terror-filled eyes.

Wrong place, wrong time. Sorry lady.

His gun exploded a second time and the impact knocked her slender body back into the room. Her legs splayed, her fingers clenched, she stared blankly at the ceiling; her night of pleasure turned abruptly into her last night on earth.

Bill Burton ran up to his kneeling partner and surveyed the carnage with incredulity, which was quickly replaced with anger.

"Are you fucking crazy!" he exploded.

"They saw my face, what the hell was I supposed to do? Make them promise not to tell? Fuck it!"

Both men's nerves were at their breaking point. Collin gripped his gun hard.

"Where is he? Was it Graham?" Burton demanded.

"I think so. He went down the fire stairs."

"So he's gone."

Collin looked at him and then stood up. "Not yet. I didn't waste two people just so he could get away." He started to take off. Burton grabbed him.

"Give me your gun, Tim."

"Goddammit, Bill, are you nuts?"

Burton shook his head, pulled out his piece and handed it to him. He took Collin's weapon.

"Now go get him. I'll try to do some damage control here." Collin ran to the door and then disappeared down the stairs. Burton looked at the two dead bodies. He recognized Sandy Lord and sucked in his breath sharply. "Goddamn. Goddamn," he said again. He turned and went quickly to Jack's office. Trailing his sprinting partner, he had found it right at the moment the first shot rang out. He opened the door and turned on the light. He surveyed the interior quickly. The guy would have the package with him. That was clear. Richmond had been right about Edwina Broome's involvement. Whitney had entrusted her with the package. Shit, they had been so close. Who knew Graham or anybody else would be here this late?

He made another sweep of the room's contents with his eyes.

They went past and slowly came back to the desk. His plan came together in a few seconds. Finally, something might be going their way. He moved toward the desk.

Jack reached the first floor and yanked on the doorknob. It didn't budge. His heart sank. They had had trouble with this before. Routine fire drills and the doors had been locked. The building management said they had fixed the problem. Right! Only now their mistake could cost him his life. And not from any inferno.

He looked back up the stairs. They were coming fast, silence was no longer an issue. Jack raced back up the stairs to the second floor, prayed silently before he grabbed the knob and a rush of relief swept over him as it turned in his sweating hand. He turned the corner, hit the elevator bank, pushed the button. He checked his backside, ran to the far corner and crouched down out of sight.

Come on! He could hear the elevator heading up. But then an awful thought ran through his mind. Whoever was following him could be on that elevator. Could have figured what Jack would try to do and attempt to checkmate him.

The car halted on his floor. At the instant the doors opened Jack heard the fire door smash against the wall. He jumped for the car, slid in between the doors and crashed against the back of the elevator. He leapt up and hit the button for the garage.

Jack felt the presence immediately, the slightly elevated breathing. He saw a flash of black, then the gun. He hurled the paperweight, and threw himself into the corner.

He heard a grunt of pain as the doors finally closed.

He ran through the dark underground parking garage, found his car and a few moments later he was through the automatic door and hit the accelerator. The car raced up the street. Jack looked back. Nothing. He looked at himself in the mirror. His face was drenched with sweat. His entire body was one large knot. He rubbed his shoulder where he had slammed into the elevator wall. Jesus, that had been so close. So close.

As he drove he wondered where he could go. They knew him, knew all about him, it seemed. He clearly couldn't go home. Where then? The police? No. Not until he knew who was after him. Who had been able to kill Luther despite all the cops. Who seemed to always know what the cops knew. For tonight he would stay someplace in town. He had his credit cards. In the morning, first thing in the morning, he would hook up with Frank. Everything would be okay then. He eyed the box. But tonight he would see what had almost cost him his life.

Russell lay underneath the sheets. Richmond had just finished on top of her. And without a word he had climbed off and left the room, her sole purpose brutally fulfilled. She rubbed her wrists where he had clenched them. She could feel the abrasions. Her breasts hurt where he had mauled them. Burton's warning came back to her. Christine Sullivan, too, had been mangled, and not just by the agents' bullets.

She slowly moved her head back and forth, fought to hold back the tears. She had wanted this so badly. Had wanted Alan Richmond to make love to her; she had imagined it would be so romantic, so idyllic. Two intelligent, powerful and dynamic people. The perfect couple. How wonderful it should have been. And then the vision of the man startled her back to reality; pounding away at her, with no more emotion on his features than if he had been masturbating alone in the toilet with the latest *Penthouse*. He had never

465

even kissed her; had never even spoken. He had just pulled off her clothes as soon as she came in the bedroom, sunk his hardened flesh into her and now he was gone. It had all taken barely ten minutes. And now she was alone. *Chief of Staff! Chief Whore more like it.*

She wanted to scream out *I fucked you! You bastard! I fucked you in that room that night and there wasn't a damn thing you could do about it, you sonofabitch.*

Her tears wet the pillow and she cursed herself for breaking down and crying yet again. She had been so sure of her abilities, so confident that she could control him. God, she had been so wrong. The man had people killed. Walter Sullivan. *Walter Sullivan* had been killed, murdered, with the knowledge, indeed the blessing, of the President of the United States. When Richmond had told her she couldn't believe it. He said he wanted to keep her fully informed. Fully terrified was more like it. She had no idea what he was up to now. She was no longer a central part of this campaign and she thanked God that she wasn't.

She sat up in bed, pulled the ripped nightgown over her quivering body. Shame rocked her again, momentarily. Of course she was now his personal whore. And his consideration for that was his unspoken promise not to crush her. But was that all? Was that really all?

She huddled the blanket around her and looked into the darkness of the room. She was an accomplice. But she was also something more. She was a *witness.* Luther Whitney had also been a witness. And now he was dead. And Richmond had calmly ordered the execution of one of his oldest and dearest friends. If he could do that, what was her life worth? The answer to that question was shockingly clear.

She bit into her hand until it hurt. She looked at

the doorway through which he had disappeared. Was he in there – in the dark, listening – thinking about what to do with her? A cold shudder of fear grabbed her and did not leave. She was caught. For once in her life she had no options. She wasn't sure if she would even survive.

Jack dropped the box on the bed, took off his coat, looked out the window of his hotel room and then sat down. He was pretty sure he hadn't been followed. He had gotten out of the building so fast. He had remembered, at the last minute, to ditch his car. He didn't really know who was pursuing him, but he assumed they were sophisticated enough to trace his car's whereabouts.

He checked his watch. The cab had dropped him off at the hotel barely fifteen minutes ago. It was a nondescript place, a hotel where tourists on the cheap would stay and then wander around the city to get their fill of the country's history before heading back home. It was out of the way but then he wanted out of the way.

Jack looked at the box and then decided he had waited long enough. A few seconds later he had it open and was staring at the object inside the plastic bag.

A knife? He looked at it more closely. No, it was a letter opener, one of the old-fashioned kind. He held the bag by its ends and examined the object minutely. He wasn't a trained forensic specialist, and thus he didn't register that the black crustings on the handle and blade were actually very old, dried blood. Nor was he aware of the fingerprints that existed within the leather.

He lay the bag carefully down and leaned back in the chair. This had something to do with the woman's murder. Of that he was certain. But what?

He looked at it again. This was obviously an important piece of physical evidence. It hadn't been the murder weapon; Christine Sullivan had been shot. But Luther had thought it critically important.

Jack jerked straight up. Because it identified who had killed Christine Sullivan! He grabbed the bag and held it up to the light, his eyes searching every inch of space. Now he could dimly make them out, like a swirl of black threads. Prints. This had the person's fingerprints on it. Jack looked at the blade closely. Blood. On the handle too. It had to be. What had Frank said? He struggled to recall. Sullivan had possibly stabbed her attacker. In the arm or the leg with a letter opener, the one in the bedroom photo. At least, that was one of the detective's theories he had shared with Jack. What Jack held in his hand seemed to bear that analysis out.

He carefully placed the bag back into the box and slid it under the bed.

He went over to the window and again looked out. The wind had picked up. The cheap window rattled and shook.

If only Luther would have told him, confided in him. But he was scared for Kate. How had they made Luther believe Kate was in danger?

He thought back. Luther had received nothing while in prison, Jack was certain of that. So what then? Had whoever it was just walked up to Luther and told him flat out: talk and your daughter dies? How would they even know he had a daughter? The two hadn't been in the same room with each other for years.

Jack lay down on the bed, closed his eyes. No, he was wrong about that. There was one time when that would have been possible. The day they had arrested Luther. That would be the only time that father and daughter would have been together. It was possible that, without saying anything, someone could have made it crystal-clear to Luther, with just a look, nothing more. Jack had handled cases that had been dismissed because witnesses were afraid to testify. No one had ever said anything to them. It was solely intimidation by the unspoken word. A silent terror, there was nothing new about that.

So who would've been there to do that? To deliver the message that had made Luther shut up like his mouth was stapled closed? But the only people who were there, as far as Jack knew, were the cops. Unless it was the person who had taken a shot at Luther. But why would he hang around? How could that person just waltz into the place, walk up to Luther, make eye contact, without anyone becoming suspicious?

Jack's eyes shot open.

Unless that person were a cop. His immediate thought hit him hard in the chest.

Seth Frank.

He dismissed it quickly. There was no motive there, not a scintilla of motive. For the life of him he couldn't imagine the detective and Christine Sullivan in any type of tryst and that's what this boiled down to, didn't it? Sullivan's lover had killed her and Luther had seen the whole thing. It couldn't be Seth Frank. He hoped to God it wasn't Seth Frank because he was counting on the man to get him out of this mess. But what if tomorrow morning Jack would be delivering the very thing Frank had been desperately searching for? He could have dropped it, left the room, Luther comes out of his hiding place, picks it up and flees. It was possible. And the place sanitized so clean a pro had to be behind it. A pro. An experienced homicide detective who knew exactly how to cleanse a crime scene.

Jack shook his head. No! Dammit no! He had to believe in something, someone. It had to be something else. Someone else. It had to be. He was just tired. His attempts at deduction were becoming ludicrous. Seth Frank was no murderer.

He closed his eyes again. For now he believed he was safe. A few minutes later he fell into an uneasy sleep.

The morning was refreshingly cold, the close, trapped air expunged by the storm of the night before.

Jack was already up; he had slept in his clothes and they looked it. He washed his face in the small bathroom, smoothed down his hair, cut the light off and went back into the bedroom. He sat on the bed and looked at his watch. Frank would not be in yet, but it wouldn't be long now. He pulled the box from under the bed, laid it beside him. It felt like a time bomb next to him.

He flicked on the small color TV that sat in the corner of the room. The early-morning local news was on. The perky blonde, no doubt aided by substantial amounts of caffeine as she waited for her break into prime time, was recounting the top stories.

Jack expected to see the litany of various world trouble spots. The Middle East was good for at least a minute each morning. Maybe Southern California had had another quake. The President fighting the Congress.

But there was only one top story this morning. Jack leaned forward as a place he knew very well flashed across the screen.

Patton, Shaw & Lord. The lobby of PS&L. What was the woman saying? People dead? *Sandy Lord murdered?* Gunned down in his office? Jack leaped across the room and turned up the volume. He watched with increasing astonishment as twin gurneys were wheeled out of the building. A picture of Lord flashed into the upper-right-hand corner of the TV screen. His distinguished career was briefly recounted. But he was dead, unmistakably dead. In his office, someone had shot him.

Jack fell back on the bed. Sandy had been there last night? But who was the other person? The other one under that sheet? He didn't know. Couldn't know that. But he believed he knew what had happened. The man after him, the man with the gun. Lord must have run into him, somehow. They were after Jack and Lord had walked right into it.

He turned off the TV and went back into the bathroom and ran cold water over his face. His hands shook, his throat had dried up. He could not believe that this had all happened. So quickly. It had not been his fault, but Jack could not help feeling enormously guilty for his partner's death. Guilty, like Kate had felt. It was a crushing emotion.

He grabbed the phone and dialed.

Seth Frank had been at his office for an hour already. A contact from D.C. Homicide had tipped him to the twin slayings at the law firm. Frank had no idea if they were connected to Sullivan. But there was a common denominator. A common denominator that had given him a throbbing headache and it was barely seven in the morning.

His direct line rang. He picked it up, his eyebrows arched in semi-disbelief.

"Jack, where the hell are you?"

There was a hard edge in the detective's tone that Jack had not expected to hear.

"Good morning to you too."

"Jack, do you know what's happened?"

"I just saw it on the news. I was there last night, Seth. They were after me; I don't know exactly how but Sandy must've walked into it and they killed him."

471

"Who? Who killed him?"

"I don't know! I was at the office, I heard a noise. The next thing I know I'm being chased through the building by someone with a gun and I barely get out of there with my head intact. Do the police have any leads?"

Frank took a deep breath. The story sounded so fantastic. He believed in Jack, trusted him. But who could be absolutely certain about anyone these days?

"Seth? Seth?"

Frank bit on his nail, thinking furiously. Depending on what he did next one of two totally different events would take place. He momentarily thought of Kate Whitney. The trap he had laid for her and her father. He had still not gotten over that. He might be a cop, but he had been a human being long before that. He trusted he still had some decent human qualities left.

"Jack, the police do have one lead, a real good lead in fact."

"Okay, what is it?"

Frank paused, then said, "It's you, Jack. You're the lead. You're the guy the entire District police force is combing the city for right this very minute."

The phone slowly slid down from Jack's hand. The blood seemed to have ceased flowing through his body.

"Jack? Jack, goddammit talk to me." The words of the detective did not register.

Jack looked out the window. Out there were people who wanted to kill him and people who wanted to arrest him for murder.

"Jack!"

Finally, with an effort, Jack spoke. "I didn't kill anybody, Seth."

The words were spoken as though they were spilling down a drain, about to be washed away.

472

Frank heard what he desperately wanted to hear. It wasn't the words – guilty people almost always lied – it was the tone with which they were spoken. Despair, disbelief, horror all rolled into one.

"I believe you, Jack," Frank said quietly.

"What the hell's going on, Seth?"

"From what I've been told the cops have you on tape going into the garage at around midnight. Apparently Lord and a ladyfriend of his were there before you."

"I never saw them."

"Well, I'm not sure that you necessarily would have." He shook his head and continued. "Seems they were found not completely clothed, especially the woman. I guess they had just finished doing it when they bought it."

"Oh God!"

"And again they have you on the video blowing out of the garage apparently right after they were killed."

"But what about the gun? Did they find the gun?"

"They did. In a trash Dumpster inside the garage."

"And?"

"And your prints were on the gun, Jack. They were the only ones on the gun. After they saw you on the videotape, the D.C. cops accessed your finger-prints from the Virginia State Bar file. A nine-point hit I'm told."

Jack slumped down in the chair.

"I never touched any gun, Seth. Somebody tried to kill me and I ran. I hit the guy, with a paperweight I pulled off my desk. That's all I know." He paused. "What do I do now?"

Frank knew that question was coming. In all honesty he wasn't sure what to answer. Technically, the man he was speaking to was wanted for murder.

As a law enforcement officer, his action should have been absolutely clear, only it wasn't.

"Wherever you are I want you to stay put. I'm gonna check this out. But don't, under any circumstances, go anywhere. Call me back in three hours. Okay?"

Jack hung up and pondered the matter. The police wanted him for murdering two people. His fingerprints were all over a weapon he had never even touched. He was a fugitive from justice. He smiled wearily, then he stiffened slightly. A fugitive. And he had just hung up from talking to a policeman. Frank hadn't asked where he was. But they could have traced the call. They could have done that easily. Only Frank wouldn't do that. But then Jack thought about Kate.

Cops never told the whole truth. The detective had suckered Kate. Then he had felt sorry about it, or at least he had said he had.

A siren blared outside and Jack's heart stopped for an instant. He raced to the window and looked out but the patrol car kept on going until the flashing lights disappeared.

But they might be coming. They might be coming for him right now. He grabbed his coat and put it on. Then he looked down at the bed.

The box.

He had never even told Frank about the damned thing. The most important thing in his life last night, now it had taken a back seat to something else.

"Aren't you busy enough out there in the boonies?" Craig Miller was a D.C. homicide detective of long standing. Big, with thick, wavy black hair and a face that betrayed his love of fine whiskey. Frank had known him for years. Their relationship was one of

474

friendship and the shared belief that murder must always be punished.

"Never too busy to come over to see if you ever got any good at this detective stuff," Frank replied, a wry grin on his face.

Miller smiled. They were in Jack's office. The crime unit was just finishing up.

Frank looked around the spacious interior. Jack was a long way from this kind of life now, he thought to himself.

Miller looked at him, a thought registering. "This Graham fellow, he was involved in the Sullivan case out your way, wasn't he?"

Frank nodded. "The suspect's defense counsel."

"That's right! Man, that's a pretty big swing. Defense counsel to future defendant." Miller smiled.

"Who found the bodies?"

"Housekeeper. She gets in around four in the morning."

"So any motive work its way through that big head of yours?"

Miller eyed his friend. "Come on. It's eight o'clock in the morning. You drove all the way in here from the middle of nowhere to pick my brain. What's up?"

Frank shrugged. "I don't know. I got to know the guy during the case. Surprised the shit out of me to see his face on the morning news. I don't know, it just stuck in my gut."

Miller eyed him closely for another few seconds and then decided not to pursue it.

"The motive, it seems, is pretty clear. Walter Sullivan was the deceased's biggest client. This fellow Graham, without talking to anybody at the firm, jumps in and represents the dude accused of murdering the guy's wife. That, obviously, didn't sit too well with Lord. Apparently, the two had a meeting at Lord's place. Maybe they tried to work things out, maybe they just made things worse."

"How'd you get all the inside scoop?"

"Managing partner of the place." Miller flipped open his notebook: "Daniel J. Kirksen. He was real helpful on all the background shit."

"So how does that lead to Graham coming in here to pop two people?"

"I didn't say it was premeditated. The video time tables show pretty clearly that the deceased was here several hours before Graham showed up."

"So?"

"So the two don't know the other's here, or maybe Graham sees Lord's office light on when he's driving by. It overlooks the street, it'd be easy enough to see someone in the office."

"Yeah, except if the man and woman were getting it on, I'm not sure they'd be showcasing it to the rest of the city. The blinds were probably down."

"Right, but come on, Lord wasn't in the best of shape so I doubt if they were doing it the whole time. In fact the office light was on when they were found and the blinds were partially open. Anyway, accidental or not, the two run into each other here. The argument is rekindled. The feelings accelerate, maybe threats are made. And bam. Heat of the moment. It could be it was Lord's gun. They struggle. Graham gets the piece away from the old guy. Shot's fired. Woman sees it all, she has to eat a round too. All over in a few seconds."

Frank shook his head. "Excuse me for saying so, Craig, but that sounds awfully farfetched."

"Oh yeah? Well we got the guy blowing out of here white as a sheet. The camera got a clear shot of him. I've seen it, there was no blood left in the guy's face, Seth, I'm telling you."

"How come Security didn't come and check things out then?"

Miller laughed. "Security? Shit. Half the time those guys aren't even looking at the monitors. They got a tape backup, you're lucky if they even review on any consistent basis. Let me tell you, it is not hard to get into one of these office buildings after hours."

"So maybe somebody did."

Miller shook his head, grinning. "Don't think so, Seth. That's your problem. You look for a complicated answer when the simple one's staring you in the face."

"So where did this gun mysteriously appear from?"

"A lot of people keep guns stashed in their office."

"A lot? Like how many is a lot, Craig?"

"You'd be surprised, Seth."

"Maybe I would!" Frank shot back.

Miller looked puzzled. "Why do you have such a bug up your ass about this?"

Frank didn't look at his friend. He stared over at the desk. "I don't know. Like I said, I got to know the guy. He didn't seem like the type. So his prints were on the weapon?"

"Two perfect hits. Right thumb and index. Never seen clearer ones."

Something in his friend's words jolted Frank. He was looking at the desk. The highly polished surface had been defaced. The small water ring was clearly visible.

"So where's the glass?"

"What's that?"

Frank pointed to the mark. "The glass that left that mark. Have you got it?"

Miller shrugged and then chuckled. "I haven't checked the dishwasher in the kitchen, if that's what you're asking. Be my guest."

Miller turned to sign off on a report. Frank took the opportunity to check out the desk more closely. In the middle of the desk was a slight dust ring.

Something had been there. Square in shape, about three inches across. The paperweight.

A few minutes later Seth Frank walked down the hallway. The gun had perfect prints on it. Too perfect more like it. Frank had also seen the weapon and the police report on it. A .44 caliber, serial numbers obliterated, untraceable. Just like the weapon found next to Walter Sullivan.

Frank had to allow himself a smile. He had been right in what he had done, or more accurately, what he had not done.

Jack Graham had been telling the truth. He hadn't killed anybody.

"You know, Burton, I'm becoming a little tired of having to devote so much time and attention to this matter. I *do* have a country to run in case you've forgotten." Richmond sat in a chair in the Oval Office in front of a blazing fire. His eyes were closed; his fingers formed a tight pyramid.

Before Burton could respond, the President continued. "Instead of having the object back safely in our possession, you have managed only to contribute two more entries to the city's homicide fiasco, and Whitney's defense attorney is out there somewhere with possibly the evidence to bury us all. I'm absolutely thrilled with the result."

"Graham's not going to the police, not unless he's real fond of prison food and wants a big, hairy man as his date for life." Burton stared down at the motionless President. The shit he, Burton, had gone through to save all their asses while this prize stayed safely behind the lines. And now he was criticizing. Like the veteran Secret Service agent had really enjoyed seeing two more innocent people die.

"I do congratulate you on that part. It showed quick thinking. However, I don't believe we can rely

478

on that as a long-term solution. If the police do take Graham into custody he'll certainly produce the letter opener, if he has it."

"But I bought us some time."

The President stood up, grabbed Burton's thick shoulders. "And in that time I know you will locate Jack Graham and persuade him that taking any action detrimental to our interests would not be in *his* best interests."

"Do you want me to tell him that before or after I put a bullet in his brain?"

The President smiled grimly. "I'll leave that to your professional judgment." He turned to his desk.

Burton stared at the President's back. For one instant Burton visualized pumping a round from his weapon into the base of the President's neck. Just end the bullshit right here and now. If anyone ever deserved it this guy did.

"Any idea where he might be, Burton?"

Burton shook his head. "No, but I've got a pretty reliable source." Burton didn't mention Jack's phone call to Seth Frank that morning. Sooner or later Jack would reveal his location to the detective. And then Burton would make his move.

Burton took a deep breath. If you loved a pressure-filled challenge it didn't get much better than this. It was the ninth inning, the home ream was up by one, there were two outs, one runner on, and a full count on the bruiser at the plate. Could Burton close it out or would they all watch as the white orb disappeared into the stands?

As Burton walked out the door, more than a small part of him hoped it was the latter.

Seth Frank was waiting at his desk, staring at the clock. As the second hand swept past the twelve the phone rang.

Jack sat in the phone booth. He thanked God it was as cold as it was outside. The heavy, hooded parka he had bought that morning fit right in with the bundled-up mass of humanity. And still he had the overwhelming impression that everyone seemed to be looking at him.

Frank picked up on the background noise. "Where the hell are you? I told you not to leave wherever you were staying."

Jack didn't respond right away.

"Jack?"

"Look, Seth, I'm not real good at being a sitting duck. And I'm not in a position where I can afford to completely rely on anyone. Understood?"

Frank started to make a protest, but then leaned back in his chair. The guy was right, flat-out right.

"Fair enough. Would you like to hear how they set you up?"

"I'm listening."

"You had a glass on your desk. Apparently you were drinking something. You remember that?"

"Yeah, Coke, so what?"

"So whoever was after you ran into Lord and the woman like you said and they had to be popped. You got away. They knew the garage video would have you leaving right about the time of the deaths. They lifted your prints off the glass and transferred them to the gun."

"You can do that?"

"You bet your ass, if you know what you're doing and you've got the right equipment, which they probably found in the supply room at your firm. If we had the glass we could show it was a forgery. Just as one person's prints are unique from another person's, your print on the gun couldn't match in every detail the print on the glass. Amount of pressure applied and so on."

"Do the D.C. cops buy that explanation?"

Frank almost laughed. "I wouldn't be counting on that, Jack. I really wouldn't. All they want to do is bring you in. They'll let other people worry about everything else."

"Great. So now what?"

"First things first. Why were they after you in the first place?"

Jack almost slapped himself. He looked down at the box.

"I got a special delivery from someone. Edwina Broome. It's something I think you'll get a real kick out of seeing."

Seth stood up, almost wishing he could reach through the phone and snatch it. "What is it?"

Jack told him.

Blood and prints. Simon would have a field day. "I can meet you anywhere, anytime."

Jack thought rapidly. Ironically, public places seemed to be more dangerous than private ones. "How about the Farragut West Metro station, 18th Street exit, around eleven tonight?"

Frank jotted the information down. "I'll be there."

Jack hung up the phone. He would be at the Metro station before the appointed time. Just in case. If he saw anything remotely suspicious he was going underground as far as he could. He checked his money. The dollars were dwindling. And his credit cards were out for now. He would risk hitting several ATM machines. That would net him a few hundred. That should be enough, for a while.

He exited the phone booth, checked the crowd. It was the typical hurried pace of Union Station. No one appeared the least bit interested in him. Jack jerked slightly. Coming his way were a pair of D.C. police officers. Jack stepped back into the phone booth until they passed.

He bought some burgers and fries at the food court and then grabbed a cab. Munching down while the cab took him through the city, Jack had a moment to reflect on his options. Once he got the letter opener to Frank would his troubles really end? Presumably the prints and blood would match up with the person in the Sullivan house that night. But then Jack's defense counsel mentality took over. And that mind-set told him there were clear, almost insurmountable obstacles in the path of such a pristine resolution.

First, the physical evidence may well be inconclusive. There may be no match because the person's DNA and prints may not be on file anywhere. Jack again remembered the look on Luther's face that night on the Mall. It was somebody important, somebody people knew. And that was another obstacle. If you made accusations against a person like that, you better make damn sure you could back it up or else your case would never see the light of day.

Second, they were looking at a mammoth chain-of-custody problem. Could they even prove the letter opener came from Sullivan's home? Sullivan was dead; the staff might not know for certain. Christine Sullivan had presumably handled it. Perhaps her killer had possessed it for a short period of time. Luther had kept it for a couple of months. Now Jack had it and would, hopefully, soon be passing it on to Seth Frank. It finally struck Jack.

The letter opener's evidentiary value was zilch. Even if they could find a match, a competent defense counsel would shred its admissibility. Hell, they probably wouldn't even get an indictment based on it. Tainted evidence was no evidence at all.

He stopped eating and lay back in the grimy vinyl seat.

But come on! They had tried to get it back! They had killed to get it back. They were prepared to kill

Jack to take possession of what he had. It must be important to them, deadly important. So regardless of its legal efficacy, it had value. And something valuable could be exploited. Maybe he had a chance.

It was ten o'clock when Jack hit the escalator heading down into the Farragut West Metro station. Part of the orange and blue lines on the Washington Metrorail system, Farragut West was a very busy station during the day due to its close proximity to the downtown business area with its myriad law and accounting firms, trade associations and corporate offices. At ten o'clock in the evening, however, it was pretty much deserted.

Jack stepped off the escalator and surveyed the area. The underground Metro stations of the system were really huge tunnels with vaulted honeycombed ceilings and floors consisting of six-sided brick. A broad corridor lined with cigarette advertisements on one side and automated ticket machines on the other culminated in a kiosk that sat in the center of the aisle with the turnstiles flanking it on either side. A huge Metro map with its multicolored rail lines, and travel time and pricing information, stood against one wall next to the dual phone booths.

One bored Metro employee leaned back in his chair in the glass-enclosed kiosk. Jack looked around and eyed the clock atop the kiosk. Then he looked back toward the escalator and froze. Coming down the escalator was a police officer. Jack willed himself to turn as casually as possible and he passed along the wall until he reached the phone booth. He flattened himself against the back of the booth, hidden behind its barrier. He caught his breath and risked peering out. The officer approached the ticket machines, nodded to the Metro guy in the kiosk and looked around the perimeter of the station entrance. Jack drew back. He would wait. The guy would move on shortly; he had to.

Time passed. A loud voice interrupted Jack's thoughts. He looked out. Coming down the escalator was a man, obviously homeless. His clothing was in tatters, a thick bundled blanket slung over one shoulder. His beard and hair were matted and unkempt. His face weather-beaten and strained. It was cold outside. The warmth of the Metro stations was always a welcome haven for the homeless until they got run out. The iron gates at the top of the escalators were to keep just such people out.

Jack looked around. The police officer had disappeared. Perhaps to check out the train platforms, shoot the breeze with the kiosk guy. Jack looked in that direction. That man too had vanished.

Jack looked back at the homeless man, who was now crumpled in one corner, inventorying his meager belongings, rubbing ungloved hands back and forth, trying to work circulation into limbs stretched to their breaking point.

A pang of guilt hit Jack. The gauntlet of such people downtown was staggering. A generous person could empty their entire pockets in the span of one city block. Jack had done that, more than once.

He checked the area one more time. No one. Another train would not arrive for about fifteen minutes. He stepped out of the booth and looked directly across at the man. He didn't seem to see Jack; his attention was focused on his own little world far away from normal reality. But then Jack thought, his own reality was no longer normal, if it ever had been. Both he and the pathetic mass across from him were involved in their own peculiar struggles. And death could claim either of them, at any time. Except that Jack's demise would probably be somewhat more violent, somewhat more sudden. But maybe that was preferable to the lingering death awaiting the other.

He shook his head clear. Thoughts like that were doing him no good. If he were going to survive this he had to remain focused, he had to believe he would outlast the forces marshaled against him.

Jack started forward and then stopped. His blood pressure almost doubled; the sudden metabolic change he was experiencing left him light-headed.

The homeless man was wearing new shoes. Soft-soled, brown leathers, which probably cost over a hundred and fifty bucks. They were revealed from out of the mass of filthy clothing like a shiny blue diamond on a bed of white sand.

And now the man was looking up at him. The eyes locked on Jack's face. They were familiar. Beneath the depths of wrinkles, filthy hair and wind-burnt cheeks, he had seen those eyes before; he was sure of it. The man was now rising off the floor. He seemed to have much more energy than when he first staggered in.

Jack frantically looked around. The place was as empty as a tomb. His tomb. He looked back. The man had already started toward him. Jack backed up, clutching the box to his chest. He thought back to his narrow escape in the elevator. The gun. He would see that gun appearing soon. It would be pointed right at him.

Jack backed down the tunnel toward the kiosk. The man's hand was going underneath his coat, a torn and beaten behemoth that spilled its woolen guts with every step. Jack looked around. He heard approaching footsteps. He looked back at the man, deciding whether he should make a run for the train or not. Then he came into sight.

Jack almost screamed in relief.

The police officer rounded the corner. Jack ran to him, pointing back down the tunnel at the homeless man who now stood stockstill, in the middle of the corridor.

"That man, he's not a homeless person. He's an imposter." The chance of him being recognized by the cop had crossed Jack's mind although the young cop's features didn't betray any such realization.

"What?" The bewildered cop stared at Jack.

"Look at his shoes." Jack realized he was making little sense, but how could he when he couldn't tell the cop the whole story?

The cop looked down the tunnel, saw the homeless man standing there, his face turned into a grimace. In his confusion he retreated to the normal inquiry.

"Has he been bothering you, sir?"

Jack hesitated, then said, "Yes."

"Hey!" The cop shouted at the man.

Jack watched as the cop ran forward. The homeless man turned and fled. He made it to the escalator, but the up escalator wasn't working. He turned and raced down the tunnel, darted around a corner and disappeared, the cop right after him.

Now Jack was alone. He looked back at the kiosk. The Metro guy hadn't returned.

Jack jerked his head. He had heard something. Like a shout, of someone in pain, from where the two men had disappeared. He moved forward. As he did, the cop, slightly out of breath, came back around the corner. He looked at Jack, motioned him to come over with slow movements of his arm. The guy looked sick, like he had seen or done something that disgusted him.

Jack hustled up next to him.

The cop gulped in air. "Goddammit! I don't know what the hell's going on, buddy." The cop again struggled to catch his breath. He put one hand out against the wall to steady himself.

486

"Did you catch him?"

The cop nodded. "You were right."

"What happened?"

"Go see for yourself. I've gotta call this in." The cop straightened up and pointed a warning finger at Jack. "But you are not to leave. I'm not explaining this one by myself and it sounds like maybe you know a helluva lot more about this than you're letting on. Understood?"

Jack nodded quickly. The cop hurried off. Jack walked around the corner. Wait. The cop had told him to wait. Wait for them to arrest him. He should bolt now. But he couldn't. He had to see who it was. He was certain he knew the guy. He had to see.

Jack looked up ahead. This was a service way for Metro personnel and equipment. In the darkness, far down the tunnel, there was a large bundle of clothing. In the dim lighting Jack strained to see more clearly. As he moved closer he saw that it was indeed the homeless man. For a few moments Jack remained motionless. He wanted the cops to show up. It was so quiet, so dark. The bundle did not move. Jack couldn't hear any breathing. Was the guy dead? Had the cop needed to kill him?

Finally, Jack moved forward. He knelt beside the man. What an elaborate disguise. Jack moved his hand briefly across the matted hair. Even the pungent odor of the street person was authentic. And then Jack saw the stream of blood as it trickled down the side of the man's head. He moved the hair away. A cut was there, a deep one. That was the sound he had heard. There had been a struggle and the cop had hit him. It was over. They had tried to trick Jack and gotten tripped up. He wanted to remove the wig and other elements of disguise, to see who the hell his pursuers had been. But that would have to wait. Maybe it was good the police were now involved.

He would give them the letter opener. He'd take his chances with them.

He stood up, turned and watched the cop striding quickly up the corridor. Jack shook his head. What a surprise this guy was about to get. Chalk it up to being your lucky day, pal.

Jack moved toward the cop and then stopped as the 9mm swiftly came out of the holster.

The cop glared at him. "Mr. Graham."

Jack shrugged and smiled. The guy had finally identified him. "In the flesh." He held up the box. "I've got something for you."

"I know you do, Jack. And that's exactly what I want."

Tim Collin watched the smile fade from Jack's lips. His hand tightened on the trigger as he moved forward.

Seth Frank could feel his pulse quicken as he drew nearer to the station. Finally, he would have it. He could envision Laura Simon devouring the evidence like it was a slab of aged beef. And Frank was almost one hundred percent certain they would score a hit on some database, somewhere. And then the case would crack open like an egg hurled from the Empire State Building. And finally his questions, the nagging, nagging questions would be answered.

Jack looked at the face, absorbing every detail. Not that it would do him any good. He glanced over at the crumpled clothing on the floor, at the new shoes covering lifeless feet. Poor guy had probably wangled his first new pair of shoes in ages and now would never enjoy them.

Jack looked back at Collin and said angrily, "The guy's dead. You killed him,"

"Let me have the box, Jack."

"Who the hell are you?"

"That really doesn't matter, does it?" Collin flipped open a compartment on his belt and pulled out a suppressor that he quickly twirled onto the barrel of his gun.

Jack eyed the hardware pointed at his chest. He thought of the gurneys wheeling out Lord and the woman. His turn would come in tomorrow's paper. Jack Graham and a homeless man. Twin gurneys. Of course they'd work it so Jack would be blamed for having done in the poor, wretched street person. Jack Graham, from partner at Patton, Shaw to deceased mass murderer.

"It matters to me."

"So?" Collin moved forward, placed both hands on the butt of his weapon.

"Fuck you, take it!" Jack flung the box at Collin's head right as the muffled explosion occurred. A bullet tore through the edge of the box and imbedded itself in the concrete wall. In the same instant, Jack hurled himself forward and made impact. Collin was solid bone and muscle but so was Jack. And they were about the same size. Jack felt the man's breath driven completely from his body as Jack's shoulder connected right at the diaphragm. Instinctively, long-ago wrestling moves came flowing back to his limbs and Jack picked up and then body-slammed the agent into the unwelcoming arms of the brick floor. By the time Collin managed to stagger to his feet, Jack had already turned the corner.

Collin grabbed his gun and then the box. He stopped for an instant as sickness enveloped him. His head hurt from having struck the hard floor. He knelt down, fighting to regain his equilibrium. Jack was long gone, but at least he had it. Finally had it. Collin's fingers closed around the box.

Jack flew past the kiosk, hurdled the turnstiles,

raced down the escalator and across the train plat-
form. He was vaguely aware of people staring. His
hood had fallen off his head. His face was clearly
exposed. There was a shout behind him. The kiosk
guy. But Jack kept running and exited the station on
the 17th Street side. He didn't think the man had
been alone. And the last thing he needed was
someone tailing him. But he doubted if they had both
exits covered. They probably figured he wouldn't be
leaving the station under his own power. His
shoulder ached from his collision and his breath came
in difficult gulps as the cold air burned his lungs. He
was two blocks away before he stopped running.
He wrapped his coat around himself tightly. And
then he remembered. He looked down at his empty
hands. The box! He had left the goddamned box
behind. He slumped against the front glass of a
darkened McDonald's.

A car's lights came down the road. Jack looked
away from them and quickly moved around the
corner. In a few minutes he hopped on a bus. To
where he wasn't sure.

The car turned off L street and onto 19th. Seth Frank
made his way up to Eye Street and then turned
toward 18th. He parked on the corner across from
the Metro station, got out of his car and went down
the escalator.

Across the street, hidden behind a collection of
trash cans, debris and metal fencing, the products of a
massive demolition project, Bill Burton watched.
Swearing under his breath, Burton put out his
cigarette, checked the street, and made his way
quickly across to the escalator.

As he got off the escalator, Frank looked around
and checked the time. He wasn't as early as he
thought he would be. His eyes fell upon a collection

of junk that lay against one wall. Then his gaze drifted over to the unmanned kiosk. There was no one else around. It was quiet. Too quiet. Frank's danger radar instantly lit up. With an automatic motion he pulled his gun. His ears had pricked up at a sound that came from his right. He moved quickly down the corridor away from the turnstiles. There a darkened corridor awaited him. He peered around and at first saw nothing. Then as his eyes adjusted to the diminished light he saw two things. One was moving, one wasn't.

Frank stared as the man slowly rose to his feet. It wasn't Jack. The guy was in a uniform, a gun in one hand, a box in the other. Frank's fingers tightened on his own weapon, his eyes locked on the other man's weapon. Frank stealthily moved forward. He hadn't done this in a long time. The image of his wife and three daughters veered across his mind until he pushed it back out. He needed to concentrate.

He was finally close enough. He prayed his accelerated breathing would not betray him. He leveled his pistol at the broad back.

"Freeze! I'm a police officer."

The man did indeed stop all motion.

"Lay the gun down, butt first. I don't want to see your finger anywhere near the trigger or I'm gonna put a hole right in the back of your head. Do it. Now!"

The gun slowly went toward the floor. Frank watched its progression, inch by inch. Then his vision became blurry. Frank's head pounded, he staggered and then he slumped to the floor.

At the sound, Collin slowly looked around to see Bill Burton standing there, holding his pistol by the barrel. He looked down at Frank.

"Let's go, Tim."

Collin shakily got to his feet, looked at the fallen

officer and put his gun to Frank's head. Burton's massive hand stopped him.

"He's a cop. We don't kill cops. We're not killing *anybody* else, Tim." Burton stared down at his colleague. Discomforting thoughts flickered in and out of Burton's head at the calm and accepting manner in which the younger man had stepped into the role of conscienceless assassin.

Collin shrugged, put his gun away.

Burton took the box, looked down at the detective and then over at the other crumpled mass of humanity. He shook his head disdainfully and looked reproachfully at his partner.

Several minutes after they were gone, Seth Frank let out a loud groan, tried to rise and then floated back into unconsciousness.

TWENTY-SEVEN

Kate lay in bed but was as far from sleep as she could possibly be. The ceiling of her bedroom had been replaced with a torrent of images, each one more terrifying than its predecessor. She looked across at the small clock on the nightstand. Three o'clock in the morning. Her window shade was open enough to reveal the pitch-black darkness outside. She could hear the raindrops on the windowpane. Normally comforting, now they simply added to the relentless pounding in her head.

When the phone rang, at first, she didn't move. Her limbs seemed too heavy for her to even attempt to budge, as if each had simultaneously lost all circulation. For one terrible moment she thought she had suffered a stroke. Finally, on the fifth ring she managed to lift the receiver.

"Hello?" Her voice was shaky, one step from oblivion; her nerves completely spent.

"Kate. I need some help."

Four hours later they sat in the front of the little deli at Founder's Park, the site of their initial rendezvous after so many years apart. The weather had worsened into a hard, pelting snow that had made driving nearly impossible and walking only for the irrationally daring.

Jack looked across at her. The hooded parka was off, but a ski cap, a few days' worth of beard and a pair of thick glasses obscured his features to such a degree

493

that Kate had to look twice before she recognized him.

"You're sure no one followed you?" He looked anxiously at her. A cup of steaming coffee partially clouded her line of vision, but she could see the strain on his face. It was clear he was near the breaking point.

"I did what you said. The subway, two cabs and a bus. If anyone kept up with me in this weather, they're not human."

Jack put his coffee down. "From what I've seen, they might not be."

He had not specifically identified the meeting place on the phone. He now assumed that they were listening to everything, to anyone connected to him. He had only mentioned the "usual" place, confident that Kate would understand, and she had. He looked out the window. Every passing face was a threat. He slid a copy of the *Post* across to her. The front page was revealing. Jack had shaken with anger when he had first read it.

Seth Frank was in a stable condition at George Washington University Hospital with a concussion. The homeless man, as yet unidentified, had not been so fortunate. And smack in the middle of the story was Jack Graham, a one-man crime wave. She looked up at him after reading the story.

"We need to keep moving." He looked at her, drained his coffee and then got up.

The cab dropped them off at Jack's motel on the outskirts of Alexandria's Old Town. His eyes looking left and right and then behind, they made their way to his room. After locking and bolting the door, he took off the ski cap and glasses.

"God, Jack, I'm so sorry you're involved in any of this." She shook; he could actually see her trembling from across the room. It took a moment for him to wrap his arms around her until he felt her body calm, relax. He looked at her.

"I got myself involved. Now I just need to get myself uninvolved." He attempted a smile, but it didn't dent the fear she was feeling for him; the awful dread that he might soon join her father.

"I left a dozen messages for you on your machine."

"I never thought to check, Kate." He took the next half hour to tell her the events of the last few days. Her eyes reflected the growing horror with each new revelation.

"My God!"

They were silent for a moment.

"Jack, do you have any idea who's behind all this?"

Jack shook his head; a small groan escaped his lips. "I've got a bunch of loose threads sliding around in my head but none of them have added up to spit so far. I'm hoping that status will change. Soon."

The finality with which the last word was spoken hit her like a sudden slap. His eyes told her. The message was clear. Despite the disguises, the elaborate travel safeguards, despite whatever innate ability he could bring to the battlefield, they would find him. Either the cops or whoever wanted to kill him. It was only a matter of time.

"But at least if they got what they wanted back?" Her voice drifted off. She looked at him, almost pleadingly.

He lay back on the bed, stretched exhausted limbs that didn't seem to belong to him any longer.

"That's not something I can really hang my hat on forever, Kate, is it?" He sat up and looked across the room. At the cheap picture of Jesus hanging on the wall. He would take a dose of divine intervention right now. A small miracle would do.

"But you didn't kill anyone, Jack. You told me

Frank's already figured that out. The D.C. cops will too."

"Will they? Frank knows me, Kate. He knows me and I could still hear the doubt in his voice at first. He picked up on the glass, but there's no evidence that anyone tampered with it or the gun. On the other hand there's clear, take-it-to-the-bank proof, pointing to me killing two people. Three if you count last night. My lawyer would recommend my negotiating a plea and hoping for twenty to life with the possibility of parole. I'd recommend it myself. If I go to trial I've got no shot. Just a bunch of speculation trying to tie Luther and Walter Sullivan and all the rest into some landscape of conspiracy of, you have to admit, mind-boggling proportions. The judge'll laugh my ass right out of court. The jury will never hear it. Really, there's nothing to hear."

He stood up and leaned against the wall, hands shoved in his pockets. He didn't look at her. Both his short- and long-term prospects had doomsday written all over them.

"I'll die an old man in prison, Kate. That is, if I make it to old age – which is a big question mark in itself."

She sat down on the bed, her hands in her lap. A gasp caught midway in her throar as the sheer hopelessness sank in, like a boulder dropped in deep, dark waters.

Seth Frank opened his eyes. At first nothing came into focus. What his brain registered resembled a large white canvas on which a few hundred gallons of black, white and gray paint had been poured to form a cloggy, mind-altering quagmire. After a few anxious moments, he was able to discern the outline of the hospital room in all its stark white, chrome and sharp angles. As he tried to sit up, a hand planted itself firmly against his shoulder.

"Uh–uh, Lieutenant. Not so fast."

Frank looked up into the face of Laura Simon. The smile did not entirely hide the worry lines around the eyes. Her sigh of relief was clearly audible.

"Your wife just left to check on the kids. She's been here all night. I told her as soon as she left you'd wake up."

"Where am I?"

"GW Hospital. I guess if you were gonna have your head pounded in, at least you picked a place close to a hospital." Simon continued to lean over the bed so Frank wouldn't have to turn his head. He stared up at her.

"Seth, do you remember what happened?"

Frank thought back to last night. Or was it last night?

"What day is it?"

"Thursday."

"So it happened last night?"

"Around eleven or so. At least they found you about then. And the other guy."

"Other guy?" Frank jerked his head around. Pain shot through his neck.

"Take it easy, Seth." Laura took a moment to prop a pillow next to Frank's head.

"There was another guy. Homeless. They haven't identified him yet. Same kind of blow to the back of the head. Probably died instantly. You were lucky."

Frank gingerly touched his throbbing temples. He didn't feel so lucky.

"Anybody else?"

"What?"

"Did they find anybody else?"

"Oh. No, but you're not going to believe this. You know the lawyer who watched the tape with us?"

Frank tensed. "Yeah, Jack Graham."

"Right. The guy kills two people at his law firm and then he's spotted running away from the Metro about the time you and the other guy get whacked. The guy's a walking nightmare. And he looked like a Mr. All-American."

"Have they found him yet? Jack? They're sure he got away?"

Laura looked at him strangely. "He got out of the Metro station if that's what you mean. But it's only a matter of time." She looked out the window, reached for her purse. "The D.C. cops want to talk with you as soon as you're able."

"I'm not sure how much help I can be. I don't remember all that much, Laura."

"Temporary amnesia. You'll probably get it back." She put on her jacket. "I have to go. Somebody's got to keep Middleton County safe for the rich and famous while you're counting sheep in here." She smiled. "Don't make a habit out of this, Seth. We were really worried we might have to hire a new detective."

"Where would you find someone as nice as me?"

Laura laughed. "Your wife will be back in a few hours. You need to get some rest anyway." She turned to go to the door.

"By the way, Seth, what were you doing at the Farragut West Metro at that time of night?"

Frank didn't answer right away. He didn't have amnesia. He recalled the night's events clearly.

"Seth?"

"I'm not sure, Laura." He closed his eyes and then reopened them. "I just don't remember."

"Don't worry, it'll come back to you. In the meantime, they'll catch Graham. That'll probably clear everything up."

After Laura left, Frank did not rest. Jack was out there. And he had probably initially thought the detective had set him up, although if Jack had seen the paper he would know that the detective had walked blindly into the ambush that had been laid for the lawyer.

But they had the letter opener now. That's what was in that box. He was certain of it. And without that, what chance did they have of nailing these people?

Frank again tried to struggle up. There was an IV in his arm. The pressure on his brain caused him to immediately lie back down. He had to get out of here. And he had to get in touch with Jack. Right now he had no idea how he would accomplish either.

"You said you needed my help. What can I do?" Kate looked directly at Jack. There were no reservations on her features.

Jack sat on the bed next to her. He looked troubled. "I've got some real serious doubts about getting you anywhere near this. In fact, I'm wondering if calling you was the right thing to do."

"Jack, I've been surrounded by rapists, armed robbers and murderers for the last four years."

"I know that. But at least you knew who they were. This could be anybody. People are getting killed left and right, Kate. This is about as serious as it gets."

"I'm not leaving unless you let me help you."

Jack hesitated, his eyes turned away from hers.

"Jack, if you don't, then I'm going to turn you in. Better you take your chances with the cops."

He looked at her. "You'd do that, wouldn't you?"

"Damn straight I would. I'm breaking all the rules by being here with you now. If you let me in on it, then I forget all about seeing you today. If you don't . . ."

There was a look in her eyes that, despite all the

horrific possibilities he was contemplating, made him somehow feel fortunate to be here at this exact moment.

"Okay. You need to be my contact with Seth. Outside of you he's the only one I can trust."

"But you lost the package. How can he help?" Kate could not hide her dislike of the homicide detective.

Jack stood up and paced. Finally he stopped and looked down at her. "You know how your dad was a freak for control? Always have a backup plan?"

Kate said dryly, "I remember."

"Well, I'm counting on that quality."

"What are you talking about?"

"That Luther had a backup plan on this one."

She stared at him, open-mouthed.

"Mrs. Broome?"

The door opened another notch as Edwina Broome peered out.

"Yes?"

"My name is Kate Whitney. Luther Whitney was my father." Kate relaxed as the old woman greeted her with a smile. "I knew I'd seen you before. Luther was always showing pictures of you. You're even prettier than your photos."

"Thank you."

Edwina jerked the door open. "What am I thinking about. You must be freezing. Please come in."

Edwina led her into the small living room where a trio of felines were cloistered on various pieces of furniture.

"I just made some fresh tea, would you like some?"

Kate hesitated. Time was short. Then she looked around the narrow confines of the home. In the corner sat a battered upright piano, thick dust on the

500

wood. Kate looked at the woman's weakened eyes; the pleasures of a musical pastime had also been taken from her. Husband passed on, her only daughter dead. How many visitors could she possibly have?

"Thank you, I would."

Both women settled into the old but comfortable furniture. Kate sipped the strong tea and she began to thaw out. She brushed the hair out of her face and looked across at the elderly woman to find a pair of sad eyes upon her.

"I'm sorry about your daddy, Kate. I really am. I know you two had your differences. But Luther was as good a man as I've come across in my life."

Kate felt herself growing warmer. "Thank you. We both have had a lot to deal with in that regard."

Edwina's eyes drifted over to a small table next to the window. Kate followed the gaze. On the table numerous photographs displayed a small shrine to Wanda Broome; capturing her in happy times. She strongly resembled her mother.

A *shrine*. With a jolt Kate recalled her father's own collection of her personal triumphs.

"Yes indeed." Edwina was looking at her again.

Kate put down her tea. "Mrs. Broome, I hate to jump right into this, but the fact is I don't have much time."

The old woman leaned forward expectantly. "This is about Luther's death, and my daughter's too, isn't it?"

Kate looked surprised. "Why do you think that?"

Edwina leaned forward even more; her voice dropped to a whisper. "Because I know Luther didn't kill Mrs. Sullivan. I know it as if I'd seen it with my own eyes.

Kate looked puzzled. "Do you have any idea who—"

501

Edwina was already shaking her head sadly. "No. No, I don't."

"Well, how do you know my father didn't do it?"

Now there was definite hesitation. Edwina leaned back in her chair and closed her eyes. When she finally reopened them, Kate had not moved a muscle.

"You're Luther's daughter and I believe you should know the truth." She paused, took a sip of her tea, pressed her lips dry with a napkin and then settled back into her chair. A black Persian drifted across and promptly went to sleep in her lap. "I knew about your father. His past, so to speak. He and Wanda got to know each other. She got into trouble years back and Luther helped her, helped her get back on her feet and get settled into a respectable life. I will always be grateful to him for that. He was always there when Wanda or I needed anything. The fact is, Kate, your father would never have been in the house that night if it weren't for Wanda."

Edwina spoke for some minutes. When she had finished Kate sat back in her chair and realized she was holding her breath. She let out a loud gasp that seemed to echo around the room.

Edwina didn't say anything but continued to watch the young woman with her large sad eyes. Finally she stirred. A thickly wrinkled hand patted Kate's knee.

"Luther loved you, child. More than anything."

"I realize that."

Edwina slowly shook her head. "He never blamed you for the way you felt. In fact, he said you were entirely right to feel that way."

"He said that?"

"He was so proud of you, your being a lawyer and all. He used to say to me, 'My daughter is a lawyer and a damned fine one. Justice is what matters for her and she's right, dead right.'"

Kate's head began to swirl. She was feeling

502

emotions she was ill-equipped right now to deal with. She rubbed the back of her neck and took a moment to look outside. A black sedan pulled down the street and then disappeared. She quickly looked back at Edwina.

"Mrs. Broome, I appreciate your telling me these things. But I really came here for a specific reason. I need your help."

"I'll do whatever I can."

"My father sent you a package."

"Yes. And I sent it on to Mr. Graham, like Luther said to."

"Yes, I know. Jack got the package. But someone . . . someone took it away from him. Now we're wondering if my father sent you something else, something else that might help us?"

Edwina's eyes no longer looked sad. They had collected into twin masses of stark intensity. She looked over Kate's shoulder.

"Behind you, Kate, in the piano seat. The hymnal on the left."

Kate opened the piano seat and lifted out the hymnal. Inside the pages was a small packet. She looked down at it.

"Luther was the most prepared man I have ever met in my life. Said if anything went wrong with my sending the package that I was to send this to Mr. Graham. I was getting ready to do that when I heard about him on the TV. Am I right in thinking Mr. Graham didn't do any of the things they say he did?"

Kate nodded. "I wish everybody thought like you did."

She started to open the package.

Edwina's voice was sharp. "Don't do that, Kate. Your father said that only Mr. Jack Graham was to see what was inside of there. Only him. I think it best if we took him at his word."

Kate hesitated, fighting her natural curiosity, and then closed the package.

"Did he tell you anything else? Whether he knew who had killed Christine Sullivan?"

"He did know."

Kate looked at her sharply. "But he didn't say who?"

Edwina shook her head vigorously. "He did say one thing though."

"What was that?"

"He said if he told me who had done it, I wouldn't have believed him."

Kate sat back, thought for several anxious moments.

"What could he have meant by that?"

"Well, it surprised me, I can tell you that."

"Why? Why did that surprise you?"

"Because Luther was the most honest man I'd ever met. I would have believed anything he would have told me. Accepted it as the gospel."

"So whatever he saw, whoever he saw, must have been someone so unlikely as to be unbelievable. Even to you."

"Exactly. That's exactly what I thought too."

Kate rose to go. "Thank you, Mrs. Broome."

"Please call me Edwina. Funny name, but it's the only one I have."

Kate smiled. "After this is all over, Edwina, I . . . I'd like to come back and visit if you don't mind. Talk about things some more."

"I'd like nothing better. Being old has its good and bad. Being old and lonely is all bad."

Kate put on her coat and went to the door. She put the package safely in her purse.

"That should narrow your search shouldn't it, Kate?"

Kate turned around. "What?"

504

"Someone that unbelievable. Can't be too many of them around I wouldn't think."

The hospital security guard was tall, beefy and uncomfortable as hell.

"I don't exactly know what happened. I was gone maybe two, three minutes tops."

"You shouldn't have been away from your post at all, Monroe." The diminutive supervisor was in Monroe's face and the big man was sweating hard.

"Like I said, the lady asked for some help with a bag, so I helped her."

"What lady?"

"I told you, just some lady. Young, good-lookin', dressed real professional." The supervisor turned away, disgusted. He had no way of knowing the lady was Kate Whitney and that she and Seth Frank were already five blocks away in Kate's car.

"Does it hurt?" Kate looked at him, with not much sympathy in either her features or her voice.

Frank gingerly touched the bandages around his head. "You kidding? My six-year-old hits me harder." He looked around the interior of the car. "You got some smokes? Since when the hell are hospitals nonsmoking?"

She rummaged in her purse and flipped him an open pack.

He lit up and eyed her over the cloud of smoke. "By the way, nice job on the rent-a-cop. You should be in the movies."

"Great! I'm in the market for a career change."

"How's our boy?"

"Safe. For now. Let's keep him that way."

She turned the corner and looked hard at him.

"You know, it wasn't exactly my plan to let your old man buy it right in front of me."

505

"That's what Jack said."

"But you don't believe him?"

"What does it matter what I believe?"

"It does. It matters to me, Kate."

She stopped for a red light. "Okay. Let's put it this way. I'm coming around to the idea that you didn't want it to happen. Is that good enough?"

"No, but it'll do for now."

Jack turned the corner and tried to relax. The latest storm front had finally wearied of the Capital City, but although there no longer was any pelting icy rain, the thermometer had remained consistently in the twenties and the wind had returned with a vengeance. He blew on stiff fingers and rubbed sleep-deprived eyes. Against a drift of black sky, a sliver of moon hung, soft and luminous. Jack checked his surroundings. The building across the street was dark and empty. The structure he was standing in front of had closed its doors a long time ago. A few passersby braved the inclement conditions, but for large chunks of time Jack stood alone. Finally he took shelter inside the doorway of the building and waited.

Three blocks away a rusting cab pulled to the curb, the back door opened and a pair of low heels touched the cement sidewalk. The cab immediately pulled off and a moment later the street was silent again. Kate tugged her coat around her and hurried off. As she passed the next block, another car, lights out, turned the corner and drifted along in her wake. Her thoughts focused on the steps that lay ahead of her, Kate did not look back.

Jack saw her turn the corner. He looked in all directions before moving, a habit he had quickly cultivated and hoped he would be able to discard very soon. He moved quickly to meet her. The street was quiet. Neither Kate nor Jack saw the sedan's nose as it crept past the corner building's front. Inside, the driver zeroed in on the couple with a night-vision device the mail-order catalogue had trumpeted as being the very latest in Soviet technology. And although the former communists had no clue as to how to run a democratic, capitalist society, they did, for the most part, build sound military hardware.

"Jesus, you're freezing, how long have you been waiting?" Kate had touched Jack's hand and the icy feel had coursed through her entire body.

"Longer than I needed to. The motel room was shrinking on me. I just had to get out. I'm going to make a lousy prisoner. Well?"

Kate opened her purse. She had called Jack from a pay phone. She couldn't tell him what she had, only that she had something. Jack had agreed with Edwina Broome that if risks had to be taken, he would take more than anyone. Kate had already done enough.

Jack grasped the packet. It wasn't that difficult to discern what was contained inside. Photographs.

Thank God, Luther, you didn't disappoint.

"Are you okay?" Jack scrutinized her.

"I'm getting there."

"Where's Seth?"

"He's around. He'll drive me home."

They stared at each other. Jack knew that the best thing was to have Kate leave, maybe leave the country for a while, until this blew over or he was convicted of murder. If the latter, then her intention of starting over somewhere else was probably the best plan anyway.

But he didn't want her to leave.

"Thank you." The words seemed wholly inadequate, like she had just dropped off lunch for him, or picked up his dry cleaning.

"Jack, what are you going to do now?"

507

"I haven't thought it all through yet. But it's coming. I'm not going down without a fight."

"Yeah, but you don't even know who it is you're fighting. That's hardly fair."

"Who said it was supposed to be fair?"

He smiled at her as the wind kicked old newspapers down the street.

"You better get going. It's not that safe around here."

"I've got my pepper mace."

"Good girl."

She turned to leave, then clutched him by the arm. "Jack, please be careful."

"I'm always careful. I'm a lawyer. CYA is SOP for us."

"Jack, I'm not kidding."

He shrugged, "I know. I promise I will be as careful as I can." As Jack said this he stepped toward Kate and took off his hood.

The night goggles fixated on Jack's exposed features and then they were lowered. Shaky hands picked up the car's cellular phone.

The two clung in an easy embrace. While Jack desperately wanted to kiss her, under the circumstances he settled for a soft brush of his lips against her neck. When they stepped back from each other, tears had begun to form in Kate's eyes. Jack turned and walked quickly away.

As Kate walked back down the street she didn't notice the car until it swerved across the street and almost ended up on the curb. She staggered back as the driver's side door flew open. In the background, the air had exploded with sirens, all coming toward her. Toward Jack. She instinctively looked behind her. There was no sign of him. When she turned back, she was staring into a pair of smug eyes, framed under bushy eyebrows.

"I thought our paths might cross again, Ms. Whitney."

Kate stared at the man, but recognition was not forthcoming.

He looked disappointed. "Bob Gavin. From the *Post*?"

She looked at his car. She had seen it before. On the street passing Edwina Broome's house.

"You've been following me."

"Yes, I have. Figured you'd eventually lead me to Graham."

"The police?" Her head jerked around as a squad car, siren blaring, tore down the street toward them. "You called them."

Gavin nodded, smiling. He was obviously pleased with himself.

"Now before the cops get here I think we can work a little deal. You give me an exclusive. The down and dirty on Jack Graham, and my story changes just enough so that instead of an accessory, you're just an innocent bystander in this whole mess."

Kate glared at the man, the rage within her, having been built up from a month of personal horrors, was near its exploding point. And Bob Gavin was standing directly over the epicenter.

Gavin looked around at the patrol car nearing them. In the background, two more squad cars were heading in their direction.

"Come on, Kate," he said urgently, "you don't have much time, You stay out of jail and I get my long-overdue Pulitzer and my fifteen minutes of fame. What's it gonna be?"

She gnashed her teeth, her response startlingly calm, as though she had practiced its delivery for months. "Pain, Mr. Gavin. Fifteen minutes of pain." As he stared at her, she pulled the palm-size canister,

509

pointed it directly at his face and squeezed the trigger. The pepper gas hit Gavin flush in the eyes and nose, marking his face with a red dye. By the time the cops exited their vehicle, Bob Gavin was on the pavement clutching at his face, trying unsuccessfully to tear his eyes out.

The first siren had sent Jack into a sprint down a side street.

He slid flat against a building sucking in air. His lungs ached, the cold tore at his face. The deserted nature of the area he was in had turned into a huge tactical disadvantage. He could keep moving, but he was like a black ant on a sheet of white paper. The sirens were coming so heavy now he couldn't ascertain from what direction.

Actually they were coming from all directions. And they were getting closer. He ran hard to the next corner, stopped and peered around. The view was not encouraging. His eyes fastened on a police blockade being set up at the end of the street. Their strategy was readily apparent. They knew his general coordinates. They would simply cordon off a wide radius and systematically close that radius in. They had the manpower and the time.

The one thing he did have was a good knowledge of the area he was in. Many of his PD clients had come from here. Their dreams set not on college, law school, good job, loving family and the suburban split-level but on how much cash they could generate from selling bags of crack, how they could survive one day at a time. Survival. It was a strong, human drive. Jack hoped his was strong enough.

As he flew down the alley, he had no idea what he would encounter, although he supposed the fierce weather had kept some of the local felons indoors. He almost laughed. Not one of his former partners at

Patton, Shaw would have come near this place, even with an armored battalion surrounding them. He might as well be running across the surface of Pluto.

He cleared the chain-link fence with one jump and landed slightly off-balance. As he put out his hand against the rugged brick wall to steady himself he heard two sounds. His own heavy breathing and the sound of running feet. Several pairs. He'd been spotted. They were homing in on him. Next the K-9's would be brought in and you didn't run away from the four-legged cops. He exploded out of the alley and made his way over to Indiana Avenue.

Jack veered down another street as the squeal of tires flew toward him. Even as he raced in the new direction, a new flank of pursuers rushed to greet him. It was only a matter of time now. He felt in his pocket for the packet. What could he do with it? He didn't trust anybody. Technically, an inventory of an arrestee's possessions taken from him would be made, with appropriate signatures and chain-of-custody safeguards, all of which meant nothing to Jack. Who-ever could kill in the middle of hundreds of law officers and disappear without a trace could certainly manage to secure a prisoner's personal possessions from the D.C. Police Department. And what he had in his pocket was the only chance he had. D.C. didn't have the death penalty but life without parole wasn't any better and in a lot of ways seemed a helluva lot worse.

He raced in between two buildings, stumbled on some ice and plunged over a stack of garbage cans and hit the pavement hard. He picked himself up and half-rolled into the street, rubbing at his elbow. He could feel the burn, and there was a looseness in his knee that was a new sensation. As he stopped rolling, he managed to sit up, then froze.

A car's headlights were coming right for him. The

511

police bubble light blasted into his eyes as the wheels came within two inches of his head. He slumped back on the asphalt. He was too winded to even move.

The car door sprang open. Jack looked up, puzzled. It was the passenger door. Then the driver's door flew open. Big hands slid under his armpits.

"Goddammit, Jack, get your ass up."

Jack looked up at Seth Frank.

TWENTY-EIGHT

Bill Burton leaned his head into the Secret Service command post. Tim Collin sat at one of the desks going over a report.

"Come on, Tim."

Collin looked up, puzzled.

Burton said quietly, "They've got him cornered down near the courthouse. I want to be there. Just in case."

Seth Frank's sedan flew down the street, the blue bubble light commanding immediate respect from a traffic population unaccustomed to conveying any whatsoever to fellow motorists.

"Where's Kate?" Jack lay in the back seat, a blanket over him.

"Right now she's probably being read her rights. Then she's gonna get booked on a slew of accessory charges for helping you."

Jack sprung up. "We've gotta go back, Seth. I'll turn myself in. They'll let her go."

"Yeah, right."

"I'm not kidding, Seth." Jack was halfway over the front seat.

"I'm not either, Jack. You go back and turn yourself in, that'll do nothing to help Kate and it'll snuff out what little shot you've got to get your life back to reality."

"But Kate—"

"I'll take care of Kate. I've already called a buddy

513

at D.C. He'll be waiting for her. He's a good guy."

Jack slumped back down. "Shit."

Frank opened his window, reached out and flicked the bubble light off and tossed it on the seat beside him.

"What the hell happened?"

Frank looked in his rearview mirror. "I'm not sure. The best I can figure is that Kate picked up a tail somewhere. I was cruising the area. We were going to meet at the Convention Center after she made the drop with you. Heard over my police radio that you had been spotted. I followed the chase over the airwaves, tried to guess where you might go. Got lucky. When I saw you blow out of the alley, I couldn't believe it. Damn near ran you down. How's the body by the way?"

"Never better. I ought to do this crap once or twice a year just to keep me limber. Get ready for the Fleeing Felon Olympics."

Frank chuckled. "You're still alive and kicking, my friend. Count your blessings. So did you get any nice presents?"

Jack swore under his breath. He had been so busy running from the police that he had never even looked. He took out the packet.

"Got a light?"

Frank flicked on the dome light.

Jack flipped through the photographs.

Frank checked the mirror. "So what do we got?"

"Photos. Of the letter opener, knife, whatever the hell you want to call it."

"Huh. Not surprising I guess. Can you make out anything?"

Jack looked closely in the poor light. "Not really. You guys must have some gadget that'll do some good."

Frank sighed. "I gotta be straight with you, Jack,

514

unless there's something else we don't have much of a shot. Even if we can somehow pull something that looks like a print off there who's to say where it came from? And you can't do DNA testing on blood from a friggin' photograph, at least not that I'm aware of."

"I know that. I didn't spend four years as a defense counsel picking my ass."

Seth slowed the car down. They were on Pennsylvania Avenue and the traffic had grown heavier. "So what's your idea then?"

Jack rubbed back his hair, dug his fingers into his leg until the pain in his knee subsided and then lay down on the seat. "Whoever's behind all this wanted the letter opener back really bad. Enough to kill you, me, anybody else that got in the way. We're talking paranoia at its peak."

"Which fits in with our theory of some big shot with a lot to lose if this comes out. So? They got it back. Where does that leave us, Jack?"

"Luther didn't make these photos just in case something happened to the original article."

"What are you talking about?"

"He came back into the country, Seth, remember? We could never figure that one out."

Frank stopped at a red light. He turned around in his seat.

"Right. He came back. You think you know why?"

Jack carefully sat up in the back seat, keeping his head below the window line. "I think so. Remember I told you that Luther wasn't the kind of guy to let something like this lie. If he could he'd do something about it."

"But he did leave the country. At first."

"I know. Maybe that was his initial plan. Maybe that was his plan all along if the job had gone according to plan. But the fact is he came back.

515

Something made him change his mind and he came back. And he had these photographs." Jack spread them fanlike.

The light turned green and Frank started up again.

"I'm not getting this, Jack. If he wanted to nail the guy why not just send the stuff in to the police?"

"I think that was his plan, eventually. But he told Edwina Broome that if he told *her* who he had seen, she wouldn't have believed him. If even she, a close friend, wouldn't have believed his story, considering he'd have to admit to burglary to convince someone, he probably thought that his credibility was zip."

"Okay, so he has a credibility problem. Where do the photos come in?"

"Let's say you're doing a straight exchange. Cash for a certain item. What's the hardest part?"

Frank's reply was immediate. "The payoff. How to get your money without getting killed or caught. You can send instructions later on for the pickup of the item. It's getting the money that's tough. That's why the number of kidnappings have plummeted."

"So how would you do it?"

Frank thought for a moment. "Since we're talking about the payoff coming from people who ain't gonna bring in the police I'd go for speed. Take minimal personal risk, and give yourself time to run."

"How would you do that?"

"EFT. Electronic Fund Transfer. A wire. I was involved in a bank embezzlement case when I was in New York. Guy did it all through the wire transfer department at his own bank. You wouldn't believe the dollars that fly through those places on a daily basis. And you also wouldn't believe how much stuff gets lost in the shuffle. A smart perp could take a little chunk here and there and by the time they caught it, he'd be long gone. You send your wire instructions. The money is sent out. Only takes a few minutes.

516

Helluva lot better than rummaging through a Dumpster in a park where somebody can take a nice little bead on your head with a cannon."

"But the sender can presumably trace the wire."

"Sure. You have to identify the bank it's going to. ABA routing number, you have to have an account at the bank. All that shit."

"So, assuming the sender is sophisticated enough, they trace the wire. Then what?"

"Then they can follow the flow of money. They might be able to dig some info on the account. Although no one would be stupid enough to use their own name or Social Security number. Besides, a real smart guy like Whitney would probably have preset instructions in place. Once the funds hit the first bank, bam they get sent out to another place, and then another and another. At some point, the trail probably disappears. It's instant money after all. Immediately available funds."

"Fair enough. I'm betting Luther did something just like that."

Frank carefully scratched around the edges of his bandage. His hat was pulled down tight and the whole thing was greatly uncomfortable. "But what I can't figure is why do it at all. He didn't need the money after the Sullivan hit. He could've just stayed disappeared. Let the whole thing blow over. After a while they figure he's permanently retired. You don't bother me, I don't bother you."

"You're right. He could've done that. Retired. Given it up. But he came back, and more than that, he came back and apparently blackmailed whoever he saw kill Christine Sullivan. And if he presumably didn't do it for money, then why?"

The detective thought for a moment. "To make 'em sweat. To let them know he was out there. With the evidence to destroy them."

"But evidence he wasn't sure was enough."

"Because the perp was so respectable?"

"Right, so what would you do, given those facts?"

Frank pulled to the curb and put the car in park. He turned around. "I'd try to get something else on them. That's what I'd do."

"How? If you're blackmailing someone?"

Frank finally threw up his hands. "I give up."

"You said the wire transfer could be traced by the sender."

"So?"

"So, what about the other way? Receiver back up the line?"

"Goddamned stupid." Frank momentarily forgot his concussion and slapped his forehead. "Whitney put a tracer on the wire, going the other way. The person sending out the money thinks all along that they're playing cat and mouse with Whitney. They're the cat, he's the mouse. He's hiding, getting ready to run."

"Only Luther didn't mention the fact that he was into role reversal. That he was the cat and they were the mouse."

"And that tracer would eventually lead right to the bad guys, probably no matter how many shields you put up, if they thought to put up any at all. Every wire in this country has to go through the Federal Reserve. You get the wire reference number from the Fed or the sending bank's wire room, you got something to hang your hat on. Even if Whitney didn't trace it back, the fact that he received the money, a certain amount, is damaging enough. If he could give that info to the cops with the name of the sender and they check it out . . ."

Jack finished the detective's thought. "And suddenly the unbelievable becomes very believable. Wire transfers do not lie. Money was sent. If it was a lot of money like I'm sure it was here, then that cannot be explained away. That is pretty damn close to bull's-eye evidence. He set them up with their own payoff."

"I just thought of something else, Jack. If Whitney was building a case against these people, then he was eventually planning to go to the police. He was going to just walk in the door and deposit himself and his evidence."

Jack nodded. "That's why he needed me. Only they were quick enough to use Kate as a way to ensure his silence. Later they used a bullet to accomplish that."

"So he was going to turn himself in."

"Right."

Frank rubbed his jaw. "You know what I'm thinking?"

Jack answered immediately. "He saw it coming." The two men looked at each other.

Frank spoke first; the words came out low, almost hushed. "He knew Kate was a setup. And he went anyway. And I thought I was so fucking clever."

"Probably figured it was the only way he'd ever get to see her again."

"Shit. I know the guy stole for a living, but I gotta tell you, my respect for him grows by the second."

"I know what you mean."

Frank put the car back in gear and pulled off.

"Okay, again, where does all this conjecture leave us?"

Jack shook his head, lay back down. "I'm not sure."

"I mean so long as we don't have a clue as to who it is, I'm not sure what we can do."

Jack exploded back up. "But we do have clues." He sat back as though all his energy had suddenly evaporated after that one thrust. "I just can't make any sense out of them."

The men drove on in silence for a few minutes.

"Jack, I know this sounds funny coming from a policeman, but I think you might want to start considering getting the hell out of here. You got some bucks saved? Maybe *you* should retire early."

"And what, leave Kate swinging in the wind? If we don't nail these guys what is she looking at? Ten to fifteen as an accessory? I don't think so, Seth, not in a million years. They can fry my ass before I let that happen."

"You're right. Sorry I brought it up."

As Seth glanced in his mirror the car next to them tried to do a U-turn directly in front of them. Frank hit the brakes and his car spun sideways, crashing into the curb with a bone-crunching impact. The Kansas license plates on the vehicle that had nearly crashed into them quickly disappeared.

"Stupid tourists. Fucking bastards!" Frank gripped the steering wheel hard, his breath coming in gasps. The shoulder restraint had done its job, but it had dug deeply into his skin. His battered head pounded.

"*Fucking bastard!*" Frank yelled again to no one in particular. Then he remembered his passenger and looked anxiously in the back seat.

"Jack, Jack, you okay?"

Jack's face was pressed up against the door glass. He was conscious; in fact, his eyes were staring at something with great intensity.

"Jack?" Frank undid his seat belt and gripped him by the shoulder. "You okay? Jack!"

Jack looked at Frank and then back out the window. Frank wondered if the impact had relieved his friend of his senses. He automatically searched Jack's head for bruises until Jack's hand stopped him and pointed out the window. Frank looked out.

Even his hardened nerves took a jolt. The rear view of the White House filled his entire line of vision.

Jack's mind raced; images hurtled across like a video montage. The vision of the President pulling back from Jennifer Baldwin, complaining of tennis elbow. Only it had been inflicted with a certain letter opener that had started this whole crazy thing. The unusual interest taken by the President and the Secret Service in Christine Sullivan's murder. Alan Richmond's timely appearance at Luther's arraignment. *Led me right to him*. That's what the detective had said their videotaping citizen had reported. *Led me right to him*. It also explained killers who killed in the middle of an army of law enforcement officers and walked away. Who would stop a Secret Service agent protecting the President? No one. No wonder Luther felt no one would believe him. The President of the United States.

And there had been a significant event right before Luther had returned to the country. Alan Richmond had held a press conference where he had told the public how terrible he felt about the tragic murder of Christine Sullivan. He was probably fucking the man's wife and somehow she had gotten killed and this slimeball was gaining political dollars showing what a sensitive and good friend he was; a man who would get tough on crime. It had been a tour de force performance. And that was truly what it had been. Nothing about it had been true. It had been broadcast to the world. What would Luther have thought, seeing that? Jack believed he knew. That was why Luther had come back. To settle the score.

All the pieces had been dangling inside Jack's head just waiting for the right catalyst to come along.

Jack looked back once more at the catalyst.

Directly under the lamplight, Tim Collin again glanced down the street at the minor traffic mishap, but could make out no details in the oncoming swarm of car headlights. Next to him Bill Burton was

521

also peering out. Collin shrugged, and then rolled the window back up on the black sedan. Burton threw his bubble light on top of the car, hit his siren, quickly drove the car through the rear White House gate and tore off in the direction of D.C. Superior Court in pursuit of Jack.

Jack looked at Seth Frank and smiled grimly as he reflected on the detective's outburst. The same phrase had erupted from Luther's mouth, right before his life had ended. Jack finally remembered where he had heard it before. The hurled newspaper at the jail. The smiling President on the front page.

Outside the courthouse, staring right at the man. Those same words had exploded out, with all the fury and venom the old man could muster.

"*Fucking bastard*," Jack said.

Alan Richmond stood by the window and wondered if he was destined to be surrounded by incompetents. Gloria Russell sat dronelike in a chair across from him. He had bedded the woman a half-dozen times and now had completely lost interest. He would catapult her away when the time was right. His next administration would be comprised of a far more capable team. Underlings who would allow him to focus on his particular vision for the country. He had not sought the presidency to sweat the details.

"I see we haven't gained an inch in the polls." He didn't look at her; he anticipated her response.

"Does it really matter so much whether you win by sixty percent or seventy percent?"

He whirled around. "Yes," he hissed. "Yes, it god-damn does matter."

She bit her lip and retreated. "I'll step up the effort, Alan. Maybe we can pull a shutout in the Electoral College."

"At a minimum, we should be able to do that, Gloria."

She looked down. After the election, she would travel. Around the world. Where she knew no one and no one knew her. A fresh start. That was what she needed. Then everything would be okay.

"Well, at least our little problem is cleared up." He was looking at her, hands clasped behind his back. Tall, lean, impeccably dressed and groomed. He looked like the commander of an invincible armada. But then again history had proven that invincible armadas were far more vulnerable than people imagined.

"It's been disposed of?"

"No, Gloria, I have it in my desk — would you like to see it? Perhaps you might wish to abscond with it again." His air was so thick with condescension she felt the urgent need to bring their consultation to a close. She rose.

"Will there be anything else?"

He shook his head and returned to the window. She had just put her hand on the doorknob when it turned and opened.

"We've got a problem." Bill Burton looked at each of them.

"So what does he want?" The President looked down at the photograph Burton had handed him.

Burton replied quickly. "Note doesn't say. I can guess that the shape the guy's in with cops on his ass, he's looking for some quick funds."

The President looked pointedly at Russell. "I'm very puzzled as to how Jack Graham knew to send the photo here."

Burton picked up on the look from the President, and while the last thing he wanted was to defend Russell they had no time to misanalyze the situation.

"It's possible Whitney told him," Burton answered.

"If that's true, he waited a long time to dance with us," the President fired back.

"Whitney may not have told him directly. Graham could've figured it out for himself. Pieced things together."

The President tossed down the photo. Russell quickly averted her eyes. The mere sight of the letter opener had paralyzed her.

"Burton, how could this possibly be damaging to us?" The President stared at him, seemingly probing through the inner areas of the agent's mind.

Burton sat down, rubbed his jaw with the palm of his hand. "I've been thinking about that. It could be Graham's grasping at straws. He's in a pretty tight fix himself. And his lady friend is cooling her heels in the lockup right now. I'd chalk it up to him being desperate. He gets a sudden inspiration, puts two and two together and takes a flyer on sending us this, hoping it's worth it to us to pay his price, whatever it might be."

The President stood up and fingered his coffee cup. "Is there any way to find him? Quickly?"

"There are always ways. How fast I don't know."

"So if we ignore his communication?"

"He may do nothing, just hightail it and take his chances."

"But again we're confronted with the possibility of the police catching up to him—"

"And him spilling his guts," Burton finished the sentence. "Yeah, that's a possibility. A real possibility."

The President picked up the photo. "With only this to back up his story?" He looked incredulous. "Why bother?"

"It's not the incriminating value of what's in the photo *per se* that bothers me."

524

"What bothers you is that his accusations, coupled with whatever ideas or leads the police can develop from the photo, might make for some very uncomfortable questions."

"Something like that. Remember, it's the allegations that can kill you. You're up for re-election. He probably sees that as an ace for him. Bad press can be just as deadly to you right now."

The President pondered for a moment. Nothing, no one would interfere with his reelection. "Buying him off is no good, Burton. You know that. So long as Graham's around, he's dangerous." Richmond looked over at Russell, who had sat the entire time, hands in her lap, eyes pointed down. His eyes bored into her. *So weak.*

The President sat down at his desk and started to sift through some papers. He said dismissively, "Do it, Burton, and do it soon."

Frank looked at the wall clock, went over and shut his door and picked up the phone. His head still ached, but the doctors predicted a full recovery.

The phone was answered. "D.C. Executive Inn."

"Room 233 please."

"Just a moment."

The seconds dragged by and Frank started to get anxious. Jack was supposed to be in his room.

"Hello?"

"It's me."

"So how's life?"

"Better than yours, I bet."

"How's Kate?"

"She's out on bail. Got 'em to let her go into my custody."

"I'm sure she's thrilled."

"That wasn't the word I was thinking of. Look, it's getting close to shit–or–get–off–the–pot time. Take my advice and run like hell. You're wasting valuable time right now."

"But Kate—"

"Come on, Jack, they've got the testimony of one guy who was trying to hit her up for an exclusive. His word against hers. Nobody else even saw you. It's a slam dunk she'll beat that charge. A slam dunk. I've talked to the Assistant U.S. Attorney. He's looking seriously at dropping the whole case."

"I don't know."

"Goddammit, Jack. Kate is gonna come out of this a whole helluva lot better than you are if you don't start thinking about your future. You've got to get out of here. That's not just me talking. That's her too."

"Kate?"

"I saw her today. We don't agree on much, but on that we do."

Jack relaxed, then let out a heavy sigh. "Okay, so where do I go and how do I get there?"

"I get off duty at nine. At ten o'clock I'll be at your room. Have your bags packed. I'll take care of the rest. In the meantime, stay put."

Frank hung up the phone and took a deep breath. The chances he was taking. It was better not to think about them.

Jack checked his watch and looked at the single bag on the bed. He wouldn't be running with much. He looked at the TV set in the corner but there wouldn't be anything on he cared to watch. Suddenly thirsty, he pulled some change from his pocket, opened the door to his room and peered out. The drink machine was just down the hallway. He plopped on his baseball cap, donned his Coke-bottle glasses and slipped out. He didn't hear the door to the stairwell at the other end of the hallway open. He had also forgotten to lock his door.

526

When he slipped back in, it struck him that the light was off. He had left it on. As his hand hit the switch, the door was slammed shut behind him and he was thrown onto the bed. As he quickly rolled over and his eyes adjusted to the light, the two men came into focus. They were not wearing masks this time, which spoke volumes in itself.

Jack started to lunge forward but twin cannons met him halfway. He sat back down, scrutinized each of their faces.

"What a coincidence. I've already made each of your acquaintance, separately." He pointed at Collin. "You tried to blow my head off." He swiveled to Burton. "And you tried to blow smoke up my ass. And succeeded. Burton, right? Bill Burton. Always remember names." He looked at Collin. "Didn't catch yours though."

Collin looked at Burton, then stared back at Jack. "Secret Service Agent Tim Collin. You pack a nice little wallop, Jack. Must've played some ball back in school."

"Yeah, my shoulder still remembers you."

Burton sat down on the bed next to Jack.

Jack looked at him. "I thought I'd covered my tracks pretty good. I'm kind of surprised you found me."

Burton looked at the ceiling. "A little bird told us, Jack."

Jack looked over at Collin and then back at Burton. "Look, I'm heading out of town, and I'm not coming back. I don't think you guys need to add me to the body count."

Burton eyed the bag on the bed and then got up and slipped his gun back in its holster. Then he grabbed Jack and flung him up against the wall. The veteran agent left nothing unprobed by the time he had finished. Burton spent the next ten minutes

527

examining every inch of the room for listening devices and other items of interest, ending his search at Jack's bag. He pulled out the photos and examined them.

Satisfied, Burton secreted them in his inner coat pocket and smiled at Jack. "Excuse me, but in my line of work paranoia is part of the mentality." He sat back down. "I would like to know, Jack, why you sent that photo to the President."

Jack shrugged. "Well, since my life here happens to be over, I thought your boss might want to contribute to my going-away fund. You could've just wired the funds, like you did with Luther."

Collin grunted, shook his head and grinned. "The world doesn't work that way, Jack, sorry. You should've found another solution to your problem."

Jack shot back, "I guess I should've followed your example. Got a problem? Just kill it."

Collin's smile evaporated. His eyes glittered darkly at the lawyer.

Burton stood up and paced around the room. He pulled out a cigarette and then crunched it up and put it in his pocket. He turned to Jack and said quietly, "You should've just gotten the hell out of town, Jack. Maybe you would've made it."

"Not with you two on my butt."

Burton shrugged. "You never know."

"How do you know I haven't given one of those photos to the cops?"

Burton pulled out the photos and looked down at them. "Polaroid OneStep camera. The film comes in a standard pack of ten shots. Whitney sent two to Russell. You sent one to the President. There are seven left here. Sorry, Jack, nice try."

"I could've just told Seth Frank what I know."

Burton shook his head. "If you had I think my little bird would've told me. But if you want to insist on the point we can just wait for the lieutenant to show up and join the party."

Jack burst up from the bed and launched himself toward the door. Right as he reached it, an iron fist slammed into his kidney. Jack crumpled to the floor. An instant later he was hustled up and thrown back on the bed.

Jack looked up into Collin's face.

"Now we're even, Jack."

Jack groaned and lay back on the bed, fighting the nausea the blow had caused. He sat back up, caught his breath as the pain subsided.

When Jack finally managed to look up, his eyes found Burton's face. Jack shook his head, the disbelief clear on his features.

Burton eyed Jack intently and said, "What?"

"I thought you were the good guys," Jack said quietly.

Burton said nothing for several long moments.

Collin's eyes went to the floor and stayed there.

Finally Burton answered, his voice faint, as if his larynx had suddenly collapsed. "So did I, Jack. So did I." He paused, swallowed painfully and went on. "I didn't ask for this problem. If Richmond could keep his dick in his pants none of this would've happened. But it did. And we had to fix it."

Burton stood up, looked at his watch. "I'm sorry about this, Jack. I really am. You probably think that's laughable but it's the way I really feel."

He looked at Collin and nodded. Collin motioned Jack to lie back on the bed.

"I hope the President appreciates what you're doing for him," Jack said bitterly.

Burton smiled ruefully. "Let's just say he expects it, Jack. Maybe they all do, in one way or another."

Jack slid slowly back and watched as the barrel moved closer and closer to his face. He could smell

529

the metal. He could envision the smoke, the projectile racing out faster than any eye could follow.

Then the door to the room was hit with an enormous blow. Collin whirled around. The second blow crashed the portal inward and a half-dozen D.C. cops bulled in, guns drawn.

"Freeze. Everybody freeze. Guns on the floor. *Now.*"

Collin and Burton quickly put their guns down on the floor. Jack lay back on the bed, his eyes closed. He touched his chest where his heart threatened to explode.

Burton looked at the men in blue. "We're United States Secret Service. IDs in our right inner pockets. We've tracked this man down. He was making threats against the President. We were just about to take him into custody."

The cops warily pulled out the IDs and scrutinized them. Two other cops pulled Jack roughly up. One began to read him his rights. Handcuffs were placed on his wrists.

The IDs were given back.

"Well, Agent Burton, you're just gonna have to wait until we get done with Mr. Graham here. Murder takes a priority even over threatening the President. Might be a long wait unless this guy's got nine lives."

The cop looked at Jack and then down at the bag on the bed.

"Shoulda taken off when you had the chance, Graham. Sooner or later we were gonna get you." He motioned for his men to take Jack out.

He looked back at the bewildered agents and smiled broadly. "We got a tip he was here. Most tips are worth shit. This one might get me that promotion I'm sorely in need of. Have a good day, gentlemen. Say hello to the President for me."

They left with their prisoner. Burton looked at Collin, and then pulled out the photos. Now Graham had nothing. He could repeat everything they had just told him to the police and they'd just get him ready for the rubber room. Poor sonofabitch. A bullet would've been a lot better than where he was headed. The two agents picked up their hardware and left.

The room was silent. Ten minutes later the door to the adjoining room was eased open and a figure slipped into Jack's room. The corner TV was swiveled around and the back was eased off. The TV was remarkably real-looking and an absolute sham. Hands reached inside and the surveillance camera was swiftly and silently removed and the cabling was pushed through the wall until it disappeared from sight.

The figure opened the adjoining door and went back through. A recording machine sat on a table next to the wall. The cable was coiled up and deposited in a bag. The figure hit a button on the recording machine and the tape slid out.

Ten minutes later the man, carrying a large back-pack, walked out of the front door of the Executive Inn, turned left and walked to the end of the parking lot where a car was parked, its engine idling. Tarr Crimson passed the car, and casually tossed the tape through the open window and onto the front seat. Then he proceeded over to his Harley-Davidson 1200cc touring bike, the joy of his life, got on, fired it up and thundered off. Setting up the video system had been child's play. Voice-activated camera. Recording machine kicked on when the camera did. Your standard VHS tape. He didn't know what was on the tape, but it must be something pretty damn valuable. Jack had promised him a year's free legal services for doing it. As he hurtled along the high-way, Tarr smiled, remembering their last meeting

531

where the lawyer had balked at the new age of surveillance technology.

Back in the parking lot, the car glided forward, one hand on the steering wheel, the other protectively around the tape. Seth Frank turned onto the main road. Not much of a moviegoer, this was one tape he was dying to watch.

Bill Burton sat in the small but cozy bedroom he had shared with his wife through the evolution of four beloved children. Twenty-four years together. They had made love countless times. In the corner by the window, Bill Burton had sat in a much worn rocker and fed his four offspring before reporting for early-morning shifts, allowing his exhausted wife a few minutes of much needed rest.

They had been good years. He had never made a lot of money, but that had never seemed to matter. His wife had gone back and finished her nursing degree after their youngest had entered high school. The added income had been nice, but it was good to see someone who had long sacrificed her personal goals to the needs of others to finally do something just for herself. All in all it had been a great life. A nice house in a quiet, picturesque neighborhood safe, so far, from the ever-expanding war zones around them. There would always be bad people. And there would always be people like Bill Burton to combat them. Or people like Burton had been.

He looked out the dormer window. Today was his day off. Dressed in jeans, bright red flannel shirt and Timberland boots, he could have easily passed as a burly lumberjack. His wife was unloading the car. Today was grocery shopping day. The same day for the last twenty years. He watched her figure admiringly as it bent low to pull out the bags. Chris, his fifteen-year-old, and Sidney, nineteen, long-legged and a real beauty, and in her sophomore year at Johns Hopkins, with her sights set on medical school, were helping their mother. His other two were out on their own and doing well. They occasionally called their old man for advice on buying a car or a house. Long-term career goals. And he loved every minute of it. He and his wife had hit four out of the park and it was a good feeling.

He sat down at the little desk in the corner, unlocked a drawer and pulled out the box. He lifted the top and stacked the five audiocassette tapes on top of the desk next to the letter he had written that morning. The name on the envelope was written in large, clear letters. "Seth Frank." Hell, he owed the guy.

Laughter floated up to him and he again went to the window. Sidney and Chris were now engaged in a pitched snowball battle with Sherry, his wife, caught in the middle. The smiles were big and the confrontation culminated in all of them landing in a heap next to the driveway.

He turned away from the window and did something he could never remember doing before. Through eight years as a cop, where tiny babies had expired in his arms, beaten to death by the ones who were supposed to love and protect them, through day after day of looking for the worst in humankind. The tears were salty. He didn't rub them away. They kept pouring. His family would be coming in soon. They were supposed to go out to dinner tonight. Ironically, today was Bill Burton's forty-fifth birthday.

He leaned across the desk, and with a quick motion, pulled the revolver from his holster. A snowball hit the window. They wanted their daddy to come join them.

I'm sorry. I love you. I wish I could be there. I'm sorry for all I've done. Please forgive your dad. Before he could lose his nerve he pushed the .357 as far down his throat as he could. It was cold and heavy. One of his gums started to bleed from a nick.

Bill Burton had done everything he could to ensure that no one would ever know the truth. He had committed crimes; he had killed an innocent person and had been involved in five other homicides. And now, seemingly in the clear, the horror behind him, after months of mounting disgust with what he had become, and after a sleepless night next to a woman he had loved with all his heart for over two decades, Bill Burton had realized that he could not accept what he had done, nor could he live with that knowledge.

The fact was that without self-respect, without his pride, his life was not worth living. And the unfailing love of his family did not help matters, it only made them worse. Because the object of that love, of that respect, knew that he deserved none of it.

He looked over at the stack of cassette tapes. His insurance policy. Now they would constitute his legacy, his own bizarre epitaph. And some good would come out of it. Thank God for that.

His lips curled into a barely perceptible smile. The Secret Service. Well, the secrets were going to fly now. He briefly thought of Alan Richmond and his eyes glistened. *Here's hoping for life without parole and you live to be a hundred, asshole.*

His finger tightened on the trigger.

Another snowball hit the window. Their voices drifted up to him. The tears started again as he thought of what he was leaving behind. "Goddammit." The word floated from his mouth, carrying with it more guilt, more anguish than he could ever hope to bear.

I'm sorry. Don't hate me. Please God don't hate me.

At the sound of the explosion, the playing stopped

as three pairs of eyes turned as one toward the house. In another minute they were inside. It only took one more minute for the screams to be heard. The quiet neighborhood was no more.

TWENTY-NINE

The knock on the door was unexpected. President Alan Richmond was in a tense conference with his Cabinet. The press had lately been lambasting the administration's domestic policies and he wanted to know why. Not that the actual policies themselves were of much interest to him. He was more concerned about the perception they conveyed. In the grand scheme of things perceptions were all that mattered. That was Politics 101.

"Who the hell are they?" The President looked angrily at the secretary. "Whoever they are, they're not on the list for today." He looked around the table. Hell, his Chief of Staff had not even bothered to show up for work today. Maybe she had done the smart thing and taken a bottle of pills. That would hurt him short-term, but he would work out an impressive spin on her suicide. Besides, she had been right about one thing: he was so far ahead in the polls, who cared?

The secretary timidly crept into the room. Her growing astonishment was evident. "It's a large group of men, Mr. President. Mr. Bayliss from the FBI, several policemen, and a gentleman from Virginia, he wouldn't give his name."

"The police? Tell them to leave and submit a request to see me. And tell Bayliss to call me tonight. He'd be cooling his heels in some Bureau outpost in the middle of nowhere if I hadn't pushed through his nomination as Director. I will not tolerate this disrespect."

"They're most insistent, sir."

The President flushed red and stood up. "Tell them to get the hell out. I'm busy, you idiot."

The woman quickly retreated. Before she could reach the door, however, it had opened. Four Secret Service agents entered, Johnson and Varney among them, followed by a contingent of D.C. police, including Police Chief Nathan Brimmer, and FBI Director Donald Bayliss, a short, thickly built man in a double-breasted suit with a face whiter than the building he was now in.

Bringing up the rear, Seth Frank quietly closed the door. In his other hand he carried a plain brown briefcase. Richmond stared at each of them, his eyes finally coming to rest on the homicide detective.

"Detective Frank, right? In case you weren't aware you are interrupting a confidential Cabinet meeting. I'm going to have to ask you to leave." He looked across at the four agents, raised his eyebrows and cocked his head toward the door. The men stared back; they didn't budge.

Frank stepped forward. He quietly slipped a paper out of his coat, unfolded it and handed it to the President. Richmond looked down at it while his Cabinet watched in utter bewilderment. Richmond finally looked back at the detective.

"Is this some kind of joke?"

"That is a copy of an arrest warrant naming you on capital murder charges for crimes committed in the Commonwealth of Virginia. Chief Brimmer here has a similar arrest warrant for murder one accessory charges that will be brought against you in the District. That is, after the commonwealth finishes with you."

The President looked over at Brimmer, who met

537

his gaze and sternly nodded. There was a cold look in the lawman's eyes that told exactly how he felt about the Chief Executive.

"I'm the President of the United States. You can't serve me with anything unless it's coffee. Now get out." The President turned to go back to his chair.

"Technically that may be true. However, I don't really care. Once the impeachment process is complete you won't be President Alan Richmond, you'll just be Alan Richmond. And when that happens I'll be back. Count on it."

The President turned back around, his face bloodless. "Impeachment?"

Frank moved forward until he was eye-to-eye with the man. On any other occasion this would have triggered prompt action on the part of the Secret Service. Now, they simply stood motionless. It was impossible to tell that each one of them was inwardly reeling over the loss of a respected colleague. Johnson and Varney seethed at having been duped as to the events of that night at the Sullivan estate. And the man they blamed for it all was now crumpling in front of them.

Frank said, "Let's cut through the bullshit. We already have Tim Collin and Gloria Russell in custody. They've both waived right to counsel and each has given detailed depositions regarding all of the events involving the homicides of Christine Sullivan, Luther Whitney, Walter Sullivan and the two killings at Patton, Shaw. I believe they've already cut deals with the prosecutors, who are really only interested in you anyway. This case is a real career-builder for a prosecutor, let me tell you."

The President staggered back a step, then righted himself.

Frank opened the briefcase and pulled out a video-tape and five audiocassette tapes. "I'm sure your

538

counsel will be interested to see these. The video is of Agents Burton and Collin when they attempted to murder Jack Graham. The tapes are of several meetings at which you were present and at which the plannings for the various crimes took place. Over six hours of testimony, Mr. President. Copies have been delivered to the Hill, the FBI, CIA, the *Post*, the Attorney General, White House counsel and anybody else I could think of – and no gaps on the tapes. Also included is the tape Walter Sullivan made of your telephone conversation on the night of his murder. It doesn't exactly coincide with the version you gave me. All compliments of Bill Burton. Said in his note he was cashing in his insurance policy."

"And where is Burton?" The President's voice was filled with rage.

"He was pronounced DOA at Fairfax Hospital at ten-thirty this morning. Self-inflicted gunshot wound."

Richmond barely made it to his chair. No one offered to assist him. He looked up at Frank.

"Anything else?"

"Yeah. Burton left behind one other paper. It's his proxy. For the next election. Sorry, but it seems you didn't get his vote."

One by one the Cabinet members got up and left. Fear of political suicide by association was alive and well in the Capital City. The lawmen and Secret Service agents followed. Only the President remained. His eyes stared blankly at the wall.

Seth Frank popped his head back in the door.

"Remember, be seeing you soon." He quietly closed the door.

EPILOGUE

The seasons of Washington followed a familiar pattern, and a bare week of spring with tolerable temperatures and humidity under fifty percent gave way abruptly to a meteoric thermometer and a humidity level that routinely delivered a full body shower whenever you walked outside. By July, the typical Washingtonian had adapted as much as they were ever going to, to air that was difficult to breathe and movements that were never slow enough to prevent a sudden burst of perspiration under one's clothing. But in all of that misery, the occasional evening was not ruined by the sudden materialization of a whipping, drenching thunderstorm with multiple branches of lightning that threatened to touch the earth with every explosion. Where the breeze was cool, the air sweet-smelling and the sky clear. Tonight was just such a night.

Jack sat on the edge of the pool set up on the building's roof. His khaki shorts revealed muscled, tanned legs, hairs curled by the sun. He was even leaner than before, all remnants of office-induced flab banished by months of physical exertion. Cords of well-toned muscle sat just beneath the surface of his white T-shirt. His hair was short, his face as brown as his legs. The water swished between his bare toes. He looked at the sky and breathed deeply. The place had been packed a mere three hours ago as office dwellers dragged tan-free, fleshy bodies to the replenishing powers of the warm waters. Now Jack sat alone. No bed beckoned him. No ringing alarm would disturb his sleep the next morning.

The door to the pool opened with a slight squeak. Jack turned and saw the beige summer suit, wrinkled and uncomfortable-looking. The man carried a brown paper bag.

"Building super told me you were back." Seth Frank smiled. "Mind some company?"

"Not if you've got what I think you've got in that bag." Frank sat down in a web chair and tossed a beer to Jack. They dinked cans and each man took a long pull.

Frank looked around. "So how was wherever you were?"

"Not bad. It was good to get away. But it's also good to be back."

"This looks like a nice place to meditate."

"It gets crowded around seven for a couple of hours. Most of the other time it's pretty much like this."

Frank looked wistfully at the pool and then started to take off his shoes. "You mind?"

"Help yourself."

Frank rolled up his pants, curled his socks into his shoes and sat down next to Jack, letting his milky-white legs sink into the water up to his knees.

"Damn, that feels good. County detectives with three daughters and a mortgage out the ying-yang rarely come into contact with swimming pools."

"So I've heard."

Frank rubbed his calves and looked at his friend. "Hey, being a bum agrees with you. You might want to think about sticking with it."

"I am thinking about it. The idea gets more appealing every day."

Frank eyed the envelope next to Jack.

"Important?" He pointed at the paper.

541

Jack picked it up, briefly reread the contents. "Ransome Baldwin. Remember him?"

Frank nodded. "What, has he decided to sue you for dumping his baby?"

Jack shook his head and smiled. He finished his beer and fished in the bag and pulled out another cold one. He tossed a second one to Frank.

"You never know, I guess. The guy basically said I was too good for Jennifer. At least for right now. That she had a lot of growing up to do. He's sending her out on some missionary duties for the Baldwin Charitable Foundation for a year or so. He said if I ever needed anything to let him know. Hell, he even said that he admired and respected me."

Frank sipped his beer. "Damn. Doesn't get much better than that."

"Yes, it does. Baldwin made Barry Alvis his chief in-house counsel. Alvis was the guy Jenn got fired at Patton, Shaw. Alvis promptly walked into Dan Kirksen's office and pulled the entire account. I think Dan was last seen on the ledge of a very tall building."

"I read where the firm closed its doors."

"All the good lawyers got snapped up right away. The bad ones ought to try something else for a living. Space is already rented out. The whole firm gone, without a trace."

"Well, same thing happened to the dinosaurs. It's just taking a little longer with you attorney types." He punched Jack in the arm.

Jack laughed. "Thanks for coming and cheering me up."

"Hell, I wouldn't miss it."

Jack looked at him, his face clouded. "So what happened?"

"Don't tell me you still haven't been reading the papers?"

"Not for months. After the gauntlet of reporters,

talk show hosts, teams of independent prosecutors, Hollywood producers and your run-of-the-mill curious person I've had to deal with I never want to know anything about anything. I changed my phone number a dozen times and the bastards kept finding it. That's why the last two months have been so sweet. No one knew me from Adam."

Frank took a moment to collect his thoughts. "Well, let's see, Collin pled to conspiracy, two counts of second-degree murder, obstruction and a half-dozen assorted lesser included offenses. That was the D.C. stuff. I think the judge felt sorry for him. Collin was a Kansas farm boy, Marine, Secret Service agent. He was just following orders. Been doing that most of his life. I mean, the President tells you to do something, you do it. He got twenty to life, which if you ask me was a sweetheart deal, but he gave a full account to the prosecution team. Maybe it was worth it. He'll probably be out in time for his fiftieth birthday. The commonwealth decided not to prosecute in return for his cooperation against Richmond."

"What about Russell?"

Frank almost choked on his beer. "Jesus, did that woman spill her guts. They must have spent a fortune on court-reporting fees. She just wouldn't stop talking. She got the best deal of all. No prison time. Thousand hours of community time. Ten years' probation. For fucking conspiracy to commit murder. Can you believe that? Between you and me, I think she's right on the borderline sanity-wise anyway. They brought in a court-appointed shrink. I think she might spend a few years in an institution before she's ready to come out and play. But I gotta tell you, Richmond brutalized her. Emotionally and physically. If half of what she said was true, Jesus . . . Mind games from hell."

"So what about Richmond?"

"You really have been on Mars, haven't you? Trial of the millennium and you slept right through it."

"Somebody had to."

"He fought right to the end, I have to admit that. Must've spent every dime he had. The guy didn't do himself any good testifying I can tell you that. He was so damn arrogant, obviously lying out his ass. And they traced the money wire straight back to the White House. Russell had pulled it from a bunch of accounts but made the mistake of assembling the five mil into one account before she wired it. Probably afraid if all of the money didn't show up at the same time Luther would go to the cops. His plan worked, even if he wasn't around to see it. Richmond didn't have an answer for that or a lot of other things. They tore him up on cross. He brought in a Who's Who of American Greatness and it didn't help him one little bit, the sonofabitch. One dangerous and sick dude if you ask me."

"And he had the nuclear codes. Real nice. So what'd he get?"

Frank stared at the ripples in the water for a few moments before answering. "He got the death penalty, Jack."

Jack stared at him. "Bullshit. How'd they manage that?"

"A little tricky from a legal-technical point of view. They prosecuted him under the murder-for-hire statute. That's the only one where the trigger man rule doesn't apply."

"How the hell did they get murder for hire to stick?"

"They argued that Burton and Collin were paid subordinates whose only job was to do what the President told them to do. He ordered them to kill. Like a Mafia hitman on the payroll. It's a stretch, but the jury returned the verdict and the sentence and the judge let it stand."

"Jesus Christ!"

"Hey, just because the guy was President doesn't mean he should be treated differently than anybody else. Hell, I don't know why we should be surprised at what happened. You know what kind of person it takes to run for President? Not normal. They could start out okay, but by the time they reach that level they've sold their soul to the devil so many times and stomped the guts out of enough people that they are definitely not like you and me, not even close."

Frank studied the depths of the pool, then finally stirred. "But they'll never execute him."

"Why not?"

"His lawyers will appeal, the ACLU will file, along with all the other death penalty opposers; you're gonna get *amicus* briefs from all over the planet. The guy took a tidal wave plunge on the popularity scale but he's still got some powerful friends. They'll find something wrong on the record. Besides, the country might agree on convicting the scumball. But I'm not sure the United States could actually execute some guy they elected to the presidency. Doesn't look real good from a global perspective either. Makes me feel kind of queasy too, although the asshole deserves it."

Jack scooped up handfuls of water and let the warm liquid run down his arms. He stared off into the night.

Frank looked keenly at Jack. "Not that some positives haven't come out of all this. Hell, Fairfax wants to make yours truly a division head. I've gotten offers from about a dozen cities to be their Chief of Police. The lead prosecutor on the Richmond case, they say, is a shoo-in for the AG slot next election."

The detective took a sip of beer. "What about you, Jack? You were the one who brought the guy down.

Setting up Burton and the President was your idea. Man, when I found my line was tapped, I thought my head was gonna explode. You were right though. So what do you get out of all this?"

Jack looked at his friend and said simply. "I'm alive. I'm not practicing rich-man law at Patton, Shaw and I'm not marrying Jennifer Baldwin. That's more than enough."

Frank studied the blue veins on his legs. "You heard from Kate?"

Jack took another swallow of beer before answering. "She's in Atlanta. At least she was last time she wrote."

"She gonna stick there?"

Jack shrugged. "She's not sure. Her letter wasn't all that clear." He paused. "Luther left her his house in his will."

"I'm surprised she'd take it. Ill-gotten gains and all that."

"Luther's father left it to him, bought and paid for. Luther knew his daughter. I think he wanted her to have. . . something. A home's not a bad place to start."

"Yeah? A home takes two if you ask me. And then some dirty diapers and infant formula to make it complete. Hell, Jack, you two were meant to be together. I'm telling you."

"I'm not sure that matters, Seth." He wiped off the thick droplets of water from his arms. "She's been through a lot. Maybe too much. I'm kind of connected to all the bad stuff. I really can't blame her for wanting to get away from it all. Wipe the slate clean."

"You weren't the problem, Jack. From what I saw everything else was."

Jack looked across at a helicopter roaring its way across the sky. "I'm a little tired of always being the

546

one to make the first step, Seth, you know what I'm saying?"

"I guess."

Frank looked at his watch. Jack caught the movement. "Got somewhere to go?"

"I was just thinking we need something a lot stronger than beer. I know this nice little place out by Dulles. Rack of ribs long as my arm, two-pound corn-on-the-cobs and tequila till the sun comes up. And some not-so-bad-looking waitresses if you're so inclined, although being married I will only watch from a respectful distance while you make a complete fool of yourself. We take a cab home because we'll both be shit-faced and you crash at my place. What do you say?"

Jack grinned. "Can I get a rain check on that? It sounds good though."

"You sure?"

"I'm sure, Seth, thanks."

"You got it." Frank stood up, rolled down his pants and flopped across to put on his shoes and socks.

"Hey, how about Saturday you come out to my place? We're grilling, burgers, fries and dogs. Got tickets to Camden Yard too."

"You got a deal on that one."

Frank stood up and headed to the door. He looked back. "Hey, Jack, don't think too much, okay? Sometimes that's not real healthy."

Jack held up his can. "Thanks for the beer."

After Frank left, Jack lay back on the cement and stared at a sky that seemed filled with more stars than there were numbers. Sometimes he would awaken from a deep sleep and realize that he'd been dreaming about the most bizarre stuff. But what he'd been dreaming about had actually happened to him. It was not a pleasant feeling. And it only added to the confusion that, at his age, he hoped would have been

547

long since eliminated from his life.

An hour-and-a-half plane ride due south was probably the surest answer to what ailed him. Kate Whitney may or may not come back. The only thing he felt sure about was that he could not go after her. That this time it would be her responsibility to return to his life. And it was not bitterness that made Jack feel such was imperative. Kate had to make up her own mind. About her life and how she wanted to spend it. The emotional trauma she had experienced with her father had been surpassed by the overwhelming guilt and grief she had endured at his death. The woman had a lot to think through. And she had made it very clear that she needed to undertake that exercise alone. And she was probably right.

He took off his shirt, slid into the water and did three quick laps. His arms cut powerfully through the water and then he pulled himself back up on the tiled apron. He grabbed his towel and wrapped it around his shoulders. The night air was cool and each droplet of water felt like a miniature air conditioner against his skin. He again looked at the sky. Not a mural in sight. But neither was Kate.

He was deciding whether to head back to his apartment for some sleep when he heard the door squeak open again. Frank must have forgotten something. He looked over. For a few seconds he couldn't move. He just sat there with the towel around his shoulders afraid to make a sound. That what was happening might not be real. Another dream that would flicker out with the sun's first rays. Finally he slowly got up, water dripping off him, and moved toward the door.

Down on the street, Seth Frank stood next to his car for a few moments admiring the simple beauty of the evening, sniffed the air that was more reminiscent of a wet spring than a humid summer. It wouldn't be that late when he got home. Maybe Mrs. Frank would like to hit the neighborhood Dairy Queen. Just the two of them. He'd heard some good reports about the butterscotch-dipped cone. That would finish off the day just fine. He climbed in his car.

As a father of three, Seth Frank knew what a wonderful and precious commodity life was. As a homicide detective he had learned how that precious commodity could be brutally ripped away. He looked up at the roof of the apartment building and smiled as he put the car in gear. But that was the great thing about being alive, he thought. Today might not be so good. But tomorrow, you got another chance to get it right.

AUTHOR'S NOTE

This novel is obviously a work of fiction and intends to be nothing more. It in no way implies that members of the United States Secret Service would do any of the acts attributed to the fictional agents in the novel. The agents in *Absolute Power* were good, loyal men put into an impossible situation. The decisions they made were decisions any one of us might have made if confronted with the total destruction of all we have worked for.

I cannot imagine a more difficult task than the one every Secret Service agent undertakes on any given day. Weeks, months, or years of tedium may, at any moment, be shattered by the actions of those who wish to harm, to kill. Secret Service agents seem, to me, to be the counterparts of football's unheralded offensive linemen. No one praises them when things go right, when the millions of logistical details making up their daily routines result in no assassination attempt, nothing newsworthy. But, of course, we do hear of them on the very rare occasion when something bad does happen. And Secret Service agents must live with that unfairness every day as they protect people whose political survival demands that they do things that make them, in essence, unprotectable. For this and many other reasons, the men and women of the United States Secret Service deserve the respect and admiration of every American. They certainly have mine.

David Baldacci
Washington, D.C.
January 1996

ACKNOWLEDGMENTS

Jennifer Karas, for being a terrific friend and avid supporter and for getting the ball rolling way back when. Karen Spiegel, my biggest fan on the West Coast, may there be many huge movies and small statuettes in your future. Jim and Everne Spiegel, for all their support and encouragement.

Aaron Priest, the man who plucked me from obscurity, my friend and agent for life, and a helluva nice guy on top of it. And his assistant, Lisa Vance, who diligently answers every one of my questions, no matter how off-the-wall. And to the Priest Agency's editor-in-residence, Frances Jalet-Miller, whose insights and thoughtful comments made me dig deeper into my characters and made the book far better in the process.

My editor, Maureen Egen, for making my freshman publication experience so painless and rewarding. And to Larry Kirshbaum, who saw something in the pages very late at night and changed my life forever.

Steven Wilmsen, a fellow writer, who well knows how hard it is, and who fed me good advice and tons of encouragement all along the way. Thank you, my friend.

Steve and Mary Jennings, for technical advice, legwork, and being the best friends anyone could hope for. Richard Marvin and Joe Barry, for technical advice on security systems.

And to Art, Lynette, Ronni, Scott, and Randy for all their love and support.

Here, the words really do fail me.

split second

David Baldacci
Published December 2003

DON'T BLINK your life might depend on it . . .
'He was the only one in the room who could see
it. His attention stayed there for one beat, two beats,
three beats, far too long. Yet who could blame him
for not being able to pull his gaze away from *that*?'

When something distracts Secret Agent Sean
King for a split second, it costs him his career and
presidential candidate Clyde Ritter his life. What
stole his attention? Why was Ritter shot? Where
were the other detail leaders?

Eight years later Michelle Maxwell is on the fast
track through the ranks of the Secret Service when
her career is stopped short: presidential candidate
John Bruno is abducted from a funeral home while
under her protection.

The similarity between the two cases drives
Michelle to re-open investigations into the Ritter
fiasco and join forces with attractive ex-agent,
King. The pair are determined to get to the bottom
of what happened in those critical moments.

Meanwhile, high-ranking members of the legal
system and key witnesses from both cases are going
missing. King is losing friends, colleagues and
clients fast and his ex-lover, Joan Dillinger, is playing curious games – she wants Sean back, but she
also owes him for something . . .

AN EXTRACT FROM THIS STUNNING
THRILLER FOLLOWS . . .

PROLOGUE

September, 1996

It only took a split second. Although, it seemed like the longest split second ever.

They were on the campaign trail at a nondescript hotel meet-and-greet in a place so far out you had to use long distance to reach the boonies. Standing behind his protectee, he had scanned the crowd, while his ear mike buzzed sporadically with unremarkable information. It had been muggy in the large room filled with excited people waving "Elect Clyde Ritter" pennants. There were more than a few infants being thrust toward the smiling candidate. He hated this because the babies could so easily shield a gun until it was too late. Yet the little ones just kept coming and Clyde kissed them all, and ulcers seemed to form in his belly as he observed this potentially dangerous spectacle.

The crowd drew closer, right up to the velvet rope on stanchions that had been placed as a line in the sand. In response, he had moved closer to Ritter. The palm of his outstretched hand rested lightly on the candidate's sweaty, coatless back, so that he could pull him down in an instant if something happened. He couldn't very well stand in front of the man, for the candidate belonged to the *people*. His catechism was set in stone: shake hands, wave, smile, nail a sound bite in time for the six o'clock news, then pucker up and kiss a fat baby. And all the time he silently watched the crowd, keeping his hand on Ritter's soaked shirt and

555

looked for threats, he hoped in all the right places.

Someone called out from the rear of the space. Ritter answered the jibe back with his own bit of humor and the crowd laughed good-naturedly, or at least most of them did. There were people here who hated Ritter and all he stood for. Faces didn't lie, not for those trained to read them, and he could read a face, as well as he could shoot a gun. That's what he spent all his working life doing: reading the hearts and souls of men and women through their eyes, their physical tics.

He keyed on two men in particular, ten feet away, on the right. They looked like potential trouble although each wore a short sleeve shirt and tight pants with no place to house a weapon, which dropped them several pegs on the danger meter. Assassins tended to favor bulky clothing and small handguns. Still, he mumbled a few words into his mic, telling others of his concern. Then his gaze flitted to the clock on the back of the wall. It was 10:32 in the morning. Five more minutes and then they were on to the next town where the handshakes, the sound bites, the baby kisses and the face reading would continue.

His gaze had turned in the direction of the new sound, and then the new sight, something totally unexpected. Standing facing the crowd and behind the hard-politicking Ritter, he was the only one in the room who could see it. His attention stayed there for one beat, two beats, three beats, far too long. Yet who could blame him for not being able to pull his gaze away from *that*? Everyone, as it turned out, including himself.

He heard the bang, like the sound of a dropped book. He could feel the moisture on his hand where it had touched Ritter's back. And now the moisture wasn't just sweat. His hand stung, where the slug had come out the body and taken a chunk off his middle finger before hitting the wall behind him. As Ritter dropped, the split second moved into maximum overdrive akin to a comet going hell-bent and still taking a billion light years to get where it was actually going.

Shrieks from the crowd poured out and then seemed to dissolve into one long, soulless moan. Faces stretched into images one only saw in carnival fun houses. Then the blur hit him like the force of an exploding grenade as feet moved and bodies gyrated and the screams came at him from all directions. People pushed, pulled and ducked to get out of the way. He remembered thinking that there was no greater chaos than when swift, violent death knocks on the door of an unsuspecting crowd.

And the now ex-presidential candidate Clyde Ritter was lying by his feet on the hardwood floor shot right through the heart. His gaze left the newly deceased and was now on the shooter, a tall, handsome man in a tweed jacket and wearing glasses. The killer's Smith & Wesson .44 was still pointing at the spot where Ritter had been standing, as though waiting for the target to get back up so he could be shot all over again. The mass of panicked people held back the guards who were fighting to get through, so that he and the killer were the only ones at the party.

He pointed his pistol at the chest of the assassin. He gave no warning, called out not one constitutional right accorded the assassin under American jurisprudence. His duty now clear, he fired once, and then again, though the first time was enough. It dropped the man right where he stood. He never said a word, as though he had expected to die for what he'd done, and accepted the terms stoically like a good martyr should. And all martyrs left behind people like him, the ones who were blamed for letting it happen in the first place. Three men had actually died that day, and he had been one of them.

Sean Ignatius King, Born August 1, 1960 – Died September 21, 1996 in a place he had never even heard of until the final day of his life. And yet he had it far worse than the other fallen. They went tidily into their coffins and were forever mourned by those who loved them or at least loved what they stood for. The soon to be ex-Secret Service agent King had no such luck. After his death, his unlikely burden was to keep right on living.

total control

ONE

The apartment was small, unattractive and possessed of an unsettling musty odor that suggested long neglect. However, the few furnishings and personal belongings were clean and well organized; several of the chairs and a small side table were clearly antiques of high quality. The largest occupant of the tiny living room was a meticulously crafted maple bookcase that might as well have rested on the moon, so out of place did it seem in the modest, unremarkable space. Most of the volumes neatly lining the shelves were financial in nature and dealt with such subjects as international monetary policy and complex investment theories.

The only light in the room came from a floor lamp next to a rumpled couch. Its small arc of illumination outlined the tall, narrow-shouldered man sitting there, his eyes closed as though he were asleep. The slender watch on his wrist showed it to be four o'clock in the morning. Conservative gray cuffed suit pants hovered over gleaming black-tasseled shoes. Hunter-green suspenders ran down the front of a rigid white dress shirt. The collar of the shirt was open, the ends of a bow tie dangled around the neck. The large bald head was like an afterthought, because what captured one's attention was the thick, steel-gray beard that fronted the wide, deeply lined face. However, when the man abruptly opened his eyes, all other physical characteristics became secondary; the eyes were chestnut brown in color

1

and piercing; they seemed to swell to a size that completely engulfed the eye sockets as they swept across the room.

Then the pain wracked the man and he ripped at his left side; actually the hurt was everywhere now. Its origins, however, had been at the spot he now attacked with a fierce, if futile, vengeance. The breaths came in gushes, the face grossly contorted.

His hand slipped down to the apparatus attached to this belt. About the shape and size of a Walkman, it was actually a CADD pump attached to a Groshong catheter that was fully hidden under the man's shirt, where its other end was embedded in his chest. His finger found the correct button and the computer resting inside the CADD pump immediately delivered an incredibly potent dose of painkilling medication over and above what it automatically dispensed at regular intervals throughout the day. As the combination of drugs flowed directly into the man's bloodstream, the pain finally retreated. But it would return; it always did.

The man lay back, exhausted, his face clammy, his freshly laundered shirt soaked with perspiration. Thank God for the pump's on-demand feature. He had an incredible tolerance for pain, as his mental prowess could easily overpower any physical discomforts, but the beast now devouring his insides had introduced him to an altogether new level of physical anguish. He wondered briefly which would come first: his death or the drugs' total and complete defeat at the hands of the enemy. He prayed for the former.

He stumbled to the bathroom and looked into the mirror. It was at that moment that Arthur Lieberman started to laugh. The near-hysterical howls continued upward, threatening to explode through the thin walls of the apartment, until the uncontrollable outburst ended in sobs and then choked vomiting. A few minutes later, having replaced his soiled shirt with a clean one, Lieberman began calmly to coax his bow tie into shape in the reflection of the bathroom mirror. The violent mood swings were to be expected, he had been told. He shook his head.

He had always taken care of himself. Exercised regularly, never smoked, never drank, watched his diet. Now, at a youthful sixty-two, he would not live to see sixty-three. That fact had been confirmed by so many specialists that, finally, even Lieberman's massive will to live had given way. But he would not go quietly. He had one card left to play. He smiled as he suddenly realized that impending death had granted him a maneuverability that had been denied in life. It would indeed be an ironic twist that such a distinguished career as his would end on such an ignoble note. But the shock waves that would accompany his exit would be worth it at this point. What did he care? He walked into the small bedroom and took a moment to glance at the photos on the desk. Tears welled up in his eyes and he quickly left the room.

At five-thirty precisely Lieberman left the apartment and rode the small elevator down to the street level, where a Crown Victoria, its government license plates a gleaming white in the wash of the streetlight, was parked at the curb, its engine idling. The chauffeur exited the car briskly and opened and held the door for Lieberman. The driver respectfully tipped his cap to this esteemed passenger and, as usual, received no response. In a few moments the car had disappeared down the street.

At about the time Lieberman's car entered the on ramp to the Beltway, the Mariner L500 jetliner was being rolled out of its hangar at Dulles International

3

Airport in preparation for the nonstop flight to Los Angeles. Maintenance checks completed, the 155-foot-long plane was now being fueled. Western Airlines subcontracted out the fueling component of its operation. The fuel truck, squat and bulky, was parked underneath the starboard wing. On the L500 the standard configuration had fuel tanks located within each wing and in the fuselage. The fuel panel under the wing, located about a third of the way out from the fuselage, had been dropped down and the long fuel hose snaked upward into the wing's interior, where it had been locked into place around the fuel intake valve. The one valve served to fuel all three tanks through a series of connecting manifolds. The solitary fueler, wearing thick gloves and dirty overalls, monitored the hose as the highly combustible mixture flowed into the tank. The man looked slowly around at the increasing activity surrounding the aircraft: mail and freight cargo were being loaded on, baggage carts were wending their way to the terminal. Satisfied that he wasn't being observed, the fueler used one gloved hand to casually spray the exposed part of the fuel tank around the intake valve with a substance in a plastic container. The metal of the fuel tank gleamed where it had been sprayed. Closer examination would have revealed a slight misting on the metal's surface, but no closer examination would be made. Even the first officer making the rounds on the preflight check would never discover this little surprise lurking within the massive machine.

The man replaced the small plastic container deep within one pocket of his overalls. He pulled from his other pocket a slender rectangular-shaped object and raised his hand up into the wing's interior. When his hand came back down, it was empty. The fueling completed, the hose was loaded back on the truck and fuel panel on the wing was reattached. The truck drove off to complete work on another jet. The man looked back once at the L500 and then continued on. He was scheduled to get off duty at seven this morning. He did not intend to stay a minute longer.

The 220,000-pound Mariner L500 lifted off the runway, easily powering through the early morning cloud cover. A single-aisle jet with twin high bypass ratio Rolls-Royce engines, the L500 was the most technologically advanced aircraft currently operating outside those flown by pilots of the U.S. Air Force.

Flight 3223 carried 174 passengers and a seven-member flight crew. Most passengers were settling into their seats with newspapers and magazines while the plane climbed swiftly over the Virginia countryside to its cruising altitude of thirty-five thousand feet. The onboard navigational computer had established a flight time to Los Angeles of five hours and five minutes.

One of the passengers in the first-class section was reading the *Wall Street Journal*. A hand played across the bushy, steel-gray beard as large, active eyes scanned the pages of financial information. Down the narrow aisle, in the coach section, other passengers sat quietly, some with hands folded across their chests, some with eyes half closed and others reading. In one seat, an old woman gripped rosary beads in her right hand, her mouth silently reciting the familiar words.

As the L500 climbed to thirty-five thousand feet and leveled off, the captain came on the loudspeaker to make her perfunctory greetings while the flight attendants went about their normal routine – a routine that was about to be interrupted.

All heads turned to the red flash that erupted on the right side of the aircraft. Those sitting in the window seats on that side watched in the starkest horror as the right wing buckled, metal skin tearing, rivets popping free. Bare seconds passed before two-thirds of the wing sheared off, carrying with it the starboard-side Rolls-Royce engine. Like savaged veins, shredded hydraulic lines and cables whipped back and forth in the fierce headwind as jet fuel from the cracked fuel tank doused the fuselage.

The L500 immediately rolled left over on its back, making a shambles of the cabin. Inside the fuselage every single human being screamed in mortal terror as the plane whipped across the sky like a tumble-weed, completely out of control. Passengers up and down the aisle were violently torn from their seats. For most of them the short trip from the seats was fatal. Screams of pain were heard as heavy pieces of luggage, disgorged from compartments torn open when the shock waves of air pressure gone wild exceeded their locking mechanism's strength limits, collided with soft human flesh.

The old woman's hand slipped open and the rosary beads slid down to the floor, which was now the ceiling of the upside-down plane. Her eyes were wide open now, but not in fear. She was one of the fortunate ones. A fatal heart attack had rescued her from the next several minutes of sheer terror.

Twin-engine commercial jetliners are certified to fly on only one engine. No jetliner, however, can fly with only one wing. The air-worthiness of Flight 3223 had been irreversibly destroyed. The L500 settled into a tight nose-to-ground death spiral.

On the flight deck the two-member crew struggled valiantly with the controls as their damaged aircraft shot downward through the overcast skies like a spear through cotton. Unsure of the precise nature of this catastrophe, they nevertheless were well aware that the aircraft and all lives on board were in significant jeopardy. As they frantically tried to regain control of the aircraft, the two pilots silently prayed they would collide with no other plane as they hurtled to earth. "Oh, my God!" The captain stared in disbelief at the altimeter as it raced on its unstoppable course to zero. Neither the most sophisticated avionics system in the world nor the most exceptional piloting skills could reverse the startling truth facing every human being on the fractured projectile: They were all going to die, and very soon. And as happens in virtually all air crashes, the two pilots would be the first to leave this world; but the others on board Flight 3223 would only be a fraction of a second behind.

Lieberman's mouth sagged open as he gripped the armrests in total disbelief. As the plane's nose dropped to six o'clock, Lieberman was looking face down at the back of the seat in front of him, as if he were at the very top of some absurd roller coaster. Unfortunately for him, Arthur Lieberman would remain conscious until the very second the aircraft met the immovable object that it was now racing toward. His exit from the living would come several months ahead of schedule and not at all according to plan. As the plane started its final descent, one word escaped from Lieberman's lips. Though monosyllabic, it was uttered in one continuous shriek that could be heard over all of the other terrifying sounds flooding the cabin.

"Noooo!"

TWO

Jason Archer, his starched shirt dirty, his tie askew, labored through the contents of the piles of boxes. A laptop sat beside him. Every few minutes he would stop, pull a piece of paper from the morass and, using a handheld device, scan the contents of the paper into his laptop. Sweat trickled down his nose. The storage warehouse he was in was hot and filthy. Suddenly a voice called out to him from somewhere within the vast space. "Jason?" Footsteps approached. "Jason, are you here?"

Jason quickly closed up the box he was working on, shut down his laptop and slid it between a crevice in the stacks of boxes. A few seconds later a man appeared. Quentin Rowe stood about five-eight, weighed perhaps a hundred fifty, with narrow shoulders; slender oval glasses rested above a hairless face. His long, thin blond hair was tied back into a neat ponytail. He was dressed casually in faded jeans and a white cotton shirt. The antenna of a cellular phone sprouted from his shirt pocket. His hands were stuffed into his back pockets. "I happened to be in the area. How's it coming?"

Jason stood up and stretched his long, muscular frame. "It's coming, Quentin, it's coming."

"The CyberCom deal is really heating up and a they want the financials ASAP. How much longer do you think it will take you?" Despite his carefree appearance, Rowe looked anxious.

Jason eyed the stack of boxes. "Another week, ten days tops."

"You're sure?"

Jason nodded and methodically wiped his hands off before resting his eyes on Rowe. "I won't let you down, Quentin. I know how important CyberCom is to you. To all of us." A twinge of guilt hit Jason between the shoulder blades, but his features were inscrutable.

Rowe relaxed somewhat. "We won't forget your efforts, Jason. What with this and the job you did on the tape backups. Gamble was particularly impressed, to the extent he can understand it."

"I think it'll be remembered for a long time," Jason agreed.

Rowe surveyed the warehouse with incredulity. "To think the contents of this entire warehouse could fit comfortably on a stack of floppy disks. What a waste."

Jason grinned. "Well, Nathan Gamble isn't the most computer literate person in the world." Rowe snorted. "His investment operations generated a lot of paper, Quentin," Jason continued, "and you can't argue with success. The man's made a lot of money over the years."

"Exactly, Jason. That's our only hope. Gamble understands money. The CyberCom deal will make all the others look puny by comparison." Rowe looked admiringly up at Jason Archer. "After all this work you've got a great future ahead of you."

Jason's eyes took on a soft gleam and then he smiled at his colleague. "My thoughts exactly."

Jason Archer climbed into the passenger seat of the Ford Explorer, leaned across and kissed his wife.

9

Sidney Archer was tall and blond. Her chiseled features had softened after the birth of their daughter. She inclined her head toward the rear seat. Jason smiled as his eyes fell upon Amy, two years old and dead asleep in her baby seat. Winnie the Pooh automatically clutched in one fist.

"Long day for her," Jason said as he unknotted his tie.

"For us all," Sidney replied. "I thought being a part-time law partner would be a breeze. Now it seems like I cram the same fifty-hour week into three days." She shook her head wearily and pulled the truck on to the road. Behind them soared the world headquarters building of Triton Global, her husband's employer and the world's undisputed leader in technologies ranging from global computer networks to children's educational software and just about everything in between.

Jason took one of his wife's hands in his and squeezed it tenderly. "I know, Sid. I know it's rough, but I might have some news soon that'll let you chuck the practice for good."

She looked at him and smiled. "You devised a computer program that'll let you pick the correct Lotto numbers?"

"Maybe something better." A grin flashed across his handsome features.

"Okay, you've definitely got my attention. What is it?"

He shook his head. "Uh-uh. Not until I know for sure."

"Jason, don't do this to me." Her mock plea brought a broader smile to his lips. He patted her hand. "You know I'm real good at keeping secrets. And I know how you love surprises."

She stopped at a red light and turned to him. "I also like opening presents on Christmas Eve. So

10

come on, talk."

"Not this time, sorry, no way, nohow. Hey, how about we go out to eat tonight?"

"I'm a very tenacious attorney, so don't try to change the subject on me. Besides, eating out is not in this month's budget. I want details." She playfully poked him as she went through the green light.

"Very, very soon, Sid. I promise. But not now, okay?" His tone had suddenly become more serious, as though he regretted bringing up the subject. She looked over at him. He was staring rigidly out the window. A trace of concern came over her face. He turned back to her, caught the look of worry, put a hand against her cheek and winked. "When we got married, I promised you the world, didn't I?"

"You've given me the world, Jason." She stared at Amy in the rearview mirror. "More than the world."

He rubbed her shoulder. "I love you, Sid, more than anything. You deserve the best. One day I'll give it to you."

She smiled at him; however, as he turned to look out the window the look of concern returned to her features.

The man was bent over the computer, his face bare inches from the screen. His fingers were pounding the keys so fiercely they resembled a column of miniature jackhammers. The battered keyboard appeared ready to disintegrate under the relentless attack. Like pouring water, digital images flowed down the computer screen too fast for the eye to follow. A weak light overhead provided illumination for the man's task. Thick droplets of sweat clustered on his face, although the room temperature hovered at a comfortable seventy degrees. He swiped at the moisture as the salty liquid slid behind his glasses and stung his already painful, bloodshot eyes.

11

So intent was he on his work that he did not notice the door to the room slowly open. Nor did he hear the three pairs of feet as they made their way in, moving across the thick carpet until they stood directly behind him. Their movements were unhurried; the intruders' superior numbers apparently provided them with overwhelming confidence.

Finally the man at the computer turned around. His limbs started to quake uncontrollably, as though he had foreseen what was about to happen to him.

He would not even have time to scream.

As the triggers snapped back simultaneously and the firing pins rammed home, the guns roared in deafening unison.

Jason Archer jerked upright in the chair where he had fallen asleep. Real sweat clung to his face while the vision of violent death clung to his mind. The damn dream, it wouldn't let go. He quickly looked around. Sidney was dozing on the couch; the TV droned on in the background. Jason rose and covered his wife with a blanket. Then he went down to Amy's room. It was almost midnight. As he peeked in the door he could hear her tossing in her sleep. He went to the edge of her bed and watched the tiny form as it moved restlessly around. She must be having a bad dream, something her father could well relate to. Jason gently rubbed his daughter's forehead and then picked her up and held her, slowly swaying from side to side in the quiet darkness. This normally chased away the nightmares; and in a few minutes Amy was back in a peaceful sleep. Jason covered her up and kissed her on the cheek. Then he went to the kitchen, scribbled a note to his wife, put it on the table next to the couch where Sidney continued to doze and headed to the garage, where he climbed into his old Cougar convertible.

As he backed out of the garage, he did not notice Sidney at the front window watching him, his note clutched in her hand. After his taillights disappeared down the street, Sidney turned from the window and read the note again. Her husband was heading back to the office to do some work. He would be home when he could. She looked at the clock on the fireplace mantel. It was nearly midnight. She checked on Amy and then put a teakettle on the stove. She suddenly slumped against the kitchen counter as a deeply buried suspicion exploded to the surface. This wasn't the first time she had awoken to find her husband backing his car out of the garage, leaving a note behind telling her he had gone back to work.

She made her tea and then on impulse raced up the stairs to the bathroom. She looked at her face in the mirror. A little fuller than when they had first married. She abruptly stripped off her sleeping gown and underwear. She looked from the front, side and, finally, the back, holding up a hand mirror to check this most depressing angle. Pregnancy had done some damage; the stomach had pretty much recovered, but her bottom was definitely not as firm. Were her breasts sagging? The hips did seem slightly wider than before. Not so unusual after giving birth. With nervous fingers she pinched the millimeter of extra skin under her chin as acute depression sunk in. Jason's body was as iron-hard as it had been when they first started dating. Her husband's amazing physique and classic good looks were only part of a very attractive package that included a remarkable intellect. The package would be immensely attractive to every woman Sidney knew and certainly most of those she didn't. As she traced her jawline she gasped as she realized what she was doing. A highly intelligent, well-respected

13

attorney, she was examining herself like a piece of meat, just as generations of men had routinely done to womankind. She threw her gown back on. She *was* attractive. Jason *loved* her. He *was* going to work to catch up on things. He was building his career rapidly. Soon, both their dreams would be fulfilled. His to run his own company; hers to be a full-time mother to Amy and the other children they expected to have. If that sounded like a 1950s sitcom, so be it, because that's exactly what the Archers wanted. And Jason, she firmly believed, was right this minute working furiously to get there.

At about the time Sidney wandered off to bed, Jason Archer stopped at a pay phone and dialed a number he had memorized long before. The call was answered immediately.

"Hello, Jason."

"I'm telling you this has to be over soon, or I may not make it."

"Bad dreams again?" The tone managed to sound sympathetic and patronizing at the same time.

"You're implying that they come and go. Actually they're always with me," Jason curtly replied.

"It won't be long now." The voice was now reassuring.

"You're sure they're not on to me? I get these funny feelings, like everyone's watching me."

"It's normal, Jason. Happens all the time. If you were in trouble, we'd know it, believe me. We've been through this before."

"I have believed you. I just hope that belief is not misplaced." Jason's voice grew more tense. "I'm not a pro at this. Dammit, it's getting to me."

"We understand that. Don't go crazy on us now. As I said, it's almost over. A few more items and then you officially retire."

14

"Look, I don't understand why we can't go with what I've already gotten."

"Jason, it's not your job to think about those things. We need to dig a little deeper and you're just going to have to accept that. Keep your head up. We're not exactly babes in the woods on things like this; we've got it all planned out. You just hold up your end and we're fine. Everybody will be fine."

"Well, I'm going to finish up tonight, that's for damn sure. Do we use the same drop routine?"

"No. This time it'll be a personal exchange."

Jason's tone registered surprise. "Why?"

"We're nearing the end and any mistakes could jeopardize the entire operation. While we have no reason to believe they're on to you, we can't be absolutely sure *we're* not being watched. Remember, we're all taking chances here. Drops are usually safe, but there's always a margin of error built in. A face-to-face out of the area with fresh people eliminates that margin, simple as that. It keeps you safer too. And your family."

"My family? What the hell do they have to do with this?"

"Don't be stupid, Jason. These are high stakes. The risks were explained to you from the start. It's a violent world. Understand?"

"Look—"

"Everything will be fine. You just have to follow the instructions to the letter." The last three words were said with particular force. "You haven't told anyone, have you? Particularly not your wife."

"No. Who the hell would I tell? Who would believe me?"

"You'd be surprised. Just remember: Anyone you tell is in danger, just as you are."

"Tell me something I don't know," Jason snapped back. "So what are the details?"

15

"Not now. Soon. The usual channels. Hang in there, Jason. We're almost through the tunnel."

"Yeah, well, let's hope the damn thing doesn't collapse on me before then."

The response drew a small chuckle and then the line went dead.

Jason slipped his thumb out of the fingerprint scanner, spoke his name into the small speaker mounted on the wall and patiently waited as the computer matched his thumb and voice prints to the ones residing in its massive files. He smiled and nodded at the uniformed security guard sitting at a large console in the middle of the eighth-floor reception area. Jason was conscious of the name TRITON GLOBAL spelled out in foot-long silver letters behind the guard's broad back.

"Too bad they don't give you the authority to just let me in, Charlie. You know, one human being to another."

Charlie was a large black man in his early sixties, with a bald head and a quick wit.

"Hell, Jason, for all I know you could be Saddam Hussein in disguise. These days you can't trust outward appearances. Nice sweater, by the way, Saddam." Charlie chuckled. "Besides, how could this big, sophisticated company possibly trust the judgment of a little old security guard like me when they got all these gadgets to tell them who's who? Computers are king, Jason. The sad truth is human beings don't measure up anymore."

"Don't sound so depressed, Charlie. Technology has its good points. Hey, I tell you what, why don't we switch jobs for a while? Then you can see the good stuff." Jason grinned.

"Sure thing, Jason. I'll play with all those million-dollar toys and you can go sniffing around the rest

16

room every thirty minutes looking for bad guys. I won't even charge you for use of the uniform. Of course, if we switch jobs we also switch paychecks. I wouldn't want you to miss out on a windfall like seven bucks an hour. It's only fair."

"You're too damn smart for your own good, Charlie."

Charlie laughed and went back to studying the numerous TV monitors mounted into the console.

As the massive door opened on whisper-quiet hinges, the smile on Jason's face abruptly disappeared. He moved through the opening. Striding down the hallway, he pulled something from his coat pocket. It was the size and shape of a typical credit card and was also made of plastic.

Jason stopped in front of a doorway. The card slid neatly into the slot in the metal box bolted to the door. The microchip buried within the card silently communicated with its counterpart attached to the portal. Jason's index finger pecked four times at the adjacent numeric pad. There was an audible click. He gripped the doorknob, turned it and the three-inch-thick door swung back into the darkened space.

As the lights came on, Jason was illuminated briefly in the doorway. He quickly closed the door; the twin dead bolts slid back into place. As he looked around the neatly arranged office, his hands were shaking and his heart was beating so hard he was absolutely certain it could be heard throughout the entire building. This was not the first time. It was far from the first time. He allowed himself a brief smile as he focused on the fact that this would be the last time. Regardless of what happened, this was it. Everyone had a limit, and tonight he had reached his.

He moved to the desk, sat down and turned on the computer. Attached to the monitor was a small microphone mounted on a long flexible metal neck that one could speak into for voice commands. Jason impatiently pushed it out of the way so he would have a clear view of the computer screen. His back ramrod straight, eyes glued to the screen, hands poised to strike, he was now clearly in his element. Like a pianist's in full swing, his fingers flashed across the keyboard. He peered at the screen, which fed instructions back to him, instructions so familiar as to be rote. Jason hit four digits on the numeric pad attached to the base of the computer's micro-processor unit, then he leaned forward and fixed his gaze at a spot in the upper right-hand corner of the monitor. Jason knew that a video camera had just that instant electronically interrogated his right iris, transmitting a host of unique discriminators con-tained within his eye to a central database, which, in turn, compared the image of his iris to the thirty thousand residing in that computerized file. The entire process had taken barely four seconds. As accustomed as he was to the ever-expanding muscle of technology, even Jason Archer had to shake his head occasionally over what was really out there. Iris scanners were also used to closely monitor worker productivity. Jason grimaced. Truth be known, Orwell had actually underestimated.

He refocused on the machine in front of him. For the next twenty minutes Jason worked away at the keyboard, pausing only when more data flashed across the screen in answer to his queries. The system was fast, yet it had a difficult time keeping up with the fluid swiftness of Jason's commands. Suddenly his head jerked around as a noise from the hallway filtered into the office. The damn dream again. Probably just Charlie making rounds. He looked at the screen. He wasn't getting much of anything. A waste of time. He wrote down a list of file names on a piece of paper, shut the computer down, rose and went to the door. Pausing, he leaned his ear against the wood. Satisfied, he slid the dead bolts back and opened the door, turning off the lights as he closed the door behind him. A moment later the dead bolts automatically moved back into locked positions.

He moved quickly down the hallway, finally stopping at the far end of the corridor in a little-used section of the office space. This door had an ordinary lock that Jason opened using a special tool. He locked the door behind him. He did not turn on the overhead light. Instead, he produced a flashlight from his coat pocket and turned it on. The computer console was in the far corner of the room next to a low filing cabinet piled three feet high with cardboard packing boxes.

Jason pulled the computer workstation away from the wall, exposing cables that dangled down from the back of the computer. He knelt down and gripped the cables while at the same time inching aside a filing cabinet adjacent to the worktable, revealing an outlet on the wall with several data ports. Jason attached a cable line from the computer into a port, making sure it was tight. Then he sat down in front of the computer and turned it on. As the computer came to life, Jason perched his flashlight on a box top so that the light shone directly on the keyboard. There was no numeric keypad on which to input a security pass code. Nor did Jason have to stare at the upper right-hand corner of the computer screen waiting to be positively identified. In fact, as far as Triton's computer network was concerned, this workstation didn't even exist.

He slipped the piece of paper from his pocket and laid it in the flashlight's beam atop the keyboard. Suddenly he was conscious of movement outside

19

the door. Holding his breath, he buried the flashlight into his armpit with his hand before hitting the off button. He dimmed the monitor until the images on the screen receded into blackness. Minutes went by as Jason sat in the darkness. A drop of sweat formed on his forehead and then lazily made its way down his nose before settling on the top of his lip. He was too afraid to wipe it away.

After five minutes of silence he turned the flashlight and computer monitor back on and resumed his work. He grinned once as a particularly stubborn firewall – an internal security system designed to prevent unauthorized access to computerized databases – collapsed under his persistent nudgings. Working quickly now, he made his way to the end of the files listed on the paper. Then he reached inside his coat and withdrew a three-and-a-half-inch micro floppy disk and placed it in the computer's disk drive. A couple of minutes later, Jason withdrew the disk, turned off the computer and left. He walked quietly back through the maze of security, said good-bye to Charlie and moved out into the night.

THREE

The moonlight drifted through the window, giving shape to certain objects in the darkened interior of the large room. On a long, solid pine bureau a number of framed photos stood in three tiers. In one photo, set in the back row, Sidney Archer, dressed in a dark blue business suit, leaned against a gleaming silver Jaguar sedan. Next to her Jason Archer wore a smile along with his suspenders and dress shirt as he looked lovingly into Sidney's eyes. Another photo showed the same couple, dressed casually, standing in front of the Eiffel Tower, their fingers pointing up, mouths opened in spontaneous laughter.

In the middle row of photos, Sidney, some years older, her face bloated, hair wet and clinging to the sides of her head, reclined in a hospital bed. A tiny bundle, eyes scrunched shut, was clutched in her arms. The picture next to that showed Jason, bleary-eyed and unshaven, wearing only a T-shirt and Looney Tunes boxer shorts, lying on the floor. The little one, the eyes now wide open and the brightest of blues, formed a small and contented hump on her father's chest.

The center photo in the front row had clearly been taken at Halloween. The little bundle was now two years old and dressed as a princess replete with tiara and slippers. Mother and father hovered proudly behind, eyes staring into the camera, their hands cradling the little girl's back and shoulders.

21

Jason and Sidney lay in the four-poster bed. Jason tossed and turned. It had been a week since the last late-night visit to his office. Now the payoff finally was here, making it impossible to sleep. Next to the bedroom door a fully packed, large and particularly ugly canvas bag with blue crisscross stripes and the initials JWA sat next to a black metal case. The clock on the nightstand limped to two A.M. Sidney's long, slender arm reached out from under the covers and glided around Jason's head, slowly pushing his hair around.

Sidney propped herself up on one elbow and continued to play with her husband's hair as she moved closer to him, finally matching his contours with her own. The flimsy nightgown clung to her. "Are you asleep?" she murmured. In the background the muted creaks and groans of the aged house were the only sounds to break the silence.

Jason rolled over to look at his wife. "Not really."

"I could tell – you've been moving around a lot. Sometimes you do it in your sleep. You and Amy."

"I hope I haven't been talking in my sleep. Don't want to give any secrets away." He smiled weakly.

Her hands to dropped to his face, which she gently stroked. "Everyone needs to keep some secrets, I guess, although I thought we agreed not to have any." She gave a little laugh, but it was hollow. Jason's mouth parted for a moment as if he were going to speak, but he quickly closed it, stretched his arms and looked at the clock. He groaned when he saw the time. "Jesus, I might as well get up now. The cab will be here at five-thirty."

Sidney glanced over at the bags by the doorway and frowned. "This trip really came out of the blue, Jason."

Jason didn't look at her. Instead he wiped his eyes and yawned. "I know. I didn't even find out about it

22

until late yesterday afternoon. When the boss says go, I go."

Sidney sighed. "I knew the day would come when we'd both be out of town at the same time."

Jason's voice was anxious as he looked at her. "But you worked it out with the day-care center?"

"I had to arrange for someone to stay past the regular closing, but that's okay. You won't be longer than three days, though, right?"

"Three tops, Sid. I promise." He rubbed vigorously at his scalp. "You couldn't get out of the New York trip?"

Sidney shook her head. "Lawyers don't get excused from business trips. It's not in the Tyler, Stone manual of being a productive attorney."

"Christ, you do more in three days than most of them do in five."

"Well, sweetie, I don't have to tell you, but in our shop, it's what did you do for me today, and, more important, what are you going to do for me tomorrow, and the day after that."

Jason pulled himself up to a sitting position. "Same at Triton; however, being in the advanced technology business, their expectations go into the next millennium. One day our ship will come in, Sid. Maybe today." He looked at her.

She shook her head. "Right. So while you're waiting down at the docks for our yacht, I'll keep depositing our paychecks and paying down debt. Deal?"

"Okay. But sometimes you have to be optimistic. Look into the future."

"Speaking of the future, have you given any more thought to working on another baby?"

"I'm more than ready. If the next one's like Amy, it'll be a breeze."

Sidney pressed her full thighs against him, quietly

23

pleased that he voiced no objection to enlarging the family. If he was seeing someone else . . . ? "Speak for yourself, Mr Male Half of this little equation." She pushed him.

"Sorry, Sid. Typical brain-dead man thing to say. It won't happen again, promise."

Sidney lay back on the pillow and stared at the ceiling as she gently rubbed his shoulder. Three years ago the thought of leaving the practice of law would have been out of the question. Now, even part-time seemed too intrusive on her life with Amy and Jason. She longed for total freedom to be with her child. Freedom they could not yet afford solely on Jason's salary, even with all the cutbacks they had made, constantly fighting the American-consumer compulsion to spend as much as they earned. But if Jason kept moving up at Triton, who knew?

Sidney had never wanted to be financially dependent on anyone else. She looked at Jason. If she was going to tie her economic survival to one person, who better than a man she had loved almost from the moment she had laid her eyes on him? As she continued to watch him, a glimmer of moisture appeared in her eyes. She sat up, leaning into him.

"Well, at least while you're in Los Angeles you can look up some of your old friends – just skip the old flames, please." She tousled his hair. "Besides, you could never leave me. My father would stalk you." Her eyes slowly drifted over his shirtless torso: abdominal muscles stacked on top of one another, cords of muscle rippling just beneath the skin of his shoulders. Sidney was once again reminded of how lucky she had been to collide with Jason Archer's life. And she also knew beyond doubt that her husband believed he was the lucky one for finding her. He didn't answer, just stared

24

off. "You know you've really been burning the midnight oil the last few months, Jason. At the office at all hours, leaving me notes in the middle of the night. I miss you." She nudged him with her hip. "You remember how much fun it is to snuggle at night, don't you?"

In response he kissed her on the cheek.

"Besides, Triton has a lot of employees. You don't have to do it all yourself," she added.

He looked at her and there was a painful weariness in his eyes. "You'd think so, wouldn't you?"

Sidney sighed. "After the CyberCom acquisition closes, you'll probably be busier than ever. Maybe I should sabotage the deal. I am lead counsel for Triton, after all." She smiled.

He chuckled halfheartedly, his mind clearly elsewhere.

"The meeting in New York should be interesting, anyway."

He abruptly focused on her. "Why's that?"

"Because we're meeting on the CyberCom deal. Nathan Gamble and your buddy Quentin Rowe will both be there."

The blood slowly drained from her husband's face. He stammered, "I – I thought the meeting was for the BelTek proposal."

"No, I was taken off that a month ago so I could focus on Triton's acquisition of CyberCom. I thought I told you."

"Why are you meeting them in New York?"

"Nathan Gamble is there this week. He has that penthouse overlooking the park. Billionaires get their way. So off I go to New York."

Jason sat up, his face so gray she thought he was going to be sick.

"Jason, what is it?" She gripped his shoulder.

He finally recovered and faced her, his expression

an acutely disturbing one to her – dominated as it was by guilt.

"Sid, I'm not exactly going to L.A. on business for Triton."

She took her hand off his shoulder and stared at him, her eyes wide with astonishment. Every suspicion she had dutifully battled during the last several months now shot back to the surface. Her throat went completely dry. "What do you mean, Jason?"

"I mean" – he took a deep breath and gripped one of her hands – "I mean, this trip is not for Triton."

"Then who exactly is it for?" she demanded, her face flushed.

"For me, us! It's for us, Sidney."

Scowling, she sat back against the headboard and crossed her arms. "Jason, you're going to tell me what's going on and you're going to do it right now."

He looked down and played with the bedcovers. She took his chin in her hand and gave him a searching look. "Jason?" She paused, sensing his inner struggle. "Pretend it's Christmas Eve, honey."

He sighed. "I'm going to L.A. to interview with another firm."

She took her hand away. "What?"

He spoke quickly. "AllegraPort Technology, they're one of the largest speciality software manufacturers in the world. They've offered me, well, they've offered me a vice presidency and would be grooming me for the top spot eventually. Triple my salary, huge year-end bonus, stock options, beautiful retirement plan, the whole ball game, Sid. A home run."

Sidney's face instantly brightened; her shoulders slumped in relief. "That was your big secret? Jason, that's wonderful. Why didn't you tell me?"

"I didn't want to put you in an awkward position.

26

You're Triton's counsel, after all. All the late hours at the office? I was trying to finish up my work. I didn't want to leave them in the lurch. Triton's a powerful company; I didn't want any hard feelings."

"Honey, there's no law against your joining another company. They'd be happy for you."

"Right!" His bitter tone puzzled her for a moment, but he hurried on before she had a chance to question him about it. "They'd also pay for all our relocation expenses. In fact, we'd make a nice profit on this place, enough to pay off all our bills."

She stiffened. "Relocation?"

"Allegra's headquarters are in Los Angeles. That's where we'd be moving. If you don't want me to take it, then I'll respect your decision."

"Jason, you know my firm has an L.A. office. It'll be perfect." She sat back against the headboard again and stared at the ceiling. She looked over at him, a twinkle in her eye. "And let's see, at triple your current salary, the profit from this house and stock options to boot, I just might be able to become a full-time mom a little sooner than I thought."

He smiled as she gave him a congratulatory hug. "That's why I was so surprised when you told me you were meeting with Triton."

She looked at him, confused.

"They think I took some time off to work around the house."

"Oh. Well, sweetie, don't worry. I'll play along. You know there's attorney-client privilege and then there's the much stronger privilege between a horny wife and her big, beautiful husband." Her soft eyes met his and she nuzzled her lips against his cheek. He swung his legs over the side of the bed. "Thanks, babe, I'm glad I told you." He shrugged. "Well, I might as well jump in the shower. Maybe I can accomplish a few things before I leave."

Before he could stand up, her arms clamped around his waist.

"I'd love to help you accomplish something, Jason."

He turned his head to look at her. She was wearing nothing; the nightgown lay over the footboard. Her large breasts pushed into his lower back. He smiled and slid one hand down her smooth back and gripped her soft bottom appreciatively.

"I've always said, you've got the world's greatest ass, Sid."

She grunted. "If you like a little additional padding, but I'm working on it."

His strong hands slid under her armpits, hoisting her up so they were face-to-face. His eyes looked deeply into hers and his mouth formed a solemn line before he spoke. "You're more beautiful now than the day I met you, Sidney Archer, and every day I love you more and more." The words came out slowly and gently, and made her tremble just as always. It wasn't the words he used that had that effect on her. You could find them in any Hallmark aisle. It was how he said them. The utter conviction in his voice, his eyes, the pressure of his touch against her skin.

Jason looked at the clock again and grinned mischievously. "I've gotta leave in three hours to make my plane."

She crooked her arm around his neck, pulled him down on top of her. "Well, three hours can be a lifetime."

Two hours later, his hair still wet from the shower, Jason Archer walked down the hallway of his home and opened the door to a small room. Set up as a home office with computer, filing cabinets, wood desk and two small bookcases, the space was cramped but tidy. One small window looked out on to the darkness.

Jason closed the door to his office, took a key from his desk drawer and unlocked the top drawer of the filing cabinet. He stopped and listened for any sound. This had become habitual even in the confines of his own house. That revelation was suddenly profoundly disturbing to him. His wife had gone back to sleep. Amy was sleeping soundly two doors down. He reached in the drawer and carefully pulled out a large old-fashioned leather briefcase with double straps, brass buckles and a worn, glossy finish. Jason opened the briefcase and pulled out a blank floppy disk. The instructions he had been given were precise. Put everything he had on one floppy disk, make one hard copy of the documents and then destroy everything else.

He put the floppy disk in the drive slot and copied all the other materials he had collected on to that same floppy. That completed, his finger hovered over the delete key as he prepared to follow his instructions on destruction of all pertinent files on his hard drive.

His finger wavered, however, and, finally, he chose to follow his instincts instead.

It took him only a few minutes to make a duplicate copy of the floppy, after which he deleted the files on his hard drive. After perusing the contents of the duplicate floppy on his screen for several moments, he took a few minutes to perform some additional functions on his computer. As he watched, the text on the screen turned to gibberish. He saved the changes, exited out of the file, slipped the duplicate disk out of the computer and inserted it in a small padded envelope, which he secreted far down in a side pouch of the leather briefcase. As instructed, he then printed out a hard copy of the contents of the original floppy and put the printed pages and the original floppy disk in the briefcase's main compartment.

Next, he took out his wallet and withdrew the plastic card he had used to enter his office earlier. He would no longer be needing it. He flipped the card into his desk drawer and shut it.

He studied the briefcase, his thoughts hovering far away from the little room. He didn't enjoy lying to his wife. He had never done that before and the feeling of prevarication was particularly repugnant to him. But it was almost over. He shuddered when he thought of all the risks he had taken. His body shook again when he dwelled on the fact that his wife knew absolutely nothing about it. He silently went over the plan again. The route he would take, the evasive steps he would employ, the code names of the people who would be meeting him. In spite of it all his mind continued to wander. He looked out the window, seeming to stare across the horizon as, behind the glasses he wore, his eyes seemed to grow larger and larger as the possibilities were swiftly sorted through. After today he could actually say for the first time that the risk had been worth it. All he had to do was survive today.

FOUR

The darkness that enveloped Dulles International Airport would soon be dispelled by the fast-approaching dawn. As the new day began stretching itself awake, a cab pulled up in front of the airport's terminal. The rear door of the cab opened and Jason Archer stepped out. He carried the leather briefcase in one hand and the black metal case, housing his laptop computer, in the other. He put a dark green wide-brimmed hat with a leather band on his head.

Jason smiled as the memory of making love to his wife commanded his thoughts. They had both showered, but the scent of recent sex lingered, and, had there been time, Jason Archer would have made love to his wife a second time.

He put down the computer case for a moment, stretched his arm back inside the cab and pulled out the oversized canvas bag, which he slung over his shoulder.

At the Western Airlines ticket counter Jason exhibited his driver's license, got his seat assignment and boarding pass and checked the canvas bag. He took a moment to smooth down the collar on his camel-hair overcoat, push his hat farther down on his head and adjust his tie, which bore soft swirls of gold, hazel and lavender. His pants were dark gray and baggy. Not that anyone would have noticed, but the socks were white athletic ones and the dark shoes were, in fact, tennis shoes. A few minutes later,

31

Jason purchased a *USA Today* and a cup of coffee along the terminal's vendors' row. He then passed through the security gates.

The shuttle to the midfield terminal was three-quarters full. Jason stood among men and women dressed much as he was: dark suits, touches of color at the neck, rolling racks stacked with bags clenched in many a weary hand.

Jason's hand never left the leather briefcase; his legs straddled the computer case. He occasionally looked round the interior of the shuttle examining its sleepy occupants. Then his eyes would eventually wander back to his newspaper as the shuttle swayed and bumped over to the midfield terminal.

Sitting in the large, open waiting area in front of Gate 11, Jason checked the time. Boarding would begin soon. He glanced outside the broad window, where a row of Western Airline jets sporting the familiar brown and yellow stripes were being readied for early morning flights. Slashes of pink streaked the sky as the sun slowly rose to illuminate the East Coast. Outside, the wind pushed fiercely against the thick glass; airline workers hunched forward against the invisible thrusts of nature. The full measure of winter would be settling in soon and the winds and icy precipitation would blanket the area until the following April.

Jason pulled out the boarding pass from his inner coat pocket and studied its contents: Western Airlines Flight 3223 from Washington's Dulles International Airport to Los Angeles International Airport with direct, nonstop service. Jason had been born and raised in the Los Angeles area but hadn't been back there in over two years. Across the aisle of the massive terminal a Western Airlines flight destined for Seattle, after a brief layover in Chicago, would also be boarding shortly. Jason licked his lips, a trickle of apprehension playing through his nervous system. He swallowed a couple of times to work through the dryness in his throat. As he finished his coffee, he thumbed through the newspaper, halfheartedly observing the collective aches and miseries of the world that poured forth from every colorful page.

As he glanced over the headlines, Jason noted a man striding resolutely down the middle of the concourse. He was a six-footer with a lean build and blond hair. He was dressed in a camel-hair overcoat and baggy gray pants. A tie identical to Jason's peeped out at his neck. Like Jason, he carried a leather briefcase and black laptop computer case. In the hand holding the computer case he also held a white envelope.

Jason quickly rose and walked to the men's room. It had just reopened after having been cleaned.

Entering the last stall, Jason locked the door, hung his overcoat on the door hook, opened the leather briefcase and extracted a large collapsible nylon bag. He pulled out a four-by-eight-inch mirror. He pushed it against the wall of the stall and it held due to its magnetized back. He next pulled out a pair of thick black glasses to replace his wire-rimmed pair, and a paste-on black mustache. A short-haired wig matched the inky darkness of the mustache. The tie and jacket came off, were stuffed in the bag and replaced with a Washington Huskies sweatshirt. The baggy pants came off, revealing matching sweats underneath. Now the tennis shoes did not look so out of place. The overcoat was reversible and, instead of camel, it became dark blue in color. Jason checked his appearance again in the mirror. The leather briefcase and the metal case disappeared into the nylon bag along with the mirror. He left the hat on the hook behind the stall door. Unlocking the door, he stepped out and walked over to the sink.

After washing his hands, Jason studied his new bespectacled face in the mirror. In the reflection the tall blond man he had seen earlier appeared in the doorway, moved over to the stall Jason had just exited and closed the door. Jason took a moment to carefully dry his hands and swipe at his new hair. By that time the man had emerged from the stall, Jason's hat perched on his head. Without his disguise Jason and the man could have passed as twins. Leaving through the exit door, they momentarily collided. Jason quickly mouthed an apology; the man never looked at him. He quickly walked away, Jason's plane ticket disappearing into his shirt pocket, while Jason tucked the white envelope into his coat.

Jason was about to return to his seat when he looked over at the bank of phones. Hesitating for an instant, he hurried over and dialed a number.

"Sid?"

"Jason?" Sidney was simultaneously dressing and feeding a struggling Amy Archer and stuffing files into her briefcase. "What's wrong? Is your flight delayed?"

"No, no, it leaves in a few minutes." He fell silent as he caught his altered reflection in the shiny face of the telephone. He felt embarrassed to be talking to his wife while disguised.

Sidney struggled with Amy's coat. "Well, is anything wrong?"

"No, I just thought I'd call, to check on things."

Sidney let out an exasperated grunt. "Well, let me give you the rundown: I'm late, *your* daughter is being uncooperative as usual, and I just realized I left my plane ticket and some documents I need at work, which means instead of having thirty minutes to spare I've got maybe ten seconds."

"I'm . . . I'm sorry, Sid. I . . ." Jason's hand tightly

34

gripped the nylon bag. Today was the last day. The last day, he kept repeating to himself. If anything were to happen to him – if for some reason, despite the precautions, he didn't make it back – she would never know, would she?

Sidney was seething now. Amy had just spilled her bowl of Cheerios all over her coat and a good part of the milk had made its way into Sidney's crammed briefcase as she struggled to hold the phone under her chin. "I've gotta go, Jason."

"No, Sid, wait, I need to tell you some—"

Sidney stood up. Her tone allowed for no compromise as she surveyed the damage wrought by her two-year-old, who now stared defiantly up at her mother with a chin sharply reminiscent of her own. "Jason, it's going to have to wait. I've got a plane to catch too. Goodbye." She hung up the phone and snatched up her writhing daughter under one arm. Cheerios and all, they headed out the door.

Jason slowly put down the phone and turned away. He let out a deep breath and for the hundredth time prayed today would end the way it had been planned to. He did not observe a man glance casually in his direction and then turn away. Earlier, the same man had passed by him before Jason had made the change in the rest room, close enough in fact to read the identification tag on his travel bag. It was one small but significant oversight on Jason's part, because the tag set forth his real name and address.

A few minutes later Jason stood in line to board his flight. He pulled out the white envelope he had been given by the man in the rest room and took out the plane ticket that was in it. He wondered what Seattle would be like. He glanced across the aisle in time to see his "twin" get on the flight to Los Angeles. Then Jason caught a glimpse of another passenger in line for the flight to Los Angeles. Tall and lean, the man had a bald pate that topped a square face partially covered by a massive beard. The expressive features looked familiar, but Jason couldn't quite place their owner, as the man disappeared through the doorway on his way to the waiting plane. Jason shrugged, dutifully handed over his boarding pass and walked down the jetwalk.

Barely half an hour later, as the jet Arthur Lieberman was on slammed into the ground and coils of black smoke soared toward white clouds, hundreds of miles to the north Jason Archer sipped a fresh cup of coffee and opened his laptop computer. Smiling, he looked out the plane's window as it rocketed on to Chicago. The first leg of his trip had gone off without a hitch, and the captain had just announced smooth sailing for the duration of the flight.

FIVE

Sidney Archer tapped the horn impatiently and the car in front of her sped through the green light. With a reflex motion she checked the backseat in her Ford Explorer's rearview mirror. Amy, her Winnie the Pooh bear clutched tightly in one tiny hand, was fast asleep in her baby seat. Amy shared her mother's thick blond hair, strong chin and slender nose. Her dancing blue eyes and much of her athletic grace came from her father, although Sidney Archer had in college been a wick-thin power forward on the women's basketball team.

She turned into the blacktop parking lot and pulled into a parking space in front of the low brick building. She got out, opened the rear door of the Ford and gently disengaged her daughter from the confines of the baby seat, taking care to bring Pooh and Amy's day bag. Sidney pulled up the hood of Amy's jacket and shielded her daughter's face from the biting wind with her overcoat. A sign over the double glass doors said JEFFERSON COUNTY DAY-CARE CENTER.

Inside, Sidney removed Amy's coat, taking a moment to wipe off the remains of the earlier cereal incident, and checked the provisions in her carry bag before handing it over to Karen, one of the day-care people. The front of Karen's white jumpsuit was already smeared with red crayon, and a large spot of what looked to be grape jelly was visible on her right sleeve.

"Hi, Amy. We've got some new toys you probably want to check out." Karen knelt down in front of her. Amy still gripped her bear, her right thumb firmly in her little mouth.

Sidney held up Amy's bag. "Beans and franks, and some juice and a banana. She's already had breakfast. Potato chips, and a brownie if she's really good. Let her sleep a little longer at nap time, Karen, she had a rough night."

Karen put out a finger for Amy to take. "Okay, Mrs. Archer. Amy's always good, aren't you?"

Sidney knelt down and pressed a small kiss on her daughter's cheek. "You've got that right. Except when she doesn't want to eat, sleep or do what she's told."

Karen was the mother of a little boy the same age as Amy. The two moms shared a knowing smile.

"I'll be here by seven-thirty tonight, Karen."

"Yes, ma'am."

"Bye-bye, Mommy. I love chu."

Sidney turned to see Amy waving at her. The little fingers floated up and down. The sharp chin had dissolved into a cute little bump and, with it, Sidney's anger from the morning's battle. Sidney returned the wave.

"I love you too. We'll get some ice cream tonight, sweetie, after dinner. And I'm sure Daddy will be calling to talk to you, okay?" A wonderful smile broke across Amy's features.

Thirty minutes later Sidney pulled into her office parking garage, grabbed her briefcase from the passenger seat and slammed the truck door as she raced to the elevator. The chilly wind funneling down the underground garage entrance brightened her thoughts. Soon the old stone fireplace in their living room would be in use. She had come to love the smell of a fire; it was comforting and made her feel safe. The coming of winter had turned her thoughts to Christmas. This would be the first December in which Amy could actually appreciate its very special time. Sidney felt herself growing more and more excited about the approaching holidays. They were going to her parents' place for Thanksgiving, but this year Jason, Sidney and Amy were staying home for Christmas. Just the three of them. In front of the popping fire flanked by a fat-bottomed white pine Christmas tree and a mountain of presents for their little girl.

Although technically only a part-timer, she was still one of the hardest working attorneys at the firm. The senior partners at Tyler, Stone smiled every time they passed Sidney Archer's office as they saw their respective pieces of the partnership pie grow even larger through her efforts. Though they probably believed they were using her, Sidney had her own agenda. The part-time scenario was only an interim measure. Sidney could always practice law; however, she only had one opportunity to be Amy's mother while Amy was still a little girl.

The old stone and brick house had been purchased at roughly half price because of all the renovation work needed. Work that Sidney and Jason and a group of subcontractors had completed at fiercely negotiated prices over the last two years. The jag had been traded in for the cranky six-year-old Ford. The last of the massive student loans were almost gone, and their monthly living expenses had been reduced by almost fifty percent through common sense and sacrifice. In another year the Archers would be almost completely debt-free.

Her thoughts went back to the early morning hours. Jason's news had been truly stunning. But she felt the tuggings of a smile as she considered the ramifications. She was proud of Jason. He deserved this kind of success, more than anyone. It was shaping up to be quite a good year. All those late nights. He had probably been putting together the details of his job. All those hours of needless worry on her part. She now felt bad about hanging up on him earlier. She would make it up to him when he got back.

Sidney stepped off the elevator, hurried down the richly appointed hallway and opened the door to her office. She checked her e-mail and voice mail; neither revealed any emergencies. She loaded her briefcase with the documents she would need for her trip, grabbed the airplane tickets from her chair where her secretary had left them and slid her laptop into a carry case. She left a stream of voice-mail instructions for her secretary and four other lawyers at the firm assisting her on various matters. Sufficiently weighed down, she managed to stagger back out to the elevator.

Sidney checked in at the USAir shuttle desk at National Airport and a few minutes later was settling into her seat on the Boeing 737. She was confident the plane would take off right on time for the barely fifty-minute trip to New York's La Guardia Airport. Unfortunately, it took almost as long to drive into the city from the airport as it did to traverse the two hundred and thirty or so miles from the nation's capital to the capital of the financial world.

The flight, as usual, was full. As she assumed her seat, she noted that sitting next to her was an elderly man dressed in an old-fashioned three-piece pin-stripe suit. A wide-knotted bright red tie shone out from the background of a crisp button-down shirt. In his lap sat a battered leather briefcase. Slender hands nervously clasped and unclasped as he looked out the window. Small tufts of white hair clung around his earlobes. The shirt collar hung loosely around the skinny neck like walls pulling loose from their foundation. Sidney noticed beads of perspiration adhering to his left temple and over his thin lips.

The plane lumbered clumsily to the main runway. The whir of wing flaps settling into the down takeoff position seemed to calm the old man. He turned to Sidney.

"That's all I listen for anymore," he said, his voice deep and rocky and laced with the front-porch drawl of a lifetime spent in the South.

Sidney looked at him curiously. "What's that?"

He pointed out the small window. "Make sure they set the damn flaps on the wings so this thing'll get off the ground. Remember that plane up in Dee-troit?" He said the word as if it were actually two. "Damn pilots forgot to set the flaps right and killed everybody on board except for that little girl."

Sidney looked out the window for a moment. "I'm sure the pilots are well aware of that," she replied. She sighed inwardly. The last thing she needed was to be sitting next to a nervous flier. Sidney turned back to her notes, doing a quick scan for her presentation before the flight attendants made everyone stow their belongings under the seats. As the flight attendants came by for another check, she slipped the papers back in her briefcase and slid it under the seat in front of her. She looked out the window at the dark, choppy waters of the Potomac. Flocks of seagulls scattered across the water; from a distance they resembled swirling pieces of paper. The captain crisply announced over the intercom that the USAir shuttle was next in line to take off.

A few seconds later the plane rose smoothly off the ground. After banking left to avoid flying over the restricted airspace above the Capitol and the White House, the plane raced to its cruising altitude.

41

Several minutes after the plane leveled off at twenty-nine thousand feet, the beverage cart rolled by and Sidney got a cup of tea and the obligatory bag of salty peanuts. The elderly man next to her shook his head when asked for his beverage request and continued to stare anxiously out the window.

Sidney reached down and pulled her briefcase from underneath the seat in anticipation of doing some work for the next half hour. She settled back in her seat and took some papers out of her briefcase. As she began to go over their contents she noticed the old man still glancing out the window; his small frame was tense as he rode every bump, obviously listening for any out-of-the-way sound that would herald a catastrophe. The veins were tight in his neck; his hands were wrapped around the armrests of his seat. The common plight of the not-so-rare white-knuckler. Her face softened. Being frightened was difficult enough. Believing you are alone in that fear merely compounded matters. She reached out and patted his arm gently and smiled. He glanced quickly over at her and returned the smile in an embarrassed fashion, his face slightly reddening.

"They do this flight so many times, I'm sure they've worked out all the kinks," she said, her voice quiet and soothing.

He smiled again and rubbed his hands to return the circulation.

"You're absolutely right . . . ma'am."

"Sidney, Sidney Archer."

"George Beard is what they call me. Glad to know you, Sidney." They firmly shook hands.

Beard abruptly looked out the window at the puffy clouds. The sunlight was sharp and penetrating. He slid the window shade down partway. "I've flown so many damn times over the years, you'd think I'd get used to it."

"It can be nerve-racking for anyone, George, no matter how often you've done it," Sidney replied kindly. "But it's not nearly as frightening as the cabs we're going to have to take into the city."

They both laughed. Then Beard jumped slightly as the plane hit a particularly stubborn air pocket and his face once again became ashen. "Do you go to New York often, George?" She tried to hold his eyes with hers. No mode of transportation had ever bothered her in the past. But ever since she'd had Amy, little cells of apprehension appeared when she boarded a plane or train, or even got in her car. She studied Beard's face as the old man tensed again while the plane bumped along. "George, it's all right. Just a little turbulence."

He took a deep breath and finally eyed her squarely. "I'm on a couple of boards of companies headquartered in New York. Have to go up twice a year."

Sidney glanced back at her documents, suddenly remembering something. She frowned. There was a mistake on the fourth page. That would need to be corrected when she got into town.

George Beard touched her arm. "I guess we're all right today at least. I mean, how often to they have two crashes in one day? Tell me that."

Preoccupied, Sidney did not answer right away. Finally she turned to him, her eyes narrowing. "Pardon?"

Beard leaned forward in a confidential manner, his voice low. "Took one of them puddle-jumpers up from Richmond early this morning. I got to National about eight o'clock. I overheard two pilots talking. Couldn't hardly believe it. They were nervous, I can tell you that. Hell, I would be too."

Sidney's face evidenced her confusion. "What are you talking about?"

43

Beard bent even closer to her. "I don't know if this is public knowledge, but my hearing aid works a lot better now with the new batteries, so those fellows might have thought I couldn't hear." He paused dramatically, his eyes glancing sharply around before settling once again on Sidney. "There was a plane crash early this morning. No survivors." He looked at her, his white, bushy eyebrows twitching like a cat's tail.

For an instant, Sidney's major organs collectively seemed to cease all functioning. "Where?"

Beard shook his head. "I didn't hear that part. It was a jet, though, a pretty big one, I gathered. Fell right out of the sky, apparently. I guess that's why those fellows were so nervous. I mean, not knowing why is just as bad, right?"

"Do you know what airline?"

He shook his head again. "Guess we'll know soon enough. It'll be on the TV when we get to New York, I would bet. I already called my wife from the airport, told her I was okay. Hell, of course she hadn't even heard about it yet, but I didn't want her to start worrying if she saw it on the TV or something."

Sidney looked at his bright red tie. It suddenly took on the image of a large, fresh wound gaping at his throat. The odds – it couldn't be possible. She shook her head and then stared straight ahead. Looking back at her was a quick resolution to her worry. She inserted her credit card in the slot in the seat in front of her, grabbed the plane phone from its niche and a moment later she was dialing Jason's SkyWord pager. She didn't have his new cell phone number; in any event, he normally turned his phone off during flights. He had been reprimanded twice by airline personnel for receiving cell calls during flights. She hoped to God he had remembered to

44

bring the pager. She checked her watch. He would be above the Midwest right about now, but bouncing its signals off a satellite, the pager was easily capable of receiving pages on planes. However, he couldn't call her back on the plane phone; the 737 she was on was not equipped with that technology yet. So she left her office number at the prompt. She would wait ten minutes and call in to her secretary.

Ten minutes passed and she called her office. Her secretary picked up on the second ring. No, her husband hadn't called. At Sidney's urging, her secretary checked Sidney's voice mail. Nothing there either. Her secretary had heard of no plane accident. Sidney began to wonder if George Beard had misunderstood the pilots' conversation. He probably sat around imagining every possible catastrophe, but she had to be sure. She frantically searched her memory for the airline her husband was on. She called information and got the number for United Airlines. She finally got through to a human being and was told that the airline did have an early morning flight to L.A. from Dulles but there had been no reports of any airline crash. The woman seemed reluctant to discuss the subject over the telephone and Sidney hung up with fresh doubts. Next she called American and, after that, Western Airlines. She could not get through to an actual person at either airline. The lines seemed to be jammed with calls. She tried again, with the same result. A numbness slowly coursed through her body. George Beard touched her arm again. "Sidney . . . ma'am, is everything okay?" Sidney didn't answer. She continued to stare ahead, oblivious to everything except the certainty that she would race off the plane as soon as it landed.

SIX

Jason Archer looked at the SkyWord pager and the number etched across its tiny screen. He rubbed at his chin and then took off his glasses and wiped them on his lunch napkin. This was his wife's direct office number. Like his wife's plane the DC-10 he was flying on also had cellular phones recessed into the backs of every other seat. He started to reach for the phone and then stopped. He knew Sidney was in her firm's New York office today, which was why the leaving of her D.C. office number puzzled him. For a terrifying instant, he thought something might be wrong with Amy. He checked his SkyWord pager again. The call had come in at nine-thirty A.M. EST. He shook his head. His wife would have been on a plane halfway to New York at that time. It wouldn't have had anything to do with Amy. Their daughter would have been at day care before eight. Was she calling to apologize for hanging up on him earlier? That, he concluded, was far from likely. That exchange didn't even qualify for minor spat status. It didn't make sense. Why on earth would she be calling him from a plane and leaving the number of an office at which he knew she would not be?

His face suddenly went pale. Unless it was not his wife who had called. Given the bizarre circumstances, Jason concluded that it was probably not his wife who had placed that call. He instinctively scanned the cabin. The in-flight movie droned on from the pull-down screen.

46

He sat back in his seat and stirred the remains of his coffee with a plastic spoon. The flight attendants were clearing away meal plates and offering pillows and blankets. Jason's hand curled protectively around the handle of the leather briefcase. He glanced at the case containing his laptop where it was stowed under the seat in front of him. Maybe her trip had been canceled; however, Gamble was already in New York and nobody canceled on Nathan Gamble, Jason knew that. Besides, the CyberCom deal was at a critical stage.

He leaned back farther in his seat, his hand fingering the SkyWord pager like a ball of putty. If he placed the call to his wife's office, what then? Would he be relayed to New York? Should he call home to check messages? Any communication option at this juncture required him to use a cellular phone. He was carrying a new, sophisticated model in his briefcase, one with latest security and scrambler capabilities; however, he was prohibited by airline regulations from using it. He would have to use the one supplied by the airline, in which case he would also have to use a credit or phone card. And it was not a secure line. That would allow opportunities, however remote, for his location to be ascertained. At the bare minimum, there would be a discernible trail. He was supposed to be heading to L.A.; instead he was thirty-one thousand feet above Denver, Colorado, on his way to the Pacific Northwest. This unexpected bump was acutely disturbing after all the careful planning. He hoped it was not a precursor of things to come.

Jason looked at the pager again. The SkyWord pager had a headline news service and late-breaking stories came across its screen several times a day. The political and financial data treading across the pager screen did not interest him at the moment. He turned the matter of the supposed page from his wife over in his mind for a few minutes more and then he deleted the page message and put the audio earphones back on. However, his mind was far away from the images drifting across the movie screen.

Sidney darted through the crowded terminal at La Guardia, her two bags clunking against her nylon-stockinged legs. She did not see the young man until he almost collided with her.

"Sidney Archer?" He was in his twenties and dressed in a black suit and tie, a chauffeur's hat perched on top of brown curly hair. She stopped and looked dully at him, fear thudding through her body as she waited for him to deliver his terrible message. Then she noticed the placard in his hand with her name on it and her entire body deflated in relief. Her firm had sent a car to take her to the Manhattan office. She had forgotten. She nodded slowly, her blood beginning to circulate again.

The young man took one of her bags and led her towards the exit. "I got a description of you from your office. Like to do that in case people don't see the sign. Everybody moves fast around here, preoccupied, y'know. You need a good backup system. Car's right outside. You might want to button your coat up, though, it's freezing out there."

As they passed the check-in counter, Sidney hesitated. Long lines streamed out from the busy airline counters as overwrought travelers tried valiantly to keep one step ahead of the demands of a world that seemed more and more to exceed human capacities. She quickly scanned the terminal for anyone who looked like an idle airline employee. All she saw were the skycaps calmly trucking luggage around amid the hysteria of panicked travelers. It was chaotic, but it was the *normal* chaos. That was good, wasn't it?

The driver looked at her. "Everything okay, Mrs Archer? You not feeling well?" She had grown even paler in the last few seconds. "I've got some Tylenol in the limo. Perk you right up. Those planes make me sick too. All that recirculated air. I tell you what, though, you get some fresh air, you'll be A-OK. That is if you can call the air in New York City fresh." He smiled.

His smile suddenly vanished as Sidney abruptly bolted away.

"Ms, Archer?" He sped after her.

Sidney caught up with the uniformed woman whose identifying badges and insignias stamped her as an employee of American Airlines. Sidney took a few seconds to get her question out. The young woman's eyes grew large.

"I haven't heard anything like that." The woman spoke in a low voice so as not to alarm passersby. "Where did you hear that?" When Sidney answered, the woman smiled. By that time, the driver had joined them. "I just got out of a briefing, ma'am. If something like that happened to one of our aircraft, we would've heard. Trust me."

"But if it had just happened? I mean—" Sidney's voice was rising.

"Ma'am, it's all right, okay? Really. There's nothing to be concerned about. It's by far the safest way to travel." The woman took one of Sidney's hands in a firm grip, looked at the driver with a reassuring smile and then turned and walked away.

Sidney stood there a few moments longer, staring after the woman. Then she took a deep breath, looked around and shook her head in dismay. She started to walk toward the exits again and looked across at the driver as if noticing him for the first time. "What's your name?"

"Tom, Tom Richards. People call me Tommy."

49

"Tommy, have you been at the airport long this morning?"

"Oh, 'bout a half hour. Like to get here early. Transportation headaches are not what businessmen – um, people need, y'know."

They reached the exit doors and the stiff, punishing wind hit Sidney flush in the face. She staggered for a moment and Tommy grabbed one of her arms to steady her.

"Ma'am, you don't look so good. You want I should drive you to a doctor or something?"

Sidney regained her balance. "I'm fine. Let's just get to the car."

He shrugged and she followed him to a gleaming black Lincoln Town Car. He held the door for her.

She lay back against the seat cushions and took several deep breaths. Tommy climbed in the driver's seat and started the engine. He looked in the rearview mirror. "Look, I don't mean to beat a dead horse, but you sure you're okay?"

She nodded and managed a brief smile. "I'm fine, thank you." She took another deep breath, unbuttoned her coat, smoothed out her dress and crossed her legs. The interior of the car was very warm and after the cold burst she had just encountered she actually wasn't feeling all that well. She looked at the back of the driver's head.

"Tommy, did you hear anything about an airplane crash today? While you were at the airport, or on the news?"

Tommy's eyebrows went up. "Crash? Not me, I ain't heard nothing like that. And I been listening to the twenty-four-hour news radio all morning. Who says a plane crashed? That's crazy. I got friends at most of the airlines. They would've told me." He looked at her warily, as if he were suddenly unsure of her mental state.

50

Sidney didn't answer but lay back against the seat. She took the cellular phone supplied by the car company out of its receptacle and dialed Tyler, Stone's New York office. She silently cursed George Beard. She knew the odds were billions to one that her husband had been in a plane crash, a purported crash that, so far, only an old, terrified man seemed to know about. She shook her head and finally smiled. The whole thing was absurd. Jason was hard at work on his laptop having a snack and a second cup of coffee or, more likely, settling in to watch the in-flight movie. Her husband's pager was probably gathering dust on his nightstand. She would give him hell about it when he got back. Jason would laugh at her when she told him this story. But that was okay. Right now she very much wanted to hear that laugh.

She spoke into the phone. "It's Sidney. Tell Paul and Harold that I'm on my way." She looked out the window at the smooth-flowing traffic. "Thirty-five minutes tops."

She replaced the phone and again stared out the window. The thick clouds were heavy with moisture and even the stout Lincoln was buffeted by powerful winds when they took the bridge over the East River on their way into Manhattan. Tommy again looked at her in the rearview mirror.

"They're calling for snow today. A lot of it. Me, I say they're blowing smoke. I can't remember the last time the weather guys got anything right. But if they do, you might have a problem getting out, ma'am. They shut La Guardia down at the drop of a hat these days."

Sidney continued to look out the tinted windows, where the army of familiar skyscrapers making up the world-famous Manhattan skyline filled the horizon. The solid and imposing buildings reaching

51

to the sky seemed to bolster her spirit. In the foreground of her mind Sidney could see that white pine Christmas tree holding court in one corner of the living room, the warmth of a cozy fire radiating outward, the touch of her husband's arm around her, his head against her shoulder. And, best of all, the shiny, enchanted eyes of their two-year-old. Poor old George Beard. He should retire from those boards. It was clearly all becoming too much for him. She told herself he wouldn't even have gotten close with his preposterous story if her husband hadn't been flying today.

She looked toward the front of the Lincoln and allowed herself to relax a little. "Actually, Tommy, I'm thinking of taking the train back."

SEVEN

In the main conference room of Tyler, Stone's New York office in midtown Manhattan, the video presentation outlining the latest business terms and legal strategies for the CyberCom deal had just ended. Sidney stopped the video and the screen returned to a pleasant blue. She scanned the large room where fifteen heads, mostly white males in their early to mid-forties, stared anxiously at one man sitting at the head of the table. The group had been sequestered in the tension-filled room for hours.

Nathan Gamble, the chairman of Triton Global, was a barrel-chested individual of medium height, in his mid-fifties, with gray-streaked hair brushed straight back and held rigidly in place with a substantial amount of gel. The expensive double-breasted suit was professionally tailored to his stocky form. His face was deeply lined and carried the remnants of an off-season tan. His voice was baritone and commanding; Sidney could easily envision the man bellowing across the conference room tables at quaking underlings. The head of a far-reaching corporate powerhouse, he certainly looked and acted the part.

From under thick gray eyebrows, Gamble's dark brown eyes were glued on her. Sidney returned the stare. "Do you have any questions, Nathan?"

"Just one."

Sidney steadied herself. She could feel it coming.

53

"What is it?" she asked pleasantly.

"Why the hell are we doing this?"

Everyone in the room, except for Sidney Archer, winced as though they had collectively sat on one gigantic needle.

"I'm not sure I understand your question."

"Sure you do, unless you're stupid, and I know you're not." Gamble spoke quietly, his features inscrutable despite the sharpness of his rhetoric.

Sidney bit her tongue hard. "I take it you don't like having to sell yourself in order to buy CyberCom?"

Gamble looked around the table. "I've offered an exorbitant amount of cash for that company. Apparently, not content with making a ten thousand percent return on their investment, now they want to go through my records. Correct?" He looked at Sidney for an answer. She nodded without speaking, and Gamble continued. "I've bought a lot of companies and no one has ever asked for those materials before. Now CyberCom does. Which gets back to my earlier question. Why are we doing this? What the hell's so special about CyberCom?" His eyes made an exacting scope of the table before settling once again on Sidney.

A man seated to the left of Gamble stirred. A laptop computer in front of him had drawn his attention throughout the meeting. Quentin Rowe was the very young president of Triton and subordinate only to Nathan Gamble. While all the other men in the room were entombed in stylish suits, he was dressed in khaki pants, worn deck shoes, a blue denim shirt and a brown vest buttoned up the front. Two diamond studs were lodged in his left earlobe. He looked more suited to appearing on an album cover than stepping into a boardroom.

"Nathan, CyberCom *is* special," Rowe said. "Without them we could well be out of business within two years. CyberCom's technology will completely reinvent and then dominate how information is processed over the Internet. And as far as the high-tech business is concerned, that's like Moses coming down the mountain with the Commandments; there's no substitute." Rowe's tone was a little weary but carried strident undertones. He did not look at Gamble.

Gamble lit up a cigar, casually leaning his expensive lighter up against a small brass sign on the table that read NO SMOKING. "You know, Rowe, that's the problem with this high-tech crap: You're king of the hill in the morning and cow shit by the afternoon. I never should have gotten into the damn business in the first place."

"Well, if money is all you care about, keep in mind that Triton is the world's dominant technology company and generates more than two billion dollars in profits per quarter," Quentin Rowe shot back.

"And cow shit by tomorrow afternoon." Gamble gave Rowe a sidelong glance filled with disgust and puffed away.

Sidney Archer cleared her throat. "Not if you acquire CyberCom, Nathan." Gamble turned to look at her. "You'll be on top for at least the next decade and your profits could well triple within five years."

"Really?" Gamble did not look convinced.

"She's right," Rowe added. "You have to understand that no one, until now, has been able to design software and related communication peripherals that will allow users to take full advantage of the Internet. Everyone's been floundering, trying to figure out how to make it all work. CyberCom has accomplished that. It's why there's been such a furious bidding war for the company. We are now in a position to close that war out. We have to unless we want to be an also-ran."

55

"I don't like them looking at our records. Period. We're a privately held company of which I'm, by far, the largest stockholder. And cash is cash." Gamble stared hard between Sidney and Rowe.

"They're going to be your partners, Nathan," Sidney said. "They're not taking your money and walking like the other acquisitions you've done. They want to know what they're getting into. Triton isn't publicly traded, so they can't go to the SEC and get the information they want. This is reasonable due diligence. They requested the same things from the other bidders."

"You presented my last cash offer?"

Sidney nodded. "We did."

"And?"

"And they were duly impressed and reiterated their request for financial and operational records on the company. If we give it to them, sweeten the purchase price some and load the back-end with better incentives, I think we've got a deal."

Gamble's face reddened and he lurched to his feet. "There's not a company out there that can touch us and this chickenshit CyberCom wants to check up on *me*?"

Rowe sighed deeply. "Nathan, it's merely perfunctory. They're not going to have any problems with Triton, we both know that. Let's just get it done. It's not like the records are unavailable. They're in the best shape they've ever been in," he said, visibly frustrated. "In fact, Jason Archer recently completed that reorganization and did a superb job. A warehouse full of paper with no rhyme or reason to it. I still can't believe that." He looked at Gamble with contempt.

"In case you forgot, I was too busy making money to piss around with a bunch of paper, Rowe. The only paper I happen to care about is the green kind."

Row ignored Gamble's response. "Because of Jason's work the due diligence can be completed very soon." He waved cigar smoke away from his face.

Gamble glared at Rowe. "Really?" Then he scowled at Sidney. "Well, would someone care to tell me why Archer isn't at this meeting, then?"

Sidney paled and for the first time all day she mentally shut down. "Um—"

Rowe stepped in. "Jason took a few days off."

Gamble rubbed his temples. "Well, let's get him on the phone and see where we stand. Maybe we have to give CyberCom some of it, maybe we don't, but what I don't want is us giving them stuff we don't have to. What if the deal doesn't go through? What then?" His fierce eyes swept the table.

Sidney's tone was calm. "Nathan, we'll have a team of attorneys check every document before they are turned over to CyberCom."

"Fine, but is there anybody who knows the records better than her husband?" Gamble looked at Rowe for an answer.

The young man shrugged. "No, not right now."

"Then let's get him on the line."

"Nathan—"

Gamble cut Rowe off. "Jesus Christ, you'd think that the chairman of the company would be able to get a status report from an employee, wouldn't you? And why is he taking time off anyway with the CyberCom deal heating up?" He jerked his head in Sidney's direction. "I can't say that I much like the idea of having husband and wife involved in the same acquisition, but you happen to be the best deal attorney that I know of."

"Thank you."

"Don't thank me, because this deal isn't done yet." Gamble sat down and took a long puff on his cigar. "Let's call your husband. He home?"

Sidney blinked rapidly and sat back down. "Well, actually he's not right now."

Gamble looked at his watch. "Well, when will he be?"

Sidney distractedly rubbed at her brow. "I'm not exactly sure. I mean, I tried him during our last break and he wasn't. In, I mean."

"Well, let's try him again."

Sidney stared at the man. She seemed suddenly all alone in the massive room. Sidney inwardly sighed and handed the TV remote to Paul Brophy, a young New York – based partner. *Dammit, Jason, I hope you really have this new job locked up because it looks like we're really going to need it, honey.*

The door to the conference room opened and a secretary poked her head in. "Ms. Archer, I hate to interrupt, but is there a problem with your plane tickets?"

Sidney looked puzzled. "Not that I know of, Jan, why?"

"Well, someone from the airline is on the phone for you."

Sidney opened her briefcase, pulled out her shuttle tickets and quickly perused them. She looked back at Jan. "It's a shuttle ticket, so it's an open return. Why would the airline be calling me about that?"

"Can we get on with the meeting?" Gamble bellowed.

Jan cleared her throat, looked anxiously at Nathan Gamble and continued speaking to Sidney. "Well, whoever it is wants to talk to you. Maybe they had to cancel the shuttle for the rest of today. It's been snowing for the last three hours."

Sidney picked up another device and hit a button. The automatic blinds covering the wall of windows slowly slid back.

"Christ!" Sidney gasped in dismay. She watched the fat snowflakes pouring down. They were so thick she couldn't see the building across the street.

Paul Brophy looked at her. "The firm still has that condo up on Park, Sid, if you need to stay over." He paused. "Maybe we could grab some dinner." His eyes were quietly hopeful.

Sidney sat down wearily without looking at him. "I can't." She was about to say that Jason was out of town but quickly caught herself. Sidney thought rapidly. Gamble was obviously not going to let this one go. She could call home, confirm what she already knew: that Jason wasn't there. They could all go out to dinner and she could slip away and start calling around L.A., starting with the office of AllegraPort. They could patch Jason through, he could satisfy Gamble's curiosity, and with a little luck she and her husband could escape with little more than a bruised ego and the beginnings of an ulcer. And if the airports were closed, she could take the last Metroliner train home. She swiftly calculated travel times. She would have to call the day care. Karen could take Amy home with her. Worse-case scenario, Amy could do a sleep-over at Karen's. This logistical nightmare only reinforced Sidney's desires for a simpler existence.

"Ms. Archer, do you want to take the call?"

Sidney snapped out of her musings. "I'm sorry, Jan, just put it through in here. And Jan, see if you can get me on the last Metroliner, just in case La Guardia's closed."

"Yes, ma'am." Jan closed the door. In another moment a red light blinked on the telephone perched on the credenza. Sidney picked it up.

Paul Brophy ejected the video and the TV came back on, voices from the screen filling the room. He quickly hit the mute button on the remote and the room was once again silent.

Sidney cradled the phone against her ear.

"This is Sidney Archer. Can I help you?"

The woman's voice on the other end was a little hesitant, but oddly soothing. "My name is Linda Freeman. I'm with Western Airlines, Ms. Archer. Your office in Washington gave me this number."

"Western? There must be a mistake. I'm ticketed on USAir. On the New York to D.C. shuttle." Sidney shook her head. A stupid mistake. She had enough on her plate right now.

"Ms. Archer, I need you to confirm that you're the spouse of Jason W. Archer, residing at 611 Morgan Lane, Jefferson County, Virginia."

Sidney's tone betrayed her confusion; however, her answer was automatic. "Yes." As soon as the word passed her lips, Sidney's entire body froze.

"Oh, my God!" Paul Brophy's voice cut through the room.

Sidney whirled around to look at him. All eyes were staring at the TV. Sidney turned slowly toward it. She didn't notice the words "Special News Report" flashing across the top of the screen, or the hearing-impaired close-captioned subtitles flowing across the bottom while the news correspondent recounted the tragic story. Her eyes were riveted on the mass of smoky, blackened wreckage that had once been a proud member of the Western Airlines fleet. George Beard's face appeared in her mind. His low, confidential tones assailed her. *There was a plane crash.*

The voice on the phone beckoned her. "Ms. Archer, I'm afraid there's been an accident involving one of our aircraft."

Sidney Archer heard no more. Her hand slowly descended to her side. Her fingers involuntarily opened and the phone receiver fell to the thickly carpeted floor.

Outside, the snow continued to pour down so forcefully it resembled one of the city's famous ticker-tape parades. The cold winds hurled themselves against the broad array of windows, and Sidney Archer continued to stare in complete disbelief at the crater containing the remains of Flight 3223.

EIGHT

One man, dark-haired, with a cleft chin below chubby cheeks, dressed in a fashionable two-piece and clearly introducing himself as William, met Jason Archer at the airport gate in Seattle. The two exchanged a couple of sentences, each composed of seemingly arbitrary words. The coded greeting successfully exchanged, they walked off together. As William went through the exit doors to signal for their ride, Jason took the opportunity to unobtrusively deposit a padded envelope into a U.S. mailbox located to the right of the exit door. Inside the envelope was the copy of the computer diskette he had made before leaving home.

Jason was quickly escorted to a limousine that had pulled up to the curb on William's signal. Inside the limo William presented identification to Jason that revealed his name actually to be Anthony DePazza. A few words of innocuous conversation were exchanged, but nothing further, as the men settled back into the deep leather. Another man, dressed in a conservative brown suit, drove. During the ride, at DePazza's suggestion, Jason took the opportunity to remove the wig and mustache.

The leather briefcase rode on Jason's lap. Occasionally DePazza would eye it and then continue to stare out the window. Had Jason observed a little more closely, he would have noticed the bulge and occasional glint of metal under DePazza's jacket. The Glock M-17 9mm was a particularly deadly piece of ordnance. The driver was similarly equipped. Even if Jason had seen the weaponry, however, it would not have surprised him. Indeed, he expected them to carry guns.

The limo headed east from Puget Sound. Jason looked out the tinted windows. The sky was overcast, and drops of rain splattered against the window. From his small pool of meteorological knowledge, Jason knew this weather was apparently a fixture for Seattle.

Within half an hour the limo had reached its destination: a collection of warehouse buildings that were accessed through an electric gate where a guard was stationed.

Jason looked around nervously, but said nothing. He had been told to expect unusual meeting conditions. They entered one of the warehouses through a metal overhead door that rose up as the limo approached. Exiting the vehicle, Jason could see the door closing. The only light came from a couple of overhead fixtures that were in need of cleaning. A set of stairs was at one end of the vast space. The men motioned for Jason to follow them. Jason looked around and felt an uneasiness start to wash over him. With an effort he brushed aside the feeling, took a deep breath and walked toward the stairs.

Up the stairs, they entered a narrow doorway to a small, windowless room. The driver waited outside. DePazza hit the light switch. Jason looked around. The furnishings consisted of one card table, a couple of chairs and a battered file cabinet with holes rusted through.

Completely unknown to Jason, a surveillance camera, activated as soon as the light in the small room had been turned on, looked out from one of the file cabinet's rusty apertures, silently recording the events.

63

DePazza sat down in one of the chairs and motioned for Jason to do likewise. "Shouldn't be long now," DePazza said in a friendly tone. He flipped out a cigarette and offered another to Jason, who shook his head. "Just remember, Jason, don't do any talking. They only want what's in that briefcase. No need to complicate matters. Okay?"

Jason nodded.

Before DePazza could light the menthol, there were three quick knocks on the door. Jason stood up, as did DePazza, who quickly put the cigarette away and opened the door. In the doorway stood a man, small in stature, his hair solid gray, his skin tanned and heavily wrinkled. Behind him were two men, dressed in cheap suits and wearing sunglasses despite the dim light. They both appeared to be in their late thirties.

The older man looked at DePazza, who in turn pointed to Jason. The man looked at him with penetrating blue eyes. Jason suddenly realized he was drenched with perspiration, although the entire warehouse was unheated and the temperature must have been close to forty degrees.

Jason glanced at DePazza, who slowly nodded. Jason quickly handed over the leather briefcase. The man looked inside the bag, briefly perusing its contents, taking a minute to scrutinize one piece of paper in particular. The older man smiled broadly and then replaced the page, closed the briefcase and handed it to one of his men. The other one handed him a silver metal case, which he held briefly and then handed over to Jason. The case was secured by an electronic lock.

The sudden roar of the airplane overhead made them all jerk their heads upward. It seemed to be landing on the building. In a few moments it had passed by and the silence returned.

The elderly man smiled, turned, and the door quietly closed behind all three.

Jason slowly let out his breath.

They waited for a minute in silence and then DePazza opened the door and motioned for Jason to walk out. DePazza and the driver followed. The lights were turned out. The surveillance camera instantly shut off as the darkness returned.

Jason climbed back into the limo, holding tightly to the silver case. It was fairly heavy. He turned to DePazza.

"I didn't expect it to go exactly like that."

DePazza shrugged. "However you count it, though, it was a success."

"Yeah, but why couldn't I say anything?"

DePazza stared at him, faintly annoyed. "What would you have said, Jason?"

Jason finally shrugged.

"If I were you, I'd focus my attention on the contents of that." DePazza pointed at the briefcase.

Jason tried to open it but without success. He raised his eyebrows at his companion.

"When you get to where you'll be staying, you can open it. I'll tell you the code when we get there. Follow the instructions inside." He added, "You won't be disappointed."

"But why Seattle?"

"It's doubtful you'd run into anyone you know here. Correct?" DePazza's calm eyes rested on Jason's face.

"And you won't need me anymore. You're sure?"

DePazza almost smiled. "As sure as I've ever been about anything." He shook Jason's hand.

DePazza leaned back in his seat. Jason put his seat belt on and felt something jab him in the side. He pulled his SkyWord pager from his belt and looked guiltily at it. What if it *had* been his wife calling earlier? He looked at the tiny screen and his face suddenly registered disbelief.

Flashing across the screen, the pager's headline feature told the story of a terrible tragedy: Western Airlines' early morning Flight 3223 from Washington to L.A. had crashed in the Virginia countryside; there were no survivors.

Jason Archer couldn't catch his breath. He tore open his black metal case and frantically reached for the phone inside.

DePazza's voice was sharp, "What the hell are you doing?"

Jason handed DePazza the pager. "My wife thinks I'm dead. Oh, Christ. That's why she was calling. Oh, my God." Jason's fingers fumbled over the phone case, trying to open it.

DePazza looked down at the pager. He read the digitized headline and the word "Shit" silently passed between his lips. Well, this would only accelerate the process slightly, he thought. He didn't like to deviate from the established plan, yet clearly he had no choice but to do exactly that. When he looked back up at Jason, his eyes were cold and deadly. One hand reached over and snatched the cellular phone from Jason's trembling hands. The other reached inside his jacket and reappeared, holding the compact shape of the deadly Glock directly at Jason's head.

Jason looked up and saw the gun.

"I'm afraid that you're not calling anybody." DePazza's eyes never left Jason's face.

Transfixed, Jason watched DePazza reach up to his face and tug at his skin. The elaborate disguise came off piece by piece. In another moment, next to Jason sat a blond-haired man in his early thirties with a long aquiline nose and fair skin. The eyes, though, remained the same blue and chilling. His

66

real name, although he rarely used it, was Kenneth Scales. He was a certifiable sociopath, with a twist. He took great pleasure in killing people, and reveled in the details that went into that terrible process. However, he never did it randomly. And he never did it for free.

NINE

It had taken the better part of five hours to contain the fire, and in the end the flames retreated of their own accord after having consumed everything combustible within their long reach. The local authorities were grateful only that the conflagration had raged in an empty, secluded dirt field.

A National Transportation Safety Board "go-team," outfitted in their blue biohazard protective suits, were now slowly walking the outside perimeter of the crash while smoke billowed skyward and small pockets of obstinate flames were attacked by diligent teams of firefighters. The entire area had been cordoned off with orange and white street barricades behind which a number of anxious area residents stood and stared in the typical mixture of horrified disbelief and morbid interest. Columns of fire trucks, police cars, ambulances, dark green National Guard trucks and other emergency vehicles were stacked along both sides of the field. The EMTs stood next to their vehicles, hands in their pockets. Their services would not be needed other than as silent transports of whatever human remains, if any, could be extracted from the holocaust.

The mayor of the nearby rural Virginia town stood next to the farmer whose land had received this terrible intrusion from above. Behind them, two Ford pickup trucks sported "I survived Pearl Harbor" license plates. And now, for the second time in their lives, their faces carried the horror of sudden, terrible and massive death.

"It's not a crash site. It's a goddamn crematory." The veteran NTSB investigator shook his head wearily, removed his cap emblazoned with the letters NTSB and wiped at his wrinkled brow with his other hand. George Kaplan was fifty-one years old with thinning, gray-edged hair that covered a wide head; he carried a small paunch on a five-foot-seven-inch-frame. As a fighter pilot in Vietnam, then a commercial pilot for many years, he had joined the NTSB after a close friend had crashed a two-seater Piper into the side of a hill after a near miss with a 727 during a heavy fog. It was then that Kaplan decided he should do less flying and more work trying to prevent accidents.

George Kaplan was the designated investigator in charge and this was absolutely the last place in the world he wanted to be; but, unfortunately, one obvious place to seek preventive safety measures was at the scene of aircraft accidents. Every night members of the NTSB crash investigative "go-teams" went to bed hoping beyond hope that no one would have need of their services, praying that there would be no reason to travel to distant places, to pick through the pieces of yet another catastrophe.

As he scanned the crash area, Kaplan grimaced and shook his head again. Starkly absent was the usual trail of aircraft and body parts, luggage, clothing and the millions of other items that routinely would be discovered, sorted, cataloged, analyzed and papered until some conclusions could be found for why a 110-ton plane had fallen out of the skies. They had no eyewitnesses, because the crash occurred in the early morning and the cloud cover was low. It would have only been seconds between the time the plane exited the clouds and when it struck the earth.

69

Where the plane had penetrated the ground, nose first, there now existed a crater that later excavation would determine to be approximately thirty feet deep, or about one-fifth as long as the aircraft itself. That fact alone was a terrifying testament to the force that had catapulted everyone on board into the hereafter with frightening ease. The entire fuselage, Kaplan figured, had collapsed like an accordion, fore and aft, and its fragments now rested in the depths of the impact crater. Not even the empennage, or tail assembly, was visible. To compound the problems, tons of dirt and rock were lying on top of the aircraft's remains.

The field and surrounding areas were peppered with bits of debris, but most of it was palm-sized, having been thrown off in the explosion when the aircraft hit the earth. Much of the plane and the passengers strapped inside would have disintegrated from the terrible weight and velocity of the impact and the igniting of the jet fuel, which would have caused another explosion bare seconds later, before thirty feet of dirt and rubble combined for an airtight mass grave.

What was left on the surface was unrecognizable as a jet aircraft. It reminded Kaplan of the inexplicable 1991 Colorado Springs crash of a United Boeing 737. He had worked that disaster too as the aviation systems specialist. For the first time in the history of the NTSB, from its inception in 1967 as an independent federal agency, it had not been able to find probable cause for a plane crash. The "tin-kickers," as the NTSB investigators referred to themselves, had never gotten over that one. The similarity of the Pittsburgh crash of a USAir Boeing 737 in 1994 had only heightened their feelings of guilt. If they solved Colorado, many of them felt, Pittsburgh might have been prevented. And now this.

George Kaplan looked at the now clear sky and his bewilderment grew. He was convinced the Colorado Springs crash had been caused, at least in part, by a freakish rotor cloud that had hit the aircraft on its final approach, a vulnerable moment for any jetliner. A rotor was a vortex of air generated about a horizontal axis by high winds over irregular terrain. In the case of United Airlines Flight 585, the irregular terrain was supplied by the mighty Rocky Mountains. But this was the East Coast. There were no Rocky Mountains here. While an abnormally severe rotor could conceivably have knocked a plane as large as an L500 out of the sky, Kaplan could not believe that was what had befallen Flight 3223. According to air traffic control, the L500 had started falling from its cruising altitude of thirty-five thousand feet and never looked back. No mountains in the United States were capable of throwing off the formation of a rotor that high. Indeed, the only mountains nearby were in the Shenandoah National Forest and were part of the relatively smallish Blue Ridge Mountain chain. They were all in the three-to-four-thousand-foot range, more hills than mountains.

Then there was the altitude factor. Normally, the roll experienced by planes flying into a rotor or other freakish atmospheric condition is controlled by aileron application. At six miles up, the Western Airlines pilots would have had time to reestablish control. Kaplan was sure the dark side of Mother Nature had not torn the jet from the peaceful confines of the sky. But something else clearly had.

His team would shortly return to their hotel, where an organizational meeting would be held. Initially, on-scene investigative groups would be formed for structures, systems, survival factors, power plants, weather and air-traffic control. Later, units would be assembled to evaluate aircraft performance, to analyze the cockpit voice recorder and the flight data recorder, crew performance, sound spectrum, maintenance records and metallurgical examinations. It was a slow, tedious and oftentimes heart-wrenching process, but Kaplan would not leave until he had examined every atom of what had recently been a state-of-the-art jetliner and almost two hundred very much alive human beings. He swore to himself that probable cause would not escape him this time.

Kaplan slowly walked toward his rental car. An early spring would come to the dirt field: soon, red flags would bloom everywhere, tiny beacons signifying the location of remnants of the flight. Darkness was settling in rapidly. He blew into his frigid hands to warm them. A hot thermos of coffee waited in the car. He hoped the FDR, the flight date recorder – known popularly as the "black box," although it was actually blazing orange – would live up to its reputation of indestructibility. An updated version had just been installed in the plane and the 121 parameters measured by the FDR would tell them one hell of a lot about what had happened to doom Flight 3223. On the L500 the FDR and the cockpit voice recorder (CVR) were located in the overhead hull between the aft galleys. An L500 had never experienced a hull loss before; this crash would certainly test the flight data recorder's invulnerability.

Too bad human beings weren't invulnerable.

As he climbed a small rise in the earth, George Kaplan froze. In the rapidly failing light a tall image stood a bare five feet from him. Sunglasses hid a pair of slate-gray eyes; the six-foot-three-inch frame supported naturally bulky shoulders, meaty arms and a thickening waistline, and featured a pair of telephone-pole-sized legs; an aging middle linebacker was the description that would probably jump to mind. The man's hands were in his pant pockets, the unmistakable silver shield pinned to the belt.

Kaplan squinted in the gathering dusk. "Lee?"

FBI Special Agent Lee Sawyer stepped forward. "Hello, George."

The men shook hands.

"What the hell are you doing here?"

Sawyer looked around at the crash site and then back at Kaplan. His angular face carried expressive, full lips. Sawyer had thinning black hair heavily laced with silver. His long forehead and slender nose that veered slightly to the right, a relic from a past case, combined with his impressive size to give him a very intense and commanding presence. "When an American plane is downed over American soil by what looks to be sabotage, the FBI gets a little excited, George." The FBI agent looked at Kaplan pointedly.

"Sabotage?" Kaplan said warily.

Sawyer looked over the expanse of the disaster again. "I checked the meteorological reports. Nothing up there that would have caused this. And the aircraft was almost brand-new."

"That doesn't mean it was sabotage, Lee. It's too early to tell. You know that. Hell, even though the odds are probably a billion to one, we could be looking at the in-flight deployment of a reverse thruster that could've knocked the plane right out of the sky."

"There's a part of the aircraft I'm particularly interested in, George. I'd like you to take a very close look at it."

Kaplan snorted. "Well, that crater's going to take some time for us to dig out. And when we do, you'll be able to hold most of the pieces in your hand."

73

Sawyer's response almost made Kaplan's knees buckle.

"This part isn't in the crater. And it's fairly large: the starboard wing and engine. We found it about thirty minutes ago."

Kaplan stood stock-still for a full minute as his wide eyes took in Sawyer's expressionless features. Then Sawyer hustled him toward the agent's vehicle.

Sawyer's rented Buick sped away as the last flames from Flight 3223 were extinguished. The darkness would soon be gathering around a thirty-foot-deep pit that represented a crude monument to the abrupt termination of 181 lives.

TEN

The Gulfstream jet streaked through the sky. The luxurious cabin resembled an upscale hotel lounge complete with wood paneling, brown leather captain's chairs and a well-stocked bar, bartender and all. Sidney Archer was curled up in one of the oversized chairs, eyes firmly closed. A cold compress curved over her forehead. When she finally opened her eyes and removed the compress, she looked as though she were sedated, so heavy were her eyelids, so sluggish her movements. In fact, she had neither taken medication nor availed herself of the bar's inventory. Her mind had shut down: Today her husband had died in a plane crash.

She looked around the cabin. It had been Quentin Rowe's suggestion that she take Triton's corporate jet home with him. At the last minute, and adding to Sidney's pain, Gamble had accompanied them. He was now in his private cabin in the rear of the aircraft. She hoped to God he would remain there for the duration. She looked up to see Richard Lucas, Triton's in-house security chief, watching her closely.

"Relax, Rich." Quentin Rowe passed in front of the security man and headed over to Sidney. He sat down next to her. "So, how're you doing?" he asked gently. "We have some Valium on board. Carry a constant supply because of Nathan."

"He uses Valium?" Sidney looked surprised.

Rowe shrugged. "Actually, it's for the people travelling with Nathan."

75

Sidney managed a weak smile in return, a smile that abruptly vanished. "Oh, God, I can't believe it." She looked out the window with reddened eyes. Her hands flew to her face. She spoke without looking at Rowe. "I know this looks bad, Quentin." Her voice was trembling.

"Hey, no law against someone traveling on his own time," Rowe said quickly.

"I don't know what to say—"

Rowe held up a hand. "Look, this isn't the time or place. I've got some things to do. You need anything, just let me know."

Sidney looked at him gratefully. After he disappeared into another part of the cabin, Sidney leaned back in her chair and once again closed her eyes. The waves of tears slid down her puffy cheeks. From the front of the cabin, Richard Lucas continued his solitary watch.

Sidney would sob anew each time she recalled her last exchange with Jason. In anger, she had hung up the phone on him. Here was a stupid little episode that didn't mean anything, an act replicated a thousand times over the life of many successful marriages, and yet was that to be his last memory of their lives together? She shuddered and gripped the armrest. All her suspicions over the last few months. God! He had been working so hard trying to land a terrific new job, and she could only see the absurd image of him bedding more attractive women. Her guilt was numbing. The rest of her life would be forever tainted by that single, terrible misjudgment of the man she loved.

When she opened her eyes, she received another shock. Nathan Gamble was sitting next to her. She was startled to see tenderness in his face, an emotion she had certainly never witnessed in him before. He offered her the glass in his hand.

"Brandy," he said gruffly, looking past her out the porthole at the dark sky. When she hesitated, he took her hand and wrapped it around the glass. "Right now you don't want to be thinking too clearly," he said. "Drink."

She put the glass to her lips and the warm liquid cascaded down her throat. Gamble sat back in the leather and motioned Lucas to leave. The Triton CEO absently rubbed the armrest as he surveyed the cabin. He had removed his suit jacket and his rolled-up shirt-sleeves revealed surprisingly muscular forearms. The plane's engines droned deep in the background. Sidney could almost feel the electrical currents running amok through her as she waited for Gamble to speak. She had seen him completely devastate people at all levels of authority with his relentless disregard for personal feelings. Now, even through the veil of utter grief, she sensed the presence of a different, more caring man next to her.

"I'm very sorry about your husband." Sidney was dimly conscious of how ill at ease Gamble seemed. His hands were constantly in motion, as though matching the maneuvers of his very active mind. Sidney glanced at him as she took another swallow of brandy.

"Thank you," she managed to say.

"I really didn't know him personally. Company as big as Triton, hell, I'm lucky if I meet even ten percent of the management-level people." Gamble sighed and, as if suddenly noticing the ceaseless dance of his hands, folded them across his lap. "Of course, I knew him by reputation and he was moving up quickly. By most accounts he would've made very good executive material."

Sidney winced at the words. She thought back to Jason's news that very morning. A new job, a vice presidency, a new life for them all. And now? She

77

quickly finished the brandy and managed to forestall a sob before it broke the surface. When she glanced again at Gamble, he was looking directly at her. "I might as well get this out now, although it's a rotten time to do it, I know." He paused and studied her face. Sidney braced herself again; her fingers instinctively gripped the armrest as she tried hard not to shake. She swallowed an enormous lump in her throat. The chairman's eyes were no longer tender.

"Your husband was on a plane to Los Angeles." He licked his lips nervously and leaned toward her. "Not at home." Sidney unconsciously nodded, as she knew exactly what the next question would be.

"You were aware of this?"

For one brief moment Sidney felt as if she were floating through the dense clouds without the benefit of a $25 million jet. Time seemed suspended, but actually only a few seconds had passed before she uttered her response. "No." She had never lied to a client before; the word had escaped her lips before she knew it. She was certain he didn't believe her. But it was too late to go back now. Gamble searched her features for a few more seconds, then sat back in his seat. For the moment he was motionless, as if satisfied he had made his point. Abruptly, he patted Sidney's arm and stood up. "When we land, I'll have my limo take you home. You have kids?"

"One daughter." Sidney stared up at him, bewildered that the interrogation had ended so suddenly.

"Just tell the driver where to go and he'll pick up her too. She in day care?" Sidney nodded. Gamble shook his head. "Every kid's in damned day care these days."

Sidney thought of her plans to stay home to raise

78

Amy. She was a single parent now. The revelation made her almost dizzy. If Gamble hadn't been there, she would have slumped to the floor in agony. She looked up to find Gamble eyeing her, one hand gingerly rubbing his forehead. "You need anything else?"

She managed to hold up the empty glass. "Thanks, this helped quite a bit."

He took the glass. "Booze usually does." He started to leave, then paused. "Triton takes good care of its employees, Sidney. You need anything – money, funeral arrangements, help with the house or kid, stuff like that – we have people to handle it. Don't be afraid to give us a call."

"I won't. Thank you."

"And if you want to talk anymore about . . . things" – his eye-brows shot up suggestively – "you know where to find me."

He walked off and Richard Lucas quietly resumed his sentry post. Shaking slightly, Sidney once again closed her eyes. The plane raced on. All she wanted to do was hold her daughter.

ELEVEN

Sitting on the side of the bed, the man stripped down to his boxers. Outside, the sun was not yet up. His body was heavily muscled. A tattoo of a coiled snake rode on his left biceps. Three packed bags stood ready by the bedroom door. A U.S. passport, a batch of airline tickets, cash and identification documents had been waiting for him as promised. They were all in a small leather pouch on top of one of the travel bags. His name would change once again, not for the first time in his crime-laden life.

He wouldn't be fueling any more planes. Not that he would ever need to work again. The electronic deposit of funds into the offshore account had been confirmed. He now had the kind of wealth that had eluded him his entire life despite all his past efforts. Even with his long experience in criminal matters, his hands still shook as he pulled the hairpiece, oval turquoise-colored eyeglasses and tinted contacts from a small bag. Although probably weeks would pass before anyone could figure out what had happened, in his line of work you always planned for worst-case scenario. That dictated running immediately and running far. He was well prepared to do both.

He thought back to recent events. He had tossed the plastic container into the Potomac River after he had rid it of its contents; it would never be found. There were no prints to pick up, no other physical evidence left behind. If they found anything tying him to the plane sabotage, he would be long gone anyway. Moreover, the name he had been living under for the last two months would lead them to a complete dead end.

He had killed before, but certainly not on such a vast and impersonal scale. He had always had a reason to kill – if not a personal one, then one supplied by whoever had hired him. This time the sheer number and complete anonymity of the murdered people managed to prick even his hardened conscience. He had not stayed around to see who had boarded the aircraft. He had been paid to do a job and he had done it. He would use the vast sums at his disposal to forget how he had earned that money. He figured it would not take him all that long.

He sat down in front of the small mirror resting on the table in the bedroom. The wig changed his curly dark hair to a wavy blond. A new suit, far removed in its sleek elegance from the clothing he had just discarded, was hanging on the door. He cupped his hand and bent his head low as he concentrated on inserting the contact lenses that would change his low-key brown eyes to a startling blue.

He rose back up to check the effect in the mirror and felt the elongated muzzle of the Sig P229 placed directly against the base of his skull. With the sharpened perception that accompanies panic, he noticed how the attached suppressor almost doubled the barrel length of the compact 9mm.

His absolute shock lasted barely a second as he felt the cold metal against his skin, saw the dark eyes staring at him in the mirror's reflection, the mouth set in a firm line. His own countenance often held a similar look right before a kill. Taking the life of another human being had always been a serious business to him. Now, in the mirror he watched, mesmerized, as another face went through his very own signature ritual. Then he watched with growing surprise as the features of the person about to kill him next turned to anger and then moved to unadulterated loathing, emotions he had never felt in the midst of an execution. The victim's eyes grew wide as he focused on the finger tightening on the trigger. His mouth moved to say something, probably an expletive; however, the words were not formed in time, as the round exploded into his brain. He jerked backward from the impact and then collapsed forward on to the little table. The killer tossed his limp body face down in the small crevice between the bed and the wall and emptied the remaining eleven shots from the Sig's magazine into the dead man's upper torso. Although the victim's heart was no longer pumping, dime-sized drops of dark blood appeared at each point of entrance, like the sprout of tiny oil wells. The auto pistol landed next to the body.

The shooter walked calmly from the room, stopping only to perform two tasks. First, he scooped up the leather bag containing the dead man's new identity. Second, out in the hallway he hit the HVAC switch on the wall and turned the air-conditioning on full blast. Ten seconds later the front door of the apartment opened and closed. The apartment was silent. In the bedroom, the beige carpet was fast becoming an ugly shade of crimson. The balance in the offshore bank account would be reduced to zero and closed within the hour, its owner no longer requiring use of the funds.

It was barely seven in the morning. Darkness still reigned outside. Sitting at the kitchen table, wearing her battered old house-robe, Sidney Archer slowly closed her eyes and once again tried to pretend this was all a nightmare and her husband was still alive and would be walking through the front door. He would have a smile on his face, a present under his arm for his daughter and a long, soothing kiss for his wife.

When she opened her eyes, nothing had changed. Sidney looked at her watch. Amy would be awake soon. Sidney had just gotten off the phone with her parents. They would be at their daughter's house at nine to drive the little girl to their home in Hanover, Virginia, where she was going to stay for a few days while Sidney tried to make some sense of what had happened. Sidney cringed at the thought of having to explain the catastrophe to her little girl when she was older, at having to relive, years later, the horror she was now feeling. How to tell her daughter that her father had died for no apparent reason other than a plane doing the unthinkable, shedding almost two hundred lives in the process, and killing the man who had helped breathe life into her.

Jason's parents had passed on years before. An only child, he had adopted Sidney's family as his own, and they had happily accepted him. Sidney's two older brothers had already called with offers of help, commiseration and, finally, quiet sobbing.

Western had offered to fly Sidney to the small town near where the crash had occurred, but she had declined. She could not bear to be with other family members of crash victims. She envisioned all of them boarding long, gray buses in silence, unable to make eye contact, exhausted limbs twitching, frail nervous systems ready to crumble from overwhelming shock. Struggling with complicated feelings of denial, grief and sorrow was terrible enough without being surrounded by people you didn't know who were going through the same ordeal. Right now, the comfort of similarly stricken folk did not sound at all appealing to her.

She headed upstairs, walked down the hallway and paused at her bedroom. As she leaned against the door, it halfway opened. She looked around the room, at all the familiar objects, each having a unique history of its own; memories inextricably tied to her life with Jason. Her gaze finally came to rest on the unmade bed. So much pleasure had occurred there. She couldn't believe that that early morning encounter before Jason had boarded the plane was to be the last time.

She closed the door quietly and walked down the hallway to Amy's room. The even breathing of her daughter was comforting, especially now. Sidney sat in the wicker rocking chair beside the trundle bed. She and Jason had recently succeeded in moving their daughter from crib to bed. The effort had required many nights of sleeping on the floor beside the little girl until she grew comfortable with the new arrangements.

While she slowly rocked in the chair, Sidney continued to watch her daughter, the tangle of blond hair, the small feet in thick socks that had kicked free from the blankets. At seven-thirty, a small cry escaped Amy's lips and she abruptly sat up, eyes tightly shut like a baby bird's. Barely a moment passed before mother had daughter in her arms. They rocked for a while longer until Amy awoke fully.

As the sun began its ascent, Sidney gave Amy a bath, dried her hair, dressed her in warm clothes and helped her down the stairs to the kitchen. While Sidney was making breakfast and brewing coffee, Amy wandered into the adjacent living room, where Sidney could hear her playing with an ever-growing pile of toys that had occupied one corner of the room for the last year. Sidney opened the cupboard and automatically pulled out two coffee cups. She stopped halfway to the coffeepot, rocking slowly back and forth on the wood floor. She bit into her lip until the urge to scream subsided. She felt as though someone had cut her in half. She put one cup back on the shelf and carried her coffee and a bowl of hot oatmeal over to the small pine kitchen table.

She looked toward the living room. "Amy. Amy, sweetie, it's time to eat." She could barely speak above a whisper. Her throat was killing her; her entire body seemed to have eroded into one large ache. The little girl hurtled through the doorway. Amy's normal speed was most other kid's top speed. She carried a stuffed Tigger and a photo frame. As she raced toward her mother, her little face was bright and shining, hair still slightly damp, straight on top with curls emerging at the bottom.

Sidney's breath suddenly left her body as Amy held up a photo of Jason. It had been taken just last month. He had been outside working in the yard. Amy had crept up on him and sprayed him with the hose. Daughter had ended up with father in a pile of bright red, orange and yellow leaves.

"Daddy?" Amy's face was anxious.

Jason was to have been out of town for three days so Sidney had already anticipated having to explain his absence to her daughter. God! Three days seemed like three seconds now. She steeled herself as she smiled at the little face.

"Daddy's away right now, sweetie," she began, unable to hide the tremble in her voice. "It's just you and me right now, okay? Are you hungry, you want to eat?"

"My daddy? Daddy working?" Amy persisted, chubby finger pointing at the photo. Sidney lifted her daughter on to her lap. "Amy, do you know who you're going to see today?"

85

Amy's face looked expectant.

"Gramps and Mimi."

The child's mouth formed a large oval and then broke into a big smile. She nodded enthusiastically and blew a kiss toward the refrigerator, where a picture of her grandparents hung with the aid of a magnet. "Gramps, Mimi."

Sidney carefully pulled the photo of Jason from Amy's hand while sliding the bowl of oatmeal over.

"Now you need to eat before you go, okay? It's got maple syrup and butter, your favorite."

"I do it. *I* do it." Amy climbed out of her mother's lap and into her own chair, carefully maneuvering the spoon as she hungrily plunged into the oatmeal.

Sidney sighed and covered her eyes. She tried to hold her body rigid, but several wracking sobs still managed to escape. She finally fled the room, carrying the photo with her. She raced up the stairs to her bedroom, put the photo on the top shelf of the closet and flung herself on the bed, muffling her sobs in the pillow.

A full five minutes went by and the outpouring of sorrow continued. Usually Sidney could lock on Amy's whereabouts like radar. This time she never heard her little girl until she felt the small hand on her shoulder, pulling at her. Amy lay down beside Sidney, burrowing her face into her mother's shoulder.

Amy saw the tears and cried out "Oh, boo-boos, boo-boos," as she touched the wetness. She cupped her mother's face between her two little hands and started to cry too as she struggled to form the words. "Mommy, sad?" Their wet faces touched, tears mixed together. After a while Sidney pulled herself up, held her daughter, rocked her back and forth on the soft mattress. A bit of oatmeal clung to Amy's mouth. Sidney silently cursed herself for breaking down, for making her daughter cry, but she had never experienced such overpowering emotion before.

Finally the spasms stopped. Sidney rubbed at her eyes for the hundredth time and finally there were no new tears to replace the old. After a few more minutes she carried Amy into the bathroom, wiped her face and kissed her.

"It's okay, baby, Mommy's okay now. No more crying."

When Amy finally calmed down, Sidney gathered some toys from the bathtub for her. While she was thus preoccupied, Sidney quickly showered and changed into a long skirt and turtleneck.

When Sidney's parents knocked on the door promptly at nine, Amy's bag was packed and she was ready to go. They walked out to the car. Sidney's father carried Amy's bag. Sidney's mother walked along with Amy.

Bill Patterson put one burly arm around her daughter's shoulder, his sunken eyes and caved-in shoulders revealing how strongly the tragedy had struck him.

"Jesus, honey, I still can't believe it. I just talked to Jason two days ago. We were going to do some ice fishing this year. Up in Minnesota. Just the two of us."

"I know, Dad, he told me. He was very excited about it."

While her father loaded Amy's bag in the car, Sidney strapped her daughter in the baby seat, handed her Winnie the Pooh, squeezed her hard and then kissed her gently.

"I'll see you very soon, babydoll. Mommy promises."

Sidney closed the door. Her mother took her hand.

"Sidney, please come down with us. You don't want to be alone right now. Please."

Sidney gripped her mother's slender hand. "I do need some time alone, Mom. I need to think things through. I won't be long. A day or two, then I'll be down."

Her mother eyed her for several more seconds and then gripped Sidney in a massive hug, her small frame shaking. When she got in the car, her round face was smeared with tears.

Sidney watched the car pull out of the driveway. She stared at the backseat where her daughter clutched her beloved stuffed bear, a thumb stuck firmly in her small mouth. In a few moments the car turned the corner and they were gone.

With the slow, unsteady motions of an elderly woman, Sidney walked back to her house. A thought suddenly struck her. With renewed energy, she rushed toward the house.

Inside, she dialed information for the Los Angeles area and obtained the number for AllegraPort Technology. Because of the time difference, she had to wait to call. The hours went by with agonizing slowness. As she punched in the number, she wondered why they hadn't called when Jason had not shown up. There had been no messages from them on the answering machine. That fact should have prepared her for AllegraPort's response, but she wasn't.

After speaking with three different people at the company, she hung up the phone and stared numbly at the kitchen wall. Jason had not been offered a vice presidency with AllegraPort. In fact, they had not heard of him. Sidney abruptly sat down on the floor, drew her knees up to her chest and wept uncontrollably. All of the suspicions she had experienced earlier swarmed back; the swiftness of their return threatened to dissolve her remaining ties to reality. She pulled herself up and ducked her head into the kitchen sink. The cold water partially revived her. She stumbled over to the table, where she covered her face in her hand. Jason had lied to her. That was indisputable now. Jason was dead. That, also, was incontrovertible. And, apparently, she would never know the truth. It was with that last thought that she finally stopped crying and looked out the window into the backyard. She and Jason had planted flowers, bushes and trees over the last two years. Working together toward a common goal: They had conducted much of their married lives along that same theme. And despite all the uncertainty she was feeling right now, one truth remained sacred to her. Jason loved her and Amy. Whatever had compelled him to lie to her, to climb aboard a doomed plane instead of remaining safely at home doing nothing more daring than prepping the kitchen walls for painting, she would find out what it was. She knew Jason's reasons would have been completely innocent. The man she knew intimately and loved with all her heart would have been capable of nothing less. Since he had been senselessly ripped from her, she at least owed it to him to track down why he had been on that plane. As soon as she was mentally able, she would take up that pursuit with every bit of energy she could muster.

TWELVE

The airplane hangar at the regional airport was small. On the walls were rows of power tools; stacks of boxes lay all over the floor. The darkness outside was turned into daylight inside by a ceiling full of overhead lights. Wind rattled against the metal walls as the sleet intensified, clanging like buckshot against the structure. The interior of the hangar was filled with the thick, pungent smell of an assortment of petroleum products.

On the concrete floor near the front of the hangar lay an enormous metal object. Bent and grossly distorted, it was the remains of the right wing of Flight 3223, with starboard engine and pylon intact. It had landed in the middle of a densely wooded area, directly on top of a ninety-foot-tall, hundred-year-old oak, which was spilt in half by the impact. Miraculously, the jet fuel had not ignited. Most of the payload had probably been lost when the tank and lines had been pierced, and the tree had cushioned some of the fall. The pieces had been removed by helicopter and brought to the hangar for examination.

A small group of men gathered closely around the wreckage. Their exhalations formed clouds in the unheated air; thick jackets kept them warm. They used powerful flashlights to probe the jagged edge of the wing where it had been torn loose from the ill-fated airliner. The nacelle housing the starboard engine was partially crushed and the right-side cowling was caved in. The flaps on the trailing edge of the wing had been ripped off on impact, but these had been recovered nearby. Examination of the engine had shown severe blade shingling, clear evidence of a major airflow disturbance while the engine was delivering power. The "disturbance" was easy to pinpoint. A great deal of debris had been ingested into the engine, essentially destroying its functionality even had it remained attached to the fuselage.

However, the attention of the men gathered around the wing was centered on where it had detached from the plane. The jagged edges of the metal were burned and blackened and, most telling, the metal was bent outward, away from the surface of the wing, with clear signs of indentation and pitting on the metal's surface. There was a short list of events that could have caused that; a bomb was clearly on that list. When Lee Sawyer had examined the wing earlier, his eyes had riveted on that area.

George Kaplan shook his head in disgust. "You're right, Lee. The changes in the metallurgy I'm seeing could only have been caused by a shock wave exerting immense but short-lived overpressure. Something exploded here, all right. It's the damnedest thing. We put detectors in airports so some crazy assholes with an agenda can't smuggle a gun or bomb on board, and now this. Jesus!"

Lee Sawyer moved forward and knelt down next to the edge of the wing. Here he was, nearly fifty years old, half of those years spent with the bureau, and again he was sifting through the catastrophic results of human pollution.

He had worked on the Lockerbie disaster, an investigation of mammoth proportion that had brought together a damned near airtight case culled from what bordered on microscopic evidence unearthed from the shattered remains of Pan Am Flight 103. With plane bombings there were usually never any "big" clues. At least Special Agent Sawyer had thought so up until now.

His observant eyes swept over the wreckage before they came to rest on the NTSB man. "What's your best list of possible scenarios right now, George?"

Kaplan rubbed his chin, scratching absently at the stubble. "We'll know a lot more when we recover the black boxes, but we do have a clear result: The wing came off a jetliner. However, those things just don't happen. We're not exactly sure when it happened, but radar indicates that a large part of the plane – now we know it was the wing – came off in-flight. When that occurred, of course, there was no possibility of recovery. The first thought is some type of catastrophic structural failure based on a faulty design. But the L500 is a state-of-the-art model from a top manufacturer, so the chances of that kind of structural failure are so remote that I wouldn't waste much time on that angle. So maybe you think it's metal fatigue. But this plane barely had two thousand cycles – takeoffs and landings – it's practically brand-new. Besides that, the metal fatigue accidents we've seen in the past all involved the fuselage because the constant contraction-expansion of cabin pressurization and depressurization seems to contribute to the problem. Aircraft wings are not pressurized. So you rule out metal fatigue. Next, you look at the environment. Lightning strike? Planes get hit by lightning more often than people think. However, planes are equipped to deal with that and because lightning needs to be grounded to do real damage, a plane up in the sky may suffer, at worst, some burning of the skin. Besides, there were no reports of lightning in the area on the morning of the crash. Birds? Show me a bird that flies at thirty-five thousand feet and is large enough to take off an L500's wing and then maybe we'll discuss it. It sure as hell didn't collide with another plane. It sure as hell didn't."

Kaplan's voice was rising with each word. He paused to catch his breath and to look once more at the metal remains.

"So where does that leave us, George?" Sawyer calmly asked.

Kaplan looked back up. He sighed. "Next we look at possible mechanical or nondesign structural failure. Catastrophic results on an aircraft usually stem from two or more failures happening almost simultaneously. I listened to the transmission record between the pilot and the tower. The captain radioed in a Mayday several minutes before the crash, although it was clear from what little she said that they were unsure what had happened. The plane's transponder was still kicking the radar signals back until impact, so at least some of the electrical systems were working up until then. But let's say we had an engine catch on fire at the same time a fuel leak occurred. Most people might assume fuel leak, flames from the engine – wham, you got yourself an explosion and there goes the wing. Or there might not have been an actual explosion, although it sure as hell looks like there was. The fire could've weakened and finally collapsed the spar and the wing gets torn off. That could explain what we think happened for Flight 3223, at least at this early stage." Kaplan did not sound convinced.

"But?" Sawyer looked at him.

Kaplan rubbed his eyes, the frustration clear in his troubled features. "There's no evidence that any-thing was wrong with the damned engine. Except for the obvious damage caused from its impact with the terrain and ingesting debris from the initial explosion, nothing leads me to believe that an engine problem played a role in the crash. If there was an engine fire, standard procedure would dictate cutting off the fuel flow to that engine and then turning off the power. The L500's engines are equipped with automatic fire detection and extinguisher systems. And, more importantly, they're mounted low, so flames would fly toward the wings or the fuselage. So even if you have twin catastrophes – a flaming engine and a fuel leak – the design features of the aircraft and the environmental conditions prevailing at thirty-five thousand feet and an airspeed of over five hundred miles per hour would pretty much ensure that the two shall not meet." He rubbed his foot against the wing. "I guess what I'm saying is I wouldn't bet the farm on a bad engine having crashed this bird." He paused. "There's something else."

Kaplan once again knelt beside the jagged edge of the wing. "Like I said, there is clear evidence of an explosion. When I first checked the wing, I was thinking some type of improvised explosive device. You know, like Semtex wired to a timer or altimeter device. Plane hits a certain altitude, the bomb goes off. The blast fractures the skin, you got almost immediate rivet failure. Hundreds-of-miles-per-hour winds hitting it, that wing's gonna open right up at the weakest point, like unzipping your fly. Spar gives way, and bam. Hell, the weight of the engine on this section of the wing would have guaranteed that result." He paused, apparently to study the interior of the wing more closely. "The twist is I don't think a typical explosive device was involved."

"Why's that?" Sawyer asked.

Kaplan pointed inside the wing to the exposed

section of the fuel tank near the fuel panel. He held his light over the spot. "Look at this."

A large hole was clearly visible. All around the perforation were light brown stains and the metal was warped and bubbled. "I noticed those earlier," Sawyer said.

"There is no way in the world a hole like this could have been naturally generated. In any event, it would've been caught on routine inspection before the plane took off," Kaplan said.

Sawyer put on his gloves before touching the area. "Maybe it happened during the explosion."

"If it did, it was the only spot it happened to. There are no other markings like this on this section of the wing, although you got fuel everywhere. That pretty much rules out the explosion having caused it. But I do believe something was put on the fuel tank wall." Kaplan paused and nervously rubbed his fingers together. "I think something was put on it deliberately to cause that hole."

"Like a corrosive acid?" Sawyer said.

Kaplan nodded. "I'll bet you dinner that's what we find, Lee. The fuel tanks are of an aluminium alloy structure consisting of the front and rear spars and the top and bottom of the wings. The thickness of the walls varies around the structure. A number of acids will eat right through a soft alloy metal like that."

"Okay, acid; but, depending on when it was applied, it was probably slow-acting, to let the plane get up in the air, right?"

Kaplan answered immediately. "Right. The transponder continually sends the plane's altitude to air traffic control, so we know the plane had reached its cruising altitude shortly before the explosion."

Sawyer continued his line of thought. "Tank gets pierced at some point during the flight. You got jet fuel spilling out. Highly flammable, highly explosive. So what ignited it? Maybe the engine wasn't on fire, but how about just the standard heat thrown off from the engine?"

"No way. You know how cold it is at thirty-five thousand feet? It'd make Alaska feel like the Sahara. Besides, the engine housing and coolant systems pretty much dissipate the heat thrown off from the engine. And any heat it does generate sure as hell ain't gonna end up *inside* the wing. Remember you got a damn fuel tank in there. It's pretty well insulated. On top of that, if you got a fuel leak, because of the plane's airspeed, the fuel will flow backward and not toward the front of the wing and below, where the engine is located. No, if I were inclined to take down a plane this way, no way would I count on engine heat being my detonator. I'd want something a lot more reliable."

Sawyer had a sudden thought. "If there was a leak, wouldn't it be contained?"

"In some sections of the fuel tank the answer to that would be yes. In other areas, including where we got this hole, the answer is no."

"Well, if it went down like you say – and right now I'm inclined to think you're right, George – we're going to have to focus on everybody who had access to that aircraft at least twenty-four hours before its final flight. We're going to need to go easy. It looks to be an insider, so the last thing we need is to spook him. If anybody else is involved in this, I want every last sonofabitch."

Sawyer and Kaplan walked back to their cars. Kaplan looked over at the FBI agent. "You seemed to accept my sabotage theory pretty readily, Lee."

Sawyer was aware of one fact that made the bombing theory infinitely more plausible. "It'll need to be substantiated," he replied without looking at the NTSB man. "But, yeah, I think you're right. I was pretty sure it was that as soon as the wing was found."

"Why the hell would someone do that? I mean, I can understand terrorists taking out an international flight, but this was a plain-vanilla domestic. I just don't get it."

As Kaplan was about to get into his car, Sawyer leaned on the door. "It might make sense if you wanted to kill someone in particular, in a spectacular fashion."

Kaplan stared at the agent. "Down an entire plane to get to one guy? Who the hell was on that thing?"

"Does the name Arthur Lieberman ring any bells?" the FBI agent asked quietly.

Kaplan searched his brain but came up empty. "Sounds damn familiar, but I can't place it."

"Well, if you were an investment banker or stockbroker, or a congressman on the Joint Economic Committee, you'd know. Actually, he's the most powerful person in America, maybe the entire world."

"I thought the most powerful person in America was the president."

Sawyer smiled grimly. "No. It's Arthur Lieberman with the big *S* on his chest."

"Who the hell was he?"

"Arthur Lieberman was the chairman of the Federal Reserve Board. Now he's a homicide victim along with a hundred and eighty others. And my hunch is, he's the only one they wanted to kill."

THIRTEEN

Jason Archer had no idea where he was. The limo had seemed to drive around for hours, he couldn't be sure, and DePazza, or whoever the hell he really was, had blindfolded him. The room he was now in was small and bare. Water dripped in once corner and the air was thick with the odor of mold. He sat on a rickety chair across from the one door. There were no windows. The only light came from a naked overhead bulb. He could hear someone on the other side of the door. They had taken his watch, so he had no idea what time it was. His captors brought him food at very irregular intervals, which made it difficult to ascertain how much time had passed.

Once, when food was brought to him, Jason had noticed his laptop computer and cellular phone resting on a small table just on the other side of the door. Other than that the outer room was much like the one he was in. The silver case had been taken from him. There had been nothing in it, he was now reasonably certain. What was going on was beginning to become clear to him. Christ, what a sucker! He thought of his wife and child, and how desperately he wanted to be with them again. What Sidney must be thinking had happened to him. He could barely comprehend the emotions she must be feeling right now. If only he had told her the truth. She would be in a position to help him. He sighed. But the bottom line was that telling her anything would have put her in danger. That was something he would never do, not even if it meant never seeing her again. He wiped the tears from his eyes as the image of eternal separation fixed itself in his head. He stood up and shook himself.

He wasn't dead yet, although the grimness of his captors was far from reassuring. However, they had made one mistake despite their obvious care. Jason took off his glasses, placed them on the concrete floor and carefully scrunched them with his foot. He picked up one ragged piece of glass, positioned it carefully in his hand, then walked over to the door and pounded on it.

"Hey, can I get something to drink?"

"Shut up in there." The voice sounded annoyed. It wasn't DePazza, probably the other man.

"Listen, dammit, I've got medication to take and I need something to take it with."

"Try your own spit." It was the same man's voice. Jason could hear a chuckle.

"The pills are too big," Jason shouted, hoping someone else might hear him.

"Too bad."

Jason could hear the pages of a magazine being leisurely turned.

"Great, I won't take them and I'll just keel over dead right here. It's for high blood pressure and right now mine's clear through the roof."

Now Jason could hear a chair scraping the floor, keys jangling. "Step back from the door."

Jason did so, but only a short distance. The door swung open. The man held the keys in one hand, his gun in the other.

"Where are the pills?" he asked, his eyes narrowing.

"In my hand."

"Show 'em to me."

Jason shook his head in disgust. "I don't believe this." As he stepped forward, he opened his hand and held it out. The man glanced at it. Jason swung his leg up, connected with the man's hand and sent the gun flying.

"Shit," the man yelled. He hurtled toward Jason, who met him with a perfect uppercut. The jagged glass caught the man right across the cheek. He howled in pain and staggered back, blood streaming down from the grisly wound.

The man was large, but his muscle had long since started to turn to fat. Jason exploded into him like a battering ram, smashing the older man flat against the wall. They briefly struggled, but the far stronger Jason was able to hurl the man around until he collided face first with the cinder-block wall. One more serious head thrust into the wall and two vicious punches to the man's kidney's and he slumped to the cold floor unconscious.

Jason picked up the gun and ran through the open doorway. With his free hand he scooped up his laptop and cell phone. Stopping for a moment to gauge his surroundings, he spotted another doorway and, pausing to listen for any sound, he hurried through it.

He stopped and let his eyes adjust to the darkness. He swore under his breath. He was in the same warehouse, or one identical to it. They must have been driving in circles. He cautiously slipped down the steps and on to the main floor. The limo was nowhere in sight. He suddenly heard a sound from the direction he had just come. He raced to the overhead door, searching frantically for the switch to open it. His head jerked around as he heard running footsteps. He ran across the warehouse to the opposite end. Hidden in a corner behind some fifty-gallon drums, he carefully placed the gun on the floor and clicked open his laptop.

The laptop was a sophisticated model complete with a built-in phone modem. He turned on the computer's power switch and used a short cable housed in his laptop's case to hook his computer's modem to his cellular phone. Sweat poured from his brow as the machine took a few seconds to warm up. Using his mouse, he clicked through the necessary function screens and then, in the darkness, his fingers guided by strong familiarity with the keys, he typed his message. So intent was he on sending it, Jason did not hear the footsteps behind him. He began to type in the e-mail address of the recipient. He was sending the message to his own America Online mailbox. Unfortunately, like people who couldn't remember their own phone number because they never called it, Jason, who never sent e-mail to himself, didn't have his e-mail address programmed into his laptop. He did remember it, but typing cost him a few precious seconds. While his finger hovered over the keys, a light flashed over him, a strong arm locked around his neck.

Jason managed to click on the send command. The message leaped electronically off the screen. For one brief moment. Then a hand slashed in front of his face, grabbed the laptop from him, the cell phone dangling precariously in the air at the end of the short cable. Jason could see the thick fingers hitting necessary keys to cancel the e-mail.

Jason swung a short, brutal punch that connected with his assailant's jaw. The grip relaxed on the laptop and Jason was able to snatch it and the cell phone away. He slammed a foot into his attacker's abdomen and raced off, leaving the man face down on the floor. Unfortunately, he left the 9mm behind as well.

Heading toward a distant corner of the ware-house, Jason now could hear racing feet coming from all directions. There would be no escape for him, that was clear. But he could still do something. He dodged behind some metal stairs, dropped to his knees and started typing. A shout nearby made him jerk his head up. His flying fingers, so accurate now, failed him as his right index finger hit the wrong keystroke when typing the recipient's e-mail address. He began typing the message, the sweat pouring down his face, stinging his eyes. His breath came in big clumps, his neck ached from the stranglehold. It was so dark, he couldn't even see the keyboard. He alternated between scanning the warehouse as the shouts and running feet came nearer and nearer to his location.

He didn't realize that the small amount of light thrown off by the computer screen was like a laser show in the dark warehouse. The sound of men running hard toward him barely ten feet away made him cut short his message. Jason hit the send button and waited for the confirming signal. Then he deleted both the file he had sent and the name of the recipient. He did not look at the e-mail address as his finger held down the delete key. He slid the laptop and cell phone across the floor underneath the steps until they stopped far back in the corner. He had time to do nothing more as multiple searchlights hit him squarely in the face. He slowly stood up, his breathing heavy but his eyes defiant.

A few minutes later the limo pulled out of the warehouse. Jason was slumped over in the backseat, several lacerations and deep bruises on his face, his breathing irregular. Kenneth Scales had the laptop open and was cursing loudly as he stared at the small screen, powerless to reverse what had occurred minutes earlier. In a fit of rage he tore Jason's cell phone free from the cable and repeatedly smashed it against the door of the limo until it dropped to the floor in jagged pieces. Then he pulled a small secured-line cellular phone from his inner pocket and punched in a number. Scales spoke slowly into the phone. Archer had contacted someone, sent some message. There were a number of possible recipients and they would all have to be checked out and appropriately dealt with. But that potential problem would just have to keep. Other matters would now demand his time. Scales clicked off and looked over at Jason. When Jason managed to look up, the pistol's muzzle was almost against his forehead.

"Who, Jason? Who'd you send the message to?"

Jason managed to catch his breath as he gripped his painfully bruised ribs. "No way. Not in a million years, pal."

Scales pushed the muzzle flush against Jason's head.

"Pull the trigger, you asshole!" Jason screamed.

Scale's finger started to press down on the Glock's trigger, but then he stopped and roughly pushed Jason back against the seat.

"Not yet, Jason. Didn't I tell you? You've got another gig to do."

Jason stared up helplessly at him as Scales smiled wickedly.

Special Agent Raymond Jackson's eyes took in the area with one efficient sweep. He moved into the room shutting the door behind him. Jackson shook his head in quiet amazement. Arthur Lieberman had been described to him as a fortune-builder with a career several decades long. This hovel did not conform to that description. He checked his watch. The forensics team would be here shortly to conduct and in-depth search. Although it seemed unlikely that Arthur Lieberman personally knew who had blown him out of a peaceful Virginia sky, on investigations of this magnitude, every possibility had to be explored.

Jackson went into the tiny kitchen and quickly determined that Arthur Lieberman did not cook or eat here. There were no dishes or pans in any of the cupboards. The only visible occupant of the refrigerator was a lightbulb. The stove, though old, showed no signs of recent use. Jackson scanned the other areas of the living room and then walked into the small bathroom. With his gloved hand he carefully edged open the door to the medicine cabinet. It contained the usual toiletries, nothing of significance. Jackson was about to close the mirrored door when his eye caught the small bottle edged in between the toothpaste and the deodorant. The prescription label had dosage and refill information and the physician who had prescribed it. Agent Jackson was unfamiliar with the name of the drug. Jackson had three kids and was an informal expert on prescription and over-the-counter drugs for a host of ailments. He wrote down the name of the medication and closed the door to the medicine cabinet.

Lieberman's sleeping chamber was small, the bed little more than a cot. A small desk sat against the wall nearest the window. After examining the closet, Jackson turned his attention to the desk.

Several photos on the desk showed two men and one woman ranging in age from what looked to be late teens to mid-twenties. The photos appeared several years old. Lieberman's kids, Jackson quickly concluded.

Three drawers confronted him. One was locked. It took Jackson only a few seconds to open the locked drawer. Inside was a bundle of handwritten letters held together with a rubber band. The handwriting was careful and precise, the contents of the letters decidedly romantic. The only strange part was that they were all unsigned. Jackson muddled over that one for a moment, then replaced the letters in the drawer. He spent a few more minutes looking around until a knock on the door announced the arrival of the forensics unit.

FOURTEEN

During the time Sidney had been alone in her house, she had explored every crevice of the place, driven by a force that she could not come close to identifying. She sat for hours in the small window seat in the kitchen, her mind racing through her years of marriage. Every detail of those years, even moments of relative insignificance, came surging up from the depths of her subconscious. At times her mouth curled in amusement as she recalled a particularly funny memory. Those instances were brief, however, and were always followed by wracking sobs as the realization that there would be no more fun times with Jason came crashing down on her.

Finally stirring, she rose and walked up the stairs, drifted slowly down the hallway and entered Jason's small study. She looked around at the spare contents, then sat down in front of the computer. She moved her hand across the glass screen. Jason had loved computers ever since she had known him. She was computer functional, but, aside from word processing and checking her e-mail, her knowledge of the world of computer hardware and software was extremely limited.

Jason did quite a bit of correspondence by e-mail and normally checked his electronic mailbox every day. Sidney hadn't checked it since the plane crash. She decided it was time to do so. Many of Jason's friends had probably sent messages. She turned the computer on and watched the screen as a series of numbers and words trooped across that were, in large part, meaningless to her. The only one she did recognize was available memory. There was a lot of it. The system had been customized for her husband and was bursting with power.

She stared at the available memory number. With a jolt she realized that the last three digits, 7, 3 and 0, constituted the date of Jason's birthday, July 30. A deep breath prevented a quick relapse into tears. She slid open the desk drawer and idly fumbled through its contents. As an attorney she well knew the number of documents and procedures that would have to be gone through as Jason's estate was settled. Most of their property was jointly held, but there were still many legal hoops. Everyone eventually had to face such things, but she couldn't believe she had to confront them so soon.

Her fingers sifted over papers and miscellaneous office paraphernalia in the drawer, closing over one object, which she pulled out. Although she was unaware of the fact, she was holding the card Jason had thrust there before leaving for the airport. She looked at it closely. It looked like a credit card, but stamped on it was the name "Triton Global," followed by "Jason Archer" and, finally, the words "Code Restricted – Level 6." Her brow furrowed. She had never seen it before. She assumed it was some type of security pass, although it did not have her husband's photo on it. She slipped it into her pocket. The company would probably want it back.

She accessed America Online and was greeted by the computerized voice announcing that mail was indeed present in their electronic mailbox. As she had thought, it contained numerous messages from their friends. She read through them, crying freely. Finally she lost all desire to complete the task and started to exit out of the computer. She jumped as another e-mail suddenly flashed on the screen; it was addressed to ArchieJW2@aol.com, which was her husband's e-mail address. In the next instant it was gone, like a mischievous inspiration scurrying through one's head before disappearing.

Sidney hit some function keys and quickly checked the computerized mailbox again. Her brow tightened into a sea of wrinkles when she discovered it was completely empty. Sidney continued to stare at the screen. A creeping sensation was pushing her to the conclusion that she had just imagined the entire episode. It had happened so damn quickly. She rubbed at her painful eyes and sat there for another few minutes, anxiously waiting to see if the performance would be repeated, although she had no idea of its meaning. The screen remained blank.

Moments after Jason Archer had re-sent his message, another e-mail was announced by the computerized voice saying, "You've got mail." This time the message held and was duly logged into the mailbox. However, this computer mailbox was not located at the old stone and brick house, nor was it at Sidney's desk at the offices of Tyler, Stone. And, currently, there was no one home to read it. The message would just have to keep.

Sidney finally rose and left the study. For some reason the sudden flash across the computer screen had given her an absurd hope, as if Jason were somehow communicating to her, from wherever he had gone after the jet had plunged into the ground. Stupid! She told herself. That was impossible.

An hour late, another episode of wrenching grief, her body dehydrated, she gripped a picture of Amy. She had to take care of herself. Amy needed her. She opened a can of soup, turned on the stove and a few minutes later ladled out a small quantity of beef barley into a bowl and carried it over to the kitchen table. She managed to ingest a few spoonfuls while she looked at the walls of the kitchen that Jason had planned to paint that weekend after much nagging from her. Everywhere she turned, a new memory, a fresh pang of guilt, battered her. How could it not? This place contained as much of them, as much of him, as was possible for an inanimate shell to hold.

She could finally feel the hot soup passing through her system, but her body still shuddered as though it were almost out of fuel. She grabbed a bottle of Gatorade from the refrigerator and drank straight from the container until the shakes stopped. Yet even as the physical side started to calm down, she could feel the inner forces building once again.

She jumped up from the table and walked into the living room; she turned on the TV. Numbly channel-hopping, she ran across the inevitable: live news coverage of the crash. She felt guilty about her curiosity regarding an event that had ripped her husband from her. However, she could not deny that she craved knowledge about the event, as if her approaching it from a coldly factual angle would at least temporarily lessen the terrible hurt that tore at her.

The newswoman was standing near the crash site. In the background the collection process was being dutifully conducted. Sidney watched the debris being carried and sorted into various piles. Suddenly she almost fell out of the chair. One worker had passed directly behind the newswoman as she rambled on with her story. The canvas bag with the crisscross pattern barely looked damaged, only singed and dirtied at the edges. She could even make out the large initials written in the bold, black print.

The bag was placed in a pile of similar items. For one awful moment, Sidney Archer couldn't move. Her limbs were completely locked. The next moment she was all action.

She ran upstairs, changed into jeans and a thick white sweater, put on low warm boots and hurriedly packed a bag. In a few minutes she was backing the Ford out of the garage. She glanced once at the Cougar convertible parked in the other garage bay. Jason had lovingly kept it running for almost ten years and its battered look had always been under-scored by their memory of the sleek elegance of the Jag. Even the Explorer looked brand-new by comparison with the Cougar. The contrast had always amused her before. Tonight it did not, as a new cascade of tears blurred her vision and made her slam on the brakes.

She beat her hands on the dashboard until jarring pain shot up to her elbows. Finally she laid her head against the steering wheel as she struggled to regain her breath. She thought she would be nauseous as the taste of beef barley made its way into her throat, but it finally receded into the depths of her quivering stomach. Moments later she was heading down the quiet street. She looked back briefly at her home. They had lived there almost three years. A wonder-ful place built almost a hundred years ago with large-proportioned rooms, wide crown moldings, random-width oak plank flooring and enough secret nooks that you didn't have to try very hard to find a quiet place to lose yourself on a gloomy Sunday afternoon. It had seemed a terrific place to raise kids, they had both decided. So much they had wanted to do. So much.

She felt another wave of sobs climbing diligently toward the surface. She sped up and turned on to a main road. In ten more minutes she was looking at the red and yellow colors of the neighborhood McDonald's. She pulled into the drive-through and ordered a large coffee. As she pressed the window button, she was staring into the freckled face of a gangly teenage girl, her long, auburn hair tied back in a ponytail, who would more than likely grow up into a lovely young woman, just as Amy would. Sidney hoped the girl still had her father. It jolted her again to think that Amy was fatherless.

Within an hour she was headed west on Route 29, a narrow black strip of road that split gentle rolling Virginia countryside as it cut a roughly forty-five degree angle through Virginia and on across the North Carolina border. Sidney had traveled the road many times while she attended law school at the University of Virginia in Charlottesville. It was a beautiful drive past long-silent Civil War battlefields and old yet still functioning family farms. In the fall and spring the colors of the foliage rivaled any painting she had ever seen. Names like Brightwood, Locust Dale, Madison and Montpelier flashed by on the road signs, and Sidney thought back to the many trips she and Jason had taken to Charlottesville to attend some function or other. Now no part of the familiar road or countryside felt comforting.

The night swept on. Sidney looked at the dashboard clock and was surprised to see it was nearing one in the morning. She accelerated and the truck flew down the empty road. Outside, the temperature continued to drop as she headed into higher elevations. Thick clouds had settled in and the spread of her headlights was the only contrast to the pitch-blackness. She turned up the truck's heat even more and hit her high beams.

An hour later, she glanced at the map resting next to her on the front seat. Her turnoff was coming up. She held her body rigid as she drew nearer to her destination. She started to count the miles on her odometer.

At Ruckersville she headed west. She was now in Greene County, Virginia, rustic and rural, far removed from the pace of life Sidney knew and had thrived in. The county seat was the town of Standardsville, whose emotional climate was now anything but, with an impact crater and scorched earth appearing on television screens all over the world.

Sidney finally pulled off the road and peered around to try to fix her location. The darkness of the countryside enveloped her. She flicked on the reading light and held the map close to her face. Getting her bearings, she continued down the slash of road another mile until she rounded a bend of partially naked slender elms, knotty maples and towering oaks, after which the vista opened up to stark, flat farmland.

At the end of the road, a police cruiser was parked near a rusted, leaning mailbox. To the right of the mailbox was a dirt road that snaked its way back, with full, well-tended evergreen hedges bordering the dirt road on either side. In the distance the earth seemed to glow like a huge phosphorous cave.

She had found the place.

In the swirl of the Explorer's headlights, Sidney noticed that it was lightly snowing. As she pulled up closer, the door of the police car opened and a uniformed officer wearing a neon-orange all-weather slicker stepped from the vehicle. He walked over to the Ford, pointing his flashlight at the license plate and then swept it over the Explorer's exterior before its beam came to rest on the driver's-side window.

Sidney took a deep breath, hit the window switch and the glass slowly slid down.

The officer's face appeared at her shoulder. His upper lip was partially covered by a bushy mustache streaked with gray, the corners of his eyes were heavily stacked with wrinkles. Even under the orange raincoat, the bulky strength of his shoulders and chest were evident. The officer made a perfunctory scan of the interior and then settled on Sidney.

"Can I help you, ma'am?" The voice was tired, and not just physically.

"I . . . I came . . ." She faltered. Her mind suddenly went blank. She looked at him, her mouth moved, but no words came out.

The cop's shoulders sagged. "Ma'am, it's been one helluva long day up here, y'know? And I've had a lot of people just happen on by here that really have no business being here." He paused and studied her features. "Are you lost?" His tone made it clear that he did not believe she had strayed one inch off her intended course.

She managed to shake her head.

He looked at his watch. "The TV trucks finally headed out on down to Charlottesville about an hour ago. They went to get some sleep. I suggest you do the same. You can see and read all you want on the TV and in the papers, believe me." He straightened back up, signaling that their conversation, oneside as it was, was at an end. "Can you find your way back out?"

Sidney slowly nodded and the cop lightly touched the brim of his cap and headed back to his car. Sidney turned the truck around and started to drive away. She looked in the rearview mirror and abruptly stopped. The strange glow beckoned to her. She opened the truck door and got out. She opened the rear door of the Ford, pulled out her overcoat and put it on.

113

The cop watched her walk toward the patrol car and he got out too. His slicker was wet from the snow's moisture. Sidney's blond hair was covered by flakes as the winter storm stepped up its intensity.

Before the cop could open his mouth, Sidney held up one hand.

"My name is Sidney Archer. My husband, Jason Archer . . ." Her voice began to waver here as the full effect of the words she was about to speak hit her. She bit her lip, hard, and continued. "He was on the plane. The airline offered to bring me down here, but . . . I decided to come down on my own. I'm really not sure why, but I did."

The cop stared at her. His eyes had softened considerably; the heavy mustache dropped like a weeping willow, his erect shoulders slumped down. "I'm really sorry, Ms. Archer. I really am. Some of the other . . . family have already come by. They didn't stay very long. The FAA people don't want anybody up there right now. They're coming back tomorrow to walk the area looking . . . looking for . . ." His voice trailed off and he looked down at the ground.

"I just came to see . . ." Her voice failed her too. She looked at him, her eyes blistering red, her cheeks hollow, her forehead frozen into a vertical column of wrinkles. Although tall, she seemed childlike in her overcoat, her shoulders hunched forward, hands plunged deeply into pockets – as though she were disappearing as well, along with Jason.

The cop looked embarrassed, his vacillation evident. He glanced up the dirt road, then down at his shoes and then back at her. "Hold on a minute, Ms. Archer." He ducked back inside his patrol car. Then his head popped back out. "Ma'am, come on in here out of the snow, please, before you catch something."

114

Sidney climbed inside the patrol car. It smelled of cigarette smoke and spilled coffee. A rolled-up *People* magazine was tucked inside a crevice in the front seat. A small computer screen sat atop a stack of electronic hardware. The cop rolled down his window and swept the patrol car's searchlight across the rear of the Explorer. He rolled the window back up and proceeded to hit a number of keys on the keyboard and then studied the screen. He looked at Sidney.

"Just punching in your license plate. Gotta confirm your identity, ma'am. Not that I don't believe you. I mean, you didn't drive up here in the middle of the night for a vacation. I know that. But I got rules to go by."

"I understand."

The screen filled with information, which the officer quickly studied. He pulled a clipboard off the dash and ran through a list of names. He looked up at her briefly, embarrassment again displayed on his features.

"You said *Jason* Archer was your husband?"

She slowly nodded. *Was?* The word was numbing to her. She felt her hands begin to shake uncontrollably, the vein in her left temple to pulse spasmodically.

"I just had to make sure. There was another Archer on the plane too. A Benjamin Archer."

For a moment her hopes soared, but reality threw her immediately back down. There had been no mistake. If there had been, Jason would have called. He had been on that plane. As much as she had willed him not to be, he had been. She looked over at the distant lights. He was there now. Still there.

She cleared her throat. "I have some photo identification, Officer." She opened her wallet and handed it across.

115

He noted the driver's license and then his eyes caught on the photo of Jason, Sidney and Amy, taken barely a month ago. He stared at it for several moments. Then he handed the wallet back quickly. "I don't need to check anything else, Ms. Archer." He looked out the window. "There's a couple of other deputies stationed along up the road, and a slew of National Guard all around. Some of the guys from Washington are still up there, that's what all the lights are for." He looked at her. "I really can't leave my post, Ms. Archer." He looked down at his hands. Her eyes trailed his. She saw the wedding ring on his left hand, the ring finger swollen by time so that the simple gold band would never come off without taking the digit with it. The officer's eyes crinkled and a faint bit of moisture appeared on his cheek. He looked away suddenly, his hand quickly rising to his face and then back down.

He started the car and put it in gear. He looked over at her. "I can understand why you came up here, but I don't recommend that you stay long, Ms. Archer. It's not . . . well, it's not that kind of a place." The patrol car swayed and bumped over the dirt road. The officer stared intently ahead, toward the blinding lights. "There's a devil in hell and a Lord God above, and, while the devil had his way with that plane, all those people are with the Lord right now, Ms. Archer, every last one of 'em. You believe that, and don't let anybody ever tell you different." Sidney found herself nodding at his words, wanting so badly to believe that they were true.

As they approached the lights, Sidney felt her mind recede farther and farther into the distance. "There was . . . a bag, canvas with blue crisscross stripes. It was my husband's. It had his initials on it. JWA. I actually bought it for him for a trip we took several years ago." She briefly smiled as the memory

116

washed over her. "It was really for a joke. We had sort of had an argument and it was the ugliest bag I could find at the time. Of course, as it turned out, he loved it."

She abruptly looked up and caught the officer's surprised look. "I . . . I saw it on the TV. It didn't even look damaged. Is there any way I could see it?"

"I'm sorry, Ms. Archer. Whatever's been collected has already been taken away. The truck came just about an hour ago to take away the last shipment for the day."

"Do you know where it goes?"

The officer shook his head. "It wouldn't matter if I did. They wouldn't let you near it. After the investigation is complete, they'll return it, I expect. But from the looks of this one, that could be years. Again, I'm sorry."

The patrol car finally stopped a few feet away from another uniformed policeman. The officer got out of the car and conferred briefly with his colleague, pointing twice in the direction of the police cruiser while Sidney sat there, unable to take her eyes off the lights.

She was startled when the officer leaned his head in the car. "Ms. Archer, you can get out here."

Sidney opened the door and got out. She briefly looked at the other officer and he nervously nodded toward her, pain in his eyes. There was pain, apparently, everywhere. These men too would have rather been home with their families. Here there was death; it was everywhere. It seemed to cling to her clothes, much like the snowfall.

"Ms. Archer, when you're ready to leave, you tell Billy over there and he'll radio me. I'll come right up and get you."

As he started to get back in his cruiser, she called to him. "What's your name?"

117

The officer looked back. "Eugene, ma'am. Deputy Eugene McKenna."

"Thank you, Eugene."

He nodded and touched the brim of his cap. "Please don't stay too long, Ms. Archer."

As the car drove away, Billy led her toward the lights. He kept his eyes straight ahead. Sidney didn't know how much Officer McKenna had told his partner, but she could feel the distress emanating from his body. He was a slender straw of a man, young, barely twenty-five, she thought, and he looked sickened and nervous.

He finally stopped walking. Up ahead Sidney could see people moving slowly across the property. Barricades and yellow police tape were everywhere. Under the artificial daylight, Sidney could see the utter devastation. It resembled a battlefield, the earth seemingly inflicted with a terrible surface wound.

The young police officer touched her arm. "Ma'am, you oughta stay back around here. Those folk from Washington are real particular about people messing around up here. They're afraid somebody might stumble over . . . you know, mess up stuff." He took a deep breath. "There's just things everywhere, ma'am. Everywhere! I ain't never seen anything like it and I hope I never do again so long as I live." He looked off in the distance again. "When you're ready, I'll be down there." He pointed in the direction from which they had come and then headed back down.

Sidney wrapped her coat around her and brushed the snow from her hair. She unconsciously moved forward, then stopped, then started advancing again. Directly under the umbrella of light, mounds of dirt had been thrown up. She had seen that on the news now countless times. The impact crater. They said the entire plane was in there, and though she knew it to be true, she could not believe it was possible.

The impact crater. Jason was in there too. It was a thought that had become so deep, so wrenching, that instead of sending her into hysterics, it simply incapacitated her. She clenched her eyes shut and then reopened them. Thick tears rolled down her cheeks, and she did not bother to wipe them away.

She did not expect to ever smile again.

Even when she forced herself to think of Amy, of the wonderful little girl Jason had left her, not a trace of happiness was able to break through her utter sorrow. She stared ahead as cold winds buffeted her, her long hair swirling around her head.

While she continued to watch, several large pieces of equipment headed over to the crater, engines whining, black, smoky exhaust gushing up from their bowls. Steam shovels and earth movers attacked the pit with great force, lifting up huge mouthfuls of earth and depositing them in waiting dump trucks, which headed out on special routes over terrain that had already been searched. Speed was the overriding concern, even paramount to the risk of further damaging the aircraft's remains. What everyone wanted desperately to uncover was the FDR. That was more important than worrying about turning a quarter-inch fragment into something smaller by the accelerated excavation work.

Sidney noticed the snow was adhering to the ground – an obvious concern to the investigators, she assumed, as she saw a number of them racing around with searchlights, only stopping long enough to stick small flags in the rapidly whitening earth. When she moved closer, she made out the green-clad figures of the National Guardsmen as they patrolled their sectors, rifles slung over their shoulders, their heads turning constantly in the direction of the crater. Like an omnipotent magnet, the crash site seemed inexorably to demand everyone's attention. The price to be paid for the innumerable joys of life, it seemed, was the constant threat of swift, inexplicable death.

As Sidney moved forward again, her foot caught on something covered by the snow. She bent down to see what it was, and the words of the young policeman came back to her. *There are things everywhere. Everywhere!* She froze, but continued to search with the innate curiosity of human beings. A moment later she was running down the dirt road, her feet fumbling and slipping in the snow, her arms jerking awkwardly forward, violent sobs exploding from her lungs.

She never saw the man until she collided headlong into him, buckling his legs. They both went down, he as surprised as she, perhaps even more so.

"Damn," Lee Sawyer grunted as he landed on a clod of dirt, the wind knocked out of him. Sidney, however, was on her feet in a second and continued sprinting down the twisting path. Sawyer started to go after her until his knee locked, a recurring condition compliments of his chasing down an athletic bank robber on hard pavement for twenty long blocks many years before. "Hey," he yelled after her as he awkwardly hopped around on one foot, rubbing at his knee. He shone his flashlight in her direction.

When Sidney Archer turned her head, he caught her profile in the arc of the light. A second later he snatched a glimpse of her horror-filled eyes. Then she was gone. He gingerly stepped over to the area where he had first spotted her. He shone his flashlight on the ground. Who the hell was she and what was she doing up here? Then he shrugged.

Probably a curious area resident who had seen something she wished she hadn't. A minute later Sawyer's light confirmed his suspicions. He bent down and picked up the small shoe. It looked tiny and helpless in his big paw. Sawyer looked back in Sidney Archer's direction and sighed deeply in the darkness. His large body began to tremble in almost uncontrollable rage as he stared at the terrible hole in the earth dead ahead. He fought back an urge to scream at the top of his lungs. There had only been a handful of times in his career with the FBI that Lee Sawyer wanted to deny the persons he had run to ground the opportunity of a trial by their peers. This was one of those times. He silently prayed that when he did find those responsible for this horrendous act of violence, they would try something, anything that would provide him with the tiniest fraction of an opening, allowing him to spare the country the cost and media circus any such trial would entail. He slipped the shoe into his coat pocket and, nursing his injured knee, walked off to check in with Kaplan. Then he would head back to town. He had an appointment in Washington that afternoon. His investigation of Arthur Lieberman would now start in earnest.

A few minutes later, Officer McKenna looked anxiously at Sidney as he helped her out of the patrol car. "Ms. Archer, are you sure you don't want me to call somebody to come get you?"

Sidney, eggshell pale, limbs convulsing, her hands and clothes dirty from where she had fallen, shook her head hard. "No! No! I'm all right." She leaned up against the cruiser. Her arms and shoulders still twitched involuntarily, but at least her balance had somewhat stabilized. She closed the door of the police cruiser and started to walk unsteadily toward her Ford. She hesitated and then turned around. Office McKenna was beside his cruiser, watching her closely.

"Eugene?"

"Yes, ma'am?"

"You were right . . . It's not a place where you should stay too long." The words were said in the hollow tone of one entirely vacant of spirit. She turned and slowly walked toward the Ford and got in.

Deputy Eugene McKenna slowly nodded, his prominent Adam's apple sliding quickly up and down as he briefly fought the tears welling in his eyes. He opened the door of the police cruiser and fell rather than sat in the front seat. He closed the door so the sounds he was about to make would go no farther.

As Sidney retraced her route back, the cellular phone in her car buzzed. The totally unexpected sound made her jerk so badly she almost lost control of the Explorer. She looked down at the phone as complete disbelief spread over her features. No one knew where she was. She looked around at the darkness as if someone were watching her. The shorn trees were the only witnesses to her journey back home. As far as she could tell, she was the only living person around. Her hand slowly reached down to pick up the phone.

FIFTEEN

"My God, Quentin, it's three in the morning."

"I wouldn't be calling unless it was really important."

"I'm not sure what you want me to say." Sidney's hand slightly trembled as she held the cellular phone. Sidney slowed the car; her foot had steadily pressed down on the accelerator as the conversation continued, until she was traveling at a dangerous rate of speed on the narrow roadway.

"Like I said, I heard you and Gamble talking on the trip back from New York. I thought you would have come to me, Sidney, not Gamble." The voice was soft but contained a certain edge.

"I'm sorry, Quentin, but he asked questions. You didn't."

"I was *trying* to give you some space."

"I appreciate that, I really do. It's just that Gamble confronted me. I mean he was nice about it, but I had to tell him something."

"And so you told him you didn't know why Jason was on that plane? That was your answer? That you had no idea he was even on the plane?" She could discern certain unspoken thoughts in his words. How could she tell Rowe something different from what she had told Gamble? And even if she revealed Jason's story for going to Los Angeles, how could she tell Rowe that she now knew Jason hadn't gone to interview with another company? She was in an

123

impossible situation and right now there seemed to be no way out of it. She decided, instead, to change the subject.

"How did you think to call me in the car, Quentin?" It made her feel slightly creepy that he had been able to trace her.

"I tried the house, then the office. Only place left was the car," he said simply. "To tell you the truth, I was kind of worried about you. And—" His voice abruptly stopped, as if he had decided an instant too late not to communicate the thought.

"And what?"

Rowe was hesitant on the line, but then he quickly finished his thought. "Sidney, you don't have to be a genius to figure out the question we all want answered. Why was Jason going to L.A.?"

Rowe's tone was clear enough. *He* wanted an answer to that question.

"Why would Triton care what he does on his own time?"

Rowe let out a deep sigh. "Sid, everything Triton does is highly proprietary. There are whole industries out there who spend all day long trying to steal our technology and people. You know that."

Sidney flushed. "Are you accusing Jason of selling Triton's technology to the highest bidder? That's absurd and you know it." Her husband was not here to defend himself and she damned sure wasn't going to let that insinuation go by.

Rowe sounded hurt. "I didn't say *I* was thinking it, but others here are."

"Jason would never, ever do anything like that. He worked his butt off for that company. You were his friend. How could you even make that allegation?"

"Okay, explain what he was doing on a plane to L.A. instead of painting the kitchen, because I'm about to make the one acquisition that will allow Triton to lead the world into the twenty-first century and I cannot allow anything or anyone to destroy that opportunity. It will never be repeated."

The tone in his voice was just enough to ignite every molecule of rage in Sidney Archer's body.

"I can't explain it. I'm not even going to try to explain it. I don't know what the hell's going on. I just lost my husband, *goddammit!* There's no body, there's no clothes. There's nothing left of him and you're sitting there telling me you think he was ripping you off? Damn you." The Ford swerved slightly off the road and she had to struggle to bring it back on. She slowed down once again as the vehicle hit a major rut. The jolt went through her entire body. It was getting harder to see in the swirling snow.

"Sid, please, please calm down." Rowe's voice was suddenly panicked. "Listen, I didn't mean to upset you further. I'm sorry." He paused, then quickly added, "Can I do anything for you?"

"Yeah, you can tell every friggin' person at Triton to drop dead. Why don't you go first?" She clicked the off button and tossed the phone down. The tears were pouring so fast she finally had to pull off the road. Shaking as if she had just been plunged into ice, Sidney finally undid her seat restraint and lay across the front seat, one arm covering her face for several minutes. Then she put the Ford back into gear and took to the road once more. Despite her evident exhaustion, her thoughts moved as fast as the V-6-powered Explorer. Jason had been terrified of her upcoming meeting with Triton. He probably had the job interview story ready in case of an emergency. Her meeting with Nathan Gamble and company had qualified as such. But why? What could he possibly have been involved in? All those late nights? His reticence? What had he been doing?

She looked at the dashboard clock and noted the time creeping relentlessly toward four A.M. While her mind was functioning in high gear, the rest of her wasn't. Her eyes would now barely stay open, and she had to address the obvious concern of where she would spend what was left of the night. She was coming up to Route 29. When she turned on to the highway, she went south instead of retracing her route north. A half hour later Sidney cruised through the empty streets of Charlottesville. She drove past the Holiday Inn and other possibilities for lodging and finally turned off Route 29 on to Ivy Road. She soon entered the parking lot of the Boar's Head Inn, one of the area's best-known resorts.

Within twenty minutes she had signed in and was slowly pushing her near-immobile limbs between the sheets in a well-appointed room with beautiful vistas that at the moment she cared nothing about. What a day of nightmares, all of them absolutely real. It was her last conscious thought. Two hours before dawn, Sidney Archer finally fell asleep.

SIXTEEN

At three o'clock in the morning, Seattle time, the thick clouds spilled open and delivered still more rain to the area. The guard huddled in the small guard shack, his feet and hands close to the floor heater. In one corner of the structure a steady stream of water trickled down the wall, forming a puddle on the ragged green carpet. The guard wearily checked the time. Four hours to go before his watch was over. He poured out the last of the hot coffee from his thermos and longed for a warm bed. Each building was leased by different companies. Some of the buildings simply stood empty, but all were secure regardless of their contents, with armed guards onsite twenty-four hours a day. The high metal fence had barbed wire at the top, although not the deadly razor wire favored at prison facilities. Video monitors were discreetly placed throughout the area. It would be a difficult place to break into.

Difficult, but far from impossible.

The figure was clad head to foot in black. It took him less than a minute to climb the fence in the back of the warehouse facility, expertly avoiding the sharp wire. Once over the fence, he slipped in and out of the shadows as the rain continued to pour down, completely covering the slight sounds that his quick-moving feet made. On his left sleeve was a miniature electronic jamming device. He passed three video cameras on the way to his destination; none of them captured his image.

Reaching the side door of Building 22, he pulled a slender wire-like device from his knapsack and inserted it in the sturdy padlock. Ten seconds later the lock hung loose.

He took the metal steps two at a time after making a visual sweep of the building's interior with his night-vision goggles. He opened the door to a room, illuminating the small space with his flashlight. He unlocked the filing cabinet and removed the surveillance camera. He placed the videotape in one part of his knapsack, reloaded the camera and replaced it in the cabinet. Five minutes later, the area was once again quiet. The guard had not yet finished his last cup of coffee.

At the crack of dawn, a Gulfstream V lifted off from the Seattle airport. The black-clad figure was now dressed in jeans and a sweatshirt and was fast asleep in one of the luxurious cabin chairs, his dark hair falling into his youthful face. Across the aisle, Frank Hardy, head of a firm specializing in corporate security, and counter-industrial espionage, intently read every page of a lengthy report as the plane soared through the now clear morning sky; the last vestiges of the previous night's storm system had finally pushed on. Inside a metal briefcase was the videotape that had been removed from the camera in the file cabinet. The case was within easy reach of his hand. A steward appeared and poured out another cup of coffee for the plane's one awake passenger. Hardy's eyes rested on the metal briefcase. His brow wrinkled and, from long habit, his fingers traced and retraced the worry lines stamped across his forehead. Then Hardy put the report down, leaned back in his seat and stared out the cabin window as the aircraft headed east. He had a lot to think about. He was not a happy man right now. Both his jaw and his gut clenched and unclenched as the sleek jet raced on.

The Gulfstream hit its cruising altitude on a flight that would culminate in Washington D.C. The rays of the rising sun reflected off the familiar company logo emblazoned on the aircraft's empenage. The soaring eagle represented an organization like no other. More recognized worldwide than even Coca-Cola, more feared than most of the world's largest conglomerates – which, by comparison, were aging dinosaurs awaiting the constant pull of extinction. It was the complete package as the twenty-first century hurtled toward them, just like the bald eagle symbol that was rapidly making its way into the four corners of the world and everywhere in between.

Triton Global would have it no other way.

129

SEVENTEEN

A uniformed security guard escorted Lee Sawyer through the massive lobby of the Marriner Eccles Building, the Constitution Avenue home of the Federal Reserve Board. Sawyer thought that the premises were in keeping with the enormous clout of their occupant. After walking up to the second floor, Sawyer and his escort stopped at a thick wooden door and the escort knocked. The words "Come in" filtered out to them. Sawyer moved through the doorway to a large, cozily furnished office. The floor-to-ceiling bookcases, dark furniture and ornate mouldings made a somber impression. The thick drapes were closed. A green banker's lamp glowed on the large, leather-topped partners desk. The smell of cigars hovered everywhere; Sawyer could almost see gray wisps of smoke hanging in the air like ghostly apparitions. It reminded him of the scholarly studies of some of his old college professors. A small fire burning in the fireplace threw both warmth and light into the room.

When a man of massive girth swiveled around in the chair behind the desk, Sawyer's attention was instantly riveted upon him. A corpulent red face housed light blue eyes hiding behind lids reduced to slits by sagging facial skin and the overgrowth of a pair of eyebrows as thick as Sawyer had ever seen. The hair was white and abundant, the nose was wide and the tip was even redder than the rest of the face. For one brief moment, Sawyer jokingly wondered if he was confronting Santa Claus.

The man rose from behind the desk, and his big, cultured voice flowing across the room to envelop Lee Sawyer dispelled all such thoughts.

"Agent Sawyer, I'm Walter Burns, vice chairman of the Federal Reserve Board."

Sawyer moved forward to grip the flabby hand. Burns matched the six-foot-three Sawyer in height, but carried at least a hundred more pounds on his frame than did the powerfully built FBI agent. Sawyer took the leather chair indicated by Burns. When Burns sat back down, Sawyer noted that he moved with a grace that was not uncommon to large men.

"I appreciate you seeing me, sir."

Burns shot the FBI man a penetrating glance. "I take it that your agency's involvement in this matter means it was not merely a mechanical or other similar problem that befell that plane?"

"We're checking through all possible scenarios. Nothing has been ruled out right now, Mr. Burns." Sawyer's features were impassive.

"My name is Walter, Agent Sawyer. Since we're both members of the sometimes unwieldy system known as the federal government, I think that allows us the pleasure of a first-name basis."

Sawyer grinned. "Mine's Lee."

"How can I help you, Lee?"

The clatter of freezing rain assaulted the window and a chill seemed suddenly to pervade the air. Burns rose and walked over to the fireplace, beckoning Sawyer to pull his chair over. While Burns placed some small pieces of kindling taken from a brass bucket on to the fire, Sawyer flipped open his notebook and briefly studied some notes. When Burns sat down across from him, Sawyer was ready.

"I realize that a lot of people have no idea what the

Fed does. I mean people outside the financial markets."

Burns rubbed at one eye and Sawyer almost heard a chuckle escape the other man's lips. "If I were a betting man, I would be inclined to lay money on the fact that fully half the population of this country have no idea of the existence of the Federal Reserve System, and that nine out of ten have no clue as to what our actual purpose is. I must confess I find that anonymity enormously comforting."

Sawyer paused and then leaned toward the older man. "Who would benefit from Arthur Lieberman's death? I don't mean personally, I'm focusing on his professional side. As chairman of the Fed."

Burns's eyes widened until the slits reached the shape of half-moons, about the limits of their range. "You're implying that someone blew up that plane in order to kill Arthur? If you don't mind my saying so, that seems awfully far-fetched."

"I didn't say that was the case. That is, we're looking at everything right now." Sawyer spoke in low tones, as though he feared he would be over-heard. "The fact is I've combed through the pass-enger manifest and your colleague was the only VIP aboard. If it was a deliberate sabotage, then one reason that jumps out would be killing the Fed chairman."

"Or just a planned terrorist attack and Arthur simply had the misfortune to be on board."

Sawyer shook his head. "If we are looking at sabotage, then I don't believe Lieberman being on the plane was a coincidence."

Burns leaned back in his chair and slowly put his feet out toward the fire. "My God!" he finally said as he stared into the fire. Although he would have looked quite at home in a three-piece suit replete with watch chain, his current attire – camel-hair sport coat, dark blue crew sweater with a white button-down shirt collar peeking out, gray pleated slacks and comfortable black loafers – did not look so out of place on his frame. Sawyer noted that the man's feet were surprisingly small for his size. Neither man spoke for at least a minute.

Sawyer finally stirred. "I know I don't have to tell you that anything I say to you tonight is extremely confidential."

Burn's head swiveled around to the FBI agent. "Secrets are something I am quite good at keeping, Lee."

"So getting back to my question: Who benefits?"

Burns considered the query for some moments and then took a deep breath. "The United States economy is the largest in the world. Hence, as America goes, so goes the world. If another country hostile to America desired to damage our economy or disrupt the world financial markets, perpetrating an atrocity such as this could well have that effect. I have no doubt that the markets will take a staggering blow if it turns out his death was premeditated." The vice chairman shook his head sadly. "I just never thought I would live to see the day."

"How about anyone in this country who might like to see the chairman dead?" Sawyer asked again.

"As long as the Fed has existed there have been conspiracy theories painted so vividly about the institution that I'm quite sure there are more than a handful of people in this country who take them, however nonsensical they are, quite seriously."

Sawyer's eyes narrowed. "Conspiracy theories?"

Burns coughed and then loudly cleared his throat. "There are those who believe that the Fed is actually a tool for wealthy families around the globe to keep the poor in their place. Or that we take our marching orders from a small group of international bankers.

I've even heard one theory that has us being the pawns of alien beings who have infiltrated all the highest positions of government. My birth certificate says Boston, Massachusetts, by the way."

Sawyer shook his head. "Christ, that's pretty wacko."

"Exactly. As if a seven-trillion-dollar economy employing well over a hundred million people could be secretly run by a handful of waistcoated tycoons."

"So one of these conspiracy groups could have plotted to kill the chairman in retaliation for perceived corruption or injustice?"

"Well, few governmental institutions are more misunderstood and feared out of ignorance than the Federal Reserve Board. When you first mentioned the possibility, I said it was far-fetched. Having thought about it for a few minutes, I have to say my initial reaction was probably not correct. But blowing up a plane . . ." Burns shook his head wearily.

Sawyer jotted down some notes. "I'd like to know more about Lieberman's background."

"Arthur Lieberman was an immensely popular man in the major financial circles. For years he was one of the top moneymakers on Wall Street, before turning to public service. Arthur called things as he saw them and he was usually right in his judgment. With a series of masterful maneuvers, he shook up the financial markets almost from the moment he became chairman. He showed them who was boss." Burns stopped to put another piece of wood on the fire. "In fact, he led the Fed in a way that I would like to think I would if ever given the opportunity."

"Any idea who might succeed Lieberman?"

Burns shook his head. "No."

"Around the time he left for Los Angeles, had

anything unusual occurred at the Fed?"

Burns shrugged. "We had our FOMC meeting on the fifteenth of November, but that was a regularly scheduled event."

Sawyer looked puzzled. "FOMC?"

"Federal Open Market Committee. It's our policy-making board."

"What goes on at those meetings?"

"Well, in a shorthand version, the seven members of the Board of Governors and the presidents of five of the twelve Federal Reserve Banks look at all pertinent financial data on the economy and decide whether any actions are required with respect to money supply and interest rates."

Sawyer nodded. "When the Fed raises or lowers interest rates, for instance, then that affects the entire economy. Contracts or expands it."

"At least we think so," Burns replied sardonically. "Although our actions have not always had the results we intended."

"So was there anything unusual at this FOMC meeting?"

"No."

"Nevertheless, could you give me a rundown of exactly what was said and by whom? It might seem irrelevant, but getting a motive could really help us track down whoever did this."

Burns voice went up an octave. "Impossible. The actual deliberations of FOMC meetings are absolutely confidential and cannot be divulged to you or anyone else."

"Walter, I won't push it now, but with all due respect, if any information discussed at these meetings is relevant to the FBI's investigation, rest assured that we will have access to it." Sawyer stared at him until Burns dropped his gaze.

"A brief report detailing the minutes of the

135

meeting is released six to eight weeks after the meeting is held," Burns said slowly, "but only after the occurrence of the next meeting. The actual results of the meetings, whether any action was taken or not, are released to the news media the same day."

"I read in the paper where the Fed left the interest rates the same."

Burns pursed his lips and then eyed Sawyer. "That's right, we didn't adjust the interest rates."

"How exactly do you adjust rates?"

"There are actually two interest rates that are directly affected by the Fed, Lee. The Federal Funds Rate is the interest rate banks charge other banks who borrow funds to meet reserve requirements. If that rate goes up or down, interest rates on bank CDs, T-bills, mortgages and commercial paper will soon follow. The Fed sets the target Federal Funds Rate at the FOMC meetings. Then the New York Federal Reserve Bank, through its Domestic Trading Desk, buy or sells government securities, which in turn restricts or expands the supply of money available to banks to ensure that that interest rate is maintained. We call that adding or subtracting liquidity. That's how Arthur took the bulls by the horns when he became chairman; by adjusting the Fed Funds Rate in ways the market didn't anticipate. The second interest rate which can be affected by the Fed is the Discount Rate, the rate charged by the Fed to banks for loans by the Fed. However, the Discount Rate is tied to loans for what amounts to emergency purposes; thus, it's known as the 'window of last resort.' Banks who frequent that window too often will come under increased regulatory scrutiny, since it's seen as a sign of weakness in banking circles. For that reason, most banks will borrow money from other banks at the slightly higher Federal Funds

Rate, since there is no stigma attached to that channel of credit."

Sawyer decided to change direction. "Okay, had Lieberman been acting strangely? Anything bothering him? Any threats that you know of?"

Burns shook his head.

"This trip to L.A. that Lieberman was taking, was it a regular thing?"

"Very regular. Arthur was meeting with Charles Tiedman, president of the San Francisco Federal Reserve Bank. Arthur was very good about making the rounds of the presidents, and he and Charles were old friends."

"Wait a minute. If Tiedman is head of the San Francisco bank, why was Lieberman flying into L.A.?"

"There is a branch office of the Fed there. Also, Charles and his wife live in Los Angeles and Arthur would stay with them."

"But he would've just seen Tiedman at the November fifteenth meeting."

"That's right. But Arthur's trip to L.A. was planned well in advance. It was only a coincidence that it occurred shortly after the FOMC meeting. However, I do know he was anxious to talk to Charles."

"Do you know what about?"

Burns shook his head. "You'd have to ask Charles."

"Anything else that might help me?"

Burns considered the question briefly and then shook his head again. "I can't think of anything in Arthur's personal background that would have led to this abomination."

Sawyer rose and shook Burns's hand. "I appreciate the information, Walter."

When Sawyer turned to leave, Burns gripped his

137

shoulder. "Agent Sawyer, the information we have at the Fed is so enormously valuable that the slightest slip could reap incredible profits for undeserving individuals. I guess I've become extremely tight-lipped over the years to prevent just such an occurrence."

"I understand."

Burns put a flabby hand on the door as Sawyer buttoned up his coat. "So, do you have any suspects yet?"

The agent turned back to Burns. "Sorry, Walter, we have secrets at the FBI too."

Henry Wharton sat behind his desk, nervously tapping his foot on the carpeted floor. The managing partner of Tyler, Stone was small in stature but large in legal ability. Partially bald with a trim gray mustache, he looked every bit the senior partner in a major law firm. After thirty-five years of representing the elite of American business, Wharton was not easily intimidated. However, if anyone came close, it was the man currently seated across from him.

"So that's all she told you? That she was unaware her husband was on the plane at all?" Wharton asked.

Nathan Gamble's eyes were half closed as he looked down at his hands. He now looked up at Wharton. The movement made the attorney jerk slightly.

"That's all I asked her."

Wharton shook his head sadly. "Oh, I see. Well, I know when I spoke with her she was devastated. Poor thing. Such a shock, right out of the blue like that. And—"

Wharton broke off speaking as Gamble stood up and went over to the window behind the lawyer's desk. He studied the Washington landscape in the late morning sunlight. "It occurred to me, Henry, that further questioning might better come from you." Gamble put one big hand on Wharton's narrow shoulder and gently squeezed.

Wharton quickly nodded. "Yes, yes, I can understand your thinking on that point."

Gamble strolled over to peruse numerous diplomas from prestigious universities neatly lining one wall of Wharton's expansive quarters. "Very impressive. I never finished high school. I don't know if you knew that or not." He looked over his shoulder at the lawyer.

"I didn't," Wharton said quietly.

"I guess I did okay for a dropout." Gamble shrugged his thick shoulders.

"Quite the understatement. Your success is unparalleled," Wharton said quickly.

"Hell, I started with nothing, probably end up that way."

"I hardly think that."

Gamble took a moment to straighten one of the diplomas. He turned back to Wharton. "Getting to particulars, it was obvious to me that Sidney Archer knew her husband *was* on that plane."

Wharton started. "You're saying you think she lied to you? No disrespect, Nathan, but I can't believe that."

Gamble returned to his chair. Wharton was about to speak again, but Gamble fixed the lawyer with a gaze that froze him. Gamble resumed speaking. "Jason Archer was working on a major project for me. Organizing all of Triton's financial records for the CyberCom deal. Guy's a friggin' computer genius. He had access to everything. Everything!" Gamble slowly pointed a finger across the desk. Wharton nervously rubbed his hands together but kept silent. "Now, Henry, you know that CyberCom is a deal I have to have – at least everyone keeps telling me that."

"Absolutely brilliant match," Wharton ventured.

"Something like that." Gamble pulled out a cigar and took a minute to light up. He blew smoke in Wharton's general direction. "Anyway, on the one hand I've got Jason Archer privy to all my stuff, and on the other I've got Sidney Archer heading up my deal team. You following me?"

Wharton's brow collapsed in puzzlement. "I'm afraid, no, I'm—"

"There are other companies out there who want CyberCom as badly as I do. They'd pay a lot of money to get their hands on my deal terms. Then they'd come in and screw me. I don't like to get fucked, as least not that way. You understand?"

"Yes, certainly, Nathan. But how—"

"And you also know that one of the companies who'd like to get their hands on CyberCom is RTG."

"Nathan, if you're suggesting—"

"Your firm also represents RTG."

"Nathan, you know we've taken care of that. This firm is not representing RTG on their bid for CyberCom in any way, shape or form."

"Philip Goldman's still a partner here, isn't he? And he's still RTG's top gun, isn't he?"

"Of course. We couldn't exactly ask him to leave. It was merely a client conflict and one that has been more than adequately compensated for. Philip Goldman is not working with RTG on its bid for CyberCom."

"You're sure?"

"Positive," Wharton said quickly.

Gamble smoothed down the front of his shirt. "Are you having Goldman followed twenty-four hours a day, his phone lines tapped, his mail read, his business associates shadowed?"

"No, of course not!"

"Then you can hardly be positive he's not working for RTG and against me, can you?"

"I have his word," Wharton said curtly. "And we have certain controls in place."

Gamble played with an elegantly shaped ring on one of his fingers. "Much the same, you can't know what your other partners are really up to, including Sidney Archer, can you?"

"She has the highest integrity of anyone I've ever met, not to mention one of the sharpest minds." Wharton was bristling now.

"And yet she's completely ignorant of her own husband climbing on a plane to Los Angeles, where RTG happens to have its U.S. headquarters. That's quite a coincidence, don't you think?"

"You can't blame her husband's actions on Sidney."

Gamble took the cigar out of his mouth and deliberately removed a bit of fuzz from his suit coat. "What are the Triton billings up to per year now, Henry? Twenty million? Forty million? I can get the exact number when I get back to the office. It's in that ballpark, wouldn't you say?" Gamble stood up. "Now, you and I go back a few years. You know my style. Somebody thinks they got the best of me, they're wrong. It may take me some time, but the knife comes back at you and cuts twice as deep as the hit I took." Gamble put the cigar on Wharton's desk, placed his hands palm down on the leather surface and leaned forward so that he was barely a foot from Wharton's face. "If I lose CyberCom because my own people sold me out, when I come back at the persons responsible it'll be like the big old Mississippi flooding its banks. A whole lot of potential victims out there, most of them entirely blameless, only I'm not going to take the time to sort them out. Do you understand me?" Gamble's tone was low and calm and yet it slammed into Wharton like a giant fist.

Wharton swallowed hard as he stared into the intense brown eyes of the Triton chief. "I believe I do, yes."

Gamble put on his overcoat and picked up his cigar stub. "Have a good day, Henry. When you talk to Sidney, tell her I said hello."

It was one o'clock in the afternoon when Sidney pulled the Ford out of the parking lot of the Boar's Head and quickly made her way back toward Route 29. She drove past the old Memorial Gymnasium where she had once grunted and sweated and hit tennis balls in between the rigors of law school. She pulled her car into a parking garage at the Corner, a favorite hangout of the college crowd, with its numerous bookstores, restaurants and bars.

She slipped into one of the cafés and purchased a cup of coffee and a copy of the day's *Washington Post*. She sat down at one of the small wooden tables and looked over the paper's headlines. She almost fell out of her chair.

The type was bold, thick and marched across the page with the urgency its contents deserved. FEDERAL RESERVE BOARD CHAIRMAN ARTHUR LIEBERMAN KILLED IN AIRPLANE CRASH. Next to the headline was a photo of Lieberman. Sidney was struck by the man's penetrating eyes.

Sidney quickly read the story. Lieberman had been a passenger on Flight 3223. He took regular monthly trips to Los Angeles to meet with the San Francisco Federal Reserve Bank president, Charles Tiedman, and the ill-fated Western Airlines flight had been one of those regular excursions. Sixty-two years old, and divorced, Lieberman had headed the Federal Reserve for the last four years. The article devoted a great deal of space to Lieberman's illustrious financial career and the respect he commanded across the globe. Indeed, the official news of his death had not been reported until now, because the government was doing its best to prevent a panic in the financial community. Despite those efforts, the financial markets all over the world had begun to suffer. The story ended with a notice of a memorial service for Lieberman the following Sunday in Washington.

There was an additional story about the plane accident farther back in the front section. There were no new developments, only that the NTSB was still investigating. It could be over a year before the world knew why Flight 3223 had ended up in a farmer's plowed-under cornfield instead of on the tarmac at LAX. Weather, mechanical failure, sabotage and everything in between was being considered, but for now it was all just speculation.

Sidney finished her coffee, discarded the newspaper and pulled her portable phone out of her bag. She dialed her parents' house and spoke for some time to her daughter, coaxing a few words out of Amy; her daughter was still shy on the phone. Then Sidney spent a few minutes talking with her mother and father. She next called her answering machine. There were numerous messages, but one that plainly stood out from the rest: Henry Wharton. Tyler, Stone had generously allowed her all the time off she needed to deal with this personal catastrophe. Sidney was convinced that the rest of her life would not be long enough. Henry had sounded worried, nervous even. She knew what that meant: Nathan Gamble had paid him a visit.

She quickly dialed the familiar number and was

put through to Wharton's office. She tried her best to steady her nerves while she waited for him to pick up. Wharton could be a holy terror or awe-inspiring mentor, depending on whether you were in favor or not. He had always been one of Sidney's biggest supporters. But now? She took a deep breath when he came on the line.

"Hello, Henry."

"Sid, how are you holding up?"

"I'm still numb, to tell you the truth."

"Maybe that's best. For now. You'll get through this. It might not seem like it, but you will. You're strong."

"Thanks for the support, Henry. I do feel bad for leaving you in the lurch. What with CyberCom and all."

"I know, Sidney. Don't worry about that."

"Who's taking the lead on it?" She wanted to avoid diving right into the Gamble issue.

Wharton didn't answer right away. When he did, his voice was lower. "Sid, what do you think of Paul Brophy?"

The question caught her by surprise, but it brought some welcome relief. Perhaps she had been wrong about Gamble talking to Wharton. "I like Paul, Henry."

"Yes, yes, I know that. He's a pleasant enough fellow, talented rainmaker, talks a good game."

Sidney spoke slowly. "You want to know whether he can head the CyberCom deal?"

"As you know, he's been involved up until now. But it's stepped up to another level. I want to keep the circle of attorneys with access as limited as possible. You know why. It's no secret about our potential problem with Goldman and his representation of RTG. I don't want even the hint of an impropriety. I also only want guns on that team that can contribute real substance to the process. I'd like your opinion on him under those circumstances."

"This conversation is confidential?"

"Absolutely."

Sidney spoke with authority, grateful to be analyzing, for the moment, something other than her personal loss. "Henry, you know as well as I do that deals as complex as this one are like chess games. You have to see five or ten moves ahead. And you don't get second chances. Paul has a bright future at the firm, but he does not possess the breadth of vision for the deal, or attention to detail. He does not belong on the final negotiation team for the CyberCom acquisition."

"Thank you, Sidney, those were my thoughts precisely."

"Henry, I don't think my comments are exactly earth-shattering news to you. Why was he being considered?"

"Let's just say he expressed a very strong interest in heading the deal. Not hard to see why; it would be a lucrative feather in anyone's cap."

"I see."

"I'm going to put Roger Egert in charge."

"He's a first-rate transaction attorney."

"He was very complimentary of your work on the matter thus far. 'Perfectly positioned,' I think were his words." Wharton paused for a moment. "I hate to ask this, Sidney, I really do."

"What, Henry?"

She heard him let out a long breath. "Well, I promised myself I wouldn't do this – it's just that you're so damn indispensable." He paused again.

"Henry, please, what is it?"

"Could you take a moment to talk to Egert? He's almost up to speed, but a few minutes with you on the strategic and tactical issues would be invaluable.

145

I know that it would. I certainly wouldn't ask it, Sidney, if it weren't vitally important. In any event, you'll also have to provide him with the pass code for the master computer file."

Sidney covered the phone and sighed. She knew Henry meant well, business always came first with him. "I'll call him today, Henry."

"I won't forget, Sidney."

Her cellular was drowning in static. Sidney walked out of the café to get a better reception. Outside, Henry Wharton's tone had changed slightly.

"I received a visit from Nathan Gamble this morning."

Sidney stopped walking and leaned up against the brick wall of the café. She closed her eyes and grit her teeth until they hurt. "I'm surprised he waited so long, Henry."

"He was a little distraught, Sid, to say the least. He firmly believes you lied to him."

"Henry, I know this looks bad." She hesitated and then decided to come clean. "Jason told me he had a job interview in Los Angeles. He obviously didn't want Triton to know. He swore me to secrecy. That's why I didn't tell Gamble."

"Sid, you're Triton's lawyer. There are no secrets—"

"Come on, Henry, this is my husband we're talking about. His taking another job isn't going to damage Triton. And he doesn't have a noncompete."

"Still, Sidney, it hurts me to say this, but I'm not sure you exercised the best judgment in the matter. Gamble suggested quite strongly to me that he suspected Jason of stealing corporate secrets."

"Jason would never do that!"

"That's not the point. It's how the client perceives it. Your having lied to Nathan Gamble does not help

146

matters. Do you know what would happen to the firm if he were to pull the Triton account? And don't think he wouldn't." Wharton's voice was rising steadily.

"Henry, when Gamble wanted to teleconference Jason in, I had maybe two seconds to think about it."

"Well, for God's sake why didn't you tell Gamble the truth? As you said, he wouldn't care."

"Because a few seconds later I found out my husband was dead!"

Neither one said anything for a moment; however, immense friction was clearly present. "Some time has passed now," Wharton reminded her. "If you didn't want to tell them, you could have confided in me. I would've taken care of it for you. Now, I believe I can still patch things up. Gamble can't hold it against *us* that your husband wanted to change jobs. I'm not sure Gamble will be too excited about your working on his matters in the future, Sidney. Perhaps it's good you're taking some time off. It'll pass over, though. I'll call him right now."

When she spoke, Sidney's voice was barely audible. It felt as though a large fist was wedged down her esophagus. "You can't tell Gamble about the job interview, Henry."

"Excuse me?"

"You can't do it."

"Would you mind telling me why not?"

"Because I found out that Jason wasn't interviewing with any other company. Apparently . . ." She paused and forced back a sob. "Apparently he lied to me."

When Wharton again spoke, his tone was one of barely suppressed anger. "I cannot tell you the irreparable damage that this situation may cause and may well already have caused."

"Henry, I don't know what's going on. All I'm

147

telling you is what I know, which isn't much."

"What exactly am I supposed to tell Gamble? He's expecting an answer."

"Put the onus on me, Henry. Tell him I can't be reached. I'm not returning calls. You're working on it and I won't be back at the office until you get to the bottom of the matter."

Wharton thought that over for a moment. "I guess that might work. At least temporarily. I appreciate your taking responsibility for the situation, Sidney. I know it's not of your making, but the *firm* certainly shouldn't suffer. That's my chief concern."

"I understand, Henry. In the meantime, I'll do my best to find out what was going on."

"You sure you're up to that?" Under the circumstances, Wharton felt compelled to ask the question, although he was certain of the answer.

"Do I have a choice, Henry?"

"Our prayers are with you, Sidney. Call if you need anything. We're a family at Tyler, Stone. We take care of each other."

Sidney clicked off her phone and put it away. Wharton's words had hurt her deeply, but maybe she was just being naïve. She and Henry were professional colleagues and friends, to a point. Their phone conversation had underscored to her just how superficial most professional relationships are. As long as you were productive, didn't cause waves, kept the sum of the whole thriving, you had nothing to worry about. Now, suddenly a single mom, she had to be careful that her legal career didn't abruptly vanish. She would have to pile that one next to all the other problems she currently had.

She took the brick walkway, cut across Ivy Road and headed over to the university's famed Rotunda building. She made her way through the equally famous Lawn portion of the campus grounds, where the university's elite students lived in one-room quarters that had changed little from Thomas Jefferson's time, with fireplaces the only source of heat. The simple beauty of the campus had enthralled her whenever she had visited before. Now, framed against a pristine late-fall morning, it was barely noticed. She had many questions, and it was time she started getting some answers. She sat down on the steps of the Rotunda and once again pulled her phone from her purse. She punched in the required numbers. The phone rang twice.

"Triton Global."

"Kay?" Sidney asked.

"Sid?" Kay Vincent was Jason's secretary. A plump woman in her fifties, she had adored Jason and had even served as a babysitter for Amy on several occasions. Sidney had liked her from the start, both sharing common perspectives on mother-hood, work and men.

"Kay, how are you? I'm sorry I haven't called before."

"How am I? Oh, Lord, Sid, I am so sorry. So damn sorry."

Sidney could hear the tears welling up in the older woman's voice.

"I know, Kay. I know. It's all been so sudden. So . . ." Sidney's voice trailed off, then she steeled herself. She had to know some things, and Kay Vincent was the most honest source she could think of. "Kay, you know that Jason took some time off from the office."

"Right. He said he was going to paint the kitchen and fix up the garage. He'd been talking about it for a week."

"He never mentioned the trip to Los Angeles to you?"

"No. I was shocked to hear he was on that plane."

149

"Has anyone been in to talk to you about Jason?"

"Lots of people. Everyone's devastated."

"How about Quentin Rowe?"

"He's been in several times." Kay paused and then said, "Sid, why all these questions?"

"Kay, this needs to be kept between us, okay?"

"All right." She sounded very reluctant.

"I thought Jason was going to L.A. for a job interview with another company because that's what he told me. I recently found out that that wasn't true."

"My God!"

While Kay slowly digested the news, Sidney ventured another question. "Kay, is there any reason you could think of why Jason would have lied about that? Was he acting strange at work?"

There was a considerable pause now. "Kay?" Sidney fidgeted on the steps. The cold from the bricks had begun to chill her. She abruptly stood up.

"Sid, we have really strict rules about discussing any of the company's business. I don't want to get into trouble."

"I know that, Kay. I'm one of Triton's attorneys, remember?"

"Well, this is a little bit different." Kay's voice abruptly disappeared from the line. Sidney wondered if she had hung up, but then the voice reappeared. "Can you call me later tonight? I don't really want to talk on company time about this. I'll be home around eight. You still have my home phone?"

"I've got it, Kay. Thanks."

Kay Vincent hung up without saying anything else.

Jason rarely discussed Triton's business with Sidney, although as an attorney at Tyler, Stone, she was immersed in numerous matters for the company. Her husband took the ethical responsibilities of his position very seriously. He had always been careful not to put his wife in an awkward situation. At least until now. She slowly walked back to the parking garage.

After paying the attendant, she started toward her car. Suddenly she turned, but by then the man had disappeared around the corner. She walked rapidly back to the street next to the garage and peered down it. No one was in sight. There were numerous shops along there, though. Someone could have disappeared into any one of them in a few seconds. She had first noticed him looking at her while she was seated on the steps of the Rotunda. He had been standing behind one of the many trees sprinkled around the Lawn. Busy talking to Kay, she had quickly dismissed him as some guy just checking her out for the obvious reason. He was tall, at least six feet, lean and dressed in a dark overcoat. His face had been partially covered by sunglasses and the overcoat's collar had been turned up, further hiding his features. A brown hat had covered his hair, although she had managed to note that it was light in color, reddish blond, perhaps. For a brief moment she wondered if paranoia had been added to her growing list of problems. She couldn't worry about it right now. She had to get home. Tomorrow she would pick up her daughter. She then remembered that her mother had mentioned a memorial service for Jason. The details of that would have to be gone over. Amid all the mystery surrounding her late husband's last day, the recollection of the memorial service had brought back the crushing knowledge that Jason was indeed dead. No matter how he had deceived her, or for what reason he had done so, he was gone. She headed back home.

EIGHTEEN

Under drifting cloud cover that was quickly overtaking the razor-blue sky, a chilly wind whipped through the crash site. Armies of people walked the grounds, marking debris with red flags, forming a mass of crimson in the cornfield. Near the crater sat a crane with a dangling bucket large enough to hold two grown men. Another such crane hovered over the crater, its long cable and bucket disappearing into the depths of this shallow hell. Other cables connected to motorized winches set on flatbed trucks snaked down into the pit. Heavy equipment was lumbering nearby in preparation for the final excavation of the impact crater. The most critical piece, the flight data recorder, had not yet been unearthed.

Outside the yellow barricades a number of tents had been raised. They served as depositories of collected evidence for on-site analysis. In one such tent George Kaplan was pouring hot coffee from his thermos into two cups. He briefly scanned the area. Luckily the snow had stopped as quickly as it had started. However, the temperature had remained cool and the weather forecast called for more precipitation. He knew that was not good. Snow would make a logistical nightmare even more daunting.

Kaplan handed one of the steaming cups to Lee Sawyer, who had followed the NTSB investigator's gaze around the crash site.

"That was a good call on the fuel tank, George.

The evidence was very slight, but lab results show it was an old reliable: hydrochloric acid. Tests indicated that it would've eaten through the aluminium alloy in about two to four hours. Faster if the acid was heated. Doesn't look like it was accidental."

Kaplan grunted loudly. "Shit, like a mechanic would be walking around with acid and just accidentally smear it on the fuel tank."

"I never thought it was an accident, George."

Kaplan threw up his hand in apology. "And you can carry hydrochloric acid in a plastic container, could even use a squirt bottle with a modified tip so you can gauge how much you're applying. Plastic won't trip a metal detector. It was a good choice." Kaplan's face twisted in disgust.

He looked out at the crash site for a few more seconds and then stirred, turning to Sawyer. "Nailing down the timing that close is good. Cuts down the list of possible suspects who would've had access."

Sawyer nodded in agreement. "We're following that up right now." He took a long sip of the coffee.

"You really think somebody blew up an entire planeload of people to take out one guy?"

"Maybe."

"Christ Almighty, I don't mean to sound callous, but if you want to kill the guy, why not just grab him off the street and put a bullet in his head? Why this?" He pointed at the crater and then slumped back in his seat, his eyes half closed, one hand rubbing viciously at his left temple.

Sawyer sat in one of the folding chairs. "We're not sure that's the case, but Lieberman was the only passenger on the plane warranting that kind of special attention."

"Why the hell go to all this trouble to kill the Fed chairman?"

Sawyer pulled his coat tighter around him as the cold wind swirled inside the tent space. "Well, the financial markets took a tremendous beating when the news broke of Lieberman's death. The Dow lost almost twelve hundred points, or about twenty-five percent of its total. In two days. That makes the Crash of 1929 look like a hiccup. The overseas markets are being battered too." Sawyer stared pointedly at Kaplan. "And wait until news leaks that the plane was sabotaged. That Lieberman might have been deliberately killed. Who the hell knows what that will trigger?"

Kaplan's eyes widened. "Jesus! All that for one guy?"

"Like I said, somebody killed Superman."

"So you got a lot of potential suspects – foreign governments, international terrorists, crap like that, right?" Kaplan shook his head as he contemplated the number of bad people on the increasingly small sphere they all called home.

Sawyer shrugged. "Let's say it's not going to be your run-of-the mill street criminal."

The two men fell silent and again stared over at the crash site. They watched the crane's cable reverse its direction, and within two minutes a bucket carrying two men appeared above the pit. The crane swung around and gently rested the bucket on the ground. The two men clambered out. Sawyer and Kaplan watched with growing excitement as the pair raced toward them.

The first to arrive was a young man whose white-blond hair partially obscured a choirboy's features. In his hand was clenched a plastic baggie. Inside the baggie was a small, metallic, rectangular object, heavily charred. The other man lumbered up behind him. He was older, and his red face and labored breathing spoke of the rarity of his finding himself

154

racing across wide cornfields.

"I couldn't believe it," the younger man almost shouted. "The starboard wing, or what was left if it, was sitting right on top, pretty much intact. I guess the left side took the brunt of the explosion with the full tank. Looks like when the nose burrowed into the ground, it created an opening slightly larger than the circumference of the fuselage. When the wings hit the sides of the pit, they crumpled back and over the fuselage. Damn miracle, if you ask me."

Kaplan took the baggie and stepped over to the table. "Where'd you find it?"

"It was attached to the wing's interior side, right next to the access panel for the fuel tank. It must have been placed inside the wing on the inboard side of the starboard engine. I'm not sure what it is, but I can damn sure tell you it doesn't belong on a plane."

"So it was placed to the left of where the wing sheared off?" Kaplan asked.

"Exactly, Chief. Another couple inches and it would've been gone too."

The older man spoke. "From the looks of it, the fuselage shielded the starboard wing from a good deal of the initial postcrash explosion. When the sides of the crater collapsed, all the dirt must've cut off the fire almost immediately." He paused and then added solemnly, "But the forward section of the cabin's gone. I mean nothing's left, like it was never there."

Kaplan handed the baggie over to Sawyer. "Do you know what the hell this is?"

Sawyer's face broke into a dark scowl. "Yeah, I do."

NINETEEN

Sidney Archer had driven to her office and was now seated at her desk; her office door was closed and locked. It was a little after eight in the evening, but she could hear the faint buzz of a fax machine in the background. She picked up the phone and dialed Kay Vincent's number at home.

A man answered.

"Kay Vincent, please. It's Sidney Archer."

"Just a minute."

As Sidney waited, she looked around the confines of her office. A place normally of deep comfort to her, it looked strangely out of focus. The diplomas on the wall were hers, but at this moment she could not seem to remember when or where she had earned them. She had become purely reactive, battered by one shock after another. She wondered if a new surprise was awaiting her at the other end of the phone line.

"Sidney?"

"Hello, Kay."

The voice sounded ashamed. "I feel so bad, I didn't even ask you this morning about Amy. How is she?"

"She's at my parents' right now." She swallowed hard and then added, "She doesn't know, of course."

"I'm sorry I acted the way I did at work. You know how that place is. They get uptight if they think you're taking personal calls on their time."

"I know, Kay. I didn't know who else to talk to

156

over there." She didn't add, *whom she could trust.*

"I understand, Sid."

Sidney took a deep breath. She might as well get right down to it. Had she looked up, she might have noticed the doorknob on her door slowly turn and then stop as the locking mechanism prohibited further movement.

"Kay, is there something you wanted to tell me? About Jason?"

There was a perceptible pause on the other end of the line before Kay answered. "I couldn't have asked for a better boss. He worked real hard, was moving up fast. But he still took the time to talk to everybody, spend time with them." Kay stopped talking, perhaps trying to collect her thoughts before plunging ahead, Sidney wasn't sure. When Kay didn't say anything, Sidney floated a question. "Well, did that change? Was Jason acting differently?"

"Yes." The word was blurted out so quickly, Sidney almost didn't catch it.

"How so?"

"It was a bunch of little things, really. The first thing that had me concerned was Jason ordering a lock for his door."

"A lock on an office door isn't unusual, Kay. I have one on mine." Sidney glanced over at her own door. The doorknob was now motionless.

"I know that, Sid. The thing is, Jason already had a lock on his door."

"I don't understand, Kay. If he already had a lock, why did he order another one?"

"The lock he had on his door was a pretty simple one, a pop-out lock on the doorknob. Yours is probably one of those."

Sidney glanced at her door. "That's right, it is. Aren't all office door locks pretty much the same?"

"Not these days, Sid. Jason had a computerized

lock put on his system that required a smart card."

"Smart card?"

"You know, a plastic card with a microchip thing in it. I'm not sure exactly how it works, but you need it to get into the building here, and certain restricted access areas, among other things."

Sidney fumbled through her purse and pulled out the plastic card she had taken from Jason's desk at home.

"Does anyone else at Triton have those kinds of locks on their office doors?"

"About a half dozen. Most of them are in finance, though."

"Did Jason tell you why he had ordered the additional security for his office?"

"I asked him, because I was concerned that maybe there had been a break-in and nobody told us. But Jason said he had taken on some additional responsibilities with the company and had some items in his keeping that he wanted additional protection for."

Tired of sitting, Sidney stood up and paced. She looked out the window into the darkness. Across the street, the lights of Spencers, a posh new restaurant, gleamed back at her. A stream of taxis and luxury cars disgorged elegantly dressed parties who sauntered into the establishment for a night of fine food, drink and the latest city gossip. Sidney pulled the blind down. She let out her breath and sat on her credenza, slipping out of her shoes and absently rubbing sore and tired feet.

"Why didn't Jason want you to tell anyone that he had taken on additional responsibilities?"

"I don't know. He's been promoted three times already in the company. So I know it wasn't that. You wouldn't be secretive about something like that anyway, would you?"

Sidney pondered this information for a few

seconds. Jason hadn't mentioned a promotion to her and it was inconceivable that he would not. "Did he tell you who had given him the additional responsibilities?"

"No. And I really didn't want to pry."

"Did you tell anyone else what Jason had told you?"

"No one," Kay said firmly.

Sidney tended to believe her. She shook her head. "What else had you concerned?"

"Well, Jason kept a lot more to himself lately. He also made excuses for missing staff meetings, things like that. This had been going on for at least a month."

Sidney stopped rubbing nervously at her foot.

"Jason never mentioned testing the waters with another company?"

"Never." Sidney could almost feel the firm shake of Kay's head through the phone line.

"Did you ever ask Jason if anything was bothering him?"

"I did once, only he wasn't real receptive. He was a good friend, but he was also my boss. I didn't want to push it."

"I understand Kay." Sidney slid off the credenza and replaced her shoes. She noticed a shadow pass under her door and then it stopped. She waited for a few more seconds, but the shadow did not budge. She clicked the button on her receiver to portable use and disconnected the cord. A thought had occurred to her.

"Kay, has anyone actually been into Jason's office?"

"Well . . ." Kay's hesitation allowed Sidney to come up with another inquiry.

"But how could they, with all the extra security measures on his office door?"

"That's the problem, Sid. No one had the code or

Jason's security card. The door's three inches of solid wood set on a steel frame. Mr. Gamble and Mr. Rowe haven't been in the office this week and I think no one else really knew what to do."

"So no one's been in Jason's office since it . . . it happened?" Sidney looked down at the smart card.

"Nobody. Mr Rowe was in late today. He's having the company that installed the lock come tomorrow to open it."

"Who else has been around?"

Sidney could hear Kay let out her breath. "They had someone over from SecurTech."

"SecurTech?" Sidney shifted the phone receiver to her other ear as she continued to eye the shadow. She inched toward the door. She was not concerned that it was an intruder. Plenty of people were still working at the office. "That's Triton's security consultant, isn't it?"

"Yes. I was wondering why they were called in. The word is it's pretty normal procedure when something happens like this."

Sidney was now to the right of the door, her free hand inching toward the doorknob.

"Sidney, I've got some things of Jason's at my workstation. Photos, a sweater of his he let me borrow one time, some books. He tried to get me interested in eighteenth- and nineteenth-century literature, although I'm afraid I never did."

"He did the same thing with Amy until I pointed out it would probably help to have her learn her ABCs before she plunged headlong into Voltaire."

The two women laughed together, which felt very good under the awful circumstances.

"You can come by whenever you want to pick them up."

"I will, Kay, maybe we can have lunch . . . and talk some more."

"I'd like that. I'd like that a lot."

"I really appreciate what you've told me, Kay. You've been a big help."

"Well, I cared a lot for Jason. He was a good, decent man."

Sidney felt the tears start to bubble to the surface, but when she looked at the shadow under her door again, her nerves hardened. "Yes, he was." The last word she uttered contained a dead-cold finality.

"Sid, you need anything, and I mean anything, you just call, you hear me?"

Sidney smiled. "Thank you, Kay. I may just take you up on that." As soon as she clicked off the phone and laid it down, Sidney yanked her office door open.

Philip Goldman did not appear startled. He stood there calmly staring at Sidney with his balding head, expressive face, protruding eyes, slender, rounded shoulders and the beginnings of a belly. His clothing appeared to be and was indeed very expensive. Standing in her shoes, Sidney was taller than Philip by two inches.

"Sidney, I was passing by and noticed the light on. I had no idea you were here."

"Hello, Philip." Sidney eyed him closely. Goldman was a slender notch below Henry Wharton in the Tyler, Stone partnership pecking order. He had a substantial client base and his life was focused on his own professional career enhancement.

"I must say I'm surprised to see you here, Sidney."

"Going home right now isn't such an appealing idea, Philip."

He slowly nodded his head. "Yes, yes, I can well understand that." He glanced over her shoulder at the phone receiver lying on the shelf of one of the bookcases. "Talking with someone?"

"Personal. There are a lot of details I need to go over now."

161

"Of course. Death is terrible enough to confront. Sudden death even more so." He continued to stare pointedly at her.

Sidney felt her face flushing. She turned way, grabbed her bag off the couch and pulled her coat from behind the door, partially closing the door on Goldman, who had to step back quickly to avoid being struck.

She put on her coat and poised her hand over the light switch. "I've got an appointment I'm late for."

Goldman stepped back into the hallway. Sidney made a show of locking her office door before shutting it.

"This may be an awkward time, Sidney, but I wanted to congratulate you on your handling of the CyberCom transaction."

She jerked her head around. "I'm certain we should not be discussing that subject, Philip."

"I know, Sidney," he said. "However, I still read the *Wall Street Journal* and your name has been mentioned several times. Nathan Gamble must be very pleased."

"Thank you, Philip." She turned to face him. "I have to go now."

"Let me know if there's anything I can do for you."

Sidney quickly nodded and then moved past Goldman. She walked down the hallway toward the firm's main entrance and disappeared around the corner.

Goldman strode quickly down the hallway in time to see Sidney enter the elevator. He then walked casually back down the corridor to Sidney's office. After looking in both directions, he pulled out a key, inserted it in the lock, opened the door and went inside. The lock clicked into place, and then there was silence.

TWENTY

Sidney pulled the Ford into Triton's vast parking lot and got out. She buttoned up her coat against the chilly wind, checked her purse once more to make sure the plastic card was there and walked as normally as she could to the fifteen-story building that housed Triton's world headquarters. She identified herself into the speaker located next to the entrance. A video camera mounted over the doorway was pointed directly at her head. Then a compartment next to the speaker swung open and she was directed to insert her thumb into the fingerprint scanner that was now revealed. Triton's after-hours security measures probably matched those of the CIA, she surmised. The glass and chrome doors slid noiselessly open. She walked into the building's lobby, which featured a soft waterfall, soaring atrium and enough polished marble to have emptied a good-sized quarry. When she walked toward the elevator, the lighting automatically illuminated her path. Gentle music also followed her and the elevator doors opened as she approached them. Triton's headquarters building had received the full benefit of the company's immense technological muscle.

She rode the elevator to the eighth floor and got off.

The security officer on duty there rose and walked over to her, grasping her hand. There was pain in the man's eyes.

"Hello, Charlie."

"Sidney, ma'am. I am so sorry."

"Thank you, Charlie."

Charlie shook her head. "On his way to the top. Worked harder than anybody here. A lot of times it was just him and me in the whole building. He'd bring me coffee and a little something to eat from the lunchroom. Never asked him to, he just did it. Wasn't like some of the big shots here who think they're better than you are."

"You're right, Jason wasn't like that."

"No, ma'am, he wasn't. Now what can I do for you? You need something? You just tell old Charlie what it is."

"Well, I was wondering if Kay Vincent was still here."

Charlie stared blankly at her. "Kay? I don't think so. I come on duty at nine. She's usually gone around seven so . . . I wouldn't have seen her leave. Let me check."

Charlie strode over to the console. The holster housing his revolver flapped against his side and the keys clipped to his gun belt jangled as he walked. He put on a headset and punched a button on the console. After a few seconds he shook his head. "I'm just getting her voice mail, Sidney."

"Oh. Well, she had some things . . . some things of Jason's that I wanted to pick up." Sidney looked down at the floor, apparently unable to continue speaking.

Charlie walked back over to her. He touched her arm. "Well, maybe she has them at her desk."

Sidney looked up at him. "She probably does, I would think."

Charlie hesitated. He knew this was against all the rules. But then, rules shouldn't always apply. He went back over to the console, hit a couple of buttons

164

and Sidney watched as the red light next to the door leading into the office corridor turned to green. He walked back over and, pulling keys from his belt, unlocked the door.

"You know how they freak out over security here, but I think this situation is a little different. Nobody's back there anyway. Usually this place is buzzing up until about ten, but it's the holiday week and all. I've gotta make rounds now on the fourth floor. You know where she sits, right?"

"I do, Charlie. I really appreciate this."

He gave her hand another squeeze. "Like I said, your husband was a good man."

Sidney moved down the softly lit corridor. Kay's cubicle was about halfway down, with Jason's office diagonally across from it. While Sidney walked down the hallway, she looked carefully around; all was quiet. She turned the corner and saw Kay's darkened cubicle. In a box next to her desk chair was a sweater and some framed photos. She probed underneath and lifted out a finely bound book with gilt edges. *David Copperfield.* It was one of Jason's favorites. She put the things back in the box and placed it next to the chair.

She looked around again. The corridor was also empty. Charlie had said everyone was gone, but then again, he hadn't been certain about Kay. Satisfied that she was alone at least for now, Sidney reached her husband's office door. Her hopes sank when she spied the numeric keypad. Kay hadn't mentioned that device. She thought for a moment, pulled the plastic card out of her pocket, looked around once more, and then slid it into the slot. A light on the keypad clicked on. Sidney read the word "Ready" next to the light. She thought quickly and punched in some numbers; however, the light didn't budge from its position. She became frustrated. She didn't even know how many digits to punch in, much less what they were. She tried a few more combinations without success.

She had almost decided to give up when she noted that there was a small digital screen in one corner of the numeric keypad. Apparently it was a time counter and it was now on eight seconds. The alarm light on the pad started to glow a brighter and brighter crimson. "Oh, shit," she hissed. An alarm! The counter was now at five seconds. She stood frozen. Flashing across her mind were all the results that would occur were she found here attempting to infiltrate her husband's office. None of them rated less than a complete disaster. As her eyes locked on the counter, which was now at three seconds, she broke out of her inertia. One more possible combination rocketed across her brain. Mouthing a silent prayer, her fingers punched in the numbers 0-6-1-6. She hit the last digit right as the counter clicked to zero. Waiting for the piercing alarm to explode, Sidney held her breath for one long instant.

The alarm light turned off and the door's locks clicked free. Sidney steadied herself against the wall as she slowly started breathing normally again. June 16 was Amy's birthday. Triton probably had a policy about not using personal numbers for security codes: too easy to crack. For Sidney, it was proof positive that the little girl was never really out of her father's thoughts.

She removed the plastic card from the slot. Before grasping the doorknob, she pulled a handkerchief from her purse and wound it around her hand to avoid leaving any prints. Acting the part of an intruder both exhilarated and terrified her. She felt her pulse hammering in her ears. She entered the office and quickly closed the door behind her.

The flashlight she pulled from her bag was small

but effective. Before turning it on, she checked to make sure that the window blinds were all the way down and completely closed. The thin light swept around the office. She had been here before, several times in fact, to have lunch with Jason, although they had not stayed long in his office. Usually it was just to snatch a quick kiss behind closed doors. Her light skipped to bookcases filled with technical tomes far beyond her realm of comprehension. The techno-crats really did rule, she mused for a moment, if only because they were the only ones who could fix the damn things when they broke down.

The light fell upon the computer and she quickly went over to it. It was off and the presence of another keypad made her decide not to push her luck in attempting to turn it on. She would be hopelessly lost even if she was fortunate enough to log on, since she had no idea what she was looking for or where to search. It wasn't worth the risk. A number of desk drawers were locked. The few that weren't revealed nothing of interest.

In stark contrast to her office at the law firm, there were no diplomas on the walls or other personal touches in her husband's office. She did note, with a glistening eye, that a photo of Jason and his family held a prominent position on his desk. As she looked around the office, it suddenly occurred to her that she had taken enormous risks for nothing. She whirled around at a sudden noise from somewhere within the office space. The flashlight collided with the microphone and, to her horror, the slender device bent in half. She stood completely still, listening for the sound to be repeated. Finally, after a minute of sheer terror, she turned her attention back to the slender microphone. She spent a couple of minutes trying to return it to its original shape without much success. Finally she gave up, wiped her prints from it, retreated to the door and turned off her flashlight. Using the handkerchief to grip the doorknob, she listened at the door for a moment and then exited the office.

She heard the footsteps coming as soon as she reached Kay's desk. For an instant she thought it might be Charlie, except there was no jangling of keys against his gun belt. She looked quickly around to determine which way the sounds were coming from. Clearly the person was back farther in the office. She slipped across to Kay's cubicle and knelt down behind her desk. Trying to breathe as quietly as possible, she waited as the footsteps came closer. Then they stopped. A minute went by and they did not resume. Then Sidney heard a slight clicking sound, as though something was being rotated back and forth, but only in a limited radius.

Unable to stop herself, she cautiously peered around the corner of Kay's cubicle. A man's back was barely six feet away from her. He was slowly turning the doorknob on Jason's office door back and forth. The man took a card out of his shirt pocket and started to insert it into the slot. Then he hesitated over the keypad as if deciding whether to chance it or not. Finally his courage failed and he put the card back in his pocket and turned away.

Quentin Rowe did not look pleased. He retreated down the hallway the way he had come.

Sidney slipped out from her hiding place and walked in the opposite direction. She was moving rapidly when she rounded the corner and her purse hit the wall. The noise, while not loud, seemed to echo like an explosion through the quiet hallways. Her breath caught in her throat when she heard the retreating footsteps stop and then turn as Quentin Row started to head rapidly in her direction. She hurried as fast as she could down the hallway, reached the main office door, was through it in an instant and found herself back in the reception area, staring at Charlie, who looked back at her anxiously.

"Sidney, you okay? You look white as a ghost."

The footsteps were nearing the door. Sidney put one finger to her lips, pointed in the direction of the door and motioned Charlie to go behind his console. He rapidly caught both the sounds of the footsteps and her meaning and quickly followed her instructions. Then Sidney slipped over to the rest room door that stood to the right of the entrance to the lobby. She opened her purse, poised herself at the door to the ladies' room, which she held partially open with one hand, and kept an eye on the door to the hallway. As soon as it opened and Rowe appeared, Sidney pretended to stroll out of the ladies' room fumbling with something in her purse. When she looked up, Rowe was staring at her. He held the door to the secured area open with one hand.

"Quentin?" She said it with as much surprise as she could muster.

Rowe looked from Sidney to Charlie, suspicion written all over his features.

"What are you doing here?" He did not try to hide his displeasure.

"I came to see Kay. We had talked earlier. She had some things of Jason's. Some personal effects she wanted me to have."

Rowe snapped back, "Nothing can leave the premises without prior authorization. Certainly nothing having to do with Jason."

Sidney looked at him squarely. "I know that, Quentin."

Her response surprised him.

She looked at Charlie, who stared at Rowe with unfriendly eyes. "Charlie already informed me of that, though in a much less offensive way than you just did. And he wouldn't let me back into the office area because we all know that's against the company's security policy."

"I apologize if I was little abrupt. I've been under a lot of pressure lately."

Charlie's voice was tense with a mixture of anger and incredulity. "And *she* hasn't? She just lost her husband, for God's sake."

Before Rowe could answer, Sidney cut in. "Quentin and I have already covered that topic, Charlie, in an earlier conversation. Haven't we, Quentin?"

Rowe seemed to dissolve under her withering gaze.

He decided it best to change subjects. "I thought I heard a noise." He again looked accusingly at Sidney.

Sidney answered immediately. "So did we. Right before I went to the ladies' room, Charlie went to check it out. I guess he heard you and you heard him. He didn't think anyone was still in the office. But you were." Her tone matched his in its accusatory implications.

Rowe bristled. "I'm the president of this company. I can be here at any time of the day or night and it's nobody's business but my own."

Sidney stared him down. "I'm sure you can. However, I would think that you would be working late on their behalf rather than conducting personal business, even though it's long after regular business hours. I'm speaking as a legal representative of the company, Quentin." Under normal circumstances, she never would have uttered those words to a client's senior executive.

Rowe started to sputter. "Well, of course, I meant I was working for the company. I know all—" Rowe

170

stopped abruptly when Sidney walked over to Charlie and took his hand.

"Thank you very much, Charlie. I understand that rules are rules." Rowe could not see the look she gave the elderly security guard, but it brought a grateful smile to Charlie's face.

As she turned to leave, Rowe said, "Good night, Sidney."

She didn't answer him, nor did she even look at him. After she disappeared into the elevator, Rowe looked angrily over at Charlie, who was getting up to head out the door.

"Where are you going?" he demanded.

Charlie's expression was calm. "I've got rounds to make. That's part of *my* job." He bent down to the smaller man's height when he said it. Charlie started out the door and then turned back. "Oh, it might help avoid confusion in the future if you let me know you're still around." He touched his sidearm. "We don't want no unfortunate accidents, you know?" Rowe went pale at the sight of the gun. "You hear any more noise, you come get me, okay, Mr. Rowe?"

After Charlie turned away, he broke out in a broad smile.

Rowe stood at the doorway for a minute longer, thinking intently. Then he turned and went back into the office.

TWENTY-ONE

Lee Sawyer eyed the small three-story apartment building, which was located about five miles from Dulles International Airport. Residents enjoyed a complete fitness center, Olympic-size pool and Jacuzzi, and huge party room. It was home to mostly young single professionals who got up early to make the traffic-stifling trek into downtown. The parking lot was littered with low-end Beemers, Saabs and the occasional Porche.

Sawyer was interested in only one of the occupants of this community. He was not a young lawyer, marketing executive or holder of an MBA. Sawyer briefly spoke into his walkie-talkie. Three other agents were seated in the sedan with him. Stationed around the area were five other teams of FBI agents. A black-clad squadron of the elite FBI Hostage Rescue Team (HRT) was also zeroing in on Sawyer's target. A battalion of local authorities was backing up the federal lawmen. A lot of innocent people were around, and great pains were being taken to ensure that if anyone was going to get hurt, it would be only the man whom Sawyer believed had already killed almost two hundred people.

Sawyer's plan of attack was textbook FBI. Bring overwhelming force to a completely unsuspecting target, force so overpowering, in a situation so totally controlled, that resistance was useless. Controlling the situation completely meant you could control the outcome too. Or so the theory went.

172

Every agent carried a 9m semiautomatic pistol with extra clips. Each team of agents also had one member with an appropriately named Franchi Law-12 semiautomatic shotgun and another member sporting a Colt assault rifle. The HRT members all carried heavy-caliber automatic weapons, most with electronic laser sights.

Sawyer gave the signal to move in and the teams moved forward. In less than one minute members of the HRT had reached the door of apartment number 321. Two other teams covered the only other possible escape, the two back windows of the apartment that overlooked the pool area. Snipers had already set up there, their laser sights fixed immovably on the twin apertures. After listening intently at the door of 321 for a few seconds, the HRT members exploded through the opening. No gunfire disturbed the peaceful stillness of the night. Within a minute, Sawyer received the all-clear signal. He and his men hurried up the stairs of the apartment building.

Sawyer was met by the leader of the HRT.

"Nest empty?" Sawyer asked.

The HRT man shook his head. "Might as well be. Someone beat us to it." He jerked his head in the direction of the small bedroom at the rear of the apartment.

Sawyer walked quickly back there. A shiver hit him right between the shoulder blades; the place was like the insides of a freezer. The overhead light in the bedroom was on. Three HRT members looked down at the small space between the bed and the wall. Sawyer followed their gaze and his spirits sank

The man was lying face down. Multiple gunshot wounds in the back and head were plainly visible; so were the firearm and the twelve pieces of brass that littered the floor. Sawyer, with the aid of two HRT

173

members, carefully lifted the body, turning it sideways before returning it exactly to the spot where it had been before.

Sawyer rose, shaking his head. He barked into his walkie-talkie. "Tell the state guys to get a medical examiner out here and I want the forensics team here yesterday."

Sawyer looked at the body. Well, at least the guy wouldn't be sabotaging any more planes, although a full clip into his body didn't seem like nearly enough punishment for what the sonofabitch had done. But a dead man couldn't talk either. Sawyer moved out of the room, his walkie-talkie squeezed tightly in his hand. In the empty hallway he noted that the air-conditioning had been turned on full blast. The apartment's temperature hovered around thirty degrees. He quickly jotted down the precise temperature setting and then, using the point of a pencil so as not to destroy any possible fingerprints, he turned the heat back on. He wasn't about to let his men freeze to death while they investigated the crime scene. He slumped against the wall, momentarily depressed. While he'd known the odds were long that they would find the suspect at his apartment, the fact that they had found him murdered clearly indicated that someone was a couple of steps ahead of the FBI. Was there a leak somewhere, or had this murder been part of some master plan?

He gripped the walkie-talkie and headed back to the bedroom.

TWENTY-TWO

S idney exited the Triton building and started across the parking lot. She was so deep in thought she didn't see the black stretch limousine until it careened to a halt directly in front of her. The rear door opened and Richard Lucas stepped out. He was dressed in a dark blue conservative single-breasted suit. His face was chiefly distinguished by a pug nose and a pair of small eyes that were too close together by about an inch. His breadth of shoulders and the omnipresent hump under his suit coat made him an imposing physical presence.

"Mr. Gamble would like to meet with you." His tone was even. He held the door open and Sidney could see the holstered pistol under his coat. She froze, swallowed hard and then her eyes blazed. "I'm not sure that fits my schedule right now."

Lucas shrugged. "As you wish. However, Mr. Gamble thought it best to speak directly with you. To get your version of the facts before he decides upon any type of action. He felt the sooner the meeting took place the better for *all* concerned."

Sidney took a deep breath and looked at the limo's black-tinted windows. "Where is the meeting to take place?"

"Mr. Gamble's estate in Middleburg." He checked his watch. "Our ETA is thirty-five minutes. We will, of course, take you back to your car after the meeting is concluded."

She eyed him sharply. "Do I really have a choice?"

"A person always has choices, Ms. Archer."

Sidney pulled her coat tighter around her and climbed in. Lucas sat across from her. She didn't ask any more questions and he ventured nothing further. His eyes, however, remained squarely upon her.

Sidney was dimly aware of an enormous house of stone surrounded by meticulously landscaped tree-lined grounds. *You can make it through this*, she thought. Interrogation was often a two-way street. If Gamble wanted answers from her, she would do her best to get some from him. She followed Lucas through a double-door entryway, down an impressive hallway and into a large chamber of polished mahogany and comfortable seating. Original oil paintings portraying distinctly masculine subjects covered the walls. A small fire burned in the hearth. On a table situated in one corner a dinner with two settings was laid out. Although she had no appetite, the aroma was enticing nevertheless. In the center of the table a bottle of wine was chilling. The door closed behind her with a click. She went over and confirmed that it was indeed locked. She whirled around as she heard a slight movement behind her.

Nathan Gamble, dressed casually in an open-collared shirt and cuffed slacks, came around the corner of a high-wingback chair that had been turned toward the far wall. His penetrating gaze made her draw her coat more closely around her. He moved over to the food. "You hungry?"

"Not really, thanks."

"Well, you change your mind, there's plenty to eat. I hope you don't mind if I do."

"It's your house."

Gamble sat down at the table and started fixing his

plate. Then she watched as he poured two glasses of wine. "When I bought this place it came with a wine cellar and two thousand very dusty bottles of wine. Now, I don't know crap about wine, but my people tell me it's a first-rate collection, not that I intend on collecting. Where I come from, you collect stamps. This stuff you drink." He held up a glass for her.

"I really don't think—"

"I hate to drink alone. Makes me think I'm the only one having fun. Besides, it worked for you on the plane, right?"

She finally nodded, slowly removed her coat and took the glass from him. The room was soothingly warm, but she remained on her guard; it was SOP when in the vicinity of active volcanoes and people like Nathan Gamble. She sat down at the dinner table and eyed him while he started eating. He looked at her and motioned at the food. "You sure you're not interested?"

She held up her glass. "This is fine, thanks."

He shrugged, gulped his wine and then proceeded to slice up a hefty piece of steak. "I talked to Henry Wharton recently. Nice guy, always looking out for his people. I appreciate that in an employer. I look out for my people too." He sopped gravy on to a roll and bit a chunk off.

"Henry has been a wonderful mentor to me."

"That's interesting. I never had a mentor, coming up. That might've been nice." He chuckled lightly.

Sidney glanced around the elegant room. "It doesn't look like it hurt you any."

Gamble raised his wineglass, tapped it to hers and then resumed eating. "You holding up? You look like you've lost some weight from the last time I saw you."

"I'm doing okay. Thanks for asking." She flicked at her hair while watching him carefully, trying to keep her nerves in check. She was waiting for the inevitable moment when the small talk would abruptly end. She would have preferred to have gotten right down to business. Gamble was merely playing with her. She had seen him do it dozens of times with other people.

Gamble poured himself another glass of wine and despite her protests, he topped off Sidney's glass. Twenty minutes of innocuous conversation later, Gamble wiped off his mouth with his napkin, stood up and led Sidney over to an oversized leather sofa in front of the fire. She sat down and crossed her legs and took an invisible deep breath. He remained standing by the fireplace mantel and looked at her from under hooded eyelids.

She studied the fire for a moment, sipped the wine and then looked up at him. If he wasn't going to start, she decided she would. "I spoke with Henry too, apparently soon after you did."

Gamble nodded absently. "I thought Henry might give you a buzz after our little talk." Underneath her opaque exterior, Sidney felt herself growing angry at how Gamble manipulated and bullied people to get what he wanted. Gamble produced a cigar from a humidor perched on the mantel. "You mind?"

"As I said, it's your house."

"Some people say cigars aren't habit-forming; I'm not so sure about that. You have to die from something, right?"

She took another sip of wine. "Lucas said you wanted to meet. I'm not privy to the agenda, so would you like to begin?"

Gamble took several short puffs on his cigar to get it going before answering. "You lied to me on the plane, didn't you?" His tone was not one of anger, which surprised her. If anything, she had assumed that a man like Nathan Gamble would have exhibited unbridled fury at such an offense.

"I wasn't completely truthful, no."

A faint twitch moved across Gamble's features. "You're so damned pretty, I keep forgetting you're an attorney. I guess there's a difference between lying and not being completely truthful, although, frankly, I'm not all that interested in the distinction. You lied to me, that's all I'm going to remember."

"I can understand that."

"Why was your husband on that plane?" The question shot out of Gamble's mouth, but his features remained impassive as he stared at her.

Sidney hesitated, then decided to answer fully. It was going to come out at some point. "Jason told me he had been offered an executive position at another technology company based in Los Angeles. He said he was going out for a last round of meetings."

"What company? RTG?"

"It wasn't RTG. It wasn't a direct competitor of yours at all. That's why I didn't think it important to tell you the truth. But as it turns out, it really doesn't matter which company it was."

"Why not?" Gamble looked surprised.

"Because what Jason told me wasn't the truth. There was no job offer, no meetings. I just found that out." She said as calmly as she could.

Gamble finished his wine and made considerable progress on his cigar before he spoke again. Sidney had noted this trait with other clients who possessed vast wealth. Nothing hurried them. Your time was their time.

"So your husband lied to you and you lied to me. And I'm now supposed to accept what you're telling me as the gospel?" His tone remained even, but his incredulity was unmistakable. Sidney remained silent. She couldn't blame him for not believing her. "You're my lawyer; advise me on how I should handle this situation, Sidney. Do I accept what the witness is saying, or not?"

Sidney spoke hurriedly. "I'm not asking you to accept anything. If you don't believe me, and you probably have reason not to, then there's nothing I can do about that."

Gamble nodded thoughtfully. "Okay. What else?"

"There is no 'what else.' I've told you all I know."

Gamble flicked his cigar into the fire. "Come on! In the course of my three divorces I've found, much to my dismay, that pillow talk does happen. Why should you be any different?"

"Jason doesn't . . . discuss Triton business with me. What he did at your company was confidential as far as I was concerned. I don't know anything. I have a lot of questions myself but no answers." Her tone was suddenly bitter, but then she quickly calmed down. "Has anything happened at Triton? Anything that involved Jason?" Gamble didn't say anything. "I'd really like an answer to that."

"I'm not inclined to tell you anything. I don't know whose side you're on, but I doubt if it's mine." Gamble was eyeing her so severely that she felt her face growing red. She uncrossed her legs and looked up at him. "I know you're suspicious—"

Gamble broke in heatedly. "You're goddamned right I'm suspicious. With RTG breathing down my neck. With everybody telling me my company will be an also-ran unless I do a deal with CyberCom. How would you feel?" He didn't allow her to answer. He swiftly sat next to her and gripped one of her hands. "Now, I'm really sorry your husband is dead, and under any other circumstances his getting on a plane wouldn't be any of my business. But when everybody starts lying to me at the same time my company's future is blowing in the wind, then it very much becomes my business." He let her hand drop.

Tears pulled at the corners of Sidney's eyes as she jumped up and grabbed her coat. "Right now I don't give a damn about your company or you, but I can tell you that neither my husband nor I have done anything wrong. You got that?" Her eyes blazed at him, her chest heaving. "And now I want to leave."

Nathan Gamble studied her for a long moment, then went over to a table in the far corner of the room and picked up the phone. She couldn't hear what he said. In a moment the door opened and Lucas appeared.

"This way, Ms. Archer."

Walking out, she looked back at Nathan Gamble. He lifted his wineglass in a salutary manner. "Let's keep in touch," he said quietly. The delivery of those four simple words sent a shiver through her entire body.

The limousine reversed its trek and less than forty-five minutes later Sidney was deposited in front of her Ford Explorer. She quickly got in and drove off. She punched a speed dial on her portable phone. A sleepy voice answered.

"Henry, it's Sidney. Sorry if I woke you."

"Sid, what time . . . Where are you?"

"I wanted you to know that I just met with Nathan Gamble."

Henry Wharton was fully awake now. "How did that come about?"

"Let's just say it was at Nathan's suggestion."

"I've been trying to cover for you."

"I know, Henry. I appreciate it."

"So how did it go?"

"Well, probably as well as it could have, under the circumstances. In fact, he was pretty civil."

"Well, that's good."

"It might not last, though, but I wanted you to know. I just left him."

"Maybe this whole thing will just blow over." He added hurriedly, "Of course, I don't mean about Jason's death. I don't mean in any way to minimize that horrible tragedy—"

Sidney quickly cut him off. "I know, I know, Henry. No offense taken."

"So how did you leave it with Nathan?"

She took a deep breath. "We agreed to keep in touch."

The Hay-Adams Hotel was only a few blocks from Tyler, Stone's offices. Sidney awoke early. The clock showed it to be barely five in the morning. She quietly reassessed the progress of the night before. The visit to her husband's office had yielded nothing useful and the meeting with Nathan Gamble had badly scared her. She hoped she had appeased Henry Wharton. For now. After grabbing a quick shower, she called room service and ordered a pot of coffee. She had to be on the road by seven to pick up Amy. She would discuss the memorial service with her parents then.

By the time she was dressed and packed, it was six-thirty. Her parents were habitual early risers and Amy did not ordinarily sleep past six. Sidney's father answered the phone.

"How is she?"

"Your mother's got her. She just finished getting a bath. Just came marching in our bedroom this morning pretty as you please like she owned the place." Sidney could hear the deep pride in her father's voice. "How you holding up, sweetie? You sound a little better."

"I'm holding, Dad. I'm holding. Finally got some sleep, I'm not sure how."

"Well, your mother and I are coming back up with you and we're not taking no for an answer. We can take care of stuff around the house, field calls, run errands, help with Amy."

"Thanks, Dad. I'll be at your place in a couple of hours."

"Here comes Amy looking like a baby chick caught in the rain. I'll put her on."

Sidney could hear the receiver being coddled by the small hands. A few chortles drifted over the line.

"Amy, sweetie, it's Mommy." In the background, Sidney could hear gentle coaxing coming from her mother and father.

"Hi. Mommy?"

"That's right, sweetie, it's Ma-ma."

"*You* talking to me?" Then the little girl laughed uncontrollably for a moment. This was a favorite phrase right now. Amy always hopped off the ground when she said it. Her daughter proceeded to cradle the phone and rattle off her own version of life, in a language most of which Sidney could easily decipher. This morning it was pancakes and bacon and a bird that she had seen go after a cat outside. Sidney smiled. Her smile abruptly vanished with Amy's next words.

"Daddy. I want my daddy."

Sidney closed her eyes. One of her hands moved across her forehead, brushing some hair back. She felt a painful mound of air muscling its way to her throat. She held her hand over the phone so the sound would not carry.

Recovered, she again spoke into the phone. "I love you, Amy. Mommy loves you more than anything. I'll see you in a little while, okay?"

"Love chu. My daddy? Come over, come over now!"

Sidney heard her father tell Amy to say bye-bye.

"Bye-bye, baby. I'll be there soon." The tears fell freely now, their salty taste very familiar to her.

"Honey?"

"Hello, Mom." Sidney rubbed her sleeve across her face. The wetness sprung back immediately, like a stubborn layer of old paint seeping through the fresh coat.

"I'm sorry, honey. I guess she can't talk to you without thinking about Jason."

"I know."

"She's been sleeping all right, at least."

"I'll see you soon, Mom." Sidney hung up the phone and sat with her head in her hands for a few minutes. Then she drifted over to the window, where she pulled open the curtains a notch and peered out. A three-quarters moon together with the multiple streetlights illuminated the area exceedingly well. Even with that, Sidney didn't see the man standing in an alleyway across the street, a small pair of binoculars held in his hands and pointed in her direction. He was dressed in the same coat and hat he had been wearing in Charlottesville. He dutifully watched as Sidney absently scanned the streets below. From years of pulling this kind of duty, his eyes took in every detail. Her face, her eyes in particular, was weary. Her neck was long and graceful, like a model's, but her neck and shoulders were arched back, obviously filled with tension. When she turned away from the window, he lowered his binoculars. A very troubled woman, he concluded. After having observed the suspicious actions of Jason Archer at the airport the morning of the plane crash, the man felt Sidney Archer had every reason to be worried, nervous, perhaps even fearful. He leaned up against the brick wall and continued his sentinel.

TWENTY-THREE

Lee Sawyer was staring out the window of his small apartment in southeast D.C. In the daylight he would be able to see the dome of Union Station from his bedroom window. But daylight was still at least thirty minutes away. Sawyer had not arrived home from investigating the plane fueler's death until almost four-thirty in the morning. He had allowed himself ten minutes under a hot shower to work out the kinks and grogginess. Then he had quickly dressed, put on a pot of coffee, cooked up a couple of eggs and a slice of ham that he probably should have tossed a week ago and toasted some bread. He ate the simple meal on a TV tray in his living room, a small table lamp the only light. The soothing darkness allowed him to sit quietly and think. With the wind rattling against the windows, Sawyer turned his head to study the simple configurations of his home. He grimaced. Home? This was not really his home, although he had been here over a year. Home was in the tree-lined Virginia suburbs: a split-level with vinyl siding, a two-car garage and a brick barbecue in the backyard. This small apartment was where he ate and occasionally slept, mainly because, after the divorce, it was really the only thing he could afford. But it was not and never would be his home, despite the few personal effects he had brought with him, chief of which were the photographs of his four children that peeked out at him from everywhere.

He picked up one of the photos. Looking back at him was his youngest. Meg – Meggie, she was called by nearly everyone. Blond and good-looking, she had inherited her father's height, slender nose and full lips. His career as an FBI agent had taken off during her formative years and he had been on the road for much of her adolescence. Paybacks were hell, though. They were not speaking now. At least she wasn't. And he, big as he was, and despite what he did for a living, was too terrified to try anymore. Besides, how many different ways could you say you were sorry?

He rinsed off the dishes, wiped the sink clean and threw some dirty laundry in a mesh bag for deposit at the cleaners. He looked around for anything else that needed to be done. Really there was nothing. He cracked a weary smile. Just killing time. He checked his watch. Almost seven. He would leave for the office shortly. Although he had regular duty shifts, he was typically there at all hours. Not too difficult to understand, since being an FBI agent was really the only thing he had left. There would always be another case. Isn't that what his wife had said that night? The night their marriage had disintegrated. She had been right, though, there would always be another case. In the end, what more could he really ask for or expect? Tired of waiting, he put on his hat, holstered his gun and walked down the stairs to his car.

Barely a five-minute ride from Sawyer's apartment sat the FBI headquarters building on Pennsylvania Avenue between Ninth and Tenth Streets, northwest. It was home to approximately seventy-five hundred employees of the FBI's total workforce of twenty-four thousand. Of the seventy-five hundred, only about one thousand were special agents; the rest were support and technical personnel. In the headquarters building one prominent special agent was sitting at a large conference room table. Other FBI personnel were scattered around the table dutifully going over stacks of files or screens on their laptops. Sawyer took a moment to look around the room and stretch his limbs. They were in the Strategic Information Operations Center, or SIOC. A restricted access area composed of a block of rooms separated by glass walls and shielded from all known types of electronic surveillance, the SIOC was used as the command post for major FBI operations. On one wall was a line of clocks delineating different time zones. A cluster of large-screen TVs lined another wall. The SIOC had secure communications to the White House Situation Room, the CIA and a myriad of federal law enforcement agencies. With no external windows, and thick-carpeting, it was a very quiet place used to organize mammoth investigations. A small galley kept the personnel here functioning through exhaustive work hours. Presently, fresh coffee was brewing. Caffeine and brainstorming seemed to go hand in hand.

Sawyer looked across the table to where David Long, a longtime member of the FBI's Bomb Squad, sat staring at a file. To the left of Long was Herb Barracks, an agent from the Charlottesville resident agency, the closest FBI office to the crash site. Next to Barracks was an agent from the Richmond office, the FBI field office in nearest proximity to the disaster. Across from them were two agents from the Washington metropolitan field office at Buzzard Point, which, until the late eighties, had been simply the Washington field office until the Alexandria, Virginia, field office had been collapsed into it.

The director of the FBI, Lawrence Malone, had left

an hour earlier after being briefed on the murder of one Robert Sinclair, most recently employed as an aircraft fueler at Vector Fueling Systems and now an occupant of a Virginia morgue. Sawyer felt sure that a fingerprint run through the FBI's Automated Fingerprint Identification System, or AFIS, would give the late Mr. Sinclair another name. Conspirators in a scheme as large as Sawyer figured this one was rarely used their real names in securing employment positions they would later use to down an airliner.

More than two hundred and fifty agents had been assigned to the bombing of Flight 3223. They were following up leads, interviewing family members of the victims and undertaking an excruciatingly detailed investigation of all persons having the motive and opportunity to sabotage the Western Airlines jet. Sawyer figured Sinclair had done the actual dirty work, but he wasn't taking any chances on overlooking an accomplice at the airport. While rumors had been floating in the press for some time, the first major story actually declaring the downing of the Western flight as being caused by an explosive device would be in the next morning's edition of the *Washington Post*. The public would demand answers and they would want them soon. That was fine with Sawyer, only results weren't always obtained as fast as one would like – in fact, they almost never were.

The FBI had latched on to the Vector line soon after the NTSB team members had found that very special piece of evidence in the crater. After that it was a simple matter to confirm that Sinclair had been the fueler on Flight 3223. Now Sinclair was dead too. Someone had made sure he would never have an opportunity to tell them why he sabotaged the plane.

Long looked at Sawyer. "You were right, Lee. It was a heavily modified version of one of those new

188

portable heating elements. The latest rage in cigarette lighters. No flame, just intense heat from a platinum coil, pretty much invisible."

"I knew I'd seen it before. Remember that arson case involving the IRS building last year?" Sawyer said.

"Right. Anyway, this thing is capable of sustaining about fifteen hundred degrees Fahrenheit. And it wouldn't be affected by wind or cold, even if doused by the jet fuel, or anything like that. Five-hour supply of fuel, rigged so that if it went out for any reason it would automatically relight. One side was affixed with a magnetic pad. It's a simple but perfect way to do it. Jet fuel comes spewing out when the tank gets penetrated. Sooner or later, it's going to get within range of the flame, and then boom." He shook his head. "Pretty damn ingenious. Carry it in your pocket; even if it's detected, on the surface it's a damned cigarette lighter." Long sifted through some more pages as the other agents closely watched him. He ventured a further analysis. "And they didn't need a timer or altimeter device. They could roughly gauge the timing by the acid's corrosiveness. They knew it would be up in the air when it went. Five-hour flight, plenty of time."

Sawyer nodded. "Kaplan and his team found the black boxes. The casing on the flight data recorder was split open, but the tape was relatively intact. Preliminary conclusions indicate that the starboard engine, and the controls running through that section of the wing, were severed from the plane seconds after the CVR recorded a strange sound. They're doing spectrum sound analysis on it now. The FDR showed no drastic change in cabin pressure, so there was definitely no explosion *inside* the fuselage, which makes sense, since we now know the sabotage occurred on the wing. Before that, everything was operating smoothly: no engine problems, level flight, ordinary control surface movements. But once things went bad, they never had a chance."

"The pilots' recording on the CVR give any clues?" Long asked.

Sawyer shook his head. "Usual expletives. The Mayday they radioed in. The FDR showed the plane was in a ninety-degree dive for almost thirty thousand feet with the left engine going at almost full power. Who knows if they could even have remained conscious under those conditions?" Sawyer paused. "Let's hope none of them were," he said solemnly.

Now that it was clear that sabotage had downed the plane, the FBI had officially taken over the investigation from the NTSB. Because of the complexities of the case and its massive organizational challenges, FBI headquarters would be the originating office and Sawyer, his first-rate work on the Lockerbie bombing still fresh in the minds of FBI leadership, would be the case agent, meaning he would run the investigation. But this bombing was a little different: It had occurred over American airspace, had left a crater on American soil. He would let others at the bureau handle the press inquiries and issue statements to the public. He much preferred doing his work in the background.

The FBI devoted large resources of personnel and money to infiltrate terrorist organizations operating in the United States, ferreting out plans and grand schemes to wreak destruction in the name of some political or religious cause before they had a chance to come to fruition. The bombing of Flight 3223 had come right out of the blue. There had been no trickles of information from the FBI's vast network that anything of this magnitude was on the horizon. Having been unable to prevent the disaster, Sawyer would now devote every waking moment, and probably suffer through many a nightmare, in his quest to bring those responsible to justice.

"Well, we know what happened to that plane," Sawyer said. "Now we just have to find out why and who else is involved. Let's start with motive. What else did you dig up on Arthur Lieberman, Ray?"

Raymond Jackson was Sawyer's young partner. He had played college football at Michigan before hanging up his cleats and eschewing an NFL career for one in law enforcement. A shade under six feet, the thick-shouldered black man possessed intelligent eyes and a soft-spoken manner. Jackson flipped open a three-ring notebook.

"A lot of info here. For starters, the guy was terminal. Pancreatic cancer. It was in an advanced stage. He had, maybe, six months. *Maybe*. All treatment had been discontinued. Dude was on massive painkillers, though. Schlesinger's Solution, a combo of morphine and a mood elevator, probably cocaine, one of its few legit uses in this country. Lieberman was outfitted with one of those portable units that dispense drugs directly into the bloodstream."

Sawyer's face betrayed his astonishment. *Walter Burns and his secrets*. "The Fed chairman has six months to live and nobody knows? Where'd you get the info?"

"I found a bottle of chemotherapy drugs in the medicine cabinet at his apartment. Then I went right to the source. His personal physician. Told him we were just doing routine background inquiries. Lieberman's personal calendar evidenced a lot of doctor visits. Some visits to Johns Hopkins, another to the Mayo Clinic. Then I mentioned the medication I'd found. The doc was nervous when I asked him about it. I subtly suggested that not telling the whole truth to the FBI could land his keister in a shitload of trouble. When I mentioned a subpoena, he cracked. He probably figured the patient was dead, what the hell would he care."

"What about the White House? They had to know."

"If they're playing straight with us, they were in the dark too. I talked with the chief of staff about Lieberman's little secret. I don't think he believed me at first. Had to remind him FBI stands for fidelity, bravery and integrity. I also sent over a copy of the medical records to him. Word is the president went ape-shit when he saw them."

"That's an interesting twist," Sawyer said. "I always understood Lieberman was some financial god. Solid as a rock. And yet he forgets to mention he's about to check out with cancer and leave the country in the lurch. That doesn't make much sense."

Jackson grinned. "Just reporting the facts. You're right about the guy's abilities. He's a bona fide legend. However, personally, he wasn't in such great shape financially."

"What do you mean?" Sawyer asked.

Jackson turned the pages of his fat notebook and then stopped. He slipped the notebook around and slid it across to Sawyer. Sawyer stared down at the information while Jackson continued his report.

"Lieberman was divorced about five years ago after twenty-five years of marriage. Apparently he was a naughty boy caught fooling around on the side. The timing could not have been worse. He was just about to go through Senate confirmation hearings for the Fed position. His wife threatened to shred him in the papers. The Fed chairmanship, which I'm told Lieberman coveted, would've gone bye-bye real quick. To get rid of the problem, Lieberman gave just about everything he had to his ex. She died just a couple of years ago. To complicate matters, rumor has it his twenty-something girlfriend had expensive tastes. The Fed job is prestigious, but it doesn't pay the Wall Street bucks, not anywhere near. Fact is, Lieberman was up to his ass in debt. Lived in a crummy apartment over on Capitol Hill while trying to crawl out of a financial hole the size of the Grand Canyon. The stack of love letters we found at the apartment apparently came from her."

"What happened to the girlfriend?" Sawyer asked.

"Not sure. It wouldn't surprise me if she'd walked out when she found out her little pot of gold was full of the big C."

"Any idea where she is now?"

Jackson shook his head. "From all accounts, she's been out of the picture for some time now. I tracked down several colleagues of Lieberman's back in New York. The woman was beautiful but brainless according to them."

"It's probably a waste of time, but make some more inquiries on her anyway, Ray."

Jackson nodded.

Sawyer looked at Barracks. "Any word from the Hill on who's going to take Lieberman's slot?"

When Barracks answered, Sawyer was rocked for the second time in less than a minute.

"General consensus: Walter Burns."

Sawyer stared at Barracks for several moments and then wrote the name "Walter Burns" in his notebook. In the margin next to it he scribbled the word "asshole" and then the word "suspect" with a question mark next to it.

Sawyer looked up from his notebook. "Sounds like our Mr. Lieberman was riding a streak of particularly bad luck. So why kill him?"

"Lots of reasons," Barracks spoke up. "The Fed chairman is the symbol of American monetary policy. Make a nice little target for some third world crap-can of a country with a big green monster on its shoulder. Or pick from about a dozen active terrorist groups who specialize in plane bombings."

Sawyer shook his head. "No group has claimed responsibility for the bombing yet."

Barracks snorted. "Give 'em time. Now that we've confirmed it was a bombing, whoever did it will be phoning in. Blowing Americans out of the sky to make a political statement, that's what those ass-holes live for."

"Goddammit!" Sawyer slammed his massive fist down on the table, stood up and started pacing, his face a sheet of vivid red. It seemed as though every ten seconds the image of the impact crater swept across his thoughts. Added to that now was the smaller but even more devastating vision of the tiny, singed shoe he had held in his hand. He had cradled each of his children in one big hand upon their birth. It could have been any of them. Any of them! He knew that vision would never leave his thoughts for as long as he remained on this earth.

The agents eyed him anxiously. Sawyer had a well-deserved reputation as being one of the sharpest agents among a legion of them at the bureau. Through twenty-five years of seeing fellow humans gallop a crimson path through the country, he had continued to attack each case with the same zeal and rigor he had shown from day one on the job. He ordinarily chose carefully worded analysis over scattergun hyperbole; however, most of the agents who had worked with him over the years under-stood crystal-clearly that his temper was contained by a very slender catch.

He stopped his pacing and looked at Barracks. "There's a problem with that theory, Herb." His voice was once again calm.

"What's that?"

Sawyer leaned against one of the glass walls, crossed his arms and rested them on his broad chest. "If you're a terrorist looking to make a big splash, you sneak a bomb on a plane – which, let's face it, isn't all that hard to do on a domestic flight – and you blow the plane into a million pieces. Bodies pouring down, crashing through roofs, interrupting Americans eating breakfast. Leave no room for doubt that it was a bombing." Sawyer paused and intently looked at the face of each agent. "That did not happen here, gentlemen."

Sawyer resumed his pacing. All eyes in the room followed his progress. "The jet was virtually intact on its way down. If the right wing hadn't come off, *all* of it would be in that crater. Mark that point. The fueler from Vector is presumably paid to sabotage the plane. Surreptitious work performed by an American who is not, at least as far as we know, linked to any terrorist group. It would be hard for me to believe that Middle Eastern terrorist groups have started admitting Americans into their ranks to perform their dirty work.

"We had the damage on the fuel tank, but that could as easily have been caused by the explosion and fire. The acid was almost all burned away. A little more heat and maybe we would have found nothing. And Kaplan has confirmed that the wing didn't have to come off the fuselage in order to crash the plane in the same manner. The starboard engine was destroyed from debris ingestion, critical flight control hydraulic lines were severed by the fire and explosion, and the aerodynamics of the wing, even if it had remained intact, was destroyed. So if we hadn't found the igniter in the crater, this thing might've gone down as some horrific mechanical failure. And make no mistake about it, it was a damned miracle that the igniter was found."

195

Sawyer looked through one of the glass walls and continued. "So you add that all up, and what do you have? Arguably, someone who blows up a plane but maybe doesn't want it to look that way. Not your typical terrorist MO. But then the picture gets even more cloudy. The logic starts to cut the other way. First, our fueler ends up with a full clip in him. His bags were packed, half a disguise on, and his employer presumably changes the plan on him. Second, we have Arthur Lieberman on the same flight." Sawyer glanced at Jackson. "The man went to L.A. every month, like clockwork, same airline, same flight each month, right?"

Jackson, eyes narrowed to slits, nodded slowly. Each agent was unconsciously leaning forward as they followed Sawyer's logic.

"So the odds of the guy being on the flight by accident are so high it's not worth debating. Looking at it cold, Lieberman had to be the target, unless we're missing something really big. Now put the two pieces together. Initially, our bombers may have tried to make it look like an accident. Then the fueler ends up dead. Why?" Sawyer looked sharply around the room.

David Long finally spoke up. "Couldn't risk it. Maybe the chances are it goes down like an accident, and maybe not. They can't wait around until the papers report it one way or another. They have to take the guy out right away. Besides, if the original plan was to have the guy take a hike, him not showing for work would raise suspicion. Even if we didn't think sabotage, the guy skipping town would sure as hell turn us in that direction."

"Agreed," Sawyer replied. "But if you want the trail to end there, why not make it look like the fueler's some fanatical zealot? Put a bullet into his temple, leave the gun and some BS suicide note

196

behind filled with I-hate-America language and let us think the guy's a loner. You fill him full of holes, leave behind evidence pointing to the guy getting ready to run, now we know there are others involved. Why the hell bring yourself that kind of trouble?" Sawyer rubbed his chin.

The other agents leaned back in their chairs, looking confused.

Sawyer finally looked at Jackson. "Any word from the ME on our dead guy?"

"They promised a top priority. We'll know soon."

"Anything else turn up at the guy's apartment?"

"One thing that didn't turn up, Lee."

Sawyer flashed a knowing look. "No I.D. docs."

"Yep," Jackson said. "Guy getting ready to hit the road after blowing up a plane will not be running as himself. Way this was probably planned out, he had to have phony docs, *good* phony docs ready."

"True, Ray, but he could've had them stashed someplace else."

"Or whoever killed him might've taken them too," Barracks ventured.

"No argument there," Sawyer said.

On those words the door to the SIOC opened and through it stepped Marsha Reid. Petite and motherly looking, with salt and pepper hair cut short and glasses riding on a chain over her black dress, she was one of the bureau's top fingerprint personnel. Reid had tracked down some of the worst criminals on the planet through the esoteric world of arches, loops and whorls.

Marsha nodded to the other agents in the room and then sat down and opened the file she had carried in.

"AFIS results, hot off the presses," she said, her tone businesslike but laced with a touch of humor. "Robert Sinclair was actually Joseph Philip Riker,

197

currently wanted in Texas and Arkansas on murder and related weapons charges. His arrest sheet is three pages long. His first arrest was for armed robbery at age sixteen. His last was for second-degree murder. He served seven years. Was released five years ago. Since then he's been implicated in numerous crimes, including two murders-for-hire. An extremely dangerous man. His trail went cold about eighteen months ago. Not a peep from him since. Until now."

Every agent at the table looked stunned.

"How does a guy like that get a job fueling planes?" Sawyer's tone was incredulous.

Jackson answered the query. "I spoke with representatives from Vector. They're a reputable company. Sinclair – or, rather Riker had been with them only about a month. He had excellent credentials. Worked at several aircraft fueling companies in the Northwest and in southern California. They did a background check on him, under the name Sinclair, of course. Everything came out okay. They were as stunned by this as anyone else."

"What about fingerprints? They had to check his fingerprints. That would've told them who the guy really was."

Reid eyed Sawyer. She spoke with authority. "Depends on who's taking the prints, Lee. A borderline competent tech can be fooled, you know that. There's synthetic material out there you'd swear was skin. You can buy prints on the street. Put it all together and a career criminal becomes a respectable citizen."

Barracks piped in. "And if the guy was wanted on all those other crimes, he probably had a new face put on. Five gets you ten the face in that morgue isn't the face on those wanted posters."

Sawyer looked at Jackson. "How did Riker end up fueling Flight 3223?"

"About a week ago he asked to be switched to the graveyard shift, twelve to seven. Flight 3223's scheduled departure time was six forty-five. Same time every day. Log shows the plane was fueled at five-fifteen. That puts it on Riker's rounds. Most people don't volunteer for that shift, so Riker got it pretty much by default."

Another question occurred to Sawyer. "So where's the real Robert Sinclair?"

"Probably dead," said Barracks. "Riker took over his identity."

No one commented on that theory until Sawyer pursued the issue with a startling query. "Or what if Robert Sinclair doesn't exist?" Now even Reid looked puzzled. Sawyer looked deep in thought when he spoke. "There are a lot of problems with taking over a real person's identity. Old photos, co-workers or friends who show up unexpectedly and blow your cover. There's another way to do it." Sawyer pursed his lips and raised his eyebrows as he thought his idea through. "I've got a gut feeling on this one that's telling me we need to redo everything that Vector did when they performed their background check on Riker. Get on that, Ray, like yesterday."

Jackson nodded and jotted down some notes.

Reid looked at Sawyer. "Are you thinking what I think you are?"

Sawyer smiled. "It wouldn't be the first time a person was invented out of whole cloth. Social Security number, job history, past residences, photo identification, bank accounts, training certifications, fake phone numbers, dummy references." He looked at Reid. "Even false prints, Marsha."

"Then we're talking some pretty sophisticated guys," she replied.

"I never doubted they were anything less, Ms. Reid," Sawyer rejoined.

Sawyer looked around the table. "I don't want to stray from SOP, so we'll still continue to conduct interviews of family members of the victims, but I don't want to waste too much time on that. Lieberman is the key to this whole thing." He suddenly changed gears. "Rapid Start running smoothly?" he asked Ray Jackson.

"Very."

Rapid Start was the FBI's version of the show on the road and Sawyer had used it successfully in the past. The premise of Rapid Start was the veracity of an electronic clearinghouse for every bit of information, leads and anonymous tips involved in an investigation that otherwise would become unorganized and muddled. With an integrated investigation and pretty close to real-time access to information, the chances of success, the bureau believed, were immeasurably increased.

The Rapid Start operation for Flight 3223 was housed in an abandoned tobacco warehouse on the outskirts of Standardsville. Instead of tobacco leaves stored floor to ceiling, the building now housed the latest in computer and telecommunications equipment manned by dozens of agents working in shifts who inputted information into the massive databases twenty-four hours a day.

"We're gonna need every miracle it can produce. And even that might not be enough." Sawyer was silent for a moment and then snapped to attention. "Let's get to work."

TWENTY-FOUR

"Quentin?" Sidney stood at the front door of her house, the surprise evident on her face.

Quentin Rowe stared back at her through his oval glasses. "May I come in?"

Sidney's parents were out grocery shopping. While Sidney and Quentin headed toward the living room, a sleepy Amy wandered into the room dragging Pooh. "Hi, Amy," Rowe said. He knelt down and put out a hand to her, but the little girl drew back. Rowe smiled at her. "I was shy when I was your age too." He looked up at Sidney. "That's probably why I turned to computers. They didn't talk back at you, or try to touch you." He paused, seemingly lost in thought. Then he started and looked up at her. "Do you have time to talk?"

Sidney hesitated.

"Please, Sidney?"

"Let me put this little girl down for a much-needed nap. I'll be back in a few minutes." Sidney carried her out.

While she was gone, Rowe slowly walked around the room. He studied the many photos of the Archer family scattered across the walls and tabletops. He looked over as Sidney came back into the room. "Beautiful little girl you have there."

"She is something. A terrific something."

"Especially now, right?"

Sidney nodded.

Rowe kept his eyes on her. "I lost both my parents in a plane crash when I was fourteen."

"Oh, Quentin."

He shrugged. "It was a long time ago. But I think I can understand a little better than most how you're feeling. I was an only child. There really wasn't anyone left for me."

"I guess I'm fortunate in that regard."

"You are, Sidney, keep reminding yourself of that."

She took a deep breath. "Would you like something to drink?"

"Tea, if you have it."

A few minutes later they were settled on the living room sofa. Rowe balanced his saucer on his knee while he sipped delicately at his tea. He put his cup down and looked over at her, his awkwardness apparent. "First, I want to apologize to you."

"Quentin—"

He put up one hand. "I know what you're going to say, but I was way out of line. The things I said, the way I treated you. I . . . Sometimes I don't think before I speak. In fact, I'm not all that good at presenting myself. I know I come off as geeky and uncaring sometimes, but I'm really not."

"I know that, Quentin. We've always had a good relationship. Everyone at Triton thinks the world of you. I know that Jason did. If it makes you feel any better, I find you far easier to relate to than Nathan Gamble."

"You and the rest of the world," Rowe said quickly. "With that said, I guess I should explain by saying that I was under a great deal of pressure, what with Gamble balking at doing CyberCom, the chance that we could lose it all."

"Well, I think Nathan understands what's at stake."

Rowe nodded absently. "The second thing I wanted to tell you is how truly sorry I am about Jason. It just shouldn't have happened. Jason was probably the one person I could truly connect to at the company. He was as talented as I was on the technology side, but he was also able to present himself well, an area, as I said, I'm lacking in."

"I think you handle yourself very well."

Rowe brightened. "You do?" Then he sighed. "Next to Gamble, most people, I guess, seem like wallflowers."

"I wouldn't disagree, but I also wouldn't recommend that you emulate him."

Rowe put his tea down. "I know it seems like he and I are strange bedfellows."

"It's hard to argue with the success you two have had."

His tone was suddenly bitter. "Right. The great measuring stick of money. When I first started out, I had ideas. Wonderful ideas, but no capital. Then along came Nathan." His expression was not a pleasant one.

"It's not only that, Quentin. You have a vision for the future. I understand that vision, to the extent a technology neophyte can. I know that vision is what's driving the CyberCom deal."

Rowe smacked his fist into the palm of his hand. "Exactly, Sidney. Exactly. The stakes are so incredibly high. CyberCom's technology is so dramatically superior, so monumental, it's like the second coming of Graham Bell." He seemed to shiver with anticipation as he looked at her. "Do you realize that the one thing holding back the limitless potential of the Internet is the fact that it's so large, so all-consuming that navigating it efficiently is often a horrendous exercise in futility for even the most adept computer users?"

"But with CyberCom, that will change?"

"Yes! Yes. Of course."

"I have to confess, despite working on this deal for so many months. I'm really not certain what exactly CyberCom has come up with. Lawyers rarely get into those nuances, particularly those who never excelled in the sciences, such as myself." She smiled.

Rowe sat back, his slender frame assuming a comfortable tilt when the conversation veered toward technical issues. "In laymen's terms CyberCom has done nothing less than create artificial intelligence, so-called intelligent agents that will initially be used to effortlessly navigate the myriad tributaries of the Internet and its progeny."

"Artificial intelligence? I thought that existed only in the movies."

"Not at all. There are degrees of artificial intelligence, of course. CyberCom's is by far the most sophisticated I've ever seen."

"How exactly does it work?"

"Let's say you want to find out about every article written on some controversial subject, and you also want a summary of those articles, listing those in favor and opposed, the reasons therefor, the analysis behind it and so on. Now, if you attempted that on your own through the unwieldy labyrinth the Internet has become, it would take you forever. As I said, the overwhelming amount of information contained on the Internet is its greatest drawback. Human beings are ill-equipped to deal with something on that scale. But you get around that obstacle and suddenly it's as though the surface of Pluto becomes alive with sunshine."

"And that's what CyberCom has done?"

"With CyberCom in our fold, we will initiate a wireless, satellite-based network that will be seamlessly coordinated with proprietary software that will soon be on every computer in America, and eventually the world. The software is easily the most user-friendly I've ever seen. It asks the user precisely what information is needed. It will ask additional questions as it deems necessary. Then, tapping into our satellite-based network, it will explore every molecule of the conglomeration of computers we call the Internet until it assembles, in picture-perfect form, the answer to every single question you asked, and many more you weren't perceptive enough to think of. Best of all, it's chameleon-like in that the intelligent agents can adapt to and communicate with any network server in existence. That's another drawback to the Internet: systems' inability to communicate with each other. And it will perform this task a billion times faster than any human could. It will be like minutely examining every drop of the Nile River in a few minutes. Even faster. Finally, the vast sources of knowledge that are out there and growing exponentially with every passing day can actually be efficiently linked up to the one entity which really needs them." He looked pointedly at her. "Humanity. And it doesn't stop there. The network interface with the Internet is only one small part of the overall puzzle. It also elevates the encryption standard to unparalleled heights. Imagine fluid responses to attempts to illegally decrypt electronic transmissions. Responses that can not only adjust to fend off a hacker's multithrust attacks, but aggressively pursue the intruder and track *him* down. Do you think that would be popular with law enforcement agencies? This is the next milestone in the technological revolution. This will dictate how all data is transmitted and used in the next century. How we build, teach, think. Just envision computers that are not merely dumb machines reacting to precise instructions keyed in by humans. Picture computers using their vast intellectual muscle to think on their own, to *problem-solve* for us in ways unthinkable today. It will make so much obsolete, including much of Triton's existing product line. It changes everything. Like the internal combustion engine did to the era of the horse-drawn carriages but even more profoundly."

"My God," Sidney exclaimed. "And I guess the potential profits—"

"Yes, yes, we'll make billions from sales of software, the network charges – every business in the world will want to be on-line with us. And that's only the beginning." Rowe sounded distinctly uninterested in this side of the equation. "And yet with all that, Gamble still won't see, is incapable of understanding . . ." He stood up in his anxiety, his arms flailing. He caught himself and sat back down, his face carrying a red sheen. "I'm . . . I'm sorry, sometimes I get carried away."

"It's okay, Quentin, I understand. Jason shared your excitement about the CyberCom deal, I know that."

"We had many pleasant discussions about it."

"And Gamble is acutely aware of the consequences of another company acquiring CyberCom. I have to believe that he will come to his senses over the records issue."

Rowe nodded. "One can only hope," he said quickly. Sidney glanced at the diamond studs in his earlobe. They seemed to be the only extravagance about the man, and a small one at that. A millionaire several hundred times over, Rowe lived much like the impoverished college student he had been ten years ago. Finally Rowe broke the silence. "Jason and I talked about the future a lot, in fact. He was a very special person." He seemed to share the depths of Sidney's misery whenever Jason's name was

206

mentioned. "I guess you won't be working on the CyberCom matter anymore?"

"The attorney who's replacing me is top-notch. You won't miss a beat."

"Oh, good." He sounded extremely unconvinced.

She rose and gripped his shoulder. "Quentin, this deal *will* get done." She noted his empty teacup. "Would you like some more tea?"

"What? Uh, no, no, thanks." He collapsed back into deep thought, rubbing his thin hands nervously. When he snatched a look at her, Sidney thought she knew what was on his mind.

"I had an impromptu meeting with Nathan recently."

Rowe slowly nodded. "He told me something of it."

"So you know about Jason's 'trip'?"

"That he told you he was going for a job interview?"

"Yes."

"What company?" The question was asked very matter-of-factly.

Sidney hesitated and then decided to answer. "AllegraPort Technology."

Rowe snorted. "I could've told you that was a joke. AllegraPort will be out of business in less than two years. They were on the cutting edge a while back, but they let the industry pass them by. You grow and keep innovating in this field or you die. Jason would never have seriously considered going with them."

"As it turned out, he didn't. They had never heard of him."

Rowe was obviously already privy to this information. "Could it have been something else . . . I don't quite know how to put this . . ."

"Personal? Another woman?"

Like an embarrassed child, Rowe mumbled, "I shouldn't have said that. It's none of my business."

"No, it's all right. I can't tell you that the thought never crossed my mind. However, our relationship recently was the best it's ever been."

"So he never indicated to you that anything was going on in his life? Nothing that would have prompted him to . . . take a trip to L.A., and not to tell you the truth about it?"

Sidney looked wary. Was this all a fishing expedition? Had Gamble perhaps sent his second-in-command over to glean some information? When she looked at Rowe's troubled expression, she swiftly concluded that he had come here on his own in an attempt to figure out what had happened to his employee and friend.

"Nothing. Jason never really talked to me about work. I have no idea what he was doing. I wish to God I did. It's the not knowing that's killing me." She debated whether to ask Rowe about the new locks on Jason's door and Kay Vincent's other concerns, but finally decided not to.

After an awkward silence, Rowe stirred. "I have those personal items of Jason's you came to the office for in the car. After I was so rude to you, I thought it best to bring them myself."

"Thank you, Quentin. Believe me when I tell you I harbor no hard feelings. It's a rough time for us all."

Rowe thanked her with a smile as he stood up. "I have to be going. I'll go get the box. If you need anything, just let me know." After bringing in the items, Rowe said his good-byes and turned to leave. Sidney touched him on the shoulder.

"Nathan Gamble won't be looking over your shoulder forever. Everyone knows who's really behind the success of Triton Global."

He looked surprised. "You really think so?"

"It's hard to hide genius."

He breathed deeply. "I don't know. Gamble seems to keep surprising me in that regard."

He turned and walked slowly back to his car.

TWENTY-FIVE

It was nearly midnight when Lee Sawyer's head hit the pillow after a hastily eaten dinner. His eyes, however, failed to close, although a massive weariness tugged at him. He looked around the tiny living space and abruptly decided to get up. He padded through the hallway in his bare feet, undershorts and T-shirt and plopped down on a beaten-up recliner in the living room. The typical career of an FBI agent didn't often lend itself to long-standing domestic tranquillity. Too many missed anniversaries, holidays, birthdays. Gone for months at a time, no end in sight. He had been severely wounded in the line of duty, a traumatic situation for any spouse. There had been threats to his family from the human waste he had dedicated his life to eradicating. All for the cause of justice, of making the world, if not better, at least momentarily safer. A noble goal that didn't sound so special when you were trying to explain to your eight-year-old over the phone why Daddy was going to miss another baseball game, another recital or school play. He had known that going in; Peg had too. Being so much in love, they truly believed they could beat the odds, and they had for a long time. Ironically, his relationship with Peg was now better than it had been in years.

The kids though, were a different matter. He had taken the full brunt of the blame for the breakup and maybe he deserved it, he thought. Only now were his three oldest kids beginning to talk to him on anything approaching a consistent basis. Meggie was completely gone from him. He didn't know what was going on in her life. That's what had hurt the most. The not knowing.

Everyone had choices to make and he had made his own. He had enjoyed a very successful career at the bureau, but that success had come with a cost. He walked to the kitchen, pulled out a cold beer and plopped back down in the recliner. His magical sleeping potion of choice. At least he wasn't into the hard liquor. Yet. He finished the beer in several large gulps, lay back in the chair and closed his eyes.

An hour later, the telephone ringing roused him from a deep sleep. He was still sitting in the recliner. He picked up the telephone receiver on the table next to his chair.

"Yeah?"

"Lee?"

Sawyer's eyelids fluttered briefly, then opened. "Frank?" Sawyer looked at his watch. "You're not with the bureau anymore, Frank, I thought the private sector lets you keep more regular hours."

On the other end of the line Frank Hardy was fully dressed and sitting in a nicely furnished office. On the wall behind him hung numerous mementos depicting a long and distinguished career with the FBI. Hardy smiled. "Too much competition out here, Lee. Just having twenty-four hours in a day doesn't seem fair."

"Well, I'm not ashamed to admit it's about my limit. What's up?"

"Your plane bombing," Hardy said simply.

Sawyer sat straight up, fully awake now, his eyes focusing in the darkness. "What?"

"I got something here you're going to need to see, Lee. I'm not clear on exactly what it all means yet.

I'm about to brew a pot of coffee. How long will it take you to get here?"

"Give me thirty minutes."

"Just like old times."

In five minutes Sawyer was fully dressed. He slipped his 10mm pistol into its holster and went down to the street to fire up his sedan. On the drive over he reported in to headquarters to alert them to this recent development. Frank Hardy had been one of the best agents the bureau had ever produced. When he left to start his own security firm, every agent had felt the loss, but no one begrudged Hardy the opportunity after his many years of service. He and Sawyer had been partners for ten years before Hardy made his exit. They had been a prolific team, beating the odds on a number of high-profile cases and bringing to justice criminals who had gone far underground. Many of their targets were now serving life sentences without parole at various maximum-security federal prisons around the country. More than a handful, several of them serial killers, had been executed.

If Hardy thought he had something on the plane bombing, then he did. Sawyer sped up and within ten minutes pulled his car into a vast parking lot. The fourteen-story building in Tysons Corner housed a number of businesses, none of them involved in anything nearly as exciting as Hardy's concern. Sawyer was cleared through security after showing his FBI credentials and rode the elevator up to the fourteenth floor. Stepping out of the elevator, he found himself in the modern-looking reception area. Soft cove lighting illuminated the otherwise darkened expanse of the area. Behind the receptionist's desk were six-inch-high white letters proclaiming the name of the establishment: SECURTECH.

212

TWENTY-SIX

Sidney Archer watched the methodical rise and fall of the small chest. Her parents were sleeping soundly in the guest bedroom down the hall while Sidney sat in the rocking chair in Amy's room. Finally Sidney rose and went to the window to look out. She had never been much of a night person. Hectic days had demanded that when the time came to sleep, she slept. Now the darkness seemed powerfully soothing to her, like a gentle cascade of warm water. It made recent events seem less real, less terrifying than she knew them actually to be. When the daylight came, though, the calming quiet of the night would leave her again. Tomorrow also would bring the memorial service for Jason. People would be coming to the house to pay their respects, to reflect on what a good life her husband had led. Sidney wasn't sure if she would be up to it, but that was a worry that she would allow to lie for a few more hours.

She kissed Amy on the cheek, quietly exited the room and moved down the hallway to Jason's small study. She reached above the doorjamb and pulled down half a bobby pin, which she inserted in the lock on the door. At two years old, Amy Archer could get into anything; mascara, pantyhose, jewelry, Jason's ties, shoes, wallets and purses. They had once found the title to Jason's Cougar crammed in the pancake mix along with the house keys they had been frantically searching for. Once she and

213

Jason had awoken to find a full box of dental floss wrapped around their four-poster bed. Turning doorknobs was a simple matter for the youngest Archer, hence most doors in the place had a bobby pin or bent paper clip riding above them.

Sidney went in and sat down in front of the desk. The computer screen stared back at her, its flat face dark and silent. A part of her waited for another e-mail to burst on the screen, hoping beyond hope, but it did not happen. She looked around the small room. Being wholly Jason's, it seemed continually to draw her. She touched certain favourite items of his as if they would, by osmosis, reveal to her the secrets her husband had left behind. The phone ringing broke her thoughts. It rang again and she quickly picked it up, not knowing what to expect. For a moment Sidney did not recognize the voice. "Paul?"

"I'm sorry for calling so late. I've been trying to reach you the last few days. I left messages."

She hesitated. "I know, Paul, I'm sorry, there's been so much—"

"Jesus, Sid, I didn't say that to make you feel guilty. I was just worried about you. Finding out about Jason like that, I don't know how you're holding up. You're stronger than I am."

She smiled weakly. "I don't feel so strong right now."

Paul Brophy's voice was earnest. "You've got a lot of people at Tyler, Stone pulling for you. And one New York-based partner in particular who is available twenty-four hours a day to help."

"The support is touching, it really is."

"I'm flying down for the memorial service tomorrow."

"You don't have to do that, Paul, you must be swamped."

"Not really. I don't know if you were aware, but I

made a run at taking the helm on the CyberCom deal."

"Really?" Sidney did her best to keep her voice even.

"Yeah, only I didn't get it. Wharton was rather blunt in rejecting my offer."

"I'm sorry, Paul." Sidney felt momentary guilt. "There will be other deals, though."

"I know, but I really thought I could do it. I really did." He paused. Sidney prayed that he would not ask her whether Wharton had sought her advice on the matter. When he finally did speak, she felt more guilty still. "I am coming tomorrow, Sid. I can't think of any place I'd rather be."

"Thank you." Sidney pulled her robe closer around her.

"Is it okay if I come directly to your house from the airport?"

"That's fine."

"Get some sleep, Sid. I'll see you first thing in the morning. You need anything, anytime, day or night, you just have to call, okay?"

"Thank you, Paul. Good night." Sidney put the phone down. She had always gotten along with Brophy, but she was certainly aware that under his ultrasmooth exterior lurked a pure opportunist. She had told Henry Wharton that Paul did not belong on the CyberCom deal and now he was coming down to be with her in her time of grief. Well, she may be grieving, but she didn't believe in coincidences that big. She wondered what his true motive could be.

As he hung up the phone, Paul Brophy surveyed the broad expanse of his luxurious apartment. When you were thirty-four, single and good-looking with a mid-six-figure income, New York City was a great place to be. He smiled and ran his hand through thick hair. Six figures that would, with a little luck, turn into seven. Much in life depended on whom you allied yourself with. He picked up the phone and dialled. The phone was answered after one ring. The voice was quick and businesslike after Brophy identified himself.

"Hello, Paul, I was hoping to hear from you tonight," Philip Goldman said.

TWENTY-SEVEN

Frank Hardy loaded the videotape into the VCR resting under the wide-screen TV in one corner of the conference room. It was almost two o'clock in the morning. Lee Sawyer sat in one of the plush chairs, nursing a cup of hot coffee and admiring the surroundings. "Damn, business must be really good, Frank. I keep forgetting how far you've risen in the world."

Hardy laughed. "Well, if you'd ever take my offer to join me, Lee, I wouldn't have to keep reminding you."

"I'm just so set in my ways, Frank."

Hardy grinned. "Renee and I are thinking of going to the Caribbean over Christmas. You could join us. Maybe even bring somebody else along." Hardy looked at his former partner expectantly.

"Sorry, Frank, there really isn't anybody right now."

"It's been two years. I just thought . . . After Sally walked out, I thought I was going to die. Didn't want to go through the dating process again. Then Renee happened along. I couldn't be happier."

"Seeing as how Renee could pass as Michelle Pfeiffer's twin, I can see how you must be a very happy man."

Hardy laughed. "You might want to reconsider. Renee has some girlfriends who adhere strictly to her level of aesthetics. And the women go nuts over you tall, strong types, I'm telling you."

Sawyer grunted. "Right. Not to detract from you,

217

handsome old buddy, but I don't have the bucks in the bank you do. Consequently, my attraction level has dimmed a little over the years. Besides, I'm still only a government employee. Coach class and Kmart are about my limit and I don't think you travel in those circles anymore."

Hardy sat down and picked up a coffee mug with one hand and the VCR remote with the other. "I was planning on picking up the whole tab, Lee," he said quietly. "Call it an early Christmas present. You're so damned hard to shop for."

"Thanks anyway. Actually, I'm thinking about trying to spend some time with the kids this year. If they'll have me."

Frank nodded. "I hear you."

"Now, what do you have for me?"

Hardy said, "We've been Triton Global's chief security consultant for the last several years."

Sawyer picked up his coffee cup. "Triton Global? Computer, telecommunications. They're a Fortune 500, aren't they?"

"Technically, they don't qualify for the list."

"Why's that?"

"They're a nonpublic company. They dominate their field, expanding like crazy, and doing it all without capital from the public markets."

"Impressive. How does that tie in to a plane taking a nosedive into the Virginia countryside?"

"Several months ago Triton suspected that certain proprietary information was being leaked to a competitor. They called us in to verify the suspicion and, if true, to discover the leak."

"Did you?"

Hardy nodded. "We first narrowed down the list of those competitors who were most likely to participate in such a scheme. Once we had those nailed down, we undertook surveillance."

"That must've been tough. Big companies, thousands of employees, hundreds of offices."

"It was a daunting challenge, at first. However, our information led us to believe the leak was fairly senior, so we kept our eye on high-level Triton people."

Lee Sawyer settled farther back in his chair and sipped his coffee. "So you identified some other 'unofficial' places where the exchange might take place and set up your snooping shop?"

Hardy smiled. "Sure you don't want that job?"

Sawyer shrugged off the compliment. "So what happened?"

"We identified a number of these 'unofficial' locations, property owned by our suspect companies and which seemed to have no legitimate operational purpose. At each of these sites we set up surveillance." Hardy smiled sardonically at his former colleague. "Don't read me the riot act over trespassing and other related legal violations, Lee. Sometimes the ends do justify the means."

"Not arguing with you there. I wish we could take shortcuts sometimes. But then we'd have a hundred lawyers screaming 'unconstitutional' and there goes my pension."

"Anyway, two days ago a routine inspection was made of a surveillance camera set up inside a warehouse building located near Seattle."

"What led you to stake out that particular warehouse?"

"Information we developed led us to believe that the building was owned, through a string of subsidiaries and partnerships, by the RTG group. They're one of Triton's major global competitors."

"What was the nature of the information Triton believed was being leaked? Technology?"

"No. Triton was involved in negotiations for the

acquisition of a very valuable software company called CyberCom. We believe that information on those negotiations was being leaked to RTG, information that RTG could use to step in and buy the company itself, since it would know Triton's terms and negotiating position. Based on the video you're about to see, we've made subtle noises to RTG. They've denied everything, of course. They're claiming that the warehouse was leased last year to an unaffiliated company. We checked out the company. It's nonexistent. Meaning RTG is lying or we've got another player in this game.

Sawyer nodded. "Okay. Tell me about the tie-in to my case."

Hardy responded by pushing a button on the remote. The largescreen TV sprung to life. Sawyer and Hardy watched as the scene in the small room in the warehouse was replayed. When the tall young man accepted the silver case from the older gentlemen, Hardy froze the screen. He looked over at Sawyer's puzzled face. Hardy pulled a laser pointer from his shirt pocket to highlight the young man.

"This man is employed by Triton Global. We didn't have him on the surveillance list because he wasn't senior-level management and he wasn't directly involved in the acquisition negotiations."

"Despite that, he's obviously your leak. Recognize anyone else?"

Hardy shook his head. "Not yet. The man's name, by the way, is Jason W. Archer of 611 Morgan Lane in Jefferson County, Virginia. Sound familiar?"

Sawyer concentrated hard. The name did seem to ring a bell. Then is suddenly hit him like a half-ton truck. "Jesus Christ!" He half rose out of his chair, eyes bulging at the face on the screen as the name shot out at him from a passenger manifest that he had scrutinized a hundred times already. The date and time stamp read NOVEMBER 17, 1995 11.15 AM PST Sawyer's quick eyes took in the information with one glance and he calculated rapidly. Seven hours after the plane had crashed in Virginia, this guy was alive and kicking in Seattle. "Jesus H. Christ!" he exclaimed again.

Hardy nodded. "That's right. Jason Archer was listed as a passenger on Flight 3223. But he obviously wasn't on the flight."

Hardy let the tape run. When the roar of the plane erupted on its sound track, Sawyer jerked his head to the window. The damn thing sounded like it was coming right at them. When he looked back at Hardy, his friend was smiling.

"I did the same thing when I heard it for the first time."

Sawyer watched as the men on the screen looked skyward until the sound of the plane in the background drifted away. Sawyer squinted at the screen. Something caught his eye; he just couldn't put his finger on it.

Hardy was watching him closely. "See something?"

Sawyer finally shook his head. "Okay, what was Archer doing in Seattle on the morning of the Virginia crash if he was supposed to be on a plane to L.A.? Company business?"

"Triton didn't even know Archer was going to L.A., much less Seattle. They thought he was taking some time off to spend at home with his family."

Sawyer narrowed his eyes, searching his memory. "Help me out here, Frank."

Hardy's answer was prompt. "Archer has a wife and young daughter. His wife, Sidney, is an attorney at Tyler, Stone, Triton's lead outside counsel. The wife works on a number of Triton's business matters, including heading up Triton's pursuit of CyberCom."

"That's real interesting, and maybe convenient for her and her husband."

"Gotta admit, that's the first thought that struck me, Lee."

"If Archer was in Seattle by, say ten or ten-thirty in the morning, Pacific time, he must've grabbed an early morning flight from D.C."

"Western Airlines had one leaving about the same time as the L.A. departure."

Sawyer stood up and walked over to the TV screen. He rewound the tape and then froze it. He scrutinized every detail of Jason Archer's face, burning it into his memory. He turned to Hardy. "We know Archer was on Flight 3223's passenger manifest, but you say his employer didn't know about the trip. How'd they find out he was on the plane? Supposedly was," Sawyer corrected himself.

Hardy poured out some more coffee and stood up, moved over to the window. Both men seemed innately to crave movement while thinking. "Airline tracks down the wife while she's on a business trip to New York and tells her the bad news. At that meeting are a bunch of people from Triton, including the chairman. They find out then. Pretty soon everyone knew. This videotape has only been shown to two other people: Nathan Gamble, the chairman of the board of Triton and Quentin Rowe, the second-in-command over there."

Sawyer rubbed a kink out of his neck, picked up the fresh cup of coffee and took a gulp. "Western confirmed that he checked in at the ticket counter and that his boarding pass was collected. They wouldn't have informed his family otherwise."

"You know as well as I do that it could've been anyone checking in there using a dummy I.D. The tickets were probably paid for ahead of time. He checks a bag, goes through security. Even with the

FAA's recent heightened security requirements, they don't require photo identification to board a plane, only at check-in or with the skycaps."

"But somebody got on the plane in Archer's place. The airline has his boarding pass, and once on, you do not get off an aircraft."

"Whoever it was, was one very stupid or one very unlucky sonofabitch. Probably both."

"Right, but if Archer was on that Seattle flight, that means he had another ticket."

"He could've checked in twice, once for each flight. He could have used an alias and dummy I.D. for the Seattle flight."

"That's true." Sawyer pondered the possibilities. "Or he could've simply switched tickets with the guy who took his place."

"Whatever the truth is, you've certainly got your work cut out for you."

Sawyer fingered his coffee mug. "Anyone talk to the wife?"

In response, Hardy opened the file he had carried in with him. "Nathan Gamble did, briefly, on two occasions. Quentin Rowe also talked to her."

"And what's her story?"

"Initially she said she didn't know her husband was on the plane."

"Initially? So her story changed."

Hardy nodded. "Next she told Nathan Gamble that her husband had lied to her. Said he told her he was going to L.A. to meet with another company."

"Who says?"

"Sidney Archer. I guess she must have called the company, probably to tell them her husband wasn't going to be making it."

"But you verified it?" asked Sawyer. Hardy nodded. "So, any progress with your investigation?"

Hardy's face took on almost a pained expression.

"Not much makes sense right now. Nathan Gamble is far from a happy man. He pays the bills and wants results. But it takes time, you know that. Still . . ." Hardy paused and studied the thick carpet. It was easy to see the man did not enjoy being puzzled about anything. "Anyway, according to Gamble and Rowe, at least, Mrs. Archer thinks her husband's dead."

"If she's telling the truth, and right now everything with me is a big *if*." Sawyer's tone was heated.

Hardy looked at him quizzically.

Sawyer caught the look and his shoulders slumped. "Just between you and me, Frank, I'm feeling a little stupid on this one."

"Why's that?"

"I had it pegged for sure that Arthur Lieberman was the target. Structured the whole investigation around that theory, mainly just going through the motions on any other angle."

"It's early on in the investigation, Lee. No harm done yet. Besides, maybe Lieberman *was* the target, in a way."

Sawyer's head jerked back. "How's that?"

"Think about it. You already answered your own question."

Hardy's point suddenly came to him. Sawyer's face grew dark. "You mean you think this guy Archer arranged to blow up the plane because we'd think Lieberman was the target? Come on, Frank, that's a helluva stretch."

Hardy countered. "Well if we hadn't lucked out with this video, that's exactly what you'd still be thinking, isn't it? Remember, there's one unique thing about an airplane crash, particularly one where the aircraft collides with the ground relatively intact, as happened here."

Sawyer's face turned ashen while he thought it

through. "No bodies. Nothing to identify, no remains."

"Exactly. Now, if the plane had been conventionally blown up in the air, you'd have a lot of bodies to identify."

Sawyer continued to look stunned at Hardy's revelation. "That issue had been bugging the hell out of me. If Archer sold out, collected his payoff and was planning to run, he'd know at some point the police would be on to him."

Hardy picked up the thread. "So to cover his tracks he sets it up like he gets on a plane which ends up thirty feet under. If evidence of sabotage is discovered, you logically think Lieberman's the target. If evidence of sabotage isn't found, you still won't be looking for a dead man. Everyone stops looking for Jason Archer. End of case."

"But Christ, Frank, why not just take the money and run? It's not that difficult to disappear. And there's another thing. The guy we're pretty sure sabotaged 3223 ended up with a bunch of holes in him."

"Would the time of death have allowed Archer to get back and do the killing?" Hardy asked.

"We don't have the autopsy results yet, but based on what I saw of the corpse, it's possible Archer could've gotten back to the East Coast in time to do it."

Hardy fingered his file while he thought through this new information.

"Come on, Frank, how much you figure Archer got for his info? Enough to bribe a fueler? This one guy who until a few days ago led a respectable life with a family? Now he's some kind of mastermind criminal blowing kids and grandmothers out of the sky?"

Frank Hardy looked at his old friend, his lips set in

a thin line. "He personally didn't blow up that plane, Lee. Besides, don't tell me you've started analyzing the depths of a person's conscience. If memory serves me correctly, some of the worst perps we ever tracked down led lives on the surface that looked like something out of *Leave It to Beaver*."

Sawyer did not look convinced. "How much?"

"Archer could've gotten several million easy for the information."

"That sounds like a lot, but you think a guy will kill a couple hundred people to cover his tracks for that? No way!"

"There's another wrinkle to all this. A wrinkle that makes me think Jason Archer was some kind of mastermind despite appearances, or maybe that he was *working* for such an organization."

"So what's the wrinkle?"

Hardy suddenly looked embarrassed. "There's some money missing from one of Triton's accounts."

"Money? How much money?"

Hardy eyed Sawyer squarely. "How does a quarter of a billion dollars grab you?"

Sawyer almost spit his coffee across the table. "What?"

"It looks like Archer wasn't just interested in selling secrets. He was also into raiding bank accounts."

"How? I mean, a company that big, it had to have controls in place."

"Triton did, only those controls were premised on it receiving correct information from the bank where the money was on deposit."

"I'm not following you," Sawyer said impatiently.

Hardy sighed and put his elbows on the table. "In this day and age, moving money from point A to point B involves the use of a computer. The banking and financial worlds are wholly dependent upon them, but that dependence comes with risks."

226

"Like there might be some glitch, the computers go down, stuff like that?" Sawyer ventured.

"Or that the bank's computers might be penetrated and manipulated for illegal purposes. It's nothing new. Hell, you know the bureau created a whole new section to deal with computer crimes."

"Is that what you think happened here?"

Hardy sat down and reopened his file, rustling through some pages until he found what he wanted. "An operating account for Triton Global Investments, Corporation, was maintained at Consolidated Bank Trust's branch here in northern Virginia. Triton Global Investments is Triton's Wall Street investment company subsidiary. The account was funded over time until the total bank balance reached two hundred and fifty million."

Sawyer interrupted. "Was Archer involved in setting up the account?"

"No. He had no access to it, in fact."

"Was there a lot of activity in the account?"

"At first, yes. However, as time went on, Triton didn't require the funds. They were sort of kept as a reserve in case Triton or its affiliated companies were in need if funding."

"What happened next?"

"Turns out a couple of months ago a new account was set up at the same bank in the name of Triton Global Investments, Limited."

"So Triton set up another account?"

Hardy was already shaking his head. "No, that's the catch. It was totally unrelated to Triton. Turns out the company is fictitious, no address, no directors or offices, no nothing."

"Do you know who set the bank account up?"

"There was only one signatory to the account. The name given to the bank was Alfred Rhone, chief financial officer. Our investigation turned up zilch on Rhone. But we did find one interesting piece of information."

"What's that?" Sawyer hunched forward in his chair.

"A number of transactions took place from the phony account. Wire transfers, deposits, things like that. The signature of Alfred Rhone appeared on each of these documents. We checked those signatures against those of all of Triton's employees. We found a match. Care to guess who?"

Sawyer's reply was immediate. "Jason Archer."

Hardy nodded.

"So what happened to the money?"

"Someone infiltrated BankTrust's computer system and did some very careful rearranging of accounts. Turns out that the legit Triton account and the phony account were assigned the same account number."

"Christ! You could drive a semi through a hole like that."

"Right. One day before Archer disappeared, a wire transfer authorization was made moving the two hundred and fifty million from the Triton account to an account set up by the phony company at another major money center bank in New York. BankTrust's wire department already had a standing authorization from our friend Alfred Rhone. The account was fully funded, all the *i*'s and *t*'s dotted and crossed. The money was transferred out the same day." Sawyer looked incredulous. "Bank people accept what the computer tells them, Lee, there's no reason not to. Besides, bank departments don't talk to each other. So long as their ass is covered, they just execute orders. Whoever was involved, they knew banking procedures down cold. Did I mention that Jason Archer used to work in the wire department of a bank a few years before he joined Triton?"

Sawyer wearily shook his head. "I knew there was

a reason I don't like computers. I still don't understand how it was done."

"Look at it this way, Lee. It was as if they cloned a rich guy and then walked the fake guy in the front door of the bank, withdrew all the rich guy's money and then walked back out. The only difference is BankTrust thought both guys were rich; however, the bank was looking at the same bank balance for both, only counting the money twice."

"Any trace of the funds?"

Hardy shook his head. "I wouldn't have expected there to be. It's gone. We've already met with members of the bureau's Financial Institutions Fraud Unit. They've commenced an investigation."

Sawyer sipped his coffee and then had a sudden thought. "You think maybe RTG was involved in both schemes? Otherwise, it would seem kind of odd that Archer would risk doing both the bank fraud and selling the secrets."

"In fact, Lee, Archer could have initiated only the theft of the company secrets and then RTG may have put him up to the bank fraud in order to further hurt Triton. He was in a perfect position to do it."

"But the bank had to make good on the loss. Triton wasn't really hurt."

"No, you're wrong there. Triton has lost the use of the money while BankTrust sorts things out and the investigation is continuing. This incident went all the way up to the board of directors. It could take months to unravel, or so Triton was told this morning. As you could imagine, Nathan Gamble is one unhappy man."

"Did Triton need the funds for something?"

"You bet they did. Triton was going to use the funds to put a good-faith deposit down on the acquisition of CyberCom, the company I was telling you about."

"So did the deal fall through?"

"Not yet. The last I heard, Nathan Gamble may provide the funds personally."

"Christ, the guy can write a check that big?"

"Gamble is a billionaire several times over. However, it's not like he wants to do it. That ties up his funds on top of losing two hundred and fifty million of Triton's cash. For him it's a five-hundred-million-dollar swing the wrong way. Even for him, that's a lot of money." Hardy winced slightly as if remembering his last encounter with Gamble. "Like I said, not a very happy man right now. His biggest concern is the secrets Archer sold to RTG, however. If RTG gets CyberCom, then the ultimate loss to Triton will be much more than a quarter billion dollars."

"But now that RTG knows you're on to them, they won't be using the info Archer slipped them."

"It's not that simple, Lee. They've denied any involvement, and while we have the video, it's far from slam-dunk evidence. RTG was already in the bidding for CyberCom. If their deal comes in a little sweeter than Triton's, who's to say how that happened?"

"It does get complicated, I guess." Sawyer wearily studied the remains of his coffee.

Hardy spread out his hands at his old partner and smiled. "Well, that's my story."

"I had faith you wouldn't get me out of bed for a simple purse snatching." Sawyer paused. "Archer must be a certifiable genius, Frank."

"Agreed."

Sawyer suddenly perked up. "Then again, everybody makes mistakes and sometimes you get lucky, like that videotape over there. Besides, it's the hard ones that make the job so gratifying. Right?" A grin spread across his face.

Hardy nodded in weary amusement. "So, where do you go from here?"

Sawyer finished his coffee and hooked the pot for a refill. He seemed reenergized as a number of possibilities on the case had now opened up.

"First, I'm going to use your phone to put out a worldwide APB on Jason Archer. Next, I'm going to pick your brain clean for the next hour. Tomorrow morning I'm going to send a team of agents to Dulles Airport to find out as much as they can about Jason Archer. While they're doing that, I'm going to follow up with a personal interview of someone who may turn out to be truly integral to this whole case."

"Who's that?"

"Sidney Archer."

TWENTY-EIGHT

"**P**aul Brophy, I'm a partner of Sidney's, Mr . . ."

Brophy stood in the foyer of the home, his overnight bag in one hand.

"Bill Patterson. I'm Sidney's father."

"She's spoken of you often, Bill. Sorry we never had a chance to meet until now. Terrible what happened. I had to come here for your daughter. She's one of my closest colleagues. A truly remarkable woman."

Bill Patterson eyed the bag Brophy deposited in one corner of the foyer. Dressed in a dark blue double-breasted suit, the latest in fashionable neckwear and glossy black shoes to go with patterned socks, the tall, lean Brophy cut quite a figure. Something about the smooth manner, though, the way he was casually moving around the stricken household, made Patterson frown. He had spent the better part of his working life with his bullshit radar set on high. His alarm was wailing now.

"She's got a lot of family here for her . . . Paul, was it?" Patterson put particular emphasis on the word *family*.

Brophy looked at him, sizing up the man quickly. "Yes. There's nothing more important than family right now. I hope you don't think I'm intruding. That's the last thing I want to do. I talked to Sidney last night. She said it was okay. I've worked with your daughter for many years. We've been through some legal deals that would send you looking for the

232

ulcer medicine. But I don't have to tell you that. You practically ran Bristol-Aluminium the last five years you were there. Read about you in the *Journal* it seems like every month. And that big spread in *Forbes* a few years ago when you retired."

"Business *is* tough," the older man agreed, relaxing his manner as he briefly recalled past triumphs from his business career.

"Well, I know that's what your competition thought." Brophy flashed the friendliest of grins.

Patterson returned it. The guy was probably okay; after all he had come all this way. Besides, this was not the morning to start any problems. "You want something to drink, or eat? You flew down from New York this morning you say?"

"First shuttle out. If you've got some coffee, that would be great . . . Sidney?" Brophy's eyes eagerly settled on the tall presence entering the room.

Dressed in black, her mother by her side and similarly attired, Sidney Archer came down the hallway.

"Hello, Paul."

Brophy walked quickly over to her, gave her a full hug and a peck on the cheek that seemed to linger for a few seconds. A little flustered, Sidney made introductions with her mother.

"So, how's little Amy taking it?" Brophy asked anxiously.

"She's staying with a friend. She doesn't understand what's happened." Sidney's mother stared at him, her eyes unfriendly.

"Right, that's right." Brophy fell back a step. He had never had kids, but that had still been a stupid question.

Sidney unwittingly helped him. She turned to her mother. "Paul flew down from New York this morning."

Her mother nodded absently and then bustled off to the kitchen to start some breakfast.

Brophy looked at Sidney. Her hair was silky, straw-colored, its color made more dramatic by the backdrop of the black dress. He found her gaunt look particularly attractive. Even though he had his own agenda, Brophy was still taken aback. The woman *was* beautiful.

"Everyone else is going directly to the chapel. After the service they'll come here." She sounded overwhelmed by the prospect.

Brophy caught the tone. "You just take it easy and when you want to go off by yourself, I'll be right here making small talk and keeping everyone's plate filled with food. If there's anything I've learned being a lawyer, it's how to use a lot of words and never really say anything."

"Don't you have to get back to New York?"

Brophy shook his head, his smile triumphant. "I'm hanging out at the D.C. office for a while." He pulled out a slender cassette recorder from his inner coat pocket. "I'm all set. Already dictated three letters and a speech I'm giving at a political fund-raiser next month. All of which means I'm here as long as you need me." He smiled tenderly, put the recorder back, reached out and took her hand.

She smiled back, a little embarrassed, while she slowly pulled her hand free. "I need to go finish up before we leave."

"Fine, I'll go make trouble in the kitchen with your parents."

She walked down the hallway to the bedroom. Brophy watched her go, a smile appearing on his face as he thought of his future prospects. A moment later Brophy walked into the large kitchen, where Sidney's mother was busily preparing eggs, toast and bacon. Bill Patterson hovered in the back, tinkering with the coffeemaker. The phone rang. Patterson took off his glasses and picked it up on the second ring.

"Hello?" He switched the receiver to his other hand. "Yes, it is. What? Oh, uh, look, can this wait? Oh, well, hold on just a minute."

Mrs. Patterson looked at her husband. "Who is it?"

"Henry Wharton." Patterson looked at Brophy. "He's the head guy at your firm, right?"

Brophy nodded. Even though his being an apostle of Goldman was a well-kept secret, Brophy was still not a favorite of Wharton's and Brophy looked forward to the day when Wharton was shoved rudely aside as the leader of Tyler, Stone. "Wonderful man, very caring of his colleagues," Brophy said.

"Yeah, well, his timing's lousy," Patterson said. He put the phone receiver down on the table and walked out of the kitchen. With a conciliatory smile, Brophy moved over to assist Mrs. Patterson.

Her father gently knocked on the door. "Honey?"

Sidney opened the door to the bedroom. Behind her Patterson could see the numerous photos of Jason and the rest of the family spread out on the bed. He took a deep breath and swallowed.

"Sweetie, there's some guy from your firm on the phone. Says it's very important that he talk to you."

"Did he give a name?"

"Henry Wharton."

Sidney's brows plunged together and then her face cleared just as suddenly. "He's probably calling to say he can't make the service. I'm not really on his top ten list right now. I'll take it in here, Dad. Tell him to give me a minute."

As her father started to close the door, he again looked at the photos. He abruptly looked up and caught his daughter staring at him, an almost ashamed expression on her face, as though she were a teenager just caught smoking in her room.

Patterson went over and kissed his daughter on the cheek and gave her a long hug.

In the kitchen Patterson picked up the phone again. "She'll be with you in a minute," he said gruffly. He put the phone back down and was about to return to the intricacies of the coffeemaker when he was interrupted by a knock on the door. All three of the kitchen's occupants looked up. Patterson looked over at his wife. "Expecting anyone this early?"

She shook her head. "It's probably just a neighbor with some more food or something. Go answer it, Bill."

Patterson obediently headed to the front door.

Brophy trailed the older man into the foyer.

Patterson opened the front door. Two gentlemen in suits stared back at him.

"Can I help you?" Patterson asked.

Lee Sawyer deliberately exhibited his credentials. The man beside him did likewise. "I'm FBI Special Agent Lee Sawyer. My partner, Raymond Jackson."

Bill Patterson's confusion was evident as he looked from the official government credentials to the men holding them. They looked steadily back at him.

Sidney quickly put the photos away, lingering over only one: from the day Amy had been born. Jason, dressed in hospital garb, was holding his minutes-old daughter. The look of absolute pride on the new father's face was wonderful to behold. She put that one in her purse. She felt certain she would need it during the course of the day when it all started to become too much, as she knew it would.

She smoothed down her dress and went over to the nightstand, sat down on the bed and picked up the phone.

"Hello, Henry."

"Sid."

If she hadn't been sitting down, Sidney would have undoubtedly toppled to the floor. As it was, her entire body collapsed. Her brain felt as though it had been crushed.

"Sid?" The voice said again, more anxiously.

One step at a time, Sidney managed to focus herself. She felt as though she were struggling to the water's surface from some terrible depths where humans could not survive. Her brain suddenly restarted and she struggled up an inch at a time. As she fought an overpowering urge to pass out, Sidney Archer managed to utter one word in a way she never thought she would again. The two syllables struggled out from between trembling lips.

"Jason?"

TWENTY-NINE

While Sidney's mother walked through the living room to join her husband at the front door, Paul Brophy discreetly retreated until he was once again in the kitchen. FBI? This was getting interesting. While he was pondering whether to contact Goldman, Brophy spotted the phone receiver lying on the counter where Bill Patterson had set it down. Henry Wharton was on the phone. Brophy wondered what they were discussing. He could certainly score some significant points with Goldman if he could find out.

Brophy edged over to the kitchen doorway. The group was still huddled in the front foyer. He hurried over to the kitchen counter, put one hand over the lower part of the receiver and lifted the telephone to his ear. His mouth dropped open and his eyes widened while he listened to two very familiar voices. He reached into his pocket. He held the Dictaphone up to the phone receiver and recorded the conversation between husband and wife.

Five minutes later, Bill Patterson again knocked on his daughter's door. When Sidney finally opened the door, her father was surprised by her appearance. The eyes were still red and weary, but there seemed to be a light in them that he had not seen since Jason's death. He was also startled by what he saw on the bed: a half-filled suitcase.

Without taking his eyes off the suitcase, Patterson said, "Sweetie, I don't know what they want, but the FBI are here. They want to talk to you."

"FBI?" She suddenly went limp and her father grabbed on to one arm.

Patterson's face was a morass of concern. "Baby, what's going on? Why are you packing?"

Sidney managed to regain her composure. "I'm all right, Dad. I . . . I just have to go somewhere after the service."

"Go? Go where? What are you talking about?"

"Dad, please, not now. I can't go into it right now."

"But Sid—"

"Please, Dad."

Under his daughter's pleading eyes, Patterson finally looked away, disappointment and something akin to fear on his features.

"All right, Sidney."

"Where are the agents, Dad?"

"In the living room. They said they want to talk to you privately. I tried to get rid of them, but, hell, they're the FBI, you know?"

"It's all right, Dad, I'll talk to them." Sidney thought for a moment. She looked over at the phone she had just put down and then checked her watch. "Take them into the den and tell them I'll be there in two minutes."

Her hands clasped together, Sidney went over and closed the suitcase, picked it up and slid it under the bed.

Her father followed her movements, then raised his thick eyebrows to ask, "You sure you know what you're doing?"

Her answer was immediate. "I'm sure."

Jason Archer was handcuffed to the chair. A smiling Kenneth Scales held the Glock against his head. Another man hovered in the background. "Good job on the phone, Jason," Scales said. "You might have had a future in the movies. Too bad you don't have a future left."

Jason glared up at him, fury in his eyes. "You sonofabitch! You hurt my wife or my daughter and I'll tear you apart. I swear to God."

Scales's smile broadened. "Is that right. Tell me, how you gonna do that?" He smacked Jason across the jaw with the pistol. The door to the small room they were in opened slightly. As Jason recovered from the blow and stared through the cracked door, a snarl escaped his lips. With a burst of strength, he flung himself across the room, chair and all. He made it to the man's feet before Scales and his associate subdued him, dragging him back across the floor.

"Goddamn you, I'll kill you, I'll kill you!" Jason shrieked at the visitor.

The man stepped into the room and closed the door behind him. He smiled while Jason was dragged up and heavy tape was placed across his mouth. "Having bad dreams again, Jason?"

After Bill Patterson had escorted the two FBI agents to the small but comfortably furnished den, he returned to find his wife and Paul Brophy in the kitchen. He stared over at the phone, puzzlement on his features. The receiver had been replaced on the wall. Brophy caught the look. "I hung it back up for you. Figured you had other things to deal with."

"Thanks, Paul."

"My pleasure." Brophy sipped at his coffee, highly pleased with himself as he fingered the small cassette tape tucked safely in his pants pocket. "Jesus" – he looked at the Pattersons – "the FBI. What could they want?"

Patterson shrugged. "I don't know and I know Sidney doesn't know." He was intensely defensive of his daughter. The worry lines were prominent on his forehead. "Lousy timing all around today, if you ask me," he muttered as he sat down at the table to scan the newspaper. He was about to say something else when he saw the front-page headline.

THIRTY

Agents Sawyer and Jackson rose when Sidney entered the room. Sawyer visibly started when he saw her. He made a conscious effort to suck in his stomach and one of his hands flew up to his hair in a feeble attempt to press his stubborn cowlick back into place. When he brought his hand back down, he looked at it for a moment as though it were not part of his body, wondering what the hell had made it do such a thing. Both agents identified themselves and again displayed their credentials. Sawyer was aware that Sidney looked intently at him before sitting down across from them.

Sawyer rapidly sized her up. A real looker with brains and spirit. But there was something else. He could have sworn they had met before. His eyes drifted over her long form. The black dress was tasteful and appropriate to such a solemn occasion; however, it also clung to her figure in several provocative locations. Her shapely legs too, sheathed in black stocking, were equally inspiring. Her face was lovely in its despair. "Ms. Archer, by any chance have we met before?"

Her surprise was genuine. "I don't think so, Mr. Sawyer."

He studied her for another moment, shrugged and quickly launched into his interview. "As I told your father, Ms. Archer, we understand that the timing of this interview couldn't be worse, but we needed to talk with you as soon as possible."

"May I ask what it concerns?" Sidney's voice was on automatic. Her eyes flitted around the room before coming to rest on Sawyer's face. She saw a big, strong wall of a man who seemed sincere. Under normal circumstances, Sidney would have co-operated fully with Lee Sawyer. Circumstances, however, were far from normal.

Her green eyes were now sparkling and Sawyer had to kick-start his brain when he found himself transfixed by those eyes. In trying to read their depths, he found himself venturing into dangerous waters. "It has to do with your husband, Ms. Archer," he said quickly.

"Please call me Sidney. What about my husband? Is this about the plane accident?"

Sawyer didn't answer right away. He was studying her again without seeming to do so. Every word, every expression, every pause was important. It was always a very tiring, often frustrating, but sometimes incredibly productive task. "It wasn't an accident, Sidney," he finally said.

Her eyes flickered briefly, like the lights in a house do when there's a thunderstorm. The mouth parted slightly, but no words emerged.

"The plane was sabotaged; all the people on board that plane every last one of them, were deliberately murdered." While Sawyer continued to watch, Sidney shut down completely for about a minute. Her features held real, not feigned horror. Her eyes suddenly lost their feverish sparkle.

After a minute, Sawyer gently said, "Sidney? Sidney?"

With a jolt, Sidney came back but then was gone again just as quickly. Her breath suddenly came out in a huge burst. For an instant she was certain she would vomit all over herself. She put her head in her lap, clutching her calves. Ironically, her movements mirrored a passenger in crash position on an airliner. When she started moaning and the rest of her body began to shake uncontrollably, Sawyer swiftly rose and sat beside her. One arm clutched her shoulder, steadying her; the other gripped one of her hands tightly.

Sawyer looked up at Jackson. "Water, tea, something, Ray. Pronto!"

Jackson raced off.

With nervous hands, Sidney's mother poured out a glass of water for Jackson. When Jackson turned to leave, Bill Patterson held up the newspaper. "This is what it's all about, right?" The paper's headlines were big, bold and deadly sounding. WESTERN AIRLINES CRASH BLAMED ON SABOTAGE. FEDERAL GOVERNMENT OFFERS TWO-MILLION-DOLLAR REWARD. "Jason and all the others were victims of a terrorist. That's why you're here, isn't it?" In the background, Mrs. Patterson covered her face in her hands, her quiet weeping pervading the room as she sat down at the table.

"Sir, not right now, okay?" Jackson's tone brooked no opposition. He left the room with the glass of water.

Paul Brophy, meanwhile, had gone into the front yard, ostensibly to smoke a cigarette, despite the cold. If anyone had looked out the living room window, they would have seen the small cellular phone pressed to the side of his face.

Sawyer virtually had to force the water down Sidney's throat, but finally she was able to sit up. After Sidney composed herself and handed back the glass of water with a grateful look, Sawyer did not return to the plane bombing. "Believe me, if this weren't very, very important, we'd leave right now, okay?"

244

Sidney nodded. She still looked ghastly. Sawyer took a moment to marshal his thoughts. Sidney seemed relieved when he asked a couple of seemingly innocuous questions about Jason's work at Triton Global. Sidney answered calmly enough, although she was clearly puzzled. He looked around the room. They had a nice home. "Any money problems?" he asked.

"Where is this going, Mr. Sawyer?" Sidney's face had regained some of its rigidity. Suddenly she softened; she had just remembered Jason's remark about giving her the world.

"Wherever it happens to lead at this point, ma'am," Sawyer answered, his eyes meeting hers without hesitation. They seemed to burn through her exterior wall, clearly reading the thoughts, the nagging doubts buried deep within. She realized she would have to tread very cautiously with him. "We're talking with all the families of the passengers on that plane. If the plane was sabotaged because of who was on it, we need to find out reasons why."

"I see." Sidney took a deep breath. "To answer your question, we're in better shape financially than we've been in years."

"You're an attorney for Triton, right?"

"Among about fifty other clients, So?"

Sawyer changed tactics. "Okay, you know that your husband had taken a few days off from work?"

"I'm his wife."

"Good, then maybe you'd like to explain why it was, if he was taking a few days off, that he happened to be on a plane to L.A."

Sawyer had almost said "allegedly" been on a plane but fortunately caught himself.

Sidney's tone was businesslike. "Look, I have to assume you've already talked to Triton. Maybe you've spoken to Henry Wharton as well. Jason told me he was going to L.A. on business for Triton. On the morning he left, I reminded him that I had a meeting in New York with Triton. That's when he told me he was travelling to L.A. regarding another employment opportunity. He didn't want me to let the fact of his L.A. trip slip to any of the Triton people. I played along. I know it wasn't exactly the most truthful thing to do, but I did it."

"But there was no other job."

Sidney slumped back. "No."

"So, being his wife and all, do you have any idea what he was actually going to L.A. for? Any suspicions?"

She shook her head.

"That's it? Nothing else? You're sure it had nothing to do with Triton?"

"Jason rarely talked about company business with me."

"Why's that?" Sawyer craved a cup of coffee. His body was starting to go down on him after the late night with Hardy.

"My firm represents some other companies who might be perceived as having competing interests with Triton. However, any potential conflict has been waived by the respective clients, including Triton, and we've constructed Chinese walls from time to time when necessary—"

"Come again?" This was Ray Jackson. "Chinese walls?"

Sidney looked at him. "That's what it's called when we cut off communications of any kind, access to files, even shop talk, shooting the breeze in the hallway, about a particular client's matters if an attorney of the firm represents another client with a possible conflict. We even maintain secure computerized databases with respect to pending deals we're handling on behalf of clients. We also do it to

246

ensure that up-to-the-minute negotiation terms are accurately maintained. Deals change fast, and we don't want clients surprised about what the principal terms are. People's memories are fallible; computer memories are a lot better. Access to those files is restricted by use of a password known only to the lead attorney on the case. The theory is that a law firm can carve itself up, upon occasion, in order to avoid problems like that. Hence the term."

Sawyer leaned in. "So what other clients does your firm represent who could possibly have a conflict with Triton?"

Sidney thought for a moment. A name had come to mind, but she was unsure of whether to give it. If she did, the interview might be hastened to a conclusion.

"RTG Group."

Sawyer and Jackson exchanged quick glances. Sawyer spoke up.

"Who at your firm represents RTG?"

Sawyer was sure he caught a twinkle in Sidney Archer's eyes before she answered. "Philip Goldman."

In front yard of the Archers' home, the cold was beginning to eat through Paul Brophy's very expensive gloves.

"No, I have no clue as to what's going on," Brophy said into the cellular phone. He jerked his head away from the handheld unit when the speaker on the other end unleashed a blistering response to Brophy's professed ignorance. "Wait a minute, Philip. It's the FBI. They carry guns, okay? You weren't expecting that to happen, why should I?"

This deference to Philip Goldman's superior intelligence apparently calmed the man down because Brophy now held the phone normally. "Yes, I'm sure it was him. I know what he sounds like and she called him by name. I've got the whole thing on tape. Pretty damn brilliant on my part, wouldn't you say? What? Yeah, you bet I plan on sticking around, see what I can find out. Right, I'll check back with you in a few hours." Brophy put the phone away, rubbed his stiff fingers together and went back in the house.

Sawyer was watching Sidney Archer carefully as she slid her hand back and forth on the armrest of the sofa. He was debating whether to drop the bombshell on her; to tell her that Jason Archer was definitely not buried in a crater in Virginia. Finally, after much internal conflict, his gut won out over his brain. He rose and offered Sidney his hand. "Thank you for your cooperation, Ms. Archer. If you think of anything that might help us, you can reach me day or night at these numbers." Sawyer handed her a card. "That's my home phone on the back. Do you have a card with numbers where you can be reached?" Sidney picked up her purse from the table, rummaged through it and produced one of her business cards. "Again, I'm sorry about your husband." He truly meant the last part. If Hardy was right, then what the woman was going through right now would seem like a day in the park compared to what was ahead for her. Ray Jackson exited the room. Sawyer was about to join him when Sidney put a hand on his shoulder.

"Mr. Sawyer—"

"You can make it Lee."

"Lee, I would have to be pretty stupid not to realize that this all looks very bad."

"And not for a minute do I think you're stupid, Sidney." They exchanged glances of mutual respect; however, Sawyer's statement was not entirely supportive.

"Do you have any reason to suspect that my husband was involved in anything . . ." – she paused and swallowed hard, preparing to utter the unthinkable – "in anything illegal?"

He looked at her, and the unmistakable sense that he had seen the woman somewhere began to nag him again until it became a certainty. "Sidney, let's just say that your husband's activities right before he left on that flight are giving us some problems."

Sidney thought back to all those late nights, Jason's trips back to the office. "Is anything amiss at Triton?"

Sawyer watched her squeezing her hands together. Normally the most tight-lipped of FBI agents, for some reason Sawyer wanted to tell her everything he knew. He resisted the temptation. "It's an on-going bureau investigation, Sidney. I really can't say."

She stepped back a bit. "I understand, of course."

"We'll be in touch."

After Sawyer left the room, Sidney felt a twinge of apprehension as she recalled Nathan Gamble's similar remark about keeping in touch. She suddenly felt enveloped by cold bands of fear. She hugged herself and drew closer to the fire.

The phone call from Jason had initially buoyed her to the highest levels of euphoria. She had never felt such joy, yet the scant details he had provided had brought her plummeting back downward. She was currently in a state of utter confusion, helplessness and unbridled loyalty to her husband; an unwieldy emotional elixir to be carrying around inside. She wondered what surprises tomorrow would bring.

On the way out of the house, the two agents were trailed by a chatty Paul Brophy. "So obviously my firm would be quite anxious to learn of any possible wrongdoing involving Jason Archer and Triton Global." He finally stopped talking and looked hopeful.

Sawyer just kept walking. "So I've heard." The FBI agent stopped behind Bill Patterson's Cadillac, which was parked in the driveway. When he put his foot up on the rear bumper to retie his shoelaces, he saw a MAINE, THE VACATIONLAND STATE bumper sticker. *When was the last time I had a vacation?* he thought. *You know you're in trouble when you can't even remember.* He hitched up his pants and turned to the attorney, who was watching him from the front sidewalk.

"What'd you say your name was again?"

Brophy glanced at the front door and then hurried over. "Brophy. Paul Brophy." He hurriedly added, "As I said, I'm a New York-based attorney, so I really have little to do with Sidney Archer."

Sawyer eyed him closely. "And yet you flew all the way down here for the memorial service. That's what you said, right?"

Brophy looked at both men. Ray Jackson's eyes narrowed as he took in Paul Brophy. Slick money and bullshit were written all over the man.

"I'm really here as the firm's representative. Sort of by default. Sidney Archer is *only* a part-time attorney, and I was in town on business anyway."

Sawyer stared at the patch of cloud above the house. "Is that right? You know, I had an opportunity to check up on Ms. Archer. From the people I spoke with, she's one of Tyler, Stone's top attorneys. Part-time or not. In fact, I asked for a list of the top five guns in your place from at least three different sources, and you know what? The lady was on every list." He looked at Brophy and added, "Funny, though, your name never came up."

Brophy sputtered for a moment, but Sawyer

wanted to move on anyway. "You been here awhile, Mr. Brophy?" He nodded in the direction of the Archer residence.

"About an hour. Why?" Brophy's whiny tone betrayed his hurt feelings.

"Anything unusual happen while you were here?"

Brophy was bursting to tell the agents he had a dead man's words captured on tape, but that information was far too valuable simply to give away. "Not really. I mean, she's tired and depressed, or at least seems so."

"What do you mean by that?" Jackson asked, taking off his sunglasses and staring at Brophy.

"Nothing. I mean, like I said, I don't know Sidney all that well. So I don't know if she and her husband really got along."

"Uh-huh." Jackson's lip curled and he put his shades back on. He eyed his partner. "You ready, Lee? This man here looks cold. Oughta go in there and warm up," he said, looking at Brophy. "Go pay your respects to your *bare* acquaintance in there."

Jackson and Sawyer turned and headed to their car.

Brophy's face was red with anger. He looked back at the house once more and then called after them. "Oh, that's right, there was the phone call she got."

Both agents turned in perfect unison. "What's that?" Sawyer asked. His temples throbbed from lack of caffeine and he was tired of listening to this jerk. "What phone call?"

Brophy approached them and spoke in a lowered tone, occasionally glancing back at the house. "About two minutes before you showed up. The caller identified himself as Henry Wharton when Sidney's father answered the phone." The agents looked puzzled. "He's the managing partner of Tyler, Stone."

251

"So?" Jackson said. "The man might be checking in on her. Seeing if she's okay."

"That's what I would've thought too, but . . ."

Sawyer's fuse was about gone. "But what?" he asked angrily.

"I'm not sure if I'm at liberty to say."

Sawyer's voice dropped back to normal, but his words took on an even more menacing tone. "It's a little cold out here for bullshit responses, Mr. Brophy, so I'm going to ask you real nicely to give me the information, and that will be the only time I'll ask real nicely." Sawyer leaned into Brophy's now frightened face while the burly Jackson crowded him from behind.

Brophy blurted out, "I called Henry Wharton at the office while Sidney was talking to you". Brophy paused dramatically. "When I asked about his talk with Sidney, he was completely surprised. He had never called her. And when she came out of the bedroom after taking the call, she was white as a sheet. I thought she was going to faint. Her father noticed it too and was greatly disturbed."

"Well, if the FBI came knocking on my door on the day of my spouse's memorial service, I'd probably look pretty bad too," Jackson responded. One hand curled and uncurled, making a very large fist that he would have given anything at that moment to let fly. "Yeah, well, according to her father, she looked that way *before* he told her you were at the front door." Brophy had made that part up, but so what? It wasn't the FBI appearing at her doorstep that had thrown Sidney Archer for a loop.

Sawyer straightened up and looked at the house. He eyed Jackson whose eyebrows clicked up a notch. Sawyer studied Brophy's face. If the guy was screwing with them . . . But no, it was obvious he was telling the truth, or at least mostly the truth. He had evidently been dying to tell them something to bounce Sidney Archer off the ceiling. Sawyer didn't care about Paul Brophy's personal vendetta. He did care about that phone call.

"Thanks for the information, Mr. Brophy. You think of anything else, here's my number." He handed the attorney his card and left him in the front yard.

Driving back into town, Sawyer glanced at his partner. "I want Sidney Archer put under immediate twenty-four-hour surveillance. And I want all calls going into her home in the last twenty-four hours checked, starting with the one Mister Fancy Pants told us about."

Jackson stared out the window. "You think that was her husband on the phone?"

"I think she's been through enough hell to where it would take something pretty big to knock her off her feet like that. Even while we were talking to her, you could see something was off. Way off."

"So she *did* think he was dead?"

Sawyer shrugged. "Right now, I'm not jumping to any conclusions. We'll just watch her and see what happens. My gut tells me Sidney Archer is going to turn out to be a pretty interesting piece to this puzzle."

"Speaking of guts, can we stop and get something to eat? I'm starving." Jackson looked at the long line of eateries they were now passing.

"Hell, I'll even buy, Ray. Nothing's too good for my partner." Sawyer smiled and turned into the parking lot of a McDonald's. Jackson looked over at Sawyer, mock disgust on his face. Then, shaking his head, he picked up the car phone and started punching in numbers.

THIRTY-ONE

The slim Learjet streaked through the skies with power to spare. Inside the luxurious cabin Philip Goldman reclined in his seat and sipped at a cup of hot tea while the remnants of a meal were cleared away by the cabin steward. Across from Goldman sat Alan Porcher, president and chief executive officer of RTG Group, the Western Europe-based global consortium. The tanned, slender Porcher cradled a glass of wine and studied the attorney intently before speaking.

"You know Triton Global claims they have concrete evidence of one of their employees handing over sensitive documents to us at one of our warehouse facilities in Seattle. We can expect to hear from their lawyers shortly, I would imagine." Porcher paused. "From *your* law firm, of course, Tyler, Stone. Ironic, isn't it?"

Goldman put down his teacup and folded his hands in his lap." And this troubles you?"

Porcher looked surprised. "Why shouldn't it?"

Goldman's reply was simple. "Because, with respect to that claim, you're not guilty." He added, "Ironic, isn't it?"

"Still, I have heard some things about the CyberCom deal that trouble me, Philip."

Goldman sighed and sat forward in his cabin chair. "Such as?"

"That perhaps the acquisition of CyberCom will occur more rapidly than we thought. That perhaps we do not know the latest offer that will be made by Triton. When we make our offer, I must be assured it will be accepted. I will not be allowed to bid again. CyberCom is inclined toward the Americans as it is."

Goldman cocked his head and absorbed the CEO's words. "I'm not so sure of that. The Internet knows no geopolitical boundaries. So who's to say the domination cannot occur from the other side of the Atlantic?"

Porcher took another sip of wine before answering. "No, other things being equal, the deal will land in the western hemisphere. Therefore, we must ensure that conditions are decidedly unequal." There was now a hard glint in Porcher's eyes.

Goldman took a moment to methodically wipe his mouth with his handkerchief before responding. "Tell me, who are your sources for this information?"

Porcher waved his hand distractedly. "It blows in the wind."

"I don't believe in winds. I believe in facts. And the facts are that we do know Triton's latest negotiating position. To the last detail."

"Yes, but Brophy is now out of the loop. I cannot be limited to old news."

"You won't be. As I've told you, I am currently very close to solving that problem. When I do, and I will, you can easily trump Triton and walk away with an acquisition that will ensure your domination of the information superhighway for the foreseeable future."

Porcher looked pointedly at the attorney. "You know, Philip, I have often been curious about your motivation regarding this matter. If, as I hope and you continue to promise, we succeed in acquiring CyberCom, Triton will most assuredly be unhappy with your law firm. They may go elsewhere."

"One can only hope." A faraway look appeared on Goldman's face as he thought of the possibility.

"I'm afraid you have lost me."

Goldman assumed a pedantic tone. "Triton Global is Tyler, Stone's largest client. Triton Global is Henry Wharton's client. That is the chief reason Henry is managing partner. If Triton ceases using the firm as counsel, would you like to guess who becomes the largest rainmaker at the firm and, therefore, the probable successor to Wharton as managing partner?"

Porcher pointed at Goldman. "And I would hope that in such a case RTG matters would be given the highest priority in the firm."

"I think I can safely promise that."

Porcher put sown his wineglass and lit a cigarette. "Now tell me exactly how you plan to solve the problem."

"Do you really care about the method, or just the results?"

"Indulge me with your brilliance. I recall you often enjoy doing that. Just don't sound so damn professorial when doing so. I have been out of university many years now."

Goldman raised an eyebrow at the CEO's remark. "You seem to know me all too well."

"You are one of the few attorneys in my acquaintance who thinks like a businessman. Winning is king. Fuck the law!"

Goldman accepted one of the cigarettes from Porcher and took a moment lighting it. "A very recent development has occurred that has given us a golden opportunity to gain firsthand, almost real-time information about Triton's proposed deal with CyberCom. We'll know Triton's best and final offer before they even have a chance to communicate it to CyberCom. Then we march in a few hours earlier, present our proposal and wait for Triton's deal to come in. CyberCom rejects it and you become the proud owner of another jewel in your far-flung empire."

Porcher slowly withdrew the cigarette from between his lips and stared wide-eyed at his companion. "You can do this?"

"I can do this."

THIRTY-TWO

"Lee, let me warn you, he can be a little abrasive at times, but that's just the man's personality." Frank Hardy glanced back at Sawyer, and the two men walked down a long corridor after exiting a private elevator on to the top floor of the Triton Global building.

"Kid gloves, I promise, Frank. I don't usually pull out my brass knuckles on the victims, you know."

While they walked, Sawyer reflected on the results of the airport queries about Jason Archer. His men had dug up two airport personnel who had recognized Jason Archer's picture. One was the Western Airlines employee who had checked in his bag on the morning of the seventeenth. The other was a janitor who had noticed Jason sitting and reading the paper. He remembered him because Jason had never let go of his leather briefcase, even while reading the paper or drinking his coffee. Jason had gone into the rest room, but the janitor had left the area and had not noticed him coming back out. The FBI agents could not question the young woman who had actually collected boarding passes from the passengers on the ill-fated plane, since she had been one of the flight attendants on Flight 3223. A number of people recalled seeing Arthur Lieberman. He had been a regular at Dulles for many years. All in all, not much useful information.

Sawyer refocused on Hardy's back; he was moving quickly down the plushly carpeted hallway.

Gaining entry to the technology giant's head-quarters had not been easy. Triton's security had been so zealous that they had even wanted to call the bureau to verify the serial number on Sawyer's credentials until Hardy sternly informed them that that would be unnecessary and that the veteran FBI special agent deserved a lot more deference than he was being shown. None of that had ever happened to Sawyer before in all his years with the bureau, and he jokingly let a sheepish Hardy know it.

"Hey, Frank, these guys hoarding gold bullion or uranium 235 in here?"

"Let's just say they're slightly paranoid."

"I'm impressed. Usually we FBI types scare the crap out of everybody. I bet they thumb their noses at the IRS guys too."

"Actually, a former head of the IRS is their top tax guru."

"Damn, they really do have all the bases covered."

An uneasy feeling crept over Sawyer the more he thought about his chosen profession. Information was king these days. Access to information was ruled by and large through computers. The private sector was so far ahead of the government realm that there was no possible way the government would ever catch up. Even the FBI, which in public sectors had state-of-the-art technology, would have existed far down the technological sophistication list in the world where Triton Global did battle. To Sawyer the revelation was not a pleasant one. One would have to be an imbecile not to realize that computer crimes would soon dwarf all other manifestations of human evil, at least in dollar terms. But dollar terms meant a lot. They translated into jobs and homes and happy families. Or not. Sawyer stopped walking. "You mind me asking how much Triton pays you a year?"

Hardy turned around and smiled. "Why? You

thinking of hanging out your own shingle and trying to steal my clients?"

"Hey, just testing the waters in case I ever take you up on that offer of a job."

Hardy glanced sharply at Sawyer. "You serious?"

"At my age, you learn never to say never."

Hardy's face resumed its serious look while he pondered his ex-partners words. "I'd rather not get into specifics, but Triton is well into the seven figures as a client, not counting a substantial retainer they pay us."

Sawyer blew a silent whistle. "Christ, I hope you see a big slice of that at the end of the day, Frank."

Hardy nodded curtly. "I do. And you could too if you'd ever wise up and join me."

"Okay, I'll bite: What are we talking salary-wise if I come on with you? Just ballpark."

"Five to six hundred thousand the first year."

Sawyer's mouth almost hit the floor. "You've got to be shitting me, Frank."

"I never joke about money, Lee. As long as crime is around, we'll never have a bad year." The men resumed walking as Hardy added, "Think about it anyway, will you?"

Sawyer rubbed his chin and thought about his mounting debt, never-ending work hours and his tiny office at the Hoover Building. "I will, Frank." He decided to change the subject. "So is Gamble a one-man show?"

"Not by a long shot. Oh, he's the undisputed leader of Triton; however, the real technology wizard is Quentin Rowe."

"What's he like? A geek?"

"Yes and no," Hardy explained. "Quentin Rowe graduated at the top of his class from Columbia University. He won a slew of awards in the technology field while working at Bell Labs, and then at

260

Intel. He started his own computer company at age twenty-eight. That company was the hottest stock on NASDAQ three years ago and was one of the most sought-after acquisitions of the decade when Nathan Gamble bought it. It's been a brilliant fit. Quentin is the true visionary at the company. He's the one pushing for the CyberCom acquisition. He and Gamble aren't the best of friends, but they've done incredibly well together and Gamble tends to listen to him if the dollars are right. Anyway, you can't argue with the success they've had."

Sawyer nodded. "By the way, we got Sidney Archer under round-the-clock surveillance."

"I take it your interview with her aroused some suspicions."

"You could say that. And something shook her up right when we got there."

"What was that?"

"A phone call."

"From who?"

"I don't know. We traced the call. It came from a phone booth in Los Angeles. Whoever placed the call could be in Australia by now."

"You think it was her husband?"

Sawyer shrugged. "Our source said the person lied about who he was to Sidney Archer's dad when he picked up the phone. And our source said Sidney Archer looked like death warmed over after the call."

Using a smart card, Hardy accessed a private elevator. While they were carried up to the top floor, Hardy took a moment to adjust his fashionable tie and flick at his hair in the reflection of the mirrored elevator doors. His thousand-dollar suit hung well on his lead frame. Gold-plated cuff links glinted at his wrists. Sawyer appraised his former partner's exterior and then looked at his own reflection. His shirt, while freshly laundered, was frayed at the collar, the tie was a relic from a decade ago. Topping it off, Sawyer's perpetual cowlick stuck up like a tiny periscope. Sawyer assumed a mock serious tone as he looked over the very polished Hardy. "You know, Frank, it's a good thing you left the bureau."

"What?" Hardy was rocked.

"You're just too damn pretty to be an FBI agent anymore." Sawyer grinned

Hardy laughed. "Speaking of pretty, I had lunch with Meggie the other day. Great head on her shoulders too. Getting into law school at Stanford isn't easy. She's going to have a great life."

"In spite of her old man, you probably want to add."

The elevator stopped and they got off. "I don't have the best track record in the world with my two, Lee, you know that. You weren't the only one who missed all those birthdays."

"I think you recovered a lot better with your kids than I did."

"Yeah? Well, Stanford isn't cheap. Think about my offer. Might speed up your recovery. Here we are." Hardy passed through elegant glass doors etched with the shape of an eagle, the glass sliding noise-lessly open at their approach. The executive secretary, a nice-looking woman with an efficient, firm manner, announced their arrival into her headset. She pressed a button set in a panel on top of a sleek wood and metal console that looked more like a piece of modern art than a desk, and motioned Hardy and Sawyer to move toward a massive wall of lacquered Macassar ebony wood. A section of the wall opened up when they approached. Sawyer shook his head in amazement, as he had done many times since entering the Triton building.

In a few moments they were standing in front of a

desk, although a more apt description would have labelled it a command center, with its wall of TV monitors, phones and other electronic gadgetry neatly built into shining tables and impressive wall units. The man behind the desk was just putting down the phone. He turned to them.

Hardy said, "Special Agent Lee Sawyer of the FBI, Nathan Gamble, chairman of Triton Global."

Sawyer could feel the strength of the grip when Nathan Gamble's fingers closed around his own and the two men exchanged perfunctory greetings.

"Do you have Archer yet?"

Sawyer was halfway to his chair when the question hit him. The tone was clearly that of a superior to a subordinate and was more than sufficient to raise every hair on the agent's thick neck. Sawyer finished sitting down and took a moment to study the man before answering. Out of the corner of his eye, Sawyer caught the apprehensive look on his former partner's face from where he stood rigidly near the doorway. Sawyer took another moment to undo the button on his suit coat and flip open his notebook before resting his steady eyes back on Gamble.

"I'll need to ask you some questions, Mr. Gamble. I hope it won't take all that long."

"You haven't answered my question." The chairman's voice was a notch deeper now.

"No, I haven't and I don't intend to." The two men's eyes locked, until Gamble finally broke it off and looked over at Hardy.

"Mr. Gamble, it's an ongoing bureau investigation. The bureau doesn't usually comment—"

Gamble cut Hardy off with an abrupt wave of his hand. "Then let's get this over with. I have to leave to catch a plane in one hour."

Sawyer didn't know who he wanted to belt more – Gamble, or Hardy for taking this kind of crap.

263

"Mr. Gamble, perhaps Quentin and Richard Lucas should be in on this discussion."

"Maybe you should have thought about that before scheduling this meeting, Hardy." Gamble punched a button on his console.

"Find Rowe and Lucas, right now."

Hardy touched Sawyer on the shoulder. "Quentin heads up the division Archer was in. Lucas is head of internal security."

"Then you're right, Frank, I'll want to speak with them."

A few minutes later the broad portal opened and two men stepped into Nathan Gamble's private domain. Sawyer ran a penetrating eye over them and quickly discerned who was who. His grim demeanour, his look of competitive reproach at Hardy, and the slight hump under his left breast labelled Richard Lucas as Triton's head of security. Sawyer pegged Quentin Rowe as early thirties. Rowe's face held a ready smile underneath a pair of large hazel eyes that were more dreamy than intense. Sawyer concluded that Nathan Gamble could not have had a more unlikely colleague. The expanded group adjourned to the large conference table housed in one corner of Gamble's mammoth office.

Gamble stared at his watch and then looked over at Sawyer. "You have fifty minutes and counting, Sawyer. I was hoping you'd have something important for me. However, I feel disappointment looming. Why don't you prove me wrong?"

Sawyer bit his lip and tensed his shoulders, then decided against taking the bait. He looked over at Lucas. "When did you first suspect Archer?"

Lucas shifted uncomfortably in his chair. Obviously, the security man felt particularly humbled by recent events. "The first definitive event was the videotape of Archer making the exchange in Seattle."

"The one Frank's people obtained?" Sawyer eyed Lucas for confirmation.

Lucas's sullen expression spoke volumes. "That's right. Although I had my own suspicion of Archer before the video was taken."

Gamble spoke up. "Is that so? I don't recall your ever voicing those suspicions before. I don't pay you all that money to keep your mouth shut."

Sawyer eyed Lucas closely. The guy had said too much with probably nothing to back it up. But Sawyer was duty-bound to follow through.

"What sort of suspicions?"

Lucas's face was still frozen on his boss, the fierce reprimand still resonating. Lucas looked dully at Sawyer. "Well, perhaps they were more hunches than anything else. Nothing concrete to go on. Just my gut. Sometimes that's more important, you know what I mean?"

"I do."

"He worked a lot. Irregular hours. His computer log-in times made for some interesting reading, I can tell you that."

Gamble stirred. "I only hire hard workers. Eighty percent of the people here pull seventy-five to ninety hours per week, every week of the year."

"I take it you don't believe in idle hands," Sawyer said.

"I work my people hard, but they're well compensated. Every senior-level manager on up to the executive level at my company is a millionaire. And most of them are under forty." He nodded at Quentin Rowe. "I won't tell you how much he got when I bought him out, but if he wanted to go buy an island somewhere, build himself a mansion, bring in a harem and a private jet, he could do it all without borrowing a dime and have enough left over to keep his great-grandchildren in Ivy League and limos. Of course, I wouldn't expect a federal bureaucrat to understand the nuances of free enterprise. You now have forty-seven minutes left."

Sawyer promised himself he would never allow Gamble an opening of that size again. "Have you confirmed the facts of the bank account scam?" Sawyer eyed Hardy.

His friend nodded. "I'll hook you up with bureau agents handling it."

Gamble erupted, slamming his fist on the table and glaring at Sawyer as though he had personally ripped off the Triton chief. "Two hundred and fifty million dollars!" Gamble was shaking with fury.

An awkward moment of silence was broken by Sawyer. "I understand Archer had some additional protective measures put on his office door."

Lucas answered, his face a shade paler. "That's right, he did."

"I'll need to look over his office later. What sort of things did he have installed?"

Everyone in the room looked at Richard Lucas. Sawyer could almost see the sweat glistening on the security chief's palms.

"A few months ago he ordered a digital numeric pad and smart card entry system wired to an alarm for his office door."

"Was that unusual or necessary?" Sawyer asked. He couldn't imagine it was necessary, considering how many damn hoops one had to jump through just to get in the place.

"I didn't think it was necessary at all. We have the most secure shop in the industry." Lucas cringed when this response was met by a loud grunt from Gamble. "But I'm not sure I could say it was unusual; other people here had similar setups on

266

their office doors."

Quentin Rowe joined in. "Not that you could have missed it, Mr. Sawyer, but everyone at Triton is terribly security conscious. It's beaten into the head of every employee here that paranoia is the proper mind-set to have when it comes to protecting proprietary technology. In fact, Frank comes in each quarter and lectures the employees on that very subject. If an employee had a problem or security concern, he or she could go either to Richard or one of his staff, or Frank. My employees all knew of Frank's illustrious career at the FBI. I feel confident that anyone with a concern about security would have no hesitation about going to either of them. In fact, employees have done that in the past, nipping some potentially big problems in the bud."

Sawyer looked over at Hardy, who nodded in agreement. "But you had trouble getting into his office after he disappeared. You must have a system to take into account employees who get sick, die or quit."

"There is a system," Lucas proclaimed.

"Jason apparently circumvented it," Rowe said with a trace of admiration.

"How?"

Rowe looked at Lucas and then sighed. "In accordance with company policy, the code to be inputted into any individual security system placed on-site had to be delivered to the head of security," Quentin explained. "To Rich. In addition, all security personnel and key management have master key cards that can access any area of the office."

"Did Archer deliver the code?"

"He delivered the code to Rich, but then he re-programmed the reader unit at his office door with a different code."

"And that switch wasn't caught before?" Sawyer looked incredulously over at Lucas.

"There was no reason to think he had changed the code," Rowe said. "During office hours Jason's office door was usually kept open. No one other than Jason had any reason to be in there after normal hours."

"Okay, the information Archer allegedly delivered to RTG, how did he get his hands on it? Was he cleared for it?"

"Some of it." Quentin Rowe shifted uneasily in his seat and slid one hand down his ponytail. "Jason was part of the acquisition team for that project. However, there were certain parts, the highest levels of the negotiation, to which he was not privy at all. They were known only to Nathan, myself, and three other senior executives at the company. And outside legal counsel, of course."

"Where was this information kept? File drawer? Safe?" Sawyer asked.

Rowe and Lucas exchanged smiles.

Rowe answered. "We have, to a significant degree, a paperless office. All key documents are stored in computerized files."

"I assume there was some sort of security on these files, then? Like a password."

Lucas said condescendingly, "It was far more than a password."

"And yet Archer broke into it anyway, it seems," Sawyer jabbed back.

Lucas scrunched his mouth up like someone had just jammed a lemon inside.

Quentin Rowe wiped at his glasses. "Yes, he did. Would you like to see how?"

The group of men filled the small, cluttered storeroom. Richard Lucas pushed away the boxes from beside the wall while Rowe, Hardy and Sawyer looked on. Nathan Gamble had declined to join them. Where the boxes had rested, the cable outlet was now exposed. Quentin Rowe moved next to the computer and held up the cables.

"Jason hardwired into our local area network through this workstation."

"Why not just use the computer in his office?"

Rowe was shaking his head before Sawyer had stopped talking. "When he logs on to his own computer," Lucas said, "he has to go through a series of security measures. Those security measures do not merely verify the user they *confirm* the user's identity. Every workstation in the place has an iris scanner, which takes an initial video image of the user's iris patterns. In addition, the scanner takes periodic sweeps of the operator to continually confirm the user's identity. If Archer had left his desk or someone had sat down in his place, then the system would have automatically shut off to that workstation."

Rowe looked steadily at Sawyer. "The important point in all that is if Archer had accessed any file from his own workstation, we would have known he had done it."

"How's that?" Sawyer asked.

"Our network has a tag feature. Most systems have some attribute of that kind. If a user accesses a file, that access is recorded by the system. By using this workstation" – Quentin pointed at the old computer – "which is not supposed to be on the network and is assigned no number through the network administrator, he bypassed that risk. For all intents and purposes, this was a phantom computer on our network. He may have used the computer in his office to find the location of certain files without accessing them. He could do that at his leisure. That would cut down on the time he needed to spend here, where he could be caught."

Sawyer shook his head. "Wait a minute. If Archer

didn't use his own workstation to access the files because it could positively identify him and used this one instead because it couldn't, how do you know it was Archer who accessed the files in the first place?"

Hardy pointed at the keyboard. "An old reliable. We lifted numerous fingerprints from here. They all matched Archer's."

Sawyer finally asked the most obvious question. "Okay, but how do you know this workstation was used to access any files?"

Lucas sat down on one of the boxes. "For a period of time we were getting unauthorized entries on to the system. Although Archer didn't need to go through the identification process to log on through this unit, he would still leave a trail if he accessed files using it unless he electronically erased his trail as he exited. That's possible to do, although tricky. In fact, I think that's what he did. Initially, at least. Then he got sloppy. We finally picked up the trail and, while it took time, we narrowed down the breach until it led us right here."

Hardy folded his arms across his chest. "You know, it's ironic. You put all this time and effort and money into securing your networks against any breaches. You have steel doors, security guards, electronic monitoring devices, smart cards – you name it, Triton has it. And yet . . ." He looked up at the ceiling. "And yet you also have drop-down ceiling panels with exposed cables connecting your entire network together, ripe for penetration." He shook his head in dismay and looked at Lucas. "I've warned you about this risk before."

"He was an insider," Lucas said heatedly. "He knew the system and he used that knowledge to hack it." Lucas brooded for a moment. "And then he took down a planeload of people in the process. Let's not forget that little fact."

Ten minutes later the men were once again in Gamble's office. He did not look up when they reappeared.

Sawyer sat down. "Okay, any further developments on the RTG end?" he asked.

Gamble's face flamed red at the mention of his competitor. "Nobody rips me off and gets away with it."

"Jason Archer's involvement with RTG hasn't been proven. It's all speculation at this point," Sawyer said evenly.

Gamble dramatically rolled his eyes. "Right! Well, you just go and jump through your little hoops so you can keep your little job and I'll take care of the tough stuff."

Sawyer closed his notebook and stood up to his full height. Hardy stood up too, and reached out to grab Sawyer's coat, until his former partner froze him with a stare that Hardy had seen him use on many an occasion at the bureau. Sawyer turned back to Gamble.

"Ten minutes, Sawyer. Since you don't appear to have anything of note to report, I'm going to catch my plane a little early." When Gamble walked past the burly FBI agent, Sawyer tightly gripped his arm and led the Triton chairman outside into the private reception area. Sawyer looked over at Gamble's executive assistant. "Excuse us for a minute, ma'am." The woman hesitated, looking at Gamble.

"I said excuse us!" Sawyer's drill-sergeant tone catapulted the woman out of her chair and she fled the room.

Sawyer turned to the chairman. "Let's get a couple of things straight, Gamble. First, I don't report to you or anyone else at this place. Second, since it looks like one of your people conspired to blow up a plane, I'll ask you as many questions as I want to and I don't give a shit about your travel schedule. And if you tell me one more time how many minutes I've got left, I'll rip that goddamned watch off your wrist and stuff it in your mouth. I'm not one of your lackey boys and don't you ever, ever talk to me that way again. I'm an FBI agent and a damn good one. I've been shot, knifed, kicked and bitten by some seriously demented assholes who would make you look like the biggest pussy in the world on your best day. So if you think your bullshit tough-guy act is gonna make me pee in my pants, then you're wasting everybody's time, including your own. Now get back in there and sit the fuck down."

Two hours later Sawyer had finished interviewing Gamble and company and spent thirty minutes looking through Jason Archer's office, ordering it off limits and calling for a investigative team to methodically analyze every molecule of the place. Sawyer checked out Jason's computer system, but he had no way of knowing that something was missing. The only remnant of the microphone was a small, silver-plated plug.

Sawyer walked to the elevator bank with Hardy.

"See, Frank, I told you there was nothing to worry about. Gamble and I got along just fine."

Hardy laughed out loud. "I don't think I've ever seen his face quite that shade of white before. What the hell did you say to the man?"

"Just told him what a great guy I thought he was. He was probably just embarrassed by my frank admiration."

At the elevators, Sawyer said, "You know, I didn't get much usable info in there. Sure, Archer pulling off the crime of the century might make for fascinating reading, but I'd prefer to have him in a jail cell."

"Well, these guys just got taken to the cleaners and they're certainly not used to that experience. They know what happened and pretty much how it happened, but all after the fact."

Sawyer leaned up against the wall and rubbed his forehead. "You realize there's no evidence tying Archer to the plane bombing."

Hardy nodded in agreement. "I said before that Archer could've used Lieberman to cover his tracks, but there's no proof of that either. If there is no connection, Archer's one helluva lucky guy for not getting on that plane."

"Well, if that's the case, then somebody else out there took down that airliner."

Sawyer was about to hit the elevator button when Hardy touched his sleeve. "Hey, Lee, if you want my humble opinion, I don't think your biggest problem will be proving Archer was involved in the plane sabotage."

"So what's my biggest problem, Frank?"

"Finding him."

Hardy walked off. As Sawyer waited for the elevator, a voice called to him.

"Mr. Sawyer? Do you have a minute?"

Sawyer turned to find Quentin Rowe walking toward him.

"What can I do for you, Mr. Rowe?"

"Please call me Quentin." Rowe paused and looked around the hallways. "Would you like to take a short tour of one of our production facilities?"

Sawyer quickly caught his meaning. "Okay. Sure."

THIRTY-THREE

The fifteen-story Triton office building was hooked to a sprawling three-story structure that covered about five acres of ground. Sawyer pinned on a visitor's badge at the main entrance to the facility and followed Rowe through a number of security checkpoints. Rowe was obviously well-known and well-liked here, as he received a number of cordial greetings from Triton personnel. At one point, through a wall of glass, Sawyer and Rowe watched lab technicians in white coats, gloves and surgical masks working in a large space.

Sawyer looked at Rowe. "Geez, looks more like an operating room than a factory."

Rowe smiled. "Actually, that room is far cleaner than any hospital operating room."

He watched Sawyer's surprised reaction with amusement. "Those technicians are testing a new generation of computer chips. The environment has to be completely sterile, absolutely dust-free. Once they're fully functional, these prototypes will be able to carry out two TIPS."

"Damn," Sawyer said absently, having no earthly idea what the acronym stood for.

"That means two trillion instructions per *second*."

Sawyer gaped at the small man. "What in the hell needs to move that fast?"

"You'd be surprised. A litany of engineering applications. Computer-aided designs of cars, aircraft, ships, space shuttles, buildings, manufacturing processes of all types. Financial markets, corporate operations. Take a company like General Motors: millions of pieces of inventory, hundreds of thousands of locations. It all adds up. We help all of them do their jobs more efficiently." He pointed to another production area. "A new line of hard drives is being tested in there. They'll be by far the most powerful and efficient in the industry when they hit the market next year. Yet a year after that they'll be obsolete." He looked at Sawyer. "What sort of system do you use at work?"

Sawyer put his hands in his pocket. "You might not have heard of it: Smith Corona?"

Rowe gaped at him. "You're kidding."

"Just got a new ribbon in it, baby runs sweet as mother's milk." Sawyer sounded very defensive.

Rowe shook his head. "A friendly warning. Anyone who doesn't know how to operate a computer in the coming years will not be able to function in society. Don't be intimidated. The systems today are not only user friendly, they are idiot friendly, no offense intended."

Sawyer sighed. "Computers getting faster all the time, this Internet thing, whatever it really is, growing like crazy, networks, paging, cellular phones, faxes. Jesus, where's it going to end?"

"Since it's the business I'm in, I hope it never does."

"Sometimes change can happen too fast."

Rowe smiled benignly. "The change we see going on today will pale in comparison to what will take place in the next five years. We're on the cusp of technological breakthroughs that would have seemed unthinkable barely ten years ago." Rowe's eyes appeared to shine ahead into the next century. "What we know as the Internet today will seem boring and quaint very soon. Triton Global will be a huge part of that happening. In fact, if things work out correctly, we will be leading the way. Education, medicine, the workplace, travel, entertainment, how we eat, socialize, consume, produce – everything human beings do or benefit from will be transformed. Poverty, prejudice, crime, injustice, disease will crumple under the sheer weight of information, of discovery. Ignorance will simply disappear. The knowledge of thousands of libraries, the sum of the world's greatest minds, all will be readily accessible by anyone. In the end, the world of computers as we know it today will metamorphose into one enormous interactive global link of limitless potential." He peered at Sawyer through his glasses. "All the world's knowledge, the solutions to every problem, will be one keystroke away. It's the natural next step."

"One person will be able to get all that from a computer." Sawyer's tone was sceptical.

"Isn't that a thrilling vision?"

"Scares the shit out of me."

Rowe's mouth dropped open. "How could that possibly be frightening to you?"

"Maybe I'm a little cynical after twenty-five years of doing what I do for a living. But you tell me one guy can get all that information and you know the first thought pops into my head?"

"No, what?"

"What if he's a *bad* guy?" Rowe didn't react. "What if with one keystroke he wipes out all the world's knowledge?" Sawyer snapped his fingers. "He destroys everything? Or just screws it all up. Then what the hell do we do?"

Rowe smiled. "The benefits of technology far surpass any potential dangers. You may not agree with me. But the coming years will prove me right."

Sawyer scratched the back of his head. "You're

probably too young to know this, but back in the fifties, nobody thought illegal drugs would ever be a big problem either. Go figure."

The two men continued their tour. "We have five of these facilities situated across the country," Rowe said.

"Must get pretty expensive."

"You could say that. We spend over ten billion dollars per year on R&D."

Sawyer whistled. "You're talking numbers I can't even begin to contemplate. Of course, I'm just a working-stiff bureaucrat who sits around picking his nose on the public dole."

Rowe smiled. "Nathan Gamble delights in making other people squirm. I think he met his match in you, though. For obvious reasons I didn't applaud your performance, but I was seriously thinking about a standing ovation."

"Hardy said you had your own company, hot stock. If you don't mind my asking, how come you hooked up with Gamble?"

"Money." Rowe waved his arm around the facility they were in. "This all costs billions of dollars. My company was doing well, but lots of tech companies were doing well *in the stock market*. What people don't seem to understand is that while my company's stock price went from nineteen dollars a share on the day it hit the market to a hundred sixty per share less than six months later, we didn't see any of that enormous markup. That went to the people who bought the stock."

"You had to keep a chunk of the company's stock, though."

"I did, but with the securities laws being what they are, and our underwriter's requirements, I couldn't really sell any of it. On paper I was worth a fortune. However, my company was still struggling,

277

R&D was eating us up, we had no earnings," he said bitterly.

"So enter Nathan Gamble?"

"Actually he was a very early investor in the company, before we went public. He gave us some seed capital. He also gave us something else we didn't have but desperately needed: respectability on Wall Street, with the capital markets. A good solid business background. A penchant for making money. When my company went public, he held on to his shares as well. Later, Gamble and I discussed the future and decided to take the company back private."

"In retrospect a good decision?"

"From a dollar perspective, an incredibly good decision."

"But money ain't everything, right, Quentin?"

"Sometimes I wonder."

Sawyer leaned up against the wall, folded his beefy arms across his chest and looked directly at Rowe. "The tour is real interesting, but I hope that wasn't all you had in mind."

"It wasn't." Rowe swiped his card through the reader on a nearby door and motioned for Sawyer to follow him in. They sat down at a small table. Rowe spent a moment collecting his thoughts before he started speaking. "You know, if you had asked me before this all happened who I would suspect of having stolen from us, Jason Archer's name would never have entered my mind." Rowe took off his glasses and rubbed them with a handkerchief pulled from his shirt pocket.

"So you trusted him?"

"Absolutely."

"And now?"

"And now I think I was wrong. I feel betrayed, in fact."

"I could see how you might feel that way. You think anybody else at the company might be involved?"

"My God, I hope not." Rowe seemed stricken by the suggestion. "I would certainly rather believe it was Jason on his own or a competitor working with him. That, to me, makes a lot more sense. Besides, Jason would have been perfectly capable of hacking into BankTrust's computer system by himself. It's really not all that hard to do."

"You sound like you speak from experience."

Rowe's face reddened. "Let's just say that I have an insatiable curiosity. Poking around databases was a favorite pastime in college. My classmates and I had quite a good time doing it, although the local authorities, on more than one occasion, voiced their displeasure. However, we never stole anything. I actually helped train some of the police technicians in methods to detect and prevent computer-related crimes."

"Any of those people working on your security detail?"

"You mean Richard Lucas? No, he's been with Gamble it seems like forever now. Again, he's very good at what he does, but not the most pleasant company to have around. However, it's not his job to be pleasant."

"But Archer still fooled him."

"He fooled all of us. I'm certainly in no position to point fingers."

"Did you notice anything about Jason Archer that in retrospect looked suspicious?"

"Most things look different in retrospect. I know that better than most. I've given it some thought and Jason did seem to take a very active interest in the CyberCom deal."

"He *was* working on it."

"I don't mean just that. Even on the segments of the deal he wasn't involved in he asked a lot of questions."

"Like what?"

"Like did I think the terms were fair. Did I think the deal was going to get done. What would be his role once it was done. That sort of thing."

"He ever ask you about any confidential records you kept regarding the deal?"

"Not directly, no."

"He apparently got everything he needed off the computer system?"

"So it would seem."

The two men sat staring off into space for a few moments.

"You have any inkling where Archer might be?"

Rowe shook his head. "I visited his wife, Sidney."

"We've met."

"It's hard to believe he would just up and leave them like that. He has a daughter too. A beautiful little girl."

"Maybe he didn't plan to leave them."

Rowe looked at him oddly. "What do you mean?"

"I mean maybe he intends to come back for them."

"He's a fugitive from justice now. Why would he come back? Besides, Sidney wouldn't go with him."

"Why not?"

"Because he's a criminal. She's an attorney."

"This may come as a big surprise to you, Quentin, but some lawyers aren't honest."

"You mean . . . you mean you suspect Sidney Archer of being involved in this whole thing?"

"I mean I haven't ruled her or anyone else out right now as a suspect. She's an attorney for Triton. She was working on the CyberCom deal. Seems like a perfect position to cherry-pick secrets and sell them to RTG. Who the hell knows? I intend to find out."

Rowe put his glasses back on and rubbed his hand nervously across the glass tabletop. "It's so hard to believe Sidney would be involved in all this." Rowe's tone betrayed the conviction of his words.

Sawyer studied him closely. "Quentin, do you want to tell me something? Maybe about Sidney Archer?"

Rowe finally sighed and looked at Sawyer. "I'm convinced that Sidney was in Jason's office at Triton after the plane crash."

Sawyer's eyes narrowed. "What proof do you have?"

"The night before Jason supposedly left for L.A. he and I were working late on a project in his office. We left together. He secured his office door behind me. His office remained locked from that moment until we had the company come to deactivate the alarm and remove the door."

"So?"

"When we entered the office, I noticed immediately that the microphone on Jason's computer was bent almost in half. Like someone had hit it and then tried to straighten it."

"Why would you think that someone was Sidney Archer? Maybe Jason came back later that night."

"If he had there would be a record of it, both electronically and with the on-site security guard." Rowe paused, dwelling on the memory of the night of Sidney's visit. Finally he threw up his hands. "I know of no other way to put it. She was sneaking around. She claimed she was not in the restricted area, and yet I'm sure she was. I think the security guard was covering for her. And Sidney told me some bogus story about meeting Jason's secretary there to get some of Jason's personal things."

"Doesn't that sound plausible?"

"It would have, except I casually asked Kay

281

Vincent, Jason's secretary, if she had spoken to Sidney recently. And she had, from her home, on the very night Sidney went down to the office. She knew Kay wasn't there."

Sawyer sat back in his chair. Rowe continued. "You need a special chip card even to begin the deactivation process on Jason's office door. In addition, you need to know a four-digit password or the alarm will go off. It happened in fact when we initially tried to enter his office. That's when we found out Jason had changed the password. I even considered attempting it the night Sidney came by, only I knew it would be futile. I had a master security card, but without the password, the alarm would've just gone off again." He paused to take a breath. "Sidney could've have had access to Jason's security card and he could've told her the password. I can't believe I'm saying this, but she's involved in something, I just don't know what."

"I just looked through Archer's office and I didn't see any microphone. What did it look like?"

"About five inches long, the thickness of a pencil, small speaker at one end. It was mounted directly on the computer's CPU on the bottom left-hand side. It's for voice-activated commands. One day it'll replace the keyboard entirely. It's a godsend for people who can't type well."

"I didn't see anything like that."

"Probably not. I'm sure it was removed from the office because it was so damaged."

Sawyer took a few minutes to jot down notes and asked Rowe a few follow-up questions. Then Rowe escorted him back to the exit. "You think of anything else, Quentin, you let me know." He handed Rowe a business card.

"I wish I knew what the hell was going on, Agent Sawyer. I have my hands full with CyberCom, and now this."

"I'm doing what I can, Quentin. Hang in there."

Rowe slowly went back inside, Sawyer's card clutched in his hand. Sawyer walked to his car; he could hear his cellular phone buzzing. Ray Jackson's voice was agitated. "You were right."

"About what?"

"Sidney Archer's on the move."

THIRTY-FOUR

A half block behind the airport cab were the two FBI tail cars. Two other sedans were running on parallel streets and would cross over at strategic points to take over the chase so as not to alert the person they were tracking. That person swept the hair from her eyes, took a deep breath and stared out the window of the cab. Sidney Archer swiftly ran through the details of her trip once more and wondered if she had just exchanged one nightmare for another.

"She came back to the house after the memorial service, stayed a little while and then the cab came and picked her up. The direction they're heading, my call is Dulles Airport," Ray Jackson said into the car phone. "She made one stop. At a bank. Probably withdrawing some cash."

Lee Sawyer pressed the phone against his ear and fought through rush-hour traffic. "Where are you now?"

Jackson relayed his position. "You shouldn't have trouble, Lee, we're crawling through traffic here."

Sawyer started looking at cross streets. "I can be up with you in about ten minutes. How many pieces of luggage she carrying?"

"One medium suitcase."

"Short trip, then."

"Probably." Jackson eyed the cab. "Oh, shit!"

"What?" Sawyer almost yelled into the phone.

In dismay Jackson watched as the cab abruptly pulled into the Vienna metro subway station. "Looks like the lady just had a change in travel arrangements. She's hopping on the subway." Jackson watched Sidney Archer step out of the cab.

"Get a couple of guys in there right now, Ray."

"Roger that, double-quick."

Sawyer turned on his grille lights and cut around the stalled traffic. When his phone buzzed again, he snatched it up. "Talk to me, Ray, only good news."

His partner's breathing was a little more normal. "Okay, we got two guys on her."

"I'm one minute from the station. Which way she headed? Wait a minute, Vienna's the end of the orange line. She must be headed into town."

"Maybe, Lee, unless she's gonna double back on us and grab another cab when she exits the subway. Dulles is the other way. And we got a potential problem with our lines of communication. The walkie-talkies don't always work so well on the metro. If she changes trains inside the metro and our guys lose her, she's gone."

Sawyer thought for a moment. "Did she take her luggage, Ray?"

"What? Damn. No, she didn't."

"Get two cars glued to that cab, Ray. I doubt Mrs. Archer is leaving behind her clean undies and her makeup kit."

"I'm on it myself. You want to pair with me?"

Sawyer was about to agree, then abruptly changed his mind. He streaked through a red light. "You hang on it, Ray, I'm gonna cover another angle. Check in every five minutes and let's hope she doesn't give us the slip."

Sawyer did a U-turn and hurtled east.

Sidney had changed trains at the Rosslyn

substation and boarded a blue-line train heading south. At Pentagon metro station, the doors on the subway opened and approximately one thousand people careered off the train cars. Sidney was carrying the white coat she had been wearing. She didn't want to stand out from the crowd. The blue sweater she wore was swiftly lost in the thickening crowds of similarly attired military personnel.

The two FBI agents pushed through the masses as they desperately tried to relocate Sidney Archer. Neither one noticed Sidney reboard the same train several cars down, and she continued on to National airport. She looked behind her several times, but the train now held no obvious pursuers.

Sawyer pulled to a halt in front of the main terminal at National Airport, flashed his credentials to a surprised parking lot attendant and raced into the building. A few seconds later he stopped dead and his shoulders sagged in frustration as he scanned the wall-to-wall people. "Shit!" The next second he flattened himself against the wall as Sidney Archer passed barely ten feet in front of him.

As soon as Sidney was safely ahead of him, Sawyer started tracking her. The short journey ended in the line at the United Airlines ticket desk, which stood twenty deep.

Out of sight of both Sawyer and Sidney, Paul Brophy rolled his luggage carrier toward an American Airlines departure gate. Inside Brophy's inner suit pocket was Sidney's entire travel itinerary gleaned from her conversation with Jason Archer. He continued on unhurriedly. He could afford that luxury as chaos swirled around him. He would even have time to check in with Goldman.

After forty-five minutes Sidney finally received her ticket and boarding pass. Sawyer watched from a distance and noted the large wad of bills she used for the purchase. As soon as she had disappeared around the corner, Sawyer swiftly sliced through the line, his FBI badge prominently held in his hand as the first wave of angry travellers quickly parted for him.

The ticket person stared at the badge and then at Sawyer.

"The woman you just sold a ticket to, Sidney Archer. Tall good-looking blond, dressed in blue with a white coat over her arm," Sawyer added just in case his prey had used an alias. "What flight is she on? Quick."

The woman froze for an instant and then started punching keys. "Flight 715 to New Orleans. It leaves in twenty minutes."

"New Orleans?" said Sawyer, more to himself than to the woman. Now he momentarily regretted having personally interviewed Sidney Archer. She would recognize him instantly. But there was no time to call in another agent. "What gate?"

"Eleven."

Sawyer leaned forward and spoke in a low tone. "Okay, what's her seat?"

The woman glanced at the screen. "Twenty-seven C."

"Is there a problem here?" The woman's supervisor had drifted over. Sawyer showed her his FBI credentials and quickly explained his situation. The supervisor picked up a phone and alerted both the boarding gate and security, who would, in turn, inform the flight crew. The last thing Sawyer needed was a flight attendant spotting his gun during the trip with the result that the New Orleans police would be waiting for him at the door when the plane landed.

A few minutes later Sawyer, wearing a beat-up hat hastily borrowed from security personnel, his coat collar turned up, strode down the terminal's broad aisle, an airline security officer in tow. Sawyer was escorted around the metal detectors while he scanned the crowds for Sidney Archer. He spotted her at the departure gate already in line to board. He immediately turned around and sat facing away from the gate. Several minutes after the last group of people moved on to the plane, Sawyer walked down the jetwalk. He settled down into first class, in one of the few available seats on the crowded jet, and allowed himself a brief smile. It was the first time he had ever flown in such luxury. He fumbled through his wallet for his phone card. His fingers closed around Sidney Archer's business card. There were phone numbers for Sidney's direct office line, pager, fax, and mobile phone. Sawyer shook his head. That was the private sector, for you. Need to know where you are every minute. He pulled out the plane phone and slid his card through it.

The flight to New Orleans was nonstop and two and a half hours later the jet was descending into New Orleans International airport. Sidney Archer had not budged from her seat the entire flight, for which Lee Sawyer was immensely grateful. Sawyer had made a number of phone calls from the plane and his team was in place at the airport. When the door to the jet opened, Sawyer was the first one off.

When Sidney exited the airport into the mugginess of the New Orleans night, she did not notice the black sedan with the tinted windows parked across the narrow roadway used to pick up or drop off passengers. Settled into her seat in the battered gray Cadillac with CAJUN CAB COMPANY stencilled on the side, Sidney loosened her collar of her shirt and wiped a bit of perspiration from her forehead. "The LaFitte Guest House, please. Bourbon Street."

As the cab drifted away from the curb, the sedan waited a moment, then followed. Inside the sedan Lee Sawyer was filling in the other agents on the situation, his eyes all the time riveted on the dirty Caddie.

Sidney stared anxiously out the cab window. They left the highway and headed to the Vieux Carre. In the background the New Orleans skyline glittered out of the darkness, the massive hump of the Superdome resting in the foreground.

Bourbon Street was narrow and lined with garish edifices of, by American standards at least, the "ancient" French Quarter. At this time of the year, the sixty-six blocks of the Quarter were relatively quiet, although the smell of beer rose powerfully from the sidewalks as casually dressed vacationers staggered around carrying large cups of the stuff. Sidney left the cab in front of the LaFitte Guest House. She took a quick look up and down the street. No cars were in sight. She walked up the steps and pushed open the heavy front door.

Inside, the comforting smell of antiques embraced her. To her left was a large and stylishly decorated drawing room. The night clerk at the small desk raised his eyebrows slightly at Sidney's lack of baggage but smiled and nodded when she explained it was coming later. She was given the choice of riding the small elevator to the third floor, but chose the broad staircase instead. Key in hand, she went up two flights of stairs to her room. Her room contained a four-poster bed, writing desk, three walls of bookshelves and a Victorian style chaise longue.

Outside, the black sedan pulled into an alleyway half a block down from the LaFitte Guest House. A man dressed in jeans and a windbreaker alighted from the rear of the car, walked nonchalantly down the street and went into the building. Five minutes later he was back in the car.

Lee Sawyer leaned anxiously over the front seat. "What's going on in there?"

The man unzipped his windbreaker, revealing the pistol in his waistband. "Sidney Archer checked in for two days. Room's on the third floor right across from the top of the stairs. Said her baggage was coming later."

The driver looked over at Sawyer. "You think she's meeting up with Jason Archer?"

"Let's put it this way: I'd be damn surprised if she flew down here just for some R&R," Sawyer replied.

"What do you want to do?"

"Discreetly surround this place. Jason Archer shows up, we grab him. In the meantime, let's see if we can get some surveillance equipment in the room next to hers. Then see if you can get a tap on her phone line. Use a male and female team so the Archers don't get their radar up. Sidney Archer isn't someone you want to underestimate." Sawyer's tone was filled with grudging admiration. He looked out the window. "Let's get out of here. I don't want to give Jason Archer any reason not to show up." The sedan pulled slowly away.

Sidney Archer sat in the chair by the bed, staring out the window of her room on to the side balcony of the LaFitte Guest House and awaiting her husband. She rose and nervously paced the room. She was fairly certain she had lost the FBI agents in the subway, but she could not be absolutely sure. If they managed to trace her? She shivered. Ever since Jason's phone call had thrown her life into a cataclysm for a second time, Sidney had felt invisible walls closing in around her.

Jason's instructions, however, had been explicit

and she intended to follow them. She adhered fiercely to the belief that her husband had done nothing wrong, which he had assured her was correct. He needed her help; that was why she had boarded that plane and was presently pacing a quaint room in the most famous Louisiana city. She still had faith in her husband, despite events that, she had to admit, had shaken that faith, and nothing short of death would stop her from helping him. Death? Her husband had escaped its complicated tentacles one time already. From the sound of his voice, she had nagging doubts about his present safety. He was unable to give her many details. Not over the phone. Only in person, he had said. She so wanted to see him, to touch him, to confirm for herself that he was no apparition.

She sat down in the chair and stared out the open window. A refreshing breeze helped to dispel the humidity. She did not hear a couple in their mid-thirties, courtesy of the FBI's New Orleans field office, move into the room next to hers. With her phone line tapped and listening devices set up in the adjoining suite recording every sound from her room, Sidney Archer finally nodded off in the chair around one in the morning. Jason Archer had still not come.

The house was dark. A layer of new-fallen snow shone under the radiant eye of a full moon. The figure alighted from the nearby woods and approached the home from the rear. A few moments at the back door and the old lock succumbed to the skilful manipulations of the darkly clad intruder. Snow boots were removed and left outside the back door. A few moments later a single arc of light cut through the deserted house. Sidney Archer's parents and Amy had left to go back to the Pattersons' home shortly after Sidney had departed for her trip.

The intruder went straight to Jason Archer's home office. The room's window looked out on to the backyard rather than the street, so the figure risked turning on the desk lamp. Several minutes were spent thoroughly searching the desk and stacks of computer floppies. Then Jason Archer's computer system was turned on. A search was made of all files on the database. Each floppy was submitted to a detailed review. With that completed, the figure slipped a hand inside the dark jacket and extracted a floppy disk of his own. This was inserted into the computer's disk drive. After several minutes the task was complete. The "sniffer" software now existing on Jason's computer would effectively capture everything coming across its threshold. Within five minutes the house was once again empty. The footprints from the edge of the woods to the back door had been obliterated.

Unknown to the Archers' nocturnal visitor, Bill Patterson had accomplished one task, however innocently, before leaving for his Hanover home. While he backed his car out of the driveway, he had eyed the familiar red, white and blue truck stopping in front of his daughter's house. After the mail truck had departed, Patterson had hesitated and then arrived at his decision. Save his daughter the trouble, anyway. He glanced at a few of the items before depositing the pile of mail in a plastic bag. He turned toward the house and then remembered he had already locked it up and the keys were in his wife's purse. The garage door was unlocked, however. Patterson went in the garage, opened the door of the Explorer and placed the bag on the front seat. He locked the car door and then pulled down the garage door and locked it.

About midway down in the stack of mail and unnoticed by Patterson was a soft-sided package specifically designed with built-in padding to send fragile items safely through the postal system. The handwriting on the package would have been familiar to Sidney Archer at even a passing glance.

Jason Archer had mailed the computer disk to himself.

THIRTY-FIVE

Across the street from the LaFitte Guest House, Lee Sawyer stared at the old hotel through the darkened window of the room he was occupying. The FBI had set up their surveillance headquarters in an abandoned brick building its owner was planning to renovate in a year or so. Sawyer sipped hot coffee and looked at his watch. Six-thirty A.M. Raindrops clattered against the window as a chilly early morning shower invaded the area.

Next to the window stood a tripod with a camera attached. The long-range lens was almost a foot long. The only pictures snapped thus far had been of the LaFitte Guest House's entryway and only to gauge focus, distance and lighting. Sawyer walked over and looked down at the series of photos on the table. The pictures did neither the face nor the emerald eyes justice. Sidney Archer had been photographed by the New Orleans FBI field office upon exiting the airport. Despite her ignorance, she looked almost posed for the camera. Her countenance was lovely, the hair full and luxuriant. Sawyer gently traced the slender nose down to the full lips. With a start he jerked his hand away from the photograph and looked around, embarrassed. Fortunately, none of the other agents in the room had been paying attention to what he was doing.

He surveyed the rest of the room. The long table was set up in the middle of the large and practically empty space with bare brick walls, dark-timbered ceilings and filthy floors. Twin PCs occupied the most prominent space on the table. A tape-recording machine was next to them. Several of the local bureau agents manned the machines. One young agent caught Sawyer's eye and removed his headphones. "Our people are all in place. From the sounds of it, she's probably still asleep."

Sawyer nodded slowly and turned to look back out the window once again. His men had ascertained that five other guest rooms were occupied in the small hotel. All couples. None of the males matched Jason Archer's description.

The next few hours passed slowly. Used to long stakeouts that netted little except a sour stomach and an aching back, Sawyer was unfazed by the tedium.

The young agent was listening intently to his headphones. "She's exiting her room right now."

Sawyer stood up, stretched and again looked at his watch. "Eleven A.M. Maybe she's going for a late breakfast."

"How do you want to handle the surveillance?"

Sawyer considered for a moment. "As we discussed. Two teams. Use the woman from the room next door as one and a pair as the other. They can alternate on the surveillance. Tell them to look sharp. Archer's gonna be on her guard. Keep in radio communication at all times. Remember, she doesn't have any luggage at the hotel. So tell them to be ready for any mode of transportation, including Archer jumping on another plane. Make sure you got vehicles nearby at all times."

"Right."

Sawyer looked out the window again while his instructions were relayed to the teams of agents. He had a feeling about all of this he couldn't quite pin down. Why New Orleans? Why, on the same day the

FBI had interrogated her, would she risk something like this? He abruptly stopped his musings as Sidney Archer appeared on the front steps of the LaFitte Guest House. She looked back over her shoulder, her eyes filled with barely concealed fright; that look was instantly familiar to the FBI agent. A quiver went up Sawyer's spine as he suddenly realized where he had seen Sidney Archer before: at the crash site. He raced across the room and snatched up a phone.

Sidney was wearing her white coat, testament to how the temperature had dropped. She had managed to check the guest registry without the clerk observing her. There had been only one check-in after her. A couple from Ames, Iowa, was in the room next to hers. The check-in time must have been near midnight if not after. It didn't strike her as likely that a couple from the Midwest would be checking into a hotel at about the hour they would normally be entering REM sleep patterns. That she had not heard them move into the room raised her suspicions even more. Weary travellers at midnight were usually not so understanding of their fellow lodgers. She had to assume that the FBI was next door to her and probably watching the entire area. Despite her precautions, they had found her. It was hardly surprising, she had to remind herself as she walked along the mostly deserted streets. The FBI did this for a living. She didn't. And if the FBI closed in? Well, she had decided from the moment she learned her husband was alive that his chances of keeping that life intact would be considerably enhanced if he would place himself in the hands of the authorities.

Sawyer paced the room, hands shoved in his pockets. He had drunk so much coffee he could feel his bladder shooting nasty signals at him. The phone rang. The young agent answered it, identified the caller as Ray Jackson, and then handed it over to Sawyer, who took off his headphones.

"Yeah?" Sawyer's voice was vibrating with anticipation. He rubbed at his bloodshot eyes; a quarter century of pulling this kind of duty didn't make it any easier on the body.

"So how's the Big Easy?" Ray Jackson sounded fresh and alert.

Sawyer looked around at the crumbling surroundings. "Well from where I'm standing, it's sorely in need of a broom and some paint."

Jackson chuckled. "Well, your tracking down Sidney Archer at the _____ is already the stuff of legend aro_____ _____n't know how you did it."

_____wore my lucky rabbit's _____Ray. Tell me you got _____tched the receiver to _____ft arm until a cramp

_____o, but my bed last _____floor, and there's _____t ache. On top of _____unless you want _____get back, start

_____ere absolutely _____sh site in the

_____ced he was _____ndent sub-

_____rd papers _____y Eugene

was now exposed. Quentin Rowe moved next to the computer and held up the cables.

"Jason hardwired into our local area network through this workstation."

"Why not just use the computer in his office?"

Rowe was shaking his head before Sawyer had stopped talking. "When he logs on to his own computer," Lucas said, "he has to go through a series of security measures. Those security measures do not merely verify the user they *confirm* the user's identity. Every workstation in the place has an iris scanner, which takes an initial video image of the user's iris patterns. In addition, the scanner takes periodic sweeps of the operator to continually confirm the user's identity. If Archer had left his desk or someone had sat down in his place, then the system would have automatically shut off to that workstation."

Rowe looked steadily at Sawyer. "The important point in all that is if Archer had accessed any file from his own workstation, we would have known he had done it."

"How's that?" Sawyer asked.

"Our network has a tag feature. Most systems have some attribute of that kind. If a user accesses a file, that access is recorded by the system. By using this workstation" – Quentin pointed at the old computer – "which is not supposed to be on the network and is assigned no number through the network administrator, he bypassed that risk. For all intents and purposes, this was a phantom computer on our network. He may have used the computer in his office to find the location of certain files without accessing them. He could do that at his leisure. That would cut down on the time he needed to spend here, where he could be caught."

Sawyer shook his head. "Wait a minute. If Archer

McKenna, was on duty that night when Sidney Archer pulls up. McKenna thinks she's just a curiosity-seeker and tells her to head on out, but then she tells him about her husband being on the place. She just wants to look around; she's all broken up. McKenna feels sorry for her, you know, driving all night to get there and all. He checks her out, confirms she is who she says she is and then drives her up near the crash site so she can at least watch what's going on." Jackson paused.

Sawyer was irritable. "So how the hell does that help us?"

"Man, you are grouchy. I'm getting to that. On the drive up, Archer asks about a canvas bag with her husband's initials on it. She had seen it on TV. I guess it had been thrown off in the crash and was found and put with the other collected debris. Bottom line: She wanted to get that bag."

Sawyer sat down, looked out the window and then refocused on the phone. "What did McKenna tell her?"

"That it was evidence and wasn't even on-site anymore. That she'd probably get it back after the investigation was complete but that would be a while, maybe years."

Sawyer stood up and absentmindedly poured himself another cup of coffee from the pot on the hot plate while he worked through this latest development. His bladder would just have to deal with it.

"Ray, what exactly did McKenna say about Archer's appearance that night?"

"I know what you're thinking. Did she really believe her husband was on that plane? McKenna said if she was faking, she'd make Katharine Hepburn look like the world's worst actress."

"Okay, we'll let that ride for now. What about the bag? You got it?"

298

---

tion to access the files identify him and used ouldn't, how do you ed the files in the first

keyboard. "An old reliable. from here. They all

obvious question. workstation was

es. "For a period authorized entries on to er didn't need to go ccess to log on through a trail if he accessed ically erased his trail ough tricky. In ally, at least. picked up the trail narrowed down the

Hardy folded his arms across his chest. "You know, it's ironic. You put all this time and effort and money into securing your networks against any breaches. You have steel doors, security guards, electronic monitoring devices, smart cards – you name it, Triton has it. And yet . . ." He looked up at the ceiling. "And yet you also have drop-down ceiling panels with exposed cables connecting your entire network together, ripe for penetration." He shook his head in dismay and looked at Lucas. "I've warned you about this risk before."

"He was an insider," Lucas said heatedly. "He knew the system and he used that knowledge to hack it." Lucas brooded for a moment. "And then he

270

"Damn straight. Right on my desk here."

"And?" Sawyer's shoulders tensed, then dropped just as suddenly at his partner's response.

"Nothing. At least nothing we can find. The lab's been through it three times. Just some clothes, a couple of travel books. Notepad with nothing written on it. No surprises, Lee."

"Why would she drive all that way in the middle of the night for that?"

"Well, maybe there was supposed to be something in it, but there wasn't."

"That would figure if her husband was double-crossing her."

"How's that?"

Sawyer sipped his coffee and then stood up. "If Archer is on the run, one would think he is either planning to bring his family along at a later date or dump them. Right?"

"Okay, I'm following you."

"So if his wife thought he was on that plane, maybe on the initial leg of his getaway run, then that would jibe with her being despondent over the plane crash. She really thinks he's dead."

"But the money?"

"Right. If Sidney Archer knew what her husband had done maybe had even helped him pull it off somehow, she would want to get her hands on the money. It would help get her over her grief, I'm thinking. Then she sees the bag on TV."

"But what could be in the bag? Not the cash."

"No, but it could have been something to point her in the direction of the money. Archer was a computer whiz. Maybe the location of a computer file on a floppy where all the info on the money is stored. A Swiss bank account number. An airport locker key card. It could be anything, Ray."

"Well, we didn't find anything remotely like that."

"It wouldn't necessarily be in that bag, She saw it on TV and thought she could get her hands on it."

"So you really think she was in on this thing from the get-go?"

Sawyer sat back down wearily. "I don't know, Ray. I've got no strong feeling either way on it." That wasn't exactly true, but Sawyer had no desire to discuss certain disturbing thoughts with his partner.

"So what about the plane crash? How does that tie in?"

Sawyer's response was abrupt. "Who knows if it does? They could be unrelated. Maybe he paid to have it sabotaged to cover his tracks. That's what Frank Hardy thinks happened." Sawyer had stepped over to the window while he was speaking. What he saw on the street outside made him want to end the phone call quickly.

"Anything else, Ray?"

"Nope, that's it."

"Good, because I gotta run." Sawyer hung up the phone, manned the camera himself and started clicking away. Then he stepped back to the window and watched while Paul Brophy, looking searchingly up and down the street, climbed the steps of the LaFitte Guest House and went inside.

THIRTY-SIX

The typical noise and merriment usually associated with Jackson Square would have made a stark contrast to the more modest proceedings of the Quarter at this time of the morning. Musicians, jugglers and unicyclists, tarot card readers and artists ranging in talent from superb to mediocre competed for the attention and dollars of the few tourists who had braved the inclement weather.

Sidney Archer walked in front of the triple-steepled St. Louis Cathedral on her way to find food. She was also following her husband's instructions: If he had not contacted her at the hotel by eleven A.M. she was to go to Jackson Square. The bronze equestrian statue of Andrew Jackson, which had lent dignity to the square for the last 140 years, loomed large over her as she made her way to the French Market Place on Decatur Street. She had visited the city several times before, during her college and law school days when she had been young enough to survive Mardis Gras and even to enjoy and participate in its atmosphere of drunken extravagance.

Minutes later she sat near the riverfront sipping hot coffee and biting unenthusiastically into a fluffy, butter-filled croissant, idly watching the barges and tugs along the mighty Mississippi as they made slow progress toward the enormous bridge in the near distance. Within a hundred yards of her, on either side, were positioned teams of FBI agents. Listening equipment discreetly pointed in her direction was capable of capturing virtually every word spoken by or to her.

For a few minutes Sidney Archer remained alone. She quietly finished her coffee and studied the muscular river with its rain-swelled banks and stiff whitecaps.

"Three dollars and fifty cents says I can tell where you got your shoes."

Sidney collapsed out of her brown study and stared up at the face. Behind her the teams of agents slightly stiffened and edged forward. They would have surged toward her at full sprint when the man began to approach except that the speaker was short, black and close to seventy. This was not Jason Archer. But it still might be something.

"What?" She shook her head clear.

"Your shoes. I know where you got your shoes. Three-fifty if I'm right. A free shine for you if I'm wrong." His snow-white mustache hung over a mouth largely absent of teeth. His clothes were more rags than anything else. She also observed the battered wooden shoeshine kit resting on the bench beside her.

"I'm sorry. I'm really not interested."

"Come on, lady. Tell you what, I'll throw in the shine if I'm right, but you still got to come up with the money. What's to lose? You get a great shine for a very reasonable price."

Sidney was about to refuse him again until she saw the ribs sticking through the worn, gauzy shirt. Her eyes drifted over his own shoes, from which bare and heavily callused toes protruded at several spots. She smiled and reached inside her purse for money.

"Uh-uh, don't do it that way, lady. Sorry. Got to play the game or we don't do business." There was

302

more than a small reserve of pride in his words. He started to pick up his box.

"Wait a minute. All right," said Sidney.

"Okay, you don't think I can tell you where you got your shoes, do you?" he said.

Sidney Archer shook her head. She had purchased them at an obscure store in southern Maine a little over two years ago. It had since gone out of business. There was no way. "Sorry, but I don't think so," she replied.

"Well, I'm gonna tell you where you got those shoes." The man paused dramatically and then almost cackled as he pointed down. "You got them on your feet."

Sidney joined in his laughter.

In the background, the two agents holding listening devices couldn't help but smile.

After performing a mock bow to his audience of one, the old man knelt down in front of Sidney and prepared her shoes for polishing. He chatted away amiably while his dexterous hands soon turned her dull black flats to lustrous ebony.

"Nice quality, lady. Last you a long time if you take care of them. Nice ankles to go with them too. That never hurts."

She smiled at the compliment as he rose and repacked his box. Sidney pulled out three dollars and rummaged in her purse for change.

He looked at her. "That's okay, ma'am, I got plenty of change," he said quickly.

In response she handed him a five and told him to keep the difference.

He shook his head. "No way, no sir. Three-fifty was the deal and three-fifty it is."

Despite her protests, he handed her back a crumpled single and a fifty-cent piece. When her hand closed around the silver, she felt the small piece of paper taped to its underside. Her eyes bulged at him. He merely smiled and tipped the brim of his raggedy cap. "Nice doing business with you, ma'am. Remember, take care of those shoes."

After he moved off, Sidney quickly put the money away in her purse, waited for several minutes and then got up and walked off as casually as she was able.

She made her way back over to the French Market Place and into the ladies' room. In one of the stalls her quivering hands unfolded the paper. The message was short and in block print. She reread it several times and then promptly flushed it down the toilet.

Making her way up Dumaine Street toward Bourbon, she paused and opened her purse for a moment. She made a show of briefly checking her watch. She looked around and noted the pay phone attached to a brick building that housed one of the largest bars in the Quarter. She crossed the street, picked up the phone and, calling card in hand, punched in a series of digits. The number she was calling was her private line at Tyler, Stone. She was bewildered, but the piece of paper had told her to do it, and she had no choice but to follow those instructions. The voice that answered after two rings did not belong to anyone at her law firm, nor was it her recorded voice announcing her absence from the office. She could not know that the call had been diverted from her office to another number located nowhere near Washington, D.C. She was now trying to remain calm while Jason Archer's voice quietly drifted over the telephone line.

The police were watching, she was told. She was not to say anything, especially not mention his name. They would have to try again. She was to go home. He would contact her again. The words were spoken in a supremely tired manner; she could almost feel the incredible strain in the timbre. He ended by saying that he loved her. And Amy. And that everything would be worked out. Eventually.

With a thousand questions assailing her that she was in absolutely no position to ask, Sidney Archer hung up the phone and walked off toward the LaFitte Guest House, deep depression seemingly hitched to every one of her strides. With a supreme effort at self-control, she held her head up and attempted to walk normally. It was incredibly important not to reflect in her physical appearance the utter terror she was feeling inside. Her husband's obvious fear of the authorities had undermined her belief that he was innocent of any wrongdoing. Despite her intense joy at knowing he was alive, she wondered at what price that joy had come to her. In this far, she had to keep going.

The recording machine was clicked off and the telephone receiver was removed from the special receptacle in the machine. Next, Kenneth Scales rewound the digital tape. He hit the start button and listened while Jason Archer's voice once again filled the room. He smiled malevolently, turned off the machine, took out the tape and left the room.

"He climbed in the window from the galleria," Sawyer was being informed by an agent stationed on a rooftop overlooking Sidney Archer's lodgings. "He's still in there," the agent whispered into his radio. "You want me to pick him up?"

"No," Sawyer answered, peering out through the blinds on to the street. The surveillance devices installed next door to Sidney's room had told them what Paul Brophy was up to. He was searching her room. Sawyer's earlier thought of an assignation between the two law partners had obviously been way off the mark.

"He's leaving now. Going out the back way," the agent reported suddenly.

"Good thing," Sawyer replied as he spotted Sidney Archer coming down the street. After she had reentered the LaFitte Guest House, Sawyer ordered a team of agents to tail a disappointed Paul Brophy, who was walking down Bourbon Street in the other direction.

Ten minutes later Sawyer was informed that Sidney Archer had placed a call from a pay phone during her morning breakfast walk. It had gone to her office. For the next five hours nothing happened. Then Sawyer snapped to attention as Sidney Archer walked out of the LaFitte Guest House. A white cab pulled up in front of the building and she got in. The cab quickly pulled away.

Sawyer hurtled down the stairs and in another minute was riding shotgun in the same black sedan in which he had followed Sidney from the airport. He was not surprised to see the cab swing on to interstate 10, or pull off at the exit for the airport about half an hour later.

"She's heading home," Sawyer muttered to no one in particular. "She didn't find whatever it was she came here for, that's for sure. Not unless Jason Archer turned himself into the invisible man." The veteran FBI man slumped back in his seat as a new and particularly troubling revelation crossed his mind. "She's on to us."

The driver jerked his head in Sawyer's direction. "No way, Lee."

"She sure as hell is," Sawyer insisted. "She flies all the way down here, hangs out, then makes a phone call and now she's on her way back home."

"I know she didn't spot our cover teams."

"I didn't say *she* did. Her husband and whoever else is involved in this did. They tipped her and she's going home."

"But we checked. The phone call was to her office."

Sawyer shook his head impatiently. "Phone calls can be diverted."

"But how did she know to call? Something prearranged?"

"Who knows? She only had that run-in with the shoeshine guy. You're sure?"

"That's it. Played the usual tourist scam on her and then shined her shoes. He was a street person, clearly enough. Gave her her change and that was it."

Sawyer abruptly eyed the man. "Change?"

"Yeah, it was a three-fifty shine. She gave him a five. He gave her a buck-fifty back. Wouldn't take her tip."

Sawyer gripped the dashboard, leaving indentations on the smooth surface. "Damn, that was it."

The driver looked bewildered. "He only gave her the change back. I got a clear look through my lens. We heard every word they said."

"Let me guess. He gave her a fifty-cent piece instead of two quarters, right?

The man gaped. "How'd you know that?"

Sawyer sighed. "How many street people you know who would refuse a buck-fifty tip and then happen to have a fifty-cent piece all ready to give as change? And doesn't it strike you as odd in the first place that it was three-fifty for the sine as opposed to three or four bucks? Why three-fifty?"

"So you gotta make change." The driver sounded depressed now that the truth was dawning on him.

"Message taped to the coin." Sawyer stared glumly ahead at the rear of Sidney Archer's cab.

"Pick up our generous shoeshine man. Just maybe he can manage a description of whoever hired him." Sawyer wasn't holding out much hope on that one.

The cars sailed toward the airport. Sawyer endured the short ride in silence, staring out the window at brightly painted jets roaring overhead. An hour later he boarded a private FBI jet for the trip back to Washington. Sidney's nonstop flight had already left. No FBI agents boarded her plane. Sawyer and his men had reviewed the passenger manifest and diligently watched every person board the aircraft. Jason Archer was not among them. Nothing could occur on the flight back, they were confident. They didn't want to tip their hand even more to an already alerted Sidney. They would pick up her trail at National Airport.

The private jet carrying Sawyer and several other FBI agents accelerated down the runway and lifted off into the dark sky over New Orleans. Sawyer began to wonder what the hell had just happened. Why the trip in the first place? It just didn't make any sense. Then his mouth dropped open. The muck had suddenly become just a shade clearer. But he had also made a mistake, maybe a big one.

THIRTY-SEVEN

Sidney Archer sipped her coffee while the beverage cart made its way down the rest of the aisle. She was reaching to pick at the sandwich on her tray when the blue markings on the paper napkin caught her eye. She focused on the writing, a jolt went through her, and she almost spilled her coffee.

The FBI are not on the plane. We need to talk.

The napkin was on the right side of her tray and her gaze automatically swerved in that direction. For a moment she couldn't even think. Then recognition slowly came to her. The man was casually drinking his soda while munching on his meal. Thinning reddish blond hair gave way to a long, clean-shaven face that had more than its share of worry lines. The man looked mid-forties and was dressed in chino pants and a white shirt. A six-footer, he had his long legs partly stuck out into the aisle. He finally put down the soda, patted his mouth with a napkin and turned to her.

"You've been following me," she said, her voice barely above a whisper. "In Charlottesville."

"I'm afraid that's not the only place. Actually, I've kept you under surveillance since shortly after the plane crash."

Sidney's hand flew to the attendant button.

"I wouldn't do that."

Her hand stopped, millimeters from summoning assistance. "Why not?" she coldly asked.

309

"Because I'm here to help you find your husband," he said simply.

She finally managed to answer him, her wariness evident. "My husband is dead."

"I'm not the FBI, and I'm not trying to entrap you. However, I can't prove a negative, so I won't even try. What I will do is give you a telephone number where you can reach me day or night." He handed her a small white card with a Virginia telephone number on it. Otherwise it was blank.

Sidney looked at the card. "Why should I call you? I don't even know who you are or what you're doing. Only that you've been following me. That does not win you confidence points in my book," she said angrily as her fear receded. He couldn't be a threat to her on a crowded plane.

The man shrugged. "I don't have a good answer to that. But I know your husband isn't dead and you know it too." He paused; Sidney Archer stared at him, unable to say anything. "Although you have no reason to believe me, I'm here to help you, and Jason, if it's not too late."

"What do you mean, 'too late'?"

The man sat back in his seat and closed his eyes. When he re-opened them, the pain evident there made her suspicions start to fade.

"Ms. Archer, I'm not exactly sure what your husband is involved in. But I do know enough to realize that, wherever he is, he could very well be in grave danger." He closed his eyes again while Sidney's heart sank to a depth she hadn't realized existed within her.

He looked over at her. "The FBI have you under round-the-clock surveillance." His next words chilled her to the bone. "You should be very thankful for that, Ms. Archer."

When she finally spoke, the words were barely

audible to the man, who bent toward her so he could hear them. "Do you know where Jason is?"

The man shook his head. "If I did, I wouldn't be sitting on this plane with you." He looked at her hopeless expression. "All I can tell you, Ms. Archer, is I'm not sure of anything." He let out a breath and passed a hand over his forehead. For the first time Sidney noticed that his hand was shaking.

"I was at Dulles Airport the same morning your husband was."

Sidney's eyes grew wide, her hand gripping the armrest. "You were following my husband? Why?"

The man looked over at her. "I didn't say I was following your husband." He sipped his drink to moisten a throat suddenly gone dry. "He was sitting in the departure area for the flight to L.A. He looked nervous and agitated. That's what drew my attention to him in the first place. He got up and went into the men's room. Another man went in after him a few minutes later."

"Why is that unusual?"

"The second man had a white envelope in his hand when he came into the departure area. That envelope was clearly visible, almost like a lantern the way the guy was swinging it. I believe it was a signal to your husband. I've seen that technique used before."

"A signal. For what?" Sidney's breathing had accelerated to such an extent that she had to make a conscious effort to slow it down.

"For your husband to act. Which he did, he went into the men's room. The other man came out a little later. I forgot to mention that he was dressed almost identically to your husband and was carrying the same sort of baggage. Your husband never did come out."

"What do you mean my husband never came out? He had to."

"I meant he never came out as Jason Archer."

Sidney looked totally confused.

He hurriedly went on. "The first thing I noticed about your husband was his shoes. He was dressed in a suit, but he had on black tennis shoes. Do you remember him putting on tennis shoes that morning?"

"I was asleep when he left."

"Well, when he came out of the rest room his appearance had completely changed. He looked like he was a college student, dressed in a sweatsuit, different hair, everything."

"How did you know it was him, then?"

"Two reasons. First, the rest room had just opened after being cleaned when your husband went in. I watched that door like a hawk. No one remotely resembling the guy who later came out had gone in there. Second, the black tennis shoes were very distinctive. He probably should have worn a more low-key pair. It was your husband, all right. And you want to know something else?"

Sidney could barely get the words out. "Tell me."

"The other guy came out wearing your husband's hat. With the hat on, he could've passed as your husband's twin."

Sidney took a deep breath as this revelation settled in.

"Your husband got in line for the flight to Seattle. He took the same white envelope the other guy had been carrying out of his pocket. In it was the plane ticket and boarding pass for the Seattle flight. The other guy got on the flight to L.A."

"Meaning they made a ticket switch in the rest room. The other man was dressed to look like Jason in case anyone was watching."

"That's right." He nodded slowly. "Your husband wanted someone to think he was on the L.A. flight."

312

"But why?" Sidney said this more to herself than to him.

The man shrugged. "I don't know. I do know that the plane your husband was supposed to be on crashed. Then I was even more suspicious."

"Did you go to the police?"

The man shook his head. "And tell them what? It's not like I saw a bomb being put on that flight. Besides, I had my own reasons for keeping quiet."

"What sort of reasons?"

The man put up one hand and shook his head. "Let's just leave it at that for now."

"How did you find out my husband's identity? I'm assuming you didn't know him by sight?"

"Never laid eyes on him before. But I made a couple of casual passes by before he went into the rest room. He had a name and address label on his briefcase. I'm really good at reading things upside down. It didn't take me long to find out where he worked, what he did for a living, more info than I'd ever need to know. I also found out the same things about you. That's when I started following you. To tell you the truth, I didn't know if you were in any danger or not." He spoke matter-of-factly; however, Sidney's blood ran cold at this unexpected intrusion in her life.

"Then while I'm down talking to a friend of mine at the Fairfax police, an APB with your husband's photo came over the wire. That's when I took up your tail in earnest. I thought you might lead me to him."

"Oh." Sidney settled back in her chair. Then a thought struck her. "How did you follow me to New Orleans?"

"The very first thing I did was tap your phone." He ignored her surprised expression. "I needed to know quickly where you were going to go. I heard your conversation with your husband. He seemed particularly evasive."

The plane droned on through the dark skies, and Sidney Archer touched the man's sleeve. "You said you weren't FBI. Who are you, then? Why are you involved in this?"

The man scanned the aisle for several seconds before answering. When he looked back at her, he sighed. "I'm a private investigator, Ms. Archer. The case that is now occupying me pretty much full-time is your husband."

"Who hired you?"

"Nobody." He looked around again before continuing. "I thought your husband might try to contact you. Eventually he did. That's why I'm here. But it seems New Orleans was a bust. That was him on the pay phone, wasn't it? The shoeshine guy slipped you a note, right?"

Sidney Archer hesitated, then nodded her head.

"Did your husband give you any clue where he might be?"

Sidney shook her head. "He said he would contact me later. When it was safer."

The man almost laughed. "That might be a long time. A real long time, Ms. Archer."

When the plane was descending into Washington National, the man turned again to Sidney. "Couple of things, Ms. Archer. When I listened to the tape of you and your husband talking on the phone, I picked up some background noise. Like water running. I can't be sure, but I think someone was listening on another line." Sidney's face froze. "Ms. Archer, you had better assume the Feds know Jason is alive too."

A little white later the plane thudded to a landing and the cabin became alive with activity.

"You said you wanted to tell me a couple of things. What's the other one?"

The man leaned down and pulled out a small briefcase from under the seat in front of him. When

314

he sat back up, he looked her directly in the eye. "People who can bring down a jetliner can do just about anything. Don't trust anyone, Ms. Archer. And be more careful than you have ever been in your entire life. Even that might not be enough. I'm sorry if that sounds like shitty advice, but it's all I have to give you."

In another few minutes the man was gone. Sidney was one of the last passengers off the plane. The airport wasn't crowded at this hour. She made her way toward the cab stand. Remembering the man's advice, she looked carefully around, trying not to be too obvious. Her sole comfort was the fact that amid all the people probably tracking her, at least some of them were FBI.

After leaving Sidney Archer, the man boarded an airport shuttle bus that deposited him at the long-term parking lot. It was almost ten o'clock. The area was deserted. He carried a bag that he had checked on to the flight from New Orleans. Its orange sticker proclaimed that it carried an unloaded firearm. As he reached his car, a late-model Grand Marquis, he opened the bag to extract his pistol with the intent of reloading it and placing it in his shoulder holster.

The stiletto blade first hit his right lung, was pulled free, and then the savage process was repeated on the left one, collapsing both and forestalling any cry for help he might otherwise have managed. The third thrust sliced neatly through the right side of his neck. The bag dropped to the concrete floor, the firearm now useless to its dying owner. In another moment he was down on the ground, his eyes already glassing over, staring up at his killer.

A van pulled alongside and Kenneth Scales climbed in. In another moment the dead man was alone.

THIRTY-EIGHT

Lee Sawyer sat at the conference table in the FBI building going over numerous reports. He put one hand through his rumpled hair, tilted back in his chair and put his feet up on the table while he mentally sorted through the new facts. The autopsy report on Riker indicated that he had been dead about forty-eight hours before his body had been discovered. Because the room temperature had hovered around freezing, however, Sawyer knew the postmortem putrefaction of the body was not nearly as accurate as it otherwise would have been.

Sawyer looked at photos of the Sig P229 auto pistol that had been recovered at the crime scene. The serial numbers on the pistol had been sanded down and then drilled out. He next looked at photos of the slugs recovered from the body. Riker had been on the receiving end of eleven more of the hollow-point projectiles than had been necessary to kill him. The lead barrage bothered the FBI agent greatly. Riker's murder had most of the hallmarks of a professional kill. Professional assassins rarely needed more than one shot. The first shot in this case had been instantly fatal, the medical examiner had concluded. The heart had not been pumping when the other bullets had entered the body.

The blood spatters on the table, chair and mirror indicated that Riker had been shot from behind while seated. The killer had apparently dragged Riker out of the chair, thrown him face down in the corner of the bedroom and proceeded to empty his clip into the dead body from directly above at a distance of about three feet. But why? Sawyer couldn't answer that question right now. He turned his thoughts elsewhere.

Despite numerous inquiries and potential leads, nothing had been turned up on Riker's movements for the last eighteen months. No addresses, no friends, no jobs, no credit card bills, nothing. While Rapid Start was processing tons of data a day on the plane crash, they couldn't get a solid lead on anything. They knew how it had been done, they had the body of the damned person responsible for actually doing it, and yet they couldn't get beyond his corpse.

In frustration, Sawyer sat up and thumbed another report. Riker had also had a great deal of cosmetic surgery. Photos taken at Riker's last arrest bore absolutely no resemblance to the man who had met his bloody end in a quiet Virginia apartment building.

Sawyer grimaced. His gut on the Sinclair alias had been right on the mark too. Riker had not taken the place of another person. Sinclair had been created out of broadcloth and computerized records, with the result that Robert Sinclair had been hired as a living, breathing person, with excellent background credentials to be a fueler for a reputable company that had contracts to service several of the major airlines operating out of Dulles International Airport, including Western. However, Vector had made some mistakes in its background checks. They had not verified the phone numbers of Sinclair's previous employers, but had merely used the numbers provided by Riker, aka Sinclair. All the references provided by the dead man had been small fueling operations in Washington state, southern

California and one in Alaska. None of those outfits actually existed. When Sawyer's men checked, they found the numbers had been disconnected. The employment addresses given by Riker on his application were phony too. His Social Security number, however, had been run through the system and had come back as valid.

His prints had also been run through the Virginia State Police AFIS. Riker had spent time in a Virginia prison and his prints were supposed to be on file there. Only they weren't. That could only mean one thing. The Social Security Administration's and the Virginia State Police's databases had been compromised. The whole system might as well have burned up. How could you be sure of anything now? Without absolute reliability, the systems were next to useless. And if someone could do that to Virginia and the SSA, who was safe? Sawyer angrily shoved the reports aside, poured himself another cup of coffee and paced around the broad space of the SIOC.

Jason Archer had been way ahead of them. There had only been one reason to have Sidney Archer travel to New Orleans. In fact, it could have been any city. The important point was that she leave town. And when she had, the FBI had gone with her. Her home had been left unguarded. Sawyer had learned from discreet inquiries with her neighbours that Sidney Archer's parents and daughter had left shortly after Sidney Archer had departed.

Sawyer clenched and unclenched his fist. A diversion. And he had fallen for it like the greenest agent in the world. He had no direct evidence supporting it, but he knew as well as he knew his own name that someone had entered the Archer home and presumably taken something from within. To go to all that risk meant that something incredibly important had slipped right through Sawyer's fingers.

It had not been a good morning and it only threatened to grow rapidly worse. He was not used to getting his butt kicked at every turn. He had filled in Frank Hardy on the results thus far. His friend was making inquiries into Paul Brophy's and Philip Goldman's backgrounds. Hardy had been understandably intrigued when he heard of Brophy's clandestine roaming through Sidney Archer's hotel room.

Sawyer flipped open the newspaper and read the headline. Sidney Archer would be heading into the panic zone right about now, he figured. Since Jason Archer was undoubtedly on to their pursuit of him, the consensus at the bureau had been to go public with his alleged crimes: corporate espionage and embezzlement of Triton's funds. His direct involvement in the plane crash was not alluded to, although the story did mention that he was listed as a passenger on the ill-fated flight but had not been on board. People could read the huge gaps between the lines on that one, Sawyer concluded. Sidney Archer's recent activities were also prominently mentioned. He looked at his watch. He was going to pay Sidney Archer a second visit. And despite his personal sympathy for the woman, this time he wasn't leaving until he got some answers.

Henry Wharton stood behind his desk, his chin sunk down on his chest as he moodily contemplated the cloudy sky outside his window. A copy of that morning's *Post* was lying face down on his desk; at least the vastly disturbing headlines were out of sight. In a chair across from his desk sat Philip Goldman. Goldman's eyes were focused on Wharton's back.

"I really don't see that we have any choice,

319

Henry." Goldman paused, a slight look of satisfaction escaping from his otherwise inscrutable features. "I understand Nathan Gamble was particularly upset when he phoned this morning. Who could really blame him? There's talk that he may pull the whole account."

Wharton winced at the remark. When he turned to face Goldman, his eyes remained downcast. Wharton was clearly wavering. Goldman leaned forward, eager to press this obvious advantage. "It's for the good of the firm, Henry. It will be painful for many people, and despite my differences with her in the past, I would have to include myself in that group, not least of which because she is a particularly strong asset for this firm." This time Goldman succeeded in restraining the smile. "But the future of the firm, the future of hundreds of people, cannot be sacrificed for the benefit of one person, Henry, you know that." Goldman leaned back in his chair, placing his hands in his lap, a placid expression on his face. He managed a sigh. "I can take care of it, Henry, if you would prefer. I know how close you two are."

Wharton finally looked up. The nod was quick, short, like the abrupt plunge of the ax it clearly was. Goldman quietly left the room.

Sidney Archer was picking up the newspaper from her front sidewalk when the phone rang. She raced back inside, the unopened *Post* in one hand. She was fairly certain it was not her husband calling, but right now she could be absolutely certain of nothing. She tossed the paper down on top of other editions she had not read yet.

Her father's voice boomed across the line. Had she read the paper? What the hell were they talking about? These accusations. He would sue, her father proclaimed angrily. He would sue everyone involved, including Triton and the FBI. By the time she got him calmed down, Sidney managed to open the paper. The headline took her breath away, as though someone had stomped on her chest. She tumbled into the chair in the semidarkness of her kitchen. She quickly read the cover story, which implicated her husband in stealing immensely valuable secrets and hundreds of millions of dollars from his employer. To top it off, Jason Archer clearly was also suspected in the plane bombing, his motive presumably to convince the authorities he was dead. Now the world knew him to be alive and on the run, according to the FBI.

When she read her own name about halfway down the page, Sidney Archer became violently sick to her stomach. She had traveled to New Orleans, the story said, shortly after her husband's memorial service, which the story made seem highly suspicious. Of course it was suspicious. Everyone, Sidney Archer included, would find such a trip fraught with dubious motives. An entire life of scrupulous honesty had just been irreversibly destroyed. In her distress she hung up on her father. She barely made it to the kitchen sink. The nausea made her dizzy. She poured cold water over her neck and forehead.

She managed to stumble back to the kitchen table, where she sobbed for some minutes. She had never felt such hopelessness. Then a sudden emotion invaded her body. Anger. She raced to her bedroom, threw on some clothes and two minutes later opened the door of the Ford Explorer. "Shit." The mail tumbled out and she bent down automatically to retrieve it. Her hands quickly sorted through the fallen pieces until she abruptly stopped as her fingers closed around the package addressed to Jason

Archer. Her husband's handwriting on the package made her legs wobble. She could feel the slender object inside. She looked at the postmark. It had been sent from Seattle on the very day Jason had left for the airport. She involuntarily shuddered. Her husband had many mailing packs like this in his home office. They were specifically designed to send computer disks safely through the mail. She did not have time to think about this latest development. She threw the mail back in the truck, climbed in and roared off.

Thirty minutes later, a disheveled Sidney Archer, escorted by Richard Lucas, entered Nathan Gamble's office. Right behind them was an astonished Quentin Rowe. Sidney marched right up to Gamble's desk and tossed the *Post* in his lap.

"I hope to hell you have some really good defamation attorneys." Her intense fury made Lucas step hastily forward until Gamble waved him off. The Triton chief gingerly picked up the paper and glanced down at the story. Then he looked up at her. "I didn't write this."

"The hell you didn't."

Gamble put out his cigarette and stood up. "Excuse me, but why am I thinking that I should be the one who's pissed off?"

"My husband blowing up planes, selling secrets, ripping you off. It's a pack of lies and you know it."

Gamble stormed around the desk to face her. "Let me tell you what I know, lady. I'm out a ton of cash, that's a fact. And your husband gave RTG everything it needs to bury my company. That's also a fact. What am I supposed to do, give you a goddamned medal?"

"It's not true."

"Oh, yeah!" Gamble wheeled a chair around. "Sit down!"

Gamble unlocked a drawer in his desk, pulled out a videotape and tossed it over to Lucas. Then he hit a button on his desk console and part of the wall moved back, revealing a large TV and VCR combination unit. While Lucas popped the tape in, Sidney, her legs shaking, sank into the chair. She looked over at Quentin Rowe, who stood stock-still in the corner of the office, his wide eyes glued to her. She nervously licked her lips and turned to the TV.

Her heart almost stopped beating when she saw her husband. Having only heard his voice ever since that horrible day, she felt as though he had been gone forever. At first she fixated on his fluid movements, so familiar to her. Then she focused on his face and gasped. She had never seen her husband more nervous, under more strain. The briefcase handed across, the plane roaring overhead, the smiles of the men, the papers examined, all of these things were in the background for her, far in the background; she kept her eyes on Jason. Her eyes drifted to the time and date stamp and her heart took another jolt when the significance of those numbers hit her. When the tape went dark, she turned to find all eyes in the room on her.

"That exchange took place in an RTG facility in Seattle long after that plane went into the ground." Gamble stood behind her. "Now if you still want to sue me for defamation, go right ahead. Of course, if we lose CyberCom you might have trouble collecting any money," he added grimly.

Sidney stood up. Gamble reached behind his desk. "Here's your paper." He tossed it to her. Although she could barely stand, she managed to catch it neatly. In another moment she had fled the room.

Sidney pulled into her garage and listened to the door winding its way back down. Her limbs quivering and lungs expunging air heavily laced with sobs every few seconds, she gripped the newspaper. When it fell open, revealing the bottom half of the front page, Sidney Archer received yet another shock. This one contained a distinct element of uncontrollable dread.

The man's photo was some years old, but there was no mistaking the face. His name was now revealed to her: Edward Page. He had been a local private detective for five years after spending ten years in New York City as a police officer. He had worked solo, his firm bearing the name Private Solutions, the story stated. Page had been the victim of a fatal robbery at a National Airport parking lot. Divorced, he left behind two teenage children, the paper reported.

The familiar eyes stared at her from the depths of the page, and a chill went through her body. It was more obvious to her than to anyone else, other than Page's killer, that his death was not the result of a search for cash and credit cards. A few minutes after talking to her, the man was dead. She would have to be damn foolish to dismiss his death as a coincidence. She jumped out of the truck and raced into the house.

She took out the gleaming silver metal Smith & Wesson Slim-Nine she had kept locked in the metal box in the bedroom closet and quickly loaded it. The Hydra-Shok hollowpoints would be highly effective against anyone wishing to perpetrate a deadly attack. She checked her wallet. Her concealed-weapon permit was still valid.

When she reached up to return the box to the top of the closet, the pistol slipped out of her pocket and hit the nightstand before settling on the carpeted floor. Thank God she'd had the safety on. As she picked it up, she noted that a small corner of the hard plastic grip had broken off from the impact, but everything else was intact. Pistol in hand, she returned to the garage and climbed back into the Ford.

She suddenly froze. A sound floated toward her from inside her house. She flipped off the pistol's safety, keeping one eye and the barrel of the Smith & Wesson on the door leading back into the house. With her free hand she struggled with her car keys, one of the keys slid across her finger, gashing it. She hit the garage door opener clipped to the truck's sun visor. Her heart pounded while she waited for the damn door to finish its agonizingly slow ascent. She kept her eyes glued to the door to the house, expecting any moment for it to burst open.

Her mind darted back to the news story detailing Edward Page's demise. Two teenagers left behind. Her features grew deadly in their own right. She was not leaving her little girl behind. Her grip tightened on the butt of the pistol. She hit a button on the driver's-side armrest and the passenger window slid down. Now she would have an unobstructed firing line at the door leading into the house. She had never used her weapon on anything other than shooting range targets. But she was going to do her best to kill whoever was about to come through that door.

She did not notice the man bending low to come through the garage door as it was opening. He stepped quickly to the driver's-side door, pistol drawn. At that instant, the door from the house into the garage started to open. Sidney's grip tightened even more on her weapon until the veins rode high on her hands. Her finger started to descend on the trigger.

"Jesus Christ, lady! Put it down. Now!" The man next to the car yelled, his pistol pointed right at the driver's window and through it to Sidney's left temple.

Sidney whirled around in the car and found herself eye to eye with Agent Ray Jackson. Suddenly the house door to the garage was thrown open and crashed against the wall. Sidney jerked her head back in that direction and watched the massive bulk of Lee Sawyer hurtle through the door, his 10mm making wide arcs in the direction of the vehicles. Sidney slumped back in her seat, sweat streaming off her forehead.

Ray Jackson, gun still in hand, threw open the door of the Explorer and eyed both Sidney Archer and the gun that had almost taken a considerable hole out of his partner. "Are you crazy?" He leaned across her lap and snatched away the pistol, flipping on the safety. Sidney made no move to stop him, but fury suddenly sprawled across her features. "What are you doing, breaking into my house? I could have shot you."

Lee Sawyer slipped his pistol back into his belt holster and moved over to the Ford.

"Front door was open, Ms. Archer. We thought something might be wrong when you didn't answer our knock." His frankness made the fury evaporate as quickly as it had surfaced. She had left the front door open when she had raced inside to answer the phone call from her father. She put her head down on the steering wheel. She struggled not to be sick. Her entire body was soaked with perspiration. She shivered as a chilly wind invaded the garage from the open door.

"Going somewhere?" Sawyer eyed the Ford and then rested his gaze on the woman who sat back up dejectedly.

"Just for a drive." Her voice was weak. She did not look at him. She ran her hands over the steering wheel. The sweat from her palms glistened on the padded surface.

Sawyer looked over at the stack of mail on the passenger seat. "You always carry your mail in your car?"

Sidney followed his stare. "I don't know how it got here. Maybe my father put it there before he left."

"That's right. Right after you left. How was New Orleans, by the way? You have a good time?"

Sidney stared dully at the man.

Sawyer placed on hand firmly under her elbow. "Let's go have a chat, Ms. Archer."

THIRTY-NINE

Before exiting the car, Sidney carefully gathered up the mail and slid the *Post* under her arm. Out of the agents' sight she slipped the disk into her jacket pocket. Climbing out of the car, she eyed the pistol Jackson had abruptly confiscated. "I have a concealed weapons permit for that." Sidney handed over the authorization.

"Mind if I unload it before I give it back?"

"If it'll make you feel safer," she said, hitting the button on the garage door opener, closing the door of the Ford and heading toward the house. "Just make sure you leave the bullets."

Jackson stared after her, amazement on his features. The two FBI agents followed her into the house.

"Would you like coffee? Something to eat? It's still pretty early." These last words Sidney said in an accusatory fashion.

"Coffee would be fine," Sawyer answered, ignoring her tone. Jackson nodded his assent.

While Sidney poured out three cups of coffee, Sawyer methodically looked her over. Her unwashed blond hair hung limply around her face, which bore no makeup and was more drawn and haggard than the last time he had been here. Her clothes hung loosely on her tall frame. Her green eyes were as bewitching as usual, however. He picked up on the slight shake in her hands while she handled the coffeepot. She was clearly on the edge.

He had to grudgingly admire how she was holding up under a nightmare that seemed to metastasize with every passing day. But then everybody had limits. He expected to learn Sidney Archer's before it was all over.

Sidney placed the cups of coffee on a tray with sugar and creamer. She reached into the breadbox and pulled out an assortment of doughnuts and muffins. She loaded the tray and placed it in the middle of the kitchen table. While the agents helped themselves, she took out some Rolaids and slowly crunched them.

"Good doughnut. Thanks. By the way, you usually carry a gun with you?" Sawyer looked at her expectantly.

"There have been some break-ins nearby. I've received professional instruction on how to use it. Besides, I'm no stranger to guns. My dad and oldest brother, Kenny, were in the Marine Corps. They're also avid hunters. Kenny has an extensive firearms collection. When I was growing up, my dad used to take me skeet and target shooting. I've fired just about every type of weapon you can think of and I'm a very good shot."

Ray Jackson said, "You were handling the piece pretty good back there in the garage." He noted the crack in the grip. "I hope you didn't drop it while it was loaded."

"I'm very careful with firearms, Mr. Jackson, but I appreciate your concern."

Jackson looked at the pistol once more before sliding it and the full magazine over to her. "Nice piece of hardware. Lightweight. I use Hydra-Shok ammo too – excellent stopping force. There's still a round in the firing chamber," he reminded her.

"It's equipped with a magazine safety. No mag, no fire." Sidney touched the pistol gingerly. "But I

329

don't like having to keep it in the house, especially with Amy, although it's kept unloaded and in a locked box."

"Not much good, then, in the event of a burglary," Sawyer said between a bite of doughnut and a gulp of hot coffee.

"Only if your get surprised. I try never to be." After the events of the morning, she struggled mightily not to perceptibly wince at that remark.

Sliding the plate of bakery goods away, he asked, "You mind telling me why you took that little trip to New Orleans?"

Sidney held up the morning's newspaper so the headline was fully exposed. "Why? Are you moon-lighting as a reporter and need to file your next story? By the way, thanks for ruining my life." She angrily tossed the paper on the table and looked away. A twitch erupted over her left eye. She gripped the edge of the weathered pine table as she felt herself trembling.

Sawyer ran his eye down the story. "I don't see anything here that isn't true. Your husband *is* suspected of being involved in a theft of secrets from his company. On top of that, he wasn't on a plane he was supposed to be on. That plane ends up in a cornfield. Your husband is alive and kicking." When she didn't respond, Sawyer reached across the table and touched her elbow. "I said your husband is alive, Ms. Archer. That doesn't seem to surprise you. You want to tell me about New Orleans now?"

She slowly turned to look at him, her features surprisingly calm. "You say he's alive?"

Sawyer nodded.

"Then why don't you tell me where he is?"

"I was about to ask you that question."

Sidney dug her fingers into her thigh. "I haven't seen my husband since that morning."

Sawyer edged closer to her. "Look, Ms. Archer, let's cut through the crap. You get a mysterious phone call and then you take a plane to New Orleans after you hold a friggin' memorial service for your dearly departed, who, as it turns out, isn't. You lose my guys and hightail it south. You check into a hotel, where I'm betting you're waiting for a rendezvous with your husband." Sidney Archer, to her credit, did not even flinch. Sawyer continued. "You take a walk, get a shoeshine from a very amiable old guy who's the only street person in my experience who refuses a tip. You make a phone call, and wham, you're back on a plane to D.C. What do you say to that?"

Sidney took an invisible breath and then stared hard at Sawyer. "You said I got a mysterious phone call. Who told you that?"

The agents exchanged looks. "We've got our sources, Ms. Archer. We also checked your phone log," Sawyer said.

Sidney crossed her legs and leaned forward. "You mean the call from Henry Wharton?"

Sawyer eyed her calmly. "You're saying you talked to Wharton?" He didn't expect her to walk into that easy a trap, and he wasn't disappointed.

"No. I'm saying someone called here identifying himself as Henry Wharton."

"But you spoke with someone."

"No."

Sawyer sighed. "We've got a record of the phone call. You were on that phone for about five minutes. Were you just listening to heavy breathing or what?"

"I don't have to sit here and be insulted by you or anyone else. Do you understand that?"

"All right, my apologies. So who was it?"

"I don't know."

Sawyer jerked upright in his chair and slammed

331

his big fist down on the table. Sidney almost jumped out of her chair. "Jesus Christ, come on—"

"I'm telling you I don't know." Sidney interrupted angrily. "I thought it was Henry, but it wasn't. The person never said anything. I hung up the phone after a few seconds." Her heart started racing as it occurred to her that she was lying to the FBI.

Sawyer looked at her wearily. "Computers don't lie, Ms. Archer." Sawyer inwardly winced at this statement as his mind dwelled for an instant on the Riker fiasco. "The phone log says five minutes."

"My father answered the phone in the kitchen and then laid it down on the counter to come and tell me. You two showed up at about the same time. Do you think it's beyond the realm of possibility that he forgot to hang it back up? Wouldn't that account for the five minutes? Maybe you'd like to call and ask him. You can use the phone right over there." Sidney pointed to the kitchen wall next to the doorway.

Sawyer looked over at the phone and took a moment to think. He felt sure the lady was lying, but what she was saying was plausible. He had forgotten he was talking to an attorney, a highly skilled one.

"Would you like to call him?" Sidney repeated. "I happen to know he's home because he called just a little while ago. The last thing I heard him scream over the phone was his plan to file a lawsuit against the FBI and Triton."

"Maybe I'll try him later."

"Fine. I just thought you'd want to do it now so you couldn't accuse me later of arranging for my father to lie to you." Her eyes dug into the agent's troubled features. "And while we're at it, let's address your other accusations. You said I somehow evaded your men. Since I was unaware I was being followed, it would seem impossible for me to 'lose'

332

anyone. My cab was stuck in traffic. I was afraid I would miss my flight, so I jumped on the subway. I haven't used the subway in years, so I got out at the Pentagon station because I couldn't remember if I had to change trains there to get to the airport. When I realized my mistake, I simply got back on the same train. I didn't take my suitcase with me because I didn't want to have to lug it around on the subway, especially if I had to run to make a plane. If I had stayed in New Orleans, I was going to arrange for it to be sent down on a later flight. I've been to New Orleans many times. I've always had good times down there. It seemed like a logical place, not that I've been thinking very logically lately. I had my shoes shined. Is that illegal?" She looked at the two men. "I hope burying your spouse when you don't even have a body is something neither of you ever have to go through."

She angrily tossed the newspaper on the floor. "The man in that story is *not* my husband. You know what our idea of a wild time was? Barbecuing in the backyard in the winter. The most reckless thing I've ever known Jason to do was occasionally drive too fast and not wear his seat belt. He couldn't have been involved in blowing up that plane. I know you don't believe me, but right now I don't really care."

She stood up and leaned against the refrigerator before continuing. "I needed to get away. Do I really have to tell you why? Do I really have to do that?" Her voice rose almost to a scream before it tapered off and she fell silent.

Sawyer started to reply but then abruptly closed his mouth as Sidney held up her hand and continued speaking, in a calmer tone. "I stayed in New Orleans all of one day. It suddenly occurred to me that I couldn't run away from the nightmare my life has become. I have a little girl who needs me. And I need her. She's all I have left. Do you understand that? Can either of you understand anything?" Tears were starting to trickle out. Her hands clenched and unclenched. Her chest rose and fell unevenly. She abruptly sat back down.

Ray Jackson nervously played with his coffee cup while he looked over at his partner. "Ms. Archer, Lee and I both have families. I can't imagine what you're going through right now. You gotta understand we're just trying to do our job. A lot of things don't make sense right now. But one thing is for certain. A planeload of people are dead and whoever is responsible for that is gonna pay."

Sidney stood up again on unsteady legs, the tears now pouring. Her voice was shrill, near hysterical, her eyes blazing. "Don't you think I know that? I went down . . . there. To that . . . that hell!" Her voice rose to an even higher pitch, the tears streaming down the front of her blouse, her eyes at their widest. "I saw it." She stared fiercely at them. "Everything. The . . . the shoe . . a baby's shoe." Moaning, Sidney fell back into her chair, the sobs wracking her frame to such a degree that it looked as though her back would erupt like a volcano spewing forth far more misery than human beings had the ability to endure.

Jackson rose to get her a paper towel.

Sighing quietly, Sawyer put his hand on Sidney's and gripped it in a gentle squeeze. The baby's shoe. The one he had held in his hand, and also shed tears over. For the first time he noted Sidney's engagement ring and wedding band. A beautiful if small setting, she would have worn it all these years with pride, he was certain of that. Whether Jason Archer had done anything wrong or not, he had a woman who loved him, believed in him. Sawyer felt himself starting to hope that Jason would turn out to be innocent, despite all the evidence to the contrary. He did not want Sidney to have to confront the reality of betrayal. He wrapped a big arm around her shoulders. His body seemed to jerk and pitch with every convulsion that raced through her. He whispered soothing words into her ear, trying desperately to get her to come around. For a very brief instant his memory skipped back to the time he had held another young woman like this. That catastrophe had been a prom date gone terribly bad. It had been one of the few times he had actually been there for one of his kids. It had felt wonderful to wrap his burly arms around the small, quaking form, letting her hurt, her embarrassment, siphon off into him. Sawyer refocused on Sidney Archer. She had been hurt enough, he decided. The raw pain he was holding on to right now was not capable of being fabricated. Regardless of anything else, Sidney Archer was telling them the truth, or at least most of it. As if sensing his thoughts, her grip tightened on his hand.

Jackson handed him the wet paper towel. Sawyer did not see his partner's worried look as Jackson watched the gentle way in which he slowly brought Sidney around. The things Sawyer said to her, to calm her down, the way he kept his arms protectively around her. Ray Jackson was clearly not happy with his partner right now.

A few minutes later Sidney was sitting in front of a fire that Jackson had quickly prepared in the living room fireplace. The warmth felt good. When Sawyer looked out the broad picture window he noticed that it was snowing again. He looked around the room and his eyes settled on the fireplace mantel, where a procession of framed photographs held forth: Jason Archer, looking anything but a participant in one of the most horrendous crimes ever committed; Amy

Archer, as pretty a little girl as Sawyer had ever seen; and Sidney Archer, beautiful and enchanting. A picture-perfect family, at least on the surface. Sawyer had spent the last twenty-five years of his life constantly probing beneath the surface. He looked forward to the day when he would not have to do that. To the time when delving into the motives and circumstances that turned human beings into monsters would be someone else's job. Today, though, that duty was his. He turned his gaze from the photo to the real thing.

"I'm sorry. I seem to lose it every time you two show up." Sidney spoke slowly, her eyes clamped shut. She seemed smaller than Sawyer had remembered, as though crisis on top of crisis were causing her to collapse inward.

"Where's your little girl?" he asked.

"With my parents," Sidney replied quickly.

Sawyer nodded slowly.

Sidney's eyes fluttered open and then closed again. "The only time she's not asking for her father is when she's asleep," she added in a hushed voice, her lips trembling.

Sawyer rubbed tired eyes and drew closer to the fire. "Sidney?" She finally opened her eyes and looked at him, gathered around her shoulders the blanket she had taken from the ottoman, lifted her knees to her chest, and settled back into the chair. "Sidney, you said you went to the crash site. I happen to know that's true. You remember running into somebody out there? My knee still aches."

Sidney started, her eyes seeming to dilate fully and then slowly recede as she stared at him.

Sawyer continued to look at her. "We also have a report from the deputy that night. Deputy McKenna?"

"Yes, he was very nice to me."

"Why did you go there, Sidney?"

Sidney didn't answer. She wrapped her arms tightly around her legs. Finally she looked up. However, her eyes were fixed on the opposite wall rather than on the two agents. She seemed to be looking over a great distance, as though she were reaching back to the painful depths of a great hole in the earth; to a dismal cavern she had thought at the time had swallowed her husband.

"I had to." She abruptly closed her mouth.

Jackson started to say something, but Sawyer stopped him.

"I had to," Sidney repeated. The tears started to tumble again, but her voice remained steady. "I saw it on TV."

"What?" Sawyer leaned forward anxiously. "What did you see?"

"I saw his bag. Jason's bag." Her mouth trembled as she said his name. One shaky hand fluttered to her mouth as though to corral the utter grief concentrated there. Her hand dropped back down. "I could still see his initials on the side." She stopped again and dabbed at a tear with the back of her hand. "It suddenly occurred to me that it was probably the only thing . . . the only thing left of him. So I went to get it. Officer McKenna told me I couldn't have it until the investigation was over. So I went back home with nothing. Nothing." She said the word slowly, as though it summarized the desolate status of the life she had left.

Sawyer leaned back in his chair and looked at his partner. The bag was a dead end. He let the silence persist for about a minute before he began speaking again. "When I said your husband was alive, you didn't seem to be surprised." Sawyer's tone was low and calming, but there was an unmistakable edge to it.

Sidney's response was biting, but the voice was tired. She was obviously running out of steam. "I had just read the article in the paper. If you wanted to see surprise, you should have shown up before the paperboy did." She wasn't about to go into the humiliating experience at Gamble's office.

Sawyer sat back. He had expected that very logical answer, but was still gratified to hear it from her lips. Liars often opted for complicated stories in their effort to avoid detection. "Okay, fair enough. I don't want to drag this conversation out, so I'm just going to ask you some questions and I want some straight answers. That's all. If you don't know the answer, so be it. Those are the ground rules. Are you willing to do that?"

Sidney didn't respond. Her weary eyes swung between the two FBI agents. Sawyer hunched forward some more. "I didn't make up those accusations against your husband. But in all honestly, the evidence we've uncovered so far does not paint a real benign picture of him."

"What evidence?" Sidney asked sharply.

Sawyer shook his head. "I'm sorry, I'm not at liberty to say. But I will tell you it's strong enough for an arrest warrant to have been issued for your husband. If you didn't already know it, every cop in the world right now is looking for him."

Sidney's eyes glistened as the incredible words sunk in. Her husband, a fugitive sought worldwide. She looked at Sawyer. "Did you know all this when you were here the first time?"

Sawyer's expression became slightly pained. He finally said, "Some of it." Sawyer shifted uneasily in his chair while Jackson picked up for his partner.

"If your husband didn't do the things he's accused of doing, then he's got nothing to worry about on our end. We can't speak for anybody else's agenda, though."

338

Sidney riveted her gaze on him. "What do you mean by that?"

Jackson shrugged his broad shoulders. "Let's say he didn't do anything wrong. We know beyond doubt that he wasn't on that plane. So where is he? If he had maybe missed the plane by accident, he would've gotten on the horn right away to you, to let you know he was okay. That didn't happen. Why? The partial answer to that is that he's got himself involved in something not exactly legit. On top of that, the kind of planning and execution we're looking at on this one leads us to believe that it's more than a one-man show." Jackson paused and looked over at Sawyer, who nodded slightly. Jackson continued. "Ms. Archer, the man we suspect actually sabotaged that plane was found murdered in his apartment. It looked like he was getting ready to leave the country, but somebody had a change in plans for him."

Sidney mouthed the world slowly. "Murdered." She thought of Edward Page lying in a vast pool of his own blood. Dying right after talking to her. She pulled the blanket tighter around her. She hesitated, debating whether to tell the agents about talking with Page. Then, for a reason she could not precisely pinpoint, she decided not to. She drew a deep breath. "What are your questions?"

"First, I'll let you in on a little theory of mine." Sawyer paused for a moment, compiling his thoughts. "For the moment, we'll accept your story that you went down to New Orleans on a whim. We followed you down there. We also know that your parents and your daughter left this house shortly after you did."

"So? Why should they stay here?" Sidney looked around the interior of her once beloved house. *What is here anymore except misery?*

339

"Right. But see, you left, we left and your parents left." He paused.

"If this has a point, I'm afraid I'm not getting it."

Sawyer abruptly rose and stood with his broad back to the fire while he looked down at Sidney. He spread his arms wide. "There was no one here, Sidney. The place was completely unguarded. Regardless of why you went to New Orleans, it had the effect of drawing us off. And that left no one watching your house. Now do you see?"

Despite the fire's warmth, a sudden chill stalked through Sidney's veins. She had been a diversion. Jason knew the authorities had been watching her. He had used her. Used her to get at something in this house.

Sawyer and Jackson watched Sidney carefully. They could almost see the powerful mental gymnastics flowing behind her forehead.

Sidney looked out the window. Her eyes swept across the gray blazer lying over the rocking chair. The disk resting in the inside pocket. She suddenly wanted to hasten this interview to an end.

"There's nothing here anyone could want."

"Nothing?" Jackson sounded skeptical. "Your husband didn't keep any files or records here? Nothing like that?"

"Not from work. Triton is very paranoid about things like that."

Sawyer slowly nodded. Based on his own experience with Triton, that was one statement he could readily believe. "Nonetheless, Sidney, you might want to give it some thought. You haven't noticed anything missing or disturbed?"

Sidney slowly shook her head. "I haven't really looked, though."

Jackson stirred. "Well, if you don't have an objection, we could search the house right now." He looked over at his partner, who had raised his eyebrows at the request. Then Jackson looked at Sidney, waiting for her answer.

When she didn't deliver one, Jackson took a step forward. "We can always get a warrant. Plenty of probable cause. You could save us a lot of time and trouble, though. And if it's like you say and there's nothing here, you shouldn't have a problem with that, right?"

"I'm an attorney, Mr. Jackson," Sidney said coldly. "I know the drill. All right, help yourself. Please excuse the dirt, I haven't really kept up the household chores." She stood up, slipped off the blanket, reached out for her blazer and put it on. "While you're doing that, I'm going for some fresh air. How long will you need?"

The two agents looked at each other. "A few hours."

"Fine, help yourself to the fridge. Searching can be very hungry work."

After she had walked out, Jackson turned to his partner. "Damn, she's a piece of work, isn't she?"

Sawyer stared after the lithe form as she headed toward the garage. "She sure is."

Several hours later Sidney Archer returned.

"Nothing?" She looked at the two disheveled men.

"Not that we could find, anyway." Jackson's tone was one of reproach.

She stared him down. "That's not my problem, is it?"

The two looked at each other for several moments. "You had some questions?" Sidney finally said.

When the two FBI agents were leaving about an hour later, Sidney touched Sawyer on the arm. "You obviously didn't know my husband. If you had, you

341

would have no doubt that he couldn't . . ." Her lips moved, but no words came out for a moment. "He could never have had anything to do with that plane crash. With all those people . . ." She closed her eyes and steadied herself against the front door.

Sawyer's features were troubled. How could anyone think someone they loved, had a child with, could be capable of anything like that? But human beings committed atrocities every minute of every day; the only living things who killed with malice.

"I understand how you feel, Sidney," the agent said quietly.

Jackson kicked a piece of gravel on the way to the car and looked over at his partner. "I don't know, Lee, things just aren't adding up with that woman. She's definitely holding back."

Sawyer shrugged. "Hell, if I were in her position, I'd do the same thing."

Jackson looked surprised. "Lie to the FBI?"

"She's caught in the middle, doesn't know which way to turn. Under those circumstances, I'd play it close to the vest too."

"I guess I'll go with your judgment on that." Jackson's words did not sound very confident as he climbed in the car.

FORTY

S idney raced to the phone but abruptly stopped. She looked at the receiver as though it were a cobra about to sink venom into her. If the late Edward Page had tapped her phone, how probable was it that others had? She put the phone back down and looked at her cellular phone, which sat recharging on the kitchen counter. How secure was that? She slammed her fist against the wall in frustration as she imagined hundreds of pairs of electronic eyes monitoring and recording her every action. She slid her alphanumeric pager into her purse, figuring that form of communication was reasonably safe. It would have to do, in any case. She put her loaded pistol in her purse and raced to the Explorer. The disk was safely in her pocket. It would have to wait for now. She had something else to do that at that moment was even more important.

The Ford pulled into the McDonald's parking lot. Sidney went inside, ordered a take-out lunch and went down the hallway toward the rest room, stopping at the pay phone. After dialing, she scanned the parking lot for signs of the FBI. She saw nothing out of the ordinary, which was good – they were supposed to be invisible. But a shiver went down her back as she wondered who else was out there.

A voice came on the other end of the phone line. It took her several minutes to calm her father down.

When she stated her request, he began to erupt all over again.

"What the hell do you want me to do that for?"

"Please, Dad. I want you and Mom to go. And I want you to take Amy with you."

"You know we never go to Maine after Labor Day."

Sidney held the receiver away from her mouth and took a deep breath. "Look, Dad, you read the paper."

He started off again. "That's the biggest bunch of bullshit I ever heard. Sid—"

"Dad, just listen to me. I don't have time to argue." She had never raised her voice to her father like that.

They were both quiet for a moment.

When she broke the silence, her voice was firm. "The FBI just left my house. Jason was involved in . . . something. I'm not exactly sure what yet. But if even half of what that story reported is true . . ." She shuddered. "On the flight back from New Orleans a man spoke to me. His name was Edward Page. He was a private investigator. He was investigating something to do with Jason."

Bill Patterson's voice was incredulous. "What was he investigating Jason for?"

"I don't know. He wouldn't tell me."

"Well, I say we go ask him and we don't take no for an answer."

"We can't ask him: He was murdered about five minutes after he left me, Dad."

Stunned, Bill Patterson could no longer find his voice.

"Will you please go to the house in Maine, Dad? Please. As soon as possible."

Patterson didn't answer for a few seconds. When he finally spoke, his voice was weak. "We'll leave after lunch. I'll pack my shotgun just in case."

Sidney's hunched shoulders relaxed in relief.

"Sidney?"

"Yes, Dad?"

"I want you to come with us."

Sidney shook her head. "I can't do that, Dad."

Her father exploded. "Why the hell not? You're up there all alone. You're Jason's wife. You could sure as hell be a target in all this."

"The FBI are watching me."

"You think they're invulnerable? You don't think they make mistakes? Don't be crazy, honey."

"I can't, Dad. The FBI probably aren't the only ones watching me. If I came with you so would they." Sidney's entire body shook as she uttered the words.

"Jesus, baby." Sidney could distinctly hear her father swallowing over the phone line. "Look, why don't I send your mother and Amy up there and I'll come stay with you."

"I don't want them or you getting involved in this. It's enough that I am. And I want you with Amy and Mom. I want you to protect *them*. I can take care of myself."

"I've never lacked for confidence in you, baby girl. But . . . but this is a little different. If these people have already killed . . ." Bill Patterson couldn't finish. He had gone numb at the prospect of losing his youngest to violent death.

"Dad, I'll be fine. I have my pistol. The FBI are out there every minute. I'll check in with you every day."

"Sid—"

"Dad, I'll be fine."

Patterson didn't answer right away. Finally he said resignedly, "Okay, but call twice a day."

"Okay, twice a day. Give Mom my love. I know the paper must have upset her. But don't tell her about our talk."

"Sid, your mother's no fool. She's gonna wonder why we're suddenly taking off for Maine at this time of year."

"Please, Dad. Just make up something."

Bill Patterson finally sighed. "Anything else?"

"Tell Amy I love her. Tell her that me and her dad love her more than anything." Wet clusters were forming around Sidney's eyes as the one thing she desperately wanted to do, be with her daughter, was now firmly beyond her. In order to keep Amy safe, Sidney had to stay away, far away.

"I'll tell her, sweetie," Bill Patterson said quietly.

Sidney devoured her lunch on the ride back home. She dashed through the house and within a minute was sitting in front of her husband's computer. She had taken the precaution of locking the door to the room and bringing her cellular phone with her just in case she had to dial 911. She slid the disk out of her jacket pocket, pulled the pistol out and laid them both down on the table next to her.

She turned on the computer and watched the screen as the computer began to wake up. When she was about to pop the disk into the floppy drive she jolted upright, her eyes transfixed by what was on the screen. The available memory figure had just come up. Something wasn't right. She hit several keys on the keyboard. The available hard disk memory again came across the screen and then held. Sidney read the figures slowly: 1,356,600 kilobytes, or about 1.3 gigs, of hard drive were available. She stared hard at the last three digits. She thought back to the last time she had sat in front of the computer. The last three digits of the available memory had been Jason's birthday – seven, zero, six, a fact that had caused her to cry. To break down once again. She had prepared herself for that again, but there was less memory available now. But how could that be? She hadn't touched the computer since . . .

Oh, Christ!

A knot erupted in her stomach as she jumped up from the chair, grabbed the pistol and put the disk back in her jacket pocket. She almost felt like putting a round right into the damned computer screen. Sawyer had been right and wrong. Right that someone had been in her house while she was in New Orleans. Wrong that they had come to take something. They had *left* something instead. Something that resided on her husband's computer. Something that she was running from now as quickly as she could.

It took her ten minutes to return to McDonald's and get back on the pay phone. Her secretary's tone was strained.

"Hello, Ms. Archer."

Ms. Archer? Her secretary had been with her almost six years and hadn't called her Ms. Archer after the second day. Sidney ignored it for the moment. "Sarah, is Jeff in today?" Jeff Fisher was Tyler, Stone's resident computer guru.

"I'm not sure. Would you like me to transfer you to his assistant, Ms. Archer?"

Sidney finally blurted out, "Sarah, what the hell is it with the Ms. Archer label?"

Sarah didn't immediately answer, but then she started to whisper furiously into the phone. "Sid, that story in the paper is all over the firm. They've faxed it to every office. The Triton people are threatening to pull the entire account from the firm. Mr. Wharton is furious. And it's no secret that all the higher-ups are blaming you."

"I'm as much in the dark as everyone else."

"Well, that story made it seem . . . you know."

Sidney sighed heavily. "You want to transfer me to Henry? I'll straighten this whole thing out."

347

Sarah's response rocked her boss. "The management committee held a meeting this morning. They teleconferenced in the partners from the other offices. Rumor has it that they're putting together a letter to send to you."

"A letter? What kind of letter?" The astonishment was rapidly growing on Sidney's face.

In the background, Sidney could hear people passing by Sarah's cubicle. After the noise drifted away, Sarah spoke, her voice even lower. "I . . . I don't know how to tell you this, but I heard it was a letter of termination."

"Termination?" Sidney put one hand up against the wall to steady herself. "I haven't even been accused of anything and they've already tried and convicted me and now they're sentencing me? All because of that one story?"

"I think everyone here is worried about the firm surviving. Most people are pointing their finger at you." Sarah added quickly, "And your husband. To find out Jason's still alive . . . People feel betrayed, they really do."

Sidney drew a large breath and her shoulders slumped down. A complete weariness dragged at her.

"My God, Sarah, how do you think I felt?" Sarah didn't say anything. Sidney fingered the disk in her pocket. The pistol made an uncomfortable lump under her jacket front. She would just have to get used to that. "Sarah, I wish I could explain it to you, but I can't. All I can tell you is I haven't done anything wrong and I don't know what the hell's happened to my life. But I don't have much time. Could you discreetly find out if Jeff's in? Please, Sarah."

Sarah paused and then said, "Hold on, Sid."

As it turned out, Jeff had taken a few days off.

Sarah gave Sidney his home number. She prayed he was not out of town. Around three o'clock, Sidney finally reached him. Her original plan had been to meet him at the firm. However, now that was out of the question. Instead, she made arrangements to meet him at his home in Alexandria. It didn't hurt that he had not been at the office the last couple of days to hear all the rumors swirling around her. When Sidney told him she had a computer problem, he was eager to assist. He had some business to take care of but would be home around eight. She would just have to wait it out.

Two hours later a knock at the door startled Sidney while she was nervously pacing through the living room. She looked through the peephole and then opened the door in mild surprise. Lee Sawyer didn't wait to be asked in. He strode through the foyer and sat down in one of the chairs next to the fireplace hearth. The fire had long since gone out.

"Where's your partner?"

Sawyer ignored her question. "I checked in at Triton," he said. "You didn't tell me you had paid a call there this morning."

She stood in front of him, her arms crossed. She had showered and changed into a black pleated skirt and white V-neck sweater. Her hair, combed straight back, was still damp. She was in her stocking feet; her pumps lay next to the sofa. "You didn't ask."

Sawyer grunted. "So what did you think of your husband's little video?"

"I really haven't given it much thought."

"Like hell you haven't.

She sat down on the sofa, drawing her legs up underneath her before responding. "What exactly do you want?" she said stiffly.

"The truth wouldn't be bad, to start with. From

349

there we might be able to move on to some solutions."

"Like putting my husband in prison for the rest of his life? That's the solution you want, isn't it?" She slung the words at him.

Sawyer absently fingered the badge on his belt. His stern expression faded. When he looked at her, his eyes were weary, his big body listing to one side. "Look, Sidney, like I said, I was at the crash site that night. I . . . I held that little shoe in my hand too." His voice started to break up. Tears appeared in Sidney's eyes, but she continued to look at him, even as her frame started to shake.

Sawyer resumed speaking, his voice low but clear. "I see photos all over your house of a very happy family. A handsome husband, one of the prettiest little girls I've ever laid my eyes on and . . ." He paused. "And a very beautiful wife and mother." Sidney's cheeks flushed at the words.

Embarrassed, Sawyer hurried on. "It makes no sense to me that your husband, even if he did steal from his employer, would have participated in blowing up that plane." A tear plunged from Sidney's cheek and stained the couch while she listened. "Now, I won't lie to you and tell you that I think your husband is completely innocent. For your sake, I hope to God he is and this whole mess can be explained somehow. But my job is to find whoever brought down that plane and killed all those people." He took a long breath. "Including the owner of that little shoe." He paused again. "And I'm going to do my job."

"Go on," Sidney encouraged him, one hand nervously gripping the hemline of her skirt.

"The best lead I have now is your husband. The only way I know to explore that lead right now is through you."

350

"So you want me to help you bring my husband in?"

"I want you to tell me anything you can that will help me get to the bottom of this. Don't you want that too?"

It took Sidney a full minute to respond. When the word finally came, it was buttressed by sobs. "Yes." She said nothing else for several moments. Finally she looked at him. "But my little girl needs me. I don't know where Jason is, and if I were to go away too . . ." Her voice trailed off.

Sawyer looked confused for a moment and then it dawned on him what she was saying. He reached across and gently took one of her hands. "Sidney, I don't believe you had anything to do with any of this. I'm sure as hell not going to arrest you and take you away from your daughter. Maybe you didn't tell me the whole story before, but Christ, you're only human. I can't even begin to imagine the pressure you've been under. Please believe me. And trust me." He let go of her hand and sat back.

She dabbed at her eyes, managed a brief smile, and composed herself. She took one last deep breath before taking the plunge. "That was my husband on the phone the day you came by." After having said it, she glanced sharply at Sawyer, as though she were still afraid that he might pull out his handcuffs. He merely hunched forward, his face a mass of wrinkles.

"What did he say? Give it to me as precisely as you can."

"He said that he knew things looked bad, but that he would explain everything as soon as he saw me. I was so thrilled to know he was alive, I didn't ask very many questions. He also called me from the airport before he got on the plane on the day of the crash." Sawyer perked up. "But I didn't have time to talk to him."

351

Sidney steeled herself for another guilt attack as the memory flooded back to her. Then she recounted to Sawyer Jason's late nights at the office and their early morning conversation before he had left for the airport.

"And he suggested the New Orleans trip?" Sawyer asked.

She nodded. "He said if he didn't contact me at the hotel that I should go to Jackson Square and he would get a message to me there."

"The shoeshine guy, right?"

Sidney nodded again.

Sawyer sighed. "So that was Jason you called from the pay phone?"

"Actually, the message said to call my office number, only Jason answered. He said not to say anything, that the police were around. He told me to go home and he would contact me when it was safe to do so."

"But he hasn't as yet?"

She slowly shook her head. "I've heard nothing."

Sawyer chose his words carefully. "You know, Sidney, your loyalty is admirable, it really is. You've lived up to your marriage vows big-time, because I don't think even God himself envisioned these kinds of 'bad times.' "

"But?" She looked at him searchingly.

"But there comes a time when you have to look beyond the devotion, beyond the feelings you have for someone and consider the cold, hard facts. I'm not very eloquent, but if your husband did something wrong – and I'm not saying he did – then you shouldn't go down with him. Like you said, you've got a little girl who needs you. I've got four kids of my own; I'm not the greatest father in the world, but I can still relate."

"So what are you proposing?" Her voice was hushed.

352

"Cooperation. Nothing more than that. You give me info, I give you info. Here's some for you. Call it a good-faith deposit. The stuff in the newspaper article pretty much sums up what we know. You saw the video. Your husband met with someone and an exchange took place. Triton is convinced it was information designed to hurt their chances at acquiring CyberCom. They also have pretty strong evidence tying Jason to the bank fraud."

"I know the evidence seems overwhelming, but I can't believe any of it. I really can't."

"Well, sometimes the clearest signposts point in the wrong direction. It's my job to figure out which way they should be pointing. I gotta admit I don't believe your husband is completely clean, but on the other hand, I don't think he's the only one out there."

"You think he's working with RTG, don't you?"

"It's possible," Sawyer frankly admitted. "We're following up that lead along with all the others. It seems the most straightforward, but then again, you never know." He paused. "Anything else you want to tell me?"

Sidney hesitated for a moment as she thought back to her conversation with Ed Page right before he was murdered. When her eyes came to rest on her tweed jacket lying over the chair, she almost jerked. The fact of the disk and her planned meeting with Jeff Fisher came rushing back to her. She swallowed and then reddened. "Not that I can think of. No."

Sawyer continued to watch her for a long moment and then slowly got to his feet. "While we're exchanging information, I thought you might like to know that your buddy Paul Brophy followed you down to Louisiana."

Sidney froze at his words.

"He searched your hotel room while you went out for coffee. Feel free to use that information however you see fit." He started to walk out the door and then turned back. "And just so there's no mistake, we have you under twenty-four-hour surveillance."

"I don't plan on taking any more trips, if that's what you're worried about."

His response surprised her. "Don't keep that pistol locked up, Sidney. Keep it within easy reach, and keep it loaded at all times. In fact . . ." Sawyer opened his coat, undid his clip-on belt holster, removed his pistol and handed the holster to Sidney. "In my experience, guns in purses aren't all that effective. Please be careful."

He left Sidney in the open doorway, her thoughts centered on the brutal fate of the last man to give her that particular piece of advice.

FORTY-ONE

Lee Sawyer looked at the carefully sculpted black-and-white marble walls and floors. They were cut in asymmetrical triangular patterns. He assumed they were supposed to convey a sophisticated artistic statement. However, they only served to give the FBI agent a throbbing headache. Through the gracefully carved lines of a birchwood double doorway with etched-glass panels and buttressed by a pair of faux Corinthian columns, the clink of dishes and silverware filtered out to him from the main dining area. He took off his overcoat, removed his hat and gave both to a pretty young woman in a short black skirt and tight blouse that managed to enhance a body that didn't need much enhancing. He was given a claim check in return, accompanied by a very warm smile. One of her fingernails had slid delicately across his palm when the claim check was passed over, digging just deep enough into his skin to make his body tingle in certain discreet places. She must do damn well in tips, he figured.

The maître d' appeared and eyed the FBI agent.

"I'm here to meet Frank Hardy."

The man again flicked his eyes over Sawyer's rumpled appearance. The severe appraisal was not lost on Sawyer, who took a moment to hitch up his pants, a duty repeated many times a day by people of Sawyer's healthy dimensions. "How're the burgers here, pal?" he inquired. He took out a stick of gum, wadded it up and popped it into his mouth.

"Burgers?" The man seemed ready to topple over at the thought. "We serve *French* cuisine here, sir. The finest in the city." His accented speech bubbled with indignation.

"French? Great, I bet your fries must be damn good, then."

Turning quickly on his heel the maître d' led Sawyer through the immense dining area, where rows of crystal chandeliers sparkled above a clientele that nearly matched the brilliance of the finely cut light fixtures.

The ever elegantly dressed Frank Hardy rose from a corner booth and inclined his head at his former partner. Their waitress appeared moments after Sawyer did.

"What're you drinking, Lee?"

Sawyer settled his bulk into the booth. "Bourbon and spit," he grumbled without looking up.

The waitress looked at him blankly. "Excuse me?"

Hardy laughed. "In his own crude way my friend means *straight* bourbon. I'll have another martini."

The waitress went off, rolling her eyes.

Sawyer blew into his handkerchief and proceeded to look around the room. "Gee, Frank, I'm glad you picked the place."

"Why's that?"

"Because if I had, we'd be at Shoneys. But maybe it's best. I hear it's tough as hell to get reservations there this time of year."

Hardy chuckled and swallowed the rest of his drink. "You just can't accept even a sliver of the good life, can you?"

"Hell, I can accept it, so long as I don't have to pay for it. I'm figuring dinner for two here would run about what I have in my retirement plan."

The two men chatted for a few minutes while the

waitress returned, situated their drinks and then stood ready to take their dinner orders.

Sawyer looked over the menu, which was written very clearly, but unfortunately only in French. He put the menu down on the table. "What's the most expensive item on the menu?" he asked the waitress. She rattled off a dish in French.

"Is it real food? Not snails or crap like that?"

With raised eyebrows and a stern expression, she assured him that snails were on the menu and were excellent, but the selection she had mentioned was not snails.

With a grin at Hardy, he said, "Then I'll have that."

After the waitress departed, Sawyer swallowed his gum, grabbed a hunk of bread from the basket in the center of the table and munched on it. "So, you find out anything on RTG?" he said between bites.

Hardy put his hands on the table, smoothing out the linen cloth. "Philip Goldman is RTG's top counsel and has been for many years now."

"Doesn't that strike you as funny?"

"What?"

"That RTG would use the same lawyers as Triton, and vice versa. I mean, I'm no attorney, but isn't that setting somebody up for a nasty fall?"

"It's not that simple, Lee."

"Gee, why am I not surprised."

Hardy ignored the remark. "Goldman has a national reputation and he's been RTG's top dog for a long time. Triton is a relative newcomer to Tyler, Stone's fold. Henry Wharton brought the account in. At the time, the two companies had no direct conflicts. Since then, there have been some tricky issues as the two companies' businesses have expanded. However, they've always worked through that – full disclosures, written waivers, all papered properly. Tyler, Stone is a top-flight firm and I think neither company wanted to lose that expertise. It takes time to build that continuity and trust."

"Trust. Now, there's a funny word to use in a case like this." Sawyer fiddled with the bread crumbs in front of him while he listened.

"Anyway, with the CyberCom deal, there was a direct conflict," Hardy continued. "Both RTG and Triton want CyberCom. Tyler, Stone was barred by the code of legal ethics from representing both clients."

"So they opted to rep Triton. How come?"

Hardy shrugged. "Wharton is managing partner. Triton is his client. Enough said? They sure as hell weren't going to let both companies be represented by someone else on this deal. Too tempting for another firm to walk away with the whole kit and caboodle."

"I take it Goldman was a little upset when the firm dissed his client like that."

"From what I could find out, homicidal was more like it."

"But who's to say he can't work behind the scenes to get RTG the prize?"

"Nothing. Nathan Gamble is no dummy; he's well aware of that. And if RTG beats out Triton, you know what might well happen, don't you?"

"Let me guess. Gamble might find some new lawyers?"

Hardy nodded. "Besides that, you read the headlines. They are mad as hell at Sidney Archer. I think her job security might be a little weak."

"Well, the lady's not too thrilled herself right now."

"You talked to her?"

Sawyer nodded and finished off his bourbon. He debated and then decided not to fill in Hardy on

358

Sidney Archer's confession to him. Hardy worked for Gamble, and Sawyer was pretty sure what Gamble would do with that information: Destroy the lady. He threw out a fact as a theory instead. "Maybe she went to New Orleans to meet her husband."

Hardy stroked his chin. "I guess it makes sense."

"That's the problem, Frank, it *doesn't* make a damned bit of sense."

"How's that?" Hardy looked surprised.

Sawyer put his elbows on the table. "Look at it this way. The FBI shows up on her doorstep asking a bunch of questions. Now, you've got to be a friggin' *zombie* not to get a little nervous when that happens. So on the same day she hops on a plane to meet her husband?"

"It's possible she didn't know she was being followed."

Sawyer shook his head. "Uh-uh. This lady is sharp, like ginzu-knife sharp. I thought I had her dead to rights on a phone call she got the morning of her husband's memorial service and she sidesteps it with a perfectly plausible explanation that she probably thought up right then and there. She did the same thing when I accused her of ditching my cover guys. She knew she had a tail on her. And she still went."

"Maybe Jason Archer didn't know you were watching."

"If the guy did pull off all this shit, you don't think he's smart enough to realize the cops *might* be watching his wife? Come on."

"But she *did* go to New Orleans, Lee. You can't get around that fact."

"I'm not trying to. I think her husband did contact her and told her to hightail it down there despite our presence."

359

"Why in the hell would he do that?"

Sawyer fiddled with his napkin and didn't respond. Then their meals arrived.

"Looks good." Sawyer eyed his meticulously arranged meal.

"It is. It'll kick your cholesterol to an all-time new high, but you'll die a happy man."

Hardy reached across and tapped Sawyer's plate with his knife. "You haven't answered my question: Why would Jason Archer have done that?"

Sawyer slid a forkful of food into his mouth. "You weren't kidding about this stuff, Frank. And to think I was going to Chef Boyardee-it when you called and asked me to dinner."

"Dammit, come on, Lee."

Sawyer put down his fork. "When Sidney Archer went to New Orleans, we pulled all our guys because we had a number of routes to cover. She still almost gave us the slip. In fact, except for me getting incredibly lucky at the airport, we wouldn't have known where the hell she went. And now I think I know the reason she did go: as a diversion."

Hardy looked incredulous. "What the hell do you mean? A diversion from what?"

"When I said we pulled all our guys, I meant we pulled *all* our guys, Frank. There wasn't anybody watching the Archer's house while we were gone."

Hardy sucked in his breath and collapsed back in his seat. "Shit!"

Sawyer eyed him wearily. "I know. A big-time screwup on my part, but it's too late to bitch and moan about it now."

"So you think—"

"I think somebody paid that house a call while the missus was cooling her high heels in the Big Easy."

"Wait a minute, you don't think it was . . ."

"Let's put it this way: Jason Archer would be on

my top-five list."

"What could he have wanted?"

"I don't know. Ray and I searched the place and didn't find anything."

"You think the wife is in on it?"

Sawyer took another bite of food before answering. "If you had asked me that question a week ago, I probably would have said yes. Now? Now I think she has no idea what's going on."

Hardy sat back. "You really believe that?"

"The newspaper shredded her. She's in deep shit with her law firm. Her husband never showed up and she comes home empty-handed. What did she gain except an even bigger headache?"

Hardy started to eat again but continued to look thoughtful.

Sawyer shook his head. "Christ, this case is like a jelly doughnut. Every time you take a bite, sticky shit squirts all over you." Sawyer stuffed a mound of food in his mouth.

Hardy laughed and looked round the dining room. His eyes suddenly focused on something. "I thought he was out of town."

Sawyer followed his gaze. "Who?"

"Quentin Rowe." He discreetly pointed. "Over there."

Rowe was halfway across the dining room, ensconced at a booth in a secluded corner. Soft candlelight gave the table an intimate feel in the expanse of the crowded restaurant. He wore a costly silk blazer, collarless shirt buttoned to the top and a pair of matching silk trousers. His ponytail flopped across the back of his neck as he engaged in an animated conversation with his dinner companion, a man in his early twenties dressed in an expensively tailored suit. The two young men were sitting side by side, their eyes firmly set on one another. They spoke in low tones, and Rowe's hand briefly flickered on top of his companion's.

Sawyer arched an eyebrow at Hardy. "They make a nice couple."

"Watch it. You're starting to sound politically incorrect."

"Hey, live and let live. That's my motto. Guy can date whoever he wants."

Hardy continued to observe the pair. "Well, Quentin Rowe is worth about three hundred million dollars, and the way things are going he'll be a billionaire well before he's forty. I'd say that makes him a very eligible bachelor."

"I'm sure there's an army of young ladies just kicking themselves over that one."

"You better believe it. But the guy's flat-out brilliant. He deserves the success."

"Yeah, he gave me a little tour of the company. I didn't understand half of what he was talking about, but it was still interesting stuff. Can't say I like where all this technology crap is going, though."

"Can't stop progress, Lee."

"I don't want to stop it, Frank, I'd just like to choose how much I have to participate in it. According to Rowe, it doesn't look like I'm going to get that opportunity."

"It is a little scary. But it sure as hell is lucrative."

Sawyer glanced again in Rowe's direction. "Speaking of couples, Rowe and Gamble sure make an odd one."

"Really, what makes you say that?" Hardy grinned. "Seriously, they just happened to run into each other at an opportune time. The rest is history."

"So I understand. Gamble had the money bags and Rowe brought along the brains?"

Hardy shook his head. "Don't sell Nathan Gamble short. It's not easy making the bucks he did on Wall

362

Street. He is one bright guy and a hell of a business-man."

Sawyer wiped his mouth with his napkin. "Good thing, because the man ain't going to get by on his charm."

FORTY-TWO

It was eight o'clock when Sidney reached Jeff Fisher's home, a restored row house on the outskirts of Old Town Alexandria's elite residential area. Dressed in MIT sweats and battered tennis shoes, a Red Sox cap perched on his nearly bald head, the short, pudgy Fisher welcomed her and led her to a large room crammed top to bottom with computer equipment of all descriptions, cables running all over the hardwood floors, and multiple electrical outlets jammed to capacity. Sidney thought the space looked as though it belonged more in the Pentagon War Room than in this quiet suburban area.

Fisher proudly watched her obvious astonishment. "Actually, I've cut back some. I thought I might be getting out of control a little bit." He grinned broadly.

Sidney pulled the disk out of her pocket. "Jeff, could you put this in your computer and read what's on it?"

Fisher took the disk, a disappointed look on his face. "Is that all you need? Your computer at work can read this floppy, Sidney."

"I know, but I was afraid I might screw it up somehow. It came in the mail and it might be damaged. I'm not in your league when it comes to computers, Jeff. I wanted to come to the best."

Fisher beamed at this ego-stroking. "Okay. It'll just take second."

He started to pop the disk into the computer.

Sidney put a hand over his, halting him. "Jeff, is that computer on-line?"

He looked at the computer and then back at her. "Yeah. I've got three different services I use, plus my own gateway on to the Internet I got through using MIT as a host. Why?"

"Could you use a computer that isn't on-line? I mean, can't other people get to things on your database if you're on-line?"

"Yeah, it's a two-way street. You send stuff out. Others can hack it. That's the trade-off. But it's a big trade-off. Although you don't have to be on-line to get hacked."

"What do you mean?" Sidney asked.

"Ever heard of Van Eck radiation?" Fisher asked. Sidney shook her head. "It's really electromagnetic eavesdropping."

Sidney's face held a blank look. "What's that?"

Fisher swiveled around in his chair and looked at the puzzled attorney. "All electrical current produces a magnetic field, thus computers emit magnetic fields, relatively strong ones. These transmissions can be easily captured and recorded. On top of it, computers also give off digital impulses. This CRT" – Fisher pointed at his computer monitor – "throws off clear video images if you have the right receiving equipment, which is widely available. I could drive through downtown D.C. with a directional antenna, a black-and-white TV and a few bucks' worth of electronic parts and steal the information off every computer network in every law firm, accounting firm and government facility in the city. Easy."

Sidney was incredulous. "You're saying if it's on someone else's screen you can see it? How is that possible?"

"Simple. The shapes and lines on a computer screen are composed of millions of tiny dots called picture elements – or pixels, for short. When you type in a command, electrons are fired at the appropriate spot on the screen to light appropriate pixels – like painting a picture. The computer screen must be continually refreshed with electrons to keep the pixels lit. Whether you're playing a computer game or doing word processing or whatever, that's how you can see things on your screen. You with me so far?" Sidney nodded.

"Okay, each time electrons are shot at the screen, they give off a high-voltage pulse of electromagnetic emission. A TV monitor can receive these pulses pixel by pixel. However, since an ordinary TV monitor can't adequately organize these pixels to reconstruct what's on your screen, an artificial synchronization signal is used so the picture can be exactly reproduced."

Fisher paused to look at his computer again and then continued. "Printer? Fax? Same thing. Cellular phones? Give me one minute with a scanner and I can have your internal electronics serial number, or ESN, your cell phone number, your station class data and the phone's maker. I program that data into another cell phone with some reconfigured chips, and I start selling long-distance service and charge it to you. Any information that flows through a computer, either through the phone lines or through the air, is fair game. And what doesn't these days? Absolutely nothing is safe.

"You know what my theory is? Pretty soon we'll stop using computers because of all the security problems. Go back to typewriters and 'snail mail.'"

Sidney looked puzzled.

"Snail mail is a techie's derogatory term for the U.S. mail. They may get the last laugh, though. Mark my words. That day is coming."

A sudden thought entered Sidney's head. "Jeff,

what about regular phones? How could it be that I call a number, say my firm number, and someone answers who I know for a fact cannot be at my firm?"

"Somebody hacked into the switch," Fisher said immediately.

"The switch?" Sidney looked completely bewildered.

"It's the electronics network over which all communications from pay phones to cellular phones travel across the United States. If you hack into it, you can communicate with impunity." Fisher turned back to his computer. "However, with all that said, I've got a really good security system on my computer, Sid."

"Is it completely foolproof? No one could break it?"

Jeff laughed. "I don't know anyone in their right mind who could make that claim, Sidney."

Sidney looked at the disk, wishing she could just tear pages out of it and read them. "I'm sorry if I sound paranoid."

"No sweat. No offense, but most lawyers I know are borderline paranoid. They must have a class in law school on it or something. But we can at least do this." He unplugged the phone line from his CPU. "Now we're officially off-line. I have a first-rate virus sweeper on this system, in case anything got on previously. I just ran a check, so I think we're safe."

He motioned Sidney to sit down. She slid a chair around and they both studied the screen. Fisher hit a series of keys and a directory of the files on the disk appeared. He looked over at Sidney. "About a dozen files – from the number of bytes listed I'd say about four hundred or so pages if it's standard text. But if there are a lot of graphics there's really no way to gauge the length." Fisher hit some more keys. When the screen filled up with images, his eyes sparkled.

Sidney's face fell as she stared at the screen. It was all gibberish, high-tech hieroglyphics.

She looked at Fisher. "Is there something wrong with your computer?"

Fisher typed rapidly. The screen went blank and then reappeared with the same mess of digital images. Then at the bottom of the screen a box appeared with the command line requesting a password. "No, and there's nothing wrong with the disk either. Where'd you get it?"

"It was sent to me. By a client," she answered lamely.

Luckily, Fisher was too engrossed in the high-tech conundrum to question her further about the origin of the disk.

His fingers flew across the keyboard for several more minutes as he tried all the other files. The gibberish on the screen always reappeared. So did the message requesting a password. Finally he turned to her, a smile on his face.

"It's encrypted," he said simply.

Sidney stared at him. "Encrypted?"

Fisher continued to stare at the screen. "Encryption is a process whereby you take readable form text and put it into a nonreadable form before you send it out."

"What good is it if the person you sent it to can't read it?"

"Ah, but they can if they have the key that allows you to decrypt the message."

"How do you get the key?"

"The sender has to forward it to you, or you have to already have it in your possession."

Sidney slumped back in the chair. Jason would have had the damned key. "I don't have it."

"That doesn't make any sense."

"Would someone send an encrypted message to himself?" she asked.

Fisher looked over at her. "He wouldn't. I mean, ordinarily he wouldn't. If you have the message already in hand, you wouldn't encrypt it and then send it across the Internet to yourself at another location. It would just give someone the opportunity to intercept it and then maybe break it. But I thought you said a client sent you this?"

Sidney suddenly shivered. "Jeff, do you have any coffee? It seems chilly in here."

"Actually, I've got a fresh pot made. I keep this room a little cooler than the rest of the house because of the heat thrown off by the equipment. I'll be back in a minute."

"Thanks."

When Fisher returned with two cups of coffee, Sidney was staring at the screen.

Fisher took a sip of the hot liquid while Sidney sat back in the chair and closed her eyes. Fisher hunched forward and studied the screen. He returned to his last train of thought. "Yeah, you wouldn't encrypt a message you meant to send to yourself." He took another sip of coffee. "You'd only do it if you were sending it to someone else."

Sidney's eyes flew open and she jolted upright. The image of the e-mail flashing across Jason's computer screen like an electronic phantom swept through her memory. It was there and then gone. The key. Was it the key? Was he sending it to her?

She gripped Fisher's arm. "Jeff, how is it possible for an e-mail to appear on your computer screen and then vanish? It's not in your mailbox. It's nowhere on the system. How can that happen?"

"Pretty easily. The sender has a window of opportunity to cancel the transmission. I mean, he couldn't do it once the mail was opened and read. But on some systems, depending on their configuration, you can recall a message up until it's opened by the receiver. In that regard it's better than the U.S. mail." Fisher grinned. "You know, you get pissed off at someone and you write them a letter and mail it, and then you regret having done it. Once it's in the metal box, you cannot get it back, no way, nohow. With electronic mail, you can. Up to a point."

"How about outside a network? Like across the Internet?"

Fisher rubbed his chin. "It's more difficult to do because of the travel chain the message has to go through. Sort of like the monkey bars on the playground." Sidney again stared at him with a blank face. "You know, you climb up one side, swing yourself across and then climb down the other side. That's a rough analogy of how mail travels over the Internet. The parts are fluid per se, but they don't necessarily form a single cohesive unit. The result is, sometimes information sent cannot be retrieved."

"But it's possible?"

"If the e-mail was sent using one on-line service through the whole route – like, for example, America Online – you can retrieve it."

Sidney thought quickly. They had American Online at home. But why would Jason have sent her the key and then taken it back? She shuddered. Unless he wasn't the one who had canceled the transmission.

"Jeff, if you're sending the e-mail and you want it to go through, but someone else doesn't, could they stop it? Cancel the transmission like you said, even if the sender wants it to go through?"

"That's kind of a weird question. But the answer is yes. All you have to do is have access to the keyboard. Why do you ask?"

"I'm just thinking out loud."

Fisher looked at her quizzically. "Is something wrong, Sidney?"

Sidney ignored the question. "Is it possible to read the message without the key?"

Fisher looked at the screen and then turned slowly back to Sidney. "There are some methods one can employ." He sounded hesitant, his tone much more formal.

"Could you try to do it, Jeff?"

He looked down. "Look, Sidney, right after you called today, I phoned the office just to check on some ongoing projects. They told me . . ." He paused and looked at her with troubled eyes. "They told me about you."

Sidney stood up, her eyes downcast.

"I also happened to read the paper before you came over. Is that what this is all about? I don't want to get into trouble."

Sidney sat back down and looked directly at Fisher, gripping his hand with one of hers. "Jeff, an e-mail came across my computer at home. I think it was from my husband. But then it vanished. I think it might have been the key for this message because Jason mailed that disk to himself. Whatever is on that disk I've got to be able to read. I haven't done anything wrong, despite what my firm or the paper or anyone says. I have no way of proving that. Yet. All you have is my word."

Fisher looked at her for a long moment and then finally nodded. "Okay, I believe you. You happen to be one of the few attorneys at the firm I like." He turned back to the screen with a determined air. "You might want to get some more coffee. If you're hungry, there's some sandwich stuff in the fridge. This could take a while."

FORTY-THREE

The dinner with Frank Hardy had been an early one and it was only about eight o'clock when Sawyer pulled up to the curb in front of his apartment. When he climbed out of the car, his stomach felt immensely comfortable. His brain, however, didn't share that pleasant feeling. This case seemed to have so many angles, he wasn't quite sure where to start grabbing.

When he slammed the car door shut, he noticed the vintage Silver Cloud Rolls-Royce high-stepping down the street toward him. His neighborhood was seldom, if ever, witness to that sort of spectacular wealth. Through the windshield Sawyer could see a black-capped chauffeur at the wheel. Sawyer had to look twice and then it hit him what was odd. The driver was on the right side – it was a British-built car. It slowed down and came to a quiet stop next to him. Sawyer couldn't see in the back of the car because the glass was tinted. He wondered if that was an original production item or had been added later. He didn't have time to wonder past that. The rear window came down and Sawyer was staring into the countenance of Nathan Gamble. In the meantime the chauffeur had exited the car and stood ready by the passenger door.

Sawyer's eyes swept the length of the massive vehicle before coming to rest on the Triton chairman again. "Nice set of wheels. How's the gas mileage?"

"Like I care. You into basketball?" Gamble used a

cutter to snip off the back end of his cigar and took a moment to light up.

"Excuse me?"

"NBA. Tall black guys running around in little shorts in return for shitloads of money."

"I catch it on the tube when I get a chance."

"Well, hop in, then."

"Why?"

"You'll see. I promise you won't be bored."

Sawyer looked up and down the street and shrugged. He jostled his car keys in his pocket and then looked at the chauffeur. "I got it, buddy." Sawyer pulled open the door and climbed in. When he settled back against the leather he noted Richard Lucas in the rear-facing seat. Sawyer inclined his head slightly. Triton's security chief returned the bare gesture. The Rolls pulled swiftly away.

"You want one?" Gamble held out a cigar. "Cuban. It's against the law to import them into this country. I think that's why I like them so much."

Sawyer took the offered cigar and snipped off the end with the cutter Gamble handed him. He looked surprised when Lucas held out a butane lighter, but accepted the service.

He took a few quick puffs and then a long one as he got it going. "Not bad. Guess I'll have to give you a break on the illegal smokes."

"Thanks tons."

"By the way, how'd you know where I lived? I hoped you weren't following me. I get real jumpy when people do that."

"I got better things to do than follow you, believe me."

"So?"

"So what?" Gamble eyed him.

"So how'd you know where I live?"

"What's it to you?"

"Actually, it's a lot to me. In my line of work you don't broadcast the place you call home."

"Okay, let me see, then. What did we do? Look you up in the phone book?" Gamble abruptly shook his head and his eyes flickered amusement at Sawyer. "No, that wasn't it."

"Good thing, since I don't happen to be listed."

"Right. Well, I guess we just knew." Gamble blew a pair of perfect smoke rings to the ceiling. "You know, all our computer technology. We're Big Brother, we know everything." Gamble chuckled while he puffed on his cigar and looked over at Lucas.

Lucas caught Sawyer's eye. "Actually, Frank Hardy told us. In confidence, of course. We don't intend to spread that information around. I understand your concern." Richard Lucas paused. "Just between us," he added, "I was with the CIA for ten years."

"Ah, Rich, I just had him going too." The smell of liquor on Gamble's breath permeated the car. He reached across and opened a small door built into the wood paneling of the Rolls. A well-stocked bar was revealed. "You look like a scotch and soda man."

"I had my fill at dinner."

Gamble filled up an etched china glass with the contents of a bottle of Johnnie Walker. Sawyer glanced over at Lucas, who looked on calmly enough. Apparently this was fairly routine.

"Actually, I didn't think I'd be hearing from you after our little chat the other day," said Sawyer.

"The simple answer to that is you took me down a peg and I probably deserved it. Actually, I *was* testing you with my big-shot asshole routine and you passed with flying colors. As you can imagine, I don't meet that many people with the balls big enough to do that. When I do, I like to get better acquainted. Plus in light of recent developments I want to talk to you about the case."

"Recent developments?"

Gamble took a sip of his drink. "You know what I'm talking about. Sidney Archer? New Orleans? RTG? I just got off the horn with Hardy."

"You work pretty fast. I just left him not more than twenty minutes ago."

Gamble pulled a tiny portable phone from a receptacle on the Rolls's rear console. "Remember, Sawyer, I operate in the private sector. You don't move fast, you don't move at all, get it?"

Sawyer pulled on his cigar before answering. "I'm beginning to. By the way, you never did say where we're going."

"Didn't I? Well, sit tight. We'll be there shortly. And then we can have ourselves a nice little talk."

USAir Arena was home to the NBA Washington Bullets and the NHL Washington Capitals, at least until the new downtown stadium was completed. The arena was packed for the Bullets-Knicks game. Nathan Gamble, Lucas and Sawyer rode the private elevator to the second floor of the arena, where the corporate luxury boxes were located. When Sawyer stepped down the hallway and through the door marked TRITON GLOBAL, he felt as if he had boarded a luxury liner. These weren't merely seats to a ball game; the place was about the size of his apartment.

A young woman was tending bar and a hot and cold buffet was laid out on a long side table. There was a private bath, closet, over-stuffed sofas and chairs and a giant-screen TV in one corner with the basketball game on. From up a flight of stairs leading to the viewing section, Sawyer could hear the crowd cheering. He looked at the TV. The home-team Bullets were up by seven over the heavily favoured Knicks.

Sawyer took off his hat and coat and followed Gamble over to the bar area.

"You've gotta have something now. Can't watch a ball game without a drink in your hand."

Sawyer nodded toward the bartender. "Bud, if you've got it."

The young woman reached in the refrigerator, popped open a can of Budweiser and started to pour it in a glass.

"Can's good enough. Thanks."

Sawyer looked around the spacious room again. No one else was there. He strayed over to the buffet. He was still full from dinner, but some chips and salsa were calling to him.

"Place usually this empty?" he asked Gamble while he grabbed up a handful. Lucas assumed a hovering presence against the wall.

"Usually it's packed," Gamble replied. "Damn good perk for the employees. Keeps 'em happy and hardworking." The bartender handed Gamble his drink. In response, Gamble flushed a wad of hundred-dollar bills out of his pocket, pulled a glass off the counter and stuffed the bills in the glass. "Here, bartender's got to have a tip jar. Go buy some growth stocks." The young woman almost fainted with joy as Gamble walked over to join Sawyer.

Sawyer pointed his beer toward the TV. "Looks like a great game. I'm surprised there aren't Triton people packed in here."

"I'd be real surprised if they were, since I instructed that no tickets be given out for tonight's game."

"Why'd you do that?" Sawyer took a sip of his beer.

Gamble hooked Sawyer's arm with his free hand. "Because I wanted to talk to you in private."

Sawyer was led up the stairs to the viewing area.

From up here the view was pretty much straight down on the playing floor. Sawyer watched with a twinge of envy as two groups of tall, muscular and very rich young men ran up and down the court. The seating area he was in was closed in on three sides by Plexiglas. On either side were the occupants of other luxury boxes. However, with the glass shield, one could conduct a very private conversation amid a crowd of fifteen thousand.

The two men settled in. Sawyer jerked his head toward where they had just come from. "Rich doesn't like basketball?"

"Lucas is on duty."

"Is he ever off duty?"

"When he's sleeping. I occasionally let him do that." Gamble sat back in the comfortable chair and gulped his drink.

Sawyer looked around curiously. He had never been in one of these things before, and after the fancy dinner with Hardy he was feeling a little out of his depth. At least he'd have some stories to tell Ray. When he glanced over at Gamble, he stopped smiling. Nada in life was free. Everything had its cost. He decided it was time to check the price tag.

"So, what'd you want to talk about?"

Gamble stared down at the sports contest without really seeing any of it. "The fact is we need CyberCom. We need it badly."

"Look, Gamble, I'm not your business consultant, I'm a cop. I don't give a damn if you get CyberCom or not."

Gamble sucked on an ice cube. He seemed not to have heard. "You work hard building something and it's never enough, you know? Always somebody trying to take it away from you. Always somebody trying to screw you."

"If you're looking for sympathy, look someplace

else. You can't spend all the money you've already got. What the hell do you care?"

Gamble exploded. "Because you damn well get used to it, that's why." He calmed down quickly. "You get used to being on top. Having everybody measure themselves against you. But a lot of it is about the money." He looked over at Sawyer. "You want to know what my total income is per year?"

Despite himself Sawyer was curious. "If I say no, why do I feel like you're going to tell me anyway?"

"One billion dollars." Gamble unceremoniously dropped the ice cube from his mouth into his glass.

Sawyer swallowed a mouthful of beer as he absorbed this stunning information.

"My federal income tax bill alone this year will come to about four hundred million dollars. With that you'd think I'd qualify for a little TLC from you Feds."

Sawyer glared at him. "If you're looking for TLC, try the hookers down on Fourteenth Street. They're a lot cheaper."

Gamble stared over at him. "Shit, you guys just don't get the big picture, do you?"

"Why don't you enlighten me as to what exactly that is."

Gamble put down his glass. "You treat everybody the same." His tone was one of disbelief.

"Excuse me – are you saying that's wrong?"

"It's not only wrong, it's stupid."

"I guess you never bothered to read the Declaration of Independence – you know, that warm, fuzzy part about all men being created equal."

"I'm talking reality. I'm talking about business."

"I don't make distinctions."

"Like I'm gonna treat the chairman of Citicorp the same as I would the janitor in the building. One guy can loan me billions of dollars and the other can scrub out my toilet."

"My job is to hunt down criminals, rich, poor, in-between. It doesn't make any difference to me."

"Yeah, well, I'm not a criminal. I'm a taxpayer, probably the biggest damned taxpayer in this whole country, and all I'm asking for is a little favor that I'd get in the private sector without even asking for it."

"Hooray for the public sector."

"That's not funny."

"Not for one second was it supposed to be." Sawyer stared him down. When Gamble finally looked away, Sawyer glanced down at his hands and then took another swallow of beer. Every time he was around this guy his heartbeat seemed to double.

Down on the court a slam dunk by the home team brought the crowd to its feet.

"By the way, you ever think there's something wrong with being richer than God?"

Gamble laughed. "Like those guys down there?" He pointed at the basketball court. "Actually, based on the world's present condition, I think I had a better year than God." He rubbed at his eyes. "Like I said, it's not the cash anymore. You're right, I have more than I'll ever need. But I like the respect being on top brings. Everybody waits to see what you'll do."

"Don't confuse respect with fear."

"In my book they go hand in hand. Look, I got where I am by being one tough sonofabitch. You hurt me I'll hurt you back, only better. I grew up poorer than dirt, took a bus to New York when I was fifteen, started on Wall Street as a courier making a few bucks a day, worked my way to the top and I never looked back. Made fortunes, lost fortunes and then made them back. Hell, I got a half dozen bullshit honorary degrees from Ivy League colleges

379

and I never finished the tenth grade. All you have to do is make donations." He arched his eyebrows and grinned.

"Congratulations." Sawyer prepared to stand up. "I guess I'll be heading on, then."

Gamble grabbed his arm and then immediately let it go. "Look, I read the paper. I've talked to Hardy. And I can feel RTG breathing down my neck."

"Like I said before, that's not my problem."

"I don't mind playing on a fair field, but I'll be damned if I'm gonna lose out because an employee sold me down the river."

"*Allegedly* sold you down the river. We haven't proven anything yet. And whether you like it or not, that's all that matters in a court of law."

"You saw the videotape. What more proof do you need? Hell, all I'm really asking you to do is your job. What's wrong with that?"

"I saw Jason Archer giving some documents to some people. I have no idea what the documents were or who the people are."

Gamble sat up. "See, the problem here is that if RTG knows my deal and outbids me for CyberCom, I'm screwed. I need you to prove they ripped me off. Once they get CyberCom, it's not going to matter how they got the deal, it's theirs. You hear where I'm coming from?"

"I'm working as hard as I can, Gamble. But there's no way in hell I'm going to tailor my investigation to fit your business agenda. The murder of a hundred and eighty-one innocent people means a lot more to me than how much you pay in income taxes." Gamble didn't answer. "You hear where *I'm* coming from?" Gamble finally shrugged. "If it turns out RTG was behind it, then you can rest assured that I'll spend every waking moment making sure I bring them down."

"But couldn't you put the screws hard to them right now? The FBI investigating them would probably knock them right out of the running for CyberCom."

"We are looking into it, Gamble. These things take time. Bureaucracy with a capital *B*, remember?"

"Time is something I don't have a lot of," he growled.

"Sorry, the answer's still no. Now, is there anything else I *can't* do for you?"

The two men watched the game in silence for a few minutes. Sawyer picked up a pair of binoculars from the table in front of him. As he watched the action up close he said. "So what's up with Tyler, Stone?"

Gamble grimaced. "If we weren't so far into the CyberCom deal, I'd fire their ass right now. But the fact is I need their legal expertise and institutional memory. For now, anyway."

"But not Sidney Archer's."

He shook his head. "Never would've figured that lady to do something like that. Helluva lawyer. A real babe on top of it too. What a waste."

"How's that?"

Gamble looked at him, amazed. "Excuse me, did we read the same newspaper? She's in it up to her nice-looking ass."

"You think so?"

"Don't you?"

Sawyer shrugged and finished her beer.

"Lady takes off after her husband's memorial service," Gamble continued. "Hardy tells me she tried to give your guys the slip. You followed her all over New Orleans. She's acting suspicious, comes right home after getting a phone call. Hardy also said you thought somebody may have gone through her house while she drew all you guys off the scent.

381

Brilliant how you let that happen, by the way."

"I'm gonna have to be careful what I tell Frank in the future."

"I pay him a hell of a lot of money. He better keep me informed."

"I'm sure he's worth every penny."

"Pennies, right! That's a joke."

Sawyer gave Gamble a sidelong glance. "For all he's done for you, you don't seem to hold Frank in very high regard."

Gamble chuckled. "Believe it or not, I have really high standards."

"Frank was one of the best agents the bureau ever produced."

"I have a short memory for good work. You have to keep showering me with it." Gamble's smile quickly turned to a glare. "On the other hand, I never forget screwups."

They watched the game in silence. Finally Sawyer stirred. "Quentin Rowe ever screw anything up for you?"

Gamble looked surprised by the question. "Why do you ask that?"

"Because the guy's your golden egg and from all accounts you treat him like crap."

"Who said he's my golden egg?"

"You saying he's not?" Sawyer sat back and crossed his arms.

Gamble didn't answer right away. He brooded over his glass of liquor. "I've had a lot of golden eggs in my career. You don't get to where I am off one racehorse."

"But Rowe is valuable to you."

"If he wasn't I wouldn't have much use for his company."

"So you tolerate him?"

"So long as the dollars keep pouring in."

"Lucky you."

Gamble's look was ferocious. "I took an ivory tower geek who couldn't raise a damned dime on his own and turned him into the country's richest thirty-something. Now, who do you think's the lucky one?"

Sawyer inclined his head toward the man. "I'm not trying to take anything away from you, Gamble. You chased a dream and made it come true. I guess that's what America's all about."

"Coming from a Fed, I'll have to really savor that compliment." Gamble once again focused on the basketball game.

Sawyer stood and crumpled his beer can.

Gamble stared up at him. "Where you going?"

"Home. It's been a long day." He held up the squashed can. "Thanks for the beer."

"I'll have my driver take you home. I'll be here awhile."

Sawyer looked around the luxury box. "I think I've had enough of the high life for one day. I'll take the bus. But thanks for the invite."

"Yeah, I really enjoyed it too," Gamble said with the heaviest of sarcasm.

The agent had started down the stairs, but Gamble's "Hey, Sawyer?" turned him around.

Gamble was looking squarely at him, and then he let out a deep sigh. "I hear where you're coming from, okay?"

Sawyer stared at him a moment before answering. "Okay."

"I wasn't always this rich. I remember real well what it's like to be penniless and powerless. Maybe that's why I'm such an asshole when it comes to business: I'm terrified of going back there."

Sawyer considered this for a moment. "Enjoy the rest of the game." He left Gamble staring into his glass, deep in thought.

As Sawyer walked down the steps, he almost bumped into Richard Lucas, who had assumed a position there. Sawyer wondered if Lucas had overheard any part of the conversation with Gamble. He nodded at Lucas and stepped down into the bar area, where he launched a hook shot and the beer can sailed through the air and neatly into the trash can.

The bartender looked at him with admiration. "Hey, maybe the Bullets should sign you up," she said with a cute smile.

"Yeah, I can be the token over-the-hill white guy."

Sawyer turned back before exiting the room. "Keep, smiling, Rich."

FORTY-FOUR

Jeff Fisher stared humbly at the screen; a weary Sidney Archer sat beside him. She had given him all the personal information she could think of about Jason in order to fathom a proper password. Nothing had worked.

Fisher shook his head. "Well, we've gone through all the easy possibilities and all variations thereof. I've run a brute-force assault and got nothing. I've tried a partial random letter and number approach, but there are just too many possibilities to conduct in our lifetime." He turned to Sidney. "I'm afraid your husband really knew what he was doing. I figure he's probably got a random number-letter combo of about twenty or thirty characters. We're not going to crack it."

Sidney's hopes plummeted. It was maddening to have a disk full of information in her hand – presumably information that would explain a lot about her husband's fate – and be absolutely unable to read it.

She stood up and paced the room while Fisher continued to peck at the keyboard. Sidney crossed the room and stopped in front of a window. On a table next to the window was a stack of mail. On top was a *Field & Stream* magazine. Sidney idly glanced down at the stack of mail, eyed the magazine and then looked over at Fisher. He hardly seemed the outdoor type, she thought. Then she looked at the address label on the front cover. It was addressed to a Fred Smithers, but the address was that of the house she was standing in. She picked up the magazine.

Fisher looked over at her while he finished his Coke. When he saw the magazine in her hands, he scowled. "I keep getting that guy's mail. A bunch of companies somehow have my address on their system for this guy. I'm 6215 Thorndike and he's 6251 Thorndrive, which is clear on the other side of Fairfax County. That whole stack is his. And that's just this week. I've told the mailman who handles this route, called the Postal Service a million times, called all the companies who have been erroneously sending his mail here. Still happens."

Sidney slowly turned toward Fisher. An improbable idea was taking shape in her head.

"Jeff, an e-mail address is like any other address or phone number, right? You type in the wrong address and it can go to someone you never intended it to go to. Like this magazine." She held up *Field & Stream*. "Right?"

"Oh, sure," Fisher replied. "That happens all the time. I have most of my frequently used e-mail addresses programmed in so I just have to point and click. That cuts down on the error rate."

"But if you had to *type* in a full e-mail address?"

"Well, there's a lot more room for error in that scenario. The addresses can get rather lengthy."

"So if you hit a wrong key, the message you intended for someone could go to God knows who?"

Fisher nodded as he munched on a potato chip. "I get misaddressed e-mail all the time."

Sidney looked at him with a puzzled expression. "What do you do when that happens?"

"Well, what happens most often is pretty simple. I only have to click on my reply-to-sender command and I send a standard message saying they got the wrong address and I send the e-mail back so they know what message I'm talking about. That way I don't need to know the address. It automatically sends it back to the originator."

"Jeff, you mean if my husband sent an e-mail to the wrong location, the person receiving the e-mail by mistake could simply reply back to Jason's e-mail address to let him know the mistake?"

"Right. I mean, if you're on the same service, say American Online, it's relatively simple."

"And if that person did reply back, the e-mail would be in Jason's computerized mailbox right now, right?"

Fisher looked up at her, a slightly fearful look in his eyes at the tone in her voice. "Well, yes."

Sidney collected her purse.

Fisher looked at her. "Where are you going?"

"To check our computer at home for the e-mail. If the password is on there, I can read this disk." Sidney popped the disk out of the floppy drive and put it in her purse.

"Sidney, if you give me your husband's user name and password, I can access his mail from right here. I have AOL on my system. It's not hardware-specific. I'll just log you on as a guest. If the key to the encryption *is* in the mailbox, we can read the disk here."

"I know, Jeff. But would your access of Jason's mail from this location be traceable?"

Fisher's eyes narrowed. "It's possible. If whoever was looking knew what they were doing."

"I think we have to assume these people know what they're doing, Jeff. It'll be a lot safer for you if no one can trace that e-mail being accessed from here."

Fisher turned a shade paler. He spoke slowly, the nervousness evident in his tone and features. "What have you gotten involved in, Sidney?"

She turned away from his as she spoke. "I'll be in touch."

After she left, Fisher sat at the screen for a few more minutes and then plugged in the phone line to his computer.

Sawyer sat down in the recliner and looked once again at the *Post* story on Jason Archer and shook his head. He flipped the paper over and as his eyes hit the other headline, he almost gagged. It took him two minutes to devour the story. He jumped on the phone and made a series of calls. That finished, he tore down the stairs. A minute later his sedan shot down the street.

Sidney parked the Ford in the driveway, hurried into her house, threw off her coat and went straight to her husband's office. She was about to access her AOL mailbox when she suddenly jumped up. "Oh, God!" She couldn't do it from here, not with whatever was on there. She thought quickly. Tyler, Stone had AOL software on its computers; she could access the mailbox from there. She grabbed her coat, raced to the front door and flung it open. Her scream was easily heard up and down the street.

Lee Sawyer was standing there, looking less than pleased.

She caught her breath and grabbed at her chest. "What are you doing here?"

In response, Sawyer held up the newspaper. "You happen to catch this story?" Sidney stared at Ed Page's picture, recognition all over her features. "I . . . I haven't, no, just—" she stammered.

Sawyer stepped inside the house and slammed the door. Sidney retreated into the living room. "I thought we had a deal. You remember? Exchange of information? Well, we're gonna talk. Right now!" he bellowed.

She pushed past him toward the door. He grabbed her arm and flung her on the couch. She jerked back up. "Get out of here!" she screamed.

He shook his head and held up the paper. "You want to go it alone out there? Then your little girl better get another mommy."

She hurtled forward, slapped him across the face and wound up to do it again. He grabbed both her arms and put her in a bear squeeze. She struggled furiously.

"Sidney, I'm not here to fight you. Whether your husband did anything wrong or not, I will still help you. But dammit, you've gotta be straight with me."

They struggled across the room and fell on to the couch, she awkwardly on his lap, trying her best to slug him. He held her tightly until the tension in her arms finally faded away. He released her and she immediately pulled away to the far end of the couch and put her face in her lap. He slumped back and waited. Sitting up, Sidney wiped away the tears with her sleeve. Licking her lips, she looked over at the newspaper on the floor. The photo of Ed Page beckoned to her.

"You talked with him on the plane from New Orleans, didn't you?" Sawyer asked the question very quietly. He had watched Page get on the plane in New Orleans. The passenger manifest revealed Page had sat right next to Sidney. That fact had not been important, until now. "Didn't you, Sidney?" She slowly nodded. "Tell me about it. And this time I mean everything."

And she did, including Page's story of Jason's switch at the airport, and Page following her and tapping her phone.

"I talked to the medical examiner's office," Sawyer

389

said when she was finished. "Page was killed, by someone who knew exactly what he was doing. One puncture wound to each lung. A precision cut through the carotid artery and jugular vein. Page died in under a minute. Whoever did it was not your typical street vermin wielding a pocketknife looking for some crack money."

Sidney took a deep breath. "That's why I almost shot you in the garage. I thought they were coming for me."

"You have no idea who 'they' are?"

Sidney shook her head and rubbed at her face again. She sat back and looked at him. "I really don't know anything other than the fact that my life has sunk far past hell."

Sawyer gripped one of her hands. "Well, let's see if we can get you back to the surface." He stood and picked up her coat from where it had fallen on the floor. "The investigative firm of Private Solutions has its headquarters in Arlington, across from the courthouse. I'm going to pay it a visit. And right now, I'd prefer to have you where I can keep an eye on you. You game?"

Sidney Archer swallowed hard as she guiltily felt the diskette in her pocket. That was one secret she could not bring herself, as yet, to reveal. "I'm game."

Edward Page's office was located in a nondescript low-rise office building opposite the Arlington County Circuit Court building. The security guard on duty could not have been more accommodating after seeing Lee Sawyer's credentials. The guard led the way to the elevators and in another minute, after being deposited on the third floor and walking down the dimly lit corridor, they stopped in front of a solid oak door with the name PRIVATE SOLUTIONS engraved on a metal plate next to it. The guard pulled out his key and tried to open the door.

"Damn!"

"What is it?" Sawyer asked.

"Key doesn't work."

"Isn't your master key supposed to open any door in the place?" Sidney asked.

" 'Supposed to' is right. We've had a problem with this guy before."

"How's that?" Sawyer asked.

The guard looked at them. "He changed the lock. Management jumped all over him. So he gave them another key that he said fit the new lock. Well, I can tell you right now it doesn't."

Sawyer looked up and down the corridor. "Any other way in?"

The guard shook his head. "Nope. I can try calling Mr. Page at his home. Tell him to come on down here and open it up. I'll ream his butt good too for pulling this crap. What if there was ever a problem and I needed to get in there?" The guard slapped his holster importantly. "You know what I mean?"

"I don't think calling Page will do any good," Sawyer said calmly. "He's dead. Murdered."

The blood slowly drained from the young man's face. "Jesus Christ! Omigod!"

"Police haven't been here, I take it?" Sawyer asked. The guard shook his head.

"How're we going to get in?" the guard asked, his voice barely above a whisper as, wide-eyed, he looked up and down the hallway for possible killers lurking there.

In response, Lee Sawyer hurled his massive bulk against the door, which splintered under the battering. One more thrust and the lock gave way and the door burst open, slamming against the inner wall of the office. Sawyer looked back at the stunned young guard while he brushed off his overcoat.

"We'll check in with you on the way out. Thanks a lot."

The guard stood openmouthed for several seconds as the two moved into the office. Then he slowly walked back toward the elevator, shaking his head.

Sidney looked at the broken door and then over at Sawyer. "I can't believe he didn't even ask you for a search warrant. By the way, do you have one?"

Sawyer looked over at her. "What's it to you?"

"As an attorney, I'm an officer of the court. I just thought I'd ask."

He shrugged his thick shoulders. "I'll make a deal with you, *Officer:* We find something, you hold on to it and I'll go get a search warrant." Under different circumstances, Sidney Archer would have burst out laughing, and as it was, Sawyer's response drew a smile out of her. That perked up his own spirits.

The office was plain but neatly and efficiently furnished. For the next half hour they searched the small space, finding nothing out of place or extraordinary. They did find some stationery with Ed Page's home address on it. An apartment over in Georgetown. Sawyer perched on the side of the desk and surveyed the small area. "I wish my office was this tidy. But I don't see anything that's going to help us." Sawyer looked around the room, his expression glum. "I'd feel better if the place were ransacked. Then at least we'd know someone else was interested."

While he was talking, Sidney had made another pass around the room. She abruptly came back to one corner of the office where a row of gunmetal-gray filing cabinets stood in a row. She looked down at the floor, which was carpeted in a decidedly dull beige. "That's odd." Sidney got down on her knees, her face almost resting on the carpet. She looked at a small gap between the two filing cabinets nearest the spot she was examining. The other cabinets were butted together. She put her shoulder against one of the cabinets and shoved. The heavy cabinet didn't budge. "Can I get some help over here?" She looked back at Sawyer. He lurched over, motioned her out of the way and shoved the cabinet clear. "Hit that light over there," Sidney said excitedly.

Sawyer did so and then joined her. "What is it?"

Sidney moved aside so the FBI agent could see. On the floor where the cabinet had been was a rust spot, not very large but now clearly visible. Perplexed, Sawyer looked at her. "So? I can show you about a dozen of these in my office. Metal rusts, leaches into the carpet. Presto. Rust spots."

Sidney's eyes twinkled. "Really?" She pointed triumphantly. There were faint but discernible indentations on the carpet, which showed that the cabinet had originally butted up against the one next to it. There should have been no gap.

She motioned to the cabinet Sawyer had moved. "Lean it over and check the bottom."

Sawyer did so. "No rust spots," he said, then looked back at her. "So somebody moved this cabinet to cover the rust spot. Why?"

"Because that rust spot came from *another* filing cabinet. A filing cabinet that isn't here anymore. Whoever took it vacuumed out as best they could the indentations the missing cabinet made on the rug but couldn't get the rust spot out. So they did the next best thing. They covered it up with another filing cabinet and hoped no one paid any attention to the gap."

"But you did," Sawyer said, more than a trace of admiration in his tone.

"I couldn't figure why a guy obviously as neat as our Mr. Page would have a gap in a wall of filing cabinets. Answer: Someone else did it for him."

"And that means someone *is* interested in Edward page and what he had in that file cabinet. Which means we're heading in the right direction." Sawyer picked up the phone on Page's desk. In a succinct request he instructed Ray Jackson to find out everything he could about Edward page. He hung up and looked over at Sidney. "Since his office didn't yield all that much, what do you say we pay a visit to the late Edward Page's humble abode."

FORTY-FIVE

Page's residence was on the ground floor of a large turn-of-the-century home in Georgetown that had been transformed into a series of quaint apartments. The sleepy owner of the property had not questioned Sawyer's desire to view the premises. The man had read of Page's death and expressed dismay over it. Two detectives had been to the apartment and interviewed the landlord and several tenants. The landlord had also received a phone call from Page's daughter in New York. The private investigator had been a model tenant. His hours were somewhat irregular, and he would sometimes be gone for days at a time, but the rent was always paid on the first of the month and he had been quiet and orderly. He had no close friends of whom the owner was aware.

Using a key provided by the owner, who lived on the premises, Sawyer unlocked the front door of the apartment and he and Sidney stepped inside; he hit the light switch and then shut the door behind them. He was hoping to at least get a base hit here, although a homer would be nice.

They had checked the security log before leaving Page's office. The filing cabinet had been removed the day before by two guys in movers' uniforms bearing a legit-looking work order and the keys to the office door. Sawyer figured the moving company was certainly a phony and the contents of Page's filing cabinet, which probably held a treasure trove of interesting info, was probably no more than a pile of ash at the bottom of some incinerator by now.

The interior of Page's residence resembled the man's office in its simplicity and neatness. Sawyer and Sidney walked through the various rooms, surveying the basic layout of the apartment. A nice fireplace with a large Victorian-style mantel dominated the living room. Bookshelves filled one wall. Edward Page had been a voracious and eclectic reader, if his collection of books was any indication. There were not, however, any journals or records or receipts that might have shown where Page had been lately or whom he might have been following other than Sidney and Jason Archer. After methodically searching the living and dining rooms, Sawyer and Sidney moved on.

The kitchen and bathroom yielded nothing of interest. Sawyer tried the usual places like the tank behind the toilet and in the refrigerator, where he checked Coke cans and heads of lettuce to make certain they were real and not actually hiding places for clues as to why Ed Page had been murdered. Sidney entered the bedroom, where she undertook a thorough search, starting under the bed and mattress and ending with the closet. The few pieces of luggage there had no old airline tags. The wastebaskets were empty. She and Sawyer sat down on the bed and scanned the room. He looked over at the small stand of photographs on the side table. Edward Page and family, obviously in happier times.

Sidney picked up one of the photos. "A nice-looking family." Her thoughts were suddenly fixated on the photos residing in her house. It seemed like a long time since that phrase had applied to her family. She handed the photo over to Sawyer.

The wife was really good-looking, he thought, the son a miniature image of the old man. The daughter was very pretty. Red-headed with long coltish legs, she looked about fourteen in the photo. The date stamp showed it was taken five years ago. She must be a real heartbreaker now, Sawyer figured. And yet according to the landlord they were all in New York and Page was down here. Why?

As Sawyer started to put the photo of the Page family back, he felt a slight bulge on the photo's backing. He opened up the back. Several photos about half the size of the framed one fell out. Sawyer picked them off the floor and studied them. They were all of the same person. A young man, mid-twenties. Good-looking, too handsome for Sawyer's taste – a pretty boy, was the FBI agent's first thought. The clothes were too fashionable, the hair too perfect. He thought he noted a trace of Ed Page along the jawline and around the deep brown eyes. Sawyer turned over all the photos. All except one were blank: "Stevie" was penned on the photo. Possibly Page's brother. If so, why where the photos hidden?

Sidney looked at him. "What do you think?"

He shrugged. "Sometimes I think this whole case is going to require more thinking than I can give it." Sawyer put all the photos back except the one with the name on the back. That one he put in his coat pocket. They looked around the room once more, then rose and left, locking the door securely behind them.

Sawyer walked Sidney to her house and then, out of an abundance of caution, conducted a search of the premises, making sure the house was empty and that every window and door was secure. "Day or night, you hear anything, you have a problem, you just want to talk, you call me. Understand?" Sidney nodded. "I've got two men outside. They can be in here in seconds." He walked to the front door. "I'm going to run some things down and I'll be back in the morning." He turned to look at her. "You going to be okay?"

"Yes." Sidney wrapped her arms around herself.

Sawyer sighed and leaned back against the door. "I hope one day I can deliver this case to you in one neat little ball, Sidney. I truly do."

"You . . . you still believe Jason is guilty, don't you? I guess I can't blame you. Everything . . . looks that way, I know." Her eyes searched Sawyer's troubled features. The big man sighed and looked away for a moment. When his eyes returned to her face, she saw a glimmer of something there.

"Let's just put it this way, Sidney," he said. "I'm starting to have some doubts."

She looked confused. "About Jason?"

"No, about everything else. I can promise you this: My top priority is finding your husband safe and sound. Then we can sort out everything else. Okay?"

She trembled slightly and then nodded at him. "Okay." When he turned to go, she touched his arm. "Thank you, Lee."

She watched Sawyer from the window. He walked over to the black sedan carrying the two FBI agents, looked back at the house, spotted her and waved. She made a feeble attempt at a wave back. She was feeling rather guilty right now, for what she was about to do. She left the window, turned out all the lights, grabbed her gray blazer and purse and raced out the back door seconds before one of Sawyer's men appeared to guard that area. Slipping through the woods at the edge of the backyard, she came out on to the road on the next block. After five minutes of brisk walking she had reached a pay phone. The cab picked her up within ten minutes.

Thirty minutes later she slipped her key in the security slot of her office building and the heavy glass door clicked open. She raced to the elevator bank. A minute later Sidney stepped out on to her floor. Inside the semidarkened space of Tyler, Stone, Sidney made her way quietly down the hallway. The library was at the end of the main hall on her floor. The double doors of frosted glass were open. Beyond this portal Sidney could plainly see shelf after shelf of books making up the firm's impressive law library. The area comprised a huge open space with a series of cubicles and adjacent enclosed work areas. Behind one partition stood a row of computer terminals, which attorneys and paralegals used for computerized legal research.

Sidney looked around the darkened interior of the library before venturing in. She heard no sound, saw no movement. Thankfully no junior associate was pulling an all-nighter. Walls of windows on two adjacent sides of the library overlooked the city streets; however, the blinds were pulled all the way down. No one could see in.

Sidney sat down in front of one of the darkened terminals and risked turning on a small lamp that sat on the computer table next to the terminal. She took the disk out of her purse and laid it on the table. In a minute the computer was warmed up. She clicked on the necessary commands to start America Online and jerked slightly as the screechy modem kicked in. After the connection was made, she typed in her husband's user name and password, silently thanking him for making her memorize them when they had signed on a couple of years ago. She stared anxiously at the screen, her breathing shallow, her features taut and her stomach queasy as though she were a defendant awaiting a verdict from a jury. The computerized voice made her jump slightly, but it was what she was hoping for. "You have mail," it said.

Down the hallway two pairs of legs quietly made their way toward the library.

Sawyer looked up at Jackson. They were in the FBI conference room. "So what'd you find out on Mr. Page, Ray?"

Jackson sat down and opened his notebook. "Had a nice chat with NYPD. Page used to be a cop up there. I also spoke with Page's ex-wife. Got her out of bed, but you said it was important. She still lives in New York. She hasn't had much to do with him since their divorce. However, he was very close to his kids. I talked with his daughter. She's eighteen, in her freshman year at college, by the way, and now she has to bury her father."

"What she have to say?" Sawyer asked.

"A lot. Like her father was nervous the last couple weeks. Didn't want them to visit him. He had started to regularly carry a gun. Hadn't done that in years. In fact he had taken a gun with him to New Orleans, Lee. It was found in a bag next to his body. Poor bastard never had a chance to use it."

"Why the move from New York down here, especially if his family stayed up there?"

Jackson nodded his head. "That's interesting. The wife wouldn't say one way or another. Just said the marriage was kaput and that was it. Page's daughter was of a different mind, though."

"She give you a reason?"

"Ed Page's younger brother also lived in New York. He committed suicide about five years ago. He was a diabetic. Gave himself a serious insulin overdose after a drinking binge. Page was close to his kid brother. His daughter said her dad was never the same after that."

400

"So he just wanted to get away from the area?"

Jackson shook his head. "I gather from talking to his daughter that Ed Page was convinced his brother's death wasn't a suicide or an accident," said Jackson.

"He thought he was murdered?"

Jackson nodded.

"Why?"

"I've requested a copy of the file from NYPD. There might be some answers in there, although I spoke briefly with the detective who worked the case and he says all the evidence points to either suicide or an accident. The guy was drunk."

"If he did kill himself, anybody know why?"

Jackson sat back. "Steven Page was a diabetic, like I said, so his health wasn't the greatest in the world. According to Page's daughter, her uncle could never get his insulin regulated. Although he was only twenty-eight when he died, his internal organs were probably much older." Jackson stopped talking and looked down at his notes for a moment. "On top of that, Steven Page had very recently tested positive for HIV."

"Shit. That explains the drinking binge," said Sawyer.

"Probably."

"And maybe the suicide."

"That's what NYPD thinks."

"How'd he contract it?"

Jackson shook his head. "No one knows. Officially, at least. I mean, the coroner's report wouldn't have been able to determine the origin. I asked the ex-wife. She wasn't any help. The daughter, however, tells me her uncle was gay. Not openly, but she was pretty sure about it and she thinks this is how he contracted HIV."

Sawyer rubbed his head and blew out a mouthful

of air. "Is there some connection between the possible murder of a gay man in New York five years ago, Jason Archer ripping off his employer and a plane going down in Virginia?"

Jackson pulled at his lip. "Maybe, for some reason we don't know, Page knew that Archer didn't get on that plane."

Sawyer felt guilt for a moment. From his conversation with Sidney – a conversation he hadn't shared with his partner – Sawyer *knew* that Page had been aware that Jason hadn't been on the plane. "So Jason Archer disappears," he said, "and Page looks to pick up the trail through the wife."

"Makes sense as far as it goes. Hey, maybe it was Triton who hired Page to check on leaks, and he sniffed out Archer."

Sawyer shook his head. "Between their in-house staff and Frank Hardy's company, they have more than enough bodies to do the job."

A woman entered the room carrying a file. "Ray, this just came in over the fax from NYPD."

Jackson accepted the file. "Thanks, Jennie." After she had gone, Jackson scrutinized the file while Sawyer made a couple of calls.

"Steven Page?" Sawyer finally asked, pointing at the file.

"Yep. Real interesting stuff."

Sawyer poured a cup of coffee and sat down next to his partner.

"Steven Page was employed by Fidelity Mutual in Manhattan," said Jackson. "It's one of the biggest investment houses in the country. He lived in a nice apartment building; place was filled with antiques, original oil paintings, closet full of Brooks Brothers; Jag in the garage down the street. He also had an extensive investment portfolio: stocks, bonds, mutual funds, money markets. Well over a million dollars' worth."

"Pretty good for a twenty-eight-year-old. But I guess those investment bankers make killings. You hear all the time about these punks making truckloads of money for doing who the hell knows what. Probably screwing the likes of you and me."

"Yeah, but Steven Page wasn't an investment banker. He was a financial analyst, a market watcher. Strictly salaried position; not big bucks either, according to this report."

Sawyer's brow furrowed. "So where did the investment portfolio come from? Embezzlement from Fidelity?"

Jackson shook his head. "NYPD checked that angle. There were no funds missing from Fidelity."

"So what did NYPD conclude?"

"I don't think NYPD ever concluded anything. Page was found alone in his apartment, door and windows locked from the inside. And once the medical examiner's report came back as a probable suicide via insulin overdose, they pretty much lost interest. In case you didn't know, they've got a bit of a backlog on homicides in the Big Apple, Lee."

"Thanks for enlightening me, Ray, on New York City's corpse problem. So who inherited?"

Jackson sifted through the report. "Steven Page didn't leave a will. His parents were dead. He had no kids. His brother, Edward Page, as his only sibling, got everything."

Sawyer took a swallow of coffee. "That's interesting."

"But I don't think Ed Page popped his younger brother to fund his kids' college education. From what I could find out, he was as surprised as anyone else that his brother was a millionaire."

"Anything in the autopsy report catch your eye?"

Jackson picked out two pages from the file and

handed them across to Sawyer. "As I said, a massive insulin overdose killed Steven Page. He injected himself in the thigh. It's a typical area of administration for diabetics. Other hypodermic entry sites around the thigh region showed it was his normal area of injection as well. Toxicology report showed a point-one-eight blood alcohol level. That didn't help his cause any when he took the overdose. *Algor mortis* indicated he had been dead about twelve hours when he was found; body temp was about eighty degrees. He was also in full rigor; that corroborates the time of death indicated by the body temperature and puts his check-out time at between three and four in the morning. Postmortem lividity was fixed. Guy died right where they found him."

"Who did find him?"

"Landlady," said Jackson. "Probably wasn't a real pretty sight."

"Death rarely is. Any note left behind?"

Jackson shook his head.

"Page make any calls before he kicked the bucket?"

"The last phone call Steven Page made from his apartment was at seven-thirty that evening."

"Who'd he call?"

"His brother."

"Did the police talk to Ed Page?"

"You bet they did. Especially after they found out about the bucks Steven Page had."

"Ed Page have an alibi?"

"A pretty damn good one. As you know, he was a police officer back then. He was working a drug bust with a squad of officers on the Lower East Side when his little brother was dying."

"The police ask Ed Page about the earlier phone conversation?"

"He said his brother was distraught. Steven told

him about having HIV. Ed Page said his brother sounded like he had already been drinking."

"He didn't try to go see him?"

"He said he wanted to, but his brother wanted no part of that. Finally hung up on him. Ed Page tried calling back, but there was no answer. He had to go on duty at nine. He said he'd thought he'd let his brother alone for the night and then try to talk to him the next day. He didn't get off duty until ten A.M. He grabbed a few hours' sleep and then went to his brother's office downtown around three. When he found out Steven had never come to work, he went directly over to his brother's apartment. He got there about the time the police did."

"Jesus. I bet he was feeling some heavy-duty guilt."

"If that had been my little brother . . ." Jackson said. "Damn. Anyway, they ruled it a suicide. All the facts sure point that way."

Sawyer rose and started pacing. "And yet with all that, Ed Page didn't think it was suicide. I wonder why."

Jackson shrugged. "Wishful thinking. Maybe he was really feeling guilty and made himself think that so he'd feel better. Who knows? NYPD didn't find any evidence of foul play, and looking at this report, neither do I."

Sawyer didn't answer. He was in deep thought.

Jackson took the report on Steven Page and put it back in the file. He looked over at Sawyer. "Find anything at Page's office?"

Sawyer focused absently on his partner. "No. But I did find something interesting at his house." He put a hand inside his suit pocket and extracted the photograph labeled "Stevie." He handed the photograph to Jackson. "Interesting, because it was kind of hidden behind some other photo. I'm pretty sure it's a picture of Steven Page."

As soon as Jackson's eyes came to rest on the photo, his mouth dropped open. "Oh, my God!" He rose from his chair. "Oh, my God!" he said again, his voice rising, his hands violently shaking as they clasped the photo. "This can't be – it's not possible."

Sawyer grabbed his shoulder. "Ray, Ray? What the hell is it?"

Jackson ran to another table in the room. He frantically grabbed files, scanned them before tossing them down and snatching up others, his movements becoming more and more frenetic. Finally he stopped, a file open in his hand, his eyes glued to something in the mass of papers within.

Sawyer was beside him in an instant. "Dammit, Ray, what is it?" he said fiercely.

In response, Jackson handed over to his partner an object from the file. Sawyer stared down at the photo in disbelief. In a different pose, the too-handsome face of Steven Page looked back at him.

Sawyer grabbed the photo he had taken from Ed Page's apartment off the table where Jackson had dropped it and looked at the picture again. His eyes swung back to the file photo. There was no doubt, it was the same man in both photos.

A wide-eyed Sawyer looked at Jackson. "Where did you get this photo, Ray?" he asked very slowly, his voice hardly above a whisper.

Jackson licked his lips nervously; his head swayed from side to side. "I can't believe this."

"Where, Ray, where?"

"Arthur Lieberman's apartment."

FORTY-SIX

Subj: Fwd: Not me.
Date: 95—11—26 08:41:52 EST
From: ArchieKW2
To: ArchieJW2

Dear Other Archie: Watch your typing.
By the way do you often send mail to
yourself? Message a little melodramatic
but a nice password nonetheless. Maybe
we can talk encryption techniques.
Heard one of the best around is the
Secret Service's racal-milgo. See you
in Cyberspace. Ciao.

Forwarded Message:
Subj: Not me
Date: 95—11—19 10:30:06 PST
From: ArchieJW2
To: ArchieKW2

sid all wrong all backwards/ disk in
mail099121.19822.29629.295111.39614
seattlewarehouse-gethelphurryI

Sidney stared at the computer screen; her mind
alternated between racing out of control and
threatening to shut down. She had been right,

407

though. Jason has mistyped, had hit the k instead of the j. Thank you, ArchieKW2, whoever you are. Fisher had also been right about the password – almost thirty characters long. She assumed that's what the numbers represented: the password.

Her heart sank as she looked at the date of the original message. Her husband had implored her to hurry. There was nothing she could have done about it, and yet she had an overwhelming sense of having let him down. She printed out the single page and put it in her pocket. At least she would finally be able to read what was on the disk. Her adrenaline soared with the thought.

It abruptly went even higher as the sound of someone entering the library reached her ears. She carefully exited the program and turned off the computer. Her hands were shaking as she put the disk back in her purse. She waited for additional sounds, her breath coming in shallow bursts, one hand on the butt of her pistol.

When a sound came from her right, she slipped out of the chair, bent low and proceeded to move quietly to her left. She rounded a corner and stopped. Staring her in the face was a bookshelf of F.2d, volumes she had spent much of law school and her first years in practice poring over. She looked through a gap in their ranks at the man in the shadows. She could not make out his face. She didn't dare move farther for fear of making any noise. Then the man started to come directly toward her. Her grip tightened on the Smith & Wesson; her index finger clicked off the safety. She pulled it from the holster as she backed away. Crouching low, she made her way behind a partition, her ears straining for any sound as she desperately tried to think of a way out. The problem was there was only one doorway leading into the library. Her only chance was to circle around, trying to keep a little ahead of whoever was out there until she reached the doorway and could run like hell. A bank of elevators was right down the hallway. If she could make it.

She proceeded to move a few feet and wait, then repeated the process. She had to assume she was making enough noise for the man to hear her but not in a manner, she felt, for him to gauge her strategy. The footsteps from behind matched her maneuvers almost perfectly. That should have been enough to set off alarm bells in her head. She was almost at the doorway and could actually see the frosted glass in the dim light. She gathered her strength and nerve to take a few more steps, and then she would make her run. Five more feet. Now she was almost at the exit. Flattened against the wall, she slowly began to count to three.

She never made it past one.

The bright lights blinded her. By the time she refocused, the man was right next to her. Pupils dilating, she instinctively swung the pistol in his direction.

"My God, have you lost your mind?" Philip Goldman blinked rapidly to adjust to the new level of brightness.

Sidney gaped at him.

"What the devil do you mean, sneaking in here like this? With a gun, no less?"

Sidney stopped shaking and straightened up. "I'm a partner in this firm, Philip. I have every right to be here." Her voice was trembling, but she met his gaze forcefully.

Goldman's voice was sneering. "Not for long, though," He withdrew an envelope from his inner pocket. "Actually, this will save the firm the cost of a messenger." He held out the envelope to Sidney. "Your termination from the firm. If you would kindly just sign it now, it would save everyone a great deal of trouble and rid the firm of an enormous embarrassment."

Sidney did not take the envelope but kept her eyes and the pistol on Goldman.

Goldman fingered the envelope before glancing at the pistol. "Would you mind putting away that gun before you add additional crimes to your résumé?"

"I haven't done a damn thing, and you know it." She spat the words out.

Goldman rolled his eyes. "Of course. I'm sure you were entirely ignorant of your loving husband's nefarious schemes."

"Jason hasn't done anything wrong either."

"Well, I'm not going to argue with you while you have a firearm pointed at me. Would you *please* put it away?"

Finally Sidney began to lower the 9mm. Then something occurred to her. Who had turned on the lights? Goldman hadn't been anywhere near a switch.

Before she had time to react, a strong hand gripped her arm and the pistol was violently jerked from her. A powerful force slammed into her and she was thrown up against a wall. She sank down to the floor, her head splitting with pain from the impact. When she looked up, a burly man dressed in a black chauffeur's uniform stood over her, pointing her own pistol at her head. From behind the gunman, another man appeared.

"Hello, Sid. Gotten anymore phone calls from dead husbands lately?" Paul Brophy laughed.

Shaking, Sidney managed to stand up and lean against the wall while she tried to get her breath back.

Goldman looked over at the burly man. "Good work, Parker. You can go get the car. We'll be down in a few minutes."

410

Parker nodded and put Sidney's pistol in his coat pocket. She noted that he carried a holstered gun of his own. Much to her dismay, he picked up her purse from the floor where it had fallen during the brief struggle and strode off.

"You've been following me!"

"I like to know the after-hours comings and goings at the firm: an electronic tap on the entry system to the building. I was quite pleased when I saw your name come over the log at one-thirty A.M." He looked at the shelves of legal tomes. "Doing some legal research, or perhaps following your husband's example and trying to steal some secrets?" Sidney would have hit Goldman flush in the face with her fist if Paul Brophy hadn't been too quick for her.

Goldman was unruffled. "Perhaps now we can get down to business." Sidney made a move to lunge through the doorway; Brophy blocked her way, however, pushing her back into the library. Sidney stared a hole through him. "Going from partner in a major firm to burglary in a New Orleans hotel is a big swing, Paul." Brophy's smile disappeared.

Sidney looked over at Goldman. "If I scream right now, someone might hear me."

Goldman responded coolly. "Actually, Sidney, you may have forgotten, but all attorneys and paralegals left earlier today for the firm's annual conference in Florida. They won't be back for several days. Unfortunately, I was called away on unexpected business and have to take an early morning flight down. Paul had a similar predicament. Everyone else is in attendance." He glanced at his watch. "Thus you can scream all you want. However, actually you have every reason to work with us."

Her eyes turned to slits, Sidney looked at both men. "What are you talking about?"

"This conversation might best be carried on in my office." Goldman motioned toward the door and then produced a small-caliber revolver of his own to reinforce the request.

Brophy closed and locked the office door. Goldman handed the gun to him and sat down behind his desk. He motioned for Sidney to sit across from him. "It's certainly been an exciting month for you, Sidney." He produced the termination letter again. "However, I'm afraid your recent excesses have resulted in your tenure at this firm coming to an end. I wouldn't be surprised if the firm and Triton Global instituted civil litigation against you. Possibly criminal action as well."

Sidney's eyes now bored in on Goldman. "You're holding me against my will at gunpoint and you're telling *me* to worry about criminal action?"

"Paul and I, both partners in this firm, observe someone, an intruder, in the firm's library doing Gods knows what. We attempt to apprehend said suspect and what does she do? She pulls a gun on us. We're able to wrestle the gun away, fortunately, before anyone is hurt, and now we are detaining that intruder until the police arrive."

"Police?"

"Oh, that's right, I haven't called the police yet, have I? How absentminded of me." Goldman reached for the phone, lifted the receiver and then sat back in his chair without dialing. "Oh, now I remember why I haven't called them." His tone was goading. "Would you like to know the reason?" Sidney didn't answer. "You're a deal lawyer, Sidney. Well, what if I were to propose a deal to you? A way for you to not only remain at liberty but also derive some economic gain, since you now happen to be unemployed."

412

"Tyler, Stone isn't the only firm in town, Phil."

Goldman winced at the abbreviation of his name. "Well, actually, in your case that's not quite correct. You see, as far as you're concerned, there are no firms left. Not here, not anywhere in this country, perhaps the world."

Sidney's face betrayed her confusion.

"Let's be rational, *Sid*." Goldman's eyes gleamed momentarily as he returned the verbal joust. "Your husband is suspected of sabotaging a plane, resulting in the murder of almost two hundred people. On top of that it's clear he stole money and secrets worth hundreds of millions of dollars from a client of this firm. Obviously these crimes were planned over a long period of time."

"I haven't heard you mention my name yet in this ridiculous scenario."

"You had high-level access to Triton Global's most important records, perhaps records to which even your husband wasn't privy."

"That was part of my job. That doesn't make it criminal."

"As they are fond of saying in legal circles, and as is embodied in the Canon of Ethics, even the 'appearance of an impropriety' must be avoided. I think that you long ago overstepped that boundary."

"How? By losing my husband? By being railroaded out of my job without a scintilla of proof? Why don't we talk about lawsuits for a minute? Like Sidney Archer versus Tyler, Stone for wrongful termination?"

Goldman looked over at Brophy and nodded slightly. Sidney turned her head to look at him. Her chin began to tremble when she saw the minicassette recorder emerge from his pocket.

"These things come in so handy, Sid," said Brophy. "Record so clear it's as if you were right

413

there in the same room." He hit the play button.

After a minute of listening to her conversation with her husband, Sidney whirled back around to face Goldman. "What the hell do you want?"

"Well, let's see. I suppose we must first establish market price. What is that tape worth? It establishes that you lied to the FBI. A felony in itself. Then there's aiding and abetting a felon. Accessory after the fact. Another nasty one. The list goes on from there. Neither of us is a criminal lawyer, but I think you get the picture. Father gone, mother in jail. Your little girl is how old? Tragic." He shook his head in mock sympathy.

Sidney jumped out of her chair. "Fuck you, Goldman. *Fuck you both.*" Sidney screamed the words in uncontrollable fury. Then she lunged across the desk, gripped Goldman's throat with both hands and would have done him serious damage had Brophy not come once again to the older man's rescue.

Goldman, coughing and gagging, looked furiously at Sidney as soon as she was pulled off. "You ever touch me again, you'll rot in jail," he sputtered.

Breathing hard, Sidney stared wildly at the man. She flung off Brophy's restraining hand but did not move as he kept the gun trained on her. Goldman smoothed down his tie and ruffled shirt and reassumed his confident tone. "Despite your crude reaction, I am actually prepared to be quite generous with you. If you would look at the matter rationally, you would be compelled to accept the offer I'm about to make to you." He cocked his head at her and glanced down at the chair.

Shaking and breathing irregularly, Sidney finally sat back down.

"Good. Now, as succinctly as possible, here is the situation: I know that you have spoken with Roger

Egert, who is now in charge of the CyberCom matter. You are privy to Triton's latest proposal regarding the CyberCom acquisition. This I also know to be fact. Now you are also still in possession of the password to the master computer file for the CyberCom transaction." Sidney looked dully at Goldman as her thoughts jumped ahead of his words. "I want both the latest terms of the proposal and the password to the computer file, just in case there are any last-minute changes in Triton's negotiation position."

Sidney's tone was slow, deliberate, her breathing now returned to normal. "RTG must really want CyberCom if they're paying you something other than your hourly rate to violate attorney-client privilege, not to mention stealing corporate secrets."

Goldman merely continued: "In return we are prepared to pay you ten million dollars, tax-free, of course."

"Ensuring my economic stability now that I'm unemployable? And my silence?"

"Something like that. You disappear to some nice little foreign country, raise your little girl in luxury. The CyberCom deal is consummated. Triton Global will continue on. Tyler, Stone will remain a viable firm. No one is the worse off. The alternative? Well, it's something considerably less pleasant. For you. However, time is of the essence. I need your answer in one minute." He stared at his watch, counting the seconds off.

Sidney sat back in her chair, her shoulders slumped as she swiftly thought through the few possibilities left to her. If she agreed, she would be rich, if she didn't she could and probably would go to jail. And Amy? She thought of Jason and all the terrible events of the past month. More than enough for several lifetimes. She suddenly stiffened as she looked at Goldman's triumphant features, felt the sneering presence of Paul Brophy behind her.

She knew what course of action she would take.

She would accept their terms and then would play her own cards. She would give Goldman the information he wanted then she would go straight to Lee Sawyer and tell him everything, including the existence of the disk. She would hope for the best deal she could get and she would expose Goldman and his client for what they were. She wouldn't be rich and she might be away from her little girl if she did any prison time, but she wasn't going to raise Amy with Goldman's extortion money. And, most important, she could live with herself.

"Time," Goldman announced.

Sidney didn't speak.

Goldman shook his head slowly and lifted up the phone receiver once more. Finally, almost imperceptibly, Sidney nodded her head. Goldman rose from behind the desk, a broad smile on his face. "Excellent. What are the terms and the password?"

Sidney shook her head. "My bargaining position is a little fragile. First the money, then the information. Or you can just go ahead and dial 911."

Goldman hesitated for a moment. "Well, as you say, your position is precarious. However, precisely because of that fact, we can be somewhat flexible. Shall we?" He stood up and motioned to the door. Sidney looked confused. "Now that we've reached agreement, I want to fully implement the deal before I let you go. You may be difficult to find later," Goldman explained.

As Sidney rose and turned, Brophy put the revolver into the back of his waistband and intentionally brushed lightly against her with his shoulder, his lips near her ear. "After you get settled down into your new life, you may want some

416

company. I see myself having a lot more free time and more money than I know what to do with. Think about it."

Sidney's knee slamming into his groin sent Brophy to the floor. "I just did, Paul, and I'm trying hard not to be sick to my stomach. Stay away from me if you want to keep what little manhood you've got left."

Sidney walked briskly down the hallway, Goldman right behind her. Brophy finally managed to pull himself up. Clutching his privates, his face pale, he staggered after them.

The limo was waiting for them on the lowest level of the garage next to the elevator bank, its engine running. Goldman held the door while Sidney climbed in. Brophy, still trying to catch his breath and painfully bent over, entered last and sat across from Goldman and Sidney; the darkened glass partition was fully raised behind him.

"It won't take long to make arrangements. You may find it's in your best interests to maintain your present domicile until things cool down a bit. Then we'll fly you to an interim destination. You can send for your daughter and live happily every after." Goldman's tone was openly jovial.

Sidney's response was all business. "What about Triton and the firm? You mentioned lawsuits?"

"I think that can all be taken care of. Why would the firm want to immerse itself in such embarrassing litigation? And Triton really can't prove anything, can it?"

"So why should I deal?"

Brophy held up the minicassette recorder, his face still flushed. "Because of this, you little bitch. Unless you want to spend the rest of your life in prison."

Sidney's manner remained calm. "I'll want that tape."

Goldman shrugged. "Impossible for now. Perhaps later, when things have returned to normal."

Goldman looked at the glass partition. "Parker?"

The partition slid down.

"Parker, we can go now."

The arm coming through the now open space between the front and back of the limo held a gun. Brophy's head exploded and he fell face down on to the floor of the limo. Goldman and Sidney were both splattered with his blood, among other things. Goldman's mouth dropped open and he yelled in disbelief as the pistol turned in his direction. "Oh, God. No! Parker!"

The bullet slammed into his forehead and Philip Goldman's long career as an exceedingly arrogant attorney came to a decisive end. He jolted backward in the seat from the bullet's impact, blood covering his face as well as the rear glass of the limo. Then he slumped over against Sidney, who screamed as the gun now swiveled in her direction. Her fingernails dug into the soft leather seat in her panic. For an instant she stared at the face that was covered by a black ski mask and then her eyes zeroed in on the gleaming muzzle that hovered barely five feet from her face. Every detail of the pistol was seared into her memory as she awaited her death.

Then the gun was pointed toward the right-side door of the limo. As Sidney sat frozen, the arm motioned more firmly toward the door. Trembling and unable to understand what was happening other than the fact that she apparently was not going to die, Sidney managed to push Goldman's limp form off her and started to climb over Brophy's body. While she awkwardly made her way across the dead lawyer, her hand slipped on a patch of blood and she fell on top of him. She instantly jerked back. As her fingers clawed for a solid grip, she felt the hard object under Brophy's shoulder. Her fingers instinctively closed around the metal. With her back to the gunman, she was able to tuck Brophy's revolver into her coat pocket without being observed.

When she opened the door, something hit her in the back. Frightened out of her mind, she managed to turn around and eyed her purse where it had fallen on top of Brophy's body after bouncing off her. Then her eyes caught hold of the computer disk Jason had sent her as the hand holding it disappeared back through the partition. With trembling hands she picked up her purse, pushed open the heavy door all the way and fell out of the car. Then she staggered up and raced away with every ounce of energy in her possession.

Back in the limo the man leaned through the partition. Next to him in the front seat, Parker was slumped over, a bullet hole in his right temple. The man carefully picked up the minicassette recorder where it had fallen on the seat of the limo and played a few seconds of it. He nodded to himself when he heard the voices and then carefully moved Brophy's body slightly to the side, slid the recorder several inches under his body and let him slump back to his original position. The disk was put away in the man's fanny pack. His last act was to carefully pick up the three shell casings ejected from the pistol. He couldn't make it too easy for the cops. Then the man exited the limo, the gun he had used to murder three people carried in a baggie for deposit in an out-of-the-way place, but not so out of the way that the police would fail to uncover it.

Kenneth Scales took off the ski mask. Under the bright lights of the empty garage the deadly blue eyes twinkled with deep satisfaction. Another night's work successfully completed.

Sidney punched the elevator button again and again until finally the doors opened. She slumped against the wall of the elevator car. She was covered in blood. She could feel it on her face, her hands. It was all she could do not to start shrieking at the top of her lungs. She just wanted to get it off her. With an unsteady hand she hit the button for the eighth floor.

As soon as she got to the ladies' room and saw her bloody image in the mirror, she threw up in the sink, then dropped to the floor, where she lay moaning, the dry heaves pounding her unmercifully. Finally she managed to pull herself up and wash off the blood as best she could. She continued to pour hot water over her face until its sting began to calm the shakes; she kept raking shaky fingers through her hair, probing for things that did not belong there.

Leaving the rest room, she ran down the hallway to her office and grabbed a spare trench coat that she kept there. It effectively covered the remnants of blood that had refused to come off. Then she picked up the phone and prepared to dial 911. She gripped the .32 with her other hand. She could not shake the feeling that at any moment that gleaming pistol would be pointed in her direction again. That the man behind the black mask would not let her live a second time. She had keyed two of the numbers. Then her hand froze as the vision hit her. In the limo: the barrel of the gun staring her in the face. Then its image as it swung toward the door. That's when she saw it.

The grip. The cracked grip. Cracked when she had dropped the gun back at her home. The man had her gun. Two men had just been murdered with her 9mm.

Another vision burned into her brain. The tape of her and Jason's conversation. That too was back there, with the dead men. The reason why she had been left alive became abundantly clear to Sidney Archer: She had been allowed to live so that she could rot in jail for murder. Like a terribly frightened child, she scrambled back into the far corner of her office and slumped across the floor, her body quivering uncontrollably, tears and moans spilling out of her, with absolutely no sign of ever stopping.

FORTY-SEVEN

Sawyer was still staring at the photo of Steven Page, the dead man's face looming larger and larger in his mind until he finally had to drop the picture and turn away before it completely engulfed him.

"I just assumed it was a photo of one of Lieberman's kids. They were all on his desk together. I never thought to connect up that he has *two*, not three children." Jackson slapped his forehead. "It just didn't seem all that important. Then when the investigation shifted away from Lieberman to Archer—" Jackson shook his head in obvious misery.

Sawyer sat on the edge of the table. Only those closest to him would realize that the veteran FBI agent was more stunned than he had ever been in his professional life.

"I'm sorry, Lee." Jackson snatched another look at the photo and cringed. Sawyer softly patted his partner on the back. "It's not your fault, Ray. Under the circumstances it wouldn't have seemed important to me either." Sawyer stood up and started pacing. "But now it sure as hell is. We'll need to verify that it is Steven Page, although I really don't have any doubt about it." He abruptly stopped pacing.

"Hey, Ray, NYPD could never figure out where Steven Page got all that money, right?"

Jackson's mind clicked into high gear. "Maybe Page was blackmailing Lieberman. Perhaps over his affair. They were both in finance, same professional circles. That would explain the money Page had."

Sawyer shook his head. "A number of people seemed to know about the mistress – not much opportunity for blackmail there. Besides, most people don't keep photos of their blackmailers on display, Ray." Jackson looked sheepish. "No, I think it cuts deeper than that." Sawyer leaned against the wall of the conference room, folded his arms and sunk his head on his chest. "By the way, what did you ever get on our elusive mistress?"

Jackson took a minute to consult a file. "A lot of nothing. I found a number of people who had heard rumors. Unsubstantiated rumors, they were quick to point out. They were terrified of being named or involved. I had to do some quick soft-shoe to calm them down. It was the damnedest thing, though: they had all heard about her, could describe her pretty well, although each description I got was a little different than the last. But—"

"But nobody could tell you definitively that they had ever actually met the mystery lady."

Jackson's face scrunched up. "Yeah, that's right. How'd you know that?"

Sawyer took a deep breath. "You ever play that game as a kid, Ray, where somebody tells you something and you tell somebody else and they tell somebody else? By the time it gets to the end of the line, the information is nothing like it started out to be. Or how a rumor gets started and spreads and everybody believes it to be the gospel, could almost swear they had personally seen whatever it was, and none of it is true."

"Hell, yes. My grandmother reads the *Star*. She believes everything in it and talks like she actually saw Liz Taylor getting it on with Elvis on the space shuttle."

423

"Right. It's not true, not one bit of it, but people will tell you it is, fervently believe that it is, simply because they've read about it or heard it, especially if they've heard it from more than one person."

"Are you saying . . ."

"I'm saying that I don't think the blond mistress ever existed, Ray. More to the point, I think she was created for a specific purpose."

"Like what?"

Sawyer took a very deep breath before answering. "To cover the fact that Arthur Lieberman and Steven Page were lovers."

Jackson dropped into a chair as he stared at Sawyer. "Are you serious?"

"The photo of Page at his apartment, next to his kids? Those love letters you found at the apartment? Why not sign them? A week's pay says the handwriting matches Steven Page's. And last but not least, Page being a millionaire on a working man's salary? Very doable if you're by chance *sleeping* with a guy who's made lots of people millionaires."

"Yeah, but why invent a story about a mistress? It could've blown Lieberman's chairmanship bid."

Sawyer was shaking his head. "In this day and age, Ray, who knows? If that were the criterion, a big chunk of the political leadership in this country would have to pack up and go home. And the fact is it didn't stop him from getting the Fed's top post. But do you think the outcome would've been the same if it was discovered Lieberman was homosexual and had a male lover less than half his age? Keep in mind that the financial community in this country is one of the most conservative you'll find anywhere."

"Okay, he would've been screwed, that's for damned sure. But talk about your double standards. It's okay to commit adultery, so long as it's with someone of the opposite sex."

"Right, you invent a phony heterosexual affair to cover the true homosexual one. They used to do that out in Hollywood with leading men who weren't attracted to the opposite sex. The studios would orchestrate phony marriages. All a complicated sham to preserve a lucrative career. Lieberman's scam wasn't a perfect fix, but it gets him the brass ring. His wife may or may not have known the truth. But she gets paid off big-time, so she's not going to talk. And she's six feet under now. So no loose lips there."

Jackson wiped his brow. "Jesus." He looked at Sawyer, puzzled. "If that's the case, then Steven Page's death *was* a suicide; there would be no reason to kill him."

Sawyer was shaking his head. "There would be every reason to kill him, Ray."

"Why?"

Sawyer paused for a moment, looked down at his hands and spoke quietly. "Want to make an educated guess as to how Steven Page contracted HIV?"

Jackson's eyes bulged. "Lieberman?"

Sawyer looked up. "I'd be real interested to find out whether Lieberman was HIV-positive."

Jackson's confusion suddenly cleared. "If Page knows he might be terminal, he'd have no reason to keep quiet."

"Right. Getting a terminal illness from one's lover doesn't normally inspire loyalty. Steven Page held Arthur Lieberman's professional future in his hands. I think that equals sufficient homicidal motive, in my book."

"So it looks like we need to approach this case from an entirely new angle."

"Agreed. Right now we have a lot of speculation, but not really a damn thing we can take to a prosecutor."

425

Jackson got out of his chair, started to tidy up the files. "So you really think Lieberman had Page killed?"

When Sawyer didn't answer, Jackson turned to find him staring off into space.

"Lee?" Sawyer finally looked over at him.

"I never said that, Ray."

"But—"

"I'll see you in the morning. Get some sleep, you're going to need it." Sawyer got up and walked to the door leading out of the conference room. "I've got somebody I need to speak to," Sawyer said.

"Who?"

Sawyer turned back momentarily. "Charles Tiedman, president of the San Francisco Federal Reserve Bank. Lieberman never got a chance to talk to him. I think it's about time somebody did."

Sawyer left Jackson bent over the stacks of files, his mind reeling.

FORTY-EIGHT

Sidney Archer picked herself up off the floor. As the twin feelings of hopelessness and fear faded away, they were slowly replaced with an even stronger impulse: survival. She unlocked one of her desk drawers and pulled out her passport. She had been called overseas on a moment's notice more than once in her legal career. But now the reason would be about as personal as one could get: her life. She went to the office next to hers. It belonged to a young associate who happened to be a rabid Atlanta Braves fan; a good portion of one of his shelving units mirrored that loyalty. She snatched the baseball cap off the shelf, bobby-pinned her long hair up, and pulled the cap down tight over her head.

She thought to check her purse. Amazingly, her wallet was still full of hundred-dollar bills from the New Orleans trip. The killer hadn't touched those. Exiting the building, she hailed a cab, gave the driver her destination and slid appreciatively into the seat as the vehicle sped away. She carefully slid the late Philip Goldman's .32 revolver out of her pocket, inserted it into the belt holster Sawyer had given her, and then buttoned up her trench coat.

The cab pulled in front of Union Station and she got out. She never would have gotten through airport security with her handgun, but she had no such worry traveling on Amtrak. Her plan, at the outset, was simple: run to a safe place and try to figure things out. She planned on contacting Lee Sawyer, but she didn't want to be in the same country as the FBI agent when she did. The problem was she *had* tried to help her husband. She *had* lied to the FBI. A stupid act in retrospect, but at the time it was the only thing she could do. She had to help her husband. She had to be there for him. Now? Her gun was at a murder scene; the tape of her conversation with Jason was there as well. Despite her coming partially clean with Sawyer, what would he think now? Now, she was certain, the handcuffs would come out. She started to sink into despair again, but she gathered her courage, turned up her collar in the face of the icy wind and entered the railway terminal.

She bought a coach ticket on the next Metroliner train bound for New York City. The train would leave in about twenty minutes and would deposit her at Penn Station in midtown New York at about five-thirty in the morning. A cab ride would take her to JFK Airport, where she would buy a one-way plane ticket on an early morning flight to some country, she wasn't sure which one yet. She went to the ATM machine on the lower level of the train station and withdrew some more cash. As soon as an APB was put out on her, the plastic would be useless. It suddenly occurred to her that she had no other clothes and that she would have to travel as much as possible incognito. The problem was that none of the innumerable clothing shops were open in the terminal at this time of night. She would have to wait until she got to New York.

She stepped inside a phone booth and consulted her small address book; Lee Sawyer's card tumbled out. She stared at it for a long moment. *Dammit!* She had to, she owed the man. She dialed Sawyer's home number. After four rings the answering machine came on. She hesitated and then slammed the phone down. She dialed another number. It seemed to ring indefinitely until a sleepy voice answered.

"Jeff?"

"Who's this?"

"Sidney Archer."

Sidney could hear Fisher fumbling in his bed-covers, probably looked for the clock. "I waited up to hear from you. Must've fallen asleep."

"Jeff, I don't have much time. Something terrible has happened."

"What? What's happened?"

"The less you know, the better." She paused and struggled through her thoughts. "Jeff, I'm going to give you the number where I can be reached right now. I want you to go to a pay phone and call me back."

"Christ, it's . . . it's after two A.M."

"Jeff, please, just do what I ask."

After a little grumbling, Fisher assented. "Give me about five minutes. What's the number?"

Barely six minutes later, the phone rang. Sidney snatched it up. "You're at the pay phone. You swear?"

"Yes! And I'm freezing my ass off. Now talk to me."

"Jeff, I've got the password. It was in Jason's e-mail. I was right, it was sent to the wrong address."

"That's fantastic. Now we can read the file."

"No, we can't."

"Why not?"

"Because I lost the disk."

"What? How did you do that?"

"It doesn't matter. It's gone. I can't get it back." Sidney's misery was evident in her voice. She collected her thoughts. She was going to tell Fisher to leave town for a while. He could be in danger, serious danger, if her experience in the parking garage was any indicator. She froze at Fisher's words.

"Well, you're in luck, lady."

"What are you talking about?"

"I'm not only security conscious, I'm anal as hell. I've lost too many files over the years that weren't backed up properly, Sid."

"Are you saying what I think you are, Jeff?"

"While you were in the kitchen when we were working on trying to decrypt the file . . ." He paused somewhat dramatically. "I made a couple copies of the files on the disk. One on my hard drive and one on another floppy."

Sidney couldn't speak at first. When she did, her response made Fisher blush. "I love you, Jeff."

"When do you want to come over so we can finally see what's on that sucker."

"I can't, Jeff."

"Why not?"

"I have to go out of town. I want you to send the disk to an address I'm about to give you. I want you to FedEx it. Drop it off first thing in the morning. First thing, Jeff."

"I don't understand, Sidney."

"Jeff, you've been a big help, but I don't want you to understand it. I don't want you involved any more than you already are. I want you to go home, get the disk and then go stay at a hotel. The Holiday Inn in Old Town is near your place. Send me the bill."

"Sid—"

"As soon as the FedEx office opens in Old Town, I want you to drop the package off," she repeated. "Then call in to the office, tell them you're extending your vacation for a few days. Where does your family live?"

430

"Boston."

"Fine. Go to Boston and stay with them. Send me the bill for your transportation. Fly first class if you want. Just go."

"Sid!"

"Jeff, I have to get off in a minute so don't argue with me. You have to do everything I've just told you. It's the only way you can be reasonably safe."

"You're not kidding, are you?"

"Do you have something to write with?"

"Yes."

She flipped through her address book. "Write down this address. Send the package there." She gave him her parents' mailing address and phone number in Bell Harbor, Maine. "I'm truly sorry I had to involve you in this at all, but you're the only one who could help me. Thank you." Sidney hung up.

Fisher put the phone back in its cradle, looked warily around the darkened area, ran to his car and drove home. He was about to park his car at the curb when he noticed a black van about a block behind him. As he squinted in the dark light, Fisher was able to discern two figures in the front seat of the van. His breathing immediately accelerated. He did a slow U-turn in the middle of the street and headed back toward the heart of Old Town. He didn't look at the driver as he passed by the van. When he checked his mirror again, the van was following him.

Fisher pulled his car to a stop in front of the two-story brick building. He looked up at the sign: CYBER@CHAT. Fisher was good friends with the owner and had even helped set up the computer systems offered at Cyber@Chat.

The bar stayed open all night and with good justification. Even at this hour it was three-quarters full, mostly with a college-age crowd who didn't have to get up and go to work the next morning.

431

However, instead of blaring music, rowdy patrons and a smoky atmosphere (because of the sensitive computer equipment, no smoking was allowed) the interior was filled with the sounds of computer games and low, often intense discussions about whatever was tripping its way across the abundance of computer monitors in the place. The age-old art of flirting still took place, and men and women roamed the room in search of companionship, however brief.

Fisher found his friend, the owner, a young man in his twenties, behind the bar and struck up a friendly conversation. Explaining enough of his situation to enable his friend to assist him, Fisher discreetly handed across the piece of paper containing the address in Maine Sidney had given him. The owner disappeared into the back room. Within five minutes Fisher was entrenched behind one of the computers. As he briefly peered out the window of the bar, the black van came to a stop in an alleyway across the street. Fisher turned back to the computer.

A waitress brought over a bottle of beer and a glass, and a plate of munchies. As she set the plate down next to the computer, she put a linen napkin next to it. Inside the carefully folded napkin was a blank three-and-a-half-inch disk. Fisher nonchalantly unfolded the napkin and quickly slid the disk into the computer's floppy drive. He typed in a series of characters and the high-decibel dialing of a phone modem could be heard. Within a minute, Fisher was connected to his computer at home. It took about thirty seconds for him to download the computer files he had copied from Sidney's disk on to the blank disk. He looked out the window again. The van had not moved.

The waitress came over to his table. Obviously privy to his plan, she asked if he needed anything else. On her tray was a padded FedEx envelope with the Bell Harbor address typed on the mailing label. Fisher looked out the window again. Then down the street he noticed two policemen standing next to their patrol cars shooting the breeze. When the waitress reached for the disk, which had been part of the plan hastily fleshed out with the bar's owner, Fisher shook his head. Sidney's warning had come back to him. He didn't want to involve his friends unnecessarily in any of this and now maybe he didn't have to. He whispered to the waitress. She nodded and took the FedEx envelope into the back room, returning barely a minute later. She handed another padded envelope across to Fisher. He looked down at it and smiled when he saw the metered postage label on the envelope. His friend had been very liberal in his estimation of what it would cost to mail the small package, even certified, return receipt requested. It was definitely not going to be returned for insufficient postage. It wasn't as fast as FedEx, but it would have to do under the circumstances, Fisher concluded. He slipped the disk into the envelope, sealed it and put it in his coat pocket. He then paid his bill, leaving a healthy tip for the waitress. He dabbed some of the beer on his face and clothes and then tipped the glass back and finished it in one gulp.

As he exited the bar and walked toward his car, the van's headlights came on and Fisher could hear the engine start up. The van headed toward him. Fisher started staggering and then singing loudly. The two cops down the street turned their heads in his direction. Fisher gave them an exaggerated salute and a bow before he collapsed into his car, started the engine and drove off toward the cops on the wrong side of the street.

As he hurtled by the police, his squealing tires

doing at least twenty over the speed limit, the cops jumped in their cruisers. The van followed at a safe distance but then turned off when the police cruisers caught up to Fisher. His hazardous driving and the smell of beer on his breath earned Fisher a pair of handcuffs and a quick trip to the police station.

"I hope you know a good lawyer, fella," the cop barked from the front seat.

Fisher's response was completely lucid and tinged with more than a trace of humor. "Actually, I know a number of them, Officer."

At the police station he was fingerprinted and his possessions inventoried. He was allowed to make one phone call. Before he did so, however, he politely asked the desk sergeant to do him a favor. A minute later Fisher watched gleefully as the padded envelope was dropped into the police station's U.S. mail chute. The "snail mail." If his techie friends could only see him now. On his way to the holding cell, Jeff Fisher actually broke into a cheerful whistle. It wasn't wise to screw around with an MIT man.

To his pleasant surprise, Lee Sawyer did not have to travel to California to speak with Charles Tiedman. After a phone call to the Federal Reserve, Sawyer learned that Tiedman was actually in Washington for a conference. Although it was almost three in the morning, Tiedman, still operating on West Coast time, had quickly agreed to speak to the agent. In fact, it seemed to Sawyer that the San Francisco Federal Reserve Bank president was very eager to talk to him.

At the Four Seasons Hotel in Georgetown where Tiedman was staying, Sawyer and Tiedman sat across from each other in a private room adjacent to the hotel restaurant, which had closed several hours earlier. Tiedman was a small, clean-shaven man in his early sixties who had a habit of nervously clasping and unclasping his hands. Even at this hour of the night, he was dressed in a somber gray pinstripe with a vest and bow tie; a tasteful gold watch chain spanned the vest. Sawyer could envision the dapper little man wearing a soft felt cap and tooling around in a roadster with the top down. His conservative appearance smacked much more of the East Coast than the West, and Sawyer learned quickly in the preliminary conversation that Tiedman had spent a good many years in New York before heading to California. For the first few minutes of their meeting he would only occasionally seek direct eye contact with the FBI agent, usually keeping his watery gray eyes, which were covered with a fragile pair of wire-rimmed spectacles, squarely on the carpeted floor.

"I take it you knew Arthur Lieberman quite well," said Sawyer.

"We attended Harvard together. We both started out at the same banking firm. I was the best man at his wedding, and he at mine. He was one of my oldest and dearest friends."

Sawyer took advantage of the opening. "His marriage ended in divorce, right?"

Tiedman eyed the agent. "That's right," he replied.

Sawyer consulted his notebook. "In fact, that was right about the time he was being considered to head the Fed?"

Tiedman nodded.

"Lousy timing."

"You could say that." Tiedman poured out a glass of water form the carafe on the table next to his chair and took a long drink. His thin lips were dry and chafed.

"I understand the divorce started out being really nasty but was soon enough settled and really didn't affect his nomination. Guess Lieberman lucked out."

Tiedman's eyes blazed. "You want to call that lucky?"

"All I meant was he got the Fed job. I assume that as a close personal friend of Arthur's you probably know more about it than just about anyone." Sawyer looked at Tiedman with frank, questioning eyes.

Tiedman didn't say anything for a full minute, then he let out a deep breath, put his glass down and settled back in his chair. Now he looked directly at Sawyer.

"While it's true that he became chairman of the Fed, it cost Arthur just about everything he had worked for over the years to make his 'nasty' little divorce go away, Mr. Sawyer. It wasn't fair after a career such as his."

"But the chairmanship paid good money. I looked up the salary. A hundred thirty-three thousand six hundred dollars per year. He was much better off than most."

Tiedman laughed. "That may be true, but before Arthur joined the Fed he earned hundreds of millions of dollars. Consequently, he had expensive tastes, and some debt."

"A lot of debt?"

Tiedman's eyes again went to the floor. "Let's just say the debt was somewhat more than he could afford on his Fed salary, despite its relatively large size."

Sawyer let that information sink in while he asked another question. "What can you tell me about Walter Burns?"

Tiedman looked sharply at Sawyer. "What do you want to know?"

"Just general background stuff," Sawyer replied innocently.

Tiedman rubbed at his lip in a distracted manner and eyed Sawyer's notebook. Sawyer caught the glance and abruptly closed the pad. "Off the record."

Tiedman looked resignedly at Sawyer. "I have no doubt Burns will succeed Arthur as chairman. It's quite fitting. He was a follower of Arthur's. However Arthur voted, Walter did too."

"Was that a bad thing?"

"Not usually."

"What does that mean?"

The little man's expression became astonishingly sharp when he focused on the agent's face. "It means that it is never wise to follow placidly along when good judgment should dictate otherwise."

Sawyer leaned back in his chair. "Meaning you didn't agree with Lieberman all the time."

Tiedman was not looking at the agent now. His features betrayed what he was thinking, however. It was clear that he now intensely regretted ever allowing this interview.

"Meaning that members of the Federal Reserve Board are placed on that board to exercise their own minds and their own judgments and not to blindly succumb to arguments that have little basis in reality and could lead to disastrous consequences."

"That's a pretty big statement."

"Well, it's a pretty big job we have."

Sawyer referred to his notes from the conversation with Walter Burns. "Burns said Lieberman took the bull by the horns early on, to get the market's attention, to shake it up. I take it you thought that wasn't such a good idea."

"Ludicrous would be a better term."

"If it was so off-the-wall, why did a majority go along?" Sawyer was a little skeptical.

"There's a phrase that critics of economic forecasting like to use: Give an economist a result you want, and he'll find the numbers to justify it. This entire city is filled with number crunchers who look at the exact same data and interpret it in widely disparate ways on everything from the federal budget deficit to the Social Security surplus."

"Meaning that data can be manipulated."

"Of course it can, depending on who's paying the meter and whose political agenda is being furthered," Tiedman said with asperity. "You've no doubt heard the principle that for every action there is an equal and opposite reaction?" Sawyer nodded. "Well, I'm convinced its genesis is political rather than scientific."

"No disrespect, but could it be they thought your views were wrong?"

"I am not omniscient, Agent Sawyer. However, I have been intimately involved in the financial markets for the last forty years. I have seen up and down markets. I have seen robust economies and ones teetering on collapse. I have seen Fed chairmen take prompt, effective action when confronted with crisis and I have seen others flounder badly, with the result that the economy gets tipped on its head. An ill-advised half-percent increase in the Fed Funds Rate can cost hundreds of thousands of jobs and absolutely devastate whole sectors of the economy. It is an enormous power that must not be exercised lightly. Arthur's zigzagging with the Fed Funds Rate placed every American citizen's economic future in serious jeopardy. I was not wrong."

"I thought you and Lieberman were close. Didn't he ask for your advice?"

Tiedman fingered his coat button nervously. "Arthur had previously sought out my counsel. Often. For a period of about three years he stopped doing that."

"Was that the period during which he played roller-coaster with the rates?"

Tiedman nodded. "I finally concluded, as did others on the board, that Arthur was punching a lazy financial market flush in the face. But that is not the board's mission, it's far too dangerous. I lived through the last stages of the Great Depression. I have no desire to do so again."

"I guess it never occurred to me how much power the board wields."

Tiedman looked sternly at him. "Do you know that when we decide to raise rates we can tell fairly precisely how many businesses will declare bankruptcy, how many people will lose their jobs, how many homes will be foreclosed? We have all that data, neatly bound, carefully studied. To us it's only numbers. We never, officially, look behind those numbers. If we did, I don't think any of us would have the stomach for the job. I know that I wouldn't. Perhaps if we started tracking suicide, murder and other criminal statistics, we would be more understanding of the vast powers that we hold over our fellow citizens."

"Murder? Suicide?" Sawyer looked at him warily.

"Surely you would be the first to admit that money is the root of all evil. Or perhaps more accurately stated, the *lack* of money is the root of all evil."

"Jesus, I never really thought of it that way. You sort of hold the power of . . ."

"God?" Tiedman's eyes sparkled. "Do you know how much money the Fed wire-transfers out to maintain its policies and to insure that the commercial banking system operates smoothly?" Sawyer shook his head. "One trillion dollars per day."

Sawyer sat back, stunned. "That's a lot of money, Charles."

"No, that's a lot of power, Agent Sawyer. We're one of this country's best-kept secrets. Indeed, if average citizens were fully aware of what we can do and have often done in the past, I believe they'd storm the walls and cast us all into dungeons, if not worse. And maybe they would be right."

Sawyer looked down at his notes. "Do you know the dates those rate changes occurred?"

Tiedman retreated from his musings. "Not offhand. An astonishing admission for a banker, but my memory isn't all that good with numbers anymore. I can get you the answer, though."

"I'd appreciate it. Could there have been another reason why Lieberman went nuts with the rates?" Now Sawyer clearly saw the twinge of anxiety mixed with fear in the man's features.

"What do you mean?"

Sawyer leaned back in his chair. "You said it was out of character for him. And then he abruptly returned to normal. Doesn't that sound mysterious to you?"

"I guess I never thought about it in that light. I'm afraid I still do not understand your point."

"Let me put this as clearly as I can. Maybe Lieberman was manipulating the rates against his will."

Tiedman's eyebrows shot up. "How could anyone make Arthur do that?"

"Blackmail," Sawyer said simply. "Any theories?"

Tiedman regrouped and began speaking nervously. "I had heard rumors that Arthur was having an affair, years ago. A woman—"

Sawyer broke in. "I don't buy that and neither do you. Lieberman paid off his wife to avoid a scandal so he could run the Fed, but it wasn't over a woman." Sawyer leaned forward so that his face was within inches of Tiedman's. "What can you tell me about Steven Page?"

Tiedman's face froze, but only for an instant. "Who?"

440

"This might jog your memory." Sawyer reached in his pocket and pulled out the photo Ray Jackson had found in Lieberman's apartment. He held the photo up in front of Tiedman.

Tiedman took the photo in quivering hands. His head bent low, his long brow a sea of creases. However, Sawyer could see the recognition in the man's eyes.

"How long have you known about this?" Sawyer asked quietly.

Tiedman's mouth moved, but no words came out. He finally handed the photo back to Sawyer and took another drink of water. He didn't look at Sawyer when he spoke, which seemed to make the words come a little easier. "I was actually the one who introduced them," was Tiedman's surprising reply. "Steven worked at Fidelity Mutual as a financial analyst. Arthur was still president of the New York Fed at that time. I was introduced to Steven at a financial symposium. Many colleagues whom I respected sang his praises loudly. He was an exceptionally bright young man with some intriguing ideas on the financial markets and the Fed's role in the evolving global economy. He was personable, cultured, attractive: he'd graduated near the top of his college class. I knew that Arthur would find him a welcome addition to his circle of intellectual acquaintances. He and Arthur quickly struck up a friendship." Tiedman faltered.

"A friendship that eventually blossomed into something else?" Sawyer prompted.

Tiedman nodded.

"Were you aware at the time that Lieberman was homosexual, or at least bisexual?"

"I knew that his marriage was troubled. I did not know, at the time, that the trouble stemmed from Arthur's sexual . . . confusion."

441

"He seemed to solve that confusion. He divorced his wife."

"I don't think that was Arthur's idea. I believe Arthur would have been perfectly happy keeping intact at least the facade of a happy heterosexual marriage. I know that more and more people 'come out' these days, but Arthur was an intensely private man and the financial community is very conservative."

"So the missus wanted the divorce. Did she know about Page?"

"His specific identity? No, I don't think so. But I believe she knew Arthur was having an affair, and that it wasn't with a woman. I believe that was why the divorce was so acrimonious and so one-sided. Arthur had to act quickly, lest his wife tell her attorneys, even, about her suspicions. It cost him every penny he had. Arthur only disclosed this information to me as the most personal secret one friend could tell another. And I only tell it to you under those same strict, confidential terms."

"I appreciate that, Charles," Sawyer said. "Only you have to understand if Lieberman was the reason that plane went down, I have to explore every possibility to solve that crime. However, I can promise you that I won't use the information you've just given me unless it directly impacts on my investigation. If it turns out Lieberman's affair is not connected, then no one will ever learn from me what you've just disclosed. Fair enough?"

"Fair enough," Tiedman finally said. "Thank you."

Sawyer noted Tiedman's exhaustion and decided to move forward quickly. "You're familiar with the circumstances of Steven Page's death?"

"I read about it in the paper."

"Did you know that he had tested positive for HIV?"

Tiedman shook his head.

Sawyer sat back. "A couple more questions. Did you know that Lieberman had terminal pancreatic cancer?" Tiedman nodded. "How did he feel about it? Devastated? Hurt?"

Tiedman didn't answer immediately. He sat quietly, his hands clasped in his lap. Then he looked at Sawyer. "Actually, Arthur seemed happy."

"The guy was terminal and he seemed happy?"

"I know it sounds strange, but it's the only way I can describe it. Happy and relieved."

The puzzled FBI agent thanked Tiedman and left, his head swimming with an entirely new set of questions and no way, as yet, to answer them.

FORTY-NINE

Sidney sat alone in the dining car as the train rumbled through the night on its way to New York. While darkened images flew past the windows, she distractedly sipped at a cup of coffee and nibbled on a microwave-warmed muffin. The steady clicking of the train wheels and the car's gentle swaying as it headed up the much-traveled northeast corridor soothed her.

For a good part of the train trip her mind focused on her daughter. It seemed like an eternity since she had held her little girl. Now she had no idea when she would see her again. The only thing keeping her away was the certainty that if she tried to see Amy, she would bring harm to her little girl. She would never do that, not even if it meant never seeing her again. She would call, though, as soon as she got into New York. She wondered how she could explain to her parents the next nightmare that awaited them: the headlines proclaiming their overachieving, cherished daughter a murderer now on the run. She could do nothing to shield them against the onslaught of attention that would be hurtling their way. That attention would find its way to Bell Harbor, Maine, she was sure, but perhaps her parents' trip north would buy them some precious time away from the hideous spotlight.

Sidney knew she had only one shot to unravel whatever it was that had come and blasted her life to hell. That opportunity lay in the information in the hard plastic shell that would soon be speeding its way north as fast as Federal Express could ship it. The disk was all she had. Jason seemed to think it vitally important. If he was wrong? She shuddered and forced her thoughts away from that potential nightmare. She had to trust her husband on that one. She peered out the window as a blur of trees, modest homes with crooked TV antennas and the cracked, ugly cinder blocks of abandoned businesses raced by. She huddled into her coat and lay back in the seat.

As the train rolled into the dark caverns of Penn Station, Sidney stood by the exit door. Her watch proclaimed it was five-thirty in the morning. She didn't really feel tired, although she couldn't remember the last time she had slept. Penn Station was fairly crowded for that hour of the morning. Sidney waited in the cab line and then decided to make a quick phone call before she went to JFK. She planned to dump the gun before leaving for the airport. However, the cold metal gave her a feeling of security she desperately needed right now. She still had not decided where she was traveling, but at least the cab ride to the airport would give her time to think of a destination.

On her way to the pay phone, she grabbed a copy of the *Washington Post* and scanned the headlines. Nothing about the murders had appeared yet; however, the bodies could have been found and the reporters might simply not have had time to file their stories before deadline. If her two former partners hadn't been found yet, it would not be long now. The parking garage opened to the public at seven A.M. but it could be accessed at any time by tenants of the building.

She dialed her parents' number in Bell Harbor. An automated message greeted her and announced that the number was not in service. She groaned as she suddenly remembered why. Her parents always had the phone turned off during the winter. Her father had probably forgotten to turn the service back on. He would certainly do so once he got up there. Since it wasn't back on, that meant they probably hadn't arrived yet.

Sidney swiftly calculated travel times. When she had been a child, her father would drive all the way through, about thirteen hours, stopping along the way only for food and gas. As he had grown older, though, he had become more patient. Ever since his retirement, he would stop along the way for the night, break the trip up into two days. If they had left early yesterday afternoon, as planned, that would put them in Bell Harbor at about midafternoon today. *If* they had left as planned. It suddenly occurred to Sidney that she had not verified her parents' departure yet. She decided to correct that oversight immediately. The phone rang three times and then the answering machine picked up. She spoke into the phone to let her parents know it was she. They often screened their calls. However, no one picked up the phone. She put the phone receiver back. She would try again from the airport. She checked her watch and decided to make one more phone call. Now that she knew of Paul Brophy's involvement with RTG, something didn't make sense to her. There was only one person she could think of to ask about it. And she had to do it before news of the murders reached the public.

"Kay? It's Sidney Archer."

The voice on the other end of the line was sleepy at first and then wide awake as Kay Vincent sat up in bed. "Sidney?"

"I'm sorry to call so early, but I really need your help on something." Kay didn't answer. "Kay, I know what all the papers have been saying about Jason."

Kay's voice cut her off. "I don't believe any of that stuff, Sidney. Jason could never have been involved in any of that."

Sidney breathed a sigh of relief. "Thank you for saying that, Kay. I was beginning to think I was the only one who hadn't lost the faith."

"Not by a long shot, Sidney. How can I help you?"

Sidney took a moment to calm her nerves, to keep her voice from shaking too much. She eyed a police officer walking down the hallway of the train station. She turned her back to him and hunched against the wall. "Kay, you know Jason never really talked to me about his work."

Kay snorted. "It's no small wonder. It's beaten into our heads here: Everything's one big secret."

"Right. But now secrets don't do me any good. I need to know what Jason was working on the last few months. Were there any big projects he was on?"

Kay shifted the phone to her other ear. Her husband was snoring on the other side of the bed. "Well, you know he was working on organizing the financial records for the CyberCom deal. That took a lot of his time."

"Right, I knew something about that one."

Kay chuckled. "He'd come back from that warehouse looking like he'd just mud-wrestled an alligator, filthy from head to toe. But he kept at it and did a great job. In fact, he really seemed to enjoy it. The other thing he spent a lot of time on was the integration of the company's tape backup system."

"You mean the computer system storing automatic copies of e-mails and documents and such?"

"Right."

"Why did they need an *integration* of the tape backup system?"

"Well, as you probably could've guessed, Quentin Rowe's company had a first-rate system before it was bought out by Triton. But Nathan Gamble and Triton didn't. Between you and me, I don't think Nathan Gamble knows what a tape backup is. Anyway, Jason's job was to integrate Triton's previous backup systems into Quentin's more sophisticated one."

"What exactly would the integration entail?"

"Going through all of Triton's backup files and formatting them into a shape that would be compatible with the new system. E-mails, documents, reports, graphs – anything created on the computer system. He finished that one too. This whole system is now fully integrated."

"Where were the old files kept? At the office?"

"Oh, no. At the storage facility over in Reston. Boxes stacked ten high. Same place where the financial records were stored. Jason spent a lot of time there."

"Who authorized those projects?"

"Quentin Rowe."

"Not Nathan Gamble?"

"I don't think he even knew about it initially. But he does now."

"How can you be sure?"

"Because Jason got an e-mail from Nathan Gamble commending him on the job he had done."

"Really? That doesn't sound like Nathan Gamble."

"Yeah, it surprised me too. But he did."

"I suppose you don't recall the date of that e-mail, do you?"

"Actually, I do, for a terrible reason."

"What do you mean?"

Kay Vincent sighed deeply. "It was the day of the plane crash."

Sidney jerked upright. "You're sure?"

"There was no way I could forget that, Sid."

"But Nathan Gamble was in New York on that

day. I was there with him."

"Oh, that doesn't matter. He has his secretary send out his e-mails on a preset schedule regardless of whether he's in the office or not."

That didn't make any sense to Sidney. "Kay, I suppose there's been no more news on the CyberCom deal, has there? The records issue is still hanging things up?"

"What records issue?"

"Gamble didn't want to turn over the financial records to CyberCom."

"I don't know anything about that. I do know that the financial records have already been turned over to CyberCom."

"What?" Sidney almost screamed out the word. "Did any attorneys at Tyler, Stone look them over first?"

"I don't know about that."

"When did they go out?"

"Ironically, same day as Nathan Gamble sent Jason that e-mail."

Sidney's head was spinning. "The day of the plane crash? You're absolutely sure of that?"

"I'm real good friends with one of the mail-room clerks. They recruited him to help transport the records to the copy department and then he helped deliver them to CyberCom. Why? Is that important for some reason?"

Sidney finally spoke. "I'm not sure if it is or not."

"Oh, well, do you need to know anything else?"

"No, Kay, you've given me plenty to think about." Sidney thanked her, hung up the phone and headed for the cab stands.

Kenneth Scales looked down at the message he was holding in his hands, his eyes narrowing. The information on the disk was encrypted. They needed

449

the password. He looked over at the one individual who they now knew had to be the recipient of that precious e-mail. Jason wouldn't have sent the disk to his wife without sending the password as well. That had to be the e-mail message Jason had sent from the warehouse. The password. Sidney stood in the cab line outside Penn Station. He should have just taken care of her in the limo. It was neither his practice nor to his liking to leave anyone alive. But orders were orders. At least she had been kept on a short leash until they knew where the e-mail had gone. Now he had marching instructions he could truly sink his deadly blade in. He moved forward.

When Sidney's cab pulled up, she caught a reflection in the window of the vehicle. The man was only focused on her for an instant, but with her nerves set on high, it was long enough. She whirled around and their eyes locked for one terrifying moment. The same devilish eyes from the limo. Scales cursed and raced forward. Sidney jumped in the cab and it roared off. Scales pushed several people waiting ahead of him in line aside, threw the protesting cab stand attendant to the pavement and leaped into the next available cab. It sped after Sidney.

Sidney looked behind her. Through the darkness and driving sleet she couldn't make out much. However, traffic was relatively light at this time of the morning and she saw a pair of headlights swiftly approaching. She turned back around. "I know this is going to sound crazy, but we're being followed." She gave the driver another destination. He made a hard left, then a sharp right and roared down an empty side street and then back out on to Fifth Avenue.

Sidney's cab pulled to a stop in front of a skyscraper. She jumped out and raced toward the entrance, pulling something out of her purse as she did so. She stuck the access card into the slot in the wall and the door clicked open. She went inside, pulling the door closed behind her.

The security guard at the granite console in the lobby looked up sleepily. Sidney dug once more in her bag and produced her Tyler, Stone ID card. The guard nodded and slumped back in his chair. Sidney glanced back once more as she hit the elevator button. Only one elevator car was activated this early in the morning. The second cab screeched to a stop in front of the building and a man jumped out and raced over to the glass doors and pounded on them. Sidney watched as the guard got up from his chair.

Sidney called to him. "I think that man was following me. He might be a nut. Please be careful."

The guard eyed her for a minute and then nodded. He looked back over at the doorway. One hand slipped down to the pistol in his holster as he strode over to the doorway. Sidney glanced back once more before she got on the elevator. The guard was looking up and down the street. Sidney breathed a sigh of relief and got on the elevator, hitting the button for the twenty-third floor. Moments later she entered the darkened Tyler, Stone suite and hurried into an office. She hit a light, pulled out her address book, consulted a phone number and dialed.

She was calling her parents' longtime neighbor and family friend, seventy-year-old Ruth Childs. Ruth answered the phone on the first ring, and from her brisk tone it was clear, despite it being a little after six in the morning, that she had been up for a while. Ruth tenderly commiserated with Sidney over her recent loss and then, in response to Sidney's query, reported that the Pattersons and Amy had left yesterday around two o'clock after hastily packing

451

for their trip. She knew Bell Harbor was the destination, but that was all.

"I saw your father put his shotgun case in the trunk, Sidney," Ruth said provocatively.

"I wonder why," was Sidney's weak response. She was about to say good-bye when Ruth said something that made Sidney's heart skip a beat.

"I have to admit I was kind of worried the night before they left. There was a car driving by at all hours. I don't sleep much, and when I do, it doesn't take much to wake me up. It's a quiet neighborhood, you know that, nothing out here unless you're going to see someone for a visit. The car was back yesterday morning."

"Did you see anyone in the car?" Sidney's voice was trembling.

"No, my eyes aren't what they used to be, even with trifocals."

"Is the car still there?"

"Oh, no. It left right after your parents did. Good riddance, I say. I've got my baseball bat by the door, though. Just let somebody try to break in my house. They'll wish they hadn't."

Before hanging up, Sidney told Ruth Childs to be careful and to call the police if the car showed up again, which Sidney was certain it wouldn't. The car was far away from Hanover, Virginia. It was, she was almost positive, on its way to Bell Harbor, Maine. And now, so was she.

She hung up the phone and turned to leave. That's when she heard the ding of the elevator car arriving at the floor she was on. She didn't stop to wonder who might be arriving this early. She immediately assumed the worst. She pulled out the .32 revolver and ran out of the office in the opposite direction from the elevator. At least she had the advantage of knowing the office layout.

Flying feet behind her confirmed her worst suspicions. She ran as hard as she could, her purse flapping against her side. She could hear the person's breath as he turned on to the darkened corridor she was on. He drew closer. She ran faster than she had since her college basketball days, but it clearly wasn't going to be fast enough. She would have to try a different tactic. She rounded a corner, stopped, spun around and knelt down in a shooting stance, the revolver pointed straight ahead. The man, charging hard, hurtled around the corner and stopped dead barely two feet from her. She glanced at the knife in his hand, the blood still gleaming on its blade. His body seemed to tense for an all-out attack. As if sensing that, Sidney sent a round sailing just past his left temple.

"The next one hits your brain." Sidney stood up, her eyes glued to his face, and motioned for him to drop the knife, which he did. "Move," she barked, pointing behind him with the gun. She backed him down the hallway until they reached a metal door.

"Open it."

The man's eyes bore into her. Even with the gun pointed right at his head, she felt like a kid with a slender stick confronting a rabid dog. He opened the door wide and looked inside. The lights automatically came on. It was the copy room, a large operation with massive machines, stacks of paper and all the other mundane items required by a busy law firm. She motioned through the doorway to another door at the far end of the copier room. "In there." He moved through the doorway. Sidney caught the door and held it open as she watched him move across the room. He looked back at her as he opened the other door. It was a storage closet for office supplies.

"That door opens, you're dead." Holding the door

open with her shoulder, the gun still trained directly on him, she reached across to a counter just inside the room and made a show of picking up a telephone. As soon as the man closed the door, Sidney put down the phone, quietly closed the copier room door and raced down he hallway to the elevators. She hit the button and the door immediately opened. Thank God it had remained on the twenty-third floor. She jumped on and pushed the button for the first floor, all the time listening for the man coming for her. She kept the revolver trained on the opening, but the office remained quiet. As soon as she reached the first floor, she hit all the buttons up to the twenty-third floor and jumped off the elevator. She let out her breath and allowed herself a small smile. It quickly turned to horror as she rounded the corner and almost fell over the security guard's body. Forcing herself not to scream, she raced out of the building and down the street.

It was seven-fifteen in the morning and Lee Sawyer had just closed his eyes when the phone rang. He flopped a big hand over and picked it up.

"Yeah?"

"Lee?"

Sawyer's groggy brain snapped into high gear and he sat up. "Sidney?"

"I don't have much time."

"Where are you?"

"Just listen!" She was once again standing at a pay phone in Penn Station.

He switched the phone to his other ear as he threw the bedcovers off. "Okay, I'm listening."

"A man just tried to kill me."

"Who? Where?" Sawyer sputtered as he grabbed a pair of pants off the bed and started to shove them on.

454

"I don't know who he is."

"Are you okay?" he asked anxiously.

Sidney looked around at the crowded train station. A number of New York's finest were in attendance. Problem was, they were the enemy now too. "Yes."

Sawyer let out a deep breath. "Okay, what's going on?"

"Jason sent an e-mail to our house after the plane crash. There was a password in that e-mail."

"What?" Sawyer stated to sputter again. "Jesus Christ, an e-mail, you said?" Sawyer's face was now blood-red. He stamped around the room, throwing on a shirt, socks and shoes while holding the cordless phone.

"I don't have time to tell you how I eventually received the e-mail, only that I now have it."

With a massive effort at self-control, Sawyer managed to calm down. "Well, what the hell did it say?"

From the pocket of her coat, Sidney pulled out the single sheet of paper containing the e-mail. "Do you have something to write with?"

"Hold on."

Sawyer ran into the kitchen and snatched a piece of paper and pen from a drawer. "Go ahead. But make sure you give it to me exactly as it appears."

Sidney did so, including the absence of spaces between certain words and the decimal points segregating portions of the password exactly as they appeared on the printed page she was holding. Sawyer stared down at what he had written. He went back through it again with her for accuracy.

"Do you have any idea what this message means, Sidney?"

"I haven't had much time to focus on it. I know that Jason said it was all wrong, and I believe him. It is all wrong."

"But what about this disk? Do you know what's on it?" He quickly read the message again. "Did you get it in the mail?"

Sidney hesitated and then said, "I haven't yet."

"Is the password for the disk? Is it an encrypted file?"

"I didn't know you were such a computer expert."

"I'm just full of surprises."

"Yes, I believe it is."

"When do you expect to get it?"

"I'm not sure. Look, I have to go."

"Wait a minute, the guy who tried to kill you. What'd he look like?"

She gave him a description. The thought of the maniacal blue eyes made her shudder. Sawyer wrote it down. "I'll run it through the system and see what comes up." He jolted upright. "Wait a minute, I've got you under surveillance. What the hell happened to my guys? Aren't you at your house?"

Sidney swallowed hard. "I'm not exactly under surveillance right now. At least not by your people. And no, I'm not at my house."

"Then would you mind telling me where you are?"

"I've got to go."

"The hell you do. Some creep just tried to punch your clock, my guys are nowhere on the scene. I want to know what's going on," he raged.

"Lee?"

He calmed down slightly. "What?" he said gruffly.

"Whatever happens, whatever you encounter, I want you to know that I haven't done anything wrong. Nothing." She choked back some tears and added softly, "Please believe that."

"What are you talking about? What the hell's that supposed to mean?"

"Good-bye."

456

"No! Wait!" The phone clicked in his ear and he angrily slammed it down. He looked at the message and then put it down on the table next to the phone. He bent over. His knees felt wobbly, his stomach more upset than normal. He went into the bathroom and gulped down some liquid Maalox. Wiping his mouth with the back of his hand, he returned to the kitchen, picked up the piece of paper he had written the e-mail down on and sat down at the small table. He silently mouthed the words as he read them. *Watch your typing*. The first portion of the message seemed to suggest that Archer had sent the message to the wrong person. Sawyer read the recipient's name and then the sender's. Sidney said Jason had sent the e-mail to their house. ArchieJW2. That had to be Jason Archer's e-mail name, his last name and initials. Then ArchieKW2 was the person the message had initially gone to. Jason Archer had hit the *K* instead of the *J*, that seemed clear enough. ArchieKW2 had sent the message back to the *sender* with a message about the mistake, but in doing so had actually delivered it to the intended *destination:* Sidney Archer.

The reference to the Seattle warehouse made sense. Jason had evidently run into some serious trouble with whomever he was meeting. The exchange had somehow gone bad. *All wrong?* Obviously, Sidney had pounced on it as proof of her husband's innocence. Sawyer wasn't so sure about that. *All backwards?* that seemed to be an awkward phrase. Next, Sawyer stared at the password. Jesus, Jason was truly a brain if he could pull that long a password off the top of his head. Sawyer could make no sense out of it. He squinted and parked his face closer to the paper. Jason obviously had not had the opportunity to finish the message.

Sawyer stretched his kinked neck from side to side

and leaned back in his chair. The disk. They had to get the disk. Or, more accurately, Sidney Archer would have to get it. His thoughts were interrupted by the ringing phone. Certain it was Sidney calling back, he snatched it up.

"Yeah?"

"Lee, it's Frank."

"Christ, Frank, can't you ever call during normal business hours?"

"It's bad, Lee. Real bad. Law firm of Tyler, Stone. The underground garage."

"What is it?"

"Triple homicide. You better get down here."

Sawyer put the phone down. Sidney's last words to him had just taken on real meaning. *Sonofabitch!*

The street leading into the underground parking garage was a sea of red and blue lights as police and emergency vehicles parked everywhere. Sawyer and Jackson flashed their badges at the security line. A concerned-looking Frank Hardy met them just inside the entrance and led them to the lowest level of the garage, four stories underground, where the temperature in the garage was well below freezing.

"Looks like the murders took place very early this morning, so the trail's reasonably fresh. The bodies are in good shape, too, except for some extra holes in them," Hardy said.

"How did you find out about it, Frank?"

"The firm's managing partner, Henry Wharton, was notified by the police in Florida, where he's on firm business. He called Nathan Gamble; Gamble, in turn, immediately informed me."

"So I take it whoever got bumped was affiliated with the law firm?" Sawyer asked.

"You can see for yourself, Lee. Everybody's still here. But let's say Triton has a particular interest in these murders. That's why Wharton called Gamble so fast. We also just found out that the security guard at Tyler, Stone's office in New York was murdered early this morning."

Sawyer stared at him. "New York?"

Hardy nodded.

"Anything else on it?"

"Not yet. But there were reports of a woman running out of the building about an hour before the body was discovered."

Sawyer digested this new development as the men walked through the throng of police and forensics personnel to the driver's side of the sleek limo. Both doors were open. Sawyer observed the print technicians completing their dusting of the limo's exterior. A crime scene photographer was snapping away, while another technician was filming the area with a video camera. The medical examiner, a middle-aged man wearing a white dress shirt with shirtsleeves rolled up, tie tucked inside the shirt, and sporting plastic gloves and a surgical mask, was consulting with two men wearing dark blue trench coats. Then the two men walked over to join Hardy and the FBI agents.

Hardy introduced Sawyer and Jackson to Royce and Holman, a pair of D.C. homicide detectives. "I've briefed them on the bureau's interest in the case, Lee."

"Who found the bodies?" Jackson asked Royce.

"Accountant who worked in the building. Arrived a little before six. His parking space is down here. He thought it was odd to see a limo here at this hour, particularly since it was blocking a bunch of other parking spaces. The glass on the vehicle is all tinted, as you can see. He tapped on the door, got no response. So he opened the passenger door. Bad decision. I think he's still upstairs puking. At least he managed to call it in."

The men moved over to the limo. Hardy motioned for the FBI agents to have a look. After peering inside the front and back, Sawyer looked up at Hardy. "Guy on the floor looks familiar."

"He should be: Paul Brophy."

Sawyer looked over at Jackson.

"Gentleman in the backseat with the third eye is Philip Goldman," Hardy stated.

"RTG's counsel," Jackson said.

Hardy nodded. "Victim in the front seat is James Parker, an employee of the local RTG subsidiary; the limo is registered to RTG, by the way."

"Hence, Triton's interest in the case," Sawyer said.

"You got it," Hardy said.

Sawyer leaned back in the limo and studied the wound on Goldman's forehead before scanning Brophy's body. Over his shoulder, Hardy continued, his tone calm and methodical. He and Sawyer had worked innumerable homicides together. At least here all body parts were intact. They had viewed many where that was not the case. "All three died from gunshot wounds. Appears to be heavy-caliber, fired from close proximity. Parker's wound is a contact one. Brophy's looked to be a near-contact, the little I was able to see of it. Goldman probably bought it from about three feet, maybe more, considering the burn pattern on the forehead."

Sawyer nodded in agreement. "So the shooter may have been in the front seat. Took out the driver first, Brophy next, and then Goldman last," he ventured.

Hardy didn't look convinced. "Maybe, although the killer could have been sitting next to Brophy, facing Goldman. Popped Parker through the partition opening, shot Brophy and then Goldman, or vice versa. We'll have to wait for the autopsy to get the exact trajectory of the shots. That may give us a better idea of the order." He paused and then added, "Along with some other residue." The interior of the limo was indeed a grisly sight.

"Got an approximate time of death yet?" Jackson asked.

Royce checked his notes. "Rigor hasn't peaked yet – far from it, actually. Lividity isn't fixed either. They're all in similar stages of postmortem, so it looks like they all bought it at roughly the same time. Coupled with the body temp. ME just gave me a preliminary of four to six hours."

Sawyer checked his watch. "Eight-thirty now. So anywhere between two and four this morning."

Royce nodded.

Jackson shivered as a cold draft swept down on them when the elevator doors opened to emit additional police. Sawyer grimaced as he watched clouds of breath floating everywhere. Hardy smiled. "I know what you're thinking, Lee. Nobody screwed with the air-conditioning like with your last corpse, but as cold as it is down here—"

"I'm not sure how accurate that time of death is going to be," Sawyer finished for him. "And I feel pretty certain that every minute we're off is gonna be real significant."

"Actually, we've got an exact time of entry for the limo into the garage, Agent Sawyer," Royce volunteered. "Access is limited to those having valid key cards. The garage's security system records who enters by the individual card used to access the premises. Goldman's card was entered at one-forty-five this morning."

"So he wouldn't have been here long before it all went down," Jackson ventured. "At least it gives us a benchmark."

Sawyer didn't answer. He rubbed his jaw as his eyes continued to dart around the crime scene. "Weapon?"

461

Detective Holman pulled out an object enclosed in a large sealed plastic bag. "One of the uniforms found this in a nearby sewer drain. Luckily it had gotten hung up on some debris lodged in there or we might never have found it." He handed the baggie to Sawyer. "Smith & Wesson nine-millimeter. Hydra-Shok rounds. Serial numbers intact. Shouldn't be much trouble tracing it. Three rounds short of a full clip. And we've preliminarily accounted for a total of three wounds in the victims." All of the men could easily see the traces of blood on the pistol, which was natural enough if it had been used to perpetrate a contact wound. "Sure looks to be the murder weapon," Holman continued. "Shooter picked up the ejected shell casings, but the slugs appear to still be in all the victims, so we'll get a definitive match from ballistics depending on projectile deformity."

Even before he was handed the pistol, Sawyer had already noted it. So had Jackson. They looked at each other with a sinking feeling: the cracked grip.

Hardy noticed the exchange. "You got something?"

Sawyer sighed. "Shit," was all he could think to say at the moment. He shoved his hands deep in his pockets, looked over at the limo and then back at the murder weapon. "I'm ninety-nine percent sure this gun belongs to Sidney Archer, Frank."

"What was that name again?" Both homicide detectives piped in almost simultaneously.

Sawyer filled the detective in on Sidney's identity and connection to the law firm.

"Right, the paper ran a story on her and her husband. I knew the name was familiar. That explains a hell of a lot," Royce said.

"How's that?" Jackson asked.

Royce consulted his notebook. "The front entrance to the building also tracks who enters and leaves after hours. One-twenty-one this morning, guess whose security card was entered?"

"Sidney Archer's," Sawyer said with a weary tone.

"Bingo. Damn, husband *and* wife. Nice couple. We'll get her, though. Bodies are fresh, not too much of a head start." Royce sounded confident. "We've already lifted a slew of partials from the limo. We'll run them against the dead men for elimination purposes and then focus on the remaining ones."

"I wouldn't be surprised if Archer's prints turned up all over the place," Holman said. He cocked his head at the limo. "Particularly with all the blood in there."

Sawyer turned to the detective. "Got a motive?"

Royce held up the record. "Found this under Brophy. It's already been dusted." The detective hit the play button. They all listened to the tape until it stopped a few minutes later. Sawyer's face flushed.

"That's Jason Archer's voice," Hardy said. "Know it well." He shook his head. "Now if we just had a body to go along with the voice."

"And that's Sidney's voice," Jackson added. He looked over at his partner, who was leaning against a support column, looking miserable.

Sawyer assimilated the new information and plugged it into the mutating landscape this case had become. Brophy had taped the conversation the morning they had gone to interview Sidney. That's why the sonofabitch had looked so pleased with himself. That also explained his trip to New Orleans and his little frolic and detour through Sidney's hotel room. Sawyer grimaced. He never would have disclosed voluntarily what Sidney had told him about the phone call. Only now the secret was out. She had lied to the FBI. Even if Sawyer testified – which he would do in a minute – that she had later disclosed to him the details of the phone call, she had still made plans to aid and abet a fugitive. Now she was looking at throw-away-the-key prison time. Amy Archer's tiny face intruded on his thoughts and his shoulders slumped even farther.

As Royce and Holman drifted away to continue their investigation, Hardy walked over to Sawyer. "You want my two cents?"

Sawyer nodded. Jackson joined them.

"I probably know a couple things that you don't. One being that Tyler, Stone was terminating Sidney Archer," Hardy said.

"Okay." Sawyer's eyes remained fixed on Hardy.

"Ironically, the letter of termination was found on Goldman's person. It could've gone down like this: Archer comes down to the office on her own for some reason. Maybe it's innocent, maybe it's not. She meets up with Goldman and Brophy, either by accident or arrangement. Goldman probably made Sidney Archer very familiar with the contents of the termination letter, and then they spring the tape on her. That's pretty heavy blackmail material."

"I agree the tape is very damaging, but what would they blackmail her for?" Sawyer's eyes were still fixed on his friend.

"Like I told you before, up until the plane crash, Sidney Archer was lead counsel on the CyberCom deal. She was privy to confidential information. Information that RTG would be dying to get their hands on. The price for that information is the tape. She either gives them the deal info or she goes to prison. The firm is terminating her anyway. What the hell does she care?"

Sawyer looked confused. "But I thought her husband had delivered that information to RTG already. The exchange on the videotape."

"Deals change, Lee. I know for a fact that since

Jason Archer's disappearance the terms of Triton's offer for CyberCom have changed. What Jason gave them was old news. They needed fresh stuff. Ironically, what the husband couldn't give them, the wife could."

"Sounds like they would've made a deal, then. So how does the killing part come in, Frank? Just because it was her gun doesn't mean she fired it." Sawyer was now being argumentative.

Hardy ignored the tone, continuing on with his analysis. "Maybe they couldn't agree to terms. Maybe things turned ugly. Maybe they decided the best way was to get the information they needed and then dispose of her. Maybe that's why they ended up in the limo. Parker was carrying a gun; it was still in his holster, unfired. There might have been a struggle. She pulls her piece, fires and kills one of them in self-defence. Horrified, she decides not to leave any witnesses."

Sawyer was shaking his head vigorously. "Three able-bodied men against one woman? Doesn't make sense that the situation would've gotten out of their control. Assuming she was in the limo, I can't believe she would've been able to kill all three and just walk away."

"Maybe she didn't just walk away, Lee. She might've been wounded, for all we know."

Sawyer looked at the concrete floor beside the limo. There were several bloodstains, but none readily visible farther away from the limo. Inconclusive at best, but Hardy's scenario was plausible.

"So, she kills all three and then leaves without the tape. Why?"

Hardy shrugged. "Tape was found under Brophy. The guy was big, at least two hundred pounds of literally dead weight. It took two heavyweight cops to move the body when they were trying to I.D. him.

That's when they spotted the tape. The simple answer may be that she physically couldn't get to it. Or maybe she didn't know it was under there. From the looks of it, it fell out of his pocket when he went down. Then she panicked and just ran. She tosses the gun in the sewer and gets the hell out of Dodge. How many times have we both seen that happen?"

Jackson looked at Sawyer. "Makes sense, Lee."

Sawyer, however, was doubtful. He walked over to Detective Royce, who was signing off on some paperwork.

"You mind if I call some of our forensics people in to check out a few things?"

"Hell, be my guest. I rarely turn down an assist from the FBI. You guys got all those federal dollars. Us? We're lucky if we have gas in the cars."

"I'd like to run a few tests on the interior of the limo. I'll have my team here within twenty minutes. I'd like them to do the exam with the bodies still in place. Then I'd like to do a more thorough search – minus the bodies, of course – back at the lab. Tow's on us."

Royce considered the request for a moment and then said, "I'll get the necessary paperwork in order." He looked suspiciously at Sawyer. "Look, I'm always glad of the bureau's help, but this *is* our jurisdiction. I'd be more than a little ticked to see credit misplaced when this one gets solved. You hear what I'm saying?"

"Loud and clear, Detective Royce. It's your case. Whatever we learn is yours to use in solving the crime. I sincerely hope it earns you a promotion and a nice raise."

"You *and* my wife."

"Can I ask a favour?"

"You can always ask." Royce replied.

"You mind having one of your techs get gunshot

residue samples from each of the three corpses? We're running out of time on that one. I can have my people analyze the samples."

"You think one of them might have fired the gun?" Royce looked highly doubtful.

"Maybe, maybe not. We can pretty much tell one way or another, though."

Royce shrugged and motioned for one of his techs to come over. After instructing her on what was wanted, they watched as she lugged over a battered, bulky crime scene kit, opened it and began preparations to perform a gunshot residue test, a GSR. However, time was running out: samples optimally had to be collected within six hours of the gun having been fired, and Sawyer was afraid they were about to miss that deadline.

The tech dipped a number of cotton swabs in a diluted nitric acid solution. Separate swabs were rubbed over the front and back of each corpse's hands. If any of them had fired a gun recently, then testing would reveal deposits of barium and antimony, primer charge components used in the manufacture of virtually all ammo. It wasn't conclusive. If a positive result came back, it wouldn't necessarily mean any of them had fired the murder weapon, only *some* firearm within the last six hours. In addition, they could have merely handled the firearm after it had been fired – for instance, in a struggle – and gotten the residue from the exterior of the weapon after it had just been fired. But a positive GSR result could conceivably help Sidney Archer's cause, Sawyer figured. Even though all the evidence seemingly pointed to her involvement in the homicides, Sawyer was dead certain she hadn't pulled the trigger.

"One more favor?" Sawyer asked Detective Royce. Royce's eyebrows shot up. "I'd like a copy of that tape."

"Sure. Whatever."

Sawyer rode the elevator back up to the lobby, walked to his car and phoned in for the FBI's forensics team. While he waited for them to arrive, one thought beat relentlessly through Sawyer's head. *Where the hell was Sidney Archer?*

FIFTY

Usually eschewing any except the most modest makeup, Sidney now took great pains to stencil in her face with considerable detail, holding up her compact as she stood in the stall in the women's rest room at Penn Station. She had concluded that the man pursuing her wouldn't have figured her to come back here. She then put on a tan leather cowboy hat, pulling the brim down low over her forehead. With enough artificial color on her face to almost qualify for hooker status and her bloody clothes in a shopping bag destined for a Dumpster, she walked out of the rest room attired in an assortment of garments she had spent the better part of the day acquiring: tight stone-washed blue jeans, pointy beige cowboy boots, thick white cotton shirt and a heavily insulated black leather bomber jacket. She looked nothing like the conservative Washington, D.C., attorney she had recently been and whom the police would soon be hunting down for murder. She made certain the .32 was carefully hidden away in an inner pocket. New York's gun laws were among the stiffest in the country.

A half-hour ride northeast on the commuter train took her to Stamford, Connecticut, one of a string of bedroom communities feeding the working New Yorker's desire to live outside the hyperkinetic metropolis. A taxicab ride of twenty minutes took her to a lovely white brick home with black shutters nestled in a quiet neighborhood of similarly high-priced residences. The name PATTERSON was stenciled on the mailbox. Sidney paid the cabdriver, but instead of going to the front door she walked around back to the garage area. Next to the garage door hung a large, ornate wooden bird feeder. Sidney looked around and then stuck her hand into the feed, pushing through the rough particles until she got to the bottom of the feeder. She pulled out the set of keys buried there, went over to the back door, put a key in the lock and the door opened. Her brother, Kenny, and his family were in France. He was incredibly bright, ran a very successful independent publishing business, but was also absent-minded as hell. He had locked himself out of every home he had ever owned, hence the keys in the bird feeder, a fact well known to every member of his family.

The home was old, solidly built and beautifully decorated, with large rooms and comfortable furnishings. Sidney did not have time to enjoy the surroundings. She went into a small study. Against one wall was a large enclosed oak cabinet. Using another key from the key ring, Sidney opened the heavy double doors and viewed the contents of the cabinet: an impressive array of shotguns and pistols loomed in front of her. She settled on a Winchester 1300 Defender. The twelve-gauge shotgun was relatively light, weighing in under seven pounds. It chambered three-inch Magnum shells that would stop anything on two legs, and, perhaps most important, sported an eight-shot magazine. She put several boxes of Magnum shells into one of her brother's ammo bags she had pulled from a drawer in the cabinet. Next she looked over the pistols hanging on special hooks mounted into the wall of the cabinet next to the shotgun collection. She had little confidence in the stopping force of the .32. She picked up several of the pistols, testing them for weight and comfort. Then she smiled as her hand closed around an old familiar: a Smith & Wesson Slim Nine complete with unblemished grip. She grabbed the pistol and a box of 9mm ammo, stuffed it in the same bag with the shotgun loads and locked the cabinet back up. Snagging a pair of binoculars off another shelf, Sidney left the room.

She ran upstairs to the master bedroom and spent several minutes going through her sister-in-law's clothing. Soon Sidney had assembled a suitcase full of warm clothing and footwear. A thought suddenly struck her. She switched on the small TV in the bedroom. She channel-surfed until she found an all-news station. The top story of the day was being recounted, and though she had been expecting it, her heart sank when her face appeared on the screen next to a picture of the limo. The news story was brief but devastating in portraying her inescapable guilt. Sidney received another shock as the screen split into two and she was joined by a photo of Jason. He looked tired in the photo, which she instantly recognized as the one on his Triton security badge. Apparently the media were finding the husband-wife master criminal angle an engaging one. Sidney studied her own face on the screen. She too looked tired, her hair plastered down on either side of her head. She and Jason looked . . . guilty, she concluded. Even if they weren't. But right now, most of the country would believe them to be villains, a modern-day Bonnie and Clyde.

She rose on unsteady legs and on a sudden impulse went into the bathroom, where she stripped off her clothes and climbed in the shower. The sight of the limo had reminded her that she still carried vestiges on her person of those horrible few moments. She had closed and locked the bathroom door upon entering. Keeping the shower curtain wide open, she never left her back exposed to the door. The loaded .32 revolver lay within easy reach. The hot water took the chill off her bones. By accident she glimpsed her exhausted, gaunt face in the small mirror affixed to the shower wall and shuddered at the sight. She felt tired and old. Emotionally and mentally spent, her body was giving way on her. She could feel the physical decline inch by miserable inch. Then she gritted her teeth and slapped herself in the face. She couldn't give up now. She was an army of one, but a damned determined one. She had Amy. That was something no one would ever take away from her.

Finished with her shower, she dressed warmly and raced to the mudroom, where she grabbed a heavy-duty flashlight off a hook. It had suddenly occurred to her that the police would be checking with all of her family and friends. She carried everything out to the garage, where she eyed the dark blue Land Rover Discovery, one of the sturdiest vehicles ever built. She put her hand under the left fender and pulled out a set of car keys. Her brother really was something. She turned off the sophisticated car security system by punching the tiny button on the car key, slightly wincing at the weird birdlike sound made by the deactivation. She was careful to place the shotgun on the floorboard of the backseat with a heavy blanket over it. The pistols were placed in the ammo bag, which was shoved under the front seat.

The V-8 engine roared to life. Sidney hit the door opener that was clipped to the visor and backed the Land Rover out of the garage. Carefully searching the street for any people or vehicles and finding none, Sidney eased the two-ton truck out of the driveway and on to the road, rapidly gathering speed as she left the quiet Stamford neighborhood.

Within twenty minutes she had reached Interstate 95. Traffic was heavy and it took her a while before she left Connecticut behind. She sliced her way through Rhode Island and made the loop around Boston by one in the morning. The Land Rover was equipped with a cellular phone; however, after her informative talk with Jeff Fisher, Sidney was reluctant to use it. Besides, who would she call? She stopped once, in New Hampshire, to grab some coffee and a candy bar and to fill the gas tank. The snow was now coming down full-tilt, but the Land Rover easily plowed through it, and the flapping sound of the windshield wipers at least was keeping her awake. By three in the morning, however, she was nodding off at the wheel so frequently that she had to pull over finally at a truck stop. She wedged the Land Rover in between two Peterbilt OTR semis, locked the doors, slid into the backseat, gripped the loaded 9mm with one hand and fell asleep. The sun was well up by the time she awoke. She grabbed a quick breakfast at the truck stop and within a few hours was well past Portsmouth, Maine. Two hours later she saw the exit she was seeking and turned off the highway. She was now on U.S. Route 1. At this time of the year, Sidney had the road pretty much to herself.

In the blur of heavy snow she passed the small sign announcing her arrival into the town of Bell Harbor, population, 1,650. While she was growing up, her family had spent many wonderful summers in the peaceful town: private, wide beaches, ice-cream sundaes and juicy sandwiches at the innumerable eateries in the resort town, a show at the town's very own playhouse, long bike rides and walks along Granite Point, where one could observe, up close, the ominous power of the Atlantic on a windy afternoon. She and Jason had planned one day to buy a beach house near her parents. They both had looked forward to spending summers up here, watching Amy run along the beach and dig pools in the sand much as Sidney had done twenty-five years before. It was a nice thought. She hoped it was still capable of becoming reality. Right now none of it seemed even remotely possible.

Sidney made her way toward the ocean, finally turning south on to Beach Street, where she slowed down. Her parents' house was a large, two-story affair of gray weathered board with dormer windows and a deck running the width of the house on both the upper-level ocean side and the street side. A garage occupied the basement level of the house. The ocean wind funneling in between the close-together beach houses managed to rock even the tanklike Land Rover. Sidney could not remember ever being in Maine at this time of year. They sky looked particularly unfriendly. When she glimpsed the endless darkness of the Atlantic, it occurred to her that she had never seen snow falling into the ocean before.

She slowed down slightly as her parents' house came into view. All of the other beach homes on the street were uninhabited. In winter, Bell Harbor was akin to a ghost town. Added to that, the Bell Harbor Police Department numbered all of one during off-season months. If the man who had calmly killed in a stretch limo in Washington and tracked her to New York decided to come after her again, he would be more than a match for Bell Harbor's finest of one. She grabbed the ammo bag from under the seat and put a clip in her 9mm. She pulled into her parents' snow-covered drive and got out. There was no sign that her parents had arrived. They must have stopped along the way because of the weather. She pulled the Land Rover into the garage and shut the door. She unloaded it and carried the items up the interior stairs leading from the garage to the house.

She had no way of knowing that the heavy snow had covered up very recent tire tracks in her parents' yard. Nor did she venture into the back bedroom, where numerous pieces of luggage were neatly stacked. As she entered the kitchen, she couldn't see the car passing slowly by the house and then continuing on.

The interior of the FBI testing facility was going full steam. The white-coated FBI technician walked around the exterior of the limo, motioning Sawyer and Jackson to follow her. The left-side rear passenger door was open. Fortunately, the limo's recent occupants had been since transported to the morgue. Set up next to the limo was a PC with a screen a full twenty-one inches across. The tech stepped in front of it and began keying in commands as she was speaking. Wide of hip, with lovely olive skin and a mouth that showed many smile lines, Liz Martin was one of the bureau's best and hardest-working lab rats.

"Before we physically removed any trace, we hit the entire interior, both front and back, with the Luma-lite, as you requested, Lee. We found some things of interest. We also videotaped the interior of the vehicle while we were conducting the exam and fed that video into the system. Makes it a lot easier for you to follow along." She handed each of the two agents a pair of goggles while she donned a pair herself. "Welcome to the theater; these are for your viewing pleasure." She smiled. "Actually, they block out different wavelengths that may have occurred during the exam and which may otherwise obscure what was captured on the film." As she spoke, the screen came alive. They were looking at the inside of the limo. It was very dark, the conditions under which a Luma-lite exam was conducted. Using a powerful laser of particularly high wattage, the test was designed to make a wide range of otherwise invisible items lurking at a crime scene visible.

Liz manipulated a mouse connected to the PC and the two agents watched as a large white arrow made its way across the screen. "We started out using a single light source, no chemicals applied. We were looking for inherent fluorescence, then we moved on to a series of dyes and powders."

"You said you found some items of interest, Liz?" Sawyer's tone was a touch impatient, his eyes glued to the screen even as he asked the question.

"Hard not to in such a contained space as that, considering what happened there." Her eyes flickered briefly over at the limo. As her fingers expertly manipulated the mouse, the white arrow came to rest on what looked to be the rear seat of the limo. Liz hit some additional keys and the area was blocked off on a series of grids appearing on the screen and magnified until it was readily visible. However, being readily discernible to the human eye and being readily identifiable were not the same thing.

Sawyer turned to Liz. "What the hell is that?" It looked like a string of some kind, but magnified and enlarged as it was, it had taken on the thickness of a pencil.

"Simply speaking, a fiber." Liz pressed another key on the computer and the fiber took on a three-dimensional shape. "From the looks of it, I'd say wool, animal, the real thing, not synthetic, gray in color. Sound familiar to either of you?"

Jackson snapped his fingers. "Sidney Archer was wearing a blazer that morning. It was gray."

Sawyer was already nodding. "That's right."

Liz looked back at the screen and nodded thoughtfully. "Wool blazer. That would fit the bill."

"Where exactly did you find it, Liz?" Sawyer asked.

"Left rear seat, more towards the middle really." Using the mouse, Liz drew a line across the screen measuring from the spot the fiber was found to the far left side of the rear seat. "Twenty-seven inches from the end of the left-side rear seat, seven inches up from the seat. With that location it would seem logical that it came from a coat. We also picked up some synthetic cloth fibers right next to the left-side door. They matched the clothing found on the deceased male sitting in that position."

She turned back to the screen. "We didn't need the laser to find these next samples. They were plainly visible." The screen changed and Liz used the arrow to point out several single strands of hair.

"Let me guess," Sawyer said. "Long and blond. Natural, not bleached. Found very near the fiber."

"Very good, Lee, we'll make a scientist out of you yet." Liz smiled pleasantly. "Next we used leuco-crystal violet to test for blood. Found a ton of it, as you can imagine. Spray patterns are pretty evident and actually very demonstrative in this case, again probably due to the tight parameters of the crime scene." They looked at the computer screen, where the interior of the limo was now glowing brightly in numerous places. For a moment it looked like they were deep in a mine and bits of gold blazed out at them from every nook and cranny. Liz marked several spots with the pointer. "My conclusion is that the gentleman found on the floor of the backseat was either sitting facing the rear or with his face partially toward the right-hand side window. Gunshot wound was near the right temple. Blood, bone and tissue throw-off was considerable. You can see the rear seat is covered with the debris."

"Yeah, but there's an evident gap there." Sawyer pointed to the left of the rear seat.

"Good eye, that's absolutely right," Liz said. She used her measuring device again. "We found samples pretty uniformly distributed on the rear seat. That's what makes me think the victim" – she glanced at some notes next to the computer – "Brophy, had turned away, toward his left. That would leave the area of the gunshot, the right temple, facing directly at the rear seat, which accounts for the considerable trace coverage on the rear seat."

"Sort of like a cannon firing," Sawyer said dryly.

"Not exactly a technical term, but not bad for a layman, Lee." Liz arched her eyebrows and then continued. "However, the left half of the rear seat is virtually absent of any trace, no blood, no tissue, no bone fragments for approximately forty-five inches, almost four feet. Why is that?" She looked at the two agents like a schoolmarm waiting for her students to start waving their hands.

Sawyer answer. "We know one of the victims was sitting on the far left side: Philip Goldman. He was found there. But he was an average-size guy. There's no way he could account for that width. From the size of the gap, and the hair and fiber trace you already picked up, another person was sitting right next to Goldman."

"That's how I read it," Liz answered. "Goldman's wound would have thrown off quite a bit of residue as well. Again, nothing on the seat next to him. That reinforces the conclusion that someone else was seated there and took the full brunt of it. Not a pleasant business, to say the least. I'd be soaking in a bath for a week if it had happened to me, knock on wood."

"Wool coat, long, blond hair—" Jackson began.

"And this," Liz broke in, and pointed at the screen. They all stared as the scene changed once more. It was the rear seat again. The leather had been torn in several spots. Three parallel jagged lines ran from front to back at a spot very near where Goldman had been found. In the middle of the damage a solitary object rested. The agents looked at Liz.

"That's part of a fingernail. We haven't had time to run a DNA typing analysis, of course, but it's definitely female."

"How do you know that?" Jackson asked.

"It's not always so complicated, Ray. Long nail, professionally manicured, fingernail polish. Men rarely put themselves through that."

"Oh."

"The parallel lines on the leather—"

"Scratches," Sawyer said. "She scratched the seat and broke a nail."

"Right. She must've been really panicked," Liz noted.

"Not surprising, is it?" Jackson added.

"Anything else, Liz?" Sawyer queried her.

"Oh, yes. Lots of goodies. Prints. We used MDB, a compound which is particularly good at fluorescing latent prints under laser light. Also used a deep blue lens on the Luma-lite. Got really good results. We did elimination typing on the three victims. Their prints were everywhere. Understandably. Found a number of other partials, though, including one that coincided with those scratches, which seems natural enough. We also found one that was of particular interest."

"What's that?" Sawyer's nose was almost quivering with anticipation.

"Brophy's clothes were heavily spotted with

479

blood and other human residue from his wound. His right shoulder, in particular, was covered in blood. Makes sense, since his right temple would have been bleeding heavily. We found a number of prints, thumb, index, pinkie, really examples of the entire hand, in the blood on his right shoulder."

"How do you account for that? Someone trying to turn him over?" Sawyer looked puzzled.

"No. I wouldn't say that, although I don't have firm evidence to support it. My gut is, judging from the palm print I was able to pull up, it was more like – and I know this sounds pretty bizarre under the circumstances – but it was like someone was trying to climb over him, or at least was straddling the guy. But the close placement of the fingers, the angle of the palm and so on, really strongly suggest that's what happened."

Sawyer looked highly skeptical. "Climb over him? That's kind of a stretch, isn't it, Liz? You can't really tell that from the prints, can you?"

"I'm not basing my conclusion simply on that. We also found this." She pointed at the screen again. A strange object appeared there. A shape or pattern of some sort. In fact, a couple of them. The dark background around the objects they were looking at made it difficult to understand what they were really observing.

"This was a shot taken of Brophy's body," Liz explained. "He's face down on the floorboard. We're looking at his back. You see in the middle of his back this shape pattern. Again, it's made possible by a patch of blood."

Jackson and Sawyer squinted and leaned close to the screen, trying to discern what the image was. They finally gave up and looked at Liz.

"A knee." She magnified the image until it spanned the entire screen. "The human knee does make a very unique shape, especially when you have a malleable background such as blood." She clicked another button and another image sprang to life. "We also have this."

Sawyer and Jackson again looked at the screen. This time the pattern was readily identifiable. "A shoe print, the heel," Jackson said.

Sawyer looked unconvinced. "Yeah, but why climb all the way over the dead guy, get blood and who knows what else all over you, leave traces of yourself behind, when you could just open the left-side passenger door and step out? I mean, the person we're probably talking about was seated right next to Goldman on the *left* side."

Jackson and Liz looked at each other. Neither one had a ready answer for that. Liz shrugged and smiled. "That's why they pay you the big bucks, guys. I'm just a lab rat."

Jackson smiled. "I'd love fifty more just like you, Liz."

She smiled at the compliment. "I'll have a written report on all this for you later today."

They all took off the goggles.

"I'm assuming you've already run the prints?" Sawyer looked at her.

"Jesus, I'm sorry, talk about leaving out the main course. All of the prints – the one we looked at on the screen, from the probable murder weapon, and all of the ones in the limo and leading from the limo and on to the eighth floor and back down – were from one person."

"Sidney Archer." Jackson said.

"That's right," Liz responded. "The office where the blood trail took us was hers as well."

Sawyer stepped over to the limo and peered inside. He motioned for Liz and Jackson to join him. "Okay, based on what we know right now, can we

481

assume that Sidney Archer was sitting about right there?" He pointed to a spot slightly left of the middle of the rear seat.

"Seems reasonable enough, based on the trace we've uncovered so far. The blood spray patterns, fiber and print evidence would certainly support that conclusion," Liz said.

"Okay, looking at where the body ended up, Brophy was most likely sitting facing the rear. You say he may have turned his head and that accounted for the heavy residue on the rear seats. Right?"

"That's right." Liz was nodding her head as she followed Sawyer's reconstruction.

"Now, Brophy's wound was of the contact variety, there's little doubt of that. How far would you say that is?" Sawyer was pointing to the space between the front and rear seats of the passenger area.

"We don't have to guess," Liz said. She walked over to her desk, pulled out a tape measure and came back over. With Jackson's assistance she measured the space. Liz looked at the result on the tape and then frowned as she now saw where Sawyer was headed with his analysis. "Six feet six inches from the middle of one seat to the other."

"Okay, based on the absence of residue on the rear seats, Archer and Goldman were sitting there, their backs flush against the seats, you agree?" Liz nodded, as did Jackson. "All right, is it possible for Sidney Archer, if she was sitting with her back *flush* against the rear seat, to have perpetrated a contact wound on Brophy's right temple?"

Liz answered first. "No, not unless her arms dragged the ground when she walked."

Sawyer was eyeing Liz carefully. "How about Brophy was leaning toward Archer, very close, and she pulls the gun and fires. His body falls on her, let's say, but she pushes him off and he lands on the floor. What's wrong with that picture?"

Liz thought for a moment. "If he was leaning forward – and he really would have had to almost leave his seat – then given the distance, the shooter would still have to be doing about the same thing: They would sort of meet in the middle, so to speak, for the contact wound to be possible. But if the shooter is leaning forward, then the spray patterns would be different, more than likely. The shooter's back is not flush with the seat. Even if her body caught most of the residue, it would be highly unlikely for some not to have ended up on the seat behind her. For her to remain flush against the seat when she fired, Brophy would most likely had to have been almost in her lap. That doesn't seem too probable, does it?"

"Agreed," Sawyer said. "Let's talk about Goldman's wound for a minute. She's sitting next to Goldman on his left side, okay? Wouldn't you think his entry wound would have been to the right temple and not in the middle of the forehead?"

"He could've turned to face her—" Liz started to say, and then stopped. "But then the blood spray patterns wouldn't make sense. Goldman was definitely looking toward the front of the limo when the bullet hit him. But it could still be possible, Lee."

"Really?" Sawyer pulled up a chair, sat down in it, held an imaginary gun in his right hand, coiled it around and pointed it backward as though he were about to shoot someone sitting on his left, in the forehead as that person stared directly ahead. He looked at Liz and Jackson. "Pretty awkward, isn't it?"

"Very," Jackson said, shaking his head.

"It gets even more awkward, guys. Sidney Archer is left-handed. Remember, Ray, her drinking coffee, handling the pistol? Left-handed." Sawyer repeated his performance, this time holding the imaginary firearm in his left hand. The result was almost laughable as the bulky agent contorted his body.

"That would be impossible," Jackson said. "She'd have to turn and face him to inflict a wound like that. Either that or she pops her arm out of the socket. Nobody would fire a pistol in that manner."

"So, if Archer is the shooter, she somehow shoots the driver in the front seat, jumps across to the rear seat, blows away Brophy, which we've already shown she couldn't have done, and then supposedly nails Goldman using a completely unnatural – in fact impossible – firing angle." Sawyer got up from the chair and shook his head.

"You've made some good points, Lee, but there's still a lot of indisputable trace tying Sidney Archer to the crime scene," Liz rejoined.

"Being *at* a crime scene and being the perpetrator of said crime are two different things, Liz," Sawyer said heatedly. Liz looked pained at the agent's sharp rebuff.

As they were leaving the lab, Sawyer had a final question. "You get an answer on the gunshot residue test yet?"

"I hope you realize the bureau's firearms section doesn't really do the GSR tests anymore, since the findings weren't typically turning up anything relevant. However, since it was you requesting the test, of course no one balked. Give me one minute, Agent Sawyer, and I'll check." Liz's tone was plainly antiseptic now. Sawyer didn't seem to notice as he moodily studied the floor.

Liz went back to her desk and picked up a phone. Sawyer was staring over at the limo, looking for the world like he wanted to make it disappear. Jackson watched his partner carefully, a trace of concern filtering through his eyes.

Liz walked back over. "Negative. None of the victims had either fired a gun or handled a recently fired weapon with their bare hands in the six hours before their death."

"You're sure? No mistake?" Sawyer asked, his brow laced with furrows.

Liz's usually pleasant face quickly turned to a scowl. "My people know how to do their job, Lee. A GSR test is not that complicated, although, as I said, it's not routinely done anymore because a positive finding may not always be that accurate; there are so many substances out there that could, in practice, give a false positive. However, that nine-millimeter would have thrown off a good deal of residue, and the test result was *negative*. I'd say the confidence level in that finding should be very high. However, just in case you didn't catch it, I did add a disclaimer about their bare hands. They could have worn gloves, of course."

"But none were found on the dead men," Jackson pointed out.

"That's right," Liz said, looking at Sawyer triumphantly.

Sawyer ignored the look. "Were there any other prints found on the nine-millimeter?" he asked.

"One thumb print, partially obscured. It belonged to Parker, the chauffeur driver."

"No one else's?" Sawyer asked. "You're sure." Liz said nothing. Her expression plainly answered the question.

"Okay, you said Parker's print was partially obscured. What about Archer's prints? How clean were they?"

"From what I recall, fairly clean. Although there was some smudging. I'm talking about the grip,

485

trigger and trigger guard. Her prints on the barrel were very clear."

"The barrel?" Sawyer said this more to himself. He looked at Liz.

"We have a report on the ballistics yet? I'm real interested in the trajectory patterns."

"The autopsies are being performed as we speak. We'll know soon enough. I've asked to be advised of the results. They'll probably call you first, but in case they don't, as soon as I hear, I'll buzz you." She added with a trace of sarcasm, "You'll want to make sure they didn't make any mistakes, of course."

Sawyer looked at her for a moment. "Thanks, Liz. You've been a big help." His sarcastic tone was not lost on either Liz or Jackson. Lost deep in thought, his massive shoulders sagging, Sawyer trudged away slowly.

Jackson stayed behind for a moment with Liz. She watched Sawyer leave and then looked over at Jackson. "What the hell's eating him, Ray? He's never treated me like that before."

Jackson didn't answer right away. He finally shrugged and turned to leave. "I'm not sure I can answer that right now, Liz. Not sure at all." He quietly followed his partner out.

FIFTY-ONE

Jackson climbed in the car and looked over at his partner. Sawyer was sitting there, his hands on the wheel, staring off into the darkness. Jackson looked at his watch. "Hey, Lee, how about some grub?" When Sawyer didn't reply, he added, "My treat? Don't pass that offer up. It may not be repeated in your lifetime." Jackson gripped Sawyer's shoulder and gave it a friendly squeeze.

Sawyer finally looked over at him. For an instant a smile appeared on his lips and then was gone. "Springing for a meal, huh? You think I'm seriously screwed up over this case, don't you, Raymond?"

"I just don't want you to get too skinny," said Jackson.

Sawyer laughed and put the car in gear.

Jackson attacked his meal with vigor while Sawyer merely played with a mug of coffee. The diner was in close proximity to the headquarters building and was thus a popular one for FBI personnel. The pair greeted a number of colleagues either grabbing a bite before heading home or fortifying themselves before going on duty.

Jackson eyed Sawyer. "That was a nice piece of work you did back at the lab. But you could've cut Liz some slack. She was just doing her job."

Sawyer's eyes suddenly burned into his partner. "You cut some slack when your kid misses curfew or puts a ding in your car. If somebody wants slack, then I would strongly suggest they don't seek employment with the FBI."

"You know what I mean. Liz is damned good at her job."

Sawyer's face softened. "I know, Ray. I'll send her some flowers. Okay?" Sawyer looked away again.

Between bites Jackson said, "So what's our next move?"

Sawyer looked over at him. "I'm not really sure. I've had cases change on me in midstream before, but not quite to this degree."

"You don't believe Sidney Archer killed those guys, do you?"

"Aside from the fact that the physical evidence says she couldn't have, no, I don't believe she did."

"But she did lie to us, Lee. The tape? She was helping her husband. You can't get around that."

Sawyer felt the guilt seep in again. He had never withheld information from a partner before. He looked over at Jackson and then decided to tell him what Sidney had revealed. Five minutes later, Jackson sat back stunned. Sawyer glanced at him anxiously. "She was scared. Didn't know what to do. I'm sure she wanted to tell us from the get-go. Damn, if we only knew where she was. She could be in real danger, Ray." Sawyer smacked a fist into his palm. "If she would only come to us. Work together. We could bust this whole case, I know it."

Jackson leaned forward, a determined expression on his face. "Look, Lee, we've done a lot of cases together. But, despite it all, you kept your distance. You saw things for what they were."

"And you think this case is different?" Sawyer's tone was steady.

"I *know* it's different. You've been sticking up for this lady almost from the start. And you've damn sure been treating her differently than you ordinarily would a major suspect in a case like this. Now you tell me she spilled to you about the tape and her talking to her husband. And you kept that info to yourself. Jesus Christ, Lee, that's grounds to get your butt kicked right out of the bureau."

"If you feel you need to report it, Ray, I'm not stopping you."

Jackson grunted and shook his head. "I'm not pissing away your career. You're doing a good enough job of that."

"This case isn't any different."

"Bullshit!" Jackson hunched forward even more. "You know it is and it's messing you up. All the evidence points, at minimum, to Sidney Archer being involved in some serious crimes, and yet you go out of your way at every opportunity to put a positive spin on it. You did it with Frank Hardy, with Liz, and now you're trying to do it with me. You're not a politician, Lee, you're a law enforcement officer. She may not be in on everything, but she's no angel either. That's for damned certain."

"You disagree with my conclusions on the triple homicide?" Sawyer shot back.

Jackson shook his head. "No. I think you're probably right. But if you expect me to believe that Archer is just an innocent babe caught up in some Kafkaesque nightmare, then you're talking to the wrong FBI agent. Remember what you said about slack? Well, I'd have to cut you a ton of it to even begin to believe that Sidney Archer, beautiful and intelligent as she might be, shouldn't spend a considerable part of her remaining years in prison." Jackson sat back.

"So that's what you think it's all about? Beautiful, brainy babe turns veteran agent to mush?" Jackson didn't respond, but the answer was clearly painted on his face. "Old, divorced fart wants to jump in her panties, Ray? And I can't do that if she's guilty. Is that what the hell you think?" Sawyer's voice was rising.

"Why don't you tell me, Lee?"

"Maybe I should throw your ass through that window over there instead."

"Maybe you should goddamn try," Jackson shot back.

"You sonofabitch." Sawyer's voice shook.

Jackson reached across and grabbed his shoulder. "I want you to get your head on right. You want to sleep with her, fine. Wait until after the case is over and she's proved not guilty!" Jackson shouted at him.

"How dare you!" Sawyer shouted back, ripping Jackson's hand away. Sawyer then jumped up and cocked a very large fist, a fist that stopped in midair as Sawyer realized what he was about to do. Several of the other restaurant patrons stared in shock at the scene. Sawyer's and Jackson's eyes remained locked until finally Sawyer, his chest heaving, his bottom lip trembling, lowered his fist and sat back down.

Neither of them spoke for several minutes. Finally Sawyer looked embarrassed and sighed. "Shit, I knew I was going to regret giving up the smokes one day." He closed his eyes. When he reopened them, he was looking squarely at Jackson.

"Lee, I'm sorry. I'm just worried about—" Jackson abruptly stopped as Sawyer held up his hand.

Sawyer began speaking slowly and softly. "You know, Ray, I've been with the bureau half my life. When I first started out, it was easy to tell the good guys from the bad. Back then, kids didn't go around killing people like they were yesterday's lunch. And you didn't have smooth-running drug empires worth hundreds of billions of dollars, enough money that just about anybody will do just about anything. They had revolvers, we had revolvers. Pretty soon they'll be toting surface-to-air missiles as standard equipment.

"While I'm at the grocery trying to decide what lousy TV dinner to eat and looking for which beer's on sale, about twenty new corpses are created for no better reason than somebody turning down the wrong street or a bunch of unemployed kids going at each other over a block-long piece of drug turf with more firepower than an Army battalion used to carry around. We play catch-up every day, but we never gain any ground."

"Come on, Lee, the thin blue line is still around. As long as there are bad buys."

"That thin blue line is a lot like the ozone layer, Ray. It's got mountain-size holes punched all though it. I've been walking that line for a long time. What do I have to show for it? I'm divorced. My kids think I'm a lousy father because I was out running down a plane bomber, or hauling in some slick-smiling butcher who likes to line his trophy case with human specimens, instead of helping them blow out candles on their birthday cakes. You know what? They were right. I was a lousy dad. Especially to Meggie. I worked ungodly hours, never around, and when I was, I was either sleeping or so zoned out on a case I probably never heard half of what they were trying to tell me. Now I live all alone in a crummy apartment and most of my paycheck I don't even see. My stomach feels like it's got a bunch of meat cleavers stuck in it and while I'm sure that's just my imagination, I do happen to have several pieces of real lead permanently embedded in me. On top of that, lately I find it real hard to go to sleep unless I've had a six-pack of beer."

"Jesus, Lee, you're always the rock at work. Everyone respects the hell out of you. You go into an investigation and see stuff I never do. Wrap the whole picture together while I'm still getting my notebook out. You've got the best instincts of any one I've ever seen."

"Good thing, Ray. Considering it's really the only thing I have left. But don't shortchange yourself. I've got twenty years on you. You know what instinct is? Seeing the same thing over and over again until you start to get a feel for things. A little extra step. You're way ahead of where I was with just a half dozen years under my belt."

"I appreciate that, Lee."

"But don't misinterpret this little episode of venting. I don't feel sorry for myself and I'm sure as hell not looking for any pity from anybody. I had choices and I made them. Just me. If my life's screwed up, it's because *I* screwed it up, nobody else."

Sawyer got up, walked over to the counter and exchanged a few words with a skinny, wrinkled waitress. In a moment he was striding back, cupping his hands together, a thin line of smoke floating up. He sat back down and held up the cigarette. "For old times' sake." Slowly grinding out the match in the ashtray, he sat back and took a long pull on the cigarette, a barely audible chuckle escaping his lips.

"I go into this case, Ray, thinking that I had it pretty much nailed from the get-go. Lieberman's the target. We figure out how the plane went down. We got a lot of motives, but no so many we can't follow up, sift through until we nail the sonofabitch responsible. Shit, we get the actual bomber gift-wrapped and delivered to us, even if he's not breathing anymore. Things are looking pretty damn good. Then the floor falls out from under us. We find out Jason Archer pulled off this incredible heist and turns up in Seattle selling secrets instead of being in a hole in the ground in Virginia. Is that his plan? Seems pretty likely.

"Only the bomber turns out to be a guy who somehow slipped right through the Virginia State Police's computer system. I get hoodwinked into going to New Orleans and something happens at Archer's house that I'm still in the dark about. Then, when you least expect it, Lieberman gets thrown back into the picture chiefly because of Steven Page's apparent suicide five years ago that doesn't seem to fit into the puzzle except for the fact that his big brother, who can probably tell us a lot, gets his throat handed to him in a parking lot. I talk to Charles Tiedman and maybe, just maybe, Lieberman is being blackmailed. If true, how the hell does that tie into Jason Archer? Do we have two unconnected cases seemingly connected through a coincidence: namely, Lieberman gets on a plane Archer has paid someone to blow up? Or is it all one case? If it is, what the hell is the connection? Because if there is one, it sure as hell has escaped yours truly."

Sawyer shook his head in unconcealed frustration and took another drag on his cigarette. He exhaled smoke up to the grimy ceiling and then put his elbows on the table and looked over at Jackson. "Now two other guys we figure are tying to rip off Triton Global check into the hereafter. And the common denominator in a hell of a lot of it is Sidney Archer." Sawyer slowly rubbed a finger across his cheek. "Sidney Archer . . . I know I respect the woman. But maybe my judgment is getting a little clouded. You're probably right to kick me in the ass over it. But I'll let you in on a little secret, friend." Sawyer tapped the end of his cigarette into the ashtray.

"What's that?"

"Sidney Archer *was* in that limo. And whoever

killed those three guys let her walk. Her pistol ends up with the police." Sawyer made an imaginary gun with his left hand and pointed at various parts of it with his cigarette as he continued to speak. "Smudged prints on the part she would've held if she had fired it. Clear prints on the barrel only. What do you make of that?"

Jackson thought quickly. "We know she handled the gun." The truth suddenly dawned on him. "If somebody else fired it, and they were using gloves, her prints would've been smudged on those areas but not the barrel."

"Right. The tape gets left behind. They probably did use it to blackmail her, I'm not arguing with you over that. She would've known they had it, they would've had to play it for her to make her know the threat was real. You think she would've left something like that behind? That's slam-dunk evidence of enough felonies to keep her in prison until she's a hundred. I'm telling you, she or anyone else in that situation would've lifted that damn limo clear up in the air to get to that tape. No, they let her go for one reason only."

"To set her up for the killings." Jackson slowly put his coffee cup down.

"And maybe to make sure our focus doesn't wander again."

"That's why you wanted the GSR test done."

Sawyer nodded. "I needed to be sure that one of the dead guys wasn't the shooter. You know, there could have been a struggle. From the looks of it, the wounds were all instantly fatal, but who the hell really can be sure? Or one of them could have done it and then committed suicide, for all we know. Freaked out over what he'd done and decided to blow his own brains out. Then Sidney, in a panic, grabs the gun and throws it down a sewer drain. But that didn't happen. None of the stiffs fired that weapon."

They sat in prolonged silence before Sawyer stirred. "I'll let you in on another secret, Ray. I'm gonna figure this sucker out, even if it takes me another twenty-five years walking that thin line. And when that day comes, you're going to find out something really enlightening."

"Such as?"

"That Sidney Archer has no more of a clue to what the hell is going on than you or I do right now. She's lost her husband, she's lost her career, she stands a better than even chance of standing trial for murder and about a dozen other felonies and spending the rest of her life in prison. Right now she's scared out of her wits and running for her life, not knowing who to trust or believe. Sidney Archer is in fact something that, if you just looked at the evidence in a superficial manner, you would conclude she couldn't possibly be."

"What's that?"

"Innocent."

"You really think that?"

"No. I *know* it. I wish I knew something else."

"What's that?"

Sawyer stabbed out his cigarette at the same time he let out a final mouthful of smoke. "Who really killed those three guys." Sawyer's mind drifted away as he said the words. *Sidney Archer might know. But where the hell is she?*

As the two rose to leave, Jackson put a hand on Sawyer's shoulder. "Hey, Lee, for what it's worth, I don't care how long the good guy/bad guy odds ever get to be. As long as you're willing to walk the line, I will too."

FIFTY-TWO

Looking through her binoculars, Sidney surveyed the street in front of her parents' house and then checked her watch. Dusk was rapidly gathering. She shook her head in disbelief. Could the FedEx shipment have been delayed because of weather? Snowfall in coastal Maine was usually heavy, and because of its proximity to the ocean, it was usually very slushy. That often made for hazardous driving conditions when the slush froze. And where were her parents? The problem was she had no way to communicate with them while they were traveling. Sidney hurried to the Land Rover, dialed information on the cellular phone and got the 800 number for Federal Express. She gave the operator the names and addresses of the sender and recipient of the package. After Sidney listened to computer keys clicking, the operator delivered her astonishing answer.

"You mean you have no record of the package?"

"No, ma'am, I mean, according to our records, we didn't receive the package."

"But that's impossible. You *had* to get it. There must be some mistake. Please check again." Sidney listened with growing impatience to the sounds, once again, of the keyboard. The response was the same.

"Ma'am, perhaps you should check with the sender to make sure the package was actually sent out."

496

Sidney hung up, got Fisher's number from her purse in the house, went back out to the Land Rover and dialed it. There was little chance that Fisher would be there – he had undoubtedly taken Sidney's warnings to heart – but he would most likely call in for messages. Her hands were shaking. What if Jeff had been unable to send out the package? The vision of the gun pointed at her in the limo blasted into her mind. Brophy and Goldman. Their heads exploding. All over her. For a moment, in her despair, she rested her head on the steering wheel, then picked up the phone and dialed.

The phone rang and then was answered. Sidney prepared to leave a message on the machine when a voice said hello.

Sidney started to speak until she realized the voice on the end was a live one.

"Hello?" The voice said again.

Sidney hesitated and then decided to go ahead. "Jeff Fisher, please."

"Who is this?"

"I'm . . . I'm a friend of his."

"Do you know where he is? I really need to find him," said the voice.

The hackles on the back of Sidney's neck went up. "Who is this?"

"Sergeant Rogers of the Alexandria Police Department."

Sidney quickly cut off the call.

The interior of Jeff Fisher's townhouse had seen drastic changes since Sidney Archer had been there, chief of which was that not one single piece of computer equipment or files was left in the place. In the middle of the day, neighbors had seen the moving truck. One of them had even talked to the movers. Thought it was all legitimate. Fisher hadn't mentioned that he was moving, but the movers had been so open about it, took their time, boxed things up, had paperwork on a clipboard, had even taken a smoke break in the middle of the job. Only after they had left did the neighbors get suspicious. When Fisher's next-door neighbor had gone inside to check on things, he had noticed that none of the furniture was gone, only Fisher's extensive computer system. That's when the police had been called.

Sergeant Rogers scratched his head. The problem was, nobody could find Jeff Fisher. They had checked at his job, with his family up in Boston, with his friends locally. No one had seen him in the last couple of days. Sergeant Rogers had received another shock during his investigation. Fisher had actually been in custody at the Alexandria Police Station on a reckless driving charge. He'd posted bail, been given a court date and been released. That was the last anyone apparently had seen of Jeff Fisher. Rogers finished writing up his report and left.

Sidney ran up the stairs and slammed and locked the bedroom door. She grabbed the shotgun off the bed, racked the action of the weapon, backed into the far corner and sat down on the floor, the gun pointed straight at the door. Tears streamed down her cheeks as she shook her head in disbelief. *Oh God!* She should never have gotten Jeff involved.

Sawyer was at his desk at the Hoover Building when Frank Hardy called. He briefly filled Hardy in on the most recent developments, chief of which was Sawyer's conclusion, based on his examination of the forensics evidence, that Sidney Archer had not killed Goldman and Brophy.

"You think it could have been Jason Archer?"

Hardy asked.

"That doesn't make any sense."

"You're right. Too big a risk for him to come back here anyway."

"Plus I can't believe he'd set up his wife for the murders." Sawyer paused as he considered his next question. "Any word from RTG?"

"I was just about to tell you. The president, Alan Porcher, is unavailable for comment. Big surprise there. The company's PR person gave the standard line vigorously denying the allegations, of course."

"How about the CyberCom deal?"

"Well, there we finally have some good news. This latest development with RTG has thrown CyberCom firmly into Triton's camp. In fact, a news conference is scheduled for later this afternoon announcing the deal. You want to attend?"

"Maybe. Nathan Gamble should be a happy camper."

"You got that right. I'll leave a couple of visitor badges for the press conference if you and Ray want to come see the show. It's at Triton's headquarters."

Sawyer considered the request for a moment. "I think you'll see us there, Frank."

Sawyer and Jackson, their yellow visitor badges riding brightly on their lapels, walked into the auditorium-sized room, which still managed to be crowded.

"Damn, this *must* be a big event." Jackson eyed the sea of reporters, industry people, financial analysts and other investment types.

"Money always is, Ray." Sawyer snagged two cups of coffee from the hospitality table and handed one to his partner. Sawyer stretched his six-foot-three-inch frame to its maximum height as he looked over the crowd.

"Looking for somebody?" Frank Hardy appeared behind the pair.

Jackson smiled. "Yeah, we were looking for some poor people. But I think we're in the wrong place."

"That you are. Gotta admit, you can feel the excitement, can't you?"

Jackson nodded and then pointed at the army of reporters. "But is one company buying out another really all that newsworthy?"

"Ray, it's a little more than that. I would be hard put to name any other company in America whose potential exceeds CyberCom."

"But if CyberCom is so special, why do they need Triton?" Jackson asked.

"With Triton they can partner with a world leader and have the billions of dollars needed to produce, market and expand their product base. The result will be that in a couple of years, Triton will dominate like GM and IBM used to – even more so, really. The flow of ninety percent of the world's information will be through hardware, software and other technology created by the business combination being formed today."

Sawyer shook his head as he gulped his coffee down. "Damn, Frank," he said, "that doesn't leave much room for everybody else. What happens to them?"

Hardy smiled weakly. "Well, that's capitalism for you. Survival of the fittest comes from the law of the jungle. You've probably watched those *National Geographic* shows. Animals eating each other, struggling to survive. It's not a pretty sight."

Hardy looked up at the small elevated stage where a podium had been situated. "It's about to start, guys. I've got us seats near the front. Come on." Hardy herded them through the crowds, entering a special roped-off section that encompassed the first three

500

rows from the stage. Sawyer looked over the occupants of a short line of chairs to the left of the podium. Quentin Rowe was there. He was a little more dressed up today, but despite his hundreds of millions of bucks in the bank the guy apparently didn't own any neckties. He was engaged in an animated conversation with three men in low-key business suits who Sawyer assumed were the CyberCom people.

Hardy seemed to be reading his mind. "From left to right, CEO, CFO and COO of CyberCom."

"And SOL, shit outta luck, for everybody else," Sawyer said.

Hardy pointed at the stage. From the right side Nathan Gamble, nattily dressed and smiling, marched across and settled in at the podium. The crowd quickly took their seats and abruptly quieted down as if Moses had just strolled down Mount Sinai with those tablets. Gamble took out a prepared speech and launched into it with considerable vigor. Sawyer didn't hear most of it. He was busy watching Quentin Rowe. The young man was looking at Gamble. Whether he was conscious of it or not, his expression was not amicable. From the little Sawyer did hear of Gamble's words, the main import was money, big money that came with market domination. After Gamble finished with a flourish – he was quite the glib salesman, Sawyer had to admit – there was a huge wave of applause. Then Quentin Rowe took his place at the podium. As Gamble passed him on his way to sit down, the two men exchanged smiles that were about as phony as Sawyer had ever seen outside a B movie.

In comparison to Gamble, Rowe's emphasis was on the limitless positive potential the two companies, Triton and CyberCom combined, could offer the planet. The issue of money never came up. At least from Sawyer's point of view, Gamble had pretty much covered that issue anyway. Now he looked over at Gamble, who was not looking at Rowe at all. He was engaged in a friendly discussion with the CyberCom acronyms. Rowe apparently noticed the exchange at one point as he glanced over, lost his train of thought for a moment and then carried on. His talk received, Sawyer thought, polite applause. The good of the world apparently took a distant backseat to Mother Green. At least with this crowd.

When the CyberCom people finished up the presentation, all of the men engaged in a hand-shaking, ringed-arm photo opportunity. Sawyer noted that Gamble and Rowe never actually touched flesh. They kept the CyberCom boys between them. Maybe that's why they were so excited about the deal; they'd have a buffer zone now.

Everyone from the stage made his way into the crowd and was instantly besieged by questions. Gamble was smiling, quipping and playing the moment for all it was worth. The CyberCom people followed in his wake. Sawyer watched as Rowe broke rank and headed over to the hospitality table, where he fixed a cup of tea and moved quickly over to a secluded corner.

Sawyer tugged on Jackson's sleeve and they headed in Rowe's direction. Hardy went over to listen to Gamble's pontificating.

"Nice speech."

Rowe looked up to see Sawyer and Jackson standing in front of him.

"What? Oh, thank you."

"My partner, Ray Jackson."

Rowe and Jackson exchanged hellos.

Sawyer looked over at the large group sur-rounding Gamble. "He seems to like the limelight."

Rowe sipped his tea and wiped his mouth delicately with his napkin. "His bottom-line approach to the business and limited knowledge of what we actually do makes for good sound bites." He said disdainfully.

Jackson sat down next to Rowe. "Personally, I liked what you were saying about the future. My kids are really into computers. It's true what you were saying: Better educational opportunities for everyone, especially the poor, translates into better jobs, less crime, better world. I really believe that."

"Thank you. I believe it too." Rowe looked up at Sawyer and smiled. "Although I don't think your partner shares that view."

Sawyer, who had been scanning the crowds, looked down at him with a hurt look on his face. "Hey, I'm for all that positive stuff. Just don't take away my pencil and paper. That's all I'm saying." Sawyer pointed his coffee cup over at the group of CyberCom people. "You seem to get along with those guys all right."

Rowe brightened. "I do. They're not as liberal-thinking as I am, but they're a long way from Gamble's money-is-everything position. I think they might bring a nice equilibrium to the place. Although now we have to endure at least two months of the lawyers taking their pound of flesh while the final documents are negotiated."

"Tyler, Stone?" Sawyer asked.

Rowe looked at Sawyer. "That's right."

"You gonna keep them as your counsel after the CyberCom deal is put to bed?"

"You'll have to ask Gamble that. It's his call. He *is* the head of the company. Excuse me, gentlemen, but I have to go." Rowe quickly got up and left them.

"What bee's up his bonnet?" Jackson asked Sawyer.

Sawyer shrugged his thick shoulders. "More like a hornets' nest. If you were partners with Nathan Gamble, you'd probably understand."

"So what now?"

"Why don't you grab another cup of coffee and mingle, Ray. I want to talk to Rowe some more." Sawyer disappeared into the crowd. Jackson looked around and then went over to the hospitality table.

By the time Sawyer had made his way through the crowd, he had lost sight of Rowe. As he swept his head back and forth, he saw Rowe go out the door. Sawyer was about to follow him when he felt a tug at his sleeve.

"Since when is a government bureaucrat interested in the goings-on of the for-profit sector?" Nathan Gamble asked.

Sawyer cast one more look in Rowe's direction, but he was already out of sight. The FBI agent turned to Gamble.

"I'm all for making a buck. Nice speech you gave, by the way. Left me kind of tingling all over."

Gamble let out a belly laugh. "Like hell it did. You want something stronger?" He pointed at Sawyer's Styrofoam cup.

"Sorry, I'm on duty. Besides, it's a little early for me."

"We're celebrating here, FBI man. Just announced the biggest damn deal of my life. I'd say that's worth getting drunk over, wouldn't you?"

"If you want to. It's not *my* deal."

"You never know," he said provocatively. "Let's take a walk."

Gamble led Sawyer up across the stage, down a short corridor and into a small room. Gamble plopped down in a chair and pulled a cigar from his coat pocket. "If you don't want to get drunk, at least have a smoke with me."

Sawyer put out his hand and the two men lit up.

Gamble slowly waved his match back and forth like a miniature flag before crumpling it under his foot. He eyed Sawyer intently through the twin walls of cigar smoke. "Hardy tells me you're thinking about joining up with him."

"To tell you the truth, I really haven't given it much thought."

"You could do a hell of a lot worse for yourself."

"Frankly, Gamble, I don't think I do all that bad for myself right where I am."

Gamble grinned. "Shit! What do you make a year?"

"That's none of your damned business."

"Jesus, I told you what I pull in. Come on, just a ballpark."

Sawyer cradled the cigar in his hand before clenching it between his teeth. There was now mild amusement in his eyes. "Okay, it's less than what you make. That narrow it down enough?"

Gamble laughed.

"Why do you care what my paycheck says?"

"The point is, I don't. But from what I've seen of you and knowing the government's way of doing business, I gotta believe it's not nearly enough."

"So? Even if it isn't, that's not your problem."

"I'm not into problems so much as I'm into problem solving. That's what chairmen do, Sawyer. They look at the big picture, or at least they're supposed to. So how about it?"

"So how about what?"

Gamble puffed on his cigar, a small twinkle in his eye.

It finally dawned on Sawyer what the man was getting at.

"Are you offering me a job?"

"Hardy says you're the best. I only hire the best."

"Exactly what position are you looking to fill?"

"Head of security, what else?"

"I thought Lucas already had that job."

Gamble shrugged. "I'll take care of him. He's more of my personal guy anyway. I *quadrupled* his government salary, by the way. I'll do better than that for you."

"I take it you blame Lucas for what happened with Archer."

"Hey, it's somebody's responsibility. So what do you say?"

"What about Hardy?"

"He's a big boy. Who say I can't bid for your services? I get you on board, maybe I don't need as much of him."

"Frank's a good friend of mine. I'm not doing anything that would screw him. That's not how I operate."

"It's not like the guy's gonna be reduced to going through trash cans. He's already made a hell of a lot of money. Most of it off me." Gamble shrugged. "But suit yourself."

Sawyer stood up. "To tell you the truth, I'm not sure you and I could ever survive each other."

Gamble eyed him steadily. "You know, you're probably right about that."

Sawyer left Gamble sitting there. When he exited the room, he came face-to-face with Richard Lucas, who had been standing outside the door.

"Hey, Rich, you certainly get around."

"It's part of my job," Lucas said brusquely.

"Well, in my book, you qualify for sainthood." Sawyer nodded toward the room where Nathan Gamble was puffing on his cigar and walked off.

Sawyer had just gotten back to his office when his line buzzed.

"Yes?"

"Charles Tiedman, Lee."

"I'll sure take that one." Sawyer hit the flashing red light on his phone. "Hello, Charles."

Tiedman's manner was brisk and businesslike. "Lee, I was getting back to you on your question."

Sawyer flipped back through his notebook until he reached the section on his previous discussion with Tiedman. "You were going to check on the dates Lieberman had raised the rates."

"I didn't want to mail or fax them to you. Even though they are technically publicly known . . . well, I wasn't certain who might see them other than yourself. No need to stir things up unnecessarily."

"I understand." *God, these Fed guys never stop with the secrecy, do they?* Sawyer thought. "Why don't you give them to me now."

Tiedman cleared his throat and began. "There were five such instances. December nineteenth, 1990, was the first change. The others occurred on February twenty-eighth of the following year, September twenty-sixth, 1992, November fifteenth of the same year, and finally April sixteenth, 1993."

Sawyer wrote them down. "What was the net effect? After all five changes?"

"The net effect was to add one-half a percentage point to the Fed Funds Rate. However, the first reduction was one percentage point. The last increase was three-quarters."

"I take it that's a lot at one time."

"If we were in the military discussing weapons systems, one percentage point would easily equate to a nuclear bomb."

"I know if early word leaked out about the Fed's decision regarding interest rates, then people could make enormous profits."

"Actually," said Tiedman, "advance notice of the

507

Fed's action on interest rates is, for all intents and purposes, worthless."

Mother of God. Sawyer closed his eyes, slapped his forehead and leaned back in his chair so far he almost toppled over. Maybe he should just plant his trusty ten-millimeter against his temple and save himself additional misery. "So, excuse my French, but why all the goddamned secrecy?"

"Don't misunderstand me. Unscrupulous people could certainly profit in innumerable ways from learning inside information about the Fed's deliberations. However, advance information of Fed action is not typically one of them. The market has an army of Fed watchers who are so adept at their job that the financial community usually knows well in advance whether the Fed is going to lower or raise interest rates and by how much. In effect, the market already knows what we'll do. Is that clear enough for you?"

"Very." Sawyer exhaled audibly. Then he jerked up in his chair. "What happens if the market is wrong?"

Tiedman's tone showed he was very pleased with the question. "Ah, that is an entirely different matter. If the market is wrong, then you could have enormous swings on the financial landscape."

"So if somebody knew ahead of time that one of these unexpected changes was coming down the pike, he could make some nice profits?"

"That's considerably understating it. Anyone with advance information of an unanticipated Fed change in interest rates could potentially make *billions* of dollars seconds after the Fed action was announced." Tiedman's response left Sawyer momentarily speechless. He wiped his brow and whistled under his breath. "There are innumerable vehicles in which to do so, Lee, the most lucrative probably being Eurodollar contracts trading on the

508

International Monetary Market in Chicago. The leverage is thousand to one. Or the stock market, of course. Rates go up, the market goes down, and vice versa, it's that simple. You can make billions if you're right, lose billions if you're wrong." Sawyer was still silent. "Lee, I believe there is one more question you want to ask me."

Sawyer cupped the phone receiver under his chin while he hurriedly wrote down some notes. "Only one? I was just getting warmed up."

"I think this query may make unimportant anything else you may want to know." Although Tiedman seemed on the surface to be toying with him, the agent sensed a true grimness behind the tone. He pushed himself to think. He almost yelled into the phone when it hit him. "The dates you just gave me, when the rates changed – were they all 'surprises' to the market?"

Tiedman paused before answering. "Yes." Sawyer could almost feel the electricity coming over the phone line. "In fact, they were the worst kind of surprises for the financial markets, because they did not occur as the result of regularly scheduled Fed meetings, but by Arthur's unilateral actions as Fed chairman."

"So he can raise rates by himself?"

"Yes, the board can give the chairman that power. It's often been done over the years. Arthur lobbied hard for it and got it. I'm sorry I didn't tell you that before. It didn't seem important."

"Forget it," Sawyer said. "And with those rate changes, maybe somebody made more money than there are stars?"

"Yes," Tiedman said very quietly. "Yes," he said again. "There's also the reality that others *lost* at least an equal amount of money."

"What do you mean?"

"Well, if you're correct that Arthur was being blackmailed to manipulate rates, the extreme steps he took – adjusting the Fed Funds Rate by as large as a percentage point at a time – leads me to conclude that damage to others was intended."

"Why?" Sawyer asked.

"Because if your goal was merely to profit from the adjustment in rates, you wouldn't need much in the way of movement to do so, so long as the direction, up or down, was a surprise to the markets. However, to the investments of others who anticipated a change in the other direction, a point adjustment *the other way* is catastrophic."

"Jesus. Any way to find out who took those kinds of hits?"

Tiedman smiled. "Lee, with the complexities of money movement today, neither you nor I would have enough years left to do that."

Tiedman didn't speak for at least another minute, and Sawyer really couldn't think of anything else to say. When Tiedman finally broke the silence, his voice was suddenly bone tired. "Until we had our earlier discussion, I never had considered the possibility that Arthur's relationship with Steven Page could have been used to coerce him into doing it. Now it seems rather obvious."

"You understand, though, that we don't have any proof that he was being blackmailed?"

"We'll probably never know the answer to that, I'm afraid," said Tiedman. "Not with Steven Page dead."

"Do you know whether Lieberman ever met Page at his apartment?"

"I don't believe that he did. Arthur mentioned to me once that he leased a cottage in Connecticut. And he cautioned me about mentioning it in front of his wife."

"You think that was the rendezvous spot for Page and Lieberman?"

"It could've been."

"I'll tell you where I'm going with this. Steven Page left behind a considerable estate when he died. Megabucks."

Tiedman's tone was one of complete shock. "I don't understand. I remember Arthur telling me more than once that Steven was always complaining about money."

"Nonetheless, it's undisputed that he died a very rich man. I'm wondering, could Lieberman have been the source of that wealth?"

"Highly unlikely. As I just said, Arthur's conversations with me indicated that he believed Steven to be far from affluent. In addition, I think it quite impossible that Arthur could have transferred that kind of money to Steven Page without his wife knowing about it."

"Then why take a risk with leasing a cottage? Couldn't they have met at Page's apartment?"

"All I can say is he never mentioned to me that he had visited Steven Page's apartment."

"Well. Maybe the cottage was Page's idea."

"Why do you say that?"

"Well, if Lieberman didn't give Page the money, someone else had to. Don't you think Lieberman would've been suspicious if he had walked into Page's apartment and saw a Picasso on the wall? Wouldn't he have wanted to know where the funds came from?"

"Absolutely!"

"Actually, I'm certain Page wasn't blackmailing Lieberman. At least not directly."

"How can you be sure?"

"Lieberman kept a picture of Page at his apartment. I don't think he would keep a blackmailer's photo around. On top of that, we also found a bunch of letters at Lieberman's apartment. They were unsigned, romantic in content. Lieberman obviously valued them highly."

"You think Page was the author of those letters?"

"I know a way to tell for sure. You were friends with Page. Do you have a sample of his writing?"

"Actually, I've kept several handwritten letters he wrote me while he was working in New York. I can send them to you." Tiedman paused. Sawyer could hear him scribbling a note. "Lee, you've adeptly pointed out ways Page could *not* have reaped his millions. So where did he get his wealth?"

"Think about it. If Page and Lieberman were having an affair, that's plenty of ammo to blackmail him with, you agree?"

"Certainly."

"Okay, what if someone else, a third party, encouraged Page to have an affair with Lieberman."

"But I introduced them. I hope you're not accusing me of perpetrating this ghastly conspiracy."

"You may have been the one to introduce them, but that's not to say Page and whoever was funding him couldn't have helped that introduction occur. Moving in the right circles, helping publicize Page's financial brilliance to the right people."

"Go on."

"So Page and Lieberman hit it off. The third party may believe that Lieberman may one day run the Fed. So Page and his backer bide their time. The backer pays Page to keep up the romance. They would've documented the relationship every which way from Sunday – taped phone calls, video, still photos – you can believe that."

"Then Steven Page was all part of a setup. He never actually cared for Arthur. I . . . I can't believe this." The little man sounded terribly depressed.

"Then Page gets HIV and allegedly commits suicide."

"Allegedly? You have doubts about his death?"

"I'm a cop, Charles, I have doubts about the Pope. Page is gone, but his accomplice is still out there. Lieberman becomes Fed chairman, and bam, the blackmail begins."

"But Arthur's death?"

"Well, your comment about him seeming almost happy that he had cancer tells me one thing."

"Which is?"

"That he was about to tell his blackmailer to take a flying leap and was going to go public with the scheme."

Tiedman rubbed his brow nervously. "It all makes perfect sense."

Sawyer lowered his voice. "You haven't mentioned any of what we've discussed to anyone, have you?"

"No, I haven't."

"Well, stick to that habit, and never let your guard down."

"What exactly are you suggesting?" There was a sudden catch in Tiedman's voice.

"I'm just recommending in the very strongest possible terms that you be very careful and do not tell anyone – not any of the Fed members, including Walter Burns, your secretary, your assistants, your wife, your friends – anything about this."

"Are you saying that you think *I'm* in danger? I find that very hard to believe."

Sawyer's tone was grim. "I'm sure Arthur Lieberman thought that too."

Charles Tiedman gripped a pencil on his desk so hard that it snapped in half. "I'll certainly follow your advice to the letter." Thoroughly frightened, Tiedman hung up.

Sawyer leaned back in his chair and longed for another cigarette as his mental engine went into overdrive. Somebody had obviously been paying off Steven Page. Sawyer thought he had a reasonable answer for why: setting up Lieberman. The question nagging at him now was who? And then the biggest question of all: who had killed Steven Page? The FBI agent was now convinced, despite evidence to the contrary, that Steven Page had been murdered. He picked up the phone. "Ray? It's Lee. I want you to give Lieberman's personal physician another call."

FIFTY-THREE

Bill Patterson looked at the dashboard clock and stretched out his large body. They were traveling *southbound* about two hours north of Bell Harbor. Next to him, his wife was sound asleep. It had been a far longer trip to the market than they were expecting. Sidney Archer had been incorrect. They had not stopped on the drive up to Bell Harbor, and had reached the beach house barely ahead of the storm. Having piled their luggage in the back bedroom, they headed out for food before the storm worsened. The market in Bell Harbor was sold out, so they were compelled to drive north to the far larger grocery in Port Vista. On the way back, their route had been closed off by a jackknifed tanker truck. Last night had been spent very uncomfortably in a motel.

Patterson now checked the backseat; Amy was also napping, her little mouth forming a perfect circle. Patterson looked at the heavily falling snow and grimaced. Fortunately, he had not been privy to the latest news flashes proclaiming his daughter to be a fugitive from justice. He was sick enough with worry as it was. In his anxiety he had chewed his fingernails until they had bled and his gut was full of acid. He wanted to be protecting Sidney now, as he had dutifully done when she was a little girl. Ghosts and bogeymen had been his chief foes back then. The current ones were far more deadly, he had to assume. At least he had Amy with him. God help the person who tried to harm his granddaughter. *And God be with you, Sidney.*

Ray Jackson stood silently in the doorway of Sawyer's cramped office. Behind his desk. Lee Sawyer was immersed in a file. A full pot of coffee was on a hot plate in front of him, a half-eaten meal next to it. Jackson could not remember the last time the man had failed at his job. However, Sawyer had been taking increasing heat – internally from the director of the FBI on down, in the press and from the White House to Capitol Hill. Jackson grimaced. Hell, if they thought it was so damn easy, why didn't they hit the streets and try to solve the case?

"Hey, Lee?"

Sawyer jerked up. "Hey, Ray. Fresh pot of coffee on the hot plate, help yourself."

Jackson poured himself a cup and sat down. "Word is you've been taking some grief from upstairs on this case."

Sawyer shrugged. "Goes with the territory."

"You want to talk about it?" Jackson settled down in a chair next to him.

"What's there to talk about? Fine, everybody wants to know who was behind that plane going down. I do too. I also want to know a hell of a lot more than that. I want to know who used Joe Riker for target practice. I want to know who killed Steve and Ed Page. I want to know who blew away those three guys in the limo. I want to know where Jason Archer is."

"And Sidney Archer?"

"Yeah, and Sidney Archer. And I'm not gonna find out by listening to all the people who just have a bunch of questions and no answers. Speaking of which, have you got any for me? Answers, that is?"

Jackson got up and closed the door to Sawyer's office.

"According to his doctor, Arthur Lieberman did not have the HIV virus."

Sawyer exploded. "That's impossible. The guy's lying his ass off."

"Don't think so, Lee."

"Why the hell not?"

"Because he showed me Lieberman's medical file." Sawyer sat back, stunned. Jackson continued. "When I asked the guy, I thought it was going to be like you and I talked about – his expression would have to tell us, because the man sure as hell wasn't going to show me any records without a subpoena in hand. But he did, Lee. No harm in his doctor proving that Lieberman *didn't* have the virus. Lieberman was some kind of health fanatic. Had yearly physicals, all sorts of preventive measures and testing. As part of the physicals, Lieberman was routinely tested for HIV. The doctor showed me the results from 1990 until last year. They were all negative, Lee. I saw them myself."

Sidney closed her bloodshot eyes for a moment, lay back on her parents' bed and took a deep breath. Wearily she made a decision. She pulled out the card from her purse and stared at it for some minutes. She felt the overpowering need to talk to someone. For a number of reasons, she decided it had to be him. She went down to the Land Rover and carefully dialed the number.

Sawyer had just opened the door to his apartment when he heard the phone start to ring. He grabbed up the phone, taking off his overcoat as he did so.

"Hello?"

The line was silent for a moment and Sawyer was just about to hang up. Then a voice came on the other end. Sawyer gripped the receiver with both hands and let his coat fall on the floor. He stood rigidly in the middle of his living room.

"Sidney?"

"Hello." The voice was small, but firm.

"Where are you?" Sawyer's question was automatic, but he instantly regretted it.

"Sorry, Lee, this is not a geography lesson."

"Okay, okay," Sawyer sat down in his battered recliner. "I don't need to know where you are. But are you safe?"

Sidney almost laughed. "Reasonably so, I guess, but it's still just a guess. I'm heavily armed, if that makes a difference." She paused for a moment. "I saw the TV news."

"I know you didn't kill them, Sidney."

"How—"

"Just trust me on that one."

Sidney let out a deep breath as the memory of that horrific night settled back down on her. "I'm sorry I didn't tell you when I called before. I . . . I just couldn't."

"Tell me what happened that night, Sidney."

Sidney was silent, debating whether to hang up or not. Sawyer sensed her deliberations. "Sidney, I'm not at the Hoover Building. I can't trace your call. And I happen to be on your side. You can talk as long as you want."

"Okay. You're the only one I happen to trust. What do you want to know?"

"Everything. Just start from the beginning."

It took Sidney about five minutes to recount the events of that night.

"You didn't see the shooter?"

"He was wearing a ski mask that covered his face. I think it was the same guy who tried to kill me later. At least I hope there aren't two guys walking around with eyes like that."

"In New York?"

"What?"

518

"The security guard, Sidney. He was murdered."
She rubbed at her forehead. "Yes. In New York."

"But definitely a man?"

"Yes, from his build and what I could see of his facial characteristics through the mask. And the bottom of his neck was exposed. I could see beard stubble."

Sawyer was impressed with her observations and said so.

"You tend to remember the smallest details when you think you're about to die."

"I know what you mean. I've actually been in that situation myself. Look, we found the tape, Sidney. Your talk with Jason?"

Sidney looked around the darkened interior of the Land Rover and the garage beyond. "So, everyone knows—"

"Don't worry about that. On the tape your husband sounded jumpy, nervous. Answered some of your questions but not all."

"Yes, he was distraught. Panicked."

"How about when you talked to him on the pay phone in New Orleans? How did he sound then? Different or the same?"

Sidney narrowed her eyes as she thought back. "Different," she said finally.

"How? Give it to me as exactly as you can."

"Well, he didn't sound nervous. In fact, it was almost a monotone. He told me I couldn't say anything, that the police were watching. He just gave me instructions and hung up. It was a monologue rather than a conversation. I never said anything."

Sawyer sighed. "Quentin Rowe is convinced that you were in Jason's office at Triton after the plane crash. Were you?"

Sidney was silent.

"Sidney, I really don't give a tinker's dam if you

were there. But if you were, I just want to ask you one question about something you might have done while you were in there."

Sidney remained silent.

"Sidney? Look, *you* called me. You said you trust me, although at this point I can understand you not wanting to trust anyone. I wouldn't recommend it, but you can hang up now, try going it alone."

"I was there," she said quietly.

"Okay, Rowe mentioned a microphone on Jason's computer."

Sidney sighed. "I accidentally hit it; it bent. I couldn't get it back straight."

Sawyer sat back in the recliner. "Did Jason ever use the microphone feature of the computer? Did he, for instance, have one at home?"

"No. He could type much faster than he could speak. Why?"

"So why did he have a microphone on his computer at work?"

Sidney thought about it for a moment. "I don't know. I think it was fairly recent. A few months or so, maybe a little longer. I've noticed them in other offices at Triton, if that helps. Why?"

"I'm getting there, Sidney, just bear with an old, tired G-man." Sawyer tugged at his top lip. "When you talked to Jason, both times, you're sure it was him?"

"Of course it was him. I know my own husband's voice."

Sawyer's tone was deliberate and steady, as though he were trying to graft those traits on to Sidney. "I didn't ask you if you were sure it was your husband's *voice*." He stopped momentarily, took a slow breath and then continued. "I asked you if you were sure it was your *husband* both times."

Sidney froze. When she finally found her own

voice, it came out in a furious whisper. "What are you suggesting?"

"I listened to your first conversation with Jason. You're right, he did sound panicked, breathing heavy, the works. You guys had a real conversation. But now you tell me the second time around, he sounded far different, that it really wasn't a conversation. He talked, you listened. No panic. Now, we know about this microphone in Jason's office, something that he never uses. If he never uses it, why is it really there?"

"I . . . What other reason would it be there?"

"A microphone, Sidney, is for recording things. Sounds . . . Voices."

Sidney gripped the cell phone so hard her hand turned red. "Are you saying . . ."

"I'm saying that I believe that you heard your husband's voice over the phone both times, all right. But I think what you heard the second time was a compilation of your husband's words derived from the recordings taken by the microphone, because that was its real purpose, I'm fairly certain. A recorder."

"That can't be possible. Why?"

"I don't know why, yet. But it seems clear enough. That explains why your second conversation with him was so different. The second time around I gather the vocabulary was pretty ordinary?" Sidney didn't answer. "Sidney?" Sawyer heard a sob come over the line.

"Then you think . . . you believe that Jason is . . dead?" Sidney fought back the tears. She had already lived through one episode of believing her husband dead, only to suddenly encounter him alive. Or so she thought. The tears started to slide down her cheeks as she contemplated having to grieve again for Jason.

"I have no way of knowing that, Sidney. The fact that I believe Jason's recorded voice was used rather than the real thing leads me to think that he was not around to speak himself. Why, I don't know. Let's leave it at that for now."

Sidney put down the phone and clutched her head. Every limb was now shaking like a slender elm in a windstorm.

Alarmed, Sawyer spoke earnestly into the phone. "Sidney? *Sidney?* Don't hang up. Please! Sidney?"

The line went dead.

Sawyer slammed down the receiver. "Dammit! Sonofabitch!"

A minute went by. Sawyer stomped around the small room. Working himself into a rage, he finally slammed a heavy fist right through the wall. He leaped for the phone when it rang again.

"Hello?" His voice was shaking with anticipation.

"Let's not talk anymore about whether Jason is . . . is alive, all right?" Sidney's voice was devoid of any emotion.

"All right," Sawyer said quietly. He sat down and paused for a moment, deciding what line of questioning to pursue.

"Lee, why would someone at Triton want to record Jason's voice and then use it to communicate with me?"

"Sidney, if I knew the answer to that, I'd be doing cartwheels down the hallway. You said a number of offices had them installed recently. That means that it could have been anyone at the company who could have jerry-built his mike into a recording device. Or maybe one of Triton's competitors could have done it somehow. I mean, if *you* know he didn't use the microphone, other people would as well. I do know that it's no longer in his office. Maybe it has something to do with the secrets he sold RTG."

Sawyer rubbed his scalp as he sorted through the additional questions he wanted to ask her.

She beat him to it. "Only Jason selling secrets to RTG doesn't make any sense now."

Amazed, Sawyer stood up. "Why not?"

"Because Paul Brophy was working on the CyberCom deal too. He was present at all the strategy sessions. He even made an attempt to take over the lead role in the transaction. Brophy, I now know, was working with Goldman and RTG to learn Triton's final negotiating position and beat them to the punch. He would've known far more about Triton's bargaining position than Jason ever would. The precise deal terms were physically maintained at Tyler, Stone, not at Triton."

Sawyer's eyes grew wide. "You're saying—"

"I'm simply saying that since Brophy was working for RTG, they wouldn't have needed Jason."

Sawyer sat down and swore under his breath. He had never made that connection. "Sidney, we both saw a video of your husband passing information to a group of men in a warehouse in Seattle on the day of the plane crash. If he wasn't giving them information on the CyberCom deal, then what the hell was it?"

Sidney shook in frustration. "I don't know! I do know that when Brophy was cut out of the final rounds of the deal, they tried to blackmail me for it. I pretended to go along. My actual plan was to go to the authorities. But then we got in the limo." Sidney shuddered. "You know the rest."

Sawyer stabbed a hand into his pocket and pulled out a cigarette. He cradled the phone under his chin while he lit up. "You find out anything else?"

"I spoke with Jason's secretary, Kay Vincent. She said the other major project Jason was working on other than CyberCom was an integration of Triton's backup files."

"Tape backups? Is that important?" Sawyer asked.

"I don't know, but Kay also told me that Triton had delivered financial records to CyberCom. On the very day of the plane crash." Sidney sounded exasperated.

"So what's unusual about that? They're involved in a deal."

On that same day I got my butt chewed out in New York by Nathan Gamble because he didn't want to turn those very same records over to CyberCom."

Sawyer rubbed at his forehead. "That doesn't make any sense. Do you think Gamble knew the records were turned over?"

"I don't know. I mean, I can't be sure about that." Sidney paused. The damp cold was starting to become painful. "In fact, I thought the CyberCom deal might blow up because of Gamble's refusal."

"Well, I can tell you for a fact that it didn't. I attended the press conference today announcing the deal. Gamble was smiling like the Cheshire cat."

"Well, with CyberCom in the fold I can understand him being very happy."

"Can't say the same for Quentin Rowe."

"They certainly are an odd pair."

"Right. Like Al Capone and Gandhi."

Sidney breathed deeply into the receiver but said nothing.

"Sidney, I know you're not going to like this, but I'm going to say it anyway. You'd be a lot better off if you came in. We can protect you."

"You mean imprison me, don't you?" she said, a bitter edge in her voice.

"Sidney, I know you didn't kill anyone."

"Can you prove it?"

"I think I can."

"You *think?* I'm sorry, Lee. I really appreciate the

vote of confidence, but I'm afraid that's not quite good enough. I know how the evidence stacks up. And the public's perception of things. They'd throw away the key."

"You could really be in danger out there." Sawyer slowly fingered the FBI shield pinned to his belt. "Listen, tell me where you are and I'll come. No one else. Not my partner, nobody, just me. To get you, they go through me first. Then, meanwhile, we can try to figure this thing out together."

"Lee, you're an FBI agent. There's a warrant for my arrest. It's your official duty to take me into custody the moment you lay eyes on me. On top of that, you've already covered for me once."

Sawyer swallowed with difficulty. In his mind a pair of captivating emerald eyes blended together into the light of a train bearing right down on him. "Then let's just call it part of my unofficial duty."

"And if it's found out, your career is over. On top of it, *you* could go to prison."

"I'm a big boy, I'll take my chances about that. I give you my word it'll just be me coming." His voice trembled with suppressed excitement. Sidney could not speak. "Sidney, I'm shooting straight with you. I . . . I really want you to be okay, all right?"

There was a catch in Sidney's throat. "I believe you, Lee. And I can't tell you how much that means to me. But I'm not going to let you throw your life away either. I'm not having that on my conscience too."

"Sidney—"

"I have to go now, Lee."

"Wait! Don't."

"I'll try to call back."

"When?"

Sidney stared straight ahead through the windshield, her face suddenly rigid, her eyes widening.

525

"I'm . . . I'm not sure," she said vaguely. Then the line went dead.

Sawyer put the phone down and fumbled in his pants pocket for the pack of Marlboros and lit another cigarette. He used his cupped hand for an ashtray while he paced around the room. He stopped and fingered the fist-sized hole in the wall and seriously contemplated giving it a twin. Instead he stepped to the window and looked out in complete despair at a frosty winter night.

As soon as Sidney had gone back into the house, the man stepped from the dark shadows of the garage. His breath frosted in the freezing environment. He opened the door to the Land Rover. As the car's interior dome light came on, the deadly blue eyes shimmered like hideously carved jewels in the soft light. Kenneth Scales's gloved hands expertly searched the car but found nothing of interest. He then picked up the cell phone and hit the redial button. The phone rang only once before Lee Sawyer's excited voice came on the line. Scales smiled as he listened to the urgent tones of the FBI agent, who evidently thought Sidney Archer had called him back. Then Scales disconnected the call, quietly closed the car door and made his way up the stairs to the house. From a leather sheath on his belt he pulled the stiletto blade he had used to kill Edward Page. He would have taken care of Sidney Archer as she stepped from the Land Rover except he was uncertain whether she was armed. He had already seen her skill with a gun. Besides, his method of killing was based on the total surprise of his victims.

He made his way through the first floor looking for the leather jacket Sidney had been wearing, but did not find it. Her purse was on the counter, but what he wanted wasn't in there. He proceeded over to the stairs leading up to the second floor. He paused at that point and cocked his head. Over the rush of the wind, the sound reaching his ears from the second floor made him smile once again. Water running in the tub. On this bitterly cold winter's night in rustic Maine, the sole occupant of the house was preparing to take a nice, hot, soothing bath. He made his way silently up the stairs. The bedroom door at the top of the landing was shut, but he could clearly hear the water running in the adjoining bathroom. Then the water was turned off. He waited a few more seconds as he envisioned Sidney Archer climbing into the tub, letting the hot water comfort her weary body. Then he stepped to the door of the bedroom. Scales would get the password first and then occupy himself for a while with the lady of the house. If he could not find what he wanted, he would promise to let her live in exchange for her secret and then he would kill her. He wondered briefly what the attractive lawyer would look like naked. From what he had seen of her, Scales concluded she would look very good indeed. And it wasn't as though he was in a rush. It had been a long, weary trip up the East Coast to Maine. He deserved a little R&R, he thought as he contemplated the upcoming event.

Scales stood to the side of the door, his back against the wall, his knife at the ready, and placed one hand on the knob, turning it virtually noiselessly.

The shotgun blast that disintegrated the door and embedded several pieces of the weapon's Magnum load in his left forearm was not nearly so quiet. He screamed and threw himself down the stairs, athletically rolling and landing virtually upright, gripping his bloody arm. He jerked his eyes upward as Sidney Archer, fully dressed, charged out of the bedroom. She racked the action of the shotgun again and Scales barely managed to throw himself out of the way before another blast hit the very spot where he had been standing. The house was almost totally dark, but if he moved again she would be able to zero in on his location. He crouched down behind the sofa, his predicament evident. At some point Sidney Archer would risk turning on a light and the deadly power of the shotgun would quickly devastate everything in the small room, including him.

Breathing quietly, he gripped his knife with his good hand, looked around the confines of the living room and waited. His arm stung terribly; Scales was far more used to inflicting pain than receiving it. He listened to Sidney's footsteps as she proceeded cautiously down the stairs. He was sure the shotgun was making wide sweeps of the area. From out of the darkness, he cautiously raised his head an inch or so above the top of the sofa. His eyes instantly riveted on her. She was halfway down the stairs. So intent was she on locating her quarry, she did not see a piece of the bedroom door that had landed on the stairs. When she unwittingly placed her weight fully on it, the piece slipped free and both her feet flew out from under her. With a scream, she tumbled down the stairs, the shotgun smashing against the railing. In an instant he pounced. As the pair rolled along the hardwood floor, he pounded her head against it. She kicked furiously against his chest and ribs with her heavy boots. Then she twisted away just as he struck savagely with his knife. The blow missed barely, tearing through the inside of her jacket instead of her flesh. A white object that had been in Sidney's pocket was dislodged from the impact of the blow and floated to the floor.

Sidney managed to grab the shotgun and delivered

a terrific blow to Scales's face with the butt of the solid Winchester, breaking his nose and knocking out several front teeth. Stunned, Scales dropped his knife and fell back for an instant. Then, furious, he wrenched the shotgun free, turning it on a dazed Sidney Archer. In a panic she hurled herself several feet away but was still easily in range. His fingers pulled the trigger, but the muzzle remained silent. The fall down the stairs and the ensuing struggle had jammed the weapon. Sidney, her head bursting with pain from the earlier blow, desperately crawled away. With a vicious snarl, Scales threw the useless shotgun away and stood up, blood streaming down his shirt from his torn mouth and rearranged nose. He picked up his knife where it had fallen and advanced with murderous eyes toward Sidney. When he lifted the blade to strike, Sidney whirled around, the 9mm pointed right at him. A split second before she fired, however, he exploded into an acrobatic leap that carried him over the dining room table. She held the trigger down, throwing the 9mm into full automatic fire, the Hydra-Shok slugs tracing an explosive pattern across the wall as she tried desperately to follow the path of his impromptu flight. Scales hit the polished wood floor hard, his momentum sending him headlong into the wall. As his torso whiplashed sideways from the impact with the wall, he crashed into the legs of an ornate mahogany sideboard. The slender mahogany legs snapped like matchsticks and the heavy piece collapsed right on top of him, spewing its contents across the room as drawers flew open from the fall. Scales did not move after that.

Sidney jumped up, ran though the kitchen, grabbed her purse off the counter and fled down the stairs to the garage. A minute later the garage door splintered and erupted outward and the Land Rover careened through the savaged opening, did a 180-degree spin in the driveway and disappeared into the snowstorm.

As Sidney looked in her rearview mirror, she saw a pair of head-lights. Her heart skipped a beat as she watched the big Cadillac pull into the driveway of the house she had just left. The blood drained from her face. Omigod! Her parents were finally here and the timing could not have been worse. She swung the truck around, plowing through a snowdrift, and raced back toward her parents' house. Then her problem was suddenly compounded as she caught sight of another pair of headlights coming down the road from the same direction her parents had come. She watched in steadily growing fear as the black sedan moved down the street, its tires slowly crunching over the path just left by the Caddie. The people who had dogged her parents from Virginia. With everything else happening, she had forgotten about them. Sidney slammed the Land Rover's accelerator to the floor. Slipping in the snow for a moment, the four-wheel drive system kicked in and the massive V-8 took hold, propelling the little tank forward like a cannonball. As she bore down on the sedan, Sidney saw the driver react. His hand went inside his coat. But he was a millisecond too late. She flew past her parents' house, veered across the road and, with a crush of metal, slammed into the smaller vehicle, pushing it across the slippery road and depositing it in a steep ditch. The air bag in the truck inflated. With a furious effort, Sidney ripped it off the steering column and slammed the truck into reverse. The sound of metal wrenching free was clearly heard as the two vehicles uncoupled.

Sidney turned the truck around and then stared in disbelief. Her swift attack had taken care of whoever was following her parents. It also had another result. She watched in dismay as the Cadillac turned off Beach Street and roared off back to Route 1. Sidney rammed the accelerator down and headed after them.

The man struggled out of the car and stared in shock at the rapidly disappearing truck.

Sidney saw the taillights of the Cadillac just ahead. At this point, Route 1 was a two-lane road. She pulled up behind her parents and blew her horn repeatedly. The Cadillac immediately accelerated. Her parents were by now probably so scared they wouldn't even stop for a state trooper in a marked car, much less a lunatic blowing her horn in a smashed-up truck. Sidney momentarily held her breath and then careened on to the wrong side of the road, mashed the gas pedal to the floor and pulled alongside her parents' car. She saw her father react to the Land Rover appearing on his left. The Caddie shimmied from side to side as it sped up, and Sidney had to keep the accelerator close to the floor to keep up, as the damaged Land Rover was sluggish to respond. As Sidney steadily gained ground, Bill Patterson planted the bulky Caddie squarely in the middle of the two-lane road, daring their pursuer to overtake them. Sidney rolled down her window and steered her vehicle halfway on to the dirt-and-gravel shoulder. Thank God the roads hadn't been plowed yet or she would have had no shoulder to travel on. As she inched up to the passenger side of the Cadillac, her father swung back on to the right side, forcing Sidney to go off the road entirely. As the Land Rover bounced and swayed over the rough terrain, Sidney looked at her speedometer; it hovered near eighty. Fear rattled through every nerve in her body. She looked up ahead. They were coming to a steep curve. She was about to run out of road. She smashed the accelerator flat to the floor. She only had seconds left. "Mom!" She screamed over the fury of the wind and the wall of pouring snow. "*Mom!*" Sidney leaned as far out the driver's window as she could while maintaining some control over the truck. She took one deep breath and screamed as loud as she ever had in her life. "MMMOOOMM!"

She saw her mother peering through the whipping snow, her eyes wide with terror, and then Sidney finally saw recognition and then relief in them. Her mother quickly turned to her father. The Cadillac slowed down immediately and allowed Sidney to move back into the road ahead of them. Her face and hair covered with snow, Sidney motioned with one hand for them to follow her. In the near-blinding swirl of white, the two cars raced down the road.

About an hour later, they veered off at an exit. Within ten minutes the Land Rover and the Cadillac pulled into the parking lot of a motel. The first thing Sidney Archer did was jump out of the truck, race to her parents' car, throw open the rear door and grab up her daughter in her arms. Tears were pouring down Sidney's face as fiercely as the snow. She gripped her sleepy daughter with fingers that promised never to let her go again. Amy had no way of knowing how close she had come to losing her mother this night. If the blade had veered one inch the other way? If Sidney's mother had recognized her daughter a second too late? But the little girl would never know that. Sidney Archer certainly did, however, and it made her squeeze her daughter to her breast as tightly as she possibly could as her own body painfully convulsed. Bill Patterson came around the car and planted a bear hug around his daughter. The big man was shaking severely too after this latest nightmare. His wife joined them and they stood in a small circle, clutching each other tightly, each of them silent. Though the snow soon covered their clothes, they didn't budge; they were just holding on.

The man had managed to free his vehicle and then ran over to the Patterson's house, where it was still quiet. A minute later the house was quiet no more as the sideboard was slowly raised off the floor and then violently hurled away with another crash and splintering of wood. Scales painfully stood up with the aid of his colleague. The look on his battered face made it abundantly clear that it was indeed fortunate for her that Sidney Archer was not presently within his deadly reach. As he went back to retrieve his knife he noticed the piece of paper Sidney had dropped – Jason's e-mail message. Scales picked it up, studying it momentarily. In another five minutes he and his associate had made their way to the damaged car. Scales picked up his cellular phone and punched in a speed-dial number. It was time to bring in reinforcements.

FIFTY-FOUR

At two-thirty in the morning, a highly agitated Lee Sawyer drove to the office through a snowstorm that threatened to hit blizzard status by that afternoon. The whole East Coast was being assaulted by a major winter storm system that threatened to hang around until Christmas.

Sawyer went directly to the conference room, where he spent the next five hours going over every aspect of the case, from the files, his notes and memory. His main goal was assembling the case as he now understood it into some semblance of logic. The problem was that not much made sense, chiefly because he was not certain whether he was confronted with one case or two: Lieberman and Archer together, or Lieberman and Archer separately. That's really what it boiled down to. He jotted down some new angles that occurred to him, but none of them seemed all that promising. Then he picked up the phone and dialed the lab asking for Liz Martin, the technician who had performed the Luma-lite exam on the limousine.

"Liz, I owe you an apology. I've been letting this case get to me a little bit and I took it out on you. I was out of line and I'm sorry."

Liz smiled. "Apology accepted. We're all under pressure. What's up?"

"I need your resident computer expert skills. What do you know about computer tape backup systems?"

"Funny you should ask. My boyfriend's a trial lawyer and he was just telling me the other day it's the hottest topic in the legal sector right now."

"Why's that?"

"Well, tape backups are potentially discoverable in litigation. For example, an employee writes an interoffice memo or e-mail that contains damaging information about the company. The employee later erases the e-mail and destroys all hard copies of the memo. You'd think it was gone for good, right? Nope, because with tape backup, the system might well have saved it before it was erased. And under the rules of discovery, they may have to turn it over to the other side. My boyfriend's firm advises clients that with documents created via computer, if you don't want someone else to ever read it, then don't create it."

"Hmmm." Sawyer thumbed through the papers in front of him. "Good thing I still opt for invisible ink."

"You're a relic, Lee, but at least you're a nice relic."

"Okay, Professor Liz, I've got another one for you." Sawyer read her the password.

"That's a pretty good password, isn't it, Liz?"

"Actually, it's not."

"What?" That was the absolute last response Sawyer had expected to her.

"It's so long that it would be easy to forget a portion of it or otherwise get it incorrect. Or if you were communicating it to someone else orally, they could easily get it wrong in the transmission, transpose a number, that sort of thing."

"But because it's so long, it wouldn't be capable of being broken, right? I thought that was the beauty of it."

"Certainly. However, you don't have to use *all* those numbers to accomplish that goal. Ten would've been ample for most purposes. With fifteen numbers you're pretty much invulnerable."

535

"But these days you've got computers that could crank those combos through."

"With fifteen numbers you're looking at well over a trillion combos and most encryption packages come with a shut-down feature if too many combos are tried at one time. Even if it didn't have the shut-down feature, the fastest computer in the world doing a numbers crunch still wouldn't pop this password because the presence and placement of those decimal points make the possible combinations so high that a traditional brute-force assault wouldn't work."

"So you're saying—"

"I'm saying whoever put together this password went way overboard. The negatives far outweigh its imperviousness to being cracked. It simply didn't need to be this complex to avoid being penetrated. Maybe whoever put it together was a novice about computers."

Sawyer shook his head. "I think this person knew exactly what he was doing."

"Well, then it wasn't solely for protection purposes."

"What else could it be?"

"I'm not sure, Lee. I've never seen one like this before."

Sawyer didn't say anything.

"Anything else?"

"What? Uh, no, Liz, that's it." Sawyer sounded very depressed.

"I'm sorry if I wasn't much help."

"No, you were. You gave me a lot to think about. Thanks, Liz." He brightened. "Hey, I owe you a lunch, okay?"

"I'm going to hold you to that one and this time I get to pick the place."

"Fine, only make sure they take the Exxon card.

That's about the only plastic I have left."

"You really know how to show a girl a good time, Lee."

Sawyer hung up and looked down at the password again. If half of what he had heard about Jason Archer's mental prowess was true, then the complexity of the password had been no accident. He looked at the numbers again. It was driving him nuts, but he couldn't shake the feeling that they somehow seemed familiar. He poured himself another cup of coffee, took a scratch piece of paper and started doodling, a habit that helped him think. This case seemed to have been with him for years. With a start he looked at the date on the e-mail message Archer had sent his wife: 95–11–19. He wrote the numbers down on the scratch paper: 95–11–19. He smiled. Figures a computer would kick it out like that, more confusing than anything else. Then he found himself staring at the numbers more intently. His smile faded. He quickly wrote them down another way: 95/11/19 then, finally, 951119. He quickly scribbled again, made a mistake, scratched it out and kept going. He looked at the finished product: 599111.

Sawyer's face turned whiter than the paper he was writing on. *Backwards*. He read the e-mail from Jason Archer again. All backwards, Archer had said. But why? If Archer were under so much pressure that he had mistyped the address and not finished the message, why take the time to type two phrases – "all wrong" and "all backwards" – if they meant the same thing? The truth suddenly dawned on Sawyer: unless the two phrases had entirely different meanings, both quite literal. He looked at the numbers comprising the password one more time and then started to write furiously. After several mistakes he finally finished. He numbly drained the last of his coffee as he took in the numbers in their true (unbackward) order: 12–19–90, 2–28–91, 9–26–92, 11–15–92 and 4–16–93. Archer had been very precise in his selection of passwords. It had actually been a clue within the password itself. Sawyer didn't need to consult his notes. He knew what the numbers represented. He took a deep breath.

The calendar dates of the five times Arthur Lieberman had changed interest rates on his own. The five times somebody out there had made enough money to buy a country or maybe lost that much.

Sawyer's question had finally been answered. He had one case, not two. There *was* a connection between Jason and Lieberman. But what was it? Another thought struck him. Edward Page had told Sidney he hadn't been following Jason Archer at the airport. The other person he could have been dogging was Lieberman. Page could have been shadowing the Fed chairman and walked right into Archer's switch. But why follow Lieberman? With a scowl, Sawyer finally put the message aside and looked at the videocasssette recording of Archer's exchange at the warehouse, which was sitting on the table. If Sidney was right about Brophy knowing far more than Jason Archer, what the hell had been passed off in that warehouse? Could that be the connection to Arthur Lieberman? He hadn't looked at the tape in a while. He decided to fix that oversight right now.

He popped the tape in a VCR that rested under a large-screen TV in one corner of the room. He poured some more coffee and hit the control; the tape started. He watched the scene twice through. Then he watched it a third time, in slow motion. A frown spread over his features. When he had watched the tape for the very first time in Hardy's office, something had made him frown then too. What the hell was it? He rewound the tape again and then hit the start button. Jason and the other man were waiting, Jason's briefcase was visible. The knock on the door, the other men came in. The old guy, the other two in sunglasses. Real cute. Sawyer looked at the two burly men again. They looked oddly familiar, but he couldn't . . . He shook his head and continued to watch. Here came the exchange, Jason looking extremely nervous. Then the plane going over. The warehouse was on a flight path to the airport, he had learned. Everyone in the room looked up at the thundering sound. Sawyer jerked so hard he spilled most of his coffee on his shirt. Only this time it wasn't from the sound of the plane.

"Holy shit!" He froze the tape. Then he planted his face a bare inch from the screen. He grabbed the phone. "Liz, I need your magic, and this time, Professor, it'll be dinner." He quickly told her what he wanted.

It took Sawyer two minutes, running flat out, to reach the lab. The equipment was all set up, a smiling Liz standing next to it. Sawyer, puffing hard, handed her the tape, which she put into another VCR. She sat down at a control panel and the tape began to play. The screen it appeared on was a good sixty inches across.

"Okay, okay, get ready, Liz. There! Right there!" Sawyer almost jumped off the floor in his excitement.

Liz froze the tape and then hit some buttons on her panel. The human figures on the screen grew until they spanned the whole screen. There was only one person Sawyer was looking at. "Liz, can you blow this part up right here?" His thick finger stabbed at a specific section of the screen. Liz did as he asked.

Sawyer shook his head in silent amazement. Liz

joined him in looking at the startling scene. She looked up at him. "You were right, Lee. What does it mean?"

Sawyer stared at the man who had identified himself to Jason Archer as Anthony DePazza on that fateful November morning in drizzling Seattle. More specifically, Sawyer zeroed in on DePazza's neck, which was clearly visible, since he had jerked his head up when the plane had gone over. In fact, Sawyer and Liz were both staring at a clear break in the neckline, real and false skin.

"I'm not sure, Liz. But why the hell is the guy with Archer wearing some sort of a disguise?"

Liz stared wistfully at the screen. "I used to be into that when I was a thespian in college."

"Into what?"

"You know, costumes, makeup, masks. For when we put on a performance. I'll have you know I was one wicked Lady Macbeth."

Sawyer looked at the screen, his mouth wide open as the word she had just uttered pounded through his head: *Performance?*

Chewing on this new information, Sawyer hustled back to the conference room. Ray Jackson was sitting there with several documents in his hand, which he waved at his partner. "By fax from Charles Tiedman. Page's handwriting samples. I've got copies of the letters I found in Lieberman's apartment. I'm no expert, but I think we've got a match."

Sawyer sat down and looked over the letters comparing the writing. "I agree with you, Ray, but get the lab to give us a definite."

"Right," Jackson started off to perform that task, but Sawyer abruptly stopped him. "Hey, Ray, let me look at those letters one more time."

Jackson handed them over.

540

Sawyer only really wanted to look at one of them. The letterhead was impressive: Columbia University Alumni Association. Tiedman hadn't mentioned that Steven Page had attended Columbia. Page had evidently, at some point, been active in alumni affairs. Sawyer did some rough arithmetic in his head. Steven Page was twenty-eight when he had died five years ago. That would make him thirty-three or thirty-four today, depending on his birthdate. So he probably would have been a 1984 graduate. Another thought suddenly flared into Sawyer's head.

"Go ahead, Ray. I've got some calls to make."

After Jackson went off with the documents, Sawyer dialed information and got the number for Columbia University's information office. Within a couple of minutes he got through. He was told that Steven Page had indeed been a 1984 graduate of the university, in fact a magna cum laude graduate. Sawyer looked down at his hands as he prepared to ask his next question. Every finger was quivering. He did his best to keep his emotions under control as he waited for the woman on the other end of the line to consult her records. Yes, Sawyer was told. The other student was also an '84 grad; indeed, this one had graduated summa cum laude. Quite impressive, the voice said, to achieve that at Columbia. He asked another question and was told he would have to talk to Student Housing for the answer. He waited, his nerves humming with electricity. When he finally got someone at Student Housing, the question was answered within a minute. Sawyer quietly thanked the person for his help and then slammed down the phone. The veteran FBI agent jumped out of his chair and yelled "Fucking bingo!" to the empty room. Under the circumstances, Sawyer's excitement was quite natural.

Quentin Rowe was also a 1984 graduate of Columbia University. And, far more importantly, Steven Page and Quentin Rowe had shared the same residence during their two years in college.

When it occurred to Sawyer a few seconds later why the two guys in sunglasses on the videotape looked so familiar, his happiness quickly faded into complete disbelief. There was just no damned way. But, yes, it did make sense. Particularly if you looked at it for what it was: a performance, all a sham. He picked up the phone. He had to find Sidney Archer as fast as possible and he knew where he wanted to start looking. *Jesus, Joseph, Mary, has this case just taken one big U-turn,* he thought.

FIFTY-FIVE

Traveling in a rental car, Mrs. Patterson and Amy were on their way to Boston, where they would stay for a few days. Despite arguing about it until the early morning hours, Sidney had been unable to persuade her father to accompany them. He had sat up all night in the motel room cleaning every speck of dirt and grit from his Remington twelve-gauge, his jaw clenched tight and his eyes staring straight ahead as Sidney had marched back and forth in front of him pleading her case.

"You know you really are impossible, Dad!" She said this as they were heading back toward Bell Harbor in her father's car; the battered Land Rover had been towed to a service shop for repairs. She breathed a quiet sigh of relief, though, as she leaned back against the seat. Right now she didn't want to be alone.

Her father looked stubbornly out the window. Whoever was after his daughter would have to kill him in order to get to her. Ghosts and bogeymen beware: Papa was back.

The white van trailing them was a good half mile behind and yet had no trouble mirroring the Cadillac's movements. One of the eight men in the van was not in particularly high spirits. "First you let Archer send an e-mail and then you let his wife get away. I can't believe this shit." Richard Lucas shook his head and angrily eyed Kenneth Scales, who sat beside him. His mouth and forearm were heavily bandaged and his nose, although reset by his own hands, was crimson-red and swollen.

Scales looked over at Lucas. "Believe it." The low voice coming through the damaged mouth carried with it enough pure menace to make even the tough-as-nails Lucas blink and quickly change tack.

Triton's internal security chief hunched forward in his seat. "All right, no good talking about what's past," he said hurriedly.

"Jeff Fisher, the computer guy from Tyler, Stone, had a copy of the contents of the disk on his hard drive. The file directory on Fisher's computer shows that it was accessed at the same time he was in the bar. He must've gotten another copy that way. Smart little sonofabitch. We had a few words with the waitress from the bar last night. She gave Fisher a certified-mail envelope addressed to Bill Patterson, Bell Harbor, Maine, Sidney Archer's father. It's on its way here, that's for sure, and above all else, we've got to get it. Understood?" The six other grim-faced men in the van nodded. Each sported a tattoo of a star with an arrow through it on the back of his hand, the insignia of a veteran mercenary group to which they all belonged – a group that had been formed from the vast dregs of the defunct Cold War. As a former CIA operative, Lucas had found it easy to rekindle the old ties with the allure of U.S. dollars. "We'll let Patterson pick up the package, wait for them to get to an isolated area and then we hit them, hard and fast." He looked around. "A million-dollar bonus per man when we get it." The men's eyes gleamed. Then Lucas looked over at the seventh man. "Do you understand, Scales?"

Kenneth Scales didn't look at him. He pulled out his knife and pointed the tip toward the front of the van and spoke slowly through his wounded mouth. "You can get the disk. I'll take care of the lady. And I'll throw in her old man for no extra charge."

"*First* the package, then you can do whatever the hell you want," Lucas said angrily. Scales didn't answer him. His eyes stared straight ahead. Lucas started to speak again and then thought better of it. He sat back and put one hand nervously through his thinning hair.

During the twenty minutes it took to drive to Alexandria, Jackson tried Fisher's number three times from the car phone, but there was no answer.

"So you think this guy was helping Sidney with the password?" Jackson watched the Potomac River meandering by as they scooted down the GW Parkway.

Sawyer glanced over at him. "According to the surveillance log, Sidney Archer came here the night of the murders at Tyler, Stone. I checked with them. Fisher is Tyler, Stone's resident computer geek."

"Yeah, but it looks like the gent's not at home."

"Lotta things in one's home that may help us out, Ray."

"I don't recall that we have a search warrant, Lee."

Sawyer turned off Washington Street and shot through the heart of Old Town Alexandria. "Details, Ray, you always get hung up on the details." Jackson snorted and fell silent.

They pulled to a stop in front of Fisher's townhouse, got out and quickly headed up the steps. A young woman, her dark hair blowing in the whirling snow, called to them as she got out of her car.

"He's not home."

Sawyer looked back at her. "You wouldn't happen to know where he is, would you?" He walked down the steps and over to the woman, who was hauling a couple of grocery bags out of her car. Sawyer helped her and then held out his official credentials. Jackson did likewise.

The woman looked confused. "FBI? I didn't think they called in the FBI for burglary."

"Burglary, Ms . . .?"

"Oh, I'm sorry – Amanda, Amanda Reynolds. We've lived here for about two years and it's the first time we had the police on the block. They stole all of Jeff's computer equipment."

"You've already talked to the police, I take it?"

She looked sheepish. "We moved down from New York City. There, you don't chain your car to an anchor it's gone in the morning. You're on your guard. Here?" she shook her head. "Still, I feel like an idiot. I thought for sure it was all on the up and up. I just didn't think stuff like that happened in an area like this."

"Have you seen Mr. Fisher recently?"

The woman's brow wilted into furrows. "Oh, three or four days ago, at least. So miserable outside this time of the year, everyone stays indoors."

They thanked her and drove over to the Alexandria Police Station. When they inquired about the burglary at Jeff Fisher's house, the desk sergeant punched some keys on his computer.

"Yeah, that's right. Fisher. In fact, I was on duty the night they brought him in." The desk sergeant stared at the screen, scrolling down some of the text with his skinny fingers while Sawyer and Jackson exchanged puzzled looks. "Came in on a reckless endangerment spewing this story about some guys following him. We thought he'd had a few too many. Did a sobriety test; he wasn't drunk but he reeked of beer. Kept him overnight just to be sure, he posted bail the next day, got his court date and left."

Sawyer stared at the man. "You're saying Jeff

546

Fisher was arrested?"

"That's right."

"And the next day his home was burglarized?"

The desk sergeant nodded his head and leaned against the counter. "Quite a run of bad luck, I'd say."

"Did he describe the people following him?" Sawyer asked.

The sergeant looked at the FBI agent as if he wanted to smell his breath as well. "There wasn't anybody following him."

"You're sure?"

The sergeant rolled his eyes and smiled.

"Okay, you said he wasn't drunk and yet you kept him overnight?" Sawyer put his hands on the counter.

"Well, you know some of these folk, those tests don't work on them. Down a twelve-pack and the breathalyzer comes back a point-oh-one. Fisher was driving crazy and *acting* drunk, anyway. We thought it best to keep him overnight. If he was intoxicated, he could at least sleep it off."

"And he didn't object?"

"Hell, no, said he'd never spent a night in jail before. Thought it might be refreshing." The sergeant shook his bald head. "Doesn't that take the cake? Refreshing, my ass!"

"You don't have any idea where he is now?"

"Hell, we couldn't even find him to tell him his place was broken into. Like I said, he posted his bail and got his court date. Only gets to be my concern if he doesn't show."

"Anything else you can think of?" Sawyer's face was full of disappointment.

The sergeant drummed his fingers on the counter, staring off into space. Finally Sawyer looked at Jackson and they started to leave. "Well, thanks for your help."

They were halfway to the door before the man broke out of his trance. "The guy gave me a package to mail for him, can you believe that crap? I mean, I know I wear a uniform, but do I *look* like a mailman?"

"A package?" Sawyer and Jackson bolted back to the counter.

The sergeant was shaking his head as he recalled the event. "I tell him he can make a phone call and he says, before he does that could I just pretty please drop this in the mail chute for him? Postage is already on it, he says, he'd really appreciate it." The sergeant laughed.

Sawyer stared at the man. "The package – did you mail it?"

The sergeant stopped chuckling and blinked at Sawyer. "What? Yes, I put it in that chute right over there. I mean, it wasn't any trouble. I figured I'd help the guy out."

"What'd it look like? The package?"

"Well, it wasn't a letter. It was in one of those brown puffy packages, you know."

"The ones with bubble packing inside," Jackson suggested.

The sergeant pointed at him. "That's right, I could feel it through the outside."

"How big was it?"

"Oh, well, not big, about yea wide and yea long." The sergeant made an eight-by-six-inch shape with his bony hands. "It was going first-class mail, return receipt requested."

Sawyer again put both hands flat on the counter and looked across at him, his heart racing at a fever pitch. "Do you remember that address on the package? Who it was sent from or going to?"

Again the man resumed his drumming. "Don't remember who sent it: just assumed it was Fisher.

548

But it was going up to, uh, Maine, that's right. Maine. I know because the wife and I just went up in that part of the country, fall a year ago. If you ever get a chance, you should go, absolutely breathtaking. You'll wear out your Kodak, that's for darn sure."

"Where in Maine?" Sawyer was trying his best to be patient.

The man shook his head. "Something Harbor, I think," he finally said.

Sawyer's hopes plummeted. Off the top of his head he could think of at least a half dozen towns in Maine with that word in the name.

"Come on, think!"

The sergeant's eyes popped wide open. "Were there drugs in that package? That Fisher fellow a dealer? I thought something was funny. That why the Feds are interested?"

Sawyer shook his head wearily. "No, no, it's nothing like that. Look, do you at least remember who it was sent to?"

The man thought for another minute and then shook his head. "I'm sorry, fellows, I just don't."

Jackson said, "How about Archer? Was it going to anyone with that last name?"

"Nope, I'd remember that one. One of the deputies here has that last name."

Jackson handed him his card. "Well, if you think of anything else, anything, give us a call immediately. It's very important."

"I'll sure do that. Right away. Count on it."

Jackson touched Sawyer on the sleeve. "Let's go, Lee."

They headed toward the exit. The sergeant went back to his work. Suddenly Sawyer whirled around, this thick finger pointing across the room like a pistol directly at the sergeant, the vision of a MAINE

549

VACATIONLAND bumper sticker on a Cadillac firmly planted in his mind. "Patterson!"

The sergeant looked up, startled.

"Was it going to someone named Patterson in Maine?" Sawyer asked.

The sergeant brightened and then snapped his fingers again. "That's right. Bill Patterson." His smile was cut short as he watched the two FBI agents sprint out of the police station.

FIFTY-SIX

Bill Patterson looked over at his daughter as they drove through the snow-covered streets. The snow had grown much heavier in the last half hour. "So you're saying this guy from your office was supposed to send a package up to me to hold for you? A copy of something on a computer disk Jason sent you?" Sidney nodded. "But you don't know what it is?"

"It's in code, Dad. I have the password now, but I had to wait for the package."

"But it never came? You're sure?"

Sidney sounded exasperated. "I called FedEx. They have no record of the package being picked up. Then I called his house and the police answered. Oh, God." Sidney shuddered as she thought of Jeff Fisher's possible fate. "If anything's happened to Jeff . . ."

"Well, have you tried your answering machine at home? He might have called and left a message."

Sidney's mouth dropped open at the brilliant simplicity of her father's suggestion. "Christ! Why didn't I think of that?"

"Because you've been running for your life the last two days, that's why." Her father's voice was gruff. He reached down and gripped the shotgun that lay on the floorboard.

Sidney pulled the Cadillac into a gas station and stopped near a phone booth. She ran over to the phone. The snow was pouring down so fast she didn't notice the white van that drove past the station, turned down a side road, made a U-turn and awaited her return to the highway.

Sidney punched in her calling card and phone numbers. It seemed an eternity before the machine picked up. There was a slew of messages. From her brothers, other family members, friends who had seen the news and called with questions, outrage, support. She waited with growing impatience as the messages plodded on. Then she sucked in her breath as the sound of a familiar voice reached her ears.

"Hello, Sidney, this is your Uncle George. Martha and I are up in Canada this week. Enjoying it very much, although it's very cold. I sent your and Amy's Christmas presents early like I said I would. But it's coming in the mail instead because we missed the damn Federal Express and didn't want to wait. Be on the lookout for it. We sent it first-class, certified mail so you have to sign for it. I hope it's what you wanted. We love you very much and look forward to seeing you soon. Kiss Amy for us."

Sidney slowly put the phone down. She didn't have an Uncle George or an Aunt Martha, but there was no mystery about the phone call. Jeff Fisher had impersonated the voice of an old man pretty well. Sidney raced back to the car and got in.

Her father looked sharply at her. "Did he call?"

Sidney nodded as she gunned the car and drove off with a squeal of tires, throwing her father back against the seat. "Where the hell are we going so damned fast?"

"The post office."

The Bell Harbor Post Office was located in the middle of the town center, its United States flag whipping back and forth in the punishing wind. Sidney pulled up to the curb and her father jumped out. He went in and then came out again a couple of minutes later, ducking his head to get back in the car.

He was empty-handed. "The day's mail shipment isn't in yet."

Sidney stared at him. "You're sure?"

He nodded. "Jerome's been the postmaster up here ever since I can remember. He said to check back around six. He'll stay open for us. You know, it may not be in today's bundle if Fisher only mailed it two days ago."

Sidney banged the steering wheel fiercely with both hands before laying her head wearily down on it. Her father put a big hand gently on her shoulder. "Sidney, it'll get here eventually. I just hope whatever's on that disk will clear up this nightmare."

Sidney looked up at him, her face pale and her eyes jumpy. "It has to, Dad. It has to." Her voice cracked painfully. *If it didn't? No, she couldn't think like that.* Brushing the hair out of her face, she put the car in gear and headed out.

The white van waited a couple of minutes and then pulled out of an alleyway and followed them.

"I can't friggin' believe this," Sawyer roared.

Jackson looked at him with clear frustration. "What can I tell you, Lee, it's a blizzard out there. National, Dulles and BWI are all shut down. Kennedy, La Guardia and Logan are closed too. So are Newark and Philly. It's tied up flights all across the country. The whole East Coast looks like Siberia. And the bureau won't release a plane to fly in this weather."

"Ray, we have got to get to Bell Harbor. We should've been there by now. How about the train?"

"Amtrak's still clearing track. Besides, I checked – the train doesn't go all the way through. We'd have to take a bus the last leg. And in this weather sections of the Interstate are bound to be down. Plus it's not all highway. We'd have to take some back roads. We're talking fifteen hours at least."

Sawyer looked as if he were about to explode. "They could all be dead in one hour, much less fifteen."

"You don't have to tell me that. If I could spread my arms and fly, I would, but dammit, I can't," Jackson angrily retorted.

Sawyer calmed down rapidly. "Okay, I'm sorry, Ray." He sat down. "Any luck getting the locals rounded up?"

"I made calls. The closest field office is Boston. Well over five hours away. And in this weather? Who knows? There are small resident agencies in Portland and Augusta. I've left messages, but I haven't heard back yet. The state police might be a possibility, although they've probably got their hands full with traffic accidents."

"Shit!" Sawyer shook his head in despair and drummed his fingers impatiently on the table. "A plane's the only way. There's got to be someone willing to fly in this crap."

Ray shook his head. "Maybe a fighter pilot. Know any?" he asked sarcastically.

Sawyer jumped up. "I sure as hell do."

The black van pulled to a stop near a small hanger at the Manasas county airport. The snow was falling so hard that it was difficult to see more than a few inches ahead. A half dozen black-clad members of the heavily armed Hostage Rescue Team, each carrying assault rifles, followed by Sawyer and Jackson, filed out rapidly and ran toward the plane that awaited them on the tarmac, engines running. The agents quickly boarded the Saab turboprop. Sawyer settled in next to the pilot while Jackson and the HRT members strapped themselves in the rear seats.

"I was hoping to see you again before this was

554

over, Lee," George Kaplan shouted over the noise of the engines, and smiled at the big man.

"Hell, I don't forget my friends, George. Besides, you're the only sonofabitch I know crazy enough to fly in this." Sawyer looked out the windshield of the Saab. Staring back at him was a blanket of white. He looked over at Kaplan, who was working the controls as the plane taxied to the runway. A bulldozer had just finished clearing the short strip of tarmac, but the runway was rapidly being covered again. No other planes were operating because officially the airport was closed. All sane people had heeded that edict.

In the back, Ray Jackson rolled his eyes and gripped the seat as he stared through the window at the near-whiteout conditions. He looked at one of the HRT members. "We're all crazy; you know that, don't you?"

Sawyer turned around in his seat and grinned. "Hey, Ray, you know you can stay here. I can tell you about all the fun when I get back."

"Then who the hell would look after your sorry ass?" Jackson shot back.

Sawyer chuckled and turned back around to look at Kaplan. The agent's smile was replaced with a sudden look of apprehension. "You gonna be able to get this baby off the ground?" Sawyer asked.

Kaplan grinned. "Try flying through napalm for a living."

Sawyer managed a weak smile, but he also noted how focused Kaplan was on the controls, how he continually looked at the driving snow. Finally Sawyer's eyes came to rest on the throbbing vein located on the NTSB man's right temple. Sawyer let out a deep breath, hitched his safety belt as tight as he could and held on to his seat with both hands as Kaplan pushed the throttle forward. The plane rapidly gathered speed, bumping and swaying along the snowy runway. Sawyer stared ahead. The plane's headlights illuminated a dirt field that signaled the end of the airstrip; it hurtled toward them. As the plane struggled against the snow and wind, Sawyer again looked over at Kaplan. The pilot's eyes constantly scanned ahead and then skipped briefly across his instrument panel. When Sawyer looked back ahead, his stomach went into his throat. They were at the end of the runway. The Saab's twin engines were at their loudest pitch. It didn't look as if it was going to be enough.

In the back, Ray Jackson and all the HRT members simultaneously closed their eyes. A silent prayer escaped Ray Jackson's lips as he thought back to another dirt field where a plane had ended its existence along with that of everyone on board. Suddenly the nose of the plane jerked skyward and it lifted off the ground. A grinning Kaplan looked over at Sawyer, who was two shades paler than he had been a minute before. "See, I told you it would be easy."

As they rose steadily through the skies, Sawyer touched Kaplan's sleeve. "This question might seem a little premature, but when we get up to Maine, do we have a place to land this thing?"

Kaplan nodded. "There's a regional airport in Portsmouth but that's several hours from Bell Harbor by car. That's in good weather. I checked the maps when I filed our flight plan. There's an abandoned military airfield ten minutes outside of Bell Harbor. I verified with the state police that transportation will be waiting for us."

"Did you say 'abandoned'?"

"It's still usable, Lee. The good thing is there's no air traffic to worry about because of the weather. We've got a pretty straight shot all the way."

"You mean nobody else is this crazy?"

Kaplan grinned. "Anyway, the bad news is there's no operating tower at the airstrip. We'll be on our own for landing purposes, although they're going to put lights out for us outlining the runway. It's okay, I've gone solo like that plenty of times."

"In weather like this?"

"Hey, there's a first time for everything. Seriously, this plane is solid as a rock, and the instrumentation is first-rate. We'll be okay."

"If you say so."

Through several thousand feet the plane bumped and swayed sickeningly as the snow and high winds pummeled it. One sudden blow seemed to halt the Saab in its tracks. All on board gasped collectively as the plane shuddered from the assault and then suddenly dropped a few hundred feet before being hit by another gust. The aircraft turned sideways, almost stalled and then dropped again, this time even farther. Sawyer looked out the window. All he saw was white: snow and clouds, he really couldn't tell which was which. His senses of direction and elevation were completely gone. For all he knew, terra firma was about six feet away and coming at them way too fast. Kaplan looked over at Sawyer. "Okay, I admit, this is pretty bad. Hang on, guys, I'm going to take us up to ten thousand feet. This storm system is really strong but not that deep. Let's see if I can get us a smoother ride."

The next few minutes were more of the same as the plane lurched up and down and occasionally to the side. Finally, they broke through the cloud cover and emerged into a rapidly darkening, clear sky. Within a minute the plane assumed a level, smooth flight pattern due north.

From a private airstrip in a rural area forty miles

557

west of Washington, D.C., a private jet had rocketed into the sky about twenty minutes ahead of Sawyer and his men. Flying at thirty-two thousand feet and at over double the speed of the Saab, the jet would arrive in Bell Harbor in less than half the time it would take the FBI to get there.

At a few minutes past six Sidney and her father pulled in front of the Bell Harbor Post Office. Bill Patterson went in and this time he exited carrying a package. The Cadillac sped off. Patterson pulled open one end of the package and peered inside. He hit the interior light so he could see better.

Sidney looked over at him. "Well?"

"It's a computer disk, all right."

Sidney relaxed slightly. She reached her hand in her pocket to pull out the paper with the password on it. Her face turned pale as her finger probed through the large hole in her pocket and, for the first time, she noted that the inside of her jacket, including the pocket, was slashed open. She stopped the car and frantically searched all of her other pockets. "Oh, my God! I don't believe this." She smashed her fists into the seat. "Dammit."

"What's wrong, Sid?" Her father grabbed one of her hands.

She slumped back in the seat. "I had the password in my jacket. Now it's gone. I must've lost it back at the house, when that guy was doing his best to carve me up."

"Can't you remember it?"

"It's too long, Dad. All numbers."

"And nobody else has it?"

Sidney nervously licked her lips. "Lee Sawyer does." She automatically checked the rearview mirror as she put the car back in gear. "I can try him."

558

"Sawyer. Isn't he the big guy who came to the house?"

"Yes."

"But the FBI's looking for you. You can't contact him."

"Dad, it's okay. He's on our side. Hang on." She turned into a gas station and pulled up to a phone booth. While her father held sentinel in the car with his shotgun, Sidney dialed Sawyer's home. As she waited for Sawyer to answer, she watched as a white van pulled into the gas station. It bore Rhode Island license plates. She eyed the van suspiciously for a moment and then completely forgot about it as she watched a car carrying two Maine state troopers pull into the station. One got out of the car. She froze as he glanced in her direction. Then he went inside the small gas station building, which also sold snacks and drinks. Sidney quickly turned away from the remaining trooper and put the collar of her coat up. A minute later she got back in the car.

"Jesus, I thought I was going to have a stroke when I saw the police pull in," Patterson said, his chest heaving.

Sidney put the car in gear and very slowly pulled out of the lot. The trooper was still in the gas station. Going for coffee, she surmised.

"Did you reach Sawyer?"

Sidney shook her head. "God, I can't believe it. First I have the disk and no password. Then I get the password and I lose the disk. Now I have the disk back and I've lost the password again. I'm losing my mind." She pulled at her hair.

"Where did you get the password in the first place?"

"From Jason's electronic mailbox on America Online. Omigod!" She sat straight up in the seat.

"What?"

"I can access the message again from Jason's mailbox." Sidney slumped back down again. "No, I'd need a computer to do that."

A smile slide across her father's face. "We've got one."

She jerked her head in his direction. "What?"

"I brought my laptop up with me. You know how Jason got me hooked on computers. I've got my Rolodex, investment portfolio, games, recipes, even medical information on there. I also have an AOL account, software all loaded on. My laptop's equipped with a phone modem."

"Dad, you're beautiful." She kissed him on the cheek.

"There's only one problem."

"What's that?"

"It's back at the beach house with all our other stuff."

Sidney slapped her forehead. "Dammit!"

"Well, let's go get it."

She shook her head violently. "Uh-uh, Dad. That's way too risky."

"Why? We're armed to the teeth. We lost whoever was following you. They probably think we're long gone from the area. It'll take me one minute to get it and then we can drive back to the motel, plug it in and get the password."

Sidney was wavering. "I don't know, Dad."

"Look, I don't know about you, but I want to see what's on this sucker." He held up the package. "Don't you?"

Sidney looked over at the package, bit her lip. Finally she clicked on her turn signal and headed back to the beach house.

The jet broke through the low cloud cover and skidded to a stop on the private airstrip. The sprawling resort on the Maine shoreline had once been a robber baron's summer retreat. It was currently a popular destination for the well-heeled. Now, in December, it was deserted except for weekly maintenance checks by a local firm. Because there was nothing within several miles, its seclusion was one of its chief attributes. Barely three hundred yards from the runway the Atlantic pitched and bellowed. A group of very grim-looking people alighted from the plane, were met by a waiting car and driven over to the resort located about a minute away. The jet turned around and taxied to the opposite end of the runway, where its door reopened and another man climbed off and walked quickly toward the resort building.

Sidney, struggling with the Cadillac, burrowed down the snowy road. The plows had made several passes over the hard surface but Mother Nature clearly had the upper hand. Even the big Cadillac pitched and swayed over the uneven surface. Sidney turned to her father. "Dad, I don't like this. Let's just drive down to Boston. We can be there in four or five hours. We'll hook up with Mom and Amy and find another computer tomorrow morning."

Her father's face assumed a very stubborn look. "In this weather? The highway's probably closed. Hell, most of the state of Maine closes down this time of year. We're almost there. You stay in the car, keep it running and I'll be back before you can count to ten."

"But Dad—"

"Sidney, there's nobody around. We're all alone. I'll take my shotgun. You think somebody would try anything? Just wait by the side of the road. Don't pull in the driveway, you'll get stuck."

Sidney finally gave in and did as she was told. Her

father got out of the car, leaned back in and, with a grin on his face, said, "Start counting to ten."

"Just hurry, Dad!"

She anxiously watched as he trudged through the snow, shotgun in hand. Then she began to scan the street. Her father was probably right. As she glanced down at the package containing the disk, she picked it up and put it in her purse. She wasn't going to lose it again. She jerked up suddenly as a light came on in the house. Then she caught her breath. Her father needed to see where he was going. They were almost there. A minute later she looked over at the house as the front door closed and footsteps approached the car. Her father had made good time.

"Sidney!" She jerked her head upward and stared in horror as her father burst on to the second-story deck. *"Run!"*

In the blinding white of the snow, she could see hands grabbing her father, pulling him roughly down. She heard him scream again over the wind and then she didn't hear him anymore. Headlights hit her in the face. As she whirled around to stare out the windshield, the white van was almost on her. It must have been driving before without its lights on.

Then she saw the shadowy figure next to the car and watched in horror as the muzzle of a machine gun started its ascent toward her head. All in one motion she hit the automatic door locks, slammed the car in reverse and hit the accelerator. As she threw herself down sideways in the seat, a burst from the machine gun strafed the front of the Cadillac, shooting out the passenger-side window and shattering half the windshield. The front end of the heavy vehicle slid sharply sideways under the sudden surge, thudded into human flesh and sent the gunman flying into a snowdrift. The wheels of the Caddie finally burned through the layers of snow, hit asphalt and leaped backward. Covered with bits of glass, Sidney sat back up, fighting to get control of the spinning car as she watched the van bearing down on her. She backed down the street until she had just passed the intersection leading away from the beach. Then she slammed the car in drive, punched the gas and fishtailed through the intersection. The car flew forward, kicking snow, salt and gravel in its wake. The next minute she was hurtling down the road; snow and wind screamed into the Cadillac's new multiple openings. She looked in the rearview mirror. Nothing. Why weren't they following her? She almost immediately answered her own question as her mind began to function again. Because now they had her father.

FIFTY-SEVEN

Here we go, guys, hang on." Kaplan cut the airspeed, manipulated the plane's controls, and the aircraft, rocking and swaying, suddenly burst through the low cloud cover. A few miles ahead, lit wands, stuck in the hard ground, signaled the outlines of the airstrip. Kaplan eyed the illuminated path to safety and a proud grin spread across his face. "Damn, I'm good."

The Saab landed barely a minute later in a swirl of snow. Sawyer had the door open before the plane had even stopped rolling. He sucked in huge amounts of the frigid air and his nausea quickly passed. The HRT members stumbled off, several of them sitting down on the ice-sheathed tarmac, breathing deeply. Jackson was the last off. A recovered Sawyer eyed him. "Damn, Ray, you almost look white." Jackson started to say something, then pointed a shaky finger at his partner, covered his mouth with his other hand and silently headed off with the HRT members to the vehicle waiting nearby; a Maine state trooper stood next to it, waving his flashlight at them as a guidepost.

Sawyer leaned his head back in the plane. "Thanks for the ride, George. You gonna hang tight here? I don't know how long this is gonna take."

Kaplan couldn't hide the grin. "Are you kidding? And miss the opportunity to chauffeur you guys back home? I'll be right here waiting."

Grunting in response, Sawyer closed the door and

564

hurried over to the vehicle. The others were gathered around waiting for him. When he saw what their transport vehicle was, he stopped dead in his tracks. They all eyed the paddy wagon.

The state trooper looked over at them. "Sorry, guys, it's all we had on such short notice to accommodate eight of you."

The FBI agents climbed into the back of the paddy wagon.

The vehicle had a small window of chicken wire and glass communicating with the front. Jackson slid it open so the trooper could hear him. "Can you turn some heat on back here?"

"Sorry," the man said, "a prisoner we were transporting went nuts and busted the vents; they haven't been fixed yet."

Huddled on the bench, Sawyer watched clouds of breath so thick it looked like a fire had broken out. He laid his rifle down and rubbed his stiff fingers together to warm them. A cold draft from some invisible crevice in the truck's body hit him right between the shoulder blades. Sawyer shivered. *Christ*, he thought, *it's like someone turned the air-conditioning on full-blast.* He hadn't been this cold since investigating Brophy's and Goldman's deaths in the parking garage. At that instant, Sawyer recalled his other recent encounter with the frigid effects of air-conditioning – the slain plane fueler's apartment. The look on his face became one of utter disbelief as he made the mental connection. "Oh, my God."

Sidney figured there was only one way for the men who had abducted her father to contact her. She pulled in to a convenience store, got out and hurried over to the phone. She dialed her home in Virginia. When the answering machine came on, she tried her

565

best to recognize the voice, but she didn't. She was given a number to call. She assumed it was a cellular phone rather than a fixed location. She took a deep breath and dialed the number. The phone was immediately answered. It was a different voice than the one on the answering machine, but again she couldn't place it. She was to drive twenty minutes north of Bell Harbor along Route 1 and take the exit for Port Haven. Then she was given detailed directions that took her to an isolated stretch of land between Port Haven and the larger town of Bath.

"I want to talk to my father." The request was refused. "Then I'm not coming. For all I know, he's already dead."

She was met with an eerie silence. Her heart thumped against her rib cage. The air rushed out of her as she heard the voice.

"Sidney, sweetie."

"Dad, are you all right?"

"Sid, get the hell out of he—"

"Dad? Dad?" Sidney screamed into the phone. A man coming out of the convenience store carrying a cup of coffee stared at her, looked over at the heavily damaged Cadillac and then back at her. Sidney stared back at him as her hand dipped instinctively to the 9mm in her pocket. The man hurried to his pickup truck and drove off.

The voice came back on. Sidney had thirty minutes to get her destination.

"How do I know you'll let him go if I give it to you?"

"You don't." The tone of voice brooked no opposition.

The attorney in Sidney, however, stomped to the surface. "That's not good enough. You want this disk so bad, then we're going to have to agree to terms."

566

"You've gotta be kidding. You want your old man back in a body bag?"

"So we meet in the middle of nowhere, I give you the disk and you let him and me go out of the goodness of your heart? Right! Under that proposal you'll have the disk and my father and I will be somewhere in the Atlantic providing nourishment for sharks. You'll have to do a lot better than that if you want what I've got."

Though the man had covered the receiver, Sidney heard voices on the other end of the line, a couple of them raised in anger.

"It's our way or nothing."

"Fine, I'm on my way to state police headquarters. Be sure to stay tuned to the evening news. I'm sure you don't want to miss anything. Good-bye."

"Wait!"

Sidney didn't say anything for a minute. When she did, she spoke with far more confidence than she was feeling at the moment. "I'll be at the intersection of Chaplain and Merchant Streets smack in the center of Bell Harbor in thirty minutes. I'll be sitting in my car. It should be easy to spot – it's the one with all the extra air-conditioning. You blink your headlights twice. You let my father out. There's a diner right across the street. I see him go there, I open the car door, place the disk on the sidewalk and drive off. Please keep in mind that I'm heavily armed and more than prepared to send as many of you as I can straight to hell."

"How do we know it's the right disk?"

"I want my father back. It'll be the right disk. I hope you choke on it. Do we have a deal?" Now *her* tone of voice brooked no opposition.

She waited anxiously for the answer. *Please, God, don't let them call my bluff.* She let out a sigh of relief when it finally came. "Thirty minutes." The line went dead.

Sidney got back in the car and gripped the dashboard in frustration. How the hell had they tracked her and her father? It was impossible. It was as if they had been watching Sidney and her father the entire time. The white van had also been at the gas station. The attack probably would have occurred there except for the timely arrival of the state troopers. She lay down across the front seat as she fought to keep her nerves in check. She moved her purse out of the way and then opened it, just to make sure the disk was still there. The disk for her father. But once the disk was gone, she would spend the rest of her life running from the police. Or at least until they caught her. Quite a choice. But there was really no choice about it.

As she sat back up she started to close her purse. Then she stopped, her thoughts drifting back to that night, the night in the limo. So much had happened since her terrifying escape. And yet it hadn't really been an escape, had it? The killer had let her go and also had courteously let her keep her purse. In fact, she would have forgotten it entirely except for him tossing it to her. She had been so happy to get out alive, she had never really considered why he would have done something so remarkable . . . She started to claw through the contents of her purse. It took a couple of minutes, but she finally found it, at the very bottom. It had been inserted through a slit in the lining of the purse. She held it up and stared at it. A tiny tracking device.

She looked behind her as a shiver thudded up her spine. Putting the car in gear again, she sped off. Up ahead, a dump truck converted into a snowplow had pulled to the curb. She looked in her mirror. There was no one behind her. She rolled down the driver's-side window, pulled up to the truck and cocked her hand back as she prepared to toss the tracking device into the back of the truck. Then, just as quickly, she stopped the swing of her arm and rolled her window back up. The tracking device was still in her hand. She hit the gas, leaving the truck quickly behind. She looked down at her tiny companion of the last few days. What did she have to lose? She quickly headed toward town. She had to get to the arranged drop-off spot as early as possible. But first she needed something from the grocery store.

The diner Sidney had mentioned in her telephone conversation was filled with hungry patrons. Two blocks over from the prearranged drop-off spot, the Cadillac, lights out, was parked at the curb next to the impressive bulk of an evergreen surrounded by a calf-high wrought-iron fence. The interior of the Cadillac was dark, the silhouette of the driver barely visible.

Two men walked quickly along the sidewalk, while another pair across the street paralleled their movements. One of the men looked down at a small instrument clutched in his hands; the small amber screen had a grid stamped on it. A red light burned brightly on the screen, pointed directly at the Cadillac. The men quickly moved in. One weapon flashed through where the passenger-side window had once been. At the same instant the driver's-side door was torn open. The gunmen looked in astonishment at the driver: a mop with a leather jacket over it, a baseball cap perched rakishly on top.

The white van was parked at the intersection of Chaplain and Merchant, its motor running. The driver checked his watch, scanned the street and then hit his headlights twice. In the back of the van, Bill Patterson lay on the floor, his feet and hands tied securely, his mouth taped shut. The driver jerked his head around as the passenger-side door was thrown open and a 9mm pistol was pointed at his head. Sidney climbed in the van. She cocked her head toward the back to make sure her father was okay. She had already seen him through the back window when she had spotted the van a minute earlier. She figured they had to be prepared to actually hand her father over. "Put your gun down on the floorboard. Take it out muzzle first. If you finger goes anywhere near the trigger, I will empty my entire clip into your head. Do it!"

The driver quickly did as he was told.

"Now get out!"

"What?"

She shoved the pistol into his neck, where it pushed painfully against a throbbing vein. "Get out!"

When he opened the door and turned his back to her, Sidney swung her legs up on the seat, coiled them back and kicked him with all her might. He sprawled on the pavement. She closed the door, jumped into the driver's seat and hit the gas. The van's tires turned the white snow black and then it rocketed off.

Ten minutes outside of town, Sidney stopped the van, jumped into the back and untied her father. The two sat for several minutes holding on to each other, their bodies quivering with a heavy mixture of fear and relief.

"We need to get another car to drive. I wouldn't put it past them to have bugged this one. And they'll be on the lookout for the van," Sidney said as they hurtled down the road.

"There's a rental place about five minutes away. But why don't we just go to the cops, Sid?" Her father rubbed his wrists. His swollen eyes and cracked knuckles testified to the struggle the old man had put up.

She breathed deeply and looked over at him. "Dad, I don't know what's on the disk. If it's not enough . . ."

Her father looked at her, the realization sinking in that he might lose his little girl after all.

"It will be enough, Sidney. If Jason took all the trouble to send it to you, it *has* to be enough."

She smiled at him and then her face went dark. "We have to split up, Dad."

"There's no way I'm leaving you now."

"Your being with me makes you an accessory. I'll tell you one thing: We're not both going to jail."

"I don't give a damn about that."

"Okay, then what about Mom? What would happen to her? And Amy? Who would be there for them?"

Patterson started to say something and then stopped. He frowned as he looked out the window. Finally he looked over at her. "We'll go to Boston together and then we'll talk about it. If you still want to split up then, so be it."

While Sidney sat outside in the van, Patterson went in to rent a car. When he came out a few minutes later and walked over to the van, Sidney rolled down the window.

"Did you rent a car?" Sidney asked.

Patterson nodded. "They'll have it ready in about five minutes. I got us a roomy four-door. You can sleep in the back; I'll drive."

"I love you, Dad." Sidney rolled the window back up and drove off. Her stunned father ran after her, but she was quickly out of sight.

"Christ!" Sawyer peered out the window into near-zero visibility. "Can't we go any faster?" he yelled through the window to the trooper. They had already seen the devastation of the Patterson beach house and were now desperately looking everywhere for Sidney Archer and her family.

The trooper yelled back, "We go any faster, we're going to end up dead in some ditch."

Dead. Is that what Sidney Archer is right now? Sawyer looked at his watch. He fumbled in his pocket for a cigarette.

Jackson was looking at him. "Damn, Lee, don't start smoking in here. It's hard enough to breathe as it is."

Sawyer's lips parted as he felt the slender object in his pocket. He slowly pulled the card out.

As Sidney headed out of town, she decided to keep her emotions in check and let longtime habits take over. For what seemed like forever, she had been merely reacting to a series of crises, without the opportunity to think things through. She was an attorney, trained to view facts logically, look at the details and then work them into an overall picture. She certainly had some information to work with. Jason had labored on Triton's records for the CyberCom deal. That she knew. Jason had disappeared under mysterious circumstances and had sent her a disk with some information on it. That, also, was a fact. Jason was not selling secrets to RTG, not with Brophy in the picture. That also was clear to her. And then there were the financial records. Apparently Triton had simply handed them over. Then why the big scene at the meeting in New York? Why had Gamble demanded to talk to Jason about his work on the records, particularly after he had sent Jason an e-mail congratulating him on a job well done? Why the big deal of getting Jason on the phone? Why put her in an impossible situation like that?

She slowed down and pulled off the road. Unless the intent all along was to put her in an impossible situation. Making it appear as though she had lied. Suspicion had followed her from that very moment. What exactly had been in those records in the warehouse? Was that what was on the disk? Something Jason had found out? That night Gamble's limo had whisked her to his estate, he had obviously wanted some answers. Could he have been attempting to find out if Jason had told her anything?

Triton had been a client for several years now. A big, powerful company with a very private past. But how did that tie in to all the other things? The deaths of the Page brothers. Triton beating out RTG for CyberCom. As Sidney thought once more of that horrible day in New York, something clicked. Ironically, she had the same thought Lee Sawyer had experienced earlier but for a different reason: *A performance.*

My God! She had to get in touch with Sawyer. She put the van in drive and got back on the road. A shrill ring interrupted her thoughts. She looked around at the interior of the van for the source until her eyes alighted on the cellular phone resting on a magnetized plate against the lower dashboard. She hadn't noticed it until just that moment. It was ringing? Her hand went instinctively down to answer it and then pulled back. Finally she picked it up. "Yes?"

"I thought you weren't interested in playing games." The voice was filled with anger.

"Right. And you just forgot to mention that you had a bug in my purse and were just waiting to jump me."

"Okay, let's talk about the future. We want the disk and you're going to bring it to us. Now!"

"What I'm going to do is hang up. Now!"

573

"If I were you, I wouldn't."

"Listen, if you're trying to keep me on the phone so you can lock on my location, it's not going—" Sidney's voice broke off and her entire body turned to putty as she listened to the small voice on the other end of the line.

"Mommy? Mommy?"

Her tongue as big as a fist, Sidney could not answer. Her foot went off the accelerator; her dead arms no longer had the strength to steer the van. The vehicle slowed down and drifted into a pile of snow on the shoulder.

"Mommy? Daddy? Come over?" The voice sounded frightened, pitiful.

Suddenly sick to her stomach, her entire body swaying uncontrollably, Sidney managed to speak. "AA-Amy. Baby."

"Mommy?"

"Baby, it's Mommy. I'm here." An avalanche of tears poured down Sidney's face.

Sidney heard the phone being taken away.

"Ten minutes. Here are the directions."

"Let me talk to her again. Please!"

"Now you have nine minutes and fifty-five seconds."

A sudden thought occurred to Sidney. What if it was a tape? "How do I know you really have her? That could be just a recording."

"Fine. If you want to take that chance, don't come." The voice sounded very confident. There was no earthly way Sidney would ever take that chance. The person on the other line knew that too.

"If you hurt her—"

"We're not interested in the kid. She can't identify us. After it's over, we'll drop her at a safe place." He paused. "You won't be joining her, though, Ms. Archer. Your safe places have just run out."

"Let her go. Please just let her go. She's only a baby." Sidney was trembling so much she could barely keep the phone pressed against her mouth.

"You better write down these directions. You don't want to get lost. If you don't show, there won't be enough left of your kid to identify."

"I'll be there," She said in a hushed voice and the line went dead. She pulled back on the road. A sudden thought leaped across her mind. Her mother! Where was her mother? Her blood seemed to be pooling in her veins as she gripped the steering wheel. Another ringing sound invaded the interior of the van. With a shaking hand, Sidney picked up the phone, but there was no one there. In fact, the ringing sound was different. She pulled off the road again and desperately searched everywhere. Her eyes finally stopped on the seat right next to her. She looked at her purse, slowly put her hand inside and pulled the object out. Written across the small screen on her pager was a phone number she didn't recognize. She turned off the pager's ringer. It was probably a wrong number. She couldn't imagine that someone from her law firm or a client was attempting to call her; she was fresh out of legal advice. She was about to erase the message, but her finger stopped. Could it be Jason? If it was Jason, then it would qualify as the worst timing in the history of the world. Her finger remained poised over the erase button. Finally she put the pager in her lap, picked up the cellular phone and dialed the number on the pager's screen.

The voice that came on the other end of the line was enough to take her breath away. Apparently, miracles did happen.

The main house of the resort was dark, its seclusion made all the more stark by a wall of bulk

575

evergreens in front. When the van pulled down the long driveway, two armed guards emerged from the entryway to meet it. The snowstorm had lightened considerably in the last few minutes. Behind the house the dark, foreboding waters of the Atlantic assaulted the land.

One of the guards jerked back as the van continued to roll toward them without any sign of slowing down. "Shit," he yelled as both men hurled themselves out of the way. The van tore past them, crashed right though the front door and came to an abrupt halt, its wheels still spinning, when it struck a four-foot-thick interior wall. A minute later, several heavily armed men surrounded the van and wrenched the damaged door open. No one inside. The men's eyes passed over the receptacle where the cellular phone would normally be kept. The phone was completely under the front seat, the phone cord pretty much invisible under the weak illumination of the dome light. They believed the phone had probably been dislodged upon impact rather than that it had deliberately been placed there.

Sidney entered the house through the rear. When the man had given her directions to the place, she had instantly recognized it. She and Jason had stayed at the resort several times, and she was very familiar with the interior layout. She had taken a shortcut and arrived in half the time her daughter's captors had alloted her. She had used those precious extra minutes to rig the van's steering wheel and accelerator with rope she had found in the back of the vehicle. She clutched her pistol, her finger resting lightly on the trigger as she stole through the dark rooms of the resort. She was ninety percent certain that Amy was not on the premises. The ten percent of doubt had led her to use the rigged van as a diversion so that she could attempt a rescue, however improbable, of her daughter. She was under no delusions that these men would let Amy go free.

Up ahead she heard the sound of raised voices and feet running toward the front of the house. She cocked her head to the left as a pair of footsteps echoed down the hallway. This person was not running; the tread was slow and methodical. She shrank back into the shadows and waited for the person to pass by. As soon as he did, she pressed the muzzle of her pistol directly against his neck.

"Make any sound at all, and you're dead," she said with a cold finality. "Hands over your head."

Her prisoner complied. He was tall, with broad shoulders. She felt for his gun and found it in a shoulder holster. She crammed the man's pistol in her jacket pocket and pushed him forward. The large room up ahead was well lit. Sidney could not hear any noise emanating from the space, but she didn't think that silence would last long. They would soon figure out her ploy, if they hadn't already. She prodded the man away from the light and down a darkened hallway.

They came to a doorway. "Open it and move inside," she told him.

He opened the door and she pushed him inside. One of her hands felt around for the light switch. When the lights came on, she shut the door behind her and looked at the man's face.

Richard Lucas stared back at her.

"You don't look surprised," Lucas said, his voice even and calm.

"Let's just say nothing surprises me anymore," Sidney replied. "Sit." She motioned with her gun to a straight-backed chair. "Where are the others?"

Lucas shrugged. "Here, there, everywhere. There are a lot of them, Sidney."

"Where's my daughter? And my mother?" Lucas kept silent. Sidney put both hands on her gun and pointed it directly at his chest. "I'm not screwing around with you. Where are they?"

"When I was a CIA operative, I was captured and tortured by the KGB for two months before I escaped. I never told them anything and I'm not telling you anything," Lucas said calmly. "And if you're thinking about using me to exchange for your daughter, forget it. So you might as well pull the trigger, Sidney."

Sidney's finger quivered on the trigger as she and Lucas engaged in a staring contest. Finally she swore under her breath and lowered the pistol. A smile cracked Lucas's lips.

She thought quickly. *All right, you sonofabitch.* "What color is the hat Amy was wearing, Rich? If you have her, you should know that."

The smile disappeared from Lucas's lips. He paused for a second and then answered. "Like a beige."

"Good answer. Neutral, could apply to lots of different colors." She paused as an enormous wave of relief washed over her. "Only Amy wasn't wearing a hat."

Lucas started to bolt out of the chair. A second faster than he, Sidney smashed her pistol across his head. Lucas went down in a heap, unconscious. She towered over his prostrate form. "You're a real asshole."

Sidney exited the room and stole down the corridor. From the direction of where she had entered the house, she heard men approaching. She changed course and once again headed toward the lit room she had spied earlier. She peered around the corner. The light from inside was enough to let her check her watch. She said a silent prayer and edged into the room, keeping low behind a long, carved wooden-backed sofa. She looked around, her eyes taking in a wall of French doors that was visible on the ocean side. The room was huge, with ceilings that soared at least twenty feet high. An interior second-story balcony ran across one side of the room. Another wall held a collection of finely bound books. Comfortable furnishings were placed throughout.

Sidney shrank back as far as she could when a group of armed men, all dressed in black fatigues, entered the room through another doorway. One of them barked into a walkie-talkie. By listening to his words, she knew they were aware of her presence. It was only a matter of time before they found her. Blood pounding in her eardrums, she made her way out of the room, keeping well out of sight behind the sofa. Once in the corridor, she walked swiftly back toward the room in which she had left Lucas, with the intent of using him as her exit card. Maybe they would not care about killing Lucas to get to her, but right now it was the only option she had.

Her plan ran into an immediate problem when she discovered Lucas was no longer in the room. She had hit him very hard, and she briefly marveled at his recuperative powers. Apparently he hadn't been kidding about the KGB. She ran out of the room and toward the door where she had entered the house. Lucas would most certainly raise the alarm. She probably only had seconds to make her getaway. She was a few feet from the door when she heard it.

"Mommy, Mommy."

Sidney jerked around. Amy's wails continued down the hallway.

"Oh, my God!" Sidney turned and sprinted toward the sound.

"Amy? *Amy!*" The doors to the large room she had earlier been in were closed. She hurled them open and burst into the room, her chest heaving, her eyes wildly searching for sight of her daughter.

Nathan Gamble stared back at her as Richard Lucas appeared behind him. He wasn't smiling. The side of his face was heavily swollen. Sidney was quickly disarmed and held by Gamble's men. The disk was taken from her purse and handed to Gamble.

Gamble held up a sophisticated recording device and Amy's voice was heard once again: "Mommy? Mommy?"

"As soon as I found out your husband was on to me," Gamble explained, "I had your house bugged. You get lots of goodies that way."

"You sonofabitch." Sidney glared at him. "I knew it was a trick."

"You should have gone with your first instinct, Sidney. I always do." Gamble shut off the tape and strolled over to a desk situated against one wall. For the first time Sidney noticed that a laptop computer was set up there. Gamble took the disk and popped it in. Then he pulled a piece of paper from his pocket and looked over at her. "Nice touch your husband had on the password. All backwards. You're sharp, but I bet you didn't figure that one out, did you?" His face crinkled into a smile as he looked from the paper to Sidney. "Always knew Jason was a smart guy." Using one finger, Gamble punched a number of keys on the keyboard and studied the screen. While doing so, he lit up a cigar. Satisfied with the contents of the disk, he sat down in the chair, folded his arms across his chest and flicked cigar ash on the floor.

She kept her eyes fixed on him. "Brains run in the family. I know it all, Gamble."

"I think you don't know shit," he calmly replied.

"How about the billions of dollars you made

trading on changes in the Fed Funds Rate? The very same billions you used to build Triton Global."

"Interesting. How did I do that?"

"You knew the answers before the tests were given out. You were blackmailing Arthur Lieberman. The mighty businessman who couldn't make a dime without cheating." She spat out the last words. Gamble's eyes glittered darkly at her. "Then Lieberman threatens to expose you and his plane crashes."

Gamble got up and advanced slowly toward Sidney: his hand an anger-laden fist. "I made billions *on my own*. Then some jealous competitors paid off a couple of my traders to secretly tank me. I couldn't prove anything, but they ended up with cushy jobs down the street and I lost everything I had. You call that fair?" He stopped walking and took a deep breath. "You're right, though. I caught on to Lieberman's little secret life. Scraped enough cash together to set up my little mole in luxury and bided my time. But it wasn't that simple." His lips curled into a wicked smile. "I waited until the people who had screwed me took their investment positions on interest rates and then I took the opposite one and told Lieberman which way to swing it. After it was over, I'm back on top and those guys couldn't afford a cup of spit. Nice and clean, and damn sweet."

His face gleamed as he recalled his personal triumph. "People mess with me, I pay them back. Only a lot worse. Like Lieberman. Nice guy that I am, I paid the sonofabitch over a hundred million dollars for doing this thing with the rates. How does he show his gratitude? He tried to take me down. Was it my fault he got cancer? He thought he could outsmart me, the big Ivy League legend. Didn't think I knew he was dying. I do business with somebody, I find out everything about him.

Everything!" Gamble's face flushed for an instant and then he broke into sly grin. "Only thing I regret is not having a picture of his face when that plane hit."

"I didn't think you were into genocide, Nathan. Men, women, babies." Gamble suddenly looked troubled and took a nervous puff on his cigar. "You think I *wanted* to do it like that? My business is making money, not killing people. If I could have come up with another way I would have. I had two problems: Lieberman and your husband. They both knew the truth, so I had to get rid of them both. The plane was the only way to tie them together: Kill Lieberman and blame your husband. If I could have bought every ticket on that plane except Lieberman's, I would have." He paused and looked at her. "If it makes you feel any better, my charitable foundation has already donated ten million dollars to the victims' families."

"Great, you score PR points off your own dirty work. You think money is the answer to everything?"

Gamble exhaled smoke. "You'd be surprised how often it is. And the fact is, I didn't *have* to do anything for them. It's like I told your buddy Wharton: When I go after somebody who screwed me, I don't care who gets in the way. Too bad."

Sidney's face suddenly hardened. "Like Jason? Where is he? Where is my husband, you sonofabitch?" She screamed the words in an out-of-control fury and would have pounced on Gamble if his men hadn't held her back.

Gamble stepped directly in front of her. His fist slammed into her jaw. "Shut up!"

Sidney swiftly recovered, ripped her arm free and slashed Gamble's face with her fingernails. Shocked, he stumbled back, clutching his torn skin. "Damn you!" he yelled. Gamble pressed his handkerchief against his face, his eyes blazing at her. Sidney stared back at him, her entire body shaking with more anger than she had felt in her entire life. Gamble finally motioned to Lucas. Lucas left the room for a minute, and when he returned, he was not alone.

Sidney instinctively jerked back as Kenneth Scales stepped into the room. He stared at Sidney Archer with eyes that bespoke intense hatred. She looked over at Gamble. He looked down and sighed while he stuffed his handkerchief back in his pocket, touching his face gingerly. "I guess I deserved that. You know, I had no intention of killing you, but you just couldn't leave it alone, could you?" He ran a hand through his hair. "Don't worry, I'll set a big trust fund up for your kid. You should be grateful I think everything through." He waved Scales forward.

Sidney shouted at him. "Oh, really? Did you think through the fact that maybe if I could figure it out, so could Sawyer?" Gamble stared blankly at her. "Like the fact that you blackmailed Arthur Lieberman by setting him up with Steven Page. But just when Lieberman was up for the Fed nomination, Page contracted HIV and threatened to blow the whole thing. What did you do? Just like you did with Lieberman. You had Page killed."

Gamble's response stunned her. "Why the hell would I have him killed? He was working for me."

"He's telling the truth, Sidney." She jerked her head around and stared at the source of those words. Quentin Rowe walked into the room.

Gamble stared at him, his eyes wide. "How the hell did you get up here?"

Rowe barely glanced at him. "I guess you forgot that I have my *own* private suite on the corporate jet.

583

Besides, I like to see projects through to their completion."

"Is she right? You had your own lover boy killed?"

Rowe looked at him calmly. "It's not any of your concern."

"It's my company. Everything concerns me."

"Your company? I don't think so. Now that we have CyberCom, I don't need you. My nightmare is finally over."

Gamble's face grew red. He motioned toward Richard Lucas. "I think we need to show this little prick some respect for his superior."

Richard Lucas pulled out his weapon.

Gamble shook his head. "Just rough the little sucker up some," he said, his eyes glowing maliciously. The glow quickly ebbed as Lucas swung the pistol in his direction and the cigar fell out of the Triton's chief's mouth. "What the hell. You sonofabitch traitor—"

"Shut up!" Lucas roared back. "Shut your mouth or I'll blow you away right here and now. I swear to God I will." Lucas's eyes tore into Gamble's face and Gamble quickly closed his mouth.

"Why, Quentin?" The words floated softly across the room. "Why?"

Rowe turned to find Sidney's eyes on him. He took a deep breath. "When he bought into my company, Gamble drew up legal documents so that he technically controlled my ideas, everything. In essence, he owned me." For a moment he stared at the now docile Gamble with ill-concealed disgust. Rowe looked back at Sidney, reading her mind. "The oddest couple in the world. I know."

He sat down at the desk in front of the computer. He stared at the screen as he continued to talk. The proximity of the high-tech equipment seemed to soothe Quentin Rowe even more. "But then Gamble lost all his money. My company was going nowhere. I pleaded with him to let me out of the deal, but he said he'd tie me up in court for years. I was stuck. Then Steven met Lieberman and the plot was hatched."

"But you had Page killed. Why?"

Rowe didn't answer.

"Did you ever try to find out who gave him HIV?"

Rowe didn't answer. Tears spilled down on to the laptop.

"Quentin?"

"I gave it to him. I did it!" Rowe exploded out of his chair, staggered for a moment and then collapsed back into the chair. In a painful voice, he continued. "When Steven told me he had tested positive, I couldn't believe it. I had always been faithful to him and he swore the same to me. We thought it might have been Lieberman. We got a copy of his medical records; he was clean. That's when I took an examination." His lips started to quiver. "And that's when I was told I was HIV-positive. The only thing I could think of was a damn blood transfusion I'd had when I was in a serious car accident. I checked with the hospital and discovered that several other surgery patients had contracted the virus during the same time period. I told Steven everything. I cared for him so much. I never felt so much guilt in all my life. I thought he would understand." Rowe took a deep breath. "Only he didn't."

"He threatened to expose you?" Sidney asked.

"We had come too far, worked too damn hard. Steven wasn't thinking clearly, he . . ." Rowe shook his head in complete despondence. "He came to my apartment one night; he had been drinking very heavily. He told me what he was going to do. He was going to tell everything about Lieberman, the blackmail scheme. We'd all go to prison. I told him he had to do what he thought was right." Rowe paused, his voice breaking. "I often gave him his daily dosages of insulin, kept a supply at my place. He was always forgetful about it." Rowe looked down at the teardrops dropping on to his hands. "Steven passed out on the couch. While he was asleep, I gave him an overdose of insulin, woke him up, and put him in a cab for home." Rowe added quietly, "And he died. We kept our relationship since college a secret. The police never even questioned me."

He looked at Sidney. "You understand, don't you? I had to do it. My dreams, my vision for the future." His voice was almost pleading. Sidney didn't answer. Finally Rowe stood up and wiped the tears away. "CyberCom was the last piece I needed. But it all came with a price. With all the secrets between us, Gamble and I were wedded for life." Rowe grimaced, then suddenly smiled as he looked at Gamble. "Fortunately, I will outlive him."

"You double-crossing bastard!" Gamble tried his best to get to Rowe, but Lucas held him back.

"But Jason found out everything when he was going through the records at the warehouse, didn't he?" Sidney said.

Rowe exploded again and directed his tirade at Gamble. "You idiot! You've never respected technology, and it was your undoing. You never realized that the secret e-mails you sent Lieberman could be captured on tape backup even if you later deleted them. You were so damn anal about money, kept your own set of books documenting the profits trading on Lieberman's actions. And your enemy's losses. It was all buried in the warehouse. You idiot!" Rowe exclaimed again, and looked over at Sidney. "I never wanted any of this to happen, please believe me."

"Quentin, if you cooperate with the police—" Sidney began.

Rowe erupted in laughter and Sidney's hopes faded completely. He went over to the laptop and popped out the disk. "I'm now the head of Triton Global. I just acquired the one asset that will enable me to accomplish a better future for us all. I don't intend to pursue that dream from a prison cell."

"Quentin . . ." She froze as he turned to Kenneth Scales.

"Make it quick, she is not to suffer. I mean it." He nodded in Gamble's direction. "The bodies go into the ocean, as far out as you can. A mysterious disappearance. In six months' time no one will even remember you," he said to Gamble. Rowe's eyes shone with that thought.

Gamble was slowly led away, struggling mightily and cursing.

"Quentin!" Sidney screamed as Scales came closer. Quentin Rowe didn't turn around.

"Quentin, please!" Finally he looked at her. "Sidney, I'm sorry. I really am." Holding the disk, he started to leave the room. As he passed by, he kindly patted her on the shoulder.

Her body and mind numb, Sidney's head dropped on her breast. When she looked up, the cold, blue eyes were floating toward her, the face completely blank of emotion. She looked around. Everyone in the room was intently watching Scales's methodical advance, waiting to see how he would kill her. Sidney gritted her teeth and backed away until she was flat against a wall. She closed her eyes and did her best to hold the image of her daughter rigidly in her mind. Amy was safe. Her parents were safe. Under the circumstances, that was the absolute best she could do. *Good-bye, baby, Mommy loves you.*

The tears spilled down her face. *Please don't forget me, Amy. Please.*

Scales lifted up his knife and a smile crept across his face as he looked down at the glistening blade. Light reflecting off it turned the metal a harsh reddish color, a color it had been many times in the past. Scales's smile receded as he looked down at the source of this colored light and saw the tiny red laser dot on his chest, and the barely visible, pencil-thin beam that emanated outward from the dot.

Scales backed away, his shocked eyes fixed on Lee Sawyer, who was pointing his assault rifle with attached laser scope directly at him. Bewildered, the mercenaries looked at the weaponry pointed at them by Sawyer, Jackson, the HRT and a contingent of the Maine State Police. "Guns down, gentleman, or start looking for your brains on the floor," Sawyer bellowed, tightening his grip on the rifle. "Guns down! *Now!*" Sawyer took a few more steps into the room, his finger closing on the trigger. The men started to put down their weapons. Out of the corner of his eye, Sawyer spotted Quentin Rowe trying to discreetly disappear. Sawyer swiveled his gun in the computer man's direction. "Don't think so, Mr. Rowe. Sit down!"

A thoroughly frightened Quentin Rowe sat down in a chair, the disk gripped against his chest. Sawyer looked at Ray Jackson. "Let's get to it." Sawyer started toward Sidney. At that instant a shot rang out and one of the FBI agents went down. Gunfire erupted as Rowe's men used the opportunity to seize their weapons and open fire. The lawmen quickly dove for cover and returned the fire. Muzzle flashes popped up all over the room as instant death spewed forth from over a dozen locations. It took only seconds for every light in the room to be shot out by gunmen on both sides, plunging the room into total darkness.

Caught in the cross fire, Sidney threw herself to the floor, her hands over her ears as bullets whizzed overhead.

Sawyer dropped to his knees and scrambled toward Sidney. From the other direction, Scales, his knife between his teeth, slid on his belly along the floor toward her. Sawyer reached her first and took her by the hand to lead her to safety. Sidney screamed as she saw Scales's blade flash through the air. Sawyer swung his arm out and took the brunt of the blow, the knife cutting through his thick jacket and slicing his forearm. Grunting in pain, he kicked at Scales, losing his balance and toppling over on his back. Scales pounced on the FBI agent and struck at his chest twice. The blade, however, met the advanced-stage Teflon mesh in Sawyer's body armor head-on and lost decisively. Scales paid for that defeat with a mouthful of one of Sawyer's massive fists and one of Sidney's elbows slamming into the back of his neck. The man howled in pain as his already battered mouth and broken nose received an additional litany of injuries.

Furious, Scales violently threw Sidney off and she slid across the floor and crashed into a wall. Scales's fist repeatedly slammed into Sawyer's face and then he raised the knife, the center of the FBI agent's broad forehead his target. Sawyer clamped his hand around Scales's wrist and slowly but surely heaved himself up. Scales felt the amazing strength in Sawyer's bulk, raw strength the much smaller man could not hope to match. Used to his victims being dead before they ever had a chance to fight back, Scales abruptly discovered he had hooked a very much alive Great White Shark. Sawyer smashed Scales's hand against the floor until the knife went flying into the darkness. Then Sawyer hauled back

589

and unleashed a haymaker that landed flush on Scales's face and Scales went backward across the room, screaming in agony, his nose now lying flat against his left cheek.

Ray Jackson was in one corner of the room exchanging fire with two of the mercenaries. Three of the HRT members had made their way to one of the balconies. With this tactical advantage they were quickly winning the shoot-out. Two of the mercenaries were dead already. Another was about to expire with a bullet wound in his leg that had severed the femoral artery. Two of the state troopers had been shot, one seriously. Two of the HRT members had taken hits but were still participating in the gun battle.

Stopping to reload, Jackson looked across the room and saw Scales get to his feet, knife raised, and sprint toward the very broad back of Lee Sawyer as the FBI agent again tried to pull Sidney to safety.

There was no time for Jackson to reload his rifle, his 9mm was empty and he was out of clips. If he tried to yell, Sawyer would be unable to hear him over the barrage of gunfire. Jackson jumped to his feet. As a star member of the University of Michigan Wolverines football team, he had rushed for thousands of hard-fought yards on the gridiron. Now he was about to make the run of his life. His thick legs exploded under him, and with bullets splattering all around Jackson reached maximum speed three steps into his sprint.

Scales was solid bone and muscle, but he carried about fifty fewer pounds on his frame than did the two-hundred-pound battering ram of an FBI agent. And despite being a very dangerous individual, Kenneth Scales had never experienced the brutally violent world of Big Ten football.

Scales's blade was barely a foot from Sawyer's

back when Jackson's iron shoulder collided with his breastbone. The resulting crack as Scales's chest collapsed could almost be heard over the gunfire. Scales's body was lifted cleanly off the ground and it didn't stop moving until it slammed against the solid oak wall almost four feet away. The second crack, while not as loud as the first, heralded Kenneth Scales's exit from the living as his neck snapped neatly in half. As he slumped to the floor and came to rest on his back, it was finally Scales's turn to stare blankly upward with a pair of dead eyes. By any yardstick, it was a long-overdue event.

Jackson paid a price for his heroics as he took a slug in his arm and another in his leg before Sawyer was able to ward off the shooter with multiple bursts from his 10mm. Sawyer grabbed Sidney's arm and hauled her to a corner behind a heavy table he had flipped on its side. He then raced over to Jackson, who was slumped against a wall breathing hard, and proceeded to drag him toward safety. A shot thudded against the wall within an inch of Sawyer's head. Then another hit him squarely in the rib cage. His pistol flew from his hand and slid across the floor as he slumped back against the wall, coughing up blood. The vest had done its job again, but he had heard the crack of some ribs upon impact. He started to pull himself up, but now he was very much a sitting duck.

Suddenly a string of shots erupted from near the overturned table. An abrupt scream from the direction of the shot that had hit Sawyer followed the lead barrage. Sawyer looked over at the table and his eyes widened in amazement as he saw Sidney Archer jam the still smoking 10mm pistol in her waistband. She raced out from behind the protective cover, and together she and Sawyer pulled Jackson safely behind the table.

They sat Jackson up against the wall.

"Damn, Ray, you shouldn't have done that, man." Sawyer's eyes quickly examined his partner, confirming that there were two wounds and no more.

"Right, and let you give me hell from the grave for the rest of my life? No way, Lee." Jackson bit his lip hard as Sawyer ripped off his tie and, using Scales's stiletto blade, made a crude tourniquet above the wound on Jackson's leg.

"Keep your hand right there, Ray." Sawyer guided his hand to the handle of the knife, pressing his fingers tightly against it.

He next tore his coat off, balled it up and stanched the bleeding on Jackson's arm wound. "Slug went right though, Ray. You're gonna be okay."

"I know, I could feel it exit." The sweat poured off Jackson's forehead. "You took a round, didn't you?"

"Nah, vest caught it, I'm okay." As he slumped back, Sawyer's savaged forearm started to pour blood again.

"Oh, God, Lee," Sidney stared at the crimson flow. "Your arm." Sidney took off her scarf and wound it around Sawyer's wounded limb.

Sawyer eyed her kindly. "Thanks. And I'm not talking about the scarf."

Sidney slumped against the wall. "Thank God we were able to fill in each other's blanks when you called. I regaled Gamble with my brilliant deductions to buy you some time. Even so, I didn't think it was going to be enough."

He sat down next to her. "For a couple of minutes, we lost the signal from the cell phone. Thank God we picked it back up again." He abruptly sat up, making the cracked rib even worse. He looked at her battered face. "You're okay, aren't you? Jesus, I didn't even think to ask."

She rubbed her swollen jaw gingerly. "Nothing

that time and makeup won't help." She touched his swollen cheek. "How about you?"

Sawyer had another jolt. "Omigod! Amy? Your mother?"

She quickly explained about the voice recording.

"Those sonofabitches," he growled.

She looked at him wistfully. "I'm not sure what would have happened if I hadn't answered your page."

"Point is, you did. I'm just glad I had one of your business cards." He smiled. "Maybe this high-tech crap has its uses. In tiny doses."

In another corner of the room Quentin Rowe huddled behind the desk. His eyes were closed and his hands were over his ears as he tried to shield out the sounds exploding all around him. He did not notice the man come up behind him until the last instant. His ponytail was jerked violently backward, forcing his chin up farther and farther. The hands then twisted his head around, and just before he heard the snap of his spine, he was staring into the vicious, grinning countenance of Nathan Gamble. The Triton chief let the limp body go and Rowe dropped to the floor, dead. He had experienced his last vision. Gamble snatched the laptop off the desk and smashed it so hard over Rowe's body that it cracked in half.

Gamble hovered over Rowe's body for a moment longer, then turned to make his escape. The bullets hit him square in the chest. He looked, wide-eyed, at his killer, disbelief and then anger racing across his features. Gamble managed to grip the man's sleeve for an instant before toppling to the floor.

The killer took the disk from where it had fallen next to Quentin Rowe and made his way out.

Rowe had fallen on his side and his body had

come to rest on its back, he head turned toward Gamble. Ironically, he and Gamble were bare inches from each other, far closer then the two men ever had been in life.

Sawyer inched his head above the table and surveyed the room. The remaining mercenaries had dropped their weapons and were coming out of hiding, their hands high. The HRT members moved in, and in a moment the men were down on the floor in handcuffs. Sawyer noticed the limp bodies of Rowe and Gamble. But then, outside the French doors he heard running feet. Sawyer turned to Sidney. "Take care of Ray. Show's not over yet." He hustled out.

FIFTY-EIGHT

The wind, snow and ocean spray assaulted Lee Sawyer on every front as he ran along the sand. His face was bloody and swollen, his injured arm and ribs throbbed like hell and his breath came in thudding fits and starts. He took a minute to strip off the heavy body armor, then he plunged on, pressing a hand firmly against his cracked ribs to hold them in place. His feet twisted and turned in the loose surface, slowing him down. He stumbled and fell twice. But he figured the person he was hunting was having the same problem. Sawyer had a flashlight, but he didn't want to use it, at least not yet. Twice he ran through frigid water as he strayed too close to the border of the pounding Atlantic. He kept his eyes straight down as he followed the set of deep footprints in the sand.

Then Sawyer was confronted with a massive outcropping of rock. It was a common enough formation along the Maine coast. For a moment he debated how to navigate the obstacle until he saw a rough path that cut through the middle of the miniature mountain. He headed up, pulling his gun out as he did so. Sawyer was hit with a wall of ocean spray as the water beat relentlessly against the ancient stone. His clothes clung to his body like plastic. Still he pushed on; his breathing came in huge bursts as he struggled up the path, which was becoming more and more vertical. He looked out to the ocean for a moment. Black and endless. Sawyer rounded a slight bend in the path and then stopped. He shone his light ahead, out to the very edge of the cliff before it disappeared straight down into the Atlantic far below.

The light illuminated the man fully. He squinted back and he put up a hand to shield his eyes from the unexpected burst of light. Sawyer sucked in air. The other man was doing the same after the long chase. Sawyer put one hand on his knee to steady himself as he half bent over, his gut heaving.

"What are you doing up here?" Sawyer's voice was wheezy but clear.

Frank Hardy stared back at him, his breath also coming in deep gusts from weary lungs. Like Sawyer's, his clothes were drenched and dirty and his hair was a wind-ravaged mess.

"Lee? That you?" Hardy said.

"It sure as hell ain't Santa Claus, Frank," Sawyer wheezed back. "Answer my question."

Hardy took a last lengthy breath. "I came up with Gamble for a meeting. Right in the middle of it, he tells me to go upstairs, that he has some personal business to conduct. The next thing I know, all hell broke loose. I got out of there as fast as I could. You mind telling me what's going on?"

Sawyer shook his head admiringly. "You always could think fast on your feet. It's what made you a great FBI agent. By the way, did you kill Gamble *and* Rowe, or did Gamble beat you to Rowe?"

Hardy looked at him grimly, his eyes narrowed.

"Frank, take out the pistol, muzzle first, and toss it over the cliff."

"What gun, Lee? I'm not armed."

"The gun you used to shoot one of my men and start that little gun battle in there." Sawyer paused and tightened his grip on his own pistol. "I won't tell you again, Frank."

Hardy slowly took the pistol out and tossed it over the cliff.

Sawyer flushed a cigarette out of his pocket and clenched it between his teeth. He pulled out a lighter and held it up. "Ever seen one of these, Frank? These suckers will stay lit in a tornado. It's like the one they used to down the plane."

"I don't know anything about the plane bombing," Hardy said angrily.

Sawyer paused to light his cigarette and then took a long puff. "You *didn't* know anything about the plane bombing. That's true. But you were in on everything else. In fact, I bet you charged Nathan Gamble a nice little premium. Did you get a piece of the quarter billion you framed Archer for stealing? Duplicated his signature and everything. Nice work."

"You're crazy! Why would Gamble steal from himself?"

"He didn't. That money's probably spread over a hundred different accounts he's got all over the world. It was perfect cover. Who'd ever suspect the guy who got taken for all that money? I'm sure Quentin Rowe handled the BankTrust piece and also breaking into Virginia's AFIS database to monkey around with Riker's prints. Jason Archer had the evidence to the whole blackmail scheme with Lieberman. He had to tell someone. Who? Richard Lucas? Don't think so. He was Gamble's man, plain and simple. The inside guy."

"So who did he tell?" Hardy's eyes were now pinpoints.

Sawyer took a long drag on his cigarette before answering. "He told you, Frank."

"Right. Prove it," Hardy said with disgust.

"He went to you. The 'outside' guy. The former FBI agent with a list of commendations as long as his

597

arm." Sawyer spat this last sentence out. "He went to you so you could help him expose the whole thing. Only you couldn't let that happen. Triton Global's your gravy train. Giving up private jets, the pretty ladies and nice clothes wasn't an option, was it?"

Sawyer continued. "Then you all took me through the dog and pony show, setting up Jason to be the bad guy. You guys must've been laughing your asses off at how you suckered me. Or *thought* you had. But when you saw I wasn't buying all of it, you got a little nervous. Was it your idea to have Gamble offer me a job? Between you and him I never felt so popular." Hardy remained silent. "But that wasn't your only performance, Frank."

Sawyer reached in his pocket and took out a pair of sunglasses and put them on. He looked quite ridiculous in the darkness. "You remember these, Frank? The two guys on the video in the warehouse in Seattle? They were wearing sunglasses, indoors, in a fairly dark room. Why would anybody do that?"

"I don't know." Hardy's voice was a mere whisper now.

"Sure you do. Jason thought he was handing over his proof . . . to the FBI. At least in the movies all Feds wear shades and the guys you hired to play the FBI agents must have liked going to the theater. You couldn't just kill Jason. You had to win his trust, make sure he hadn't told anyone. A top priority was getting back all the hard evidence he had. The videotape of the exchange had to be in pristine condition because you knew you'd be giving it to us as evidence of Jason's guilt. You only had one shot to get it right. But Archer was still suspicious. That's why he kept a copy of the information on another disk and later sent it to his wife. Did you tell him he'd get a big reward from the government? Was that it? Probably told him it was the biggest damned sting in the history of the FBI."

Hardy remained silent.

Sawyer looked at his old partner. "But unknown to you, Frank, Gamble had his own big problem. Namely that Arthur Lieberman was about to spill his guts. So he hires Riker to sabotage Lieberman's plane. I'm sure you didn't know about that part of the plan. On Gamble's orders you arrange for Archer to get ticketed on the flight to Los Angeles, and then you had him pull a switch and he gets on the flight to Seattle instead so you could film your little videotape of the exchange. Rich Lucas is ex-CIA, he probably had lots of ties to former Eastern European operatives with no families, no past. The guy who went down in Archer's place wouldn't be missed. You had no idea Lieberman was on the L.A. flight or that Gamble was going to kill him. But Gamble knew it was the only way the blame for Lieberman's death could be thrown on Archer. And with it, Gamble kills two birds with one stone: Archer and Lieberman. You bring me the video and I switch all my efforts to catching Jason and I forget all about poor old Arthur Lieberman. Except for Ed Page wandering into the picture, I don't think I would've ever picked up Lieberman's thread again.

"And let's not forget old RTG, who got blamed for everything, with Triton conveniently ending up with CyberCom. I told you about Brophy being in New Orleans. You found out he was actually connected to RTG and that they might actually accomplish what you'd set Jason up for: working with RTG. So you had Brophy and Goldman followed and when the opportunity arose, you took them both out and set up Sidney Archer to take the fall. Why not? You'd already done the same thing to her husband." Sawyer paused. "That's a hell of a transition, Frank: FBI agent to participation in a

599

massive criminal conspiracy. Maybe I should take you on a visit to the crash site. You want to do that?"

"I didn't have anything to do with the plane bombing, I swear," Hardy yelled out.

"I know. But you were involved in one regard." Sawyer took off his sunglasses. "You killed the bomber."

"Would you care to prove that?" Hardy's eyes blazed at him.

"You told me, Frank." Hardy's face froze. "Down in the parking garage where Goldman and Brophy checked out. The place was freezing. I was concerned about the decomposition of the bodies, that the frigid temperatures might make ascertaining the time of death impossible. Remember what you said, Frank? You said it was the same problem with the bomber. That the air-conditioning had made the apartment freeze just like the outside air did to the parking garage."

"So?"

"I never told you the air-conditioning was turned on in Riker's apartment. In fact, I turned the heat back on right after we found the body. There was no mention of the A/C being turned on in any of the bureau reports – not that you would've been privy to them anyway." Hardy's face had turned ashen. "You knew, Frank, because you were the one who turned the A/C on. When you found out about the bombing, you knew Gamble had used you. Hell, maybe they planned to kill Riker all along. But you were more than willing to do the honors. It didn't hit me until I was freezing my ass off in a police paddywagon driving over here."

Sawyer moved forward. "Twelve shots, Frank. I admit, that one really puzzled me. You were so furious at the guy for what he'd done that you went a little beserk. Emptied your whole clip into him. I guess you still had a *little* bit of the cop left in you. But now it's over."

Hardy swallowed hard, struggling to keep his nerves under control. "Look, Lee, everybody who knows about my involvement is dead."

"What about Jason Archer?"

Hardy laughed. "Jason Archer was a fool. He wanted the money, just like all of us. Only he didn't have the nerve, you know, not like you and me. He kept having *bad dreams*." Hardy edged forward. "You look the other way, Lee. That's all I'm asking. You start work at my company next month. One million dollars a year. Stock options, the works. You'll be set for life."

Sawyer flicked his cigarette away. "Frank, let me make this real clear to you. I don't like ordering my food in foreign languages, and I wouldn't know a damned stock option if it jumped up and clamped me right on the balls." Sawyer raised his gun. "Where you're going, the only *option* will be top or bottom bunk."

Hardy snarled. "Not by a long shot, old *buddy*." He pulled the disk from his pocket. "You want this, then put your gun down."

"You've gotta be kidding me—"

"Put it down," Hardy screamed. "Or I throw your whole case into the Atlantic. You let me go, I'll mail it to you from parts unknown."

Hardy started to smile as Sawyer's pistol began dropping. Then, as Sawyer stared into the grinning countenance, he abruptly returned the pistol to its original position. "First, I want an answer to one question, and I want it now."

"What is it?"

Sawyer moved forward, his hand tightening on the trigger. "What happened to Jason Archer?"

"Look, Lee, what does it matter—"

"Where is Jason Archer?" Sawyer roared over the crash of the waves. "Because that is exactly what the lady back there wants to know, and dammit, you're going to tell me, Frank. By the way, you can throw that disk as far as you want. Rich Lucas is alive," Sawyer lied. He had seen Lucas lying dead in the middle of the battlefield the hotel lobby had become. The silent sentinel was now forever silent. "Want to bet how anxious he is to rat on your ass?"

Hardy's face went stone cold as he realized his exit option had just evaporated. "Take me back to the house, Lee. I want to call my lawyer." Hardy started forward and then suddenly stopped as Sawyer assumed a textbook shooting stance.

"Now, Frank. Tell me right now."

"Go to hell! Read me my rights if you want, but get out of my damned face."

Sawyer's response was to shift his pistol slightly to the left and fire one round. Hardy screamed as the slug took off skin and the top part of his right ear. Blood poured down the side of his face. He fell to the ground. "Are you crazy?" Sawyer now aimed the gun directly at Hardy's head. "I'll have your badge and your pension, and your ass will be in jail for more years than you've got left, you sonofabitch," Hardy screamed. "You'll lose everything."

"No I wont. You're not the only person who can manipulate a crime scene, *old buddy*." Hardy watched in growing astonishment as Sawyer popped open the gun bag riding above his belt and took out another 10mm. He held it up. "This will be the gun you'll have gotten away from me in the struggle. They'll find it clutched in your hand. It'll have several shots fired from it, evidencing your homicidal intent." He pointed toward the vast ocean. "Kind of hard to find the slugs out there." He held up the other pistol. "You used to be a first-rate investigator,

FIFTY-NINE

The funeral that finally laid Jason Archer to rest in peace occurred on a clear December day atop a quiet knoll about twenty minutes from his brick and stone home. During the graveside service Sawyer had stayed in the background as family and close friends attended the once again grieving widow. The FBI agent had stayed at the grave site after all of them had gone. As he stared at the newly etched tombstone, Sawyer rested his bulk on one of the folding chairs that had been used for this simple, brief burial ritual. Jason Archer had occupied the agent's every waking moment for over a month and yet the two men had never met. That was often the case in his line of work; however, this time the emotions wending their way through the veteran agent's psyche were far different. Sawyer knew he had been powerless to prevent the man's death. And yet he still felt crushed that he had let the man's wife and little girl down, that the Archer family had been irretrievably destroyed because of his inability to get at the truth in time.

He covered his face in his hands. When he removed them some minutes later, the tears still glimmered in his eyes. He had successfully completed the case of a lifetime, yet he had never felt like more of a failure. He stood up, put on his hat and headed slowly toward his car. Then he froze. The long black limo was parked at the curb. It had come back. Sawyer watched the face peering out from the limo's rear window. Sidney was looking at the fresh hump of dirt in the earth. She turned her head in Sawyer's direction as he stood there trembling, unable to move, his heart pounding, his lungs heaving, and wishing more than anything else on earth to be able to reach into that cold soil and return Jason Archer to her. The glass slid back up as the limousine drove away.

The night before Christmas Eve, Lee Sawyer rolled his sedan slowly down Morgan Lane. The houses along the street were beautifully decorated with lights, wreaths, all-weather Santa Clauses and their trusty reindeer. Down the block a group of bundled-up carolers were performing. The area was in a festive mood, all except for one house, which was dark but for one light on in the front room.

Sawyer pulled into the Archer's driveway and got out of his car. He was dressed in a new suit, his cowlick plastered down as much as it could be. He pulled a small gift-wrapped box out the car and walked up to the house. His gait was a little stiff; his ribs were still on the mend.

Sidney Archer answered his knock. She was dressed in dark slacks and a white blouse, her hair flowing down over her shoulders. She had gained some weight back, but her features were still gaunt. The cuts and bruises had healed, though.

They sat in the living room in front of the fire. Sawyer accepted her offer of cider and looked around the room while she went to get it. On the side table was a box of computer disks with a red bow on top. He put the box he had brought with him on the coffee table, since there was no Christmas tree to put it under.

"Going somewhere for the holidays, I hope?" he asked as she sat down across from him. They each took a sip of the warm cider.

"My parents'. They've got the place fixed up for Christmas. Big tree, decorations. My father's going to dress up like Santa. My brothers and their families will be there. It'll be good for Amy."

Sawyer looked over at the box of disks. "I hope that's a gag gift."

Sidney followed his gaze and briefly smiled. "Jeff Fisher. He thanked me for the most exciting night of his life and offered me free computer advice in perpetuity." Sawyer then eyed the small, damp towel Sidney had brought back with her and placed on the coffee table. He slid the present across. "Slip this under the tree for Amy, will you? It's from me and Ray. His wife picked it out. It's a doll that does a bunch of stuff, you know, it talks and pee-pees—" He abruptly stopped and looked embarrassed. He took another sip of cider.

Sidney smiled. "Thank you very much, Lee. She'll love it. I'd give it to her now, except she's asleep."

"It's better to open presents on Christmas anyway."

"How is Ray?"

"Hell, you couldn't hurt him if you tried. He's already off the crutches—"

Sidney turned green and quickly reached for the towel. She held it against her mouth, got up and raced out of the room. Sawyer stood up but didn't follow. He sat back down. In a couple of minutes she had rejoined him. "I'm sorry, I must have caught a bug."

"How long have you known you were pregnant?" Sawyer asked. She sat back, stunned. "I've got four kids, Sidney. Believe me, I know morning sickness when I see it."

Sidney's voice was strained. "About two weeks. The morning Jason left . . ." She started to rock back

607

and forth, one hand pressed across her face. "God, I can't believe this. Why did he do it? Why didn't he tell me? He shouldn't be dead. Dammit! He shouldn't!"

Sawyer looked down at the cup in his hands. "He tried to do the right thing, Sidney. He could've just ignored what he'd found, like most people would have. But he decided to do something about it instead. A real hero. He took a lot of risks, but I know he did it for you and Amy. I never had the opportunity to meet him, but I know he loved you." Sawyer was not about to disclose to Sidney that the hopes of a government reward had played a prominent role in Jason Archer's decision to gather evidence against Triton.

She looked at him through tear-filled eyes. "If he loved us so much, why did he choose to do something that was so dangerous, so . . . It doesn't make any sense. God, it's like I lost him twice. Do you know how that feels?"

Sawyer considered this for a minute, cleared his throat and started speaking very quietly. "I have this friend who's kind of contradictory. He loved his wife and kids so much he would've done anything for them. I mean anything."

"Lee—"

He held up a hand. "Please, Sidney, let me finish. Believe me, it took a lot to get to this point." She sat back as Sawyer continued. "He loved them so much he spent all his time trying to make the world a safer place for them. So much time, in fact, that he ended up hurting terribly the very people he loved so much. And he didn't see it until it was too late." He took a sip of the cider as a massive lump formed in his throat. "So you see, sometimes people do the dumbest things for the very best reasons." His eyes shimmered. "Jason loved you, Sidney. Hell, at the end of the day, that's all that really matters. That's the only memory you ever have to keep."

Neither broke the silence for several minutes as they both stared into the flames.

Finally Sawyer looked at her. "So what're you going to do now?"

Sidney shrugged. "Tyler, Stone lost its two biggest clients, Triton and RTG. However, Henry Wharton was very nice; he said I could come back, but I don't know if I'm up to it." She covered her mouth with her towel and then her hand dropped to her lap. "I probably don't have a choice, though. Jason didn't have much life insurance. We've pretty much run through our savings. With the new baby on the way . . ." She shook her head in misery.

Sawyer waited for a moment and then reached in his suit pocket and slowly took out an envelope. "Maybe this'll help."

She dabbed at her eyes. "What is it?"

"Open it."

She pulled out the slip of paper inside. She finally looked up at Sawyer. "What is this?"

"It's a check made out to you for two million dollars. I don't think it'll bounce, considering it was issued by the United States Treasury."

"I don't understand, Lee."

"There was a two-million-dollar reward from the government for information leading to the capture of the person or persons responsible for the plane bombing."

"But I didn't do anything. I haven't done anything to earn this."

"Actually, I'm absolutely certain it will be the only time in my life that I'll give anyone a check for that much money and then tell them what I'm about to tell you."

"What's that?"

"That it doesn't even come close to being enough. That there's not enough money in the whole world that could be enough."

"Lee, I can't accept his."

"You already have. The check itself is ceremonial. The funds have already been deposited into a special account set up under your name. Charles Tiedman – he's the president of the San Francisco Federal Reserve Bank – has already put together a team of top financial advisers to invest the funds for you. All gratis. Tiedman was Lieberman's closest friend. He asked me to convey to you his sincerest condolences and heartfelt thanks."

The United States government had initially been reluctant to give the reward to Sidney Archer. It had taken Lee Sawyer a full day with congressional and White House representatives to make them change their minds. Everyone was adamant that the full details of the deliberate manipulation of America's financial markets must not come out. Sawyer's less-than-subtle suggestion that he would join with Sidney Archer in auctioning off the disk he had taken from Frank Hardy while on the cliff in Maine to the highest bidder had caused them to abruptly change their minds on the reward. That and his flinging a chair the length of the attorney general's office.

"The funds are all tax-free," he added. "You're pretty much set for life."

Sidney wiped at her eyes and put the check back in the envelope. Neither one of them said anything for several minutes. The fire popped and crackled in the grate. Finally Sawyer looked at his watch and put down the cup of cider. "It's getting late. I'm sure you've got things to do. And I've got some work back at the office." He stood up.

"Don't you ever take a break?"

"Not if I can help it. Besides, what else am I gonna do?"

She stood up too and before he could say good-bye she wrapped her arms around his thick shoulders and pressed herself against him. "Thank you." He could barely hear the words, not that he needed to. The sentiments were emanating from Sidney Archer like the warmth from the fire. He put his arms around her, and for several minutes they stood there in front of the flickering firelight holding each other as the sounds of the carolers grew closer.

When they finally drew apart, Sawyer gently took her hand in his. "I'll always be there for you, Sidney. Always."

"I know," she finally said, her voice only a whisper.

As he started to the door, she called to him. "This friend of yours, Lee . . . you might want to tell him it's never too late."

Driving down the street, Lee Sawyer spotted a full moon planted against a clear black sky. He proceeded to hum quietly a Christmas carol of his own. He wasn't going back to the office. He'd go over and hassle Ray Jackson for a while, play with his kids and maybe drink some egg nog with his partner and his wife. Tomorrow he'd do some late shopping for presents. Max out the old plastic and surprise his kids. What the hell, it was Christmas. He unclipped the FBI badge from his belt and took his pistol out of its holster. He laid them both on the seat next to him. He allowed himself a weary smile as the sedan drifted down the road. The next case was just going to have to wait.

AUTHOR'S NOTE

The aircraft featured in the preceding pages, the Mariner L500, is fictitious, although some of the general specifications noted in the book are based on actual commercial airplanes. Given that acknowledgment, aircraft enthusiasts may quickly point out that the sabotage of Flight 3223 is rather far-fetched. My goal in writing this book was not to prepare an instructional manual for deranged persons.

With respect to the Federal Reserve Board, suffice it to say the idea of this country's economic destiny being, in large measure, controlled by a handful of people who meet in secrecy without much in the way of supervision by anyone was irresistible to me from a storytelling point of view. Truth to be known, I've probably *understated* the Fed's iron grip on all our lives. To be fair, though, over the years, the Fed has navigated this country's economy extremely well through some very tough waters. Their job isn't easy, and it's far from an exact science. While the results of Fed action can be painful for many of us, we can be reasonably certain these actions are taken with the good of the country, as a whole, in mind. Still, with such enormous power concentrated in such a small, isolated sphere, the temptation to reap oceans of illegal profit can never be far from the surface. And the stories one can write!

Regarding the computer-technological aspects of *Total Control*, all of them, to the best of my research ability, are perfectly plausible if they are not already in full-scale use or perhaps even, if you can believe it, obsolete. The numerous benefits of computer technology are undeniably significant; however, with benefits of such scale, there is inevitably a downside. As the world's computers become increasingly linked into a global network, the risk that one person may one day exercise "total control" over certain important aspects of our lives also increases proportionately. And as Lee Sawyer queried in the novel, "What if he's a bad guy?"

David Baldacci
Washington, D.C.
January 1997